A
CONFEDERATION
OF VALOR

A CONFEDERATION OF VALOR

VALOR'S CHOICE

THE BETTER PART OF VALOR

Tanya Huff

DAW BOOKS, INC.

DONALD A. WOLLHEIM, FOUNDER

375 Hudson Street, New York, NY 10014

ELIZABETH R. WOLLHEIM
SHEILA E. GILBERT
PUBLISHERS

www.dawbooks.com

First Trade Paperback Printing, February 2015

1 2 3 4 5 6 7 8 9

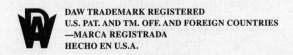

DAW TRADEMARK REGISTERED
U.S. PAT. AND TM. OFF. AND FOREIGN COUNTRIES
—MARCA REGISTRADA
HECHO EN U.S.A.

PRINTED IN THE U.S.A.

VALOR'S
CHOICE

This one's for Sheila, 'cause she was willing to take a chance.

And for Gord Rose and David Sutton and Leslie Dicker and all the other men and women who actually do the work in military organizations world-wide.

Also for my father who, during the Korean War, made Chief Petty Officer. Twice.

Prologue

A writer and philosopher of the late twentieth century once said, *"Space is big."* There are three well-known corollaries to this. The first is that the number of planets where biological accidents occurred in the correct order to create life is small. The second is that the number of planets where life managed to overcome the odds and achieve sentience is smaller still. And the third is that many of these sentient life-forms blow themselves into extinction before they ever make it off their planet of origin.

If space is big and mostly uninhabited, it should be safe to assume that any life-forms who really didn't get along could avoid spending time in each other's company.

Unfortunately, the fact that said life-forms *could* avoid each other doesn't necessarily mean that they would.

When the Others attacked systems on the borders of Confederation territory, Parliament sent out a team of negotiators to point out that expansion in any other direction would be more practical as it would not result in conflict. The negotiators were returned in a number of very small pieces, their ship cleverly rigged to explode when it would do the most damage.

The Confederation found itself at a disadvantage. Its member races had achieved an interstellar presence only after they'd overcome the urge to destroy themselves or any strangers they ran into. Evidence suggested the Others had flung themselves into space without reaching this level of maturity. Clearly, in order to survive, the Confederation would have to recruit some more aggressive members.

Humans had a bare-bones space station and a shaky toe-hold on Mars when the Confederation ships appeared. Some fairly basic technology by Confederation standards, combined with the information that the Others were heading Earth's way, convinced humanity to throw its military apparatus into space where they took to interstellar warfare the way the H'san took to cheese.

Some one and a half centuries of intermittent war later, borders had shifted, and Humans had been joined by first the di'Taykan and then the Krai. Much of the military terminology introduced into the Confederation's common tongue remained Human although, as the three races became increasingly more integrated, di'Taykan and Krai words began creeping in. The Krai, for example, had sixteen useful adjectives describing the impact of an antipersonnel weapon on a soft target.

Although the induction of younger and more aggressive species had undeniably solved the problem presented by the Others, it had also irrevocably changed the face of the Confederation. Feeling just a little overwhelmed, many of the original species spent their spare time sighing and reminiscing about the good old days.

ONE

Reveille was not the best thing to have reverberating through one's skull after a night of too much and too little in various combinations. Making a mental note to change the program to something less painfully intrusive, Torin tongued the implant and tried to remember how to open her eyes during the five blessed seconds of silence before the first of her messages came in.

At the chime, it will be 0530.

The chime set up interesting patterns on the inside of her lids. What *had* she been drinking?

Your liberty will be over at 0600.

Which might be a problem, considering how much trouble she was having with basic bodily functions. Groping for the panel beside the bed, she applied what she hoped was enough pressure for dim lighting and cautiously cracked an eye. From the little she could see, these were not her quarters. The less than state-of-the-art wall utility suggested station guest quarters—for a not particularly important guest.

Finally managing to sort current sensation from memory, she turned her head toward the warm body pressed up against her side. The di'Taykan's short lilac hair swayed gently in response to her exhalation, the pointed tip of an ear covered and uncovered by the moving strands.

A di'Taykan.

That explained things. It wasn't a hangover, she had pheromone head.

Sliding out from under the blanket, Torin stood, stretched carefully, and filled her lungs with air that hadn't been warmed by the di'Taykan's body heat. As memories returned, she smiled. Not only did Humans find the Taykan incredibly attractive, but a Taykan in the di' phase was one of the most indiscriminately enthusiastic life-forms in the Galaxy and offered the perfect and uncomplicated way to chase the memories of that last horrible planetfall right back to the galactic core.

Captain Rose wants to see you in his office at 0800.

There were two piles of clothing on the room's one chair, both folded into neatly squared-off piles. *He must've been raised by one strict* sheshan, Torin thought, grabbing her service uniform and ducking into the bathroom. It had taken most of her nine years in the Corps to achieve that precise a fold, regardless of distraction.

When she emerged a few moments later, fully dressed, all she could see of her companion was a lithe lump under the blanket and a moving fringe of uncovered hair. Relieved, she moved silently toward the door, pausing only long enough to turn off the lights. A di'Taykan considered, *"Once more before breakfast?"* to be a reasonable substitute for *"Good morning."* And, with no time to spare, she was just as happy not to have to test her willpower.

Outside in the corridor, the familiar "something's leaking somewhere" smell of the station's recycled air drove the last of the pheromone-induced haze from her head.

0547 her implant announced when she prodded. Thirteen minutes before her liberty ended and her flasher came back up on screen. Thirteen minutes to get to a part of the station that wouldn't incite prurient speculation among the duty staff.

"I should've reset wake-up for five. What was I *thinking?*" she muttered, diving into the vertical—fortunately empty at this hour—and freefalling two levels. Grabbing a handhold, she swung out onto the lock level. Easy answer, actually. She'd been thinking that she needed to forget the carnage, forget those they lost limping back to the station on a ship that had won its battle but nearly lost its own little slice of the war, forget the messages she'd sent to family and friends, and forget that new faces, always new faces, would soon be arriving to replace those they'd lost.

And she had been able to forget. For a while.

A di'Taykan wouldn't feel used. She didn't think they could.

Considering the time, it was a good thing station guest quarters were on the same side of the core as the barracks. Another vertical, another lock, and she was in NCO country.

0600.

Heading for her own quarters, Staff Sergeant Torin Kerr had her implant scan the night's reports for any of the names she kept flagged. Apparently, no one had died and no one had gotten arrested.

Things hadn't fallen apart while she was gone.

No harm done, and it wasn't as if she'd ever see that particular di'Taykan again . . .

At 0758, showered, changed, and carrying her slate, Torin approached the captain's door, turning over the possible reasons he'd moved their morning meeting up an hour. As senior surviving NCO, she'd been his acting First Sergeant since the battered remnant of Sh'quo Company had arrived back at the station. Clearly that wasn't going to last, but it was unlikely Battalion HQ would send out a new First before the recruits needed to bring the company up to strength—unlikely but possible, she admitted after a moment's reflection. Battalion HQ had shown what could only be called *unique* leadership in the past.

It was also possible that they were promoting her and the captain needed to tell her in time for her to make the 1000 shuttle. With a war on, it didn't take long to make sergeant, but after that, promotions tended to slow down, common wisdom suggesting that by the time a grunt got that third chevron, they'd learned to duck. Still, with the company losing their First, there'd be a gunny moving up and that'd leave room for her.

She'd have rather had First Sergeant Chigma back. The few Krai who went into the Marines usually opted for armored platoons or air support—their feet just weren't built for infantry—so those few who not only chose to be grunts but rose in the ranks left big shoes to fill in more than merely the literal sense. Unfortunately, since Chigma had ended up on the wrong end of an enemy projectile weapon their last planetfall . . .

0759.

Maybe Med-op had scheduled the captain for new treatments at nine.

Look at the bright side, she reminded herself, laying her palm against the sensor pad centered in the door. *We're in no condition to be sent back out.*

The presence of a two-star general in the captain's office did not come as a pleasant surprise. In Torin's experience, when generals ignored the chain of command to speak directly to sergeants, it was never good news. And smiling generals were the worst kind.

"You must be Staff Sergeant Kerr."

She nodded as he stepped forward. "Sir."

"Staff, this is General Morris." The regeneration tank around the lower half of his left leg kept Captain Rose from standing, but his voice, unexpectedly deep from such a small man, was enough to stop the general's advance. "He has new orders for you."

"Say rather an opportunity. But don't let me interrupt." He gestured at the slate under Torin's arm. "I understand you've been acting First. We'll talk once you've finished your morning report."

"Sir." Her face expressionless under the general's smiling regard, she crossed to the desk and downloaded the relevant files. Right now, with no more information to go on than his smile and two dozen words delivered in an annoying *we're-all-in-this-together* tone, she'd be willing to bet that, first of all, General Morris had never seen combat and, second, that Captain Rose liked him even less than she did. As the captain appeared to know what was going on, her sense of impending disaster strengthened.

"Doctorow's no longer critical?"

"Regained consciousness at 0300. Woke up and demanded to know what . . ." Given the general's presence, she rephrased the quote. ". . . idiot had taken his implant off line."

"Good news." Quickly scanning the rest of the report, the captain looked up, brows rising. "No one got arrested?"

"Apparently some vacuum jockeys off the *Redoubt* got into a disagreement with some of our air support in Haligan's, and betting on the fight provided a sufficient diversion."

"Wait a minute," the general interrupted, one hand raised as if to physically stop further discussion. "Am I to understand that you expected your people to get arrested?"

Together, Torin and the captain turned, Torin shifting position slightly, unable to move to the captain's side but making it quite clear where she stood as he answered. "I'm sure I don't need to tell the general what kind of planetfall we had. After something like that, I expect my people to need to blow off."

The general's broad cheeks flushed nearly maroon. "You've been on station for six days."

"Half of us have. Sir." Like many combat officers, Captain Rose had come up through the ranks and he'd retained the NCO's ability to place inflection on that final *sir.*

The two men locked eyes.

General Morris looked away first. "They say another company wouldn't have got that many out," he admitted.

"I have good people, sir. And I lost good people." The quiet reminder drew Torin's gaze down to the captain's face, and she frowned slightly. He looked tired; his fair skin had developed a grayish cast, and there were dark circles under his eyes. Had they been alone, she'd have asked how the regeneration was going; as it was, she made a mental note to check his condition with Med-op as soon as possible. As acting First, he was as much her concern as the company.

"Yes. Good people." General Morris straightened and cleared his throat. "Which leads us nicely into what I'm here for."

Oh, shit. Here it comes. Torin braced herself as he aimed that *I'm looking for someone to get their tail shot off* smile directly at her.

"I need a platoon for a special duty, shipping out ASAP."

"I haven't got a platoon, sir."

He looked momentarily nonplussed, then the smile returned. "Of course, I see. I should have said, I need you to put together a platoon out of the available Marines."

"Out of what's left of Sh'quo Company, sir?"

"Yes."

"Out of the survivors, sir?"

"Yes." The general's smile had begun to tighten.

Torin figured she'd gotten as much satisfaction from that line of inquiry as she was likely to. "A lot of them have leave coming, sir, but we should have new recruits arriving shortly."

"No. Even if I had time to wait for new recruits, I couldn't use them." Folding his hands behind his back in what Torin thought she recognized as parade ground rest—it had been a *long* time since she'd seen a parade ground—the general fixed her with an imposing stare. "I'm fully aware of your situation, Staff Sergeant Kerr, yours and Sh'quo Company's, and I wouldn't be canceling leaves if it wasn't absolutely necessary. The problem, Sergeant, is this: I'm putting together a very important diplomatic mission intended to convince a new race, the Silsviss, to join the Confederation and I need an honor guard. A military escort is absolutely essential because the political leadership of the Silsviss is dominated by a powerful warrior caste that we most certainly do not want to insult. After careful consideration, I've decided that Sh'quo Company is the best available unit."

"As an honor guard?" Torin glanced from the general to her captain—who looked so noncommittal that the hope it was some kind of a joke died unborn—and back to the general again. "We're ground combat, sir, not a ceremonial unit."

"You'll do fine. All you have to do, Sergeant, is have the troops apply a little spit and polish and then stand around and look menacing. You'll see new worlds, meet new life-forms, and not shoot at them for a change." He paused for laughter that never came, then continued gruffly. "It's a win/win situation. I won't have to pull a company out of their rotation for planetfall—which means Sh'quo Company won't be rotated in before it's their turn. As there's no need for heavy artillery, company equipment can still get the overhaul it requires."

"A full platoon makes quite an honor guard, sir."

"It's essential we make a strong impression, Sergeant." For less than an instant, an honest emotion showed in the general's eyes, but before Torin could identify it, he added, "Besides, it'll give you a chance to break in your new second lieutenant."

"My new . . ." Unable to think of anything to say to the general that wouldn't get her court-martialed, she turned to Captain Rose. "Sir?"

"He arrived yesterday afternoon. I asked him to meet us here at 0900. The general thought you should receive your orders first and then he could give the lieutenant the overview."

Officers handled the big picture, NCOs handled the minutia. Part of a staff sergeant's minutia was handling new officers in charge of their first platoon. This would be Torin's third, staff sergeants having a slightly longer life expectancy than second lieutenants.

The captain's door announced an arrival just as her implant proclaimed 0900.

"Open."

The door slid back into the wall and a di'Taykan wearing the uniform of a second lieutenant, Confederation Marine Corps, walked into the office, pheromone masker prominently displayed at his throat. It could have been any di'Taykan; Torin was no better than most Humans at telling them apart. Male and female, they were all tall, slender, and pointy and, even when heavily armed, moved like they were dancing. Their hair, which wasn't really hair but a protein-based sensor array, grew a uniform three inches long so they all looked as if they went to the same barber, and with their somewhat eclectic taste in clothing removed by the Corps . . .

It *could* have been any di'Taykan, but it wasn't.

The lilac eyes, exactly one shade darker than his hair, widened slightly when he saw her and slightly more when he spotted the general. "Second Lieutenant di'Ka Jarret reporting as ordered, Captain."

"Welcome to Sh'quo Company, Lieutenant. General Morris will begin your briefing in a moment, but in the meantime, I'd like you to meet Staff Sergeant Kerr. She'll be your senior NCO."

The corners of the wide mouth curled slightly. "Staff."

"Sir." There were a number of things Torin figured she should be thinking about now, but all that came to mind was, *so that explains why he folded his clothes so neatly*, which wasn't even remotely relevant. She only hoped she'd managed to control her expression by the time Captain Rose turned his too-perceptive attention her way.

"Sergeant, if you could start forming that platoon . . . see if you can do it without splitting up any fireteams. The three of us . . ."

She had to admire how that *us* definitively excluded the general.

". . . will go over what you've got this afternoon."

"Yes, sir." Turning toward General Morris, she stiffened not quite to attention. "Begging the general's pardon, but if I'm to cancel liberties, I need to know exactly how soon ASAP is."

"Forty-eight hours."

She should've known—a desk jockey's version of *as soon as possible*, or in other words, no real rush. "Thank you, sir." Retrieving her slate from the captain's desk, she nodded at all three officers, turned on her heel, and left the room.

The general's hearty voice followed her out into the corridor.

"Lieutenant, I've got a proposal I think you'll . . ."

Then she stepped beyond the proximity grid and the door slid shut.

"Figures," Torin sighed. "Officers get a proposal and the rest of us just get screwed."

Technically, she could've worked at the First's desk in the small office right next to the captain's. All Chigma's personal files had been deleted, every trace of his occupancy removed—it was just a desk. Smarter than any other she'd have access to, but still, just a desk. Which was why she didn't want to use it. Sometimes it was just too depressing to contemplate how quickly the Corps moved on.

The verticals were crowded at this hour of the morning, so she grabbed the first available loop for the descent down to C deck, exchanging a disgusted look with a Navy Warrant one loop over; both of them in full agreement that their careful progress represented an irritating waste of time. By the time she finally swung out onto the deck, Torin was ready to kill the idiot in station programming who'd decided to inflict insipid music on trapped personnel.

" 'Morning, Staff."

The cheerful greeting brought her up short, and she turned toward the Marine kneeling by the edges of the lock with a degrimer, turquoise hair flattened by the vibrations. The grooves could have been scrubbed automatically, but on a station designed to house thousands of Marines, manual labor became a useful discipline. "Maintenance duties again, Haysole?"

The di'Taykan grinned. "I was only cutting across the core. I figured I'd be there and back before anyone noticed I wasn't wearing my masker."

"You crossed the core on a Fivesday evening unmasked—and you're only on maintenance?"

"I kept moving, it wasn't too bad." Turquoise eyes sparkled. "Unfortunately, Sergeant Glicksohn was also crossing the core. Uh, Staff . . ." He paused while a pair of Human engineers came through the lock, waiting until they'd moved beyond their ability to overhear. ". . . I heard you were seeing stars in the captain's office."

Torin folded her arms around her slate. Many di'Taykan worked in Intelligence—most species had to make a conscious effort not to confide in them. She had no idea how need-to-know General Morris had intended to keep the status of his visit, but it was irrelevant now. "What else have you heard, Haysole?"

He grinned, taking her lack of denial for confirmation. "I've heard that the general's looking for a chance to be, oh, let's say, more than he is."

"A promotion?"

"No one used that exact word, but . . ." His voice trailed off suggestively.

Torin ignored the suggestion. "That's it?"

"About the general. But I've also heard that the new *trilinshy* is a di'Ka."

She frowned, and his grin disappeared as he realized she'd translated *trilinshy* to something approximating its distinctly uncomplimentary meaning.

"That is," he corrected hastily, "the new second lieutenant is a di'Ka, Staff Sergeant. High family. Not going to be easy to work with."

"For me or for you?" Private First Class Haysole was a di'Stenjic. Five more letters in a Taykan family name made for a considerable difference in class.

"You know me, Staff . . ." His gesture suggested she could know him better any time it was convenient. ". . . I *try* to get along with everybody."

"Staff Sergeant Kerr?"

Torin started, suddenly aware she'd been staring at nothing for a few moments too long, the implications of shepherding an aristocratic second lieutenant and a combat platoon through a planetfall where no one got to shoot anything suddenly sinking in. *And just in case that doesn't seem like enough fun, let's not forget you slept with said lieutenant.* The one bright light in her morning was that that particular little tidbit hadn't been picked up by the gossip net. "You missed a spot," she said, pointing, and left him to it.

The desire for stimulants following hard on the heels of sentience, coffee had been one of Earth's prime agricultural exports to the Confederation almost from the moment of contact. Most days, Torin appreciated the history of being able to drink exactly the same beverage that her several-times-great-grandmother had back in the dark ages, but today she'd give her right arm for a cup of Krai *sah* and its highly illegal effect on the Human nervous system.

"Staff? I got that download you wanted on the Silsviss."

Resisting the urge to yawn, she leaned into the video pickup. "Thank you, Corporal. Send it to the desk."

"Sending," the tiny image of the Admin corporal acknowledged, and disappeared.

There wasn't much.

In an effort to secure a section of the front, the Confederation planned to lay a new pattern of defense satellites with the optimum pattern placing one satellite directly in the center of 7RG6 or what was now to be called the Silsviss System. Unfortunately, the Silsviss, a warm-blooded reptilian race, had developed a limited intrasystem space travel. Both their moon and the nearest neighboring planet had been reached and they were in the process of building an orbiting space station—although Torin wondered how they'd found room for it given the number of weapons platforms already in orbit. Their technology, while crude by Confederation standards, was more than sufficient to destroy anything put into place without their cooperation—making it essential to get their cooperation.

"Thus the suck-up mission," Torin muttered, refilling her mug from the dispenser in the desk. She didn't know what General Morris had been drinking but spit and polish was not a high priority for a combat unit. If Haysole's sources were right—which they usually were—and the general intended this mission to push him toward promotion, the man was a bigger idiot than she'd first thought.

Unfortunately, he was a *two-star* idiot.

Not counting Lieutenant Jarret and herself, she needed to find thirty-nine Marines—nine four-person fireteams and three sergeants—who had not only been cleared by Med-op for planetfall but who wouldn't inadvertently turn a diplomatic mission into a bloodbath. Even had Sh'quo Company's three infantry platoons been at full strength, choosing nine from the twenty-seven fireteams wouldn't have been easy. Choosing from among the seventeen teams Med-op *had* cleared was a nearly impossible task.

It was a choice that didn't involve the kind of parameters a computer could handle.

First Sergeant Chigma would've called his three Staff Sergeants together. *To pick our brains*, Torin thought darkly. It wasn't a phrase she could say aloud, given the Krai's unfortunate taste for Human tissue. Unfortunately, with her acting as First that left only two platoon NCOs and Med-op had Greg Reghubir tanked for the foreseeable future. Down to one. After a moment's thought, she keyed Sergeant Sagarha's implant code into the desk. He'd taken over what was left of Reghubir's platoon. While it was likely he only knew the fireteams in his own squad, he was still the best source she had. Then she leaned around the edge of the dividing wall and into the next Staff cubicle.

"When you've got a moment, Amanda, I need you at my desk."

"You're running heavy on Humans here; there's got to be another di'Taykan or two available somewhere." Amanda tapped a fingertip against her screen until it protested. "What about Haysole?"

"I'm a little concerned about the class difference with our new lieutenant."

Sh'quo Company's other surviving staff sergeant raised an auburn brow. "You'd rather they worked it out in combat?"

"I'd rather they didn't work it out in front of a dozen diplomats and a species we're trying to impress." Leaning back in her chair, Torin turned toward the other person at the desk. "What do you think, Sagarha?"

Sergeant di'Garn Sagarha frowned thoughtfully. "Might be trouble if di'Ka wasn't an officer. Since he is, that shouldn't be a problem. I'll tell you what I would be concerned about, though: Haysole's a fuk-up. He's fine in combat, but the moment no one's shooting at him, he gets bored, and the next thing you know, he's got three days' latrine duty."

"Nothing wrong with clean toilets," Amanda pointed out.

"Is there anyone *else?*"

The three of them rechecked the lists.

"Not in a complete fireteam, no."

"Then I guess Haysole's going." Torin moved the di'Taykan's fireteam over to the platoon file. "If he gets too bored, I'll shoot at him myself."

"You're a little low on Krai."

"Only four of the six are available, and I'm taking one of them," she pointed out.

"Why not take Ressk?"

"I'd love to. It'd be nice to have a few more brains along on this trip." One of Sergeant Sagarha's squad, Ressk had been known to make secure military programming sit up and beg. Intelligence wanted him, but fortunately for the company, he didn't want Intelligence.

"You take Ressk, you also get Binti Mashona. I've recommended her for sniper school twice, but we keep shipping out before Admin clears the file."

"Like I said, I'd love to, but isn't their team leader still out?"

Sagarha checked his slate. "My Med-op download has Corporal Hollice cleared for duty in thirty-six hours."

"I wonder why mine doesn't," Torin muttered, tracing a path through the icons. "Some idiot probably sent it to the First's desk."

"Some idiot probably thought that's where you'd be," Amanda pointed out, adding, "I thought Hollice lost a thumb?"

"He did, but Ressk dropped it in a cold box, and the corpsmen had it reattached before we got back to the station."

"Bet Ressk was pissed at losing his snack," she snickered.

"Marines do not eat other Marines," Torin muttered absently. The eight teams they'd managed to come up with had used up all the "A" list and taken a few off the "B." Pickings were getting slim. Finally, she sighed. "I don't see any way around it. We're going to have to use Corporal Conn's team."

"No." Amanda shook her head. "I promised him some time to see his daughter. He's got leave coming."

"Point one, General Morris canceled all leaves. Point two, he's all we've got left. It can't be Algress, not with a reptilian life-form on the planet—not after Rarna IV."

"I thought Psych took care of that."

After a pregnant pause, the three NCOs snorted simultaneously.

"It'll have to be Conn," Torin repeated.

"But his daughter . . ."

With life expectancy at around a hundred and twenty old Earth years, most Human Marines put off having kids until they were either out of the Corps or had decided to make it a career. Corporal Grad Conn had fallen in love, applied for married quarters on station, and started a family. His daughter Myrna Troi had become Sh'quo Company's unofficial mascot and everyone took a turn at spoiling her. Even Torin, who usually found kids about as inexplicable as the H'san, thought she was pretty cute. And it was hard not to admire a four-year-old who could disassemble a hygiene unit into so many pieces it took three engineers most of a duty shift to put it back together.

"Extend his liberty until we assemble for boarding."

"On whose authority?"

"Mine."

Voice conspiratorially lowered, Amanda leaned toward the di'Taykan. "She's even beginning to sound like a First Sergeant."

"Very dominant," Sagarha agreed, smiling broadly.

"Very in charge of your butts," Torin reminded them.

"Crap." Amanda straightened, a sudden realization drawing her brows in over the bridge of her nose. "This means I'm going to be acting First while you're gone. If I find out you've volunteered for this mission to get out of processing those new recruits . . ."

"Shall I tell the captain you're volunteering to go in my place?"

"Not fukking likely."

"What about sergeants?" Sagarha wondered.

"Are you volunteering?"

He grinned. "Not fukking likely."

"I'd like to take Doctorow; he's a pain in the ass, but he's a socially apt pain in the ass and that could come in handy. Unfortunately, Med-op won't release him until Psych has a chance to go in and do some dirty work."

"You should tell them he's always like that."

"I did. They didn't listen. That said, I want Glicksohn, Chou, and Trey."

"Two humans and a di'Taykan?"

"The lieutenant's di'Taykan. We'll balance."

The three of them stared down at the final list of thirty-nine names. "You think the captain'll rubber stamp this?" Amanda asked.

"He'd better."

"Something I've always wondered. . . . what's a rubber stamp?"

Torin shrugged, uploading the list into her slate. "Damned if I know."

A short visit to the armory turned into over an hour of listening to complaints. *I should've bailed when I heard "Hey, Kerr, aren't you acting First?" I can't believe Chig put up with that.*

Running late, Torin grabbed lunch at a species-neutral cantina in the core. Her day thus far called out for a big dish of poutine and a beer; unfortunately duty called out louder and she settled for a bowl of noodles garnished not very liberally with an indeterminate mix of greens and meat. *There are times*, she thought, deciding it might be best if the meat remained unidentified, *when I almost wish I'd stayed on the farm.*

"Can I join you?"

Then there were those times when there was no *almost* about it. "It's a public cantina, sir."

Pulling up a stool, Lieutenant Jarret rested his elbows on the table and smiled. "And if it wasn't?"

"Fraternization between the ranks is discouraged for a good reason, Lieutenant—di'Taykan with di'Taykan excepted, of course. It undermines the structure of command and it can lead to distorted judgment in life-and-death situations."

"Are you telling me last night—you and I—never happened?"

"No, sir, I'm telling you it won't happen again." She stared into her noodles. "Although it would certainly help my position with, oh, just about everyone, if we both pretend it never happened."

"Why?"

"Because every time I look at you I'm going to think of . . ." Lilac eyes glittered, and she smiled in spite of herself. "Yeah, all right, it's a pleasant memory, but . . ."

". . . you can't have every Human in the platoon thinking about it every time you pass on one of my orders." He returned the smile. "I understand the species parameters, Staff Sergeant Kerr, as regrettable as I may find them, which is what I actually sat down to tell you."

"Oh." A sudden burst of giggles from across the cantina gave Torin an excuse to move her attention to a small table overwhelmed by three Human teenagers.

"What is it?"

"You're being watched, sir."

He glanced over his shoulder at them, and, after a moment of stunned silence, one teen sighed, "Elves," while the other two just sighed.

The off-the-record reaction of the First Human Contact Team upon meeting the di'Taykan had been, "Holy fuk, they're elves!" To the horror of right thinking xenoanthropologists everywhere, the name stuck. Once exposed to the mythology that had engendered the remark, the di'Taykan as a whole didn't seem to mind, and a number of the di'Taykan had embraced the lifestyle wholeheartedly. During basic training, Torin had actually met a di'Taykan who'd been named Celeborn after a character in an old Terran book.

The sighs turned to giggles.

"I think you may need to readjust your masker, sir."

"I think you've forgotten what it's like to be their age."

"And happy to have forgotten." She pushed the empty container into the recycling chute and stood. "It's 1340, sir. The captain wants to see us at 1400."

Lieutenant Jarret stood as well and nodded toward her slate as they crossed the cantina in step. "Is there anything specific I should know about the people you've chosen?"

"They all would've preferred that I'd chosen someone else, but other than that, no." Torin considered it a good sign that the lieutenant was asking her for information. Too many officers came out of training thinking they were going to win the war single-handedly. Fortunately, that kind of officer usually didn't last long in front of a combat unit—sometimes the enemy even got a chance to remove them. She frowned thoughtfully as they took the stairs up a deck. "They're all good people to have at your side in a fight, sir, but I'm not sure how well they'll manage ceremonial duties."

"General Morris seemed to think that the Silsviss would be more impressed by your battle honors than by an ability to march in straight lines."

"Lucky for us."

"However, he did suggest that we run over some basic drill while in transit."

Torin snorted.

"You don't think it's necessary, Sergeant."

"Necessary? Yes, sir. Survivable?" She shrugged.

"The general seems to think that the platoon can consider this a sort of working leave."

"Does he, sir?"

"You don't?"

"Either we're working, or we're on leave. We can't logically do both."

"Good point, but the general thinks . . ."

Pausing outside the captain's door, Torin sighed and turned to face the lieutenant. It was easy to forget, given their maturity in other areas, that a di'Taykan second lieutenant was as young and inexperienced as a Human one. "Begging your pardon, sir, but you'll be giving orders to this platoon, not to the general. It might be best if you think for yourself."

His ear points drooped slightly, but his tone showed none of the embarrassment he was clearly feeling. "I'll take that under consideration, Sergeant."

"Thank you, sir." She meant it sincerely and made it sound as much like *thank you for listening* as she could. Nobody liked to be patronized, second lieutenants uncertain of their own power least of all.

Lieutenant Jarret studied her face, then suddenly smiled. "You know the general also told me that a good Staff Sergeant is worth her weight in charge canisters."

"I suspect General Morris has never been in combat, sir."

"Why?"

"Because if that's all he's getting for a good staff sergeant, he's getting screwed . . ." Returning his smile, she stepped aside as the captain's door opened. ". . . sir."

Two

"Is this all of them?"

"All but one, sir."

Lieutenant Jarret, who'd been studying the Marines milling about below him in the loading bay, turned to face his staff sergeant. "One?" he asked.

The emphasis made his actual question unmistakable. Torin, who'd been trying to avoid mentioning names, no longer had a choice. "Corporal Conn, sir."

"The man whose extended liberty you authorized?"

"Yes, sir."

"He does know we're leaving this morning?"

Torin winced at the deceptively mild tone. There was something about the way the di'Taykan used sarcasm that could cut through bulkheads. Before she could answer, an imperious voice demanding to be put down rose above the general noise, and she smiled. "That's him now, sir."

Jarret watched the big man lift a flame-haired child off his shoulders and set her carefully on the deck. "He brought his daughter?"

"Yes, sir, Myrna Troi. She always comes to see the company off."

"I can't get over what Humans are willing to expose their children to," Jarret mused as the little girl ran about, accepting the homage of the platoon as her due. "Until they reach di' phase, Taykan are a lot more sheltered."

"We're a pretty flexible species, sir."

"And we're not?" Lilac hair lifted, adding entendre.

"Lieutenant . . ."

"Sorry." He grinned, clearly not at all sorry, and headed for the stairs. "Since Corporal Conn has decided to join us, let's get started."

*   *   *

"Probably I'll be bigger when you get back. Probably I'll be this big." Up on her toes, Myrna Troi waved her hand in the air as high as she could, which was just barely higher than the top of her crouching father's head. "Probably I gonna be a surgent," she told him sternly, russet brows drawn in over emerald eyes. "And then you gotta do what I say and then you gotta not leave."

"I'm sorry, sweetie. Daddy doesn't want to go, he has to."

She stared at him for a long moment, then leaned into his shoulder and sighed deeply. "I know."

"Take care of your mama while I'm gone."

"Probably Mama will cry. Mama says you shouldn't be a Marine no more. Mama says you should work on the station. Mama says probably Trisha got her boobs done."

Looking a little taken aback by the last confidence, Corporal Conn kissed the top of his daughter's head.

"You know what else? Probably my tooth will fall out when you're gone."

Torin moved past the two and went to stand by the huge double lock. *At least this time we know he'll be coming back to her*, she thought as she had the platoon fall in. And then, just so as not to tempt fate, she added a prudent *probably*.

Three days out from the station, the Marine package of living quarters, mess, gym, armory, and air support locked on to the Confederation Ship *Berganitan* bringing the diplomatic party from in-sector.

Moments after the all clear sounded, the entire ship folded into Susumi space and everyone but the plasma engineers settled in to wait. Time in Susumi space was pretty much irrelevant to everyone but those who spent it working out the calculations that would bring the ship back into real space at essentially the moment it left, although a considerable number of light-years away.

"Good news. Second Lieutenant Jarret graduated in the middle of his class."

Several members of number one squad glanced up, and someone asked, "Why is that good news, Res?"

Bare feet up on one of the tables filling the area between the double row of bunks, Ressk stretched out his toes and grinned toothily up at Juan Checya, his fireteam's heavy gunner. "Top of the class would've made him an insufferable overachiever and bottom of the class would've made him a *chrick*."

"Edible?"

"Edible."

Checya snorted and dropped onto his bunk. "What the fuk don't you consider edible?"

"Not much," Ressk admitted, fingers dancing over his slate. "Oh, my, this is interesting. One of the lieutenant's parental units was Admiral di'Ka Tereal, now ex-Admiral qui'Ka Tereal, and she tried to block his application to Ventris Station."

"Wanted him in the fukking Navy?"

"Wanted him out of the fighting entirely."

Corporal di'Merk Mysho tossed her brush into her locker and leaned over Ressk's shoulder. "It's a qui'Taykan thing," she explained. "There's nothing more conservative than a breeder. Aren't those restricted files?"

"Depends on what you mean by restricted."

"Not intended to be accessed by all and sundry."

"Which am I, all or sundry?"

She smacked him on the back of the head. "Didn't Staff Sergeant Kerr specifically tell you not to invade classified areas while we're on the *Berganitan*?"

"Technically, she told me not to invade classified areas *of* the *Berganitan*. I'm in Division records; all Marine, no Navy, no problem."

"Unless you get caught."

He brought a cup of *sah* to his mouth with one foot and took a long swallow. "Do I ever?"

"Do you ever what? Regret not eating Hollice's thumb when you had the chance?" Pulling the cup from his toes, Binti Mashona, the fourth member of the fireteam, set it back on the table. "You know I hate it when you do that with food."

"You're just jealous my species has more opposable parts than yours."

"I'm just thinking that foot spent most of the day in boots doing drill."

"Speaking of opposable parts," Juan interrupted, leaning down from his bunk. "You get lucky with that service tech back on station?"

"Nah." Binti pulled a game biscuit out of her locker and slid it into the side of her slate. "She didn't want to get involved with someone from a combat unit."

"Involved? Fuk, I thought you just wanted to get laid."

"If you wanted to get laid, why didn't you ask a di'Taykan?" Mysho wondered.

"Because once you pop your masker, I don't have a choice. Couldn't change my mind if I wanted to."

"But if you *wanted* sex . . ."

Ressk snorted. "It's a Human thing, Mysho, you wouldn't understand."

"Speaking of Human things, you guys hear what the staff is up to tonight?" Binti grinned, her teeth startlingly white against the rich mahogany of her skin. "Big fancy reception to meet these diplomats we're supposed to honor guard. Little tiny bits of food on platters, dress blacks, and polite conversation."

There was a moment of startled silence, then Juan slowly shook his head. "Staff's gonna fukking hate that."

"Anyone want to see how badly she hates it?" Ressk tapped his slate suggestively. "I can tap into the ship's security vids . . ." He let his voice trail off as the Marines gathered around the table exchanged speculative glances and then turned in unison toward Mysho.

"What?"

"You rank, Mysh."

"Oh, no, Conn got his second hook long before I did."

"Conn's off trying to rabbit something shiny for Myrna. Your decision."

She muttered something in her own language, then threw up her hands. "Why not. You're going to do it anyway, Ressk, so we might as well all get a look at it."

"Can one of you give me a hand with this? I can't get the jacket to hang straight."

Nearest the hatch separating the staff sergeants' quarters from the NCO Common, Sergeant Mike Glicksohn stood and beckoned Torin closer. "And aren't you just the picture of martial elegance."

"Aren't I just," she agreed, handing him her belt. "I can't remember the last time I got this tarted up."

"When you made Staff?"

"No, that was a field promotion—I was covered in Staff Sergeant

Guntah's guts and the only thing black on me was my fingernails where frostbite had started to set in."

"I remember." Anne Chou looked up from her slate. "Planet was barely habitable—we'd have ignored it if the Others hadn't tried to set up a mining base."

"So now *we* have a mining base there, and someday we'll have to go back to the frozen hole in the ass end of space to protect it."

"War is progress," Glicksohn muttered, stepping back. "That's got it."

"Thanks." Moving to the wall, Torin polarized the vid screen. "You think there's a reason they make these collars so uncomfortable?" she asked, checking her reflection. "Does it seem hot in here?" Working her shoulders under the black cloth, she wondered why she suddenly felt so . . . "Trey!"

The three Humans turned toward the other end of the room where the di'Taykan sergeant had just come through from the showers.

"Give me a break," she sighed, as she walked naked to her room. "What am I supposed to clip it to? Besides, you're Human, repression's good for you. And you," she continued, pausing to grin at Torin, "should thank me because before the Corps absorbed the di'Taykan, you would've had to wear a hat with that."

"Thank you," Torin told the closed door. "And thank *you*," she added as Chou turned the air recyclers on high. "Speaking of maskers, anyone know where Haysole is? I've barely seen him since we locked."

"Zero gee bubble. He said something about trying to work his way through the *Berganitan*'s crew."

"Vacuum jockeys, too?"

"Not all of them." Glicksohn settled back in his chair and picked up the pouch of beer he'd discarded earlier. "I've got a game set up at 2130, and a few showed interest."

"Playing on neutral ground?"

"Close as you can get on this flying fish tank."

"Who's going with you in case the vjs get ugly?"

Glicksohn snorted. "Is there any other kind?"

"Mike . . ."

"Sam Austin's going and Esket from the aircrew. Happy?" When she nodded, he grinned. "You worry too much."

"It's my job. And speaking of my job, did either of you . . . any of you," she corrected as Trey came out of her quarters, "manage a species check on the diplomats?"

"Dornagain and Mictok," Trey told her, dropping into a chair.

Glicksohn tossed her a beer. "I thought the Silsviss were reptilian; why not send Raszar or Niln? Let them know they're not the only lizards around before they join up."

"Or why not H'san?" Chou wondered. "Everybody likes the H'san."

"I'm guessing that they're not sending reptilians because they don't want to suggest competition." Torin flicked a bit of lint off her campaign ribbons. "And there was a H'san on the first contact team; the Silsviss kept remarking on how much it smelled like food."

"That's what I said, everybody likes the H'san."

"I know the Mictok are supposed to be these great diplomats," Glicksohn muttered, "but every time I see one, this little voice inside my head keeps screaming, *Get it off me! Get it off me!*"

Before she could answer, Torin's implant chimed.

Lieutenant Jarret is waiting for you in the corridor.

Before the di'Taykan, both the Marine Corps and the Navy had worn dress blues, but the induction of a race with pastel-colored hair and eyes had demanded a change. The Navy chose gray—dove gray for their pilots, slightly darker for the engineers who made Susumi space possible, and charcoal gray for everyone else. The Corps wore black. Regardless of trade or rank or designation, a Marine was first a Marine.

Fortunately, those with low tolerances for pastel over camouflage didn't tend to go into combat units.

Lieutenant Jarret was waiting for her by the ladder that connected the platoon to their air support, one deck up. The Corps prided itself on the flexibility of its packaging as well as its people and could snap together transportation units to match any configuration of troops. As Torin joined him, pilot and copilot slid down the ladder from above.

"Captain Fiona Daniels, Second Lieutenant Ghard, this is Staff Sergeant Torin Kerr. The sergeant will be joining us tonight at the request of Captain Carveg of the *Berganitan*."

"Glad to have you with us, Staff. The vjs are going to have us severely outnumbered."

Torin returned the captain's smile. "Happy to be providing backup, Captain." Fiona Daniels had the kind of rakish good looks that showed up on Human recruiting posters. Dark hair, green eyes, one deep dimple

punctuating straight white teeth—only someone who'd seen Med-op reconstruction up close could tell from the slight difference in tone that
the skin over the entire left side of her face had recently been replaced.
She'd been one of the pilots who'd got Sh'quo Company off the ground
after that last disastrous planetfall, and if backup extended to smacking
around a few vacuum jockeys for her, Torin would be more than happy
to oblige.

On the other side of the lock, the walls changed to Navy colors and their
implants simultaneously asked their destination.

Lieutenant Jarret's hair flattened slightly in irritation, but he answered
politely. "Wardroom."

*At the end of this passageway, take the vertical to deck seven. The
wardroom is three doors from the vertical on the left. Please proceed.*

"Don't let it bother you, Jarret," Captain Daniels advised as they began
walking. "It's a Navy thing. The vjs can't find their ass without a homing
beacon."

"What's going on?"

"Ressk's tapping into that fancy party Staff's going to." Juan ducked as
Binti swung at him. "Well, I'm not going to fukking lie."

Corporal Hollice shouldered in beside Mysho and leaned over the curve
of the Krai's head. "Those are . . . okay, were . . . Navy security codes."

"He's in?" Someone at the back of the pack demanded.

"I'm in." Ressk reached out and very carefully shoved his slate into the
port on the wall vid. The screen went black, then gray, then slowly focused.

Hollice sighed. "I'd just like to go on record as being out of the room
the whole time this access was being forced."

"Seduced," Ressk corrected, fiddling with the contrast.

"Hey, look, Mictok."

The Humans present suppressed a racial shudder as a trio of Mictok
accepted drinks from one of the commissariat.

The camera angle changed.

"I see Navy all over the fukking place," Juan complained. "Where's our
team?"

"There, at the hatch."

*   *   *

As the two pilots led the way into the room, Torin glanced over at Jarret. Given the constant movement of his hair and the way he carried his weight forward on the balls of his feet, he was nervous. She didn't blame him. Most second lieutenants learned how to command with their platoon hidden in the midst of a battalion planetfall—not out in full view of a ceremonial mission. It couldn't help that every chest in the room but his and the diplomats carried a rainbow of campaign ribbons.

"Remember that the Navy's on our side, no matter how it sounds," she murmured as they crossed toward Captain Carveg. "We're sort of like siblings; bottom line, we stand together. As for the civilians, the older races think we're savages because we're willing to fight to maintain the Confederation, so the most rudimentary of social skills impresses them. Gracious manners'll knock them right back on their collective tails."

He half turned and his hair lifted slightly.

She shrugged. "Or spinnerets. Whatever."

When the officers had been introduced and greeted, Captain Carveg turned to Torin, smiling broadly. "The staff sergeant and I have met, although she was a sergeant at the time and I, a mere commander."

Although Torin could have picked the half-dozen Krai in Sh'quo Company out of a crowd, for the most part, they all looked alike to her. She knew it was speciesist but the facial ridges, so easily identifiable to another Krai, told her gender and nothing more. Skin tones never left the mid-range of Human norm, neither as dark as Binti Mashona nor as light as Captain Rose. The few bristles of hair around the base of the broad skull were no help at all. The di'Taykan, who used scent as much as appearance, had a distinct advantage.

So, at least four years ago, she'd met a female commander named Carveg . . .

"The *CS Charest*, leaving Sai Genist?"

The captain nodded. "I'm surprised you remember."

Torin grinned, careful not to show too much tooth. "You skipped a battle cruiser into the atmosphere and fried a fighting wedge of Other ships, saving at least a dozen of your pilots. From where I stood, it was an impressive light show."

"My captain had been killed in the attack, and this was the first battle where the Others had used the new cluster technology," Carveg explained to the listening officers. "I took a gamble that paid off, although considering the mess it made of the hull, I don't think the engineers ever forgave me. Meanwhile, dirtside, Sergeant Kerr and her squad pulled three of my downed pilots out of the wreckage of their escape pods and kept them alive at some risk to her squad until we cleared the system for med-evac."

"What's so dangerous about carrying stretchers?" a di'Taykan naval officer wondered.

Lieutenant Jarret answered before Torin had a chance. "When you're carrying stretchers," he said, in a tone so pleasant the other di'Taykan's eyes lightened, "you can't use your weapon. Three stretchers meant a minimum of six Marines were defenseless and the strength of the squad almost halved. But we don't leave *anyone* behind to die." The emphasis was a gentle, aristocratic chastisement.

Bet that's a di'Taykan with more than two letters in her name, Torin thought, hiding a smile. The most junior officer in the room had been born into a family who'd been holding power from the beginning of their civilization. *He might be starting from scratch with the rest of us, but he can handle his own species just fine.*

"And never think we don't appreciate that," Captain Carveg told him, not bothering to mask her approval. "Come, let me make you known to the people you'll be accompanying."

"What's happening now?"

"More introductions."

On the screen, one of the Dornagain unfolded to his full height and bowed gravely.

"Fuk, those guys are big."

"That's likely why they're sending them, in case there's trouble."

"Nah, that's why they're sending us. The Dornagain don't fight."

"And even if they did, you ever seen one move fast enough to scratch his butt before the itch moved?"

"If they don't fight, whadda they use them fukking claws for?"

"Shellfish." The squad turned toward Hollice, who shrugged, "Don't you guys remember those 'Founders of the Confederation' vids we got in school?"

"All I remember is that the H'san sing every morning at sunrise. No matter what sun."

"No kidding. All I remember is that the H'san like cheese."

"Everyone remembers *that*."

* * *

"Lieutenant Jarret, Sergeant Kerr, this is Ambassador Krik'vir." Captain Carveg replaced the mandible clash in the middle of the name with a snap of her teeth Torin couldn't help but envy. Krai tooth enamel was so tough, bioengineers kept trying to replicate it as atmospheric shielding on the Confederation's vacuum-to-atmosphere vehicles.

The Mictok ambassador dipped her antennae in greeting. "We are very pleased to meet you both. We appreciate so many of you being able to accommodate us on such short notice."

Lieutenant Jarret inclined his head. "General Morris' orders, ma'am."

"Yes, of course." Amused, her outer mandibles clattered softly against the inner. "We forget you had no need to achieve consensus. We sometimes wish we had the same freedom. Allow us to introduce you to our staff; those you will also be guarding."

Get it off me! Get it off me! Torin had little success in putting Glick-sohn's words out of her head as the next level of introductions were made. Although the beauty of Mictok art touched almost every known species and their diplomatic skills had been instrumental in creating the Confederation, Humans looked at them and saw giant spiders. Fortunately for Human/Mictok relations, the latter were almost impossible to insult.

Ambassador Krik'vir's staff consisted of only three other Mictok, a surprisingly small number for a communal species, although one more than the minimum. Under the right conditions, three Mictok could begin a new nest, one becoming Queen, one a breeding male, and the third providing for the happy couple until the first eggs could hatch. If necessary, the male also became the incubator. Torin had often wondered how they chose but had never quite had the nerve to ask.

Introductions to the Dornagain ambassador and his staff followed with much mutual bowing and exchanging of meaningless pleasantries. Dornagain names sounded strange to Human ears since they referred to personality traits or physical descriptions and changed several times over the course of a long life. The ambassador currently bore the apt although unwieldy name of Listens Wisely And Considers All.

Her rank, or rather lack of rank, exempting her from much of the social ritual, Torin was able to stand back and appreciate the way Lieutenant Jarret handled the situation. His hair had stilled as his apprehension had dissipated and he seemed to be enjoying himself. As a member of an ancient house, his background made him perfectly suited to do the pretty with their civilian charges, and she had to admit that, green though he might be in combat experience, he was the perfect choice to command this mission.

And he won't be quite so green by the time someone starts shooting at us. An officer who'd had command experience of any kind before going into combat created a win/win situation as far as Torin was concerned, and it helped her to think more kindly of General Morris—in spite of the stranglehold her dress uniform had achieved.

Parity with the Mictok necessitated that there be four Dornagain. Well aware that their size made them intimidating to smaller species—which, from their perspective, was just about everyone else in the Confederation— they moved slowly apart when the introductions were over.

The four Marines in tow, Captain Carveg interrupted an argument on cellular plasticity to make them known to Dr. Planton Leor . . .

". . . the environmental physician who'll be ensuring that you'll all remain healthy during your stay on Silsvah. He's predominantly a research physician," she added sotto voce as they moved away. "I'll be sending a couple of corpsmen down as well, just in case."

The rest of the civilian party consisted of the Charge d'Affaires and her two assistants, all three Rakva like the doctor.

"There was a Rakva who had a canteen on station back when I was with the 9th," Ressk mused. "Great cook."

"Why would you care?" Binti wondered, looking up from her slate. "You'll eat anything you can wrestle down your throat two falls out of three."

"There's a difference between eat and enjoy," the Krai reminded her. "This guy could make a *juklae* so light you were convinced you were eating it in zero gee."

"Yeah? Too bad he's not here instead of this environmental physician guy." She snorted. "Like we never made a strange planetfall before." Shaking a finger in the air, she raised her voice into an approximation of a Rakva whistle. "Now don't touch that, we don't know where it's been."

"I, for one, am not looking a gift physician in the mouth."

Grinning, Binti glanced toward the dark rectangle of Corporal Hollice's bunk. "I don't think you *can* look a Rakva in the mouth, Hol. Those beaky things aren't set up that way."

A hand appeared long enough to flash a very Human response. "Short-sighted. That's why you're still a private."

"You won't die. That's why I'm still a private."

"You're my reason to live."

"I'm honored."

"You should be. Now, shut up, I'm trying to sleep."

Still grinning, Binti turned her attention back to her slate.

The rest of the squad had gotten bored with watching diplomacy in action—even illegally obtained. Most had wandered off to the mess, but Ressk had stayed by the screen. As the introductions ended and Captain Carveg left the Marines by the refreshment table, he hastily reset the security vid parameters to follow the *Berganitan*'s captain.

"Now that's what I call a set of *amalork*," he murmured, settling back in his chair.

He could watch Staff Sergeant Kerr any time; female Krai in the infantry were few and far between.

Chewing on something vaguely kelplike, Torin watched Lieutenant Jarret work the crowd and wondered why he'd opted for combat when he was so good at . . . she supposed diplomacy was the politest thing to call it, although the phrase "kissing butt" kept coming to mind. And why wasn't *he* being strangled by *his* dress uniform? She ran a finger under her collar, then reached for another kelp thing.

"We are pleased to welcome another reptilian species into the Confederation."

Torin hadn't heard the Mictok come up behind her, but there could be no mistaking the accent—mandibles were just not made to deal with the softer consonants. Forcing herself to turn slowly, she found herself face-to-essentially-face with the ambassador.

"The first contact team indicated that the Silsviss have a very vibrant and vital culture. We are looking forward to exploring it."

There didn't seem to be much to say to that, so Torin merely smiled and nodded. As it was a little disconcerting to see her reflection in the nearer of the ambassador's eyestalks, she dropped her gaze to the brilliant design painted onto the exoskeleton.

The eyestalk turned to follow her line of sight. "Do you like it, Staff Sergeant?"

"It's beautiful, ma'am."

"We think so, too, but we were not sure how it would appear to a biocular species." The foreleg with the least number of differentiated digits rose and tapped Torin's ribbon bar. "These are more than decoration, yes?"

"Yes, ma'am. They represent where I've been and what I've done." A barely remembered lecture on interspecies relations had suggested it was best to keep cultural explanations simple. She doubted she could make it much simpler than that.

"In reference to the fighting that you do?"

"Yes, ma'am."

The Mictok sighed—at least Torin assumed that's what the sound meant. "We do not understand why the Others insist on pushing into Confederation space. We do not like to think of sentient species having to die, even if it is the few dying to protect the many."

"We don't exactly like to think of it either, ma'am."

She made the noise again. "No, we don't suppose you do. We have often wondered why a smart weapon could not be created . . ."

"Begging your pardon, ma'am," Torin interrupted stiffly, "but you've got forty-two smart weapons on board right now. Forty-five, including our air support," she amended, hearing Captain Daniels' voice rise across the room. "You couldn't possibly program a computer to consider all the variables that can occur in combat."

"And when there is finally the development of a true A-I?"

"You'd just be sending a different sentient species to die."

Ambassador Krik'vir tapped Torin's ribbon bar again. "If one of these is not for debate, Staff Sergeant Kerr, we think it should be. Lieutenant Jarret wears no colors," she continued, not waiting for a response. "He is very new."

It wasn't a question, so Torin waited for the ambassador to make her point.

"He knows how important the Silsviss are to our defenses in this sector?"

"Yes, ma'am, he knows."

"We understand the Silsviss to be impressed by warriors. General Morris has made an interesting choice."

"General Morris knows what he's doing, ma'am." Personal opinion of the general aside, Torin wasn't about to have him criticized by a non-Marine. Besides, this evening's exercise had pretty much convinced her that Jarret had been chosen to deal with the diplomats, and the *rest* of them had been chosen to impress the Silsviss. When the ambassador repeated her thought aloud, she was startled enough to actually meet the Mictok's eyes where eight reflections stared back at her in astonishment. Unable to avoid realizing that she looked like an idiot, she closed her mouth and the eight reflections closed theirs.

Ambassador Krik'vir's outer mandibles clattered against the inner. "We do not read minds, Staff Sergeant, but it was not hard for us to guess your thoughts." The sweep of a foreleg indicated the rest of the room. "Here tonight there are four Marines as well as four Mictok, four Dornagain, and in order to be equal, four Rakva. It is, as you Humans say, appallingly politically correct. We think you will have an easier time fulfilling your commission than your lieutenant will fulfilling his. You, after all, have only one species to impress."

It might have been a warning. "And we will, ma'am."

"Good. We apologize for interrupting you while you were feeding, but we are pleased we had this opportunity to talk."

As the ambassador scuttled back into the crowd, Torin snagged a drink off a passing tray and took a long swallow. *Get it off me*, she sighed silently.

"I'm a little surprised you're coming back with us." Hand on the identity plate, Captain Daniels stood aside while the other three went through the lock, then followed and cycled it closed. "I'd have thought you'd have hooked up with another di'Taykan and spent the night away."

"Actually, I was wondering what would happen if I unmasked around a Dornagain."

"A Dornagain?"

"Most sentient carbon-based mammals react."

"Are you out of your mind? The females have got to weigh close to two hundred kilos and the males aren't much smaller. If you weren't crushed, you'd be . . ." Then she caught sight of the expression on Jarret's face. "I can't believe I fell for that."

The grin broadened. "Fell for what?"

Trouble is, Torin mused, following along behind the three officers, *with a di'Taykan there's no way to be sure they're kidding*. Some of them, given the opportunity, would pop their maskers in front of a Dornagain just to see what would happen. Lieutenant Jarret didn't seem to be the type, but their previous contact certainly proved he could pop it off fast enough when a willing partner appeared. *And you're never going to think of that again*, she reminded herself, tonguing her implant for the duty report.

"What do you think, Staff?"

Attention abruptly switched back to her companions, she tongued her implant off and shrugged apologetically. "Sorry, sir. I wasn't listening."

"Checking on the children?" Jarret wondered.

"Yes, sir."

He nodded, satisfied. Torin was impressed. A great many junior officers took months to realize that no news was good news. Some of the more officious never caught on.

"I was wondering," Captain Daniels asked, catching her eye, "if you had an opinion on the evening."

Torin had overheard more conversations than she'd been a part of. Most of them had been amazingly inane. "A military opinion?"

"Please. I think we've all heard as many uninformed opinions on the state of the buffet, the other species present, and the new season of *All My Offspring* as we can stomach."

"There's nothing like having a Mictok overanalyze your favorite vid," Lieutenant Ghard sighed.

Nothing Torin could think of anyway. "The civilians seem concerned that the Silsviss come in on our side," she began, organizing her impressions as she spoke, "although the doctor isn't pleased about bringing a fourth aggressive species into the Confederation."

Representatives of the three other aggressive species snorted.

"The Navy seems concerned that the Others will figure out what we're doing and blow this new defensive array into atoms before it's up and running. And one of the vjs who took the first contact team in said we'd better recruit the Silsviss before the Others do because she wouldn't, and I quote, want to meet those s.o.bs in battle."

Jarret nodded. "I heard that, too. Good thing we're going in as friends."

"All right, people, the clock is running again; we're forty-nine hours to planetfall. You've all seen the vids on the Silsviss, you've heard how important it is to impress them enough so that they join the Confederation before the Others move in. Given that, over the next forty-nine hours we'll be practicing ceremonial drill morning, afternoon, and evening. Or the shipboard equivalent thereof."

"Aw, Staff, we've been drilling . . ."

"I know." Torin fixed Haysole with a basilisk smile. "I've seen you." She lifted her gaze to include the entire platoon. "I've seen all of you. And that's why you're doing *more* drill."

"I thought the Silsviss were supposed to be impressed by our military prowess," a Human voice muttered.

"I've got a better idea, Drake . . ."

The heavy gunner started, while those around him snickered at his discomfort.

". . . let's start by impressing them with how well you can tell your left foot from your right. All of you; flight deck, with your weapon, 0830. Dismissed."

She stepped back to stand by the lieutenant as the platoon moved muttering out of the mess.

"Do they really need more drill?" he asked quietly.

"Not really. Considering that none of them have done it since basic, they're surprisingly good."

"Then why?"

"You don't want them thinking too much before a planetfall."

"But this isn't like other planetfalls."

"None of them are, sir. None of them are."

THREE

"**N**ot a bad looking place." Through the cloud cover, the orbital view of Silsvah showed two large land masses and half a dozen smaller ones. Although a little smaller than Terra with a little less ocean, Torin found the planet had a comfortable familiarity—even though she'd been born on Paradise, the first of the colony worlds, and had never personally seen the Human home world from space.

"Mind you," she muttered thoughtfully to no one in particular, "the fact that no one'll be trying to shoot us out of the sky as we land adds to the attraction."

As the *Berganitan* began passing over a storm that seemed to involve half the southern hemisphere, her implant chimed.

DIGNITARIES APPROACHING.

Wincing, she tongued the volume down and hurried across the flight deck to join Lieutenant Jarret. Sergeants and above had received the Silsviss translation program and the upload had scrambled her defaults, forcing her to reset almost every function. Her next promotion would net her a new implant and she had to admit that, as little as she enjoyed the techs cracking her jaw, she was looking forward to the new hardware. Among other things, she'd gain direct access to the Navy net and power enough to reach any ship not in Susumi space should the company need to be pulled out. Her next promotion would also get her a few years away from combat and she had to admit she was looking forward to that as well.

"Did you hear, sir?"

Jarret grinned, lilac hair flicking back and forth. "I heard. Get them ready, Staff Sergeant."

"Yes, sir." She called the platoon to attention as the hatch cycled open. She'd intended to have them tucked safely away on the VTA before the civilians boarded but the lieutenant had wanted everyone to get a look at each other before they left the ship. It was a good idea—the fewer surprises dirtside, the better—although she'd been a little surprised that her brand-new second lieutenant had been the one to have it.

The platoon looked good; not quite so dangerous as it did fully loaded, but good. And if there were a few nonregulation weapons tucked away in nonregulation places, well, these people were used to using every trick it took to stay alive, and she wasn't going to take that edge away.

The Mictok and the Rakva arrived at the top of the gangway before the four Dornagain had ambled across half the flight deck. Face expressionless, Torin amused herself by watching how every deliberate movement rippled new highlights through their thick fur. Then she amused herself by imagining them attempting to outrun enemy fire. Then she wasn't amused.

Captain Carveg should've sent them down an hour ago—then maybe we'd have left on schedule.

The Dornagain ambassador reached the bottom of the gangway.

Maybe two hours ago.

The ramp had been designed for loading—and off-loading—armored personnel carriers. After some discussion of weight ratios and stress factors, the Dornagain went up it in pairs.

Somehow I doubt the Honorable Listens Wisely And Considers All has considered what a pain in the ass this lack of speed is going to be for the rest of us.

When the last rippling highlight had disappeared into the forward compartment, Torin double-timed the platoon up into the belly of the beast, past the two APCs, past the armory, and into the troop compartment.

"Sergeants, sound off when squads are webbed in."

"Squad One, secure."

"Squad Two, secure."

"Haysole, secure your feet or I'll cut them off," Glicksohn growled as the di'Taykan kicked a strap free.

Turquoise eyes narrowed, hair flat against his head, Haysole retrieved the strap. "I don't like it when I can't move my feet, Sarge."

"What you like has crap all to do with life. Tie them down." Cinching his own webbing tight, Glicksohn shot a "Why me?" look at Torin and snapped, "Squad Three, secure."

"Platoon secured for drop, sir."

Lieutenant Jarret had barely passed the information along to the pilot when the VTA dropped free of the *Berganitan.* "Making up for the Dornagain?" he wondered aloud as the platoon bounced against its webbing. "Or just trying to beat that storm in the southern hemisphere?"

"More likely force of habit," Torin told him. "General Morris, in his infinite two-starred wisdom, assigned a combat pilot to this mission— probably still trying to impress the Silsviss with our military might. Combat pilots flying VTA troop carriers hit dirt as quickly as possible in an attempt not to get themselves and their cargo blown out of the air on the way down."

"And in your experience, when they hit dirt, is their cargo able to walk away?"

"Yes, sir." She grinned, teeth together so as not to bite chunks off her tongue during a particularly vigorous bit of atmospheric buffering. "Most of the time." A quick check on the platoon showed everyone more or less enjoying the flight. "Whatever it is you're eating, Ressk, swallow it before we land."

"No problem, Staff."

"More like *whoever* he's eating," Binti muttered beside him.

"You ought to count your fingers," he suggested. "You're too *serley* stupid to notice one missing."

"Maybe you ought to *gren sa talamec to.*"

"That's enough, people."

When the Confederation first started integrating the di'Taykan and the Krai into what was predominantly a Human military system, xenopsychologists among the elder races expected a number of problems. For the most part, those expectations fell short. After having dealt with the Mictok and the H'san, none of three younger races—all bipedal mammals—had any real difficulty with each other's appearance. Cultural differences were absorbed into the prevailing military culture and the remaining problems were dealt with in the age-old military tradition of learning to say "up yours" in the other races' languages. The "us against them" mentality of war made for strange bedfellows.

Conscious of Lieutenant Jarret webbed in close beside her, Torin shied away from that last thought. Not that sex with a di'Taykan could be considered anything but the default . . .

Is that going to keep cropping up during the entire mission, she wondered. *'Cause if it does, a therapeutic mind wipe is going to start looking pretty damned good.*

"We're over Shurlantec and have picked up an escort—they look like short-range fighters from here. Ground in seventeen minutes."

Captain Daniels' announcement drew her attention back to the situation at hand. "Listen up, people, and I'll go over our dispersement pattern one last time. Squad One down to the ramp to the left, Two to the right, Three along both sides. When our civilians move out, Squad Three falls in behind, One and Two spread out enough to cover full flanking positions. Remember we're supposed to be a ceremonial guard, so weapons remain at parade rest. I don't care if the Silsviss come up and bite you on the ass, do *not* respond. We're here to make friends, and we do not blow away, blow up, or just generally put holes in our friends. Is that clear? What is it, Checya?"

The heavy gunner lifted a miserable gaze to her face. "I feel naked without my exoskeleton. I never fukking landed without it before."

Throughout the platoon, the other eight HGs nodded in agreement. "And thinkin' of Checya naked ain't helpin'," one muttered.

"I know how you feel, but orders say small arms only." She glanced aside at her own KC-7 and smothered a smile. Small was a relative term— the KC just happened to be the smallest weapon they carried, excluding knives, fists, boots, teeth, and brain. A Marine was expected to survive dropped naked into enemy territory and that expectation had kept a few alive. It had probably killed a few, too, Torin realized, but since the Others didn't take prisoners, it really came down to whether or not a person died trying.

And that's just cheerful enough to make thinking of sex with the lieutenant a preferred option.

Her implant chimed, and she hit the master webbing release. "We're down. Let's go."

Under cover of the resulting noise, Lieutenant Jarret leaned close and murmured, "I'm not questioning your decisions, Staff, but why such a complicated procedure? Why not just march them down and line them up."

"Two reasons, sir. First, the Silsviss are impressed by military prowess, so we're showing them we have every intention of defending our civilians even though we won't have to. Second, if we leave this lot standing around for too long with nothing to do, it won't be pretty. I said, swallow it by landing, Ressk!" She sighed. "I did warn General Morris that we were a combat unit."

"You worry too much, Staff. This'll be a break for them."

The word *break* had occurred to her although not in that context. Break bones, break bottles, break up negotiations; yes. Enjoy standing around in a dress uniform while diplomats made decisions that eventually they'd have to risk their butts to enforce; no. But all she said was, "Yes, sir."

At the base of the ramp, the local version of concrete stretched off into the distance until it met with a wall of what looked like the same material. Except for the lack of burns and pitting—the place had obviously been resurfaced for their arrival—it could have been any friendly landing field in the Confederation.

Except for the giant lizards approaching at one o'clock, Torin amended. They were too far away for details, and she knew how the heavy gunners had felt about leaving their exoskeletons behind because she really missed her helmet. With its scanner, she could have counted the striations on each scale. Without it, she wasn't entirely certain they had scales, although the claws protruding from each foot were uncomfortably large enough to see.

They didn't seem to be wearing much, but considering the damp heat that was hardly surprising. The heat would make the Krai happy and was within Human tolerances, but she'd have to see that the di'Taykan got extra water.

A quick glance at Lieutenant Jarret showed his hair flat against his head and his nostrils flared. "When you can smell a planet over the landing fumes," he said, stroking the temperature controls on his cuff down to their lowest setting, "you know it's going to be bad."

"Pity about the Human sense of smell, sir." The di'Taykan made no secret of how useless they considered Human noses.

He looked at her then. "Nobody likes a smartass, Staff."

"Very true, sir."

The Mictok were the first on the field, then the Rakva, then, to no one's surprise, the Dornagain. By the time the Dornagain had lumbered off the ramp and the Third Squad had fallen in behind, the Silsviss welcoming committee had taken up position between two brilliantly colored banners and a formation of their own soldiers, matching the Marines exactly in numbers and mirroring their position.

They knew how many of us were coming . . . One painfully constricted heartbeat later, she remembered *this* time that wasn't a problem.

Off to one side of the soldiers, a small cluster of what could only be reporters recorded the moment for posterity. Their technology might be unfamiliar, but their attitude was unmistakable.

Beyond checking that her translation program was working properly, Torin didn't actually pay much attention to the opening exchange. Nothing of substance would be discussed on the landing field anyway so, after catching Ressk's eye and glaring at him until he brought his upper lip back down over his teeth, she used the time to size up their potential allies.

The Dornagain were still the biggest species on the ground by a considerable margin. The Silsviss present were about as tall as a tall Human or an average di'Taykan, although Torin had no idea if this group was representative of the species as a whole. Maybe short Silsviss didn't go into the army or the civil service. It did seem, however, that larger Silsviss went into the army, as only one or two of the civilians matched the size of the soldiers. They all had short muzzles, a little larger than those of the Krai, and thick necks with minor dorsal ridges. Like the two other reptilian species in the Confederation, they used their tongues a lot when they spoke, flicking them about an impressive array of teeth.

Those present were a mottled shade of grayish-green—slightly more monochrome on the front—but Torin expected that this was merely the local coloring. They'd be making another four regional stops before the "all Silsvah" meeting and, unless the Silsviss were truly unique in the galaxy, there'd be a number of variations on the theme.

Their tails were about as big around as their upper arms, not significantly larger at the base than the tip, and they never stopped moving. A number of the civilians wore bright metallic bands, and although the distance made it difficult to tell for certain, it seemed the soldiers wore duller bands not so much as decoration but to reinforce their tails as weapons.

Hand to hand to tail; good thing they're coming in on our side. One of the Other's subordinate species had been tailed, and old mindsets had needed to be reworked when an attempt to save as much of the research station as possible led to close-quarters fighting. After half a dozen Marines had been taken down by what amounted to a smack upside the head with a rubber truncheon, they learned not to relax when they saw both hands raised in surrender.

The Silsviss had similar tails. Similar reinforced tails.

They had round eyes set wide apart that seemed to be as unrelieved a black as those of the Mictok although the Silsviss had the more standard two. Evolutionary science hadn't managed to come up with a good reason for it but sentience seemed to lean toward bi-structural development. Their hands were long fingered, and although they obviously had to have opposable digits, Torin wasn't close enough to see how they opposed.

Unable to identify any sexual characteristics, she had no way of telling if the placement of the minimal clothing was merely decorative or gender specific. Not even the soldiers were wearing much, although the harnesses and the impressive amount of hardware clearly added up to uniform. Considering the heat and humidity that thickened the air almost to the consistency of soup, minimal clothing seemed wise. The exposed skin on her face and hands was already greasy with sweat.

She'd added, "Have sergeants remind the Humans in their squads to be careful about losing their grip on their weapons," to a mental list when she remembered General Morris' words: *"You'll see new worlds, meet new life-forms, and not shoot at them for a change."*

And that just feels wrong, she realized. *I really need to get out of combat for a while.*

". . . walk in parade ssso our people may sssee sssome of the many typesss of life the Galaxy offersss."

Walk in parade? Her gaze flicked over to the Dornagain and she wondered if there was a diplomatic way to say, "You've got to be fukking kidding."

Apparently, there was, and transportation was arranged.

Torin's translator insisted on calling the three vehicles flatbed trucks—or more specifically, trucksss—although they didn't look like any truck she'd ever seen. They looked a little like a cross between the sleds they used to move the heavy artillery and most of the farm machinery she'd left behind: functional and far from comfortable. Both military escorts were clearly expected to walk.

"I think the di'Taykan should ride as an honor guard for our diplomats, sir. They—you—don't handle this kind of heat well," she added when the lieutenant's hair rose in inquiry. "There's no need for any of us to be unnecessarily uncomfortable."

"You don't think the Silsviss will object?"

"I think the Silsviss will assume we're being cautious in a strange place and slap an equal number of their people on board."

With the Dornagain climbing into place surprisingly quickly, they didn't have time to discuss it.

"Very well, but I walk with the rest of the platoon."

She considered arguing but nodded instead. Rank had its responsibilities as well as its privileges. Besides, if he walked, the Silsviss wouldn't leap to the conclusion that the other di'Taykan were riding because they couldn't walk. It was something *she'd* suspect were their positions reversed, but with Lieutenant Jarret on the ground, the whole thing could be chalked up to weird alien ritual. *And if they plan on joining the Confederation, the Silsviss had best get used to dealing with that* . . . Remembering the first time she'd ever seen the Krai sit down to a festival meal, she suppressed a shudder. She'd barely been able to stop herself from freeing the appetizers before they reached the table.

During the delicate diplomatic maneuvering of boarding the trucks—while both the Silsviss officials and the Confederation delegates worked out which aliens it would be in their best political interest to ride with—she made sure that all the di'Taykan had their temperature controls at the lowest possible setting. The Silsviss did indeed match the Confederation guards with their own and Torin exchanged a glance of recognition with the soldier arranging it. Senior NCOs shared a bond that went beyond species affiliation and could recognize an expression that said, *"Who the hell came up with this brilliant idea?"* on any arrangement of features.

Lieutenant Jarret and the Silsviss officer were standing together off to one side, very probably being polite in that "we're above all this" way that officers had. The two were of a height, and di'Taykan body language seemed to suggest there had been no determination of which was the superior force. Silsviss body language seemed to be saying the same thing, but Torin had long since learned not to jump to cross-species conclusions.

As she approached, reinforced bootheels stamping emphasis into the landing field, she saw her reptilian counterpart moving in on a parallel course. Fully aware of what the other was about to do, and under no obligation of rank to make nice, they ignored one another.

Torin stopped a body-length back of the officers in time to hear the Silsviss say, ". . . no fear of the crowdsss. The citizensss in and around Shurlantec are very much in favor of usss joining with the Confederation."

And did that mean, Torin wondered, *that citizens in other areas are less in favor?* When the lieutenant turned toward her, she stiffened to attention. "The platoon is in position, sir."

"Thank you, Staff Sergeant."

"Ret Assslar." The Silsviss NCO tapped the metal band near the end of his tail sharply against the pavement. "Our troopsss are likewissse posssitioned."

The translation program left names and titles alone but changed everything else to its closest Confederation equivalent. Torin didn't know why it had decided to maintain the elongated sibilants, but she suspected all that hissing was going to get old pretty damned quick.

Ret Aslar acknowledged the information, then turned back to Lieutenant Jarret. "We will, no doubt, have further opportunity to ssspeak at the Embasssy, Lieutenant." His tail hit the pavement much as his NCO's had. "Until then."

"He's definitely done diplomatic work before," Jarret murmured as they moved toward their position.

"He, sir?"

"Ret Aslar. You can only develop his skill with small talk crammed into a room full of strangers who've been told to be polite."

"How could you tell he was male, sir?"

"Smell. The big ones are male. All the soldiers are male."

Only a di'Taykan could scent the sex of species not even in the same phylum. Torin made a mental note to keep an eye on Haysole, who seemed determined to be more di'Taykan than most.

"First impressions, Staff?"

It took her a moment to realize he meant the Silsviss. "They look like they fought to get to where they are and have no intention of giving any of it up."

Lieutenant Jarret shot her a confused glance. "Any of what?"

"Of who and what they are."

"The Confederation never asks that."

"When was the last time you went out without your masker?" When he opened his mouth to answer, she added, "In an area not controlled by the di'Taykan. When you get right down to it, sir, the Confederation is essentially an agreement to compromise, and I don't get the impression the Silsviss play well with others."

"You got all that . . ." His nod somehow managed to take in both the civil servants and the soldiers. ". . . from watching this lot stand around for an hour?"

"Yes, sir."

His eyes lightened as he glanced down at her. "So staff sergeants really do have super powers?"

Torin *had* been about to explain that survivors learned from experience to recognize those species likely to follow up their first shot with a second and a third but decided instead just to answer his question, responding to his teasing smile with as bland an expression as she could manage.

"Yes, sir."

Outside the high walls of the landing field, huge, fernlike trees not only made it impossible to see more than a few meters from the road but explained why the city had been so difficult to spot from space. Torin only hoped that the defense satellites were as good as tech thought they were, because should the Others break through, take Silsvah, and attempt to enslave the Silsviss, it would be a nasty job taking all these overgrown bits of it back.

Not that the Silsviss would be particularly easy to enslave, she acknowledged, listening to the soft rhythm of claws impacting with pavement.

They hadn't gone far when the burned concrete smell of the landing began to clear from her nose and Torin got her first unimpeded whiff of Silsvah. It reminded her of hot summer afternoons spent turning the compost pile, of anaerobic bacteria, and of scrubbing the algae out of the water troughs. It reminded her of one of the many reasons she'd left the farm.

The crowds lining the roads hissed and pointed and occasionally clusters of them would break into high-pitched ululating cries. It didn't sound friendly, but Torin was willing to allow that Ret Aslar knew his people better than she did—H'san cheering for the home team sounded like they were being skinned alive. Although some of the platoon were looking just a bit twitchy by the time the parade came to a stop at the edge of a wide plaza, they managed to form up without incident.

Taking her place at the rear, behind the three sergeants, Torin made a note of rigid shoulders and flattened hair and hoped that whatever was about to happen wouldn't take long.

They were facing an enormous colonnaded building set off from the plaza by a set of steps broad enough to be used as a graduated dais. The two groups of diplomats stood between their military escorts and the stairs. The media occupied the outer edges of the first two sections and standing on the top were those Silsviss too high ranking to be bothered with a trip to the landing field. A male and three females, judging by size alone, or a large male and three smaller males, or two smaller males and a female, or two females and a smaller male or . . . *Now* this *is a species that could use a little pink and blue.* The actual genders were of no immediate importance, Torin just liked to know. They wore robes—the first she'd seen—of some pale, diaphanous fabric that glittered in the sunlight and all four exuded nearly visible arrogance.

At least half the media seemed to be pointing their recording devices upward, and everyone seemed to be waiting for something to happen.

The big male at the top of the stairs stepped forward.

Inflated a brilliant yellow throat pouch.

And roared.

Shit! Torin couldn't hear anything over the pounding of her heart, but she saw at least three weapons snap up into firing position and her own muscles trembled with an instinctive need to respond. Lieutenant Jarret stepping forward brought her back to herself, and she marched around to take up his vacated position, thankful for the chance to move. This, at least, had been covered in the briefing.

"*At some point in the ceremony we'll be asked for our battle honors.*" Lieutenant Jarret had gazed earnestly at his sergeants as he passed on the bare details of the day. "*Staff Sergeant Kerr will take the platoon while I answer.*"

If it turned out that the lieutenant had known just what form that question would take and hadn't told her, Torin planned on kicking his aristocratic derriere right back to Ventris Station where he could repeat the course on keeping his NCOs informed.

Standing on the first step, he raised his head and began. "We are of Sh'quo Company . . ."

He clearly knew he couldn't match volume for volume so he played with tone, answering the heat of the Silsviss challenge with cold. As he detailed the company's history, his subtext clearly said: *We have nothing we need prove to you.* Torin was impressed. She could feel the mood of the platoon behind her change, until, when he finished speaking, the Silsviss were in the least amount of danger they'd been in since the Marines had landed.

Then he spun on one heel and walked back to his platoon.

At that moment, they *were* his.

Pity it won't last, Torin thought, returning to her original position.

The rest of the ceremony maintained a more conventional tone. Two of the three high-ranking females—or smaller males—gave speeches of welcome, the two ambassadors reciprocated, and finally the third of the smaller Silsviss at the top of the stairs announced they were giving over an entire wing of the Cirsarvas for the visitors to use while they were in Shurlantec.

Then the press moved in to take one final image of their leaders standing beside aliens from the stars.

"Well, that wasn't so bad," Ressk grunted, kicking off his boots and stretching his toes.

"Speak for yourself." Mysho pulled off her tunic and threw it over a stool. "I feel like I've been cooked."

"Ready for seasoning and serving," one of the other di'Taykan groaned.

Stripped down to his masker hanging from a thong around his neck, Haysole fell back onto a bunk. "Look at the bright side, these mattresses are wide enough for two."

"Species with tails need more room," Corporal Hollice said, coming in from the hall. "You should see the design of the crapper. It's not just the tail either," he went on, moving out of the way so the curious could go take a look, "they're up on their toes so their legs bend high, like the Dornagain's."

"You an' Kleers are gonna need a fukking stool," Juan snickered to Ressk when he returned. "Good thing there's so many of them around."

"Tails," Hollice said again, one hand absently rubbing Mysho's shoulder as he spoke. "You can't use a chair with a back when you've got a tail."

"So, corporal got-all-the-answers, how do you explain that the showers are bang on identical to the fukking showers back up on the vacuum pack?"

"They've never been used; I'd say someone sent down the specs and the Silsviss built them special for us."

"Must've smelled you coming, Juan." Grinning, Mysho stepped away from the heavy gunner's swing and backed right into Binti's arms.

The other woman inhaled deeply and her steadying hand moved slowly around the di'Taykan's waist. "I think you need to turn up your masker," she murmured, face buried in the moving strands of pale hair.

"Unfortunately, I think I need to take a cold shower." Sighing, she untangled herself. "It's the heat, I've got to bring my body temperature down, or I'll keep over-emitting."

Binti snorted and slapped Haysole on a bare thigh. "So how come the pheromone kid here isn't any more enticing than usual?" she asked over his protest.

"I don't know—maybe I'm from farther north, maybe the recruiting sergeant checked his psych profile and gave him an industrial strength masker, or maybe . . ." Her tone grew distinctly dry. ". . . becuase not all members of the same species react to heat the same way."

"Or maybe," Juan continued before anyone else could respond, "your climate controls are fukked." He held out his hand. "L'me look at your tunic while you shower."

"We're on duty."

"So get permission from the sergeant—just do it in your shirtsleeves so I can look at your tunic. It's not doin' you any fukking good and anyway, the regs say dress c's are uniform of the day unless on parade or on guard. What?" he added when everyone in earshot turned to stare. "You never read in the crapper?"

"Just great, if her climate controls go . . ."

"She'll be miserable, but she'll survive." Hands on her hips, Trey turned a slow circle in the middle of the small room assigned to the NCOs. "I can't get over how quiet everything sounds in here."

"Old building, thick walls," Torin told her shortly. "Power grids are all surface mounted, so this place is probably at least a hundred years old. And I wasn't thinking so much of Mysho but of the effect on the rest of the platoon."

"So *they'll* be miserable on duty and in the sack off duty, but they'll survive, too. Haysole'll probably consider it license to turn his masker off at every opportunity, but other than that I don't see much of a problem." Fuschia eyes narrowed. "You don't usually worry this much about the di'Taykan. This have something to do with the lieutenant?"

"Like what?" Torin asked, wondering if that last night of liberty was finally coming home to roost.

"Like a little sucking up to the species in charge."

Hoping the relief didn't show, Torin raised both brows. "In charge?" she repeated with heavy emphasis.

Trey grinned. "Good point. Anyway, I wouldn't worry about an over-heated masker. Considering what we usually face eight hours into a planetfall, it's minor."

Torin grunted an agreement and dropped onto a stool, grabbing the edge of the desk just barely in time to stop herself from tipping over back-ward. Chairs with no backs, desks with no brains, and a climate that clung—all inconveniences that could be ignored under fire but under the current circumstances . . . "So is it a sign of pure intentions that this 'em-bassy' is pretty much completely indefensible or have we deliberately been given the weaker position?"

"Or are you completely paranoid?"

"Just doing my job."

"Hey, Torin." One hand on the heavily carved and overly ornate wooden door, Mike Glicksohn leaned into the room. "Sled's finally here from the VTA."

"About time. Hold down the fort," she tossed over her shoulder at Trey as she headed out into the hall. "I'm going for my slate. And you," she threw at Glicksohn as she passed, "get a work detail together and get every-thing unloaded before the Silsviss offer to help."

The two sergeants exchanged a speaking glance as Torin's footsteps faded out toward the courtyard.

"Is she completely paranoid?" Glicksohn asked after a moment.

Trey shrugged. "Apparently, it's her job."

"Hey, did any of you guys notice that some of the Silsviss soldiers inflated those throat pouch things when that big guy on the step roared?"

"Not me." Ressk wrapped his feet around the bar at the end of his bunk, toe joints cracking. "I was too busy trying not to overload the moisture sensors in my uniform."

Frowning, Juan looked up from the sensor array exposed in the armpit seam of Mysho's tunic. "What the fuk does that mean?"

"It means he was trying not to piss himself," Binti explained from her bunk. "Me, I was just glad my brain came back on line before my finger squeezed the trigger." She reached up and stroked the stock of her KC. "And civilians wonder why we're not hardwired into our weapons. Mama does like having her baby this close, though."

Each bunk had a weapons rack built in. Or what looked like a weapons rack. The platoon had decided, individually and collectively, that they didn't much care what the Silsviss used it for.

A sudden cheer from the dice game in the back corner drew everyone's attention.

Corporal Hollice ducked his head so that he could look through the line of bunks at the players. "Hey, Drake, you win back that fifty you owe me yet?"

"As if!"

"Then keep it down before one of the sergeants shows up."

A Human, his skin only a little lighter than Binti's, rose up out of his crouch and flicked a good-natured finger in the corporal's direction. "Why don't I owe you this, too?" Then he froze. "Or not."

The Marines closer to the door turned to see what had caught his attention.

Sergeant Glicksohn smiled. "You're not gambling back there, are you, Drake?"

"Uh, no, Sarge."

"Glad to hear it. Outside, now. The sled's here from the VTA, and it needs unloading." His smile broadened. "Bring your friends. And if you . . ." A finger jabbed at Haysole. ". . . aren't back in uniform in three seconds and heading up to the sled, I'm coming over there to kick your bare butt. You're standing down, you're not off duty."

"But, Sarge, it's hot."

"So."

"The Silsviss aren't wearing clothes."

"Grow a tail and we'll talk." As the dice players filed past him, he frowned thoughtfully. "In the interests of expediency, you three . . ." The frown lit on Hollice, Juan, and Ressk. ". . . can join the detail, too."

"Aw, Sarge, I'm fixing Mysho's fukking tunic."

"What's wrong with it?"

"Cooling system's fukked. She's getting too warm for her masker to handle."

"That's just what we need. All right, Mashona, up top in his place."

Binti dropped off her bunk, muttering under her breath just low enough for the sergeant to ignore.

"What're we unloading, Sarge?" Ressk asked, shoving his boots back on.

"Personal effects and rations," Glicksohn told him. "Not that it matters, you'd be unloading it regardless."

"So you find out what the Silsviss drink for fun yet, Sarge?" Ressk asked as they started up the stairs to the courtyard, side by side.

"Beer. Local brewery supplies the army with its own brands. There's a light and a dark and a green."

"Green?"

Glicksohn grinned. "Maybe they're Irish."

"Irish?"

"Skip it. Alcohol content's low by our standards and since there's nothing in any of it that'll hurt us, once we get used to the taste, we'll be able to drink the Silsviss under the table. Officers and ranking civilians'll be drinking a distilled, fruit liqueur that packs more of a punch but smells like socks after a month in combat boots and will build up toxins in both Human and di'Taykan. You Krai, as usual, can handle it."

Following close behind, Hollice and Binti exchanged an identical, questioning glance.

"We've only been here a few hours, and we spent most of that time playing toy soldiers. How did the sergeant find that stuff out so fast?"

Hollice shrugged. "It's a gift. Let's just hope he never uses it for evil."

"Half the time, I don't know what the hell you're talking about," Binti muttered, shaking her head.

Although the door was open, the lieutenant wasn't alone. Moving quietly across the wide hall—an action made more difficult by the steel-reinforced heels of her dress boots—Torin paused in the open door. Rank had gotten Lieutenant Jarret a pair of adjoining rooms on the upper floor. Out of the half dozen available, he chose two at the top of the central stairs and Torin had to admit she liked the symbolism. Enemies of the Confederation would have to go through him to get to the civilians.

She liked the symbolism of the doctor and the corpsmen setting up shop directly across the hall a little less.

The room the lieutenant had decided to use as his headquarters was huge, painted a deep, under-the-canopy green, and mostly empty. It held what passed for a desk on Silsvah, a long, low table along one wall, a number of stools of varying heights, the lieutenant, and a Silsviss male. At least Torin assumed it was a male; it was difficult to tell the genders apart without either a size comparison or an inflated throat pouch.

He was standing with his back to her, facing the lieutenant across the desk. A pair of scars ran parallel across the dark gray of his right hip and another marked his right shoulder.

Left-handed, Torin thought. *Weaker on the right.*

He wore three narrow metal rings spaced evenly around the lower end of his tail and a military-style harness with about half the hardware that had been attached to the soldiers who'd met them at the landing field.

"Of courssse there'sss no intention of making thisss your permanent embasssy should we decide to join your Confederation." His voice, while still annoyingly sibilant, was deep and, allowing for the variables of translation, he spoke with a confidence Torin rather liked.

She cleared her throat.

The Silsviss reacted a fraction of a second before the lieutenant but waited for his host to look up before he turned.

Retired officer, she decided. *One of the good ones.* Catching the lieutenant's eye she said, "Excuse me, sir, but you wanted to go over the duty roster."

Lieutenant Jarret had clearly forgotten he'd ever given her such an order, but he recovered quickly and beckoned her into the room. "Yes, of course. Staff, I'd like you to meet Cri Sawyes, our Silsviss liaison. Cri Sawyes, Staff Sergeant Kerr."

"Ah, yes, your Rissstak." The flat black gaze weighed and measured. Whistling softly—it was a quieter version of the sound the crowd had been making, so Torin assumed he approved—Cri Sawyes turned back to the lieutenant. "Here we have a sssaying that a good Rissstak isss the equal of location *and* sssuperior numbersss."

"We have a similar saying."

"Sssoldiersss are sssoldiersss whatever their ssspeciesss." Tapping his tail lightly against the floor, Cri Sawyes moved toward the door. "I will leave you two to your dutiess. When you need me . . ." He indicated the squat, pale green box on the desk. ". . . you have only to call. A pleasure to meet you, Ssstaff Sssergeant."

"Sir." Torin waited until the sound of his claws faded, then leaned over the desk. "And this is?"

"A communications device." Lieutenant Jarret looked speculatively down at the pattern of slots. "It's set up for claws, but I expect I can make do with a stylus." He held out his hand for her slate. His fingers were warm where they brushed against hers—a quick glance at his cuff showed his climate controls still at the lowest setting. He couldn't be comfortable, but it didn't show. "You have fireteams with di'Taykan standing watch at night when it's cooler?"

"Yes, sir."

"Good." He downloaded the schedule into his own slate and handed hers back. "Everything looks in order. Let me know if you make any changes."

"Yes, sir."

"The desks are somewhat less than we're used to, aren't they?"

"Yes, sir."

He drummed his fingertips against the wood and sighed. "In fact, I'd have to say that, officially, they suck."

Torin smiled, more at his indignation than anything, but he didn't need to know that. "Yes, sir, they most certainly do suck."

"The doctor says we're all on rations tonight until he finishes testing the local food, so I've had a reprieve."

"A reprieve?"

"The local versions of state dinners." Jarret dropped down onto a stool. "I'd rather be shot at."

"That's because you've never been shot at, sir."

His hair lifted. "And how many state dinners have you attended, Staff?"

"None, sir."

"Then I'd say neither of us have a basis for comparison." Smiling up at her, he leaned back and caught himself just before he fell off the stool.

FOUR

The week in Shurlantec went remarkably quickly. To Torin's surprise, the entire platoon kept their off duty behavior within acceptable parameters—no one got arrested, eaten, or shot. She didn't want to know how Haysole's shoulders got gouged and since Sergeant Glicksohn assured her that both the di'Taykan and diplomatic relations were essentially unaffected, she didn't have to ask.

Although he had a tendency to make enthusiastic and inappropriate suggestions, Lieutenant Jarret allowed her to do her job without unnecessary interference. By the time they reboarded the modified VTA, Torin had to admit that, so far, she had no complaints. The lieutenant would make a fine addition to any Intelligence or Administration unit. Whether he could command a combat unit was still open to question.

With minor geographic differences, experiences at the next two cities on the Silsvah Marine Corps tour were much the same.

Daarges, the largest city in the Southern Hemisphere, took hot and humid up a notch to hot and raining. Cri Sawyes, now traveling with them, explained that the south was in the midst of their rainy season. During a discussion over a jar of green beer, one of the local NCOs shot a disgusted look at the sky and told Torin it didn't actually get much dryer.

"Agriculture down here, technology up north." He sorted through a bowl of small amphibians and tossed a pale yellow one into his mouth. "Not an entirely fair sssysssstem, but it worksss."

The citizens of Daarges were more green than gray, and both fingers and toes were webbed. Torin had never seen a species as good as the Silsviss at waterproofing; exposed metals were coated in an organic sealant and even hand weapons could be fired underwater. Once she got a look at some of the things that lived in the water, she understood why.

"In the old daysss in thisss part of the world, the young malesss went into the water with only a knife to prove themssselvesss against the *karn* and win the right to breed. Thisss hasss not been allowed for sssome time."

Torin looked where Cri Sawyes pointed and only just managed to stop herself from backing off the other side of the narrow boardwalk and right into the swamp.

"That's the biggest snake I've ever seen." Lieutenant Jarret's tone suggested polite interest—his hair, flattened to his head, suggested a slightly less sanguine reaction.

"That isss the more mobile sssection of the *karn*. The greater part of itsss body isss buried in the mud."

The thought of going up against such a monster with only a knife drew both Torin's brows up almost to her hairline. A handheld missile launcher with soft target impact detonating charges, yes. A knife, no. The expression on the lieutenant's face indicated a similar thought.

"I can see why they put a stop to it," he murmured.

Cri Sawyes made a sound between a sigh and a hiss and his claws curled into the damp wood. "The *karn* isss now a protected ssspeciesss. One by one, our young lossse the challengesss that help them to mature."

Torin was impressed that the *karn* had needed protecting and, not for the first time, gave thanks that the Silsviss were coming in on the right side. The last thing she wanted was to face off against someone who went up against something the size of a *karn* with only a knife. Those kinds of crazy people were dead to reason and nearly impossible to stop.

The third city, Ra Navahsis, was a pleasant surprise. The temperature still hovered between uncomfortable and slow roast, but the air was dry and even the di'Taykan found it bearable. The city was inland and everything, including the Silsviss, was more gold than green.

Given to flashy colors and brilliant displays, the inhabitants kept everyone moving so quickly between ceremonies that Torin barely had a moment to call her own and, at that, she had a significantly better time than the lieutenant. After his first Ra Navahsis banquet, he'd staggered into their temporary barracks, gazed glassily at his assembled NCOs and was suddenly, noisily, sick. Not at all sympathetic, Dr. Leor suggested he try eating perhaps half as much the next time.

"There wasn't actually a chance to turn anything down," Jarrett explained as Torin helped him back to his quarters after the doctor had done what he could. "They knew what local foods each of us could eat and they were determined to feed it to us. The Dornagain seemed to enjoy it—I think one of the ambassador's assistants changed her name to Well If You Insist Just One More—the Rakva can't eat enough of the local food to have a problem, Ambassador Krik'vir and her lot switched to external digestion and that got them off the hook, but it was up to me to uphold the honor of the Marines."

"The Marines appreciate it, sir."

"Don't patronize me, Staff, or I'll puke on your boots."

"Sorry, sir."

"Maybe I should deputize one of the Krai to eat in my place."

Torin eased him down onto his bed. "I'm not sure any of our Krai would be up to that kind of a ceremonial function."

"Ceremonial function, my brass. More like competitive gluttony."

"That, they'd be up to."

He belched, exhaling a breath redolent with Silsvah spices, and fell back against the ridge in the top of the mattress that passed for a pillow. "Don't think for a moment they weren't judging my abilities, throwing food at me until they knew exactly where I stood." One hand clutching his masker, he closed his eyes. "See if you can get them to shoot at me instead. I'm sure I'd feel a lot better if I'd just been shot."

"I stand by my theory that that's only because you've never been shot, sir."

"Fine. You shoot me."

Torin had no idea how the lieutenant managed to survive the continuing round of banquets his rank obligated him to attend, but the only shooting involved an elaborate display of military marksmanship where the visitors outscored the home team over two to one with their own weapons and then proved themselves laughingly inept with the Silsviss small arms.

The Silsviss, on the other hand, took to the KC like a H'san to cheese.

"Sorry, Staff." Ressk pulled his slate back from Torin's jaw and ruefully shook his head. "I can't get a clear enough interface with your implant. The data I'm getting's so scrambled, I can't find what needs fixing."

"So I'm stuck with the sibilants?"

"'Fraid so. Bottom line, you need an upgrade."

Her hand rose to protectively cup her left cheek. The tech team insisted that the installation was essentially painless, but Torin had found a lot of leeway within that qualifier. "There's an automatic upgrade coming with my next promotion. Can't it wait?"

He shrugged, a Krai adaptation of a Human gesture. "That depends."

"On?"

"Time frame. Your opstem's on the downward slide. Eventually, it'll degrade into piss and wind and even your primary programming won't run. Now, if it was up to me, I wouldn't wait for that piece of shit the techs'll put in; I'd get me a Bg347 with a direct cerebral uplink."

Torin snorted. "And if I could afford that, why would I be here, wasting my time with you lot?" She headed for the door without waiting for an answer. "Thanks for the diagnostic, Ressk."

"There'll be a little something added to my pay chit?"

"No." Pausing just inside the door's sensor range, she grinned back over her shoulder as it cycled. "But I'll ignore your little excursion up on the *Berganitan*."

"How did you . . . ?"

"I'm a staff sergeant. I know everything." She stepped over the hatch's raised edge and added, as the door cycled shut behind her, "And don't ever do it again."

"I told you she'd find out," Binti muttered, lightly smacking the back of his head as she passed behind him.

"No, you didn't."

"Yes, I did."

"Didn't."

"Did."

"Would you two shut your fukking holes." Arms stiff, Checya glared at them in mid-push-up and jerked his chin toward Conn. "You think the poor bastard doesn't already miss his four-year-old? You two have to remind him of her?"

The corporal looked a little startled at suddenly being the center of attention. "Were you guys talking to me?" He held up his slate. "I was just writing to Myrna. Captain Daniels told me she'd squirt a letter up to the *Berganitan* when we land."

"Tell her I said hi." Stepping over the heavy gunner, Binti hung her tunic over the back of her assigned position and continued toward the hatch in the back of the troop compartment that led to the APCs.

"Where are you heading?"

"I thought I'd go play with the di'Taykan."

Corporal Hollice cracked one eye and glanced up at the board. "You've got half a standard hour before we're to strap back in."

"Plenty of time if we skip the small talk."

Hollice opened the other eye and glanced around the troop compartment, counting Marines. "There's four of them in there."

"So?"

"Hey, if you can march after that, more power to you, but you know the rules about other races joining in with the di'Taykan. No allowances made. You play, you pay. And your basic Human bits are just not . . ."

"All right, killjoy, I get it." Binti frowned, turned, and dropped back into her seat. "Maybe I'll just play a level of Goopa Elite instead."

Hollice smiled and closed his eyes again. "Probably wise."

"I think it's time someone took his sergeant's exam," she muttered, shoving a game biscuit into her slate.

The Silsviss had asked that they stay within the atmosphere while traveling between cities so that as many people as possible could see the alien ship. As they were willing to provide the extra fuel it burned, Captain Daniels flew the fine line between too close to the ground and insulting their hosts.

Distances that could have been covered in a hop and skip out of the atmosphere took hours.

Torin had pulled the NCOs out of the troop compartment as soon as the VTA had reached its cruising altitude. Too much off-duty time spent with the troops tended to turn even the most levelheaded sergeant into a playground supervisor—which left no one happy.

She'd have ignored the game in the armory, but the sight of a Rakva perched behind the ammo case they were using as a table pulled her in for a closer look.

"For the sake of our beginner here, we'll keep it simple." Mike dealt one card up and four down to all six players. "The game's five card draw. Jack bets."

The junior Rakva extended a slender digit and tapped the plastic square. "This is a jack?"

"That's a jack."

"Ah." He scooped up his other four cards and fluffed out his crest as he studied them. "This one thinks that this one understands but would like to know one small thing again."

Scratching his cheek where the follicle suppressant was beginning to wear off, Mike shrugged. "Anything."

"What is it that beats a pair of eights?"

Torin grinned as the sergeant tossed his hand down in disgust. The metal ammo case had reflected the cards far too fast for Human eyes but not for Rakva. "You're not gambling in here, are you, Sergeant Glicksohn?"

"Wouldn't think of it, Staff. We're just involving our feathered friend here in a cross-cultural exchange."

The Rakva's crest fell. "This one thought you were teaching him to play poker?"

Torin left him to explain.

Her rounds bringing her back into the civilians' seating behind the bridge, she straightened her tunic and put on her best company expression before stepping into the sensor field. Although about half the size of the troop compartment for significantly fewer people, the four Dornagain made the area seem cramped and overcrowded. Her nose twitched. And, in spite of the best efforts of the ventilation system, just a little rank.

The lieutenant was talking to the Dornagain ambassador, and she wondered how he was coping. Breathing through his mouth wouldn't help—the most sensitive scent receptors were along the edge of his soft palate. Did he need rescuing?

Given the way the ends of his hair were flicking back and forth, she'd say that would be a yes.

Fortunately, Listens Well And Considers All spoke significantly faster than he moved, and at the first natural pause, Torin stepped forward. "Excuse me, Ambassador, Lieutenant. Sergeant Trey needs to speak to you at the APCs, sir."

"Thank you, Staff Sergeant." To have shown that much relief in his voice would have been rude, but Torin read it in the sudden stillness of his hair. "Excuse me, Ambassador, duty calls." He bowed and turned, and mouthed a second, silent *thank you* as he passed.

"Staff Sergeant Kerr."

"Yes, Ambassador?" She thought he was smiling at her, but she wasn't as familiar with Dornagain social cues as she should be. His ears were up, only his bottom teeth were showing, and he was resting back on his haunches—although that last bit was more an indication of the compartment height than any sort of mood.

"How are *you* finding the Silsviss thus far?"

I don't have to find them, they're all over the bloody place. "I think they'll make fine allies against the Others, sir."

"Ah, yes, the Others." Long claws dug absently at a tangle of his cream-colored fur. "You are aware that their ships have been seen approaching this sector?"

"Approaching? How close?" she demanded, then added a quick, "Sir."

"I am afraid I am not aware of their exact position, Staff Sergeant, only that the nearness of the enemy prods us to make our decisions based on expediency rather than what might be best for both the Confederation and the Silsviss."

Torin ran that through her translator one more time, just to be sure she understood. "You think we're letting the Silsviss into the Confederation too soon?"

"They are not as sociologically advanced as I would like."

"They're at about the same level Humans were, and you let us in."

"Because we required someone to fight our battles."

"Still do," Torin reminded him.

"Yes." The Dornagain nodded slowly, smoothing his whiskers with the back of one hand. "I had much the same conversation with your lieutenant, only he used the di'Taykan as his example. So I will ask you what I asked him: Do you not think it would be better if we learned to fight our own battles?"

"It's a little too late for that, Ambassador. It's now our battle, too. On the other hand, we wouldn't say no if you wanted to help."

"Help?"

"Fight."

"Ah. Yes." Eyes half closed, he began grooming again. "I will have to think about that."

Hoping he hadn't considered it a personal invitation—while amateur soldiers weren't the last thing she wanted, they were low on the list—Torin bowed and left him to his deliberations.

As near as she could figure, the approaching Others were still a diplomatic situation, not yet a military one. With any luck, someone would let her know if that changed. Hopefully, *before* the shooting started.

The other three Dornagain appeared to be asleep, the doctor was studying his slate, the Charge d'Affaires and her remaining assistant were having a low-voiced discussion—hopefully not about their missing team member, now involved in Sergeant Glicksohn's cross-cultural exchange—and all four Mictok had webbed themselves into a corner. Torin didn't know what they were doing and she wasn't going to ask.

Carefully skirting one of the sleeping Dornagain and the surrounding musky atmosphere, she joined Cri Sawyes at the vid screen. It wasn't until they reached the edge of the forest that she realized the mottled green field they'd been flying over was actually the tops of trees. "We seem to be above a whole lot of nothing."

"One of the wildernesss pressservesss," the Silsviss explained. "Our governmentsss put large areasss assside to ensure our young malesss are properly challenged."

Torin knew better than to be drawn into a discussion of alien gender issues but she couldn't stop herself from asking, "Only your males?"

"We only have a sssurplusss of malesss."

"So challenged means . . ."

"Exactly what you think it meansss, Sssergeant. We have too many malesss not to weed out the weak."

They were passing over low hills. Something moved down in one of the valleys, something big, but they were by too quickly for Torin to see exactly what it was.

"Young malesss reach an age when their body chemisssstry requiresss them to essstablish their posssition. They . . ." He glanced over at Torin and his tongue flicked out. "*We* will fight any other male we meet. It isss much easssier on sssociety if malesss during that time are placed where they can do the leassst damage."

"To everything but each other."

"Yesss. Within the pressservesss, we form packsss, continually challenging for the leadership. A good leader throwsss pack againssst pack, keeping hisss followersss too preoccupied to take him down. Eventually, chemisssstry changesss again and the sssurvivorsss realize there isss more to life than fighting."

"Like sex?"

His tongue flicked out again. "Sssex is much like fighting for my people, Sssergeant, but if you mean reproduction, then yesss. And that requiresss a sssocial posssition you cannot gain by tooth and claw in the wildernesss."

"Your females don't fight?"

"Not without cause. Our malesss outnumber our femalesss almosssst twenty to one. There may have been a reason for such dissscrepancy once—I don't know, I'm not an anthropologissst—but technology overtook evolution and now we do what we mussst to maintain civilization."

"Which is why all your soldiers are male?"

"Yesss; It helpsss integrate the young malesss back into sssociety, maintaining the hierarchy ssstructure they're familiar with and teachesss them waysss to advance that don't involve biting off an opponent'sss tail and ssstrangling him with it."

"But armies are just bigger packs."

Cri Sawyes nodded and drummed his claw tips against the edge of the screen. "Thisss will be an interesssting transssition for my people. The arrival of your Confederation ssstopped a major war and half a dozen border actionsss. Thanksss to your Confederation, we are becoming one."

"It was much the same with my people," Torin admitted. "Well, not the gender differences," she amended as he turned to stare, "but the becoming one part."

"And was it difficult for Humans?"

She shrugged. "We're an us-against-them kind of species, Cri Sawyes. As far as I can tell, and I'm no more an anthropologist than you are, we just redefined us and them."

"I sssee." He turned to stare back down at the screen, muscles tensing as they passed over an area burned clear. "I think it will be harder for usss."

They'd been to three large cities, each run by a male and two or three females. Remembering the scars on the males, Torin wondered if the delegates were being given the tour of Silsvah while the overall leadership of the planet was being determined.

And then cleaned up after.

Not my species, not my problem.

On the screen, the wilderness was replaced by cultivated land.

There was a band at the landing field in Hahraas. At least, Torin assumed it was a band. Although she couldn't hear anything that might resemble a melodic line, there was a beat that could be marched to and she didn't actually ask for more than that.

Besides the band, there was a mirror image platoon, a number of civilian dignitaries matching theirs, a banner, and a new team. The landing field had been resurfaced for their visit.

Same old, same old, Torin thought as Mike took his squad down the ramp. It was amazing how quickly the strange became the familiar and how soon after that familiarity bred contempt. As she followed Squad Three out of the VTA, she made a mental note to try and keep her troublemakers too exhausted to make trouble.

"You wanted to see me, sir?"

Lieutenant Jarret glanced up from his slate and waved Torin into the room. "Captain Daniels is on her way in from the landing field with a message from the *Berganitan.*"

"Is there a problem with the link?" The captain had the access codes to both her slate and the lieutenant's—if there was a problem, her maintenance programs hadn't flagged it.

"No, no problem." He tossed his slate onto the desk and stood, rolling his shoulders forward and back. "We're not entirely certain our communications are secure, so she's bringing it personally."

Torin frowned, trying to remember all the contact she'd had with the aircrew since they'd landed. "You think the Silsviss have cracked our link?"

"Not really, no. But it doesn't hurt to be careful." Grinning, he grabbed his left elbow behind his back and stretched. "Actually, I suspect Captain Daniels is bored spitless and is taking advantage of a loophole in her orders to stay with the VTA." Switching elbows, he continued to stretch.

"Are you stiff, sir?" The words were barely out of her mouth before she realized what she'd said. *What a question to ask a di'Taykan! Especially one you've got a history with.* As his eyes brightened and his grin broadened, she raised a cautioning hand. "Not an invitation, sir. I was just asking about your back."

"My back?" For a moment, she thought he wouldn't let the innuendo go and then he smiled. "It's nothing, I've just been sitting in one position for too long."

"Should I get Dr. Leor?" she asked, when her imagination kept filling the silence with other suggestions. She was *not* going to offer to rub it.

The lieutenant looked confused. "For a stiff back?"

"Of course not. Sorry, sir." Clearly, the troops weren't the only ones getting restless. She needed something to do. Something real. Something physical. All this ceremonial standing around left her far too much free time. And if she felt that way, she'd better start keeping a closer eye on the troops. "Any idea what Captain Daniels' message is?"

"She didn't say." The sound of approaching bootheels ringing against the polished stone floor drew the lieutenant around to the front of his desk. "But I think we're about to find out."

"Captain Carveg sends her regrets, but the *Berganitan* was the closest ship."

"If long-range sensors have detected a possibility of the Others near the edge of the sector, her responsibility is clearly to investigate." Lieutenant Jarret sounded as sincere as only a young officer with his first command could. "We're perfectly safe down here until they get back."

Torin wondered if considering that statement to be a fine example of famous last words made her unduly paranoid or just conscious of historical precedent.

"I hope your civilians take it as well."

"I don't think they'll be surprised," Torin offered, remembering her conversation with the Dornagain ambassador. "They knew the Others were approaching."

"If they're just making a recon flight, it's nothing the *Berganitan* can't handle."

If, Torin added silently.

Captain Daniels ran a hand back through thick, black hair, standing it up from her scalp in damp spikes. "Have these people never heard of air-conditioning?"

The lieutenant snorted. "Modern buildings have all the conveniences, but we keep getting billeted in these historic piles of stone. Not," he added afer a moment's reflection, "that the Silsviss are big on cooling things down at the best of times. You and your crew have it easy. All the comforts of home and you got to show off in that air show."

"Oh, yeah, that was fun. Flying a VTA in atmosphere is like wrestling a H'san—let your mind wander for an instant and you're eating dirt." The pilot wandered from window to window, peering down into the empty courtyard, and finally settled one thigh on the broad stone sill. "So, still managing to hold up under the weight of the ceremonial circuit?"

"Honestly?" Lieutenant Jarret dropped down onto a stool, caught himself with a practiced motion, and leaned carefully back against the wall. "I'm beginning to wish they'd sent me into battle instead."

"Be careful what you wish for." The captain waved a chiding finger and then turned to Torin. "And what about you, Staff? How're the troops holding up?"

"No casualties so far, sir. Which reminds me . . ." She nodded toward the lieutenant. ". . . I should go check on Haysole and tell the platoon about the *Berganitan.*"

"How do you think they'll react?"

"To the Navy buggering off and leaving them on their own?" She grinned at the two officers. "Same old, same old."

"It sure is boring being a guard." Binti tossed her tunic across the end of her bunk and collapsed down onto the bag of heated sand the Silsviss in this part of the world used as a mattress. "And what the hell are we guarding against anyway? I thought the Silsviss were supposed to be our allies?"

Various forms of grunted assent answered her as Squad One filed into their temporary barracks and found their bunks.

"It's for fukking show," Juan grunted, carefully racking his weapon before dropping onto his own sandbag. "Lets them lizards see we're ready to fight if we have to be."

Ressk hissed through his teeth as he stretched out his toes. "Staff better not hear you calling them lizards."

"But they *are* fukking lizards."

"Who's fukking lizards?" Haysole asked, coming in from the shower. He shook his head to settle his hair back into place and glanced around at the bodies on the bunks. "Come on, who?"

"Besides you?" Binti snickered.

"It was an adjective, not a verb," Corporal Hollice interrupted. "Not that you morons would know what that means." A raised hand cut off the protests of his fireteam and those other squad members close enough to hear. "Don't bother proving it."

"This is a new low. We're arguing about grammar." Punching his sand into shape, Ressk settled back. "Me, I pray to all the gods of my *tarlige* that this will be over soon."

"Might not."

All heads turned toward Haysole.

"Staff came in as I finished the crappers, just before Squad Two headed out to replace you. The *Berganitan* has left orbit."

"What?"

"Sensors read Others at the edge of the sector and they took off."

"Leaving us here, ass-deep in ceremonial fukking duties?" Juan struggled up into a sitting position and glared at the di'Taykan. "You're fukking kidding, right?"

"Wish I was. Staff told me to let you guys know when you came in."

"You know what this means? This means we could be finished with this gig before they get back and we could be stuck here. This could just go on and on and on and on."

"What if they never come back?" someone muttered.

"Okay, that's it." Binti stood up and grabbed her tunic. "I can't stand it anymore, I'm out of here."

"Mess is right next door. Big change."

"I'm not going to the mess. I'm taking my souvenir Silsvah money in my souvenir Silsvah belt pouch—which appears to have been made from a souvenir Silsviss—and I'm going out for a drink and a little action."

Ressk's eyes snapped open. "You're what?"

"Look, we know they drink, we've had the beer, and that means they have to have places they drink in."

"Maybe they drink alone."

"Did you pay no attention in school?" she demanded, smacking him on the side of the leg. "So far, only social species have achieved sentience . . ."

"Oh, yeah. Big achievement."

Binti ignored him. "The Silsviss are sentient, which makes them social, which means somewhere in this godforsaken town there's a bar."

"At the risk of sounding like the voice of reason," Hollice interrupted, "our orders are to stay put."

"No one's saying you have to come."

He snorted. "You think I'd let you run around without adult supervision?"

Ressk stared up at the corporal, then sighed and began putting his boots back on. "Come on, Juan. Looks like we're moving out."

"Praise the fukking lord."

"Anyone else want to come?"

The other Marines in the room declined. One or two expressed opinions about the wisdom of the trip, but no one raised any major objections. They all knew that someone had to be the first over the wall.

"Haysole?"

"I should get some sleep. My team's got the last watch."

"And your point is?"

"Give me a minute to get dressed."

It took very little more than a minute and then the five of them slipped into the hall and past the mess, heading for the boiler room at the end of the corridor.

"Of course I know that door leads outside the compound," Haysole muttered when asked. "You think I was cleaning the crappers because I wanted to?"

"And where do you lot think you're going?"

Hearts in their throats, the five turned as one, falling instinctively into a defensive position, the heavy gunner out in front.

Mysho grinned at them. "From the spreading stain in Juan's crotch, I guess I've got that impersonation of Staff Sergeant Kerr down pat."

"Fukking *trilinshy*," Juan muttered, unable to stop himself from looking down.

"*Trilin*sha," Haysole corrected, scowling darkly over his head at the corporal. "Female tense. But other than that . . ."

"Name-calling; very mature. It's a good thing I'm going with you."

"You don't even know where we're going," Binti pointed out, shuffling impatiently from foot to foot.

"You're going out to find a bar and get stinking with the natives. I don't need to be a H'san to figure that out." Mysho's grin slipped, and she jerked her head back toward the mess. "If I have to spend another evening in there listening to Justin analyze old Earth entertainment, I'm going to deactivate my masker and give us all something more interesting to do."

"Hey, he makes some very good points about *Babylon Space Five*."

"Moron. It's *Deep Babylon Nine*."

"Whatever."

A sudden noise from the mess moved them toward the boiler room again. Slipping single file past the storage tanks, they reached a heavy metal door.

"Wonder what the fukking sign says." Juan flicked the painted letters with a finger.

"Keep out. Authorized personnel only."

In the silence that followed, five heads turned toward Ressk—only Haysole kept his attention on the lock.

"You read Silsvah?" Binti asked after a moment.

Ressk snorted. "Don't need to. That's what it always says on these sorts of doors."

"Okay, we're through." Haysole straightened, twisting a pair of connections together. "This is what gave me away the last time."

"Security system?"

"I think Staff said it was a fire alarm."

"You think?"

"Doesn't matter." He closed the door behind them, careful not to let the connections slip. "I've fixed it."

They were in a long corridor, wide enough to hold three Marines walking abreast. It appeared to be made of Silsvah's poreless concrete and it sloped gently up toward a blue light—the only source of illumination.

"The upper door leads out onto the street that runs behind the compound," Haysole murmured as they climbed. "It's mostly an access alley, so there's no windows overlooking it. Unfortunately, Sergeant Glicksohn was standing there waiting for me, so I don't know where the road goes."

Binti reached the door first. "I'm assuming the letters on that light say exit—which reminds me, we have a small problem. No translation program."

"Not entirely accurate. And quit looking at me like that!" Ressk snapped as all six pairs of eyes turned toward him. He pulled his slate off his belt. "Staff's implant's acting up, so she asked me to have a look at her translation program. The data was too scrambled for me to fix the problem, but . . ." He finished keying in his entry and from the small speaker came an extended string of sibilants.

"And that means?" Binti demanded.

"I'll have whatever he's drinking."

She beamed down at him. "You know, for a short, hairless troll, you're pretty damned smart."

"I still say it wasn't very smart not to bring our fukking weapons," Juan muttered as Haysole worked on the door.

"We're going out for a drink, not to start a war," Hollice reminded him. "Besides—anyone who's not actually armed in some way, speak up now."

The silence stretched and lengthened, broken finally by Haysole standing and cracking open the door. The air that pushed in was significantly hotter than the air in the tunnel.

"It doesn't even fukking cool down here at night."

"Ra Navahsis was cool at night."

"And that would mean something if we were *in* Ra Navahsis."

Mouth slightly open, Mysho waved a hand vigorously in front of her face. "I really hate the way this place smells."

"What?" Juan demanded. "Your fukking nose plugs aren't working either?"

"They're working. But I still hate the smell."

One by one they slipped outside, the two di'Taykan, eyes at their darkest to utilize the minimal amount of light, on point.

As they rounded the first corner, two dark figures slipped out of the shadows and followed.

FIVE

Silsviss street lighting consisted of dim globes bulging out of the sides of concrete pillars, designed to imitate the phosphorescent fungus that grew on many of their trees. It shed a diffused green light that didn't so much pierce the swirling mist as it was absorbed and reemitted by it.

"Why are the streets so empty?" Binti asked as they hurried from pillar to pillar. "There aren't even any vehicles moving around out here."

"You don't think they put potentially dangerous aliens near where people live, do you?"

She reached out and lightly smacked the back of Ressk's head. "Who are you calling *potentially* dangerous?"

Maintaining defensive positions, they crossed a narrow parklike strip of short vegetation, every step disturbing a cloud of tiny insects that buzzed around their knees before settling back to the ground.

"Fukking bloodsuckers," Juan muttered and crushed one against his thigh.

"They're not sucking your blood," Hollice told him, "so leave them alone. And since we're speaking of alone—Haysole! There's nothing out here. Where are we going?"

The di'Taykan pointed through a masking screen of giant ferns toward a cluster of low-lying buildings skirting what looked like the Silsviss version of a chain-link fence. The buildings behind the fence had the unmistakable appearance of barracks. "This is the direction the soldiers came from when we went through maneuvers today," Haysole explained. "And where you find soldiers, some enterprising sort has to have built . . ."

"A bar," Mysho finished.

"Do we really want to drink with Silsviss soldiers?" Ressk wondered.

"Would you rather drink with civilians?"

"Good point."

"Stop skulking." Hollice grabbed Juan's shirt and hauled him upright. "You skulk and you attract attention."

"So if I don't skulk, are they going to fukking ignore us?" he demanded, yanking the bunched fabric down.

"Probably not, but at least they won't think we're up to something."

"We're *not* up to something."

"The Silsviss don't know that."

"Binti's right," Ressk snickered. "It's time you took your sergeant's exam. That kind of paranoia isn't normal."

"Look, you walk like a tourist out seeing the sights, that's how you're treated. You walk like you're heading into enemy territory . . ." The corporal shrugged, his point clear.

As they emerged from the ferns and stepped out onto another road, the two di'Taykan slowed, allowing the rest of the group to bunch up at their backs. "We've been spotted," Mysho murmured. "A pair of soldiers, over against the end of that building."

"Officers?"

"No, their harnesses are too plain. They're just a couple of regular grunts."

"I wonder how *they* think we're walking?" Binti asked sarcastically.

"Here they come."

The six Marines split into three pairs and moved far enough apart to maneuver should it come to a fight.

One of the Silsviss soldiers spoke, and a moment later Ressk's slate demanded to know where they were going. Everyone looked at Hollice, who looked at Binti.

"Your idea," he reminded her.

She rolled her eyes and stepped closer to the Krai. "We're looking for the real Silsvah, not what the politicians decide to show us."

The soldier who'd spoken before snorted and no one needed the slate to translate, *fukking politicians.*

"Not likely," Binti snorted. "Probably catch something."

The translation program seemed up to the play on words and both Silsviss hissed appreciatively. After a quiet conversation the slate couldn't pick up, they came to an obvious agreement.

"We're heading to our *savara* . . ."

It took the slate an extra moment to translate the new word into the closest Confederation equivalent.

". . . frequently visited drinking establishment. You can come as our trophies."

"Trophies?" Hands dropped toward hidden weapons and Ressk's lips curled back.

The translation program tried again. "Guests."

Raising an eyebrow at Ressk, Binti accepted for all six. "Love to. Frequently visited drinking establishment?" she asked a moment later when names had been exchanged and the Marines had fallen in behind their new friends. "Trophies? What the hell is that all about?"

"I pulled the program out of Staff's head while doing a diagnostic. I may be missing a few variables. At least it's not hissing."

"You ever think that we're only hearing what the program wants us to hear?" Mysho mused. "I mean, when those oxymorons in Military Intelligence get through with it, how do we know that Silsviss doesn't go in one end and complete garbage comes out the other?"

"You sure you want to be a corporal?" Ressk asked Binti dryly. "It'll only make you paranoid."

"Mysho's got a point," Hollice objected.

"See?"

"We don't know what we're saying to them any more than we know what they're saying to us." Hollice lowered his voice further. "Look at their throat pouches."

Both pouches were slightly distended, the stretched skin startlingly pale in the darkness.

"They're fukking pleased with themselves, aren't they?"

"Hey, they're kids," Binti reminded them. "Remember the first time *you* met an alien up close and personal?"

The two di'Taykan exchanged a meaningful snicker.

"At the risk of being species specific," she muttered, "not quite what I meant."

They could hear the *savara* before they reached it, and even the Humans could smell it soon after that.

"Outside patio," the Silsviss who introduced himself as Sooton explained, leaning in close to the slate. "We'll wait here and Hairken can go around and give them some warning. The known fellow soldiers have been drinking—if they're startled, they might take a shot at you."

"Don't want that," Binti agreed. "Known fellow soldiers?" She sighed when Hairken had disappeared around the corner and Sooton had moved to a vantage point where he could watch both his friend and the Marines. "That sort of thing's going to get old fast."

"'Specially if you fukking repeat it every time," Juan muttered.

Hairken reappeared and waved. Sooton beckoned them forward.

"Once more into the breach, dear friends," Hollice declaimed quietly.

The other five turned to stare.

"It's a Human reference."

Juan snorted. Binti rolled her eyes.

Hollice sighed. "Just forget I said anything."

Taking a step toward them, Sooton hissed and beckoned impatiently. The Marines hurried to his side. "Look, all the fellow soldiers want to meet you, but there's six members of my *partizay* there—eight counting Hairken and me—I think we should join them. There are assurances of less violence in numbers."

"Safety in numbers?" Binti hazarded.

The translator hissed her question back at the Silsviss who nodded, "Yes."

Turning the corner onto the patio brought them under the scrutiny of between thirty and forty pairs of eyes. Only the four throwing steel darts at a dangling target ignored the new arrivals. The background music didn't quite fill in the sudden silence.

After a moment, about half of the staring Silsviss decided it was beneath them to seem impressed by the same aliens they saw daily on the parade square, and conversations started up again, defiantly loud. The remaining eyes tracked them as they moved single file through the gate in the simulated woodgrain plastic fencing and threaded a careful path through tails to a large round table off to one side.

A shuffling of stools gained everyone a space about the same time Hairken arrived from the service window with a tray of beer.

"Thanks." As his slate spat out the Silsviss translation, Ressk slid it out onto the table.

One of the soldiers stopped clawing an obscene sketch into the tabletop to poke the slate with a finger. "This will allow us to speak to each other?" he asked.

Ressk swallowed his first mouthful of beer with a happy sigh. "More or less," he acknowledged, wiping foam out of his lower nasal ridges. "But the program's set up for officers, so it'll probably add in a lot of bullshit."

The flickering tongues around the table spread throughout the room as those near enough to hear passed on the quip. Tension levels eased somewhat.

"Hey, *artras!*"

"You like *artras*?" a scarred soldier asked, passing the platter so that the Marines could help themselves to the salty pastry. When the answer came back a solid affirmative, his tongue flickered out and he said, "Then you should try a *kritkar.* Yrs!" The smaller male beside him jerked erect so quickly he almost spilled his beer. "Go to the place in this building where the food is prepared . . ."

Hollice kicked Binti under the table before she could either repeat the phrase or roll her eyes and get them all eviscerated. Somehow he doubted that the damage to the side of the Silsviss' face was the only reason the big soldier appeared to be snarling.

". . . and get a big bowl of *kritkar* for our alien friends."

Clearly feeling responsible, Sooton and Hairken indulged in a brief shoving match. Sooton lost. "Wait a minute, Yrs." He turned to the scarred soldier. "You said it yourself, Plaskry, these are aliens. Why would they eat *kritkar*?"

"Why wouldn't they?" Plaskry's throat pouch inflated slightly. "Do they refuse my hospitality? Or do they not have the male equipment to eat soldiers' food?"

Wondering what Plaskry had actually said before the translation program mangled it, Hollice touched Sooton lightly on one arm. "We can handle it," he said, then added more loudly, "bring on the *kritkar.*"

Yrs continued to hesitate.

"What?" Plaskry demanded.

"*Kritkar's* expensive, Plas, and I got my pay chit docked for a moldy tail guard."

The snarl broadened. "I'll pay."

"Hey, it's his *partizay*, and he'll pay if he wants to," Hollice said brightly as the smaller Silsviss scurried away.

Everyone in earshot turned to stare.

"Just fukking ignore him," Juan advised.

Moving between the pockets of deep shadow created by the dim street lighting, the pair of dark figures had followed the Marines from the embassy to the bar. There'd been a brief exchange when the six had met up with the two Silsviss soldiers, but they hadn't interfered. Seconds after the Marines had followed Sooton and Hairken onto the patio, they'd slipped into the *savara* by a side door. The taller of the two had pulled the proprietor aside for a hurried conversation and, after an official bit of hardware had been flashed, they'd been led along the edges of the room and up a flight of stairs to an empty loft overlooking the patio.

Down below, the Marines were waiting for the *kritkar* to arrive.

"I see why no one uses this place," Torin complained, pulling off the leather cap that had hidden her hair and reshaped her head to a vaguely Silsviss silhouette. "It's hotter than bloody blue blazes up here."

"How hot isss bloody blue blazesss?" Cri Sawyes wondered, settling himself at the edge of the loft.

"Not as hot as this. Are you sure they can't see you?"

He pulled his tail back into the shadows, "Posssitive. I would, however, be more concerned that they don't sssee you. I very much doubt that any of your lot would recognize me at this dissstance."

"The two di'Taykan might. They have a highly developed sense of smell."

"Even over thisss?" His gesture took in the nearly visible miasma of beer, greasy food, and heated bodies rising from the patio.

"Probably not." Torin made a note of both exits, then settled down beside him. "Should I be worried about the Silsviss we passed downstairs? One or two of them seemed to be giving me what I could only call a flat, unfriendly stare."

"We interrupted their drinking. Thossse inssside are not necessssarily here for a good time. They're the ssseriousss drinkersssss."

"From the scars, they looked like serious fighters."

"Yesss . . ." Cri Sawyes fingered the scar on his hip. "They're the type who challenge and losssse and challenge and losssse—they can't win, but they can't ssstop challenging either. I expect it'sss why they drink. Pitiful really."

"And the boys on the patio?"

"I doubt there hasss ever been a ssseriousss challenge made by any of them."

"How can you tell?"

"Few ssscarsss. And besssidesss . . ." His tongue flicked out. "I helped to ssselect the sssoldiersss who would guard the politiciansss who would meet with the aliensss."

"Ah." A quick glance over the railing showed Ressk had slaved his slate to Binti's. "It's not going to be hard to keep an eye on my lot, is it? Given sizes and colors, they stick out like half a dozen sore thumbs."

Cri Sawyes glanced down at his hand, looking more than a little puzzled. Then he shook his head, having clearly decided it didn't matter. "To be perfectly honessst, I'm amazed your Lieutenant Jarret allowed you to go through with thisss."

"Our orders state that we're to report on how the Marines and Silsviss interact. We can't do that unless we have some actual interaction." Torin nodded toward the patio. "Besides, there're three Humans, two di'Taykan, and a Krai down there, and if any one of them can't get along with your common Silsviss soldier—or vice versa—I want to know now. Not when we're facing the Others and it might cause a problem."

"And you don't think it will caussse a problem now?"

She shrugged. "It'll cause a bigger problem if it's accompanied by live ammunition."

"True. But ssssupossse the right combination of Marinesss hadn't decided to go over the wall?"

"I'd have sent them back until they got it right."

"Ssstaff Sssergeant . . ."

"All right, when it came down to it, this is essentially the group I expected to make the break. Everyone's rapidly reaching the point where they need to do something that doesn't involve standing guard at an unused door, but these six are a little closer to that point than the rest." Torin swiped at the sweat on her neck, then rubbed her hand dry against her hip. "It's also why four of them are in the same fireteam—complementary temperaments ensures they work well as a unit."

"And their copy of the transsslation program? You planned that asss well?"

"I made it available to Ressk. He did the rest."

"I sssee." Cri Sawyes sat quietly for a moment, tail tip twitching as he thought. "You know your people," he said at last.

Torin nodded. "They're *my* people."

The *kritkar* arrived in a covered dish. An expectant silence followed its path from the kitchen to the table as the Silsviss on the patio waited to see what these alien soldiers would do.

A few tongues flicked out as Plaskry elbowed Yrs out of the way the moment he'd set the dish down. It was the bigger male's joke, after all, and he wanted to deliver the punch line.

"Help yourself," he said and lifted the lid.

A claw, about half an inch long, appeared over the edge of the bowl as the first of the *kritkar* attempted a last-minute escape.

The tongue flickering grew more pronounced.

"Like this," Plaskry hissed, scooping up a handful of the tiny live crustaceans and popping them into his mouth.

"Oh, like *that*." Ressk looked around at the others as though he'd only been waiting for instruction. "Not one at a time . . ." He scooped an equally large handful out of the bowl. ". . . like this."

Plaskry stopped chewing to watch and forgot about chewing altogether when Ressk reached for seconds, thirds, fourths, and finally picked out and ate the last three. Suddenly conscious of everyone staring at him, the Krai flushed and stopped digging at a bit of shell caught between his teeth. "Oh. Sorry. Did the rest of you want some?"

The silence lasted another two heartbeats, then erupted. Sooton and Hairken thumped each other on the chest and whacked tails, triumphantly reminding each other that they'd brought the aliens to the *savara* in the first place. After a moment of pulling the loudest phrases from the air, the two slates now holding the program spat out mostly unintelligible congratulations and a few insults thrown toward Plaskry.

"Just once I'd like to go some place where they didn't try to gross us out with the local delicacy," Binti muttered under the noise. "So, what'd they taste like?"

Ressk shrugged. "*Chrick*. Crunchy—but then all seafood tastes the same to me."

"Pity you didn't leave enough to run past a slate," Hollice grunted. "We could've checked to see if they were poisonous to the rest of us."

"And you'd have eaten a handful?"

"Hey, I once ate two dozen raw oysters to impress my best friend's date and crunchy could only be an improvement over that phlegm on the half shell."

"You figure tall, tailed, and ugly over there is going to spring for another bowl?" Binti wondered.

On cue, Plaskry rounded the table and clamped one hand down on Ressk's shoulder. "Your little food eaten before the main meal . . ."

Binti snarled and hooked her slate back on her belt.

". . . cost me a third of my pay chit!"

Continuing to dig at the bit of shell, Ressk grinned. "Guess there's no chance of seconds, then."

The big Silsviss hissed, and his tail whacked Ressk's stool at the spot where a tail would usually have hung. "Seconds? You aliens have got more male equipment than a large carnivorous quadruped!"

Ressk snatched his slate to safety before Binti could edit the program with her fist. "Then I guess I owe you a beer. Yrs!"

Attention jerked away from his mournful examination of the empty bowl, Yrs looked first to the slate and then up at Ressk.

He tossed over his souvenir credit chit. "Beer for the *partizay* on me!"

"Deftly done," Cri Sawyes acknowledged as Yrs left the patio to renewed noise.

"It's an old shtick," Torin told him. "The Krai can eat almost anything on almost any world. They have the Galaxy's most efficient gut."

"I wasss referring more to the way they usssed that efficient gut to manipulate the sssituation. Only the Krai, who asss you sssay can eat anything, had to eat the *kritkar* and yet all the Marinesss benefit. They have been accepted by the sssoldiersss."

"So far," Torin agreed. "But don't forget they're also buying a round. That helped."

"True. You do realize that the sssoldiersss will now attempt to get your people drunk."

"I realize."

"And?"

"It should be interesting."

The high-pitched beeping cut through the ambient noise like a hot knife through field rations and fell right smack in the middle of the tonal range guaranteed to produce maximum irritation. Swearing in three languages, all six Marines dropped their attention to their slates.

"Mine," Sooton muttered, plucking a black rubber cylinder off his harness. He flicked out an antenna, opened his auditory ridge to insert a round knob and bent the rest of the cylinder around by his mouth. "Yeah . . . Just a minute, I'm getting interference from the buildings . . ." Pushing back his stool, he walked over to the edge of the patio, talking as he moved.

"You think they operate on fukking radio waves?" Juan wondered, eyes gleaming.

"That's always been the cheapest." Mysho waved her beer around at the Silsviss. "And they've got to be cheap. Almost everyone seems to have one."

"Low tech," he sneered. "They've only got audio."

"Give them a break, Juan. They'd barely got off the planet before the Confederation contacted them."

Grunting a reluctant agreement, Juan moved over beside Sooton when he returned to the table and asked if he could see the cylinder.

"Sure. It was Blarnic," he added to the table at large. "Wanted to know if anything was happening here tonight."

Tongues flickered.

Squinting down at the handset, Juan rubbed a finger over the rubberized controls. "How does it work?"

"You mean inside?"

"No, I mean how does it fukking break rocks. Yeah, I mean inside."

"No idea." Sooton looked around, then pointed. "But Hars over there is a tech. He should know."

Juan grabbed for his slate as he stood, but Ressk blocked his hand. "Not yet. I've only copied half the translation program."

"You haven't even started copyin' it onto Haysole's slate, and he seems to be fukking managin' without it."

They both looked over to a dark corner where the di'Taykan had gathered a small group of his own.

"He's probably playing 'I'll show you mine if you show me yours.' I doubt he's talking much."

"Wonder if he's winning."

Ressk snickered.

"What isss the young male with the blue hair doing?"

"Plopping his pecker on the table, as near as I can tell from up here."

Cri Sawyes turned from the view below to stare at Torin. "I beg your pardon, Ssstaff Sssergeant."

"It's a di'Taykan thing. They like to know where they stand."

"He isss comparing the sssize of his reproductive organ to thossse of the sssoldiersss?"

"Yeah. Don't Silsviss do that?"

"Yesss, when we are young in the pressservesss but not usssually at thisss age."

"The di'Taykan can be pretty persuasive, and he's probably curious because nothing shows." Her gaze dropped. She didn't intend it to, but she couldn't help it.

Cri Sawyes' tongue flicked out. "I am *not* going to show you mine."

"No, sir." Ears burning, she returned her attention back to the patio.

". . . so we've got them pinned down in this small village, the civilians cleared out when they saw trouble coming, so it's just them and a couple of nasty artillery pieces that don't seem to be running out of their powering medium any time soon, and those egg suckers with the most metal send us in to clear the place residence by residence!"

"Idiots!" Hollice slapped the table for emphasis. "Why didn't they just call in an air strike?"

Sooton hissed and smacked his hand down beside the corporal's. "That's what we wanted to know!"

Juan grabbed a small electrical component just before it rolled though a puddle of beer and tried to snap it back into Hars' headset. "So this goes here?"

"No." A somewhat unsteady claw tapped the rubber. "Here."

"That's what I fukking said, *here.*"

Hars belched.

"But you're a mammal!"

Mysho's eyes lightened. "Your point?"

Binti's third dart hit the spinning target on the outer edge and during the instant between the cancellation of the old momentum and the application of the new, her fourth dart hit the black triangle in the middle.

"*Harttag!*" roared her partner, smacking her in the backs of the legs with his tail. He hissed, disappointment coloring his glee, and smacked her again. "How can we celebrate *harttag* when you have no tail!"

"I don't have a tail," Binti agreed, moving inside the painful blows. "But I do have hips." Her answering blow lifted him over an empty stool and into the lap of a Silsviss who'd been watching the game.

After a moment's stunned silence, tongues began to flick.

With his own tongue flicking so fast he could hardly breathe, Binti had to help her fallen partner to his feet.

"Your people ssseem to be drinking in moderation."

"Moderation might be a bit of an overstatement." Torin tracked Mysho's path from the bar to the table and noted whom she unloaded the beer in front of. "But they're being careful." It helped that the Silsviss beer contained less alcohol than they were used to, but she saw no need to pass that information on. "It shouldn't be long now."

Cri Sawyes blew out his throat pouch impatiently. "What shouldn't?"

"See that group over in the corner? I'm guessing they're a different *partizay* than the group my lot hooked up with and that the two don't get along. Maybe one *partizay* feels like they've been pulling more crap duties than the other, maybe it's personal, it doesn't really matter—they've been glaring across the patio all night."

"Maybe they just don't like aliensss."

"No, they'd like aliens fine if those aliens were with them, but since they're not, they've become a convenient excuse."

"For a fight?"

"Yes."

His throat pouch inflated slightly as he studied the movements in the crowd below. "And the fight becomesss a ssstudy in the sssocial interplay between ssspeciesss."

Torin shrugged. "When something is inevitable, you might as well learn what you can from it."

"We are not Human, Ssstaff Sssergeant." He turned his golden gaze from the patio to her. "Nor are we Krai, nor are we di'Taykan."

"No, but you *are* a social species with a paid fighting force who share intoxicants in a social setting." She shrugged again. "If it walks like a duck . . ."

The movement of his inner eyelids made him look momentarily cross-eyed. "What," he demanded, "isss a duck?"

"A medium-sized water bird from Terra."

He opened his mouth, clearly thought better of what he was about to say, and shook his head. "You really are a most confusssing sssspeciesss."

Hollice felt something compact under his foot, wasted a second wondering where that something had come from, as the floor had been clear when he'd started the step, and then suddenly realized what that something had to be.

"That was my tail!" A large Silsviss, nearly Plaskry's size, rose off his stool and spun around to face the Marine. "Clumsy alien, egg sucker," he snarled into the silence that had answered his first bellow. "Clumsy alien, tailless, egg sucker."

From the reactions around him, Hollice suspected the insults had lost a little in the translation. "Sorry. Didn't see it. Let me buy you a beer to take your mind off the pain."

"You think that is all my tail means to me!" The throat pouch began to distend. "I will rip your miserable alien heart out and eat it!"

He felt more than heard Binti move from the dart game into place behind him. The others were too far away to add much initial backup, and he couldn't see Haysole at all. "Look, I said I was sorry and I offered to buy you a beer. I don't know what else I can . . ." The blow glanced off his left shoulder. It threw him sideways without doing any real damage, and he came up smiling. First contact had been made.

His return blow took the Silsviss in the belly and would've had more impact had he not been avoiding a swinging tail when he made it.

The Silsviss' companions rose as one.

Hollice heard the high trill of a di'Taykan attack cry, saw Binti smash a tray into a Silsviss face, and then had time to notice nothing beyond his immediate survival.

"There, see! The us-against-them split isn't Silsviss, non-Silsviss. There." Torin pointed. "And there. Silsviss fighting beside Marines."

"Thisss isss what you wanted to sssee happen?"

"This is exactly what I wanted to see. The lieutenant will be pleased."

"Then if you have the information you need, we'd bessst ssstop the fight before sssomeone isss . . . before sssomeone elssse isss . . ." Nostrils flaring, Cri Sawyes glared down at the battle. "When you sssaid the Krai would eat anything, I never assumed that included tailsss."

"Your boy bit him first." Torin watched a Silsviss who'd been thrown down onto the floor bring the claws on both feet into play and nodded thoughtfully. "But you're right, we should stop it before an outside authority arrives."

They turned together and came face-to-face with two of the uglier customers from the room below. A little surprised they'd been able to move into position so quietly, Torin ducked the fist blow.

The second connected.

Had the rail been an inch shorter, she'd have gone over it. As it was, she dropped, rolled, and came up holding a Silsviss tail in both hands. A yank and a kick toppled her attacker sideways, his claws barely tearing the fabric across her thigh.

He was fast, she acknowledged as she leaped into an answering kick.

Son of a . . . I should never have let go of that tail! Sucking a painful breath in through her teeth, she wondered if her ribs were broken.

The Silsviss responded to her pain by inflating his throat pouch and roaring.

Heart pounding, the taste of her own blood in her mouth, Torin scooped up her stool and smashed it into the side of his head.

He finished the roar on the way down, and it ended with impact.

"Well done, Ssstaff Sssergeant." Throat pouch still slightly extended, Cri Sawyes cleaned his claws against a bit of his opponent's harness. "You were certainly not what he expected."

"Oh?"

"A challenge isss alwaysss anssswered before the fight continuesss."

She poked the prone body with her foot until he moaned, reassuring her he was still alive. "I *answered* the challenge."

"In your own way, yesss. Are you hurt?"

Shallow gouge, bruises, one rib possibly cracked. "I'm fine. What about you?"

His tongue flicked out, and he tapped his fallen opponent lightly with his tail. "I told you, they challenge and lossse and challenge again."

Torin grinned. "Pitiful really."

"Indeed."

Which was when she noticed it had gotten very quiet down below. "Wonderful, looks like the authorities have arrived."

"*Tarvar ssselk.*" After a moment, her translator came up with, "Military police."

"You, alien, tell me who issued challenge."

Hollice shifted his weight off his swelling right knee. "I didn't notice."

The Silsviss swept his gaze over the rest of the Marines.

"And I suppose none of you other aliens noticed either?" When he received the expected negative chorus, he turned his attention to his own people. "Well?"

Wiping his claws off on his leg, Plaskry snarled, "Happened too fast."

"What about you, Yrs?"

"Didn't see nothing."

"Really?" The MP smacked his tail guard against the floor as he swept his gaze over the rest of the room. "Ranscur. Looks like you took a few hits. You wouldn't know who hit who first would you?"

The big Silsviss who'd made first contact gazed over the heads of his companions at the Marines, then at the MP. "No idea."

"Don't give me that *ara srev crovmirs shartlerg*!"

All six slates hissed and sputtered but surrendered the attempt at a translation.

"Someone challenged first, and we're all going to stay right here until I find out who!"

Standing just off the patio, Torin watched Cri Sawyes walk over to the MP and show his credentials. Their discussion didn't last long. The MP wasn't happy, but Torin suspected his unhappiness didn't come close to how the Marines felt when they were escorted out of the *savara* and found their Staff Sergeant waiting.

Haysole finally broke the silence. "Did you know your leg is bleeding, Staff?"

"Yes. I know."

"Were you fighting?"

"I'd worry less about what I was doing, Private, and more about what you've been doing." Eyes narrowed, she very deliberately examined each of them. Injuries seemed minor although they'd all been marked by Silsviss claws.

"The military police officer tellsss me that none of your people will sssay who ssstarted the fight."

Torin looked past the Marines to Cri Sawyes and past him to the Silsviss standing quietly on the patio. "Is that true, Corporal Hollice?"

"Yes, Staff Sergeant."

"And do you know who started the fight?"

"It all happened so fast, Staff Sergeant."

She snapped her gaze down to meet Hollice's level stare—slightly less level than usual due to a rapidly spreading black eye—and smiled. "Of course it did, Corporal." Still holding his eyes with hers, she raised her voice. "Cri Sawyes, if you could please see that things are settled here, I'll take my people back where they belong."

"Of courssse."

He caught up just before they reached the embassy. "The proprietor hasss been paid for damagesss, the military police officer hasss left—nothing will come of thisss adventure."

Torin grinned as a certain amount of tension left the shoulders of the six Marines marching in front of her. "Nothing will come of it from the Silsviss," she amended.

The shoulders tensed again.

She marched them to the west door, managed not to laugh at the faces of the two Marines on guard, and waved them through. "Lieutenant Jarret wants to speak with you."

"Now, Staff Sergeant?"

"Do any of you need to see the doctor immediately?"

"No, Staff Sergeant."

"Then the lieutenant would like to speak with you *now*."

Just inside the door, she paused to watch them climb the stairs and note who was favoring what. Her own injuries had died to a dull throb, easy to ignore. As she followed, she realized she actually felt better than she had in days.

"You enjoyed that, didn't you?"

Torin glanced up at Cri Sawyes. He could be requesting information, but she suspected that he'd learned to read Human reactions fairly accu-

rately during the last few weeks and was, in fact, asking only for confirmation. "Yes," she told him, trying not to smile as broadly as her mood
demanded, "I did."

He nodded thoughtfully. "Remember how you told me you knew what
would happen tonight becaussse you knew your people?"

"Yes."

His tongue flicked out. "I would say that your lieutenant knows *his*
people, too."

Six

"*I would say that your lieutenant knows his people too.*"

Torin frowned as she limped up the stairs to Lieutenant Jarret's office. Their orders *had* wanted them to report on the interaction between the Marines and the Silsviss. To do that, they *had* needed interaction to occur but, more importantly, they'd needed to control the inevitable rebellion born of inactivity that was brewing in the platoon.

"Inevitable?" the lieutenant had repeated.

"Yes, sir. The Marines have trained these people to survive on the edge. It's what they're used to, and, after a while, it's what they'll go looking for. They need the rush that comes with facing the unknown."

"You think I should let them look for that rush."

"Yes, sir. I think you can use whatever they find to make field observations and to bleed off the excess energy before the whole system blows." She'd shifted her weight from foot to foot as she considered how much more she should say, then, finally, had added, "I told the general right from the beginning that this was no job for a combat unit."

"You don't think that sending a group of boredom-crazed Marines out among the Silsviss will set diplomatic relations back to square one?"

"No, sir. Not if we maintain control."

"So, you believe that since something's going to happen anyway, it shouldn't happen randomly?"

"Yes, sir."

Lieutenant Jarret had stared at her in silence for a few moments. "How do you suggest we control the situation?" he asked at last.

"When a group large enough to make observations valid goes out the lock, Cri Sawyes and I will follow them, observe them, and keep them out of trouble if need be."

"No. I don't think we should involve the Silsviss."

"I don't think we should let our people out without involving the Silsviss," Torin told him dryly. "And Cri Sawyes has the authority to stop anything that might start."

Although he clearly hadn't liked the idea, he reluctantly nodded. "All right. Cri Sawyes goes, but why you? Why not one of the sergeants?"

"The sergeants are specific to each squad, sir, and we can't be certain which squad will go over."

"Whereas you've put the fear of the gods into the whole platoon?"

"Yes, sir."

He'd stared at her a moment longer, lilac eyes dark. "I see."

At the time, Torin had considered his response nothing more than a noncommittal way to end the conversation. Now, though, she wondered what he'd seen. Had he seen past her reasoned arguments, noticing that the forced inactivity and the pointless ceremonial duties were driving her just as crazy as the six Marines now leading the way up the stairs? Had the night's adventure been as much for her to release pressure as for the platoon or for their orders?

Was he actually a good enough officer to see what she needed, or had that one unfortunate night together taught him more about her than he had any right to know?

Give it up. He's a di'Taykan. Sex may be a large part of their lives, but they keep it separate. Is it so hard to believe that he might actually be becoming a good officer?

It seemed a little early, but she supposed it was possible. It was always a difficult transition to begin thinking of second lieutenants as more than merely warm bodies in a uniform, to realize they were actually beginning to take command.

He's got a lot of bloody nerve trying to manipulate me, battled with *they grow up so fast.*

Her half-dozen malcontents/observational subjects were waiting in the hall outside Lieutenant Jarret's door. Torin walked through them, looking neither left nor right as they shuffled out of her way, and she knocked on the worn wood.

When the lieutenant's voice told them to enter, she turned to the Marines. "Form a line, single file, along the south wall under the row of high windows." Fortunately, the latch—its dimensions uncomfortable in human hands—gave her no trouble. Few things undermined authority like public fumbling. "Private Mashona . . ."

Binti paused in the doorway and Ressk turned sideways to get around her.

". . . the gash on your shoulder is bleeding again. You should see the doctor immediately."

"What about your leg, Staff?"

"What about it?"

"It's bleeding again, too."

Torin looked down at her leg and up at Binti. The younger woman's expression was easy to read: *If you don't need to see the doctor immediately, neither do I, so I'm not abandoning my team. And besides, if I'm standing there bleeding on his floor, the lieutenant'll keep it short.*

There were just the two of them and the Silsviss in the hall now. Her own face expressionless, Torin moved out of the way. "Get in there, then."

When she turned to Cri Sawyes, he shook his head.

"Thisss isss no busssinesss of mine. I will wait and ssspeak with the lieutenant later."

"Thank you for your help."

"You're very welcome, Ssstaff Sssergeant. It wasss not unenjoyable. I sssusssspect I learned asss much about your people asss you did about mine." He slapped the floor with his tail.

Good thing you're on our side, then, Torin mused, entering the office, and taking her position to the right of the line.

The lieutenant's outer office was empty of everything except an unplugged and therefore inoperative vending machine the Silsviss had considered either too heavy or too unintrusive to move. Because the triple banks of lights buzzed continually, Lieutenant Jarret preferred to work in one of the inner rooms.

Almost immediately upon Torin taking her place, the door to the next room opened and the lieutenant emerged in full dress, gloves tucked into his belt.

"Shouldn't I be waiting for them?"

"No, sir. They wait for you. You don't wait for them."

He didn't look any more perceptive than he ever had—no matter how much circumstances seemed to support Cri Sawyes' observation.

"These are the six?"

"Yes, sir."

The ceiling was so high, the room so large and empty, that their voices echoed slightly.

As Lieutenant Jarret walked slowly down the line, Torin was pleased to see that all eyes were locked on a position about six inches above his left shoulder—all eyes except for Corporal Hollice's shiner, which had swollen shut. After a second pass, where he tersely told Haysole to adjust his masker, the lieutenant paused and said before he turned to face them, "I gave orders that no one was to leave our assigned area."

He pivoted on one heel, the ends of his hair flicking back and forth. "You six chose to disobey that order." A lilac gaze raked them up, down, and side to side. "What happened after is not my concern, but if the Silsviss chose to make an issue of it, I shall have no choice but to let them. Do you understand?"

"Yes, sir." The unison was a little ragged. Although the question was no doubt right out of the officer's handbook, Torin hoped he wouldn't ask any more—this lot was just as likely to start giving him answers he didn't expect.

"Three days' stoppage of pay. As your entire fireteam was involved, Corporal Hollice, you will all be standing night two until we leave Silsvah. Corporal di'Merk Mysho, you'll be using your off-duty time to help the doctor scan his specimens. Private di'Stenjic Haysole, you may continue cleaning the sanitary facilities. When you're dismissed, you're all to go directly to the doctor. He's expecting you. You can dismiss them now, Staff."

"Yes, sir." Torin gave the one word order but watched the lieutenant as the Marines obeyed. Had she been close enough, she suspected she'd have been able to hear his hearts pounding. Fortunately, everyone else in the room had been focused over his left shoulder and on their own predicament, so they hadn't noticed how nervous he'd been. There was nothing like a discipline parade to make a junior officer realize the power he held over the forty-odd lives in his platoon.

It was also the place where a junior officer could abuse that power were he so inclined, and senior NCOs had learned to watch them closely at such times.

"Staff?"

"Yes, sir?" Torin shifted her weight back onto both legs and straightened.

"Do you think I . . ." He took a deep breath. His hair stilled. "How do you think it went?"

How did I do? They weren't the words he'd used, but it was the question he'd asked. She hid a smile. Her baby wasn't quite ready to leave the nest. "It went well, sir. You didn't waste time talking at them and at no point did you talk down to them. The punishments were fair, hard enough so they'll think twice about going out the lock again, not so hard they'll say 'fuk you' and go just to show you they can."

"We came up with punishments together."

"Yes, sir. But you *could* have overruled me."

Relief made him smile. "Really?"

Torin lifted a brow and said, in the dry tone her second lieutenant expected, "Not easily, sir."

"Thank you, Staff Sergeant. You'd better go see the doctor about your leg."

"Yes, sir."

"Staff?"

"Sir?" She turned, sucking air through her teeth as the movement pulled the damaged muscle.

"Did we win?"

She paused, waiting until she was certain she wouldn't be overheard. "We kicked lizard butt, sir."

"Good work, Staff."

"Thank you, sir."

"Three days' loss of pay." Binti sighed and poked at her shoulder. "That sucks."

"We're stuck on this *serley* mudhole until the *Berganitan* comes back," Ressk reminded her. "Where are you going to spend it?"

"Maybe I'm saving it for my retirement, asshole."

"Maybe *cark*'ll fly, but I doubt it. Stop poking at the sealant or it won't heal clean."

"Stop telling me what to do."

Upper lip curled, he smacked her hand away from the wound. "Then stop poking."

"*Private di'Stenjic Haysole, you may continue cleaning the sanitary facilities,*" Haysole snorted. "Guess Second Lieutenant di'Ka Jarret's too high class to call it a crapper like everyone else."

"Poor baby." Juan patted his cheek as he rose to take his turn with the doctor. "You think the lieutenant was too fukking hard on you?"

Haysole looked confused. "No. I just think he should've called it a crapper."

"He ought to thank us for dragging him out of whatever sexless diplomatic function he was at," Mysho grumbled. "But he won't."

By the time they got back to the barracks, the rest of the platoon was waiting only for specific details. Military structure inadvertently encouraged gossip and di'Taykans practically considered it a competitive sport. With the two combined, facts chased speculation through the troops at full speed.

Once the story had been told—and embellished—the unanimous belief, freely expressed, was that they'd gotten off easy.

"Then you can stand fukking night two for as long as we're on this rock," Juan muttered, checking the spare clip on his belt.

On station or on board ship, the second night watch, or night two, lasted from 2700 hours until 0430—a twenty-seven-hour day being the compromise among the three species who made up the military arm of the Confederation. No one liked it. Night one was at worst a late night. Night three was an early morning. Night two was a convenient punishment watch. On Silsviss it lasted four standard hours and twelve minutes.

"Too easy," Drake repeated, tossing a six-sided die from hand to hand. "Nothing on your record—clean a few toilets, help the doctor, lose some sleep, then finished and forgotten. If that's all you're getting, we can all go out the lock."

"Won't be as easy the next time," Hollice grunted, shrugging into his tunic. "They let us go. Haysole already went out that door once. You don't think they'd have taken care of a known weak spot in the perimeter?"

"Corporals." Ressk shook his head. "Paranoid."

Binti frowned. "No. He's got a point. Who told Staff where we were?"

"No mystery, the Silsviss who ran the *savara* obviously called someone when we arrived."

"Who? Who would a bartender call to report aliens walking in? The local cops?"

"The military cops."

"Yeah, right. Hello, Officer, I'd like to report aliens in my bar. They're not going to bother someone high enough to talk to our people until they know it's not a false alarm."

"Probably been a lot of them since we landed," Mysho said thoughtfully, fingering her masker.

"Right. So the MPs go to the bar, see us, then the news starts heading up the chain of command until it gets to someone who can open a diplomatic channel."

"But the MPs were *at* the bar."

"Because of the fight. Staff showed up on the patio way, way too fukking fast unless she already knew we were there."

"Probably wanted to see us interacting with the Silsviss. There's been some concern about the lack of one-on-one unsupervised action."

Everyone turned to look at Haysole, who grinned. "Hey, you overhear a lot when you're always cleaning the crapper."

"All right, you want paranoid, think about this," Hollice suggested, taking his weapon down off its rack. "Staff and our assigned lizard were in a fight."

After a brief pause, where those who'd seen the staff sergeant filled in visuals for those who hadn't, Corporal Conn set aside his latest letter home, and said thoughtfully, "Maybe he didn't want her to take you guys away from Silsviss authorities."

"They weren't fighting with each other." Hollice checked his charge and hitched the strap up onto his shoulder. "Use your brains for more than insulation; they were coming to get us and they got jumped. I think there's some Silsviss who don't want us here."

Binti reached out and smacked his shoulder. "Hey! *We* got jumped in the bar."

"That was a bar fight, nothing more. But Staff wasn't with us when she got jumped." A jerk of Hollice's chin got his fireteam moving out the door.

The Marines still in the room passed confusion back and forth until, at the last minute, one of the di'Taykan called out, "Which means?"

"I think there's something going on here."

"I don't think so," Torin snorted. "Cri Sawyes says they were the type who keeps challenging and losing and are too stupid to stop challenging."

"I don't like it." Cradling a jar of beer between both hands, Mike frowned up at the senior NCO. "I don't like that they were in the same bar you were in. Too convenient."

"I got the impression that every bar has a few." She poked at the sealant on her thigh and did a few experimental deep knee bends.

Holding the destroyed uniform trousers between thumb and forefinger, Anne Chou snorted. "Gee, I can't wait until I'm a staff sergeant and I get to be beaten up by the locals in the name of cultural interaction."

"Yeah? Well, when you're a staff sergeant, you'll know that staff sergeants beat up the locals in the name of cultural interaction, not the other way around."

"So essentially what you're saying is, you should see the other guy?"

Torin grinned. "Essentially."

Cultural interaction had an immediate result.

"All right, people, let's get this place packed up, we're moving out!"

Jerked out of his bunk and onto his feet by Sergeant Glicksohn's bellow, Haysole grabbed for his pants. "I thought we were supposed to stay here for another three days."

"And that would be relevant, Private Haysole, if the Silsviss cared what you thought. Since they don't, get moving. Sleds are on the way in from the VTA."

"What about breakfast, Sarge?" Ressk asked as the room of Marines began resembling an anthill stirred with a stick. "Squad Three hasn't eaten yet."

"We pack the mess up last. You get in there as soon as Squad Two gets out." He paused and they could hear Sergeant Trey's voice rising and falling in the next room. "If I were you, I wouldn't worry about chewing everything a hundred times. Hollice, your team sees to it that the personal effects of Corporal Conn's team are packed up and put on the sleds."

"Come on, Sarge," Hollice protested, "we stood night two."

"And your point?"

"Get someone else to do it."

Sergeant Glicksohn stopped talking long enough to smile broadly. "No." Then he fell back into the familiar cadence. "Once our sled's loaded, we load the civilians', then the whole platoon forms up in the square. Lieutenant Jarret wants us leaving for the landing field at 0930."

Juan glanced down at the time on his slate. "Fuk."

"Well put. Fortunately, the Dornagain are already moving." His eyes unfocused for a moment. "Sleds are here. You can start humping gear outside any time."

"Hey, Sarge?"

He paused in the doorway.

"You know why we're leaving?"

"Yes, I do, Haysole. Because the lieutenant gave us an order."

The di'Taykan closed the distance between them. "Aw, come on, Sarge."

"Don't even try it, Haysole. And turn up your masker."

"He knows," Binti snorted as the sound of the sergeant's bootheels faded. "He's just not going to tell us."

"Ours is not to reason why," Hollice muttered.

"You think this has something to do with last night?"

The answering silence was a clear affirmative.

"You think the Silsviss are pissed?" Binti wondered.

This time the silence wasn't so sure.

"Do we fukking care?" Juan snarled under his breath.

As two billion Silsviss significantly outnumbered one lone platoon of Confederation Marines, everyone ignored him.

"I think they've come to a decision," Hollice answered at last.

Ressk picked up a game biscuit with his toes, checked the number, and tossed it at Binti. "Don't I keep saying he's too paranoid to be a corporal?"

As the VTA shuddered into the air, Torin watched Lieutenant Jarret unhook his harness and make his way to the front of the troop compartment. In spite of the uneven ride, he moved well, and she had to admit he looked good. Of course, from a Human perspective, it was difficult for a di'Taykan to look anything but.

I wonder what would happen if we did it again . . .

Frowning, Torin denied ownership of the stray thought. They weren't going to do it again, end of discussion.

"The Silsviss have decided," the lieutenant began when he had everyone's attention, "to begin the final series of meetings intended to result in a decision about joining—or not joining—the Confederation two days early. We are therefore moving to the location of these meetings, two days early. Unofficially, it seems very likely the Silsviss will join as I was approached this morning by one of their commanders and asked to develop a simulation that would begin integrating our fighting styles."

"Is this all 'cause we proved we could kick ass, sir?"

Although he looked a little startled by it, he took the interruption in stride. "In what way, Private Mashona?"

Binti smiled broadly, her teeth gleaming against the mahogany of her face. "Things are happening today, sir. Things weren't happening yesterday. The only difference seems to be what happened last night."

"I know this is hard for a Marine to believe, Private, but it isn't always about us." There were a few snickers, and he raised a hand to forestall any other interruptions. "That said, while we're traveling, Ambassador Krik'vir wants to speak one on one with the six Marines who went out the lock. Sergeant Glicksohn . . ."

"Sir?"

"Arrange an order and send the first person up now."

"Sir."

Which does make it seem, Torin thought, as Lieutenant Jarret walked to the door and motioned for her to join him, *that the events of last night gave diplomacy a boot in the ass.* Remembering the long, boring hours of ceremonial duties, of standing for hours in damp heat while cadres of dignitaries hissed speeches about historical importance, she snorted. "If I'd known how much it would move things along," she said, following the lieutenant out of the troop compartment, "I'd have smacked someone with a stool weeks ago."

"And I'd have ordered it." He paused to allow her to fall into step. "The Silsviss seem unduly impressed by a little force, don't they?"

"Alien species, sir. All things considered, I'm just glad we found them before the Others did."

"We have already interviewed the enlisted personnel who participated in yesterday's cultural interaction . . ."

Trying not to stare at her reflection in Ambassador Krik'vir's eyestalks, Torin wondered which of the enlisted personnel had used that particular phrase. Somehow, she doubted it had also been the diplomatic label for the exercise.

". . . and have heard a startling amount of minutia but very little of substance. As you are in possession of the overview, we would now like to hear from you, Staff Sergeant Kerr." The ambassador settled back on her lower four legs while behind her, taking up most of the remaining space in the large storage locker, one of her assistants stroked the controls of a Mictok recording device. At least that's what Torin assumed it was, although it might have been anything from a musical instrument to a sex aid for all she knew. "Please, Staff Sergeant, begin at the beginning."

"The beginning?" *My family were farmers and I hated farming . . .* "A combat unit deprived of stimulus creates its own . . ." She told the ambassador how she'd discussed the inevitability of the situation with Lieutenant Jarret, his decision to allow herself and Cri Sawyes to follow and observe rather than stop it from happening, the situation as she saw it down on the patio, the fight, what she'd observed as well as her personal battle, and finally the aftermath.

"You tell the story well, Staff Sergeant."

"I've given a lot of reports, ma'am."

"Until today we have found the Silsviss to be distant, putting on a—how did Corporal Hollice put it?—a dog and pony show for our benefit."

"A dog and pony show, ma'am?" Dogs had settled Paradise with Humans but Torin had never seen a pony.

"Apparently it is an old Human term." Her outer mandibles clicked together gently. "We understand that it refers to matters of no substance. Today, we touched on substance for the first time, and we are hurried toward greater substance still. We know that the leaders of the various factions have been meeting with each other as we were shown the dogs and ponies, and perhaps the decisions they have come to are the only reason for our sudden movement. However, we cannot ignore that it may be because of the actions of last night."

"If I may, Ambassador, the Silsviss are a warrior species. General Morris made that very clear when he ordered a combat troop to a ceremonial post. Perhaps they were waiting to see some tangible indication they weren't about to hook up with a bunch of *paygari*." It was a di'Taykan word meaning *mewling infants* and the least profane description Torin could come up with on the spur of the moment.

The clicking became louder and faster. "We can think of few things more tangible than a stool to the head, Staff Sergeant."

Given the alternative, Torin supposed she was glad Ambassador Krik'vir chose to find the situation amusing.

Except for the two Mictok using the dubious privacy of the storage locker, the civilians were in their seats when Torin finally walked into their compartment. Only Madame Britt, the Rakva Charge D'Affaires, was actually working; the rest seemed to be skirting sleep. Whether they were tired of the assignment, tired of each other, or merely conserving strength for the deliberations to come, she had no idea. Fortunately, Cri Sawyes stood at his usual place by the view screen.

"Another wilderness preserve?" she asked, rounding the bulk of a Dornagain and joining him.

"Not yet, but shortly. Thisss isss one of the leassst civilized areasss of my planet. To a certain extent, the challenge rulesss outside the pressserve as well. To sssurvive here . . ." He shook his head.

"We're over it now," he said a few moments later, although Torin couldn't see a change in the terrain. "I sssussspect your Captain Danielsss hasss been given thisss flight path in order to show the young malesss that timesss are changing. That we are not alone in the universsse."

"That must have been comforting. When you found out you weren't alone," she added in response to his murmured question.

"Not really, no."

"No?" Torin, fourth generation post-contact, couldn't imagine not knowing. As far as she was concerned, space was quite empty enough, even with seventy-two known species. "It was what, then? Disturbing?"

"For me persssonally?" Cri Sawyes kept his gaze on the screen but his inner eyelids slid shut then open again. "I wasss never one of thossse who assssumed that we were the only intelligent life, that the great biological accident of our creation had happened only the once. But yesss, it wasss. It is a great blow to the ego, Sssergeant, to disssscover that you are, after all, not unique." He looked up, his tongue flickering. "I am, however, mossstly recovered."

"Glad to hear it, sir." As she made her way up to the cockpit, Torin acknowledged that she had come to quite like the big lizard. She had no idea how representative he was of his species as a whole—his willingness to be thrust into close contact with so many alien races logically suggested he was culturally flexible—but based on their time together, she thought the Silsviss would function quite well within the structure of the Confederation Marine Corps. The whole lack of female things still weirded her out a little, but she supposed she'd get used to it in time.

The cockpit on the VTA had been designed for efficiency rather than comfort, and Captain Daniels, Lieutenant Ghard, and two members of their

flight crew were just about a capacity crowd. Under the more normal circumstances of a drop from ship to ground Torin wouldn't have gone near
it, but since the Silsviss continued to insist on atmospheric travel, she had
time to kill. There was only so much ship to patrol and only so long she
could spend in a pressurized chamber with four Dornagain.

The upper third of the front wall of the cockpit was made of the same
clear silicon the Confederation used in the observatories on their deep
space ships. According to the sales pitch, the absolutely transparent material was stronger than the metals in the rest of the ship, and were it not for
the vertigo many species were subject to—not to mention the price of
production—it could have been the only material used to build the entire
fleet. Advertisements insisted it could emerge unscathed from the heart of
a star, but Torin suspected that claim had never actually been tested—not
by the advertising department anyway.

Steadying herself against the back of Captain Daniels' chair, she
squinted at the greenish-brown smear that obscured part of the view. "What
happened there?"

"Bird." Both hands continuing to work the controls, the captain flashed
a smile back over her shoulder. "Or something flying anyway."

"Something stupid," Lieutenant Ghard added. "I think it was challenging us."

Allowing for fluid dispersement, Torin put the bird at no more than half
a meter from wingtip to wingtip. "Maybe it was depressed."

"Sir." One of the aircrew looked up from her instruments. "We are
reaching the midpoint . . ." She paused, eyes unfocused. ". . . now . . ."

Torin's implant chimed midpoint.

". . . and our Silsviss escorts are peeling off. They say, good luck and
that they'll be interested to see how it turns out."

"They did?"

"Well, that's more or less how it translated, sir."

Captain Daniels shook her head. "That's new. Usually they just wish us
luck and clear skies."

"We're heading to the decision this time," Torin reminded her. Leaning
forward, she peered around at the crystal blue arc of sky. "Do we have no
escort at all now?"

"Not for another few minutes, Staff," Lieutenant Ghard told her. "We're
as far from the last place as our escort goes and not yet to the point where
our new escort picks us up."

In the silence that followed, everyone turned to look at him.

Finally, Captain Daniels snickered. "Can we blame that on the translator, airman?"

She grinned at the back of the lieutenant's head. "No, sir."

"You know what I meant," Ghard muttered, slumping over his panel. Then, almost as a continuation of the same move, he straightened again. "Hey, there they are."

"I'm not picking them up on scanners, sir."

Torin turned to look at the other airman who was frowning down at his screen, and turned back to the window again. Just at the edge of vision, she could see a pair of yellow/white flares. Sunlight reflecting from polished metal.

"All this atmospheric travel's gummed them up. We've probably got bird bits in the external sensors."

"That shouldn't make a difference, Captain."

The flares grew brighter, larger, and Torin felt the hair lift off the back of her neck. "Those aren't planes," she said softly.

"The Silsviss have some interesting design specs," Lieutenant Ghard reassured her, sounding not entirely sure himself. "They're planes."

Torin tongued her implant. "Sir, we're under attack. Missiles approaching." She didn't bother to subvocalize.

"*What?!*"

Eyes locked on the sky, she tongued the implant again. "Sir, I repeat, we're under attack." And then more emphatically, to the cockpit crew, "Those are missiles."

"They're planes," Ghard repeated.

"No." The VTA slid sideways as Captain Daniels slapped the controls. "They're not." The *Secure All* sounded. "Where are you going, Staff?"

"Back to my platoon, sir."

She was through the hatch and had it dogged shut behind her before the captain could answer.

The civilian compartment was complete chaos. Only the Mictok seemed to have realized the gravity of the situation—all four were webbing themselves into their usual corner.

The ship twisted. A Rakva slammed into her, clutching desperately at her shoulders. "What is it? This one wants to know what is happening!" She threw him toward his seat, snapping, "Strap in, damn it!"

Another Rakva went flying by, avian bone structure providing little ballast. Torin ducked instinctively but saw Cri Sawyes grab Madame Britt's assistant and stuff her into a seat.

"Shit on a stick!" The three sergeants had keyed in an acknowledgment of the situation. There wasn't anything she could do for the platoon that they weren't doing. Someone had to take charge here.

"*Staff?!*"

Bone amplified or not, she could barely hear Lieutenant Jarret over the noise. Grabbing the safety strap from a Dornagain, she snapped it into place and turned to his companion, who was moving with the same deliberate, slow speed. Winning the brief tug of war, she jerked the strap tight before tonguing her implant. "Sir, I am securing civilians."

The VTA shuddered and she would have fallen had the Dornagain ambassador not wrapped one huge arm around her and pulled her against his stomach fur. "A noble attempt, Staff Sergeant," he said, hunkering down, his slow tones in direct contrast to the shrieking all around. "But now it ends."

Struggling to free herself, she saw his claws dig into the deck plating.

Impact.

I don't want to die with civilians. . . .

SEVEN

As near as Torin could tell from within the protective embrace of the Dornagain ambassador, only one of the two missiles hit the VTA. When, to her great surprise, she was still alive two heartbeats after impact, she began to hope.

Clamped tight against the ambassador's side, fingers hooked desperately into his safety straps, her world had been reduced to soft, pungent fur and the shriek of tortured metals laid over a thousand and one other unhappy sounds.

The world turned upside down.

One leg, flung free, tried to bend against the joint. The pain forced a gasp.

Then, miraculously, the ship leveled and the leg straightened.

Torin spat out a curse and with it a mouthful of fur.

She should be with her platoon. She should be *doing* something. Fighting something.

A slate biscuit bounced off her lower lip. She tasted blood.

A Rakva was screaming. The high-pitched sound drilled into her head, singing a shrill descant to the sudden wail of the proximity sirens.

Proximity . . . ? Oh, no . . .

Her implant chimed.

*Planetary surface in five, four, three, two, one . . . *

The second impact was in every way worse than the first. Torin could feel the deck plates buckle, hear metal already twisted shriek a protest as new forces twisted it again, smell . . . she didn't know what she was smelling, but it grew stronger and stronger as the VTA finally shuddered itself still.

Compared to the chaos of an instant before, the civilian compartment had fallen silent enough for her to hear her pulse slamming against the sides of her skull.

Forcing reluctant fingers to release their grip, Torin shifted her weight onto her feet and pushed gently against the furry bulk of the ambassador. Just as panic began to chew at the edges of her control, the arm holding her sagged and she staggered back.

"Well." His ears slowly unfurled. "We seem to have survived." Blinking twice, he focused on her face. "Are you injured, Staff Sergeant?"

She coughed, dabbing crimson against the back of her hand. "Split lip. Wrenched knee. You?"

Two of the claws he'd driven into the deck had broken off, leaving a ragged, bloody edge at each fingertip. "I am bruised but essentially intact."

Her implant chimed. The lieutenant's implant, reading his vital signs, informed her he was unconscious but alive and in no immediate danger of dying. The weight of one in thirty-nine lives lifted off her shoulders.

"Thank you for securing me, sir. If you could see to your people . . . ?"

His whiskers fluffed forward. "Go where you're needed, Staff Sergeant."

The other three Dornagain were alive, but beyond that she couldn't tell; the emergency lighting threw shadows that masqueraded as injuries. Squeezing past them, sifting sounds into *deal with* and *ignore*, she tongued her implant.

Across the compartment, Cri Sawyes had unstrapped and was attempting to free the doctor from the ruins of his seat. Crest flat against his skull, Dr. Leor looked shaken but not visibly injured. The Rakva beside him, however, was clearly dead, head lolling on a broken neck. A closer look at the body and she recognized the young male who'd been learning to play poker. She knew his name, Aarik Slayir, but nothing else about him. And now, there was nothing more to know . . .

Two of the sergeants keyed in. Glicksohn and Chou. Thirty-six lives to go.

All she could see of the Mictok was webbing, but as the structural integrity of their corner seemed intact, she could only assume they were alive.

Still no response from Sergeant Trey.

The controls of the hatch to the cockpit were out. Fighting with the manual override, she tongued her implant again and subvocalized, *Sergeant Glicksohn, report.*

Staff, multiple casualties, three dead and Sergeant Trey. "Clear that space and set him down! Careful, watch his head!" The microphone in his jaw picked up the shouted order; then he began subvocalizing again. *Sensors read half VTA under mud. Can't evac down here.*

Four dead. So far. But it could have been so much worse. It seemed that one of Silsvah's ubiquitous swamps had saved them. The hatch began to give. *Doctor's alive. Will send.* She wanted to send him immediately, but unless the universe had really buggered them, the *Berganitan*'s two corpsmen were in the troop compartment and she had no idea of what she'd find in the cockpit.

Levering the seals with a steady stream of profanity, she finally opened the hatch enough to squeeze through.

"Staff!" Lieutenant Ghard looked up from the captain's body, facial ridges almost white, both hands red. "I can't stop the bleeding!"

Torin turned her head. "Doctor Leor!"

To her surprise, he was at her side in a moment, and, after one look at the situation, at Captain Daniels' side a moment later. She'd expected him to protest, or hesitate, or have hysterics or do any of the other useless things civilians did in an emergency—that he hadn't was encouraging. Torin gratefully shifted him from "civilian" to a "will do his job so don't worry about him" category.

Moving back to let the doctor work, the lieutenant stared down at his hands, his mouth working but no sound emerging. Given the way that both control panels were flashing, they didn't have time for him to go into shock.

"Lieutenant Ghard!"

Her tone blew much of the confusion off his face. He blinked and swallowed, a little color coming back into his ridges as he scrubbed his palms against his flight suit. "Staff Sergeant?"

"The VTA needs seeing to, sir."

Facing forward, his shoulders stiffened. "The engines were hit . . ." Both hands and a foot began flying over the board. Torin didn't understand the steady stream of what sounded like prayer, but behind her the female Krai aircrew gasped.

Turning, she frowned. "You all right?"

"I guess . . ." Blood ran down the lower ridges of her nose, dripping onto her uniform. She stared wide-eyed up at Torin.

"You *guess?*"

Once again, the tone did its job. "I'm all right, Staff Sergeant." Straightening, she blotted the blood into her sleeve.

"Good. And him?"

Propped up against a canted wall, the other member of the bridge crew answered for himself. "Bumped head, Staff. Spinning . . ."

"Stay there. The doctor will take a look when he's done with the captain. You, Aircrew . . . ?"

"Trenkik, Staff."

"Aircrew Trenkik. Are the external scanners functioning?"

Stepping across her fallen comrade to the other station, Trenkik scowled down at the board. "Topside bow seems fine, the rest . . ."

"Topside bow'll have to do, then. I need you to scan for enemy activity."

She dragged her thumb up a pressure bar. "Enemy, Staff?"

"Unless those missiles were launched accidentally."

"You don't think . . ." Then she caught sight of Torin's expression and flushed. "Oh. Right. There's nothing out there, Staff. Scanners show Silsviss life signs about thirty kilometers away. Our landing probably killed most of the local fauna."

They were right side up and essentially in one piece. Torin decided she'd count that as a landing, and the moment she got the chance she was buying Captain Daniels a beer. Deliberately looking past the doctor and the captain's prone body, she scowled at the mud covering the window. "Trenkik, are we still sinking?"

"Yes, but slowly."

The VTA was designed to withstand vacuum. With its physical integrity unbreached it could certainly handle a little mud. Unfortunately, the engine room had taken the brunt of the attack and the landing had pretty much finished it off.

"Fortunately, the mud seems to be containing most of the leakage."

"Fortunately," Torin agreed dryly. "Are the topside hatches usable?"

"Only the forward hatch."

"Then that'll have to do. Give me internal speakers." She glanced over at the lieutenant. "With your permission, sir?"

Ghard started, glanced down at the captain and suddenly realized what that meant. "Yes. Of course, Staff Sergeant."

". . . the situation as it stands. As Captain Daniels is badly injured and Lieutenant Ghard has his hands full with the VTA, until Lieutenant Jarret regains consciousness, you will be taking your orders from me."

"She had to tell us that?" Ressk snorted.

"Idiot." Binti smacked him on the back of the head. "She's telling the civilians. Now they know we know, they can't argue."

The staff sergeant's omnipresent voice continued. "When the doctor has done what he can for Captain Daniels, he'll come below. Sergeant Glicksohn, I want three fireteams, fully armed, at the forward hatch in ten. Once the area is secured, we'll begin evacuation. That is all."

In the moment's silence that followed, Mysho sighed deeply. "I don't know about the rest of you," she said in a voice that carried, "but I feel better knowing there's someone in charge."

"Someone who knows her fukking ass from a mudhole in the ground," Juan agreed.

Even the wounded laughed. It would clearly take more than a couple of missiles and a swamp to suck a VTA out from under Staff Sergeant Kerr.

Up in the cockpit, Torin stroked off the communication board with a steady hand. Later, once those she was responsible for were safe from both enemy action and their own damaged equipment, she'd allow herself the luxury of a reaction. Right now, she didn't have the time.

"The communications array is badly damaged, Staff, but I may be able to jury-rig something that'll enable us to send a . . ." The expression on her face cut Lieutenant Ghard off short. "What?"

"Send a message to who, sir? The *Berganitan* is not in orbit."

"We have to send a message to the Silsviss, let them know what happened and where we . . ." Once again he stopped without finishing. "There's only us and the Silsviss on this planet, isn't there, Staff?"

"As far as I know, sir."

The silence in the cockpit was so complete, Torin could hear the gentle hum of the doctor's bonder reattaching a piece of Captain Daniels' scalp.

"Why would the Silsviss shoot us down, Staff?"

"I don't know, sir. But I intend to find out." Reaching up over Trenkik's head, Torin pressed her right thumb into the dimple at the edge of the weapons locker.

"You're going to question Cri Sawyes?"

"Yes, sir." Wrapping her fingers around the familiar stock of a KC-7, she lifted it out and checked the clip.

"I'll go with you." He started to stand.

"Lieutenant!" Trenkik's voice held a touch of panic. "The rerouting you put in is failing! Leakage is rising!"

He hovered for a moment, clearly wanting to be a part of any questioning, then finally, he sat. "Be careful."

Torin felt her lip lift, then decided it was just one of those things officers said. "Yes, sir."

I should never have left that lizard alone in there. I should have got up and taken him out when he least expected it. If anything's happened . . . She'd got too used to thinking of Cri Sawyes as a friend.

The stink still lingered in the civilian compartment and her short absence made it quite clear that it lingered most strongly around the Dornagain. Breathing shallowly, as she squeezed through the partially open hatch, Torin had to admit that she wasn't surprised considering the way they smelled just generally.

She *was* surprised to find Cri Sawyes had already been taken care of. Curiosity replaced anger as she tried to take in this astonishing development.

The Silsviss had been barricaded into a corner behind several seats ripped out of the deck and webbed together. The largest of the Dornagain squatted on her haunches watching the barricade like an oversized cat watching a mouse hole. Resting her weapon on her hip, Torin cautiously approached. As no one seemed to have taken any injuries from tooth or claw, she could only assume the Silsviss was in there because he'd agreed to the captivity.

Why?

As a gesture of goodwill, obviously. Given that he was presently trapped in a VTA with a platoon of Marines his people had just shot down, he was going to need all the goodwill he could get.

Halfway across the compartment, the Mictok ambassador scuttled out to meet her. "Staff Sergeant Kerr, is it safe to assume that our vehicle has been disabled and we are confined to the ground?"

"Yes, ma'am. It is." The ambassador seemed relatively calm about the whole thing. In fact, as Torin looked around, none of the civilians seemed to be panicking—at least not within species parameters she understood.

"We have assured the others that the military is in control of the situation."

"Thank you, ma'am." That explained it. They were used to being taken care of. If she could herd them like sheep, she had a chance of keeping them alive. Unfortunately, as sheep wouldn't have taken the initiative of confining Cri Sawyers, she suspected it wasn't going to be that easy. *More's the pity.*

"We hope you have sustained no serious injuries."

"Not personally, ma'am, but I have four dead including one of my sergeants. Both aircrew tending the engines were probably killed instantly. Lieutenant Jarret is unconscious. Captain Daniels is also unconscious and more seriously injured. I don't yet know the extent of the other injuries. You?"

"We have sustained no damage, Staff Sergeant. Our protection was sufficient."

Torin stopped at the barricade. "And this?"

"Upon emerging from our protection, we realized that, except for the Confederation members on board this vehicle, the Silsviss are the only missile-using species on this planet. Therefore it must have been Silsviss who shot us down and perhaps Cri Sawyes is not to be trusted." One eyestalk swayed from side to side. "Strength Of Arm volunteered to guard him."

They were so proud of themselves that, in spite of everything, Torin had to hide a smile.

The Dornagain's ears went up, feathery tips brushing the ceiling. "He gave us no trouble, Staff Sergeant."

"No reasssson why I should," Cri Sawyes remarked dryly, framed in the triangular space between a seat top and bottom. "I am not your enemy. Thossse were not our misssilesss."

Torin snorted. "How do you know?"

His inner eyelids flicked closed and he pointed through the barricade toward the view screen. "I sssaw them approach."

"And a quick glimpse at a missile moving at just under supersonic speeds allowed you to make a positive identification?" It wasn't quite sarcasm.

"I wasss in the military for mossst of my adult life, Ssstaff Sssergeant, and at war for much of that time. Alliancesss change quickly on Sssilsss-vah, an ability to make a fassst, posssitive identification of incoming ordinance isss necesssary for sssurvival."

From what little Silsvah history she'd learned, that was certainly true. Still . . . "I doubt you can identify every single missile on the entire planet. You'd know your own, and your closest allies' or enemies'."

His tongue flicked out. "You ssseem to be making my argument for me.

If it was a Sssilsssvah misssile that I couldn't identify, it'sss clearly from a group I have no affiliation with. Will I be held ressssponsssible for the actionsss of my entire planet?"

Son of a . . . He was making way too much sense. "For the moment," Torin began, then paused as her implant chimed.

Contamination levels now at 2.5 and rising.

Humans could stand a contamination level of 5.7, di'Taykan a little more, Krai a little less. An initial warning at 2.5 gave everyone time to get clear. At least that was the theory. She had no idea how much time the three species of civilians would need, although the information was probably buried somewhere in her slate. *Best just to hurry.*

"You I'll deal with later." She nodded toward their captive, more than willing to let Cri Sawyes' loyalties slide for the moment. "Or the lieutenant will deal with you when he wakes up. The rest of you . . ." She found the massed attention of the civilians—particularly the massed attention of the Mictok—a little disconcerting and had to clear her throat before she could continue. ". . . get into your storage compartments and put together everything you'll need for personal and species survival in the wilds of Silsvah. We've only got one working exit and we can't get the sleds out of it, so you'll be carrying your gear over some rough terrain. Remember that when you put it together."

They wouldn't, but that could be dealt with later. It was more important now to get them moving, to give them enough to do that they wouldn't start thinking about the situation. Which, as far as she could tell, didn't bear thinking about.

"Staff Sergeant?"

Halfway out the hatch to the central axis, Torin turned. Grieving for her dead assistant, Madame Britt had broken the central feather in her crest. "Ma'am?"

"This one wonders if it wouldn't be safer to stay with the VTA?"

"No. The engines were hit. The mud is containing most of the leakage for the moment, but that won't last. We have to get clear."

"This one wonders if there is not enemy outside."

"Not according to the scanners, ma'am. But I'm heading out there now to check." She offered the only bit of comfort she had. "Don't worry. You're with the Marines."

*   *   *

The fireteams were waiting for her by the forward hatch. They'd managed to put together modified combat gear out of the limited supplies in the armory: helmets, vests, and belts over dress uniforms. The three heavy gunners were carrying KC-12s and, although the upper body exoskeletons they wore provided less than half of their usual amendments, they looked happier than they had since leaving the station.

Ressk stepped away from the panel as she approached. "Ship's scanners say there's nothing out there, Staff. Well, nothing alive bigger than two-and-a-half centimeters anyway."

"Right. Let's open it up and take a look."

Hollice tossed her a helmet, and she put it on as the hatch slid open.

The VTA's moving parts were not particularly thrilled to be moving. The reason became obvious as mud first trickled and then poured through the opening.

The Marines retreated.

"Topside's not supposed to be buried!"

"Get back here." Torin braced herself against the flood, and by the time she finished speaking it was over. Mud had filled the corridor ankle-deep, but the hatch was clear and the sky outside was a brilliant blue. "It was just debris from the landing." Ignoring the unpleasant sucking sounds, Torin stepped outside, flipping her helmet scanner down over her left eye. The grid remained empty. "Area's clear. Now let's find a way off this thing before that leakage gets worse and we run out of original chromosomes."

"This reminds me of a meal I had once," Binti muttered as they waded back to the hatch.

Ressk lifted his boot and stared down at the dripping, viscous brown mess ruining his shine. "I don't want to hear any more comments about what I eat if this reminds you of a meal."

"Specifically, it reminds me of a couple of hours after the meal."

"I needed to hear that?"

The area immediately around the VTA was a desolate, dripping mess. Beyond that was swamp. Torin sent teams out along both of the broad delta wings and up to the bow to scan for dry land. There wasn't much point in abandoning ship if it didn't improve the situation.

*   *   *

"All right, I'm getting something." Squinting through his helmet scanner, Hollice ran the terrain program through one more time with the magnification on full. "That way."

Squatting at the edge of the wing, Binti stared out at destruction that looked no different than any of the rest and then up at the corporal. "You're kidding, right?"

"No. That way. Twenty meters, then there's a ridge. We can follow it all the way to high ground."

"Your helmet's fukked, Hollice." Juan pointed his weapon along the line indicated. "I can see twenty meters and there's no ridge."

"There's a ridge, it's just covered in more *serley* mud." Ressk flipped his own scanner up and sighed. "And the way our day's been going, it'll be the only way out."

Mud lapped at the edge of the wing. Either they'd hit bottom or the broader surfaces were keeping them from sinking any deeper. Since the result was the same, it didn't matter much to Torin either way. The ridge would get them out of the swamp, but getting to the ridge . . .

"Never an engineer around when you need one," she muttered, glancing up at the sky. Just after noon. The sky was still clear, but at this time of the year in this part of the world, it usually rained after dark. Traveling with wounded and civilians, they had to be able to put up shelters by then. "Aylex!"

Head turned into the breeze, the di'Taykan started. "Staff?"

"You're the closest thing to an engineer we've got."

"I am?"

"You came up with a way to get us over that canyon back on Junnas."

"Well, yeah, but I could see the other side. This stuff . . ." He waved out at the mud. "It all looks the same. The scanners are all that's telling us there's solid land out there. I can't even smell a difference."

"Your point?"

He stared at her for a moment, then he sighed. "I suppose I could shoot a cable across to those stumps and string a bridge off that."

"Do what you have to. Remember, we've got wounded to evac, and it's got to hold four Dornagain." His eyes widened, but Torin kept talking, preventing the protest. Protesting wouldn't change the fact that whatever he built had to stand up to the slow-moving weight of four very large responsibilities. "Corporal Ng, you're in charge of the work detail. Defer to Private Aylex when it comes to the actual construction." For a moment, she indulged baser instincts by wishing that one of the Dornagain had died instead of the birdboned Rakva and then reminded herself that the Dornagain could eat more of the local food and weren't likely to blow away in the first bad storm. Not to mention that one of them had just saved her life. "I'll send out as much help as I can. Corporal Hollice, as soon as there's a way across, I want your team on recon. Check back when you've gone a kilometer up the ridge. Let's go, people, we're running out of time."

"Uh, Staff."

"What is it, Aylex?"

"What am I supposed to build a bridge of?"

Torin snorted and stamped one foot, her bootheel ringing against the metal skin of the VTA. "You're standing on a few tons of scrap. Improvise."

Her implant chimed as she stepped back into the muddy corridor.

Contamination levels now at 2.9 and rising.

"Oh, shut up."

"Staff?"

"Not you. Just go get the cables."

The civilian compartment had the appearance of a jumble sale with gear piled haphazardly on every conceivable surface and various arguments in progress. Captain Daniels lay on a stretcher by the door beside the covered body of the young Rakva—their island of quiet a foreboding contrast to the surrounding noise. Frowning, Torin knelt beside her and touched fingers to her throat. She was still alive. Torin straightened, feeling lighter by a life, then leaned forward again to examine the straps holding her in place. They almost looked like . . .

"Webbing. We felt it would better hold her without impairing her circulation. Dr. Leor is quite concerned about her," the ambassador continued, when Torin looked up. "We are watching her while the doctor sees to the other injured."

"Thank you." Webbing . . . Standing, she pulled her helmet off and tucked it under one arm. "Madame Ambassador, I apologize in advance if this is insulting, but I've got Marines out on the wing attempting to bridge twenty meters of essentially bottomless mud and . . ." All eight eyes were focused on her. She stared down the multiple reflections accusing her of breaking every rule of protocol in the book. ". . . a little webbing might help a whole lot."

"We don't see how."

Fortunately staff sergeants were stronger than a little embarrassment. If they weren't, that incredible night spent with Lieutenant Jarret would've been truly unfortunate. Torin gestured toward the improvised cell. "It holds things together."

Two eyestalks turned. "Yes, it does."

A few moments later, one of the ambassador's assistants was scurrying out to the wing followed by the slowly moving bulk of Strength of Arm. With the blessings of her ambassador, the Dornagain had volunteered her services. "If you think strength will be needed," she'd added shyly.

Torin stood once again by the hole in the barricade and watched Cri Sawyes watching her. "You're taking this very well," she said after a moment.

The tip of his tail drew a figure eight in the air. "Thisss isss no more than a temporary inconvenience. You will need me out there to sssurvive."

"I can survive without you." From the single flicker of his tongue, that seemed to amuse him. *Next time he sticks it out, I'm tying a knot in it.*

"I have no doubt you can sssurvive, Ssstaff Sssergeant, but you have wounded and civiliansss, and for them to sssurvive you'll need my help."

Torin glanced from Captain Daniels, lying too still by the hatch, to the Charge d'Affaires and her young assistant adding yet another container to their pile of gear and realized Cri Sawyes was not merely offering to help carry things through the mud. "We're still in the wilderness preserve, aren't we?"

"Yesss."

"Your wild boys will investigate the crash."

"Yesss."

"Will we be in any danger from them?"

"That dependsss on how you answer their challenge." He leaned forward, claws digging into a seat back, face so close to the hole that she thought she could feel the heat of his breath on her cheek. "I am not your enemy."

Not *her* enemy. Which didn't necessarily mean he wasn't the Confederation's enemy, did it? "Stay there for now. I've got enough to worry about."

Nostrils flared, he reared back, throat pouch expanding. "I have told you thossse were not our misssilesss, I have told you I am not your enemy, and ssstill you worry about what I may do? I tell you now for the lassst time that unless sssussspicion wearsss away my ssself-control, you and your people are in no danger from me!"

Half-turned away, Torin paused and came to a decision. "I believe you."

His throat pouch deflated so quickly he sneezed.

"Even if it *was* a Silsviss missile, you certainly didn't fire it. But there are another thirty-five Marines who may not see it that way," she continued, "and, right now, I don't have time to change their minds. You stay there, and I guarantee no one'll take a shot at you. You start wandering around . . ." She shrugged.

"I will ssstay here." His tongue flickered again and her hand rose; she forced it back down before anything came of it. "Thank you."

"You're welcome."

She'd taken two steps toward the argument in the middle of the room when her implant chimed.

Lieutenant Jarret has regained consciousness.

Contamination levels now at 3.1 and rising.

Torin stepped into the troop compartment; and stopped dead. Outwardly, she was surveying the activity, inwardly, she was drawing strength from being back where she belonged; no matter how bad it looked. *I should have been here . . .*

The right wall had buckled. Impact had loosened one of the sleds and it had slammed through from the vehicle bay. There were four body bags lying beside the wreckage and three stretchers beside them. Not exactly encouraging for the three injured but the best use of the available space. Two of the three were clearly sedated; the doctor was bending over the third. One of the two corpsmen was finishing a wrist-to-elbow field dressing on the arm of a corporal from Sergeant Chou's squad, and the other was putting together a second pack from the medical supply locker. There were field packs against the left wall and the armory hatch was open. She couldn't see the lieutenant.

She *could* see Corporal Conn, and she thanked any gods who were listening that she didn't have to tell a four-year-old why her daddy wasn't coming home.

"Staff."

She took another step into the compartment and turned. "Mike."

Sergeant Glicksohn held out his slate. "You want to download the full report?"

Reaching down she thumbed her input but didn't bother actually looking at the screen. "Highlights?"

"Sergeant Trey, Privates Drake . . ."

Did he die with his dice in his hand, she wondered.

". . . and Damon . . ."

Probably reading when it happened. Torin had approved extra memory for her slate so she could carry more books.

". . . and Corporal Sutton are dead."

She'd been planning on scheduling his sergeant's exam the day General Morris had given them their new orders. With Sergeant Trey dead, he'd have probably gotten a field promotion. Except that he was dead, too.

Torin added their names to the others she'd started carrying since she got her third hook. She knew there wasn't anything she could have done even if she'd been in the troop compartment, but that knowledge made her feel no less responsible.

"We had eight other injuries, three serious." His lips pressed into a thin line, then he snarled, "Haysole got both legs caught, the stupid bastard."

The doctor shifted position and Torin caught her first sight of turquoise hair lying still and unmoving. Before she could ask for an explanation, Mike spat it out, the words growing louder and crowding up against each other as he spoke.

"He was in the sled with Trey. They strapped in there, but that didn't do them any good when we hit ground." One fist slammed against the back of a seat. "Should have been in his seat. Goddamn di'Taykan, can't keep it in their pants . . ."

Torin laid her hand on his arm, and the diatribe cut off like she'd touched a switch.

The sergeant drew in a deep breath and let it out slowly. "Doc says he'll get new legs and a trip home." He lifted his head and met her gaze. "All we have to do is keep him alive until someone comes to get us. But the *Berganitan*'s gone and the Silsviss are shooting at us, so who the fuk is that going to be?"

"It's not our fault."

"He's in my squad. I should've tied him to his seat."

"We'll keep him alive."

"Goddamned right we will." He drew in another deep breath and seemed to exhale his anger with it, his voice sounding no more than weary when he added, "Ceremonial duties, my ass."

Contamination levels now at 3.5 and rising.

"You heard."

He nodded. "I heard."

"Get the stretchers topside before it gets any worse. Then I want half the able-bodied humping packs and the other half working on the bridge. Put the walking wounded on guard."

"The lieutenant's awake."

"I know."

"He seems to think it might be a better idea to stay with the VTA."

"Does he?" Torin spotted lilac hair coming into the troop compartment from behind the ruined wall. "I'll deal with him, you get moving on evac."

"Staff . . ."

She began threading her way between the remaining seats. "Don't worry. I'll be polite."

"Lieutenant Jarret." When he turned toward her, Torin could see that the side of his face was badly bruised and she was willing to bet that his cheekbone had been broken. "I'm glad to see you back on your feet, sir. Has the doctor taken a look at you?"

"No. I had the corpsman give me a pain block."

Only the unbruised side of his face moved when he spoke. If it was a side effect of the pain block, it was a new one. Given di'Taykan muscle control, Torin suspected he was still in pain and attempting to minimize it. "You should have the doctor rebond that bone, sir."

"There are Marines who need the doctor a lot more than I do, Staff Sergeant," Lieutenant Jarret told her stiffly. "He can take care of this . . ." His hand rose and two fingers lightly touched his cheek. ". . . when he's finished with them."

"Yes, sir." It was the textbook "good officer" response—*See to my men first.*—but there was a world of difference between those officers who made the declaration because they felt they should and those who meant it. The lieutenant seemed honestly insulted that she'd even made the suggestion, as though she should know him better than that. All things considered, she supposed he had grounds. "Sergeant Glicksohn has filled you in on the state of the platoon, sir?"

"Yes." He looked past her, eyes focused on the bodies across the room. "Four dead. Three badly injured. Seven others injured but mobile."

"Seven? I thought eight . . ."

As he turned toward her, she realized he hadn't counted himself among the injured, and she really hoped he wasn't so young that he'd consider *I'm fine* to be the last word on the subject. "Sir . . ."

"I'm fine."

Her expression provoked a smile on both sides of his mouth.

"For now," he added before she could speak. Then the smile vanished. "I hear you took command while I was unconscious."

"Yes, sir. Captain Daniels was badly injured and Lieutenant Ghard felt he should concentrate on the VTA. We lost one of the civilians, but the others have only minor injuries. Although contamination levels are rising quickly, we'll be able to get all personnel clear of the ship before any irreversible damage is done. There's a bridge being built from the ship to what passes for dry land in these parts, Hollice's team is scouting a route out of the swamp, and the wounded are being evacuated topside before the leakage gets any higher."

"What?"

She chose to misunderstand. "Topside, sir. We've settled so deeply into the mud that only the forward hatch topside is working."

"What I meant, Staff Sergeant, is *why* are you evacuating the wounded?"

Under other circumstances she'd have admired the edge in his voice; under these circumstances she really hoped he wasn't about to pull rank. "Sir, as I said, contamination levels are rising quickly."

He shook his head and didn't quite manage to hide the pain the motion caused. "No. I've just had a look, and the engine room wall hasn't been breached. If we're under attack, the VTA is the safest place to be. The Silsviss haven't the technology to get us out."

"With all due respect, sir, just because you can't see a breach, doesn't mean there isn't one." Her protest emerged as unchallenging as she could make it. The trick was not to sound as if she were talking to a three-year-old. "Your implant may not be functioning; we've been getting readings . . ."

"My implant is functioning fine, Sergeant. The last reading was at 3.5. That's still not enough of a threat for us to take civilians out into hostile territory." His gaze focused past her shoulder again. "Corporal Mysho! Leave that stretcher where it is!"

"Sir?"

So much for being polite, Torin decided. This had to be stopped before it got messy. "Sir, the reading was 3.5 and *rising . . .*"

He cut her off. "Still well within species tolerances. The Mictok can take levels as high as 9.2."

"Good for them. I can't. Neither can you. Neither can any other Marine under your command." His mouth opened, but she continued in the same low voice before he could speak. "The engine *has* been breached, there's *no* telling how high the contamination will rise and, according to the ship's long-range scanner, the *only* hostiles are a primitive band of male adolescents thirty kilometers away. Sir."

In this particular instance, "sir" meant: *"These are the facts. I suggest you adjust your decision making accordingly."*

Torin could feel the corporal waiting for new orders. With any luck, she was the only witness to this standoff. With any luck, it wouldn't be the first of many.

"Primitive band of male adolescents?" the lieutenant repeated at last.

"We came down in a wilderness preserve." As understanding dawned, she added, "Sir, I realize that shepherding a group of mixed species diplomats through a swamp fills you with justifiable aversion, but killing them slowly isn't the answer."

For a moment she thought he wasn't going to see the humor in that last statement, but then the uninjured side of his mouth twisted up into a crooked smile. "It isn't?"

"No, sir, it isn't."

The smile twisted a little more. "You have everything under control, don't you?"

There were a number of ways to deal with that kind of incipient self-pity in a junior officer. "Thank you, sir," she said brightly.

"That wasn't . . ." He paused.

Torin met his gaze levelly. She could almost see the wheels turning behind his eyes.

His smile untwisted and turned to honest amusement. "All right, Staff Sergeant, you win. Upon considering all the options, I've decided to continue the evacuation. Corporal Mysho!"

"Sir?"

"Carry on."

"Yes, sir."

By a mutual, albeit silent, agreement they ignored the relief in the corporal's voice.

"All right . . ." Lieutenant Jarret gestured at the rapidly emptying compartment. "The Marines are taken care of. What about the civilians?"

"Two of them are helping build the bridge, the rest are packing."

"Packing? To march through a swamp?"

"Yes, sir."

"On their own?"

"Yes, sir."

He began to shake his head but stopped, hair flat, before the motion really got started. "Send one of the walking wounded up to supervise their choices, or the doctor will want to take along his specimens and the Mictok will be packing art supplies."

"Yes, sir." Half turning, she beckoned the last of the minor casualties away from the corpsman and passed on the lieutenant's order. "Anything else, sir?"

"I think we'd better go have a look at that bridge." He swayed as he stepped forward, and without thinking, Torin reached out and slipped an arm around his waist, holding him until he steadied. When she released him, he stared at her for a heartbeat, eyes dark, and she wondered if she'd overstepped the line. It was one thing to keep him from making stupid mistakes—in fact, that was essentially her job description concerning second lieutenants—and another thing entirely to imply he couldn't stand on his own two feet. Young males of any species tended to be overly proud and young male officers . . . *Fuk it.* "Are you all right, sir?"

Twitching his tunic down into place, he pushed past her. "I'm fine."

Ready to catch him if it came to it, Torin fell into step behind him. "Yes, sir."

EIGHT

As they made their way up the central axis, Torin glanced over at the lieutenant and frowned thoughtfully. Although the bruising made it difficult to tell for certain, he seemed to be carrying what she called a "once more into the breach" expression on top of stiff shoulders and as close to a graceless walk as a di'Taykan could manage. From this point on, he'd do or die trying. And that had to be nipped in the bud before it was exactly what happened.

"Crisis of confidence, sir?"

Anyone but a di'Taykan would have tripped. "What?"

"You think you're off to a bad start. Through no fault of your own, you were unconscious when you should have taken command, and when you finally joined the party, you think you made the wrong decision." He *had* made the wrong decision, but reminding him of that wouldn't help. "You're determined to prove yourself because even though you're a trained combat officer and not a diplomatic babysitter—no matter how perfectly your background prepared you for the latter—you're afraid there's nothing you can do that I can't do better." She timed the pause so that he barely got his mouth open before she continued. "And you're beginning to wish that you'd had the doctor bond that bone because your head hurts like hell."

He'd stopped walking, so she stopped as well and turned to face him, counting silently to herself. If she got to twenty before he spoke, she'd begin an apology.

At nine, his eyes narrowed.

"There's a reason telepathic races are universally hated," he growled. "Do you always speak your mind so freely, Staff Sergeant Kerr? Because if this is some Human response to having sex . . ."

"Not at all, sir. It's part of my job description."

"Keeping me in my place?"

"No, sir. Keeping good officers alive by not letting them get trapped inside their own heads."

This time she only got to five.

"Good officers?"

"Yes, sir." She kept her answer matter-of-fact, as though he shouldn't have had to ask, and was rewarded by a long exhalation, a visible release of tension, and a grateful smile.

"Suck up."

"Yes, sir."

"Staff, why do you think the Silsviss shot us down?"

Torin shrugged. "They may not have, sir. Cri Sawyes was at the vid screen when it happened, and he says they weren't Silsviss missiles."

Jarret jerked to a stop and reached out to grab her arm, only barely managing to keep his fingers from closing—the situation had not yet deteriorated to the point where he'd be excused for panic-clutching his senior NCO. "Cri Sawyes!"

"Contained, sir."

"Contained?" When she nodded, he started breathing again. "I can't *believe* I forgot there was a Silsviss on board."

"Well, I wasn't the one who contained him," Torin admitted dryly, figuring one confession deserved another. "The Mictok ambassador arranged it while I was in the cockpit."

"Really?"

"Not something I'd be likely to make up, sir. And you, at least, had the excuse of having been knocked unconscious."

Fingertips lightly touched the bruise purpling his cheek. "Careless of us both, Staff Sergeant."

"Yes, sir."

He held her gaze for a moment, then started walking again. "Strangely enough," he said, his matter-of-fact tone an almost exact copy of her earlier one, "the discovery that you're not perfect is making me feel significantly more confident."

Unable to decide if she was insulted or amused, Torin fell back into step beside him. "I'm glad I could help, sir."

"Do you believe Cri Sawyes when he says the missiles weren't Silsviss?"

"I believe him when he says he doesn't recognize them, sir. As to whether or not they're Silsviss . . ." She shrugged. "I don't know. He also points out that we can't hold him responsible for the actions of the entire planet."

"We can," the lieutenant corrected wryly. "The question is whether or not we should."

"He says he isn't our enemy."

"And do you believe *that?*"

"Well, lying is in his best interests right now, but I don't think he was."

"Why not? Because you like him?"

"Essentially, sir, yes." When Lieutenant Jarret shot her a questioning glance, she shrugged again. "Not much to go on," she admitted, acknowledging his expression.

"I wouldn't say that." He nodded toward the rank insignia on her collar. "You didn't get those by being a bad judge of character."

Surprised at the depth of her reaction, Torin touched the stacked chevrons over the crossed KC silhouettes. "Thank you, sir." For no good reason, she found herself feeling better about the unmitigated mess they were all facing.

Contamination levels now 3.9 and rising.

A little better. Not a lot.

"Pontoons?"

"The empty storage units float, sir, and they'll hold the Dornagain."

Standing just behind the lieutenant's left shoulder, Torin leaned around him and glanced pointedly at Strength of Arm's muddy haunches.

"Well, they will now," Aylex amended, grinning. "As long as they cross one at a time."

Stepping onto the first of the completed sections, Lieutenant Jarret bounced thoughtfully. Dried mud flaked off the sides of the containers into slow moving ripples as the bridge undulated along its entire length. The omnipresent odor of rotting vegetation grew momentarily stronger. After one final bounce, he turned, stepped back onto the VTA, and yelled, "Well done!" over the sudden crash of two more units bouncing down the wing. "How soon can you have it finished?"

Aylex looked over at his crew and shrugged. "Well, sir, as long as Strength of Arm keeps tearing things apart and Gar'itac keep tying them together . . ."

The Mictok was actually tying the storage units together with cable but doing it with a speed and dexterity impossible to match with only two arms.

". . . it'll be done before it's time to leave."

"Talk about out of the frying pan into the fire," Hollice muttered. He squatted and stared into the water, but nothing had changed over the last fifteen seconds—suspended organic matter still made it impossible to see below the surface. "Damn."

Once they'd slogged their way out of the splatter zone, the ground, although not much higher than the swamp around it, had been relatively dry. Relative to the swamp. Given the unfamiliar terrain and the massed vegetation, they'd made slow but steady time.

Until now.

It looked as if something had taken a gigantic bite out of the ridge they'd been following and the swamp had seeped into the hollow. There was no way around it that didn't involve a significantly worse scenario and the end of the kilometer they were scouting was on the other side.

"Ground gets a lot higher over there," Ressk assured him, squinting through his scanner and pointing at the opposite shore nearly six meters away.

"Yeah. But we're over here."

"My scanner says the bottom's solid."

"Yeah. So does mine."

"It's only just over a meter deep."

"Good. Then it won't be over your head."

Ressk snorted. "Oh, that makes sense, send the short guy."

Juan fanned a cloud of tiny insects away from his face and swiped at a dribble of sweat with the backstroke. "Would one of you just get your ass into the water! I killed the fukking snake and we haven't seen another one!"

"Haven't *seen* another one." Straightening, Hollice stepped back, staggering a little as the ground reluctantly released his boots. "Bin, take a look at those trees over there." They didn't look much like trees, more like giant sticks topped off with a tuft of fern, but they were the tallest vegetation in the area, and after a few planetfalls he'd learned to be flexible. At least they weren't moving under their own power. "Scanner says they're tall enough to bridge this—you think you can take them down from this side?"

"Sure." Weapon resting on her hip, Binti squinted across the gap. "But it'll attract attention."

"We're still showing no unfriendlies."

"Great, just one thing; I can't make them fall where you want them from here. It's got to be done from that side."

"You positive?"

"I'm positive. So, as much as I hate to agree with Juan, get your ass in the water."

"You should . . ."

"No, I shouldn't," she interrupted emphatically. "That's lumberjack work, and you want the best shot on guard in case that snake had friends."

He couldn't argue with that. Snapping his scanner down, Hollice took another look at the water. The organic soup remained too thick for a clear reading. "I ever mention how much I hate snakes?" he muttered, stepping back to the edge. "That whole legless thing they've got going just wigs me right out." Lifting his weapon over his head, he lurched forward, bumped into Ressk's arm, and stopped. "What?"

"I'll go."

"Oh, that makes sense," Hollice snorted. "Send the short guy. No, I'm in charge here, I'll do it. Just make sure you shoot anything that moves."

"But the snakes . . ."

"Especially shoot the fukking snakes!"

The water was warm, almost body temperature. Unfortunately, dress uniforms, while essentially waterproof, hadn't been designed for walking in a swamp. Combat gear presented one impermeable surface to the outside world. At the moment, his pack, vest, and helmet would stay dry, no matter what, but he could feel water seeping into his boots and pushing up under his tunic to pour down inside the waistband of his trousers. Placing one foot carefully in front of the other, he tried not to think of what might be seeping, pushing, and pouring in with it.

The moisture dribbling down his sides he at least knew the source of. If the brains at R&D had come up with an environmental control strong enough to handle fear sweat, he'd never worn it.

Halfway across. He was wet, and every ripple added another layer to the stink of the place that lined the inside of his nose, but so far so good.

Then something brushed against the back of his leg.

The next thing he knew, he was scrambling out on the opposite shore, heart beating so violently he couldn't believe it hadn't triggered his med-alert. Flopping over onto his back, he jerked up and pointed his weapon back along his path.

Nothing. His passage had whipped up a greenish-brown foam, but whatever had touched him was still below the surface.

"Hollice? You all right?"

"Did you see it?"

They hadn't. And nothing had shown up on Ressk's scanner.

"Are you all right?" Binti repeated.

"Yeah. Fine." Breathing beginning to calm, he stood, slowly, and watched a small orange blob slide off his legs to splat against the mud below. When it started to move away from him, he stepped on it. At the moment, building impossible bridges and humping gear back at the VTA held a definite attraction.

"Hey, Staff, you know what I heard?"

Torin dropped to one knee by Haysole's stretcher and linked her fingers through his. With their lower body temperature, di'Taykans usually felt cool to Humans, but his skin was warm. "What have you heard?"

"After I get my new legs, I can go home."

"Some people'll do anything to get out of cleaning toilets."

Haysole flashed her a fraction of his usual grin. "Cleaning the crappers wasn't so bad, but all that marching up and down in straight lines was really beginning to weigh."

They winced in unison as another supply container crashed against the wing.

"Staff, after I get my new legs, will I be able to dance?"

"Sure."

"That's great, 'cause I can't dance now."

Torin had always found it amazing how much bad humor transcended species parameters. She smiled even though Haysole's eyes were so pale she doubted he could see more than a silhouette of her against the sky. "I know a sergeant who got busted down a rank for that joke."

"Good thing I've got no rank to bust, then." He sucked at the straw the doctor had tucked into the corner of his mouth, and when he'd finished swallowing, sighed deeply. "I never meant to be such a screwup."

"Yes, you did."

His eyes darkened as he forced himself to focus.

"And don't try to tell me you regret a thing because I won't believe it. You enjoyed bucking the system, even if it meant being a private for your entire time in. There're too many corporals around anyway. And way too many sergeants."

This time the grin lit up most of his face. "All after your job."

"Every damn one of them." She tightened her grip for a moment and then released his hand. "Speaking of my job, I should get back to it."

"Staff?"

She paused at the foot of his stretcher. "What?"

"If I die, take off the masker before you bag me."

"You're not going to die."

"Hey, even *you* can't guarantee that."

He laughed at her overly indignant reaction, and she carried the sound away with her, adding it to her armaments.

"How's Private Haysole?"

Torin shook her head, although she wasn't certain what she was denying. "His hair was so still . . ."

"It's the sedatives."

"The sedatives? Of course . . ." It wasn't like she'd never seen an injured di'Taykan before. She felt herself flush under Lieutenant Jarret's steady gaze. Every man and woman in the platoon was her responsibility. She wasn't supposed to have favorites. *And we weren't supposed to face any combat on this trip either. And generals aren't supposed to send their troops in unprepared. And* . . . As the lieutenant's hair fanned out from his head—and she noticed he'd finally let the doctor attend to his face—she cut short her silent soliloquy and found a new subject. "They're securing the last floats to the bridge, sir."

"Good. Has Corporal Hollice's team reported back yet?"

"Not yet, sir." The communication system built into her helmet—into everyone's helmet—buzzed. "I expect this is them now."

"Not an especially fast kilometer."

Torin looked past the mud drying and cracking on everything in sight to the tangled mass of vegetation beyond. "Not especially," she agreed, thumbing the receive.

*   *   *

". . . last of the kilometer took us out of the swamp. We're sitting high, dry, and defensible."

"Unfriendlies?"

"Nothing on scanner, Staff."

Torin glanced at the sky. The sun had moved past its zenith some time before but was still a distance above the horizon. "Can we get there before dark? Carrying wounded?"

"Piece of cake."

"Corporal?"

"That's an affirmative on arriving before dark with wounded."

Lieutenant Jarret reached out and touched her arm.

"Sir?"

"Have them start back." The lieutenant's gaze swept over the VTA, over the civilians, over the wounded, over the dead. "We're going to need all hands."

"Back?" Ressk swallowed and wiped his mouth on the back of his hand. "Is she kidding?"

"Lieutenant's orders," Hollice told them, flipping the tiny microphone back up into its recess. "We're to set out a perimeter and leave the packs."

"We'll be walking it three fukking times while everyone else walks it once!" Juan protested loudly.

"Yeah, and back at the VTA they've been sitting on their collective ass while we've been working." Activating his perimeter pin, Hollice pushed it into the ground. "Set up and let's get moving."

Brows down and hair up, Lieutenant Jarret swept a questioning gaze up one side of the armory and down the other. "We seem to be exceptionally well armed for a ceremonial mission, Staff."

"Standard armory on a VTA this size, sir."

"But two extra lockers of KCs?"

Torin had wondered about that herself. The KC-7 was a Marine's personal weapon, and it made no sense that they were carrying enough to outfit a second platoon. "Supply back on the station told me they were part of the diplomatic mission and not our concern."

Jarret shot her an incredulous stare. "They were going to arm the Silsviss?"

"That's certainly what it looks like."

"Has the Parliament completely lost its collective mind?"

That was probably a rhetorical question, but Torin chose to answer it anyway. "I believe they thought the Silsviss were on our side."

"Still . . ." He sighed and stretched out a hand toward the closest locker. "Not a total loss, we can use them to arm the diplomats." Then he paused, thumb over the lock. "Why *haven't* you armed the diplomats, Staff?"

"The diplomats refused to be armed, sir."

His arm fell back to his side as he turned toward her. "Can't say as I'm surprised. What are we . . ."

Contamination now at 4.2 and rising.

". . . leaving behind?" he finished as their implants quieted.

Torin ran her hand along the edge of a weapons locker and sighed. "Everything here, sir. We're limited without the sleds."

"Everything? What about mortars?"

"I've sent two of the EM223s up, sir. Two ammo packs each."

"Two emmies? Is that all?"

"Even an emmy weighs in at 21 kilograms, sir, and we're already carrying food, water, and wounded."

"We're surrounded by water, Staff."

"Yes, sir, and we're carrying a purifier. Counting the two sergeants, we have fifteen uninjured Marines," she continued when he opened his mouth to protest further. "We'll need six to carry the three stretchers and four to carry the emmies. That leaves only five with their hands free for their weapons *if* Corporal Hollice's team makes it back before we leave. Granted, some of the injuries aren't serious—they'll be carrying the ammo packs and riding herd on the civilians."

"The aircrew . . ."

"The two surviving aircrew will be carrying Captain Daniels."

"Lieutenant Ghard . . ."

"Is not my responsibility, sir."

He drummed his fingertips against the curve of the helmet tucked into the crook of his elbow. Reading his mood in the rhythm, Torin decided not to remind him about fingerprints smudging the photoelectric receptors. Some things it was better just to let happen.

"All right." The drumming stopped. "Standard operating procedure has us making camp a minimum of three kilometers away from a downed VTA."

"Yes, sir."

"Once we've established a defensive position, we can send a team back to pick up more weapons."

She found that such an inane thing to say she had to step on the urge to ask him about his head injury. "First of all, sir, the contamination . . ."

"May never rise above the levels a di'Taykan can handle." His eyes narrowed. "And second?"

"Second, standing orders are to blow the armory." When she'd asked him to come down here with her, she'd said nothing to him but *"Sir, the armory,"* and now she wondered what the hell he'd thought they were going to do. Given that he was di'Taykan, she decided not to speculate.

"When evacuating in territory held by the enemy."

"Sir?"

"I am familiar with standing orders, Staff Sergeant." His expression made it quite clear he found it insulting that she'd assumed he wasn't. "The armory is to be blown when evacuating in territory held by the enemy. We don't know who the enemy is, so we certainly don't know what territory they're holding. Do we?"

"No, sir," she admitted reluctantly, "we don't. But we are in a wilderness preserve, filled with hormonally hopped-up young males attempting to prove themselves by combat. If they get their hands on our weapons . . ."

"I think that Marine Corps security protocols are sufficient to keep out a boarding party of adolescent lizards, don't you?"

"With all due respect, sir, those sound like famous last words."

"Good." His tone drew a line and suggested she not step over it. "Because those were my last words on the subject. We *are* not losing a chance to add an SW46, and one of these sammies to our defenses." He stretched out a hand toward the locker holding the surface-to-air missile launcher and then, reluctantly, let it fall. "We don't know how long we'll be here or what we'll be up against."

For some reason the phrase *hormonally hopped-up young males* kept repeating itself in Torin's head.

The lieutenant stepped out of the armory into the empty crew compartment, motioning for her to follow. "Lock up behind us, Staff Sergeant." When she hesitated, he caught her gaze and held it. "You have your orders, Staff Sergeant Kerr."

The evacuation was a factual necessity. This was a difference of opinion, and he'd made it quite clear that she wasn't going to be able to change his mind.

"Locking up behind us, sir."

"Sergeant Glicksohn reports that everyone's topside, sir."

"Good."

As Torin followed the lieutenant into the civilian compartment, she frowned at a subtle difference in his gait. Was he strutting? And if so, was it because he felt he'd emerged triumphant from the armory? Or did he merely feel more confident because he'd given his senior NCO an order she'd disagreed with but she'd followed it anyway? The former meant he saw them in an adversarial position—either consciously or unconsciously—and that would be a bad thing. The latter was a part of the care and feeding of second lieutenants.

I think I've had as many bad things as I can cope with today. She decided to give him the benefit of the doubt.

"I wasss beginning to think you'd forgotten about me." Cri Sawyes peered through a hole in the barricade, the claws on his right hand embedded in the seat cushion that provided the bottom boundary of the space.

Lieutenant Jarret stopped well back out of arm's reach. "I needed to get my people out and all in one place so that we can find out where you stand, together. If they're all clear on your status, there'll be no unhappy accidents."

"On my ssstatusss? The Ssstaff Sssergeant told you that the misssilesss weren't oursss?"

"She told me that you didn't recognize them as yours and that she believes you."

"And what do you believe, Lieutenant?"

"After considering all the information . . ."

Which, since we know squat, couldn't have taken more than about five seconds, Torin added silently.

". . . I have come to believe that you, personally, are not a threat and that nothing will be served by leaving you here. Although, just to be on the safe side, we will not be immediately issuing you with a weapon."

Cri Sawyes' tongue flickered out. "Not immediately?"

The lieutenant smiled—the expression charming in a di'Taykan way and therefore open to any number of interpretations. "The situation may change."

"Ssssituationsss alwaysss do."

"Staff . . ."

Torin stepped forward, pulling the heavy bladed combat knife off her belt and hoping that it would actually cut through the Mictok webbing.

"Allow me, Ssstaff Ssssergeant Kerr." Cri Sawyes bent out of view and a lower section of the barricade swung out into the room, using four thick strands of webbing as hinges. "I had plenty of time to ssstudy the consstruction of my prissson," he explained, emerging out into the compartment. "And no intention of going down with the ship."

Sheathing her blade, Torin examined the exit. "You cut through the chairs."

"Yesss."

"With your clawsss?"

"Not entirely." As he straightened, he snapped open a piece of his harness and pulled out a slender knife.

The lieutenant shot an incredulous look at Torin. "No one searched him for weapons?"

"It'sss not a weapon, it'sss a tool."

Torin wasn't looking forward to taking it away from him.

"I see." Arms folded, the lieutenant swept an angry lilac gaze over the Silsviss. "Just so we're clear on it, what other tools are you carrying?"

Cri Sawyes patted a slender cylinder snapped into one of the diagonal belts. "Jussst my cellular phone. But don't worry, it'sss ussselesss here; we're out of area."

Contamination level now 5.3 and rising.

Levels were at 4.2 moments before in the armory—they were rising faster.

"Sir."

"I heard." He started back toward the door, indicating that Cri Sawyes should fall in beside him. "Since we'll be spending some unexpected time on Silsvah, we'd appreciate any assistance you care to give."

"I would be more than happy to help out, Lieutenant."

Torin rolled her eyes at the quiet, conversational exchange. Still, with Lieutenant Jarret now handling the big picture, she was free to remember that Cri Sawyes was weaker on his right. Just in case.

Taking a final look at the barricade, she followed the two males from the room—staying well back from the Silsviss' tail.

Given the patterns of the webbing over the stacked seats, she was afraid that the Mictok made better artists than engineers. Given that there was a Mictok working on the bridge, she hoped that observation was as inaccurate as most species generalizations tended to be.

As she stepped out onto the VTA, Torin put her helmet back on and flipped her scanner down. Thirty-four live Marines, four bodies, four Dornagain, four Mictok, three Rakva, one Rakva body. No unfriendlies in range, no sign of Corporal Hollice's team. She'd have been told if it was any different, but she liked to check for herself.

Picking up her pace, she moved out and drew even with Lieutenant Jarret. "What's he doing here?"

Lieutenant Ghard's yell had a parade ground carry that drew every eye.

A number of Marines stood. A number of weapons were readied. Torin raised a hand, and that was as far as it went.

Lieutenant Jarret snorted quietly and murmured, "I'll handle this, Staff."

Torin answered in the same low voice. "Just making certain you don't get shot while you do, sir."

If he had a response, Lieutenant Ghard prevented him from making it.

"This," he snarled up at Cri Sawyes, "is the reason we're on the ground! His people shot us down! They killed two of my aircrew and almost killed Captain Daniels!"

The Silsviss' inner eyelids flickered out and in, but he made no other movement. Even his tail was completely still. Torin kept half an eye on his throat pouch.

"Yours weren't the only casualties," Lieutenant Jarret began.

"No, they weren't," Ghard interrupted, bare feet scuffing at the skin of the VTA as though he could barely hold himself back. "And his people are responsible for your dead as well!"

"Whatever his people may or may not be responsible for, Cri Sawyes is not responsible for them."

"Isn't he?" Ghard snarled. "Not everyone on Silsvah thought it was such a great idea to join the Confederation."

Which was the first Torin had heard of it, but she wasn't surprised.

"Not wanting to join the Confederation is one thing," Jarret pointed out evenly. "One lone planet starting a war with a sizable piece of the Galaxy is something else again."

"Maybe they're not one lone planet, did you ever think of that? Maybe the Others got farther into this sector than we knew!"

Torin felt her stomach muscles tighten. She hadn't considered that. Hadn't wanted to consider it. *Didn't* want to consider it. From the sudden, total silence, neither did anyone else.

"Maybe," Ghard continued, driving the point home, "he was planted on board to ensure that any survivors of the crash died later, after we stupidly assumed he was on our side."

Jarret's expression suddenly cleared. "So he and all the Silsviss have been our enemy from the beginning?"

"Yes!"

"And I, being new, wouldn't have recognized this."

A little unsure if he was actually being asked a question, Ghard frowned. "Well, you . . ."

"And Staff Sergeant Kerr?"

"Wha . . ."

"And all three sergeants? And an entire platoon of combat-tested Marines; they wouldn't have recognized it either?"

Torin fought the urge to stare at the lieutenant in admiration as every listening Marine suddenly realized that *they* would have noticed something. And since they hadn't . . .

"I don't know who shot us down, or why." Jarret raised his voice slightly, ensuring everyone could hear. "But here and now, Cri Sawyes is not our enemy."

Because Staff Sergeant Kerr doesn't think he is. Torin finished the sentence in her head, sucked in a lungful of humid air, and exhaled sharply. *And I'm right. Because this would be a very bad time to be wrong.*

"So you're just going to let him walk around? Free?"

The lieutenant looked from the Krai to the Silsviss and back again. "Yes. Given the unfamiliar terrain, I expect we're going to need his help."

Ridges flushed, Ghard jerked around to face Torin. "Do you agree with this, Staff Sergeant Kerr?"

"I believe Lieutenant Jarret has made his position quite clear, sir."

"But do you agree?"

She gave him her best this-question-makes-no-sense look and threw enough of it into her voice that the listening Marines would have no doubt where her loyalties lay—which was also exactly what she would have done had she not agreed. If they were to get through this, there could be no question of who was in charge. "Yes, sir."

He stared at her for a moment, then nodded. "All right. Fine."

"If we might perhaps express an opinion . . ."

"No!" Ghard spun around to face Ambassador Krik'vir, who'd moved silently closer during the argument. "This is military business now, Ambassador, and has been from the moment the Silsviss opened fire." Back facing Jarret, he threw his arms out from his body, hands open wide. "I didn't want to have to do this . . ."

Torin shifted her weight forward onto the balls of her feet. If he attacked, she'd take him out and worry about the consequences later.

". . . when did you receive your commission?"

She blinked. Not what she'd been expecting.

Not what Lieutenant Jarret had been expecting either. "You don't mean . . ." When it became quite clear that was exactly what Ghard meant, he sighed. "The sixth day of the fifth month, Confederation twelve thousand, five hundred, and four. It was also the second of *Mon gleen*, for what that's worth." He flashed a brilliant di'Taykan smile.

"You?"

"Later." Nose flaps opened and closed. "Which puts you in command." The pause spoke volumes. "Sir."

Gods save me from junior officers, Torin pleaded silently and decided it was time to step in. "Begging your pardon, sirs, but General Morris' orders put Lieutenant Jarret in command, regardless. Unless," she added as both men turned, "the VTA takes off again. In the air, as long as Captain Daniels is unavailable, Lieutenant Ghard will be in command."

It was an inarguable position. And there shouldn't have been an argument to start with. Torin only hoped that Ghard was still off-balance from the crash and the casualties and wasn't planning on being a commissioned pain in the ass until rescue arrived.

The next words out of his mouth didn't show much promise. It wasn't what he said, but how he said it.

"Then if Cri Sawyes isn't our enemy, who is?"

"You were probably on the right track when you mentioned the Others," Jarret told him. "They've been reported in this sector—the *Berganitan* is off chasing them. With our ship out of orbit, they could easily drop a small force through the Silsviss defenses."

"Not easssily," Cri Sawyes protested, throat pouch extending slightly.

"Easily," Jarret repeated.

Heads nodded up and down the surface of the VTA.

"And what better way to keep the Silsviss from signing the treaty," the lieutenant continued, "than by setting them up to take the blame for shoot-ing us down. Had Cri Sawyes not seen the missiles, it might have worked."

It fit all the facts and most of the speculation, Torin reflected.

"Or a group of Silsviss from this part of the world, who would logically have weapons that Cri Sawyes from another part of the world wouldn't recognize, shot us down because they don't want their planet to join the Confederation. It won't work that way, but fanatics seldom realize they can't win."

So did that. *And where there's two viable theories*, Torin silently sighed, *there could easily be a third or a fourth.*

Lieutenant Ghard stared up at the di'Taykan lieutenant. "So which is it?"

Jarret snorted, a sound so unlike him it caught and held any wandering attention. "What difference does it make? We're ground combat troops and we're on the ground. We'll handle whatever the situation throws at us."

"Hoorah," Torin agreed, just loud enough to be heard and ignored by both officers.

Ghard looked from the lieutenant to Torin and back again. "Good thing you'll have Staff Sergeant Kerr to hold your *kayt*." he muttered softly as he turned away.

Which was an insult in Human or Krai, but he'd used the Taykan word and a di'-phase Taykan would be quite happy to have anyone hold his *kayt* without it affecting anything but his *kayt*. On the other hand, Torin rea-soned, intent had to count for something.

"Let it be, Staff."

She hadn't realized she'd stepped forward until the lieutenant's quiet command stopped her. "Yes, sir."

"And, Staff?" He'd moved up beside her, close enough to hold a private conversation, while those who'd witnessed him taking command dispersed.

"Sir?"

"Cri Sawyes may not be our enemy, but I'd appreciate it if you'd keep an eye on him anyway."

"I'd fully intended to, sir. And Lieutenant Ghard?"

"As you said earlier, not your problem."

A few moments later, she found herself beside Cri Sawyes as Lieu-tenant Jarret spoke with the civilians. The Silsviss' tail cut figure eight patterns through the humid air. "What?"

"Among my people, a challenge sssuch asss that would have drawn blood."

"Which should make it interesting to integrate your people into our military."

"Interesssting?" His tongue flickered out. "You have a way with underssstatement, Ssstaff Sssergeant."

"Just part of the job."

"How close is Hollice's team, Staff?"

"They'll be here in ten, sir."

The lieutenant glanced down at the bags lying on the highest curve of the VTA. "Then we'll wait."

Torin checked the seals and stepped back. Waiting for the absent fireteam had been a fine gesture, but if they were going to reach their first camp before dark—with the Dornagain—they'd have to hurry.

The Rakva had refused the use of a bag and moments before had slipped the weighted body of Aarik Slayir into the mud.

But the Marines didn't leave their people behind.

Lieutenant Jarret spoke the first acknowledgment of loss. *"Fraishin sha aren. Valynk sha haren."*

Beside him, Lieutenant Ghard bit a small piece from the back of his forearm. *"Kal danic dir kadir. Kri ta chrikdan."*

"We will not forget. We will not fail you." It wasn't the first time Torin had been the ranking Human. It never got easier.

"Staff."

But then it shouldn't get easier. She held out her slate and sent the command.

The bags stiffened, then flattened.

The ash fit into small cylinders that slid into measured spaces inside Torin's vest. The cylinders were virtually indestructible. Even if her body was destroyed in combat, the remains of these dead Marines would still be recovered. She found that strangely comforting.

Calculating how much longer it would be until he could get his *serley* boots off, Kleers took three steps to the Dornagain's one. A collarbone broken in the crash had gotten him assigned to escort duty even though the doc had put things pretty much back together. Since the walking sucked just as much at the front of the column as at the rear, he didn't really mind.

"There are those who say you can judge a civilization by how much respect they grant their dead."

"Really?" He pulled a handful of soft fruit off a vine as big around as his wrist, wiped off a few splatters of mud against his vest, gave them a thorough sniff, and popped them into his mouth.

"If the dead has a large family, an internment on Dornage can take many days."

Kleers took another three steps and reached for some more fruit. "Can't say as I'm surprised."

"How do the Krai treat their dead?"

"We cook them and we eat them."

Thinks Deeply walked in silence for a moment or two. "And that is a sign of respect?" she asked at last.

"Well, I'd have to say that depends on who does the cooking."

NINE

"If the ridge joinsss up with higher ground here . . ." Cri Sawyes drew a curved line in the dirt and then crossed it, ". . . then the buildingsss I sssaw from the air are here." He drew a square toward the end of the crosspiece. "They could be asss near asss three kilometers or asss far asss five."

"If this is a wilderness preserve, why are there buildings at all?" The nose filters the di'Taykan had been forced to wear made Lieutenant Jarret's voice sound flat and angry.

It was a good question, though. Since the lines in the dirt were telling Torin nothing much, she looked up at Cri Sawyes.

"I have no idea."

The lieutenant's eyes narrowed. "Why not?"

"I'm not from around here." His tongue flicked out. When neither the two officers nor the three NCOs squatting around the crude map seemed to appreciate the humor, he expanded his explanation. "Sssome of what we Sssilsssvisss do isss bound by biology and therefore relatively ssstandard planet-wide. All our young malesss are sssegregated until hormonal balance isss achieved and they—we—are able to control our aggresssion. Behavior within that sssegregation fallsss within biologically determined parametersss." He glanced around the circle of light, checking that his listeners understood. When no one indicated otherwise, he continued. "There are, asss I'm sure you're aware, many cultural differencesss even within a planet'sss dominant ssspeciesss and I believe that the buildingsss are one of thossse differencesss."

"A useful difference if we can get to them," Sergeant Chou muttered.

Heads nodded around the circle.

"The long-range scanner on the VTA placed the closest Silsviss at thirty kilometers to the northwest." Lieutenant Jarret jabbed a stick into the ground. "Approximately here. As the buildings are southeast of our position, we can assume they're empty." He frowned up at Cri Sawyes. "Could you tell if they were intact?"

"At that altitude and that ssspeed? No. I only sssaw them for a moment."

"But you're sure of where they are?"

"Within reason."

"Staff?"

Torin sat back on her heels and exhaled slowly. All things considered, it could have been worse. That she was fairly certain it was going to *get* worse didn't actually impact on the current decision. "We can't run away from a fight because of the wounded, so I'd prefer to have something solid between me and the enemy if we have to dig in."

"So would I. At first light, send a fireteam out to scout the position."

"Yes, sir." A sudden commotion in the darkness on the other side of the camp pulled Torin's attention.

"That sounds like Hollice," Mike muttered, head cocked to better separate the voices.

The unmistakable sound of a KC discharging brought everyone to their feet.

"Sergeant Glicksohn!"

"On my way, sir." He slapped down his helmet scanner and broke into a run.

Ghard shook off the lethargy he'd worn since abandoning the contaminated VTA to the swamp, dropped his weapon off his shoulder, and jerked the muzzle around toward Cri Sawyes. "Are they attacking?"

"Are who attacking?" Jarret demanded.

"His people!"

"It's not the Silsviss, sir." Torin turned slowly so as not to startle him into pulling the trigger. Tentative friendship aside, they needed Cri Sawyes alive—he'd already proved a valuable resource. "We're close enough to the VTA that all implants are still online and mine registered no perimeter violations."

"Nor did mine." Jarret stepped forward and gently pushed the other lieutenant's weapon down toward the ground. "And the sentry's helmet scanners are slaved to Staff Sergeant Kerr's. If there was anything, anyone advancing toward us, we'd know."

Ghard reluctantly moved his hand away from the trigger. "Then what was Corporal Hollice shooting at?"

"A snake, Sarge."

"A snake?" Glicksohn repeated.

Hollice nodded and moved aside.

"Holy fuk."

"You know, Sarge, that's just about exactly what I said."

The snake was as big around as a man's arm and over three meters long. A tight beam of light played down its length picked out dull green diamonds bordered in mud brown. Difficult to spot in daylight, it would have been almost impossible to see at night. Almost. The tip of its tail was a brilliant orange, and it had two stubby orange legs a handspan back from the bloody stump where its head had been.

"It must've crawled up from the swamp, Sarge. I heard it slithering." Hollice kicked at the body and shivered when the dead weight merely rocked slightly, absorbing the blow. "I hate snakes."

"Was it poisonous?"

"What's left of it isn't," Ressk answered from the shadows.

There were a number of regulations pertaining to the use of weapons within a camp perimeter. Looking down at the snake, Sergeant Glicksohn considered and discarded all of them. "Nice shot," he said.

The night passed without further incident.

"Sleep well?" Mysho asked, passing a red-eyed Hollice on her way from the di'Taykan's communal tent to the latrine.

Hollice shoved his fist up against a yawn. "I'm not sleeping until we're off this stinking planet," he snarled.

The Krai and Cri Sawyes had snake for breakfast.

It was midday by the time they finally got clear of the swamp. Torin didn't know who the morning had been harder on: the Dornagain, who'd struggled to keep moving at nearly twice their normal speed, or everyone else who'd had to fight the urge to leave all four of them behind. Even the stretcher bearers had been moving faster, and she'd be willing to swear they'd been passed by the local equivalent of a slug at least twice during the early part of the morning's march.

Having seen to the security of their makeshift camp, Torin stood and looked back down the ridge into the shallow valley that held the swamp. From her vantage point, she could see that dumb luck had dropped the VTA right next to one of only three fingers of higher land. Torin had never been a great believer in luck, preferring to trust in training, preparation, and strong artillery support, but it was impossible to deny the good fortune that had caused them to crash precisely where they had.

Good fortune and crash in the same sentence . . . that's something you don't hear every day.

Running her hand back through damp hair, she tried not to think of how wonderful a bath would feel or how badly they all needed one. Even one of the torrential downpours they'd been pummeled by at every *other* landing site on the planet would have helped, but the sky was almost painfully clear. Designed to repel dirt, the uniforms were surprisingly clean—the Marines wearing them were not. Even with an only Human sense of smell, Torin suspected the di'Taykan had removed their nose filters a little early.

Over the years she'd fought the Others on every sort of terrain imaginable, a number of them significantly more dangerous than the ground they'd just crossed, but she couldn't think of a battlefield that had smelled worse. Fortunately, as the land had risen, the ground had dried and thick stands of sharp-edged grasses had begun to take over from the multilayers of rotting vegetation. By the time they reached what turned out to be the edge of a low plateau, the ground cover had become nothing but grass and an occasional clump of low bushes. Nothing in the immediate area smelled worse than they did.

Which was a mixed blessing at best.

At least the lieutenant's scavenging parties won't have any trouble finding their way back to the VTA. She could see the muddy scar of their crash from where she stood.

And if she could see it, so could anyone else.

Reluctantly replacing her helmet, she flipped down the scanner and pivoted slowly a hundred and eighty degrees. There were no registered species—Confederation species or Other—within the five-kilometer range. Which had to be considered good news although Torin would have preferred to know exactly how close the young males of the preserve had come during the night. Only an idiot would assume they weren't planning to investigate the crash. *And I can guarantee they're making better time than we are.*

Glancing over at the Dornagain, she watched Strength of Arm lick up the last dregs of something they'd reconstituted the moment the lieutenant had called a rest. Finishing, she set the large bowl carefully aside and sagged almost instantly into sleep. From the state of her companions' bowls, it looked as though exhaustion had won out over hunger.

In contrast, the Mictok, affected by neither the mud, nor the heat, nor the distance were chittering cheerfully to themselves just out of range of her translator.

Well, it sounds cheerful anyway, Torin acknowledged. They could have been discussing ways to bisect the politician who'd sent them to Silsviss and was therefore responsible for getting them into this mess.

The Charge d'Affaires and her one surviving aide were grooming matted feathers. Dr. Leor was at the stretchers—every now and then Torin could hear Haysole's voice rising in a question. She hoped it was distance and position muting the doctor's answers and not the seriousness of Haysole's situation. Cri Sawyes had stretched out in the sun and, except for the team on watch, the Marines were stretched out by the stretchers, sharing a thin slice of shade. Lieutenant Jarret had given the di'Taykan specific orders not to wander off in search of a little privacy.

And considering how little privacy a di'Taykan needs . . . Torin cut off the thought before it took her places she didn't have time to go.

Thumbing a dribble of sweat out of her eyebrow, she decided that a few moments in the shade might be a good idea. As she walked past the piles of discarded gear, the pair of boxed emmies caught her attention. The targeting scanner on an EM223 covered between fifteen and twenty kilometers depending on conditions. Unfortunately, since the Silsviss had been considered an ally . . .

"Ressk."

The Krai lifted his head and blinked blearily at her. "Staff?"

"Can you download the data on the Silsviss from your slate into the emmy?"

"Sure." As he rolled up onto his feet, he pulled his slate from his belt. "But it's not targeting data."

"Can you reprogram the scanner to work with it?"

That stopped him cold, and a number of the others raised their heads to better follow the exchange.

"You want me to reprogram the scanner?"

"That's right."

"To target an allied species?"

"Yes."

"It's against regs," Ressk reminded her gleefully.

"So's being overwhelmed by a pack of adolescent liz . . . Silsviss," she corrected quickly, "and being beaten to death with sticks. Do what you can and do it quickly. The lieutenant wants us to move out as soon as the report's in on those buildings."

"The lieutenant wants?"

Torin caught his gaze, held it, and slowly lifted a brow. It had taken an implanted learning program to teach her the trick, but she'd never regretted the lost sleep.

Ressk's ridges flushed. "Sorry, Staff. I'll, uh, start working on the emmy."

The fireteam sent out to recon Cri Sawyes' buildings reported both intact and one nearly filled with large cloth bags of grain.

"And water?" Torin asked.

"There's a well, of sorts. Not a lot of water, but what's there is clean. The Krai can probably drink it straight."

Jarret flipped down his own mike. "Is it a position we can defend if we have to?"

"It's the best position I've seen since we grounded, sir."

Which wasn't saying much.

Before reprogramming, the targeting scanner found no enemies to lock onto. Had the Others shot down the VTA, they were apparently satisfied with the result and seemed uninterested in finishing the job.

That was the good news.

After reprogramming, it showed Silsviss only 7.3 kilometers away.

"Trouble is," Ressk admitted, around the disassembled piece of the emmy he had clamped between his teeth, "I can't get the program to tell me if that's one Silsviss or a hundred."

"Or if it's the local teenagers or the local army," Ghard added.

"I've already considered that, sir." Torin stepped between the lieutenant and Ressk before Ghard could make a grab for the targeting screen. "The Silsviss military knows what we're capable of; we've been doing demonstrations all over the planet. If that"—she jerked her head toward the screen—"was an army, they'd be opening fire with artillery by now."

"You're sure?"

He needed her to be sure, so she showed him her lower teeth, as close to a Krai social cue as she could manage. "Yes, sir. The only thing we have to worry about is how many teenagers are approaching."

"Probably clossse to a hundred," Cri Sawyes announced. When both officers, Torin, and Ressk locked eyes on his face, he lightly tapped the ground with his tail. "The leader of the nearessst pack would never allow hisss sssubordinatesss to examine the crash without him for fear they'd find sssomething that would enable them to take power," he explained. "Nor would thossse sssubordinatesss allow the pack leader to invessstigate on hisss own. They're all coming."

"And quickly." Torin squinted toward the northwest wondering how much dust a hundred Silsviss would raise. "We'll never reach those buildings before they catch up. Are you sure they'll attack?"

"Yesss. As I told you, a good leader throwsss pack againssst pack, keeping hisss followersss too preoccupied to take him down. However, I think you'll have time; they'll check out the crash sssite firssst."

"Are you sure?" Jarret demanded.

"Not one hundred percent sure, no, but classe. We are on their ground, as sssoon ass they crosss our path"—all eyes turned from Cri Sawyes to the broad, muddy trail that led back into the swamp—"they'll know they outnumber usss. They'll believe they can take usss out any time, ssso firssst they'll sssatisssfy their curiosssity about the crash."

"Their weapons?"

"Pre-technology. Only what they can make from materialsss in the pressserve. Once at the buildingsss, we should be able to hold them off indefinitely."

"Then we have to reach the buildings. Staff."

"Listen up, people!" Her voice carried to the far edge of the camp, stopping both movement and conversations. "Pack up and get ready to move. If you brought it in, carry it out!"

"Hey, Staff! What about them?" Mysho pointed downwind at the four immobile heaps of multihued golden fur.

"I'll wake the Dornagain." They were large, they had claws, and for all Torin knew, they woke up cranky. She started toward them, deciding it might be safest to begin with Thinks Deeply.

"Wait!" Ghard blocked her way with an outstretched arm.

Rocking to a stop, she stared down at the Krai. She thought they'd settled that whole chain of command thing. Apparently, Lieutenant Ghard thought otherwise. While she had some sympathy for his insecurities—grounded pilots were all a bit squiggy having been forcibly ejected from their natural element—she had none whatsoever for his timing. Fortunately, the platoon continued readying themselves for the march, paying no attention. "Sir, I have my orders."

"But what if the Silsviss don't go to the crash site first?" he demanded. Without giving her a chance to answer, he jerked his head around to face Jarret and Cri Sawyes. "If they don't go to the crash site and we start for the buildings now, they'll catch us spread out and unable to defend ourselves. Maybe that's what *he* wants."

The emphasis aimed the pronoun directly at Cri Sawyes.

"If the march isss overrun, I alssso will be overrun," he pointed out, his voice as impatient as Torin had ever heard it.

"So? You're one of them!"

"No, I am not." His throat pouch swelled enough to flash a crescent of lighter skin and then deflated. "Firstly, I am an adult and secondly, I am not of their pack." One hand swept down the length of his torso, drawing attention to gray-on-gray markings. "And although I may be of the sssame ssspeciesss, I'm not of their race. I am in thisss with you, Lieutenant Ghard, whether you want me there or not."

"Lieutenant Jarret . . ."

"I've made my decision." Eyes dark, Jarret stared at Ghard a heartbeat longer. Then, without moving his head, he snapped his gaze over to Torin. "You have your orders, Staff Sergeant."

"Yes, sir."

"A word with you in private, Lieutenant Ghard."

Judging from his tone, Lieutenant Jarret was about to give his junior officer a well-deserved reaming out.

"What're you looking so approving about?" Mike asked as she passed.

Torin paused and nodded back toward the two officers. Ghard's shoulders had slumped, but as Jarret continued talking, they began to straighten. "I like the way Lieutenant Jarret is taking command."

"As opposed to the way twoies usually take command?" He squeezed his voice into a shrill falsetto. "I'm an officer and I'm in charge, so you've got to do what I say, no matter what!" Then his voice dropped back down into its normal range. "And I'm inclined to think that's better than the overly earnest—if some idiot just out of college is going to get me killed, I'd as soon not die thinking at least their intentions were good."

"So this time we got lucky."

"We've been lucky before."

"So this time let's keep him alive."

The sergeant sighed. "That's the trick, isn't it?" Head to one side, he looked up at Torin through thick lashes. "If I were a betting man . . ."

She snorted.

Grinning, he continued. ". . . I'd say you liked him."

Just for a moment, she wondered what he knew. *She* hadn't given anything away. Had the lieutenant? Then the moment passed. If she wasn't hearing about her unfortunate indiscretion from the other di'Taykan, then no one knew. "I appreciate his ability as an officer . . ." Which she did. ". . . and I appreciate his appearance . . ." Safe enough, after all, she wasn't blind. ". . . but he's very young . . ." Not that age was relevant with a di'Taykan. ". . . and that's as far as it goes." Regardless of how far it had gone.

The grin broadened. "Yeah. That's what I meant. You like him."

Torin rolled her eyes. "I have an idea. Instead of making crude innuendoes . . ."

"You have a dirty mind, Staff."

". . . find us some stretcher bearers and four grunts to hump those emmies." Continuing toward the sleepers, she added, "I don't want to hear any complaints about who's had to carry what the whole way."

"Lieutenant, while my people are not in the habit of violence, we are more capable of defending ourselves than the wounded. If you hold the march to our speed, you delay getting them to safety. Four Marines, one Marine for each of us, will certainly be sufficient protection."

"I appreciate your offer, Ambassador, but it's just too dangerous."

The Dornagain ambassador stroked the back of one hand over his whiskers. "Come now, Lieutenant, it's only three kilometers to the buildings. Even we can cover that much ground in the time it will take our young Silsviss friends to travel over twice that, pause to examine the VTA, and then come after us."

Jarret frowned. "What do you think, Staff?"

"The ambassador makes a good point, sir. It *is* only three kilometers."

"True. But I don't like dividing our march."

"We will fall behind regardless, Lieutenant. Would it not be best to work with the inevitable?" The ambassador smiled down at the Marines, showing an impressive double ridge of teeth. "There is no need for everyone else to be made uncomfortable by the pace we set and no need for my people to be made guilty realizing that."

The lieutenant still looked unconvinced, and they were running out of time to convince him. From where Torin stood, the Dornagain were realists. She appreciated that in a species.

Dr. Leor, who'd been listening to the discussion, arms crossed and feathers flat, suddenly stepped forward. "This one would like the wounded under cover as soon as possible," he announced, "so that this one will be able to perform therapies impossible to attempt while on the move."

All eyes turned to the stretchers and quickly slid away again.

"All right." One hand raised, palm out, the lieutenant surrendered. "The Dornagain can set their own pace, but I'm sending Marines back to deepen your escort as soon they've dropped packs."

"I find that an acceptable compromise."

The doctor fixed the lieutenant with a gleaming black stare. "Then if the decision has been made, this one wonders why there is no forward movement."

"A good question, Doctor. Staff, assign a fireteam to the Dornagain and let's get this . . ."

Torin thought of several less than diplomatic descriptions.

". . . show on the road."

"Yes, sir."

With the stretcher bearers setting the pace, the column pulled rapidly away from the Dornagain and their escort. The ground was dry and firm and the vegetation short enough to make walking easy—especially compared to the mess they'd spent the morning in.

Walking near the front of the column, Jarret leaned down and plucked a stalk of Silsvah grass. "There's a lot of silicate in this," he said, rubbing it between thumb and forefinger.

Given the way it crunched, Torin acknowledged that seemed like a reasonable observation.

"But that doesn't explain why it's so short."

"Grazing, sir."

"Grazing?" he repeated, flicking the pulp away.

"Yes, sir. Pasture fields all over look pretty much like this. It's a dead giveaway when the only plants over a certain height are woody and too tough to chew."

"Too tough for *what* to chew, Staff?" His mouth opened to check the scent on a breeze and closed again significantly faster. "What the *sanLi* is that?"

Torin grinned as her less efficient sense of smell picked up the only possible odor bad enough to make a di'Taykan who'd just crawled through a swamp blaspheme. "I suspect your second question is about to answer your first."

As di'Taykan profanity moved down the line, she scanned the area upwind and finally pointed. "There. Under the cloud of insects."

Jarret's eyes darkened, but he shook his head. "I don't see . . ."

"It's a pile of shit, sir. If I can have a closer look, I'll be able to tell for certain if it's out of our grazer."

"How can you tell that from *shit?*"

"Herbivores are fairly distinctive. And if there's something walking around here big enough to drop that, I'd like to find out what I can about it."

"What about Cri Sawyes?"

They could hear the Silsviss behind them, arguing points of the Confederation treaty with the Charge d'Affaires.

"He's not from around here, sir. And he's a city boy, besides."

"Fine. Go." He waved her on, looking so appalled that she couldn't stop herself from snickering as she double-timed over to the pile, pack bouncing against the small of her back. As expected, the insects ignored her. Across the planet, Silsvah insects had ignored every species in the party except the Mictok. The non-Mictok carefully refused to speculate on a reason.

Almost two meters in diameter, the pile was half that high and had definitely come out of the back end of a single herbivore. In spite of the heat it had barely crusted, leaving Torin to believe said herbivore either hadn't gone far or had moved one hell of a lot faster than the cows back home.

Returning to the column, she filled in the lieutenant, adding, "It's heading off due west, about forty-five degrees to our line of march. I think we can safely ignore it for now."

"Well, I'm convinced; staff sergeants *do* know everything."

"You should never have doubted it, sir."

They walked in silence for a few moments.

"Staff . . ."

"I grew up on a farm, and farming and shit are pretty much synonymous."

"A farm?"

She nodded. His voice and expression suggested he'd never even seen a farm. Hardly surprising given his family's rank.

"So why did you leave?"

Torin grinned. "I just told you, sir."

It took him a moment to make the connection. He smiled when he did but refused to drop the subject. "All right, then, why did you join the Marines?"

Their shared past granted him an honest response. Torin wasn't sure why; it had, after all, lasted only one night and was never to be referred to again, but somehow it kept her from throwing out any number of the slick answers she kept ready. "I had a fight with my father, about crop rotations if you can believe it. I was sick of the farm, but it defined his whole life. Next thing I knew, I was standing in a recruiting office having a blood test, and twenty-four hours after that I shipped out. Crop rotations." She sighed. "A truly stupid reason to kill and be killed for."

"Then why do you stay? Why make it a career?"

Again, that shared past kept her from a glib response. And if it didn't entitle him to the part of the truth that involved love and honor, duty and sacrifice, it at least ensured that the truth be present. Because it sounded like he really wanted to know, she thought about it a moment. "Well, sir, it's a dirty job, but someone *has* to do it."

When he nodded, she knew he'd understood the emphasis. Unfortunately, understanding didn't stop the questions. "But why you?"

"Why me?" She considered saying, *Why not me?* and being done with it, but found herself saying instead, "I'm good at it. In fact, I'm better at it than most. Parts of it I enjoy. All of it, I feel fulfilled by." This was getting perilously close to the line a single night's sex didn't get to cross. "There's a whole lot of people in this universe who wish they could say the same."

"And no one's shooting at them."

"Maybe that's their problem, sir," Torin said dryly.

"My whole family was career military," he told her after a dozen paces when it became clear she wasn't going to ask. "Every single di'Ka since contact has served the Confederation, and we served at home before that. It was a di'Ka who kept the military from shooting down the First Contact ship, and the first di'Taykans to swear into both the Confederation Marine Corps and Navy were di'Ka. One of my progenitors even remained on the Admiralty staff in an advisory role after she shifted to qui'."

"So you're a professional soldier, sir."

"I suppose." He kicked at a purple bloom, beheading the flower and infuriating a large, yellow bug, who spat or possibly excreted something on his boot, and flew off. "All I know is that every time I give an order I can feel them all lined up behind me passing judgment."

"I wouldn't worry about them, sir."

Squinting slightly in the sunlight, the shadow of his hair not quite deep enough to block the glare, he snorted. "You don't have to worry about them. They're not your family."

"Very true, sir," she admitted so seriously he jerked around to face her. "But I don't think *you* should worry about them either."

"And why not, Staff?"

She smiled broadly at him. "Because *they're* not here."

Two paces later, he returned the smile. "And you are?"

"I certainly seem to be, sir."

"Why us? That's what I fukking want to know."

"Why not us?" Hollice shrugged. "Ours is not to question why."

Juan turned to stare at him, lip curled. "Why the fuk not?" He turned a little farther, just far enough to watch the Dornagain lumbering slowly toward them, and sighed. "How's this for an idea—you bet your next pay packet that I can run around them three times before they make it to this spot."

"How's this for a better idea—you stay here and I'll move on to the next corner."

"Fukking corporals," Juan muttered as Hollice moved away. He shoved his helmet to the back of his head and scratched at the damp line of exposed hair. "Rest of the platoon's probably nearly to the buildings by now." Squinting along the line of crushed vegetation they were following, he raised his voice as he added, "Probably sitting in the fukking shade."

Although he heard, Hollice didn't bother responding to the heavy gunner's observation. He didn't see the point; it wouldn't get them moving any faster and it would only encourage more complaints. Given the difficulty of maintaining the same pace as the Dornagain, he kept his team rotating around the four corners of the march. After twenty paces, number one corner moved up to number two, two moved to three, three to four, four to one, and twenty paces later they did it all again. It not only gave them a chance to stretch their legs, but it helped stop terminal boredom from setting in.

"Binti."

She covered a yawn with the back of her fist as he fell into step beside her. "Is it that time again?"

"It is."

"You know Ressk's got his boots off."

Hollice flipped down his helmet scanner and glanced back at the Krai's position. "Can't hurt."

Binti snorted, turned around, and began walking backward. "The Dornagain aren't talking much today."

They both glanced over at their four charges, sunlit highlights rippling from shoulder to haunch as the huge bodies moved slowly forward.

"Maybe they're saving their breath to maintain this speed."

White teeth flashed in a sarcastic smile. "Oh, yeah, baby, *this* is speed."

"Staff Sergeant Kerr, we were wondering if we might ask you a question."

Torin thanked the training that had kept her from shrieking at the sudden, totally silent appearance of the Mictok and turned a polite smile toward the closest eyestalk. "Of course, Ambassador."

"We were wondering about the stretchers."

"The stretchers?"

"Yes. We cannot help but notice that they seem to be nothing more than a pair of lightweight poles with a piece of fabric stretched between."

"Essentially, ma'am, although there are legs snapped down against the underside of the poles and a certain amount of monitoring equipment built into both poles and fabric." More familiar than she wanted to be with the Corps stretchers, she glanced over at the four carried in the center of the column. Although she hadn't done it deliberately—or at least, consciously—she'd been flanking Haysole for most of the march. They had his environmental controls up as high as possible, but he still looked hot and uncomfortable. Shadows encircled his closed eyes, and his lips were so dark they were almost purple. If the ends of his hair hadn't been moving slowly, Torin would have feared the worst.

"We were wondering why."

A little confused, Torin brought her attention back to the ambassador. "Why what, ma'am."

"Why use such simple equipment? Hospitals throughout the Confederation use stretchers that operate by pushing against the planetary gravity. Granted, the Ghazix Generators making that possible would have to be calibrated for each planet you land on, but we're certain you would find them much more efficient than this." One foreleg gestured disdainfully toward the equipment under discussion. Had Mictok the features for it, Torin was certain the ambassador would have been frowning. "A modern stretcher would put none of your people at risk. Once up and running, it could be tethered, leaving all hands free."

"Unfortunately, ma'am, unless they're very large—VTA large—Ghazix Generators can be easily knocked out with a simple electromagnetic pulse, leaving us with an extremely heavy and completely useless piece of scrap."

"The Others would attack the wounded?" Her mandibles snapped together so hard heads up and down the line turned at the sound.

Torin decided not to get into that. Had the elder races been able to understand war, they wouldn't have needed the Humans, the di'Taykan, and the Krai. And now the Silsviss. "They disable our equipment, ma'am. Just like we disable theirs. The more damage we can do from a distance, the less risk when we get up close and personal."

"So our forces also attack the wounded?"

Not for the first time, Torin realized she probably had more in common with the people she was fighting than the people she was fighting for. Dissembling seemed the order of the day. "The Others use something similar to a Ghazix Generator, ma'am, similar enough that they know how to disable one. We know they know that, so we use stretchers they can't affect because Marines don't leave Marines behind. We use primitive projectile weapons that have to be physically smashed to stop working for the same reason. So do they. Our helmets may contain complicated communication and surveillance equipment, but they're still fully functional as helmets should either or both be knocked out."

"We noticed that you did not answer our question, Staff Sergeant Kerr." She raised a foreleg to prevent an answer. "But we suspect we would be happier not knowing. We are diplomats and we spend much time dealing with the results of the war, but we have never spent so much time speaking to one actually within it." She paused. "Usually, we speak with officers."

"Lieutenant Jarret . . ."

"Is not near the rank we usually associate with."

Under those circumstances, Torin granted her the point.

"We must consider this conversation, but we would like to speak with you again, Staff Sergeant Kerr."

As the Mictok ambassador scuttled back to her companions, Mike moved up into the place she'd vacated, muttering, "Get it off me." And then a little louder. "What were you two talking about?"

Torin snorted. "Reality."

"Yours or hers?"

"Bit of both. Looks like we've arrived safely."

He squinted along the line of her finger and shook his head. "I can barely see a roof. We've still got lots of time to be descended on and slaughtered."

"If you know something I don't, now would be the time to tell me."

"I don't like this shoot-us-down-and-ignore-us crap. I keep waiting for the other shoe to drop."

"Did you hear something?"

"No, sir."

The Dornagain's ears swiveled, moving in progressively smaller arcs and, after a moment, he pointed almost due north. "That way. I suggest you use your scanner, Corporal."

Hollice screwed the cap on his water bottle, sighed, and crammed his helmet back on. Intellectually, he knew that the environmental controls would keep his head a lot cooler than any breeze, but emotionally, if he was wearing a hat, he felt hot. Flicking down the scanner, he swung around toward the north and froze. "Shit on a stick."

"May I assume from your colloquial expression that there is something there?"

"Something?" He thumbed the controls, trying to bring in a more precise reading. "I bloody well wish it was just something! Unfriendlies! Thirty of them!"

"How far?" Ressk demanded, as the unwelcome information prodded the Marines up onto their feet.

"Between one and one and a half kilometers. Make that point eight and one point three of a kilometer."

Shoving one of the exoskeleton's pins in deeper, Juan muttered, "Fuk, they're fast."

"And we aren't." Raising his scanner, Hollice swept a practiced gaze over their surroundings. "There! Those rocks!" The planet's bones jutted up dark purple to pink, out of the green, offering the only protection in the immediate area. Swinging his pack up on his back, he turned to the Dornagain ambassador. "Sir, can your people run?"

"For short distances only."

"To those rocks?"

"I am not certain . . ."

"Well, *I'm* certain we can't protect you against thirty unfriendlies on open ground."

"You make a convincing argument, Corporal. We will run."

To the Marine's surprise, the Dornagain flung himself forward, body stretching in the air, long, muscular arms extending, knuckles hitting the ground, claws curled under. Then, with a shimmer of golden fur, his body seemed to fold in on itself until his feet dug in just behind his knuckles and he leaped forward again, heavy pack swinging and banging but somehow staying on.

"This is going to destroy my manicure," Thinks Deeply sighed as she followed the ambassador.

"They're not exactly running."

"Fuk it," Juan advised, swinging his weapon from side to side as he worked the kinks out of his shoulders. "It's getting the job done."

Hollice dragged his fascinated gaze off the Dornagain. "Binti, get to the rocks! Take the high ground!"

"On my way." The sharpshooter sped forward, her long legs making short work of the ground the Dornagain had already covered.

"And we're going to?" Ressk asked.

"Try not to get a pointy stick in the back," Hollice grunted as they started to jog after their charges.

"Be a lot fukking safer on the other side of the Dornagain."

"Yeah." Carrying his weapon one-handed, he reached up to flip down his microphone. "I've considered that . . ."

TEN

Only standing beside the buildings did it become obvious that they'd been built in a shallow valley.

"An enemy on those hills would have the high ground," Torin muttered. "Not good."

"Not bad," Cri Sawyes corrected. "From here, those hillsss are in easssy range of your weaponsss, but on the hillsss your enemy hasss no weaponsss that will reach you. Againssst greater numbersss, it isss far better to have a wall at your back."

Torin couldn't argue with that.

Both buildings were a single story high. Rectangular, they were set so that the end of one angled off the side of the other with fifteen meters between them on the north and thirty on the south. If there was a reason for their placement, Torin couldn't see it. The walls were made of thick mud bricks coated in a facing layer of mud and were topped with shallow-angled thatch roofs. Inside they'd been divided into thirds, rooms closed off from each other by a surprisingly heavy wooden door. A narrow window high in each room's outside wall let in light. One building, as reported, was empty. The other was filled with large fabric sacks of grain.

In spite of their rustic setting, the waterproof, vermin-proof sacks were clearly the product of a technological society.

"I expect the grain isss brought in for the young malesss," Cri Sawyes explained to Torin, pouring a sample from one hand to the other. "We are, like all of you, omnivorousss."

An eyebrow rose of its own volition. "You intended for them to kill each other, but you don't want them to starve to death?"

"It isss more complicated than that, Ssstaff Sssergeant, but esssentially, yesss."

"So for the packs, this is neutral ground?" When he agreed that it was, Torin sighed. "And we've moved in. That's going to piss them off but good."

Chewing the grain he'd been examining, Cri Sawyes followed her out of the building. "If I undersssstand your comment correctly, it does sssum up the problem."

"Maybe we should leave."

"That would be wissse—were there anywhere to go. Asss there isss not . . ."

They joined the lieutenant at the well just as Dr. Leor finished testing the grain.

"As usual, the Krai may eat it although they will need to supplement for the amino acids it lacks."

"And the rest of us?"

"This one thinks not. And now, this one has patients to settle. That building is empty? Then this one will use the farthest room for those already injured and the nearest room to treat those about to be injured."

"And the middle room?" Torin wondered.

"If there is to be fighting," the doctor pointed out disapprovingly, "the middle room will fill quickly enough." He minced off, shouting orders to the two corpsmen as he went.

Torin peered into the well. She could see her reflection shimmering in the darkness about six meters down. "Bad news about the grain, sir."

"We have food, Staff. The bags of grain are a lot more useful as part of our defenses."

"We'll use them to buy our way out of a fight?" she asked, straightening.

"Wouldn't work," Cri Sawyes said shortly. "They will attack regardless."

"We use the bags to build walls between the buildings." Jarret turned and pointed. "There and there. It'll give us one unbroken front with the well safely inside."

"There's certainly enough," Torin admitted, mentally converting the stored grain into walls. "An excellent idea, sir."

"I'm not totally helpless without you, Staff."

"Since you're smiling, sir, I'll accept that ludicrous observation in the spirit in which it was offered."

His smile began to broaden, then cut off completely at the unmistakable alarm sounding from the helmet tucked under his arm. "Staff!"

"On my way, sir. Mysho! Conn! Get your teams and follow me!" As she ran past her pack, she grabbed her own helmet and crammed it onto her head. Without turning, she raced back along the path of trampled vegetation, eight pairs of boots pounding the dry ground behind her.

"They're so fast!" Binti squeezed off another round prone from her vantage point on top of the largest boulder. It bit into the dirt directly behind where a Silsviss had been.

"Where are they fukking going?"

To everyone's surprise, the Dornagain ambassador answered. "They are using the contours of the land. Every hollow, every rise."

"But we went over that land! It's fukking flat!" The slightly louder whomp of the heavy gun sent every Silsviss in sight, out of sight.

"Apparently not so flat as you assume and, with their coloring, they lie like shadows on the ground."

"If they'd clump up a little more, I'd launch a fukking grenade or two at them. I don't need to see them to blow them up. And why do they keep yelling?"

"I believe they are issuing challenges."

"Well, they can just fukking stop."

Sitting back on his haunches behind the largest of the boulders, presenting the smallest target possible, the ambassador studied the Marine curiously. "Later, Private Checya, when we have time, I would like to discuss the psychological determinates in your use of copulative profanity."

Juan shot a short but incredulous glance back over his shoulder. "Yeah. Later. If we fukking survive." His eyes widened as he faced front again. "Incoming!"

Short arrows flung off the ends of whiplike branches filled the air on Juan's side of the boulders. Most fell short, but the rest rattled against the stone like hard rain.

"They gotta stop doing that soon!" Tucked as far into his crevasse as he could get, he winced as one of the arrows bounced off the protruding muzzle of his gun. "How many of those fukking things did they bring!"

"You want to know, you go count them," Binti advised, taking aim at the last of the archers to duck. "Got him!"

"I'm hit!"

The two statements came so close together that for a moment no one knew how to respond. Then Binti squirmed around to peer down the south side of her perch. "Ressk?"

The Krai said something in his own language that could have been either prayer or profanity and added, "A spear knocked my helmet off. My ears are ringing, but I'm all right." Gingerly replacing the helmet, he glanced up at the sharpshooter. "Binti, ignore the arrows from now on. The Silsviss are using them to draw your fire so they can get close enough to toss the heavy artillery at the other two sides."

"Ressk's right," Hollice called, hidden from view by the four Dornagain. "I had spear throwers this side as well."

"Then why didn't you fukking shoot him?"

"You try it, asshole. They throw and duck in the same motion." He wiped one sweaty palm after another against his thighs. "Okay, next time: arrow side ducks, spear sides will spray the whole area."

"Waste of ammunition," Binti cautioned.

Juan snorted. "Show of fukking force."

"I believe you are both correct," the ambassador offered. When the silence stretched, he added, "And what is Private Mashona to do?"

"Fire at anything that shows itself . . . Incoming!"

When the noise died and the varying projectiles had settled one way or another, three Silsviss were down and the rest had fallen completely silent.

"Well, that's a nice fukking change," Juan muttered, squinting out into the setting sun.

Ears ringing, Hollice risked a look back at their charges. "Everyone . . . oh, crap. You're hit."

"Who's hit?" Ressk demanded.

"One of the Dornagain. Uh . . ." He screwed up his face trying to remember the younger male's name. "It's Walks In Thought." He hadn't been able to see much beyond Thinks Deeply's bulk, but he had seen golden fur streaked with red and dark fluid glistening on a raised spear point. "Hey!"

Think Deeply turned at his nudge.

"Is he hurt badly?"

"No. It is a flesh wound only. I am sure it looks worse than it is."

"Speaking of flesh wounds," Binti called down from her vantage point. "One of those lizards just got winged and his buddy's crawling over to him. I've got a clear shot at the buddy."

"Leave it," Hollice told her. "We're not going to shoot them as they tend their wounded."

Moving frighteningly quickly in spite of his awkward position, the crawling Silsviss reached his wounded comrade, ripped out his throat with a vicious sweep of extended claws, and dove into the hollow the dying male no longer needed as bright red arterial blood arced up and sank down.

"I think tend *to* would be the more accurate phrase," Binti observed dryly. "The wounded Silsviss is now dead and buddy has his spot and his weapons."

"Odds are good they don't take prisoners either," Ressk noted.

Exhaling forcefully, Hollice sagged and banged his helmet lightly against the rock. "One more thing to worry about."

"Two more," Thinks Deeply corrected, extending her hand into the corporal's field of vision. Held pincerlike between her claws was one of the arrows. "Do you see this discoloration here?"

An orange/brown stain covered the pointed end.

"Don't tell me . . ."

"I believe the arrows are poisoned."

Her words carried clearly over the new challenges rising around them. "Poisoned?" Binti repeated. She laid her head down on her forearm. "Can this day get any worse?"

"Poisoned for lizards doesn't necessarily mean poisoned for us," Ressk reminded them.

"Do you wish to bet your life on that?" Thinks Deeply wondered. It sounded as though she actually wanted to know the answer, that she hadn't been asking a rhetorical question.

Ressk sighed, blowing out his cheeks until his ridges spread. "As long as we're having a lull, why don't I try running it through the sla . . ."

"Incoming!"

"Or not."

Lying prone just below the crest of a long undulation in the ground—she couldn't bring herself to call it a hill—Torin stared down at the half-dozen boulders and the surrounding Silsviss. Her helmet scanner placed Privates Mashona and Checya and two of the Dornagain, but the rocks prevented her from reading the rest. She knew they were alive, but she'd have felt better had she been able to see them.

Early evening breezes brought with them the sounds of Silsviss shrieking. It might have helped had they known what was actually being said, but Torin's translator held only the common trade language and under these circumstances was completely useless.

"Sounds mocking," Conn observed thoughtfully beside her.

"Mocking?"

"Yeah, you know, *Come out here and try that, you big pissant, I just dare you!*"

On Torin's other side, Mysho snorted. "I think you've been spending too much time with four-year-olds."

"Hey, my daughter does not say pissant."

Torin raised a hand before the argument could escalate. "Taking into consideration all the warnings about not reading familiar motivations into an alien species, blah, blah, blah, I think Conn's right. It does sound like they're taunting."

"Trying to get them to come out from behind the rocks?"

"Very likely."

"So they think we're stupid."

"I suspect no one ever warned them about reading familiar motivations into an alien species."

Mysho and Conn exchanged an identical look over her back.

"So you're saying the Silsviss are stupid?" Mysho said after a moment.

"No. I'm saying that taunting must work on another Silsviss since they're putting so much effort into it."

"Unless it's a case of hope springing eternal," Conn offered.

"Unless," Torin agreed.

The ground between their hiding place and the rocks was superficially flat but actually pocketed with small irregularities into and behind which a single Silsviss could hide. Torin could see four of the enemy quite clearly—three were definitely hittable from where they were, and the fourth was about a fifty/fifty chance. Binti Mashona could have made it a sure thing, but she was currently perched on a boulder almost half a kilometer away. All four shots would have to be taken simultaneously so as not to give warning. And then what?

"Well, Staff, what do we do?" Mysho asked, as though she'd been reading Torin's mind.

"Hollice says they're surrounded and that of the original thirty unfriendlies, nine have been shot, leaving approximately twenty-one continuing to attack."

"Approximately twenty-one?" Conn shook his head in disbelief. "Even Myrna could do the math."

"They've spread out, and I expect they're moving too fast to get an exact count without actually having the Silsviss programmed into the scanners."

"If they've shot nine, it doesn't sound like they need us. At this rate they'll be able to walk out of there before dark."

"Unless this lot decides to stop showing themselves and just hold them there until their buddies arrive." Cri Sawyes had insisted that all the Silsviss would go first to the VTA. Torin couldn't help but wonder if that had been an innocent miscalculation or something more serious. Was he as much on their side as he argued he was?

Drop it. Just drop it. Her instincts said to trust him and she wasn't about to start questioning her instincts now. "All right, here's what we're going to do: we form a line, fire simultaneously at the four we can see, aiming as close as possible without hitting them. That'll get their attention in a big way and with any luck when they see a line of Marines coming over the hill, they'll run like hell."

"And if they don't? Or if they run like hell toward us?"

"Then we shoot them. According to Hollice, their maximum range isn't much more than twenty meters—ours is considerably more than that. By the time we're close enough to be hit, they'll all be dead. Anchor both ends of the line with the heavy gunners; they can take care of any Silsviss who try to flank us."

"They're that fast?"

"Corporal Hollice's exact phrase was *like shit through a H'san.*"

Mysho pursed her lips, impressed. "That's fast."

"Just tell your heavies they're not to use the flamers under any circumstances." Torin tore a handful of dead grass out from under the living and waved it for emphasis. "I don't want this whole area on fire."

"But what happens if the Silsviss stay hidden?" Conn protested. "We can't hit them if we can't see them. If they lie still until we're close enough for their weapons, it becomes a crap shoot as to who gets their shot off first."

"There's two solutions to that," Torin told him. "First, everyone keeps their scanner down. I know it's a pain when you're moving, but it *will* see things your eyes won't. The closer we get, the harder it will be for the Silsviss to hide. Second, make sure you get your shot off first."

"Yeah, well that's the trick, isn't it," Conn muttered.

"Oh, come on, even Kleers can shoot faster than some primitive."

Torin glanced over her shoulder at the young Krai, who, hearing Mysho use his name, looked up and grinned. A sudden flurry of shots turned her attention back to the problem at hand. "Bottom line, we have to get our people and the civilians out of there before enough Silsviss show up to simply overwhelm them with numbers. Mysho, go left. Conn, go right. I'll hold the center. The two Marines to either side of me will be taking those first four shots across the bow, as it were, so place your people accordingly. Once the shooting starts, make every round count; we don't know how long we're going to have to make our ammunition last. Remember there's nine of us and only twenty-one . . ." Another shot rang out from the rocks. ". . . twenty of them." Reaching up, she snapped her helmet mike down against the corner of her mouth. "I'll let Corporal Hollice know we're on our way."

Rather than have her taken out by friendly fire, Hollice rearranged the Dornagain and had Binti relinquish her perch for a crevice by Juan. "When the Silsviss hear an attack on the south, they're liable to attack us on the north—they'll think our attention is fixed away from them, and if they've got any brains at all, they'll want into the shelter of these rocks."

"If they have any brains at all, they'll run away," Binti muttered, settling herself in her new position.

"Yeah?" Juan looked up from checking a wrist point and grinned. "If I'd had any brains, I'd have been a fukking beautician like my mama wanted."

"Look alive, people!" Hollice's voice bounced from boulder to boulder. "The cavalry's on its way in."

Binti shot a questioning glance toward the heavy gunner. "Cavalry?"

Juan shrugged, a minimalist movement to keep the exoskeleton from turning it into something more destructive. "I don't know what the fuk he's talkin' about most of the time either."

"All right, Marines, keep alert. If you spot an unfriendly running away from you, let him. Otherwise, shoot." Torin wanted to say shoot to wound but given Hollice's recent report of Silsviss first aid, she didn't see much point. While she had no desire to be a part of the Silsvah culling program, neither did she want to leave injured teenagers scattered about waiting in pain for their comrades to return and finish them off. Which meant they'd have to take care of the wounded. Since she had no idea of how they were supposed to manage that, better there weren't that many wounded to take care of.

If war was fun, everybody'd be doing it.

And this action was only a sidebar to the actual war. If they'd been shot down anywhere but over the preserve . . . For a moment, Torin wondered if maybe the whole incident *was* a part of the Silsvah culling program, then she dismissed the thought. Now wasn't the time.

"Keep your scanners down and watch out for Silsviss staying hidden until we're on them and they can use their spears," she continued, barely vocalizing into her helmet mike. "Remember that you're just as dead if they kill you with a pointy stick."

She felt a smile run both ways down the line of prone Marines—strange things were funny right before combat. "Rise on three. Make those first four close enough to scare the piss out of them. Wait for my command before moving ahead. One . . ." Knees brought up under the body.

"Two."

Weight back off her elbows, onto her legs.

"Three."

The nine Marines stood as one and took two long steps to the crest of the rise. Three of the warning shots sprayed dirt over wedge-shaped heads. The fourth went through a tail unexpectedly moved.

The enraged shriek of pain attracted the desired attention.

All four leaped up and raced toward the Marines.

They were just as fast as Hollice had described.

Like shit through a H'san.

They died long before they were close enough to do any return damage.

"Marines, at the walk, advance."

The line moved forward.

When the second attempt to flank the line failed—the shot that stopped it coming from within the jumble of rock—the Silsviss began to realize they couldn't survive the fight. Instead of attacking, they stood and shrieked, banging their spear butts against the hard ground.

To Torin, it sounded as if they were shouting, *"Come on, I dare you!"*

*   *   *

"I could take them all out," Binti muttered, lifting her weapon and miming the shots. "Bang. Bang. Bang."

"Staff says to leave them alone," Hollice reminded her.

"I don't see why."

"Perhaps because the Silsviss are our allies," the Dornagain ambassador suggested calmly—in spite of the volume necessary to be heard above the surrounding shrieks of defiance. "Although," he admitted when heads craned and all eyes turned toward him, "the treaty is not yet signed."

The line moved closer to one of the standing Silsviss.

Still shrieking, he dropped the spear and slid a slender branch out of the open weave of his harness.

They've learned we won't shoot if they don't attack and they're using that to lure us into range of their arrows. Time for a new lesson. Torin put a shot into the ground between the archer's legs.

His tongue flicked out. He pulled an arrow out of the weave and set it in the end of the whip.

Wondering if he were brave or stupid, Torin shot him.

Two of the shriekers finally broke and ran.

When their companions saw they were allowed to retreat, five more joined them.

The Marines were now on the south side of the rocks, the Silsviss on the north.

"Listen up, everyone—we're going to form a large half circle around the north side of those rocks so that when the Dornagain break cover, they'll have as much protection as possible. We'll break the line to my right; outside positions move in, double time. Now."

As military maneuvers went, it could have gone better.

Moving in closer to the rocks, his eyes on the enemy, Kleers tripped over a dead Silsviss who turned out not to be. As he staggered, fighting to regain his balance, he took a tail blow across the backs of both knees. Falling, the Krai fired and missed and had no chance to get off a second shot before the Silsviss was on him, pinning him to the dirt with one set of claws, slashing with the other.

A moment later, Kleers kicked the headless corpse away and spat a mouthful of blood into the dirt.

"Any of that yours?" Torin asked, extending a hand. His med-alert hadn't gone off, but the chips had been set to trip only when they read too much damage to carry on. Combat soldiers learned early there was a whole lot of hurt between damage and *too much* damage.

"Some," Kleers admitted, sounding more confused than in pain. "My shoulder . . ."

As he stood, the right sleeve of his dress uniform tunic fell away in three perfectly parallel lines that stopped at the edge of the combat vest. Three slices of shirt fell away under the tunic. It quickly became apparent that the blood soaking the remains of his sleeve was his.

Torin sat him back down again. "Get a field dressing on that! The rest of you, fill in the line."

Encouraged by the success of one of their number, another two Silsviss charged and died.

The remaining eight retreated . . .

. . . and then followed Marines and Dornagain all the long, slow way back to the buildings. Lightning-fast charges that ended before they came close enough to be considered an attack wore at the defenders' nerves. But worst of all, was the noise; singly and collectively, the shrieking never let up.

"Ssso. Sssuccesss."

"Did you do that on purpose," Torin muttered, as the extended sibilants cut a painful path from ear to ear.

Cri Sawyes stopped and looked around. When he saw there was no one else in the immediate area, he frowned. "Do what?"

"Never mind." Guards had been posted, the injured and the civilians were safely inside, and the grain-bag walls were going up as quickly as the Marines could build them. She winced as the background shrieking hit a new high note. "Do you think they'll stay out there all night?"

"No. I don't underssstand the actual language, but it'sss clear they're building up their courage for an attack."

"But there's only eight of them."

"I know."

Standing with one hand on the top of the northern barricade, she listened to the night and tried, without much success, to think like a hormonally hopped-up teenage lizard. "We have weapons on both roofs. We're covering all approaches."

"Yesss. But they are fasst and very hard to sssee in the dark. They don't know about your ssscanners, so they'll asssume they can ssslip in, ssslit a few throatsss, and ssslip out, none the wissser."

On cue, the lookout on the north end of the west roof shouted, "Lieutenant! There's a Silsviss approaching from the north. Damn, he's fast!"

Cri Sawyes' tongue flickered out at the suspicious expression on Torin's face. "It isss what I would have done," he explained. Then he sighed as her expression remained fixed. "Would I have sssaid anything if I'd wanted them to sssucceed?"

"I suppose not," Torin allowed.

"You could conssssider it a lessson in our tacticsss."

"True."

"Or a warning."

"All right!" She raised her hand. "I get it. You've made your point."

Crossing the compound on the run, drawn by the lookout's shout, Jarret slid to a stop at Torin's side. "Can you stop him without killing him?" he called toward the roof.

"I can try, sir."

"Do it, then."

"Yes, sir!"

"Without killing him?" Torin asked softly.

"We're trying to make the Silsviss our allies, Staff Sergeant." He glanced over at Cri Sawyes as he spoke. "I'm not playing whatever game the Others think they set up when they brought us down in here."

"You believe it was the Others?"

"Don't you?"

She shrugged, unwilling to commit.

Two shots rang out, so close together the echoes back off the hill overlapped into one sound.

"He's down, sir! About fifteen meters off the end of the building."

"Corpsmen!"

"Sir?"

"Let's go!"

Jarret vaulted over the grain bags and paused on the other side. "You coming, Staff?"

"Yes, sir." She contemplated saying something like, *"You're in command, sir. You shouldn't be wandering around outside the perimeter in the dark with the enemy nearby."* But since he knew that and was out there anyway, there didn't seem to be much point. "Corporal Conn! Bring your team!"

"I don't think that's necessary, Staff."

"I don't want to lose you, sir. It'd look bad on my record."

They found the injured Silsviss without any difficulty but approaching him was another matter.

"Watch his tail! He's got some kind of thorny vine wrapped around it! Damn it, Conn! I said, watch his tail! Are you all right?"

"He caught my pants, Staff. Didn't break the skin."

Hissing through his teeth, one leg flopping uselessly by his side, the young Silsviss lashed out with the spear he still held, missed, and barely stopped himself from toppling over.

"Calm down, kid." Jarret held out his empty hands in a gesture common to all tool-using species. "We want to help you. We'll patch you up and send you back to your friends, and you can tell them we're not the bad guys."

We'll send you back to your friends, and you can attack us again, Torin thought, but she didn't say it because it looked as if the lieutenant's approach was working.

His weight on the spear, the Silsviss sank slowly to the ground, staring up at the surrounding Marines through half-lidded eyes. He roused himself to make a couple more halfhearted feints but Lieutenant Jarret kept talking, quietly and calmly, and finally the spear slid from slack fingers.

"All right, corpsmen, move in."

Breathing rapidly, he ignored them as they put the stretcher down by his good side.

When they bent to lift him, he attacked.

One of the corpsmen was thrown like a rag doll into two of the Marines. The other screamed.

As Torin moved to get a clear shot, the lieutenant fired. The Silsviss flew back missing half his head, the corpsman still impaled on his claws.

Grabbing the cooling wrists, Torin yanked the claws straight out of their entry wounds, took a look at the extent of the abdominal damage and didn't like what she saw. "Get him in to the doctor. Now!"

With the other corpsman staggering alongside the stretcher, Conn's team raced toward the nearer of the two buildings. The doctor met them at the door.

When it closed, and she could hear the sound of expletive-laced explanation rising in the compound, she turned to the lieutenant.

He was staring down at the body, still holding his sidearm. di'Taykan didn't have the best night sight, but there was starlight enough for him to separate the shadows and the dead.

"I've never actually . . ." he began, then shook his head instead of finishing.

"I know." The troops knew as well. Torin could feel the weight of them watching, waiting to see how their young officer would handle his first kill, but they were far enough away that she could cover for him if she had to.

When he finally looked at her, his eyes were so dark she could see no color at all. "I had the only clear shot."

"Yes, sir. You did." And considering that it was a partially blocked, moving target, it had been one hell of a shot, too. But he wouldn't be ready to hear that for a while.

"Do you . . ." A deep breath and he tried again. "Do you ever get used to it?"

Torin looked down at the body, then up at the lieutenant. She could see that he half wanted her to lie, but this was part of the job also so she told him the truth. "Yes, sir, I'm afraid that you do."

He held her gaze with his for a long moment, drew in a deep breath, and let it out slowly, almost as if it was his first since pulling the trigger. "Let's get back inside, Staff. I have a feeling it's going to be a long night."

"Yes, sir."

Before going over the grain bags, he paused and turned to look down the way they'd come. The shrieking, silenced by the shots, had started up again.

Torin waited, wondering what he saw.

"Staff Sergeant Kerr."

"Sir."

"Tell the lookouts to shoot to kill."

The lieutenant's feeling had been wrong. It was a short night. Before the first moon had risen a handspan above the horizon, all eight of the Silsviss who'd attacked the Dornagain's escort were dead.

The grain-bag walls were finished at almost the same time the Silsviss were. Torin went over watch schedules with the sergeants, made sure everyone had taken the time to clean their weapons, sent all nonessential personnel to bed, then went for a walk around the perimeter.

She found herself standing at the same place at the north wall staring out into the now quiet night. She could almost understand about the attacks on the buildings. What she was having difficulty getting her head around was the reaction to the overwhelming odds of the afternoon.

"You look troubled, Ssstaff Sssergeant."

One moment she was alone, the next Cri Sawyes was standing beside her.

"You're lucky I heard you coming," she growled. She hadn't, but she wouldn't give him the satisfaction. "If you have a minute, I'd like to hear your take on what happened today."

"The attacksss?"

"No, during the rescue of the Dornagain."

"I sssee." He leaned against the wall and stared out into the darkness. "It hasss been a long time sssince I wasss that young, Ssstaff Sssergeant, but I will give you what enlightenment I can."

She mirrored his position. "When we fired those first four warning shots, we were giving them a chance to get away. Why did they charge us?"

"Becaussse they sssaw your arrival asss a challenge and a challenge mussst be anssswered."

"But by then they *knew* we could kill from a greater distance than they could. What were they thinking?"

"They weren't thinking." Cri Sawyes dug a thumb into the top bag of grain, pushing into the yielding surface. Torin watched him and waited. "At that age," he said at last, "we merely react. A ssstrong leader can make usss do anything. I sssusssspect that the attack this afternoon wasss a way for the local leader to get rid of hisss worssst troublemakersss."

"He was hoping they'd be killed?"

"Yesss. He probably goaded them into attacking what he knew to be a sssuperior force. He couldn't have known that a sssmall group would have ssseparated. Had my people won thisss afternoon, the ressstructuring of the pack would have kept them from attacking the ressst of usss for three or four daysss."

"A mixed blessing at best," Torin observed.

His tongue flickered out. "Yesss. Also, I sssusssspect that the local leader wasss keeping the troublemakersss from sharing in whatever advantage he acquired at the VTA."

"There's no advantage he can acquire. Everything we left behind is locked up tighter than a H'san's grandmother."

"And that'sss tight?"

"Yeah. That's tight." She dug a hole of her own into the grain. "If a strong leader can make you do anything . . ."

"We'd be quite an addition to the Othersss' forcesss, wouldn't we? If the Othersss are asss unprincipled as your Confederation diplomatsss sssuggessst . . ."

"Trust me, they're the bad guys."

". . . imagine what they could do with an army of our young."

"Thanks, but I'd rather not." Out in the darkness, vegetation rustled, and a small something squeaked its last. "I take it this means you, your people, were definitely going to join up?"

"Trust *me*, Ssstaff Ssssergeant . . ."

When she turned to face him, she could see the stars reflected in his eyes.

". . . we want our young to die no more than you do."

Eleven

Torin lay, barely breathing, wondering what had roused her. One moment she'd been dreaming about leading a charge on the Confederation's Parliament and replacing the politicians with the remarkably lively bodies of all the Marines who'd died under her care—her subconscious had never been particularly subtle—and the next she was wide awake. She could hear the quiet breathing of the surrounding sleepers and smell the faintest trace of the Dornagain, two rooms away. Opening her eyes, she stared up past the rafters into the thatch. A small, dusty green lizard, almost the exact same color as the Silsviss of the area, stared unblinkingly back.

After a moment, its tongue flickered and it scurried out of sight.

She wasted another moment working out the odds it might be spying for the Silsviss, and when they turned out to be too small to bother about, tongued her implant.

0513

It didn't seem worth going back to sleep for another seventeen minutes—not when she'd managed to grab nearly two full hours.

The morning had dawned surprisingly cold with a dense fog that hung close to the ground. Stroking her environmental controls to a warmer setting as she stepped outside, Torin made her way to the well where a di'Taykan, stripped to the waist, had his head in a bucket of water. As much as she appreciated the view, she couldn't prevent an involuntary shiver.

It wasn't until he emerged from the bucket, water dripping from lilac hair, that she realized it was the lieutenant—looking more cheerful than he had in days.

"Good morning, Staff. Looks like we finally got some decent weather."

"Yes, sir. You're up early."

"I thought the platoon would be impressed if I was already up and working when they woke."

"Really?"

"No, not really." He flashed her a smile. "I couldn't sleep." The smile faded. "I kept thinking about all the things I still have to do before we're attacked."

Since he'd probably been thinking about that as well, Torin let it go since he'd clearly come to terms with the order he'd had to give. *One down, and one to go.* And sending others out to die was the harder order of the two.

Knowing what she'd see, she glanced around the compound. There were two Marines stationed on the roof of each building and the walls between were waist-high and a half a meter thick. They had food, they had water, they certainly had more artillery than the enemy. They had a medical station set up, and an actual doctor on site. "There's nothing more you can do, sir. Nothing but wait."

"I know. And it's strange, in spite of what happened last night, waiting's still the hard part."

Torin found herself taking a step forward, aching to physically comfort him. Fortunately, she recognized the impetus. "Sir. Your masker."

It was lying on the side of the well.

"My . . ." He followed her line of sight. "Oh. Sorry, Staff."

He sounded more amused than sorry.

At least he's got his good mood back, Torin thought, waiting until the masker was safely hooked to the lieutenant's belt before she drew another breath.

"I thought there'd be no problem, what with being outside and the lower temperature and, well, being alone."

"Understandable, sir."

"Of course you'd be more susceptible, having been exposed . . . that time that didn't happen," he finished sheepishly, his original thought stopped cold by her expression. "So, according to the emmy's targeting scanner, the Silsviss are only just leaving the swamp. There's a chance that the authorities will find us first."

"The authorities?" Not the *Berganitan*. If the ship had returned to a planetary orbit, they'd have already been found.

"The Silsviss authorities." His hair emerged from its rubdown flying off in all directions, and it took him a moment to bring it under control. "Even if Captain Daniels didn't get off a message they could read, they certainly know we're missing and, as primitive as their planetary satellite system is, they must know where we are by now."

"Unless the Others drew the *Berganitan* off so that they could slip in and overthrow the planetary governments unopposed."

"I think the Silsviss would oppose, don't you?"

"Yes, sir." She firmly squelched an unvoiced offer to dry his back. "But that would leave them too busy to come for us. And if we were shot down by a non-Confederation faction within the Silsviss . . ." He shook his head, but she continued, still unwilling to elevate one theory over the others. ". . . there'll be fighting going on as well."

"So no matter how we look at it, no rescue."

"Not this morning, sir."

Draping his towel over the side of the well, he shrugged into his shirt and moved his masker from his belt back to his throat. "You know, Staff . . ." He shot her a sideways glance from under long lashes. ". . . I was actually enjoying the morning until you showed up."

"Sorry, sir."

"But I'm sure it's part of your job to keep my feet on the ground, to examine all possibilities, to keep me from unwarranted optimism."

A di'Taykan in a teasing mood was damned near impossible to resist. In spite of herself, she smiled. "Yes, sir."

"You're doing a good job."

"Thank you, sir." She fell into step beside him as he carried the bucket toward the north wall. "Uh, Lieutenant, where are we going?"

"I'm just dumping my wash water, Staff. There's no point in making mud inside the compound."

He had a point, Torin acknowledged, especially since anticipation of an attack would place a second latrine pit inside the barricades.

Angling away from the place he'd gone over the wall the night before, Jarret braced his legs against the grain bags and threw the water from his bucket.

It arced through the air, hit the ground, and . . .

A brilliant flash of light erupted into the northeastern sky, visible in spite of distance and in spite of fog. A few seconds later, a sharp crack of sound split the morning, then died to a low, lingering rumble felt in bones and teeth more than heard. The silence that followed came without any ambient noise at all. The dawn songs of birds and insects that had been providing a background so constant it could be ignored were gone.

Drifting down from the roof of the west building came an incredulous, "What the fuk was that?"

"The self-destruct on the armory," Torin answered grimly.

Hair flat against his head, Jarret turned wide lilac eyes toward her. "Our armory? On the VTA?"

"Yes, sir." If there was another armory in the immediate area, no one had told her about it.

He stared into the distance, as though waiting for debris to come falling through the fog. "I guess we won't be making that supply run," he said at last.

Half expecting some kind of angry outburst, Torin was impressed by his calm. A calm officer was a good thing for a besieged Marine awakened by an explosion to see. "We'd have had to run *through* the Silsviss," she pointed out, her tone matching his.

"Very true." The ends of his hair started to lift. "Well, let's look at the bright side, shall we? At least we know they didn't get through the security protocols. And that explosion very likely took out a number of Silsviss. If it took out enough, they might think twice about attacking."

"You told me that the tracking scanner on the emmy put most of the Silsviss on their way out of the swamp," Torin reminded him. "The VTA would have contained all but the vertical blast, so I expect it deafened more than it killed."

A tentative birdcall broke the silence. And then another. A moment later, the morning refilled with sound. A moment after that, Torin winced as her implant went off-line. The techs insisted it wasn't supposed to hurt. What did they know?

"Did your . . . ?"

"Yes, sir."

"Do you think they left someone behind? Told him to keep trying while most of them started out after us?"

"No, sir." From what Torin understood about pack leadership, she didn't think that was likely. "Perhaps someone, thinking to challenge the leader, went back on his own. Even one of our weapons would significantly change the balance of power."

"Then it's a good thing they didn't get one, isn't it?" As they turned together to face a compound full of questioning Marines, he added, "And you were right, Staff. We should have blown it ourselves."

"Thank you, sir."

Of course she'd been right. She only wished she felt better about hearing him admit it.

"They will try to draw you out into battle, to goad you into attacking them out where their numbersss will give them the advantage even over your weaponsss." Cri Sawyes stared out over the north wall, his head slightly cocked. Torin wondered what he could hear. Was he listening to the small clump of Marines grouped around the emmy or beyond that to the approaching battle?

"Cri Sawyes, regardless of who or what shot us down, these adolescents are not the enemy. We have every intention of fighting a purely defensive battle and causing as few casualties as possible."

Wearing her best noncommittal expression, Torin turned to face the lieutenant and realized he sincerely meant what he'd just said. The deaths of eight individual Silsviss didn't add up to actually being in combat and he still had no firsthand experience of how fast good intentions got blown to kingdom come. She kept her own opinion on the type of battle they'd be fighting locked firmly behind her lips. He'd learn soon enough; she had no desire to rush the lesson. Provided that they weren't endangering her Marines, she always found it a little sad when second lieutenants lost the last of their shiny, untried ideals.

Cri Sawyes had been a soldier. "Thossse are good intentionsss, Lieutenant Jarret, but asss we sssay where I come from, it takesss two to *haylisss*, and I doubt the pack will cooperate." He continued watching the crest of the low purple hill to the north. "If you won't come out, they will come in after you."

"But we have an entrenched position . . ." Jarret's gesture took in the buildings, the compound, and the black-clad Marines filling it with shadow. ". . . and they have only primitive weapons."

"Yesss. Sssso?"

"And it's the same entrenched position they threw themselves at one at a time last night, isn't it?"

"Yesss."

"They won't be thinking, sir, they'll be reacting." Torin echoed Cri Sawyes' explanation for the lieutenant. "As far as they're concerned, we're another pack. The reaction to another pack is to defeat it. Our weapons alone are a prize worth the risk. If taken, they'd allow the pack to rule the preserve."

"Then we'll have to see they aren't taken."

All officers liked to state the obvious. In Torin's experience it was a habit they never outgrew. "Yes, sir."

His gaze shifted out to the Marines at the emmy, and Jarret exhaled loudly. "Looks like you were right again, Staff."

Again, he states the obvious.

"The sun's been up for three hours, and there's no sign of the authorities. Any authorities."

The fog had quickly burned off with the rising of the sun, and the temperature had begun to rise. The early damp had long since dried. There was already a promise of scorching heat in the still air. Torin suspected that as the day progressed, the di'Taykan would be pushing the limits of their environmental controls.

"The fact that we have not been ressscued . . ." When both Marines turned to glare, his tongue flicked out and he amended his statement. ". . . sssay rather dissscovered, leadsss me to believe it wasss not the Othersss who shot down the VTA but a disssident group of my own people. That would mossst certainly keep the variousss governmentsss at each othersss' throatsss for daysss."

"Based on what I've seen, I don't think your people have the technology to take us out."

The tongue flicked out again. "And you think you sssaw everything?" He raised a hand to cut off the lieutenant's answer. "Of courssse you don't. My apologiesss." When the lieutenant graciously allowed that the apology would be accepted, he continued. "I, persssonally, am more curiousss about why the pack hasssn't arrived. At that age, we *run* to a fight."

"Run to a *fight?*" Torin repeated, changing the emphasis. "Teenagers." She closed her teeth on what usually followed when sergeants got together to complain about new recruits. *Can't live with them, can't use them for target practice.* From the sound of it, they'd be using them for target practice today.

"Yesss. Teenagersss. Ssstill, they should be here by now."

"The explosion probably slowed them."

"Perhapsss." But he turned to stare over the north wall again.

"Sir! We have a reading!"

The ambient noise in the compound dropped as Binti yelled in the results from the emmy.

This was it. The beginning of it, at any rate. Torin felt her heart begin to beat a little faster as Lieutenant Jarret asked, "And?"

"The Silsviss are just under two kilometers away."

"How many of them?"

"Just a minute, sir." Binti reached down and gave Ressk a shove.

The Krai glared at her, then turned his attention back to the data in the emmy's targeting scanner. He frowned as he used his slate to work the program, shook his head, and stood. "I can't tell, sir. But since there's Silsviss reading at both two and three kilometers, I'd say there's more than a few."

"I'd say there's a whole fukking lot," Juan muttered.

Haysole was awake and smiling when Torin walked over to his corner of the infirmary, although she suspected that had more to do with Corporal Mysho's having just left than with *her* arrival. According to one of the corpsmen, everything but the di'Taykan's legs worked fine.

"Morning, Staff. I hear about three million underaged liz . . . Silsviss are about to come bouncing down on our heads."

"That's an exaggeration, Private. No more than two million, tops."

"Is that all?" He snorted. "Well, you won't be needing me, then."

"Good thing, since the doctor seems to think I should give you another day off." She squatted down beside his stretcher, one hand on the metal edge for balance, the other resting lightly on the back of his wrist. His skin still felt warm even though the temperature within the thick-walled building was noticeably cooler than outside in the compound. When she checked his environmental controls, they'd been set almost as low as they'd go. "How are you feeling?"

His smile crumbled a little at the edges and long fingers plucked at the hem of his tunic. "Like I'd give almost anything to get up and clean a crapper." The pause wasn't quite long enough for Torin to reply, even if she'd known what to say. "Or these days I guess it'd be digging a latrine."

"I don't think so, Private. We need that latrine dug before the Silsviss attack, and you," she added wryly, "are a galaxy-class master in the fine art of looking like you're working when you're really doing piss all."

"It's a skill," he admitted smugly, looking pleased with himself.

Torin snorted and held her hand by his head. She didn't bother hiding her relief when the turquoise hair lifted and stroked gently across her palm.

"The lieutenant was in earlier."

"Was he?"

"Yeah." Turquoise eyes sparkled. "He's a cutie. Even if he is from a high family—talk about people doing piss all. He asked me what he could do to make me feel better."

Which, given the patient, was either very naive or very di'Taykan. "And you made an explicit suggestion."

"Oh, yeah."

"And he said?"

"Later." When Torin raised an eyebrow at him, Haysole gave her a look of wounded innocence. "I wouldn't lie to you, Staff." Wounded innocence became something more salacious. "Ask him yourself."

"I don't think so." She touched her slate to the stretcher, downloading the data on his condition. "And if the lieutenant is coming back later, I'd better go so you can rest up."

"You think I'll need it?"

He's only speculating, Torin reminded herself as she straightened. *He can't know.* She flashed him her best *staff sergeants know everything* smile as she moved away. "Not as much as *he* will."

Neither of the other Marines who'd been injured in the crash of the VTA were as coherent. Torin spent a moment with each, discovered the lieutenant had spoken to them as well, and then moved on to Captain Daniels. The pilot still hadn't regained consciousness, and according to the stretcher, her vital signs were barely holding. If not for the near constant attention of her aircrew . . .

Torin chased the thought away. This was a diplomatic mission. No one was supposed to die. She thought about saying something to Aircrew Trenkik, who was spooning a gruellike food into the captain's open mouth and then massaging her throat until she swallowed, but she'd long ago overcome the need to speak meaningless comfort in order not to feel helpless in the face of inevitability.

Her helmet chirped a summons, so she headed for the door.

"Staff?" When he saw he had her attention, Haysole touched the masker at his throat. "Remember your promise."

"If I die, take off the masker before you bag me."

She could have reminded him that she hadn't actually agreed. Instead, feeling the weight of the four cylinders over her heart, she said only, "I remember."

This time, she found the lieutenant standing with six or seven other Marines by the south wall near the site of the protected latrine.

"Make sure that dirt pile is away from the wall," she said, pausing. "Let's not be building access ramps for the enemy."

"How about I dump it there, Staff?" Stripped down to a sleeveless vest over her exoskeleton, Chandra Dar pointed a heavily laden shovel back into the compound.

"There's fine."

"How deep do you want it?" the heavy gunner asked, dumping her load and driving the blade in for another.

Torin glanced over her shoulder, but the lieutenant had his attention firmly fixed on something outside the wall. "How deep were you told to dig it?"

"Not as deep as the water table."

"Then I suggest you follow the lieutenant's orders."

Dar looked down at dirt so dry she couldn't have got the blade into it without her augmentation and then up at the staff sergeant. "Well, yeah, but he's . . ."

"Your commanding officer."

Golden-brown skin blanched at Torin's tone. "I didn't mean anything against him, Staff."

"Good." A gesture suggested the heavy gunner return to work. Torin watched another shovel load removed, then continued toward Lieutenant Jarret. It wasn't difficult to fill in the end of Dar's protest.

Yeah, but he's never done this before and you have.

Heading into combat, that sort of attitude was going to crop up a lot more often. With some justification. It hadn't mattered while they were marching up and down before various governments, but no one wanted to die because a brand-new second lieutenant gave the wrong order. *So I'll just have to see that he gives the right orders. After all, if the job was easy, everybody'd be doing it.* "You wanted to see me, si . . ."

The ground under her boots trembled.

"What was that?"

"That," Jarret told her, smiling, "was what I wanted you to see."

She followed his pointing finger, moving close enough to the wall so that the eastern building didn't cut off her line of sight. "That's . . ."

"Your herbivore. I apologize for ever doubting your ability to correctly identify a pile of shit."

"Thank you, sir," she answered absently, her gaze locked on the creature chewing a path through the vegetation. From the lines of drying mud high on its haunches, it had recently come up out of the swamp. "That thing's bigger than our sleds."

"It'sss a *ghartivatrampasss,*" Cri Sawyes announced, joining them. "I've heard of them, but thisss isss the firssst I've ever ssseen. Video doesssn't do it jusssstice."

"Couldn't possibly," Torin agreed.

A glistening purple tongue emerged from a lipless mouth, wrapped around a square meter or so of stems, and scooped the grasses up into its mouth. The background rasp Torin had assumed was insects moved to the foreground and was identified as the sound of the silicates being ground between whatever served the creature for teeth. The ground trembled as it took another step. Then it continued to placidly feed, ignoring its audience. In spite of its size, it was a performance that could only hold the attention for so long.

"All right." Torin turned to the cluster of Marines. "Who told you lot to stop working?"

By the time the *ghartivatrampas* had moved out of sight behind the west building, only Cri Sawyes was still watching it. "I've been told they're extremely tasssty," he explained, when Lieutenant Jarret asked him why.

"Tasty?" Lieutenant Ghard looked intrigued. "I'll just go have another look, then." He glanced over at Jarret, who waved him off.

"That's the most enthusiasm he's shown about anything since Captain Daniels was wounded," Jarret murmured as they watched the Krai run into the building where a window would give him a framed view.

"I believe he wasss jussst asss enthusssiasssstic about taking me apart," Cri Sawyes mentioned offhandedly.

"Staff Sergeant Kerr, have you a moment?"

"Of course, Ambassador Krik'vir." Torin stood and snapped her slate back onto her belt. She'd made her preparations. If the Silsviss didn't attack soon she'd have moved right through anticipation and into annoyance. *And an annoyed staff sergeant is an ugly thing.* "How can I help you?"

"Actually, we wished to know how we could help you. We have never been in a battle before and we are uncertain of how to behave."

"The best thing a noncombatant can do in a battle is to stay out of the way."

"We were actually thinking more of transporting your wounded to the doctor's position. Using one of the wounded in the infirmary, we have determined we are strong enough working together to lift a stretcher and a Marine as well. We are capable of great speed and our movements are not restricted by bilateral symmetry."

It took Torin a moment to work out which "we" involved all four Mictok and which were merely part of a communal speech pattern. "It sounds like you've really thought this through."

"We have." The ambassador paused, left antennae running up and down the right. "We did not agree with this battle," she said at last. "As we are here, we will be of use."

Did not agree? *Diplomats,* Torin thought. *Can't have a battle without filling in the paperwork.* "You should speak with the lieutenant, ma'am."

"Lieutenant Jarret is concerned with keeping us safe, Staff Sergeant. We find that admirable . . ." Her mandibles clicked a time or two. ". . . but stifling. We are civilians, yes, but we are also adults and able to make our own decisions. We understand you have survived many battles."

"Yes, ma'am. But it wouldn't be wise to remind the lieutenant that he hasn't."

"Of course not, but we hoped you would be willing to use that experience to put our offer in its best light."

If the Silsviss ever arrived, they'd be vastly outnumbered.

If there were enough Silsviss, some of them would get through.

If some of them got through, Marines would be wounded.

If the Mictok acted as stretcher bearers, the one remaining corpsman could assist the doctor and she could keep all her Marines in the fight.

"I'll speak to the lieutenant."

"Thank you, Staff Serg . . ."

"Oh, yeah? You wanna fukking make something of it!"

"Tough guy! You weren't plugged in, I'd flatten your ass!"

"Well, if that's all that's fukking stopping you!" Juan shrugged out of his vest and tunic in the same motion and was working on the fasteners of his shirt when he went down.

"If you'll excuse me, Ambassador." A dozen steps took Torin to the fight. Leaning away from a wild swing, she grabbed first Juan's upper arm between two of the exoskeleton's contact points and then mirrored the grip on the other Marine. Using their own momentum, she slammed their bodies together. "That will be quite enough of that."

More surprised than stunned by the impact, they staggered apart, turned toward her, and began to simultaneously yell out their reasons for the fight.

Torin raised her hand and the yelling stopped. "I don't care why," she said. "If you two want to beat the snot out of each other on your own time, well, you're adults, feel free. But, in case you hadn't noticed, we're at combat readiness right now, which puts you on my time. You start up again and I will personally throw your sorry butts over the wall at the first Silsviss I see. Do you understand me, Private Checya?"

"Yes, Staff Sergeant." He fiddled with his wrist point, looked as though he wanted to add something, and clearly thought better of it.

"Do you understand me, Private Anderson?"

"Yes, Staff Sergeant."

"Good. Now, since you're clearly bored, I can always find something for you to do . . ."

To no one's surprise, they both suddenly remembered urgent preparations they needed to make.

"All right, you lot, show's over." Sergeant Glicksohn's voice scattered the small audience. "You enjoyed that too much," he said to Torin when they were alone.

"Nothing breaks up the morning like banging a couple of heads together."

He nodded toward the place where Torin had been standing. "What did the sp . . ." When that raised an eyebrow, he finished, ". . . speaking Mictok want?"

"Oh, nice recovery."

"Best you'll get."

"The ambassador was offering her party's services as stretcher bearers."

"And you said . . ."

"It's not up to me, it's up to the lieutenant."

"Yeah, right."

"I said I'd present their offer in the best possible light."

"Well, here's your chance. I think our fearless leader wants to know what all the shouting was about." He sighed. "God save me from twoie looies who need to be kept informed about every little detail."

"Give him a break, Mike. He's not doing too badly."

"He's doing what you tell him."

"No. He's making his own decisions, but he's listening to what I tell him."

"It's a start. Hey, Torin." He stopped her as she turned away. "If I get hit, I don't want a Mictok to be the last thing I see."

"Easy solution. Don't get hit." She couldn't make out the words, but from the tone his response was decidedly insulting. She was still smiling when she reached Lieutenant Jarret. "Yes, sir?"

"There was a fight . . . ?"

"Not really, sir. Just a disagreement brought on by the waiting."

"It does feel like we've been waiting forever, doesn't it? Half the platoon's asleep."

A quick glance around the compound showed slightly more than half the platoon with their helmets pulled forward to shade their eyes. Corporal Conn appeared to be writing home—again—and from the faint sound of dramatic music, Binti Mashona had a game biscuit in her slate. Strictly speaking, during combat readiness the slates were for military use only, but Torin trusted her people to be ready when the fighting started.

"Old soldier's trick, sir. Sleep when you can."

"You're not sleeping, Staff."

"Staff sergeants never sleep, sir."

"Ever vigilant?"

"You've been reading the brochure."

He smiled, and she had a sudden memory of those incredible lips tracing a cool, moist line from her throat to her navel.

"Staff?"

It had to have been triggered by the heat. Or the waiting. Or that hit of pheromone she'd taken at dawn was still working on her. She buried the memory before the lips moved any lower and she embarrassed herself. *And none too soon. My heart's pounding like a . . . wait a minute.* "Can you hear that?"

Jarret nodded, head cocked, hair fluffed fully out. "It sounds like an engine of some kind. An old one. Maybe internal combustion."

It was a steady, regular thrum that seemed to thicken the air. The sleepers woke. The lookouts up on the roofs began twisting around, trying to pinpoint the direction. There *was* no direction. It came from all around them.

Weapon ready, Torin slowly turned in place. The civilians had spilled out of their building and stood in the compound, unmoving. Listening. Cri Sawyes, still unarmed, was standing by the well, tail lashing from side to side, throat pouch fully extended.

When she faced the north again, she understood.

Throat pouch fully extended . . .

"I don't think it's an engine, sir."

"Then what else could it . . ."

One moment the surrounding low hills were merely an empty, purple horizon. The next, they were crowned with Silsviss. The thrumming from a thousand throats grew louder and ended in a bass note so deep, it continued to buzz through the silence that followed.

"Holy fuk."

Lieutenant Jarret snorted. "Private Checya, I think you've just expressed the official reaction."

Laughter banished the last of the buzz, and Torin threw a silent *well done* to the lieutenant. His ear points flushed slightly.

"Thisss explainsss why they took ssso long to arrive."

"And if you could share that explanation," Jarret suggested pointedly.

Cri Sawyes' pouch had deflated by half but was still a pale circle at his throat. "They were waiting for the ressst. Thisss"—he scanned the horizon—"hasss to be every male in the pressserve."

"Drawn by our crash?"

"I don't know. Doesss it really matter *why* they're here?"

"No. I guess not."

"Why were they thrumming?" Torin wanted to know. "The Silsviss we fought yesterday shrieked."

"Thossse you fought yesssterday were having fun. Thisss lot, however, meansss busssinesss."

As the thrumming started up again, Lieutenant Jarret's eyes darkened and his lips moved silently. Counting or praying, Torin figured, and given the situation, the latter would probably be more useful. "Everyone's in position, sir."

"Good. Get Cri Sawyes a weapon."

"Thank you." He slapped his tail against the ground. "Although, ultimately, I doubt it will make much difference."

"Maybe not," Jarret agreed, gaze locked on the surrounding Silsviss. "But it certainly can't hurt."

TWELVE

"Why are they just standing there?"

"I believe they're making a point, sir."

"A point?"

"That there's more of them than there are of us."

"Point taken." Jarret flipped up his scanner and slid his helmet off so that his hair could move.

"Sir . . ."

"I know. Setting a bad example." Sighing, he put it back on. "May I ask you a personal question, Staff?"

That was enough to move Torin's gaze from the surrounding Silsviss to the lieutenant. At some point in their working relationship, usually while the shit was hitting the afterburners, junior officers always wanted to get to *know* their senior NCOs. She didn't understand it, but she'd come to accept the inevitability. Unfortunately, Lieutenant Jarret had a better base to ask questions from than most. "You can *ask*, sir."

"Are you afraid?"

And that moved her gaze back to the Silsviss again. Hundreds, maybe thousands of them; they couldn't get a clear reading. Granted, they were attacking an entrenched position with primitive weapons, but the numbers . . .

"I'd be a fool if I wasn't, sir."

"And as you're not . . ." He smiled. "Neither am I."

"Glad to hear it." More for something to do than because it had changed, she checked the tiny line of data running across the bottom of her scanner. "They're well within range of the emmies, sir."

"I know." He rocked forward onto the balls of his feet and then back again. "But as Cri Sawyes insists it won't scare them off, I'd just as soon keep the slaughter to a minimum. We still need the Silsviss to sign that treaty when this is all over."

Whatever this *is*, Torin added silently. She'd seen enough combat to know that there were a limited number of reasons why sentient species killed each other en masse; patterns always evolved. The pattern currently evolving was so blatant, so slap-in-the-face obvious that she couldn't help think it was hiding something. Eyes narrowed, she stared out at the enemy. Unfortunately, an awareness that there were a thousand or more eyes staring back kept the analysis from progressing very far.

"Why aren't they making any noise?"

Torin and Lieutenant Jarret turned together to watch Lieutenant Ghard crossing the compound.

"I don't get it," he continued as he reached them. "Why are they just standing there? It's unnerving."

"I think that's the idea, sir. Is this your first ground combat?"

Ghard looked sheepish. "Is it that noticeable? I don't mind admitting I'd feel better if I was just a little more mobile and about thirty thousand feet up."

"Look at the bright side, sir. If you get shot down here, it'll hurt a lot less when you hit the ground."

After a startled moment, he found a smile. "Thank you, Staff Sergeant."

"You're welcome, sir."

"And thank you." He turned toward the other lieutenant. "Firing from the infirmary windows will allow us to keep an eye on Captain Daniels."

"Is she . . . ?"

"No change."

A sudden clatter from inside the building sheltering the civilians spun him around with enough force to drop his weapon strap off his shoulder. Torin caught it before it hit the ground.

"Thanks again, Staff. You know . . ." Both hands closed tightly around the grips. ". . . I'll be fine once something starts. Why don't we nail them with the emmy? Surely we're in range."

Excusing herself, Torin left for a walk around the perimeter as Lieutenant Jarret began explaining his first-strike policy.

Halfway along the south wall, she paused.

"Aylex."

The di'Taykan glanced up from his position, looking guilty.

"Put your helmet on."

"But, Staff, my hair . . ."

It was standing straight out, a pale pink aurora.

"Your hair won't protect your head. Put the helmet on."

"But . . ."

"Now. And keep it on," she added, continuing around the compound.

A heat shimmer made the distant Silsviss seem vaguely unreal. Facing them, the waiting Marines looked like the toy soldiers she'd played with as a child. They looked confident in their abilities, certain they could do what was necessary. No one fidgeted, no one spoke. She'd built this platoon out of the best Sh'quo Company had to offer—this was where it showed.

At the north wall, she paused again and peered toward the highest of the hills. There was something . . . Swarming up the grain bags stair-stepped by the side of the eastern building, she crawled over the thick thatch and stretched out belly-down on the roof. In a perfect world she'd have been able to exploit the advantage of height with more than just one fireteam per building, but she didn't think the thatch would safely hold more than four bodies. *Just hold me. That's all I ask.* "Mashona, get over here."

Binti exchanged a speaking glance with the rest of her team—she'd been waiting for the summons ever since the four of them had been sent up.

"What's the word, Staff?"

"Mashona, can you see that group, there, on the high point?"

Binti squirmed into place on the northeast corner of the building, squinted, and shrugged. "Sure."

"What's the guy in the middle holding?"

"Looks like—wait a minute, he's moving—like a staff with a skull on it."

"Silsviss skull?"

"Could be."

"Can you take him out?"

Raising her weapon, Binti squinted through the scope. "This is just a standard KC," she murmured, adjusting her sights. "I don't even have a sniper scope on this thing."

"If you'd had the scope, I wouldn't have asked if you could take him out. I'd have assumed you could."

"Thank you for that . . ." She dug her elbows further into the thatch. ". . . vote of confidence, Staff. Yeah, I think I can hit him." Maintaining the position of the gun, she flashed a dazzling white smile back over her shoulder. "Do you want me to try?"

"I'll let you know in a minute." Crawling back to the side of the building, Torin spit out a mouthful of chaff, and called for the lieutenant. She could have used her helmet mike, but since he was barely ten meters away, there didn't seem to be much point.

"What is it, Staff?"

"Excuse me, sir, but I think we've pinpointed the pack leader." She dropped her voice as he came closer. "Mashona says he's hittable. What do you want to do?"

"How do you know he's the leader?"

"Just a guess—he's holding a staff with a skull on it."

"Yesss." Cri Sawyes came up behind Lieutenant Jarret and flipped his head back almost ninety degrees to look up at Torin. "That isss the leader. Although, how it wasss decided with ssso many . . ." His voice trailed off as he lost himself in silent speculation.

"What would happen if he were killed?"

"Under normal circumsssstancesss, it would throw a *carreg* in the nessst . . ."

If they got out of this alive, Torin planned on asking just what the hell that meant.

". . . but thessse are not normal circumsssstancesss." He shrugged. "At besssst, they'll fight amongssst themsssselvesss and forget usss. At worssst, we'll have one lesss enemy and our action will be taken asss a challenge and will prod them to attack."

Torin watched the lieutenant weighing the odds. She could almost read his mind. *One death now could save the platoon. But the longer they delayed attacking, the greater the chance the* Berganitan *would return and pull them out without a battle ever occurring at all. There was no point in provoking an attack and losing that chance. On the other hand, one death now could save the platoon.*

She watched the thoughts chasing each other around on his face and knew which one he kept returning to. Had she been on the ground beside him, she might have said something to help him decide. She might have said, *One way or another, they're going to attack and one death now could save the platoon.* But she wasn't on the ground and she couldn't very well shout advice to the commanding officer in front of his command. He was on his own.

"Do it," he said, at last.

"Yes, sir." Flipping over, Torin crawled back to the peak and repeated the order. "Head shot if you're sure," she added, "but if not, their hearts are pretty much dead center." Scanner at maximum magnification, she waited.

Binti drew in a deep breath, held it, and squeezed the trigger.

An instant later the Silsviss' head exploded, spraying everyone within three or four meters with brain, bone, and blood. He stood there for a moment, headless, then slowly collapsed backward.

"She's got him, sir." And moving her mouth away from the mike. "What have you got in your clip?"

"Impact boomers, Staff Sergeant."

"The 462s?"

"Yep."

"That explains it."

The skull-topped staff remained upright for a moment longer, the bone gleaming in the bright sunlight; then it too crashed to the ground. Unfortunately, it didn't stay there long. The battle for possession was brief, but bloody.

"Did that guy just lose a leg?"

"I think so, Staff."

There were two more bodies when the skull was raised again, but the vast majority of the Silsviss didn't even seem to notice. The whole thing, from shot to recovery, took less than four minutes.

"Well, bugger that," Torin muttered.

"I could take him out, too," Binti offered, taking aim.

"Doesn't seem like it would do any good," Torin told her. "Watch the sun on your scope and scanner," she said, crawling away in a cloud of dust rising up out of the crushed thatch. "It wouldn't take much to set this stuff alight."

"We may not have stopped anything, but at least we didn't set anything off," Jarret observed as she dropped off the wall at his feet.

"Sir!" Mysho's voice caroled over the compound from the west building. "There's something happening!"

One after another, sections of the line boomed from expanded throat pouches, ran about ten meters forward, stopped, and boomed again.

"You were saying, sir?"

For the first time it became obvious that the line of Silsviss was four or five bodies deep. Six deep on the more uneven ground.

"Do the ones in front look smaller to you?" Torin asked quietly.

Cri Sawyes nodded. "They're probably the youngessst, the mossst rash. The mossst eager to show their courage."

Boom. Run. Boom.

Eventually, all the layers of the entire circle had moved in.

"Enough of this," Hollice muttered. "Shit or get off the pot!"

The booming stopped and the shrieking started as the inner ring of the circle charged forward.

"I think they heard you." Juan swung the heavy gun around and slipped his finger over the trigger. "Now, try telling them to go fuk themselves."

Down on the ground, Torin moved to the north wall.

In the middle of the compound, Jarret drew in a deep breath. "Marines, ready!"

His helmet modified the volume and made sure that every other helmet got the message, but Torin was pleased that the mechanical assistance hadn't been necessary. It took some new officers a while to realize that in combat the equipment backed up the verbal order and not the other way around.

"Mark your targets," she said quietly, walking behind the line of kneeling Marines. "We haven't got the ammo to waste on wild firing."

The ring of shrieking Silsviss charged closer.

"Aim!"

And closer.

"Fire!"

Technology had made the KC essentially noiseless when fired. R&D had been thrilled but the people actually using the weapons had been less than happy. They'd compromised somewhere between a good old bang and ear protection.

Thirty-six of them going off at once made satisfactory noise.

Silsviss began to fall.

"Heavy gunners! Switch to grenades!"

Up on the roof, Juan snapped his upper receiver into a new position. "Fukking A."

Clusters of Silsviss were blown into pieces.

The shrieking changed in pitch.

Leaving the fallen, the ring pulled back until it rejoined the rest of the circle.

"Cease firing!"

They were surrounded by the dead, but there didn't seem to be many wounded. A ragged keening drew Torin's attention to a Silsviss thrashing from side to side in a bloody froth. She turned to the lieutenant.

His eyes so dark they held almost no color, he nodded.

"Mashona!"

When Binti looked over the edge of the roof, Torin pointed.

A single shot.

The thrashing stopped.

"With any luck," Lieutenant Jarret said as she reached his side, "that was enough to discourage them."

Torin understood how he felt—it hadn't been a fight, it had been a slaughter—but it didn't feel over to her. "Sir, I'd like to check out the reaction of that command group." When he nodded, she ran for the roof.

They were crouched down, drawing in the dirt, the skull keeping watch overhead. One of them looked up, pointed toward the buildings, then began to draw again.

Feeling a little sick, she realized what they were doing. What they'd done.

"I don't know what they're planning to do next, sir," she said, joining the two lieutenants and Cri Sawyes at the well. "But I think I know what that charge was for. They were mapping our weapons. Looking for weak spots in the defense."

"They were sending kids out to be shot?" Jarret shook his head in mute denial—not of her theory, she was pleased to note, but of the very idea. "They were deliberately using the deaths of their own to plan their offense?"

She kept her tone matter-of-fact to better absorb the pain in his. "It's just a guess, sir."

"But an accurate guesss." Cri Sawyes whistled his approval. "The low-essst membersss in a pack hierarchy have little worth."

His ridges white, Ghard took a step away. "I can't believe you people! You're savages!"

The Silsviss shrugged, his tail moving from side to side. "And thisss isss why you need usss on your ssside."

"We don't *need* you!"

"No?" His voice was calm, but the movement of his tail sped up. "Then why are you here?"

"Enough!" Jarret threw the word between them. "Our fight is out there!"

"And he should be out there with them, not in here with us," Ghard snarled, his upper lip pulled back off large, ivory teeth.

"Lieutenant . . ."

Torin was impressed by the amount of quiet warning in that single word.

". . . you are so far out of line that if we didn't need every weapon for our defense, I'd relieve you of yours. For the last time, Cri Sawyes is our ally." He took a step toward the Krai, using the difference in their height to his advantage. "And I mean it, Ghard; that *was* the last ti—"

Torin knocked Lieutenant Jarret flat a second before the well exploded. Their faces were inches apart as small bits of debris rained down around them and the proximity made her head swim. Before the lieutenant had quite recovered from his surprise, she cranked his masker up another notch.

"What the . . . !"

"I heard it coming in, sir." She rolled off him and stood, half expecting a salacious comment to ignore. Most di'Taykan wouldn't have been able to resist, regardless of circumstances, but the lieutenant got quickly and quietly to his feet.

The well had contained most of the blast. One of the head-sized rocks had been flung inches into the mud brick of the western building but the rest hadn't traveled far. Torin picked her way to the edge of the blast zone, retreating quickly when the ground shifted underfoot. "The good news, a foot in either direction and we'd have had casualties. The bad news, we won't be using that well again."

"That was one of our weapons."

"Yes, sir. It was. An emmy if I'm not mistaken." Tone and expression made it quite clear that she wasn't. Which was when the next logical assumption occurred to them both.

Jarret straightened, dropping the pieces of rock he'd just picked up. "Marines! Off those roofs! Now!"

Training put eight bodies in motion before the emphasis was added.

Not fast enough.

Hollice cried out, spun sideways, landed flat against the thatch, and slid. Torin caught him before he hit the ground, ignoring the background warning from her slate that his med-alert had gone off. She didn't need a computer implant to tell her that his right shoulder would probably need to be replaced—would definitely need to be rebuilt.

"Nice catch . . . Staff." His voice was surprisingly strong, but his eyes were glassy as she lowered him to the ground.

"I try not to let my people bounce, Corporal. Stretcher!"

To give the Mictok credit, they arrived with admirable speed. In spite of everything, Torin's mouth twitched at the pattern of crimson crosses painted onto their carapaces and she wondered whose idea that had been.

Not until Hollice gasped, "Mine," did she realize she'd asked the question out loud. "From the medics of old Earth," he added weakly. "They were . . . bored."

Torin assumed he meant the Mictok, not the medics of old Earth.

Another explosion pounded them with dirt clods as she helped lift him onto the stretcher.

"Our own . . . weapons?" he asked, sucking air through his teeth.

"Our own weapons," Torin told him.

"Adding insult to . . . injury," he muttered as the Mictok carried him away.

The third explosion fell short and hit a cluster of Silsviss bodies. From the sudden screaming, one of them hadn't been dead.

With no order given, three shots rang out and the screaming stopped.

Wiping her hands against her thighs, Torin crossed the compound to the lieutenant, wondering idly how much blood a pair of dress uniform trousers could absorb.

"Everyone keep your head down!" he shouted as she stopped beside him. "Staff, with the roofs denied us, we've got to open firing holes in those walls."

"Yes, sir. If I could suggest we send the di'Taykan inside; without water, we're going to have to keep them cool."

"Them?"

"Are you willing to go inside, sir?"

"No."

Torin shrugged, silently but eloquently saying, "*I thought not,*" and began barking orders. She sent fourteen of the fifteen di'Taykan inside and set a twenty-minute chime into her slate to rotate the fifteenth. Lieutenant Ghard and his two aircrew moved reluctantly to crouch behind the south barricade.

Sporadic KC fire tore chunks out of the walls without penetrating the building, a few slammed into the grain bags, and some whistled by overhead.

"Staff?"

She frowned and held up a hand. A moment later she lowered it. "Sorry, sir, I was counting. I think the Silsviss only got the one locker open. That would make twenty-eight KCs spread pretty much all around us, but no heavy guns and no sidearms."

"How can you tell?"

"There's no heavies firing because they'd be going right through both the walls and the grain bags. I'm assuming there's no sidearms because they were in the locker with the heavies."

"But they have an emmy."

"Yes, sir. The evidence certainly points that way."

She heard him sigh, the sound eerily audible even over all the surrounding noise.

"Go ahead, Staff," he said without looking at her. "Say it."

"Say what, sir?" Attempting unsuccessfully to work out the actual position of the guns, she was only half paying attention.

"That you were right and I was wrong." His hands curled into fists at his sides. "We should have blown the locker."

That brought her back to the moment. Torin looked from the clenched hands to the muscle jumping in his jaw and pitched her voice for his ears alone. "Sir, I will give you my opinion—occasionally, whether you want it or not—before you give an order, but after, I will support you, totally. *We* should have blown the locker. *We* didn't. So now *we* deal."

He turned to face her, and she saw the knowledge that he was responsible for Hollice's injury in his expression. Well, he was. But if he was going to be a combat officer, he'd be responsible for a whole lot more soon enough.

"Looking at the bright side, sir—they could have grabbed a box of impact boomers instead of standard ammo."

They both flattened as a shell whistled overhead but blew thirty meters on the other side of the south wall.

"And," she added as they stood again, "they're lousy shots."

"I expect that they'll get better," Jarret observed dryly, dusting himself off. "We've got to take that thing out."

"From the trajectory, I'd say that they're moving it between shots and pretty damned quickly, too. If we can't pick it up on a targeting scanner . . . Ressk!"

The Krai ran in from his position at the north wall. "Staff?"

"Can we target one of our own pieces?"

"Our own . . . ?" Understanding dawned. "I don't think so. The specs aren't in the scanner, Staff. We don't usually shoot at ourselves."

"Can you reprogram it?"

He shook his head. "That's not exactly how it works."

"I don't care *how* it works, as long as it works."

"Okay . . ." Shoving his helmet back on his head, he thought for a moment, then he smiled. "If I convince it that the other emmy is a captured piece, it can input the specs from that." The smile faded. "But that'll mean we'll have one less weapon because the second emmy can't be fired or the first'll lock on."

"It'll also mean they'll have one less weapon out there," Lieutenant Jarret reminded him. "Do it."

"Yes, sir!"

The next shell exploded just outside the south wall, the concussion knocking several grain bags into the compound.

"Ressk! Hurry up!" Ears ringing, Torin raced for the wall, grabbed one end of a grain bag and, together with Cri Sawyes, swung it off a downed Marine. "Are you all right?"

"Bruised, but I think so . . ." She blinked as a round from a KC whistled past her nose, then managed a strained smile. "I guess that one wasn't for me."

"Good." Torin clapped her on the shoulder as she stood, then jumped as the lieutenant's voice rang out behind her.

"Cover that south hill with fire. I want their heads kept down while we rebuild this wall!"

"Sir, you should be back in the center of the compound. It's too dangerous out here."

"Stop arguing and start stacking, Staff. This wall has to be repaired before the dust settles and they can see to aim."

And if you take a random shot in the head, you'll be just as dead, Torin thought, wrestling one of the bags back into position.

Hurriedly repaired, the wall was neither as straight, nor as secure, but it was a solid barrier again and that was what mattered. The lieutenant was sweating freely by the time they were done. Torin racked her brains for a way to get him inside and out of the worst of the day's heat.

"Should I go check on the civilians, sir?"

He glanced toward the western building and squared his shoulders. "No, thank you, Staff. I'd better do it. There's going to be a lot of explaining to do when this is over, and I'd like us all to be telling the same story."

"Well done," Cri Sawyes murmured as they watched the lieutenant walk away. "If you'd sssuggesssted he go inssside, he'd have thought you were trying to coddle him and never agreed."

Torin shot him a look from the under the edge of her helmet and led the way back into the center of the compound. "I don't know what you're talking about."

"No. Of courssse not. He'sss coming along very nicely, Ssstaff Sssergeant. He isss learning to take command, and your Marinesss will notice that he wasss willing to put himssself at risssk to sssee that the wall protecting them wasss rebuilt."

Another shell whistled by overhead, very nearly exploding within the opposite curve of the Silsviss circle. Torin shook her head ruefully at the miss. It'd make the day so much easier if they'd just start killing each other and leave her Marines alone.

"One would almossst think that thisss whole incident had been ssset up."

"Set up for what?"

"A training exercissse, Ssstaff Sssergeant. Diplomacy, then combat. Show, then sssubsssstance. Who could ask for more?"

That sort of accusation was just what she needed. She glared at him through narrowed eyes. "I don't know how your people train, Cri Sawyes, but Marines do *not* set up training exercises where other Marines get shot."

"Of courssse not." He bowed, his tail rising. "I apologissse."

"Good."

After a moment's silence, he said, "Ssspeaking of Marinesss being shot, I wasss impresssed with the way you caught Corporal Hollice. And with the way you handled thossse grain bagsss jusssst now. You're much ssstronger than you look."

The last was said in such a hopefully speculative tone that Torin reluctantly replied. "It's an easy answer—Paradise, where I was born, is 1.14 Earth gravity. Silsvah, is .92 Earth gravity. It's a small difference, but it comes in handy."

He looked around the compound. With all but one of the di'Taykan inside and only two Krai in the platoon, the Marines looked as though they were a single species force once again. "Ssso all the Humansss have at leassst the advantage of that .08 difference?"

"Well, yes . . ." She started moving toward Ressk and the emmy. ". . . but I'm also much stronger than I look."

Out on the low ring of hills, any Silsviss who showed his head for long enough—whether he was rising up to take aim or just having a look around, died. And for every Silsviss who died, there seemed to be an infinite number to take his place. Not exactly infinite, but . . .

"Any sufficiently large number might as well be infinite," Torin muttered.

"What was that, Staff?"

"Just talking to myself, Ressk."

"The only way you can have an intelligent conversation?"

"Don't step on my lines, Private," she advised with mock severity. "It makes me cranky. We're under fire and no one would ever notice another casualty." Then in her normal tone, she added, "How's it coming?"

He steadied the cover with his left foot. "Almost done."

"Good. Because . . ." A faint whistle drew her eyes upward. Time slowed to a crawl. Impossibly, she could see the shell arcing down from a painfully bright sky directly at . . .

Time regained its proper pace.

"MARINES, DOWN!" One arm grabbing for Ressk, the other for the emmy, Torin managed four, five, six long strides, before the explosion threw her to the ground, her body half covering both the weapon and the Krai. Something smashed into the back of her helmet. Something else drew a line of pain across the top of her right shoulder. Something else dug into her right thigh.

Under her, the ground shook.

Above her, hundreds of deadly pieces of shrapnel filled the air sounding like a swarm of angry wasps.

Someone screamed, the sound strangely blunted.

It couldn't have lasted even a full minute, but Torin felt as though she'd been lying there for at least an hour when she finally lifted her head.

Distant figures moved through a nearly impenetrable cloud of dust.

A touch on her arm brought her attention down to the Marine beneath her and she shifted until he could free himself. His mouth moved, she could hear sound but not content. From the panicked expression on his face, he couldn't hear himself at all.

Her hand closed around his chin and she turned his head until he was looking directly at her.

"We were very close," she said, forming each word carefully. "Don't worry." She left him to draw his own conclusions from that. As much as she wanted to give him more comfort, there wasn't much point. Her hearing would return. But he was Krai, and she couldn't be positive about his.

Favoring her right side, she slowly stood and held out her hand. Ressk took it, and when he was standing, they turned together.

The shell had hit the second emmy and both ammo cases. Had the ammunition actually detonated instead of merely blowing to pieces, Torin doubted anyone in the compound would have survived. As it was . . .

The Mictok appeared for a moment, carrying a stretcher between them. Then two Marines, one supporting the other. Then the Mictok again.

They really are fast.

She heard Sergeant Glicksohn shouting orders, his voice sounding as though it had been squeezed into her head through a small hole. Other voices followed, growing clearer and louder as the hole stretched.

"Staff!"

A hand grabbed her right shoulder and turned her around.

The sudden pain snapped the world back into focus.

"Sir."

"You're alive!" Jarret looked down at his hand covered in her blood and his eyes darkened. "You're wounded!"

She poked a finger through the hole in her uniform sleeve, dragging the edges of the fabric apart. "It's nothing much, sir. It's a clean slice."

"It needs taping."

Sucking air through her teeth, she agreed.

"Is that the only place you were hit?" he asked as though he couldn't believe that was possible.

It wasn't.

They both looked down at the four inches of metal fragment sticking out of the back of her upper thigh.

"Good thing I was lying so that it hit the vest," Torin grunted. "Slowed it enough to keep it from going right through me."

"There's another in the back of your helmet." Jarret reached up and tugged it free, then stood staring down at a shard of an ammo box. "This could have killed you."

It wasn't the first time Torin had seen her own death. Familiarity had bred, if not contempt, a certain fatalism. "Point is, sir, it didn't." Twisting around, careful of the edges, she grabbed the piece in her hip and yanked it free. "Son of a fukking bitch!" Breathing heavily, she threw the triangular bit of metal on the ground, and pressed the heel of her hand against the wound.

"You need to see the doctor!"

"Or the corpsman, but not right now." Her other hand on his shoulder, she turned him to face the chaos around them. "Right now, we have work to do."

"Yes . . ." He visibly gathered himself, then nodded once, determinedly, and strode off. "Sergeant Glicksohn, report!"

Ressk had escaped without a scratch, although by the time Torin turned her attention back to him, his hearing had only partially returned. "STAFF! YOU SAVED MY LIFE!"

"You're shouting, Ressk."

"SOR-ry."

Frowning, Ressk's fingers danced over the screen of the surviving emmy. "IT SHOULD fire, STAff, and the tarGET lock shoULD WORK."

Torin glanced over at the hole where the ammunition had been and snorted. "It doesn't matter."

Following her gaze, Ressk smiled and flipped open the cover of the chamber.

All things considered, she decided not to give him the standard chew out on reprogramming a loaded weapon. Running her tongue over the front of her teeth and tasting grit, she nodded. "Make it count."

The explosion in the ranks of the Silsviss was very nearly as large as the explosion in the compound had been.

Torin didn't know about anyone else, but it made her feel better.

THIRTEEN

Another Marine was dead. Two more badly wounded. Half a dozen others had taken injuries similar to Torin's—not bad enough to be disabling but bad enough to need help. Walking into the med station out of the heat and the dust, she found the building cool enough inside that the familiar smell of blood wasn't entirely overwhelming. Mictok webbing crossed and recrossed the ceiling holding a quartet of mirrors in such a way that light angled in from the windows and bounced between them, illuminating the bodies below.

Only the Mictok would pack mirrors during an emergency evacuation.

Doctor Leor, his feathers matted together, worked long fingers within the belly of one of the wounded Marines. Beside him, the unwounded corpsman worked a jagged hunk of metal out of the shoulder and past the exoskeleton of a heavy gunner while one of the Mictok held her forelegs down on the pressure points. Both stretchers were balanced on a rectangular pile of grain bags stacked high enough to ease access.

One hand still pressed against the hole in her thigh, Torin's eyes narrowed. She had half a dozen Marines who needed nothing more than a patch job, who were needed back on the walls, able to fight.

A commotion at the doorway into the middle room drew her attention in time for her to see the other corpsman, the one who'd taken the brunt of the injured Silsviss' attack, slide to the floor. Before she could move, one of the di'Taykan she'd sent inside to shoot through the walls scooped him up.

When he straightened, staggering a little under his burden, she saw a pale fringe of pink under the helmet's edge.

Becoming aware of her scrutiny, Aylex met her gaze. "He said he wanted to help, Staff. Stupid *ablin gon savit* can hardly stand."

"Get him back to bed." Ignoring the only possible di'Taykan's response, Torin flipped down her helmet mike. "Sergeant Chou!"

"Staff?"

"Bring the Charge d'Affaires and her assistant to the med station on the double."

"I thought Lieutenant Jarret wanted the civilians safely tucked away."

"I'll deal with the lieutenant." She bent carefully and picked up a med kit. "You just get their tail feathers in here."

"On my way."

She took another look at the situation. "Anderson!"

The Marine, sitting on a bag by the wall, looked up, tossing light hair back off her face. "Staff Sergeant?"

"You still got one working hand?"

Anderson looked down at the long gash along her left forearm barely held together by the grip of her right fingers. She opened and closed her left hand. "Sort of."

"Good." Torin set the kit down beside her on the bag and bent awkwardly forward. "You twist, I'll pull." Someday, with any luck, she'd find the stupid son of a bitch who'd designed a latch on a med kit that needed to be opened with two hands and be able to give their ass the kicking it deserved.

By the time they'd fought it open, she could hear the two Rakva approaching. And from the sound of it, they weren't alone.

"Your staff sergeant has no authority to have this one dragged out of the dubious security of that hovel, Lieutenant. This one is not in a uniform and this one is not hers to order around. Neither is Purain."

"I'm sure she has a good reason for sending for you both. Why don't we hear what she has to say?"

"All this one wishes to hear," the Rakva insisted, stepping into the room and halting just over the threshold, "is you ordering her to apologize."

Lieutenant Jarret slid past the indignant civilian and turned to Torin, looking significantly unimpressed. "Staff Sergeant Kerr, Sergeant Chou says you directed her to bring Madame Britt and her assistant to the med station."

The assistant looked frightened, but whether of Madame Britt or the situation, Torin couldn't tell. "Yes, sir, I did. We have Marines that need a minimum of attention so they can get back to their positions, but our medical personnel have serious injuries to deal with. Madame Britt and her assistant each have two working hands the right size to handle the equipment and should both be capable of operating an aid station."

"Capable is not at question, Staff Sergeant," Madame Britt snapped. "If you need an aid station, this one suggests you use a Dornagain—from what this one has heard, they wish to help but are unable to see a way they can."

"The Dornagain's fingers are too big."

"Then use a Marine."

"All able-bodied Marines are needed to defend the compound." Torin narrowed her eyes and swept both Rakva with a speculative look. "If you'd rather pick up a weapon . . ."

Her crest rose, the stub of the broken feather jutting straight up. "This one does *not* become involved in the business of the military. Lieutenant!"

Jarret nodded. "An aid station is a good idea, Staff Sergeant. Carry on." As the astounded Charge d'Affaires stared after him, he walked out of the building calling for Sergeant Chou.

"All right." Torin showed the open med kit to the two Rakva. "It's not hard. Use one of these to wipe the edges of the wound clean, lay down a line of bonder, pinch the edges together, then spray on a coat of sealant."

Madame Britt took a step back, vestigal beak snapping open and shut a time or two before she could find a suitable protest. "This one does not . . ."

A torrent of high-pitched, fingernails-on-slate sound cut her off. It wasn't necessary to understand Rakva to catch the point of the doctor's tirade. When he finished, young Purain was looking appalled and Madame Britt slightly stunned.

"Fine," she said, taking the kit from Torin's hand. "This one will help."

"Good." Torin undid her dress pants and dropped them down around her knees, ripping fabric out of the line of blood that had dried down the back of her leg. "You can practice on me."

Still favoring her right leg, Torin stepped back out into the compound and realized the environmental unit in her tunic had shut down—probably because of the slice in the sleeve. As the afternoon heat wrapped around her, insinuating dry fingers in under her clothes, she added the name of the idiot who hadn't included combat backup systems in the dress uniforms to her hit list—currently consisting of the med-kit designer and General Morris. The latter was there mostly on principle; he *had* given the order that had sent the platoon to Silsvah.

And the way things have turned out, it's a good thing he didn't let us wait for those new recruits. They were in a tough enough fight for seasoned combat troops. Green Marines would have turned a bad situation into a nightmare.

Glancing around the perimeter as she crossed to her lieutenant's side, she realized that the atmosphere had darkened since the explosion. The easy confidence had been replaced by an edged intensity acknowledging the deaths that had already occurred as well as those that were likely to and, on an individual basis said, *I, at least, am not leaving here bagged.*

By the time she reached the shade of the other building, where Lieutenant Jarret and the Dornagain ambassador were talking, Torin could feel warm lines of sweat running down her sides, her shirt clinging to her damp back. Glancing over at the slate-gray clouds piling up in the west, she sighed. From the look of things, she was going to get wetter still.

". . . very sorry, Ambassador, but your hands are simply too large to deal easily with our medical supplies."

"And we are too slow to carry stretchers as the Mictok do."

"Yes, sir. I'm afraid so." It hadn't been a question, but Lieutenant Jarret answered it anyway. "Stretcher bearers are very vulnerable. I wouldn't have allowed the Mictok to assist were they not so very fast. It is our job to keep you—all of you—safe."

"Yes." The ambassador sighed. "All of us. An entire Confederation of ancient cultures hides behind the deaths of its youngest members." Stroking back his whiskers with his broken claw, he stared out over the lieutenant's head at the surrounding litter of reptilian bodies. "We are like the Silsviss in this, I fear, only we are old enough to know better." He sighed again, and turned his bulk toward the building that sheltered his people. "You will tell us if there is anything we can do, Lieutenant Jarret?"

"Yes, sir, I will."

"Good. Staff Sergeant Kerr." He nodded in Torin's direction and disappeared inside.

Jarret's gaze flicked to her shoulder and hip. "Are you all right?"

"Yes sir, I'm fine. Thank you."

"You'll have a little trouble sitting."

Torin waited for the echoes of a sudden flurry of shots to die down. "I don't think I'll have much chance to sit for a while, sir."

*　　*　　*

Sunset painted bands of orange and gold across the bottom of the clouds in such brilliant hues that only the di'Taykan could look to the west without their scanners. When the Silsviss charged out of the sunset, the di'Taykan stopped them.

"The lieutenant took a chance, not moving some of the others over," Mike murmured as he passed Torin a pouch of food. "You should've said something."

She broke the self-heating unit across the bottom of the bag and waited, tossing it from hand to hand. "No di'Taykan were injured in the explosion or the first charge. They felt like they weren't doing their share."

"That's ridiculous."

"Still, that's how they felt."

"Trey's dead and Haysole's legs are paralyzed."

Torin waited; she could feel the weight of more words that needed to be said filling the space between them.

"He always hated not being able to move his legs. He hated it when he had to be secured during a drop. He gave me more damn trouble than everyone else in the squad combined, but put him in combat and he settled right down." The sergeant stared into his food, not seeing it. "I should have tied him into his seat."

Torin reached out and lightly clasped his arm. When he lifted his head, she tightened her grip. "It wasn't your fault."

"I know."

"Really?"

"Yeah." His pause suggested Torin not push. So she didn't. "I could really use a beer."

Torin stared up at a cloud-covered sky, willing one of the hidden points of light to be the *Berganitan* returning before anyone else got bagged. "Me, too."

"Hey, what've you got?"

"Same fukking thing as you," Juan grunted. "Hot bag of balanced nutrients in a tasty fukking paste."

Binti snorted, eyes and teeth alone visible in the darkness. "I meant, what flavor have you got, asshole?"

"What flavor asshole?"

"Don't go there," she warned. "Just answer my question—dark or light."

"Dark."

"Figures. I pulled a light; you want to trade?"

Juan sucked paste out of the pouch, swallowed and smiled. "Are you fukking nuts? Nobody likes the light ones."

"I don't mind them," Ressk offered from Juan's other side.

"Big surprise." Leaning out from the grain bags, Binti tossed the pouch past the heavy gunner toward the outline of the Krai as showing on her scanner. "Go ahead and suck it back, Ressk. I'm not going to eat it."

"I can't trade, I've already finished mine."

"Again, big surprise." Adjusting an already perfectly adjusted sight, Binti flinched when a huge drop of water splashed against the back of her hand. "Oh, that's the perfect end to a perfect day."

"We need the water; the fukking liz . . . Silsviss blew the well."

"We need a lot of things," Binti snorted. "We need the rest of the company, including full artillery and air support. We need the luck of the H'san. We need to defeat the Others once and for all. We don't need to get wet."

Less than a minute later, scattered drops had turned into a steady downpour.

"And," she sighed, "I think it's getting colder, too."

"It's not gettin' fukking colder, it's just less warm."

"The Silsviss aren't going to attack in this," Ressk declared as water ran off the curve of his helmet and down the back of his neck. "I think the lieutenant should call it a night."

"Oh, yeah. And everyone who thinks that's going to fukking happen, don't speak up all at once."

Ressk turned a worried frown on the heavy gunner. "So you think they're going to attack?"

"No, I think we should all curl up in our little beds and be buddies until morning. How the fuk should I know?"

Sighing heavily, Ressk stared out into the night. "This is beginning to remind me of Hallack IV. You remember, we got pinned down covering the *serley* evacuation of those H'san colonists?"

"I remember. I was trying not to fukking think about it."

They listened to the rain for a while.

"You guys think Hollice is going to make it?" Binti asked at last.

"We've all seen worse," Ressk reminded them. There was no need for him to go into more detail; some things couldn't be forgotten.

Juan sighed. "Yeah, and some of them didn't fukking . . . did you hear that?"

"There's nothing out there but dead Silsviss, Juan."

"Fuk you, too. Something out there is alive. And moving."

Peering through his scanner, Ressk muttered, "Got it. I hate it when you're right."

Binti snapped down her helmet mike. "Staff? There's something happening over here."

"Sir? Private Mashona reports movement to the north about halfway between us and the hills."

Jarret resealed the top of his food pouch and stuffed it in his pocket as he stood. "Could the Silsviss have moved up without our scanners seeing them?" he asked, picking up his helmet and tucking it under his arm.

"I don't think so, sir." Torin kept her voice as low as the pounding rain allowed as together they hurried toward the north wall. "We couldn't have missed seeing them come down those hills."

"There's a lot of bodies out there, maybe it's scavengers."

"That's the most likely explanation, sir."

"Staff? This is Conn at the south wall. We've got movement."

Torin passed the new message on to the lieutenant, mentioned that his helmet would be of more use on his head, then asked Conn, "Are they at about the halfway point?"

"About that, Staff. Between the speed they're moving at and the rain, it's hard to get a solid fix. Whatever they are, they're staying awful close to the ground."

Torin checked that the lieutenant had heard just as her scanner picked up movement no more than five meters from the north wall. From Jarret's expression, he'd seen it as well.

Frowning, he stared into the darkness. "I think I'd like some light on this."

"Yes, sir. Heavy gunners! By number, illuminate!"

From the westernmost end of the south wall, a voice bellowed, "One!" Then, from high above, the compound was lit by brilliant while light.

"Don't stare directly at the flare!" Torin warned, turning slowly in place so that she could examine all approaches. "And remember to . . . son of a . . . !"

One moment, the night had been a solid presence on the other side of the wall, the next, a Silsviss leaped into the light, landing on top of the grain bags howling at full voice and brandishing a short spear in one rain-slick hand.

Ressk threw himself backward into the mud and fired.

The howl lingered for a moment after the body fell.

"You're lucky the stupid fuk paused to pose," Juan noted, ignoring the spray of blood dribbling down his cheek as he snapped his upper receiver over to flares. "If these kids were real soldiers, you'd be fukking dead." He took a step back from the wall. "Cover." When the Marines to either side shifted position slightly, he aimed at the sky. "Two!"

The second flare.

Another six Silsviss.

None of them made it to the top of the wall.

"They spent the day hiding behind their dead," Jarret yelled over the mixed sound of challenge and gunfire and pounding rain. "We were scanning the hill for them, and they were already halfway here."

"Smart kids," Torin acknowledged.

The third flare.

Only Cri Sawyes saw the arrows arching over the south wall. Grabbing Torin's arm, he swung her around.

Her eyes widened and her reaction changed from an enraged snarl to, "Arrows incoming!"

Most buried their points in the ground. A few skidded off the impenetrable curve of a helmet. Only one Marine was hit.

When Torin reached his side, Aylex had his hand pressed to his forehead. At sunset she'd started cycling the di'Taykan out to positions on the wall—maybe she should have been keeping a better eye on them. "Where's your helmet?"

"There." di'Taykan hair shed water as though it were made of plastic instead of protein, but pain had clamped Aylex's tightly to his head.

Squatting by his side, Torin softened her voice. "Let me see."

He slowly moved his hand away.

Another flare went up, illuminating an ugly red line running diagonally from the inside corner of his right eyebrow up into his hairline, blood running in unbroken watered lines down his face.

"Looks like it hit the bone and skidded. It's nothing serious."

Aylex's eyes lightened. "di'Taykan have hard heads."

"I am *fully* aware of that, Private. Now pick up your damned helmet and go get that cut sealed." She backed out of his way. "And I want the helmet on your head when you come out of the med station."

"Yes, Staff." Looking considerably less stunned now that someone had taken charge of the situation, he dumped the water out of his helmet, hung it from his belt, and began to move away from the wall.

Torin paralleled him for a moment, both of them bending low. *Which'll get us an arrow in the ass,* Torin thought, *but does bugger all otherwise.* Still, instincts insisted that when under fire the only intelligent response was to duck.

When she was satisfied he could make it on his own, she began to angle away. She could hear shouting from the south, Mike's distinctive parade ground bellow bludgeoning back the Silsviss challenges. Aylex didn't need her any longer, but there were others who . . .

She saw him fall from the corner of her eye, the brilliant pink hair drawing an almost visible arc through the night as he pitched forward and landed facedown in the mud. By the time she had him rolled over on his back, the Mictok were there.

"Allow us, Staff Sergeant Kerr."

Eight forelegs slid under the fallen di'Taykan and, in spite of the tremors beginning to rack his body, lifted him easily onto the stretcher. Torin had to run full out to keep up.

After picking off a Silsviss archer too slow to drop back down behind his shielding corpse, Binti stared at the arrow buried deep in the mud by her leg. "You guys think Hollice told anyone about what the Dornagain believed?"

"What? That traveling faster than fukking snails is impossible?"

"No, asshole, that these arrows might be poisoned."

Juan and Ressk exchanged worried frowns.

"If the brass knew, they'd have told the platoon," Ressk said at last. "We'd have got some kind of warning."

"You better fukking tell somebody," Juan pointed out, firing twice at a suspicious break in the rain.

There wasn't any point in asking why *she* should tell, Binti realized. With Hollice wounded, she was next senior, so the shit jobs came automatically to her. Beginning to rethink her desire to get her corporal's hook, she flipped down her mike. "Sergeant Glicksohn?"

*   *   *

Torin paused dripping inside the door of the med station while the Mictok
slid the now thrashing Aylex onto Dr. Leor's table and answered her helmet's insistent call. "What is it, Mike?"

"Mashona says the Dornagain think the arrows might be poisoned."

Back arced, Aylex began to fling his arms from side to side. A loop of
webbing gently restrained him.

Torin's stomach clenched. "Tell the lieutenant." Spinning around, she
raced back out into the rain. The north wall was closest, but the few arrows
that had made it over were buried point down in mud. She didn't even slow.
Ignoring the lieutenant's voice in her helmet ordering the Marines to treat
the arrows like the death threats they were, she placed her left hand flat on
the top bag, propelling herself up and over. She grabbed the first two arrows she saw sticking into the grain, and, fully aware of the sudden flurry
of shots her activity had provoked, jumped back.

She had the slate off her belt before she'd taken two steps. The first
arrow had only traces of toxins too small to read, but the second . . .

"Doctor! It's poison!"

Dr. Leor kept his eyes on the needle going into Aylex's throat. "This one
is aware of that, Staff Sergeant."

"I've done an analysis."

"And you want this one to do what?" He removed the needle and closed
his fist around the body of the syringe. "Create an antidote? With what?"
He turned to face her then, fist raised. "With these primitive tools? This one
is not a miracle worker, Staff Sergeant!" His voice rose with every word.
"This one has no proper equipment! No proper light! This one has patients
dying!"

Torin took another look at the body on the table and realized it was just
that—a body on the table. "He's dead."

"Yes! Dead! This one does not have patients die!" All at once, his crest
fell and he sagged. "This one," he said softly, laying one hand against
Aylex's cheek, "is an environmental physician. This one does the research
that allows members of the Confederation to live safely on new planets."

"Then do it." Torin held out her slate. "If I understand this stuff correctly, it can kill every Marine in the compound with a scratch. Humans,

Krai . . ." The pause was barely noticeable. ". . . and di'Taykan. I can't worry about scratches, not and keep my people alive."

"But you are not keeping your people alive, are you, Staff Sergeant? You can perform miracles no more than this one can."

"Performing miracles is part of my job, Doctor." She understood his distress; she didn't give a damn about it, not if it was putting her people in danger, but she understood. "And whether you like it or not, it's part of your job, too."

He stared down at the slate, then slowly pulled it out of her hand. "This one will try to find an antidote."

"No. Trying isn't good enough. Find one."

"And if this one doesn't have the right drugs?"

"Then find another. Find one that uses the drugs you have."

"Ah." He glanced down at Aylex and over at her again. "It will not bring the dead back to life."

Torin drew in a deep breath and let it out slowly. "It never does," she said, and walked out into the rain, rubbing the falling water off her face with the palm of one hand.

"You hear that?" Hollice asked, head turned toward the next stretcher.

"My ears still work," Haysole muttered.

"Sounded like Staff ripped a few feathers out of the doctor."

"Sounded like someone just died."

Hollice sighed. "Yeah, that, too."

The stretchers had been moved to the center of the room. A Marine stood on a grain bag against each wall, weapon resting on the thick lower edge of the window, attention fixed on any movement in the night. The room behind them could have been empty for all the attention they paid it.

"You know why they won't look at us?" Haysole asked suddenly. "They're afraid that our bad luck will rub off on them. See the dying, become the dying."

"I'm not dying," Hollice snapped. "I'm just missing a shoulder." Under a thick layer of sealant, blood vessels had been stretched across the damaged area in an attempt to save the arm. He felt nothing at all since the corpsmen had numbed the part of his brain that would have acknowledged the pain, and if he had his way, it would stay numb until they slipped him into a tank back on the *Berganitan*. Actually, he felt pretty good—which, all things considered, was just a little too weird.

On the other side of his injury, Haysole sighed.

The only light in the room came from the two corpsmen who were tending to one of the Marines unconscious since the crash, but it was enough for him to see the di'Taykan's hair had flattened tightly to his skull. "And you're not dying either," he added sharply.

"I'm not living."

"Oh, for fuk's sake, Haysole, it's just your legs. They're easy enough to rebuild."

"If the *Berganitan* comes back."

"If it doesn't, another ship will. Marines don't abandon their own. And I'll tell you something," he continued quickly before Haysole could make another melancholy objection, "if no one comes back for us soon, Staff'll build a ship out of lizard shit and . . . and . . ."

"And bones."

"Yeah, and bones. Sounds like there's enough of them piling up out there. She'll build a ship and kick it off this planet with her own dainty foot before she lets us rot here."

"You're probably right." The di'Taykan sighed again, and his hair began to make a few tentative movements.

"No probably about it." Hollice firmly believed that after a point living and dying was as much a state of mind as anything and no one was dying right next to him. Not if he had anything to say about it. "You feeling better?"

"Why not try groping it and find out?"

"Oh, yeah, you're feeling better. My work here is done."

"Does that mean you're not going to . . ."

"Yes."

"You are?"

"No."

"But . . ."

"Get some sleep, Haysole." A grenade exploded not far from the building and bits of chaff drifted down from the thatched roof, lightly dusting both men. "Or not."

By the time Torin reached Lieutenant Jarret, grenades were exploding all around the compound.

"I ordered the heavies to blow up the closest bodies," he told her. "Everything within the illumination of the flares. If we can keep them back out of arrow range, we don't have a lot to worry about." Then he caught sight of her expression. "What is it?"

"Aylex is dead. Poisoned. The doctor's working on an antidote."

"Too late."

"Yes, sir, for Aylex, but there are plenty more Marines in this compound."

Jarret looked around, squinting as the rain drove up under the edge of his helmet and into his face. "We can only react, can't we?"

"It *is* the problem with a defensive position, sir."

He nodded and waited for the sounds of another grenade to fade before saying solemnly, "I never expected my first command to be like this."

Torin reached out and lightly grasped his arm. The di'Taykan needed touch for comfort. Humans kept insisting they didn't. They were wrong. "No one ever does, sir."

The rain stopped shortly after midnight. The Silsviss didn't.

An arrow, its forward momentum almost spent, scraped across the abraded knuckles of a Human Marine. Humans proved to be significantly more susceptible than the di'Taykan. She died instantly, looking surprised.

About to fire a flare into the air, the heavy gunner by her side fired at the Silsviss archer instead. He also died instantly, but the smoke rising up from the burning hole in his chest made it impossible to see his expression before he fell.

Torin snuggled down into the clean sheets with a contented sigh. The feeling defined safety for her and had her whole life. As a child, it meant she was free of her father's expectation that she'd take over the stupefying drudgery of the farm. As an adult, it meant she'd survived the filth and horror of combat once again, that *she* at least had survived. By then, she wasn't always alone between the sheets because there was no point in survival unshared by those she cared for. Or was responsible for. Or, bottom line, both.

Sometimes it got a little crowded.

Today she was alone. She stretched out, thankful for the space, and smiled as the cool fabric slid across her skin.

"Staff Sergeant Kerr?"

"Sir!" Forcing her eyes to focus on the concerned gaze of Lieutenant Jarret, she realized to her intense embarrassment that she'd been asleep. "I'm sorry, sir. I just closed my eyes for a moment."

"It's all right, Staff. No harm done. It's not like you were awake for the last thirty-two hours or anything." Smiling, he handed her a pouch of coffee, already warmed. "Sun's rising, the Silsviss seem to be having a lie in, and an old friend's back."

"An old friend?" She sucked at the spout as she stood, sliding the webbed strap of her KC up onto her shoulder. About to ask him what he was talking about, and hoping she could be polite about it, she felt the ground vibrate slightly. "Ah."

The *ghartivatrampas* stood looking confused, forelegs shifting from one massive foot to the other, tail sweeping back and forth.

The wispy remains of an early morning fog laid a surreal perspective over the ring of carnage around the compound. The grenades had torn up the ground and scattered Silsviss body parts far and wide. One or two whole bodies, missed in the darkness and rain, punctuated the scene, beginning to bloat in the rising heat of the morning. Small scavengers scuttled about feasting on bits of flesh, occasionally squabbling over choice chunks, although there was certainly enough for all. Hundred of thousands of carrion flies provided a constant background buzz.

"Why did it come back?" Jarret wondered as they watched the giant creature's distress.

"This is probably a regular trail. I'm guessing it sleeps in the swamp at night where the water can support some of its bulk and heads out every morning to its grazing ground. At night it goes back to the swamp by a different route."

"But why stay on a trail that leads through this?"

"It's operating on instinct, sir. Look at the size of its brain case compared to its body. These things were designed to be eaten."

Jarret swept a lilac gaze over the huge creature and whistled softly. "Eaten by what?"

"Once there were carnivoresss on Sssilsssvah of equal ssstature to a *ghartivatrampasss.*"

Jarret jumped, flushed, and tried to look as though he hadn't reacted. Torin turned a bland gaze on the Silsviss, secure in the knowledge that no one could hear her heart slamming against her ribs. "What happened to them?" she asked.

Cri Sawyes shrugged. "A few ssstill exissst in zoosss. There'sss been much dissscussion lately about whether or not there should be a breeding program in place aimed at releasssing them back into the wild."

"I can see how releasing something big enough to eat *that* might cause a few second thoughts."

"Well, yesss, but the problem isss more one of ssspace. They'd need large pressservesss of their own. If they were released in with the young malesss they wouldn't lassst a week." His inner eyelids flicked across. "Defeating the *ravatarasss* was historically the choice way to prove manhood. Which, incidentally, isss why they're very nearly extinct."

"The young males killed them?"

"It took sssome time, of courssse, but, yesss."

Jarret sucked thoughtfully on his coffee for a moment. "Could they kill that?"

"For food, yesss. A ssstrong leader could organize a hunt, but . . ."

"There's a strong leader out there."

All three heads turned toward the surrounding hills.

"Unless they've gone," Torin offered, more because someone had to than because she believed it.

"No. They're ssstill out there. Once the challenge hasss been given, they will not, cannot, back down."

Torin snorted. "I'm amazed the *Silsviss* aren't extinct."

"We have a better breeding program," Cri Sawyes explained dryly.

"All right." Jarret tossed his hair back, spreading it out like a lilac corona around his head. "We need time to regroup. If we frighten that thing up into the hills, they'll have to kill it to keep it from trampling them. Once dead, it becomes food and they'll all want some. Sharing it out will take some time."

"And causssse a few fightsss asss well."

"Which will buy us some more time."

Torin nodded, understanding where the lieutenant was going. "Enough time and you never know, the horse may talk."

"What?"

"Sorry, sir, an old Terran expression I picked up from Hollice. It means that given enough time, anything could happen. The *Berganitan* could return."

"Exactly." He frowned. "I thought Humans were the only verbal species on your home world?"

"Yes, sir."

"Then horses don't . . ."

"No, sir."

Surrendering for the moment, he flashed her a brilliant smile. "Once we're clear of this situation, will you explain it to me?"

"Sir, once we're clear of this . . . situation . . ." And only an officer would use so politely nondescript a word for the carnage they found themselves at the center of. ". . . I will happily deliver Corporal Hollice to you and he can explain not only that expression but a thousand more."

"A thousand?"

"And he knows all the lyrics to something called ALW."

"Thank you for the offer, Staff, but I'll pass."

"Look at those two," Ressk grumbled, sucking vigorously at a bag of rations. "Sun's barely up and they're cheerfully planning the day. Don't they ever sleep?"

"They can't," Binti yawned, trying scratch an itch in the center of her back. "He's an officer and has to be an example to us all. And do you have to look like you're enjoying that stuff?"

Ressk shrugged. "*Chrick's chrick.* She's not an officer."

"Yeah, but it's worse for her. She has to be an example to him. Fortunately, by the time you make staff, you're so evolved you can piss into the wind and not get wet."

"Mashona!"

Binti turned to see the staff sergeant beckoning her over.

"Looks like you're wanted."

"Looks like."

"You want me to hit it where, sir?"

"Just under the base of its tail. It'll be sensitive there and that should send it stampeding up into the hills. What?"

"Sorry, sir." She took a deep breath and managed to stop laughing. Then she caught the staff sergeant's eye and it almost sent her off again. "I didn't get much sleep."

"That's all right, Private, none of us did. Can you do it?"

"Yes, sir." The big thing carried its tail out from its body—not very far but far enough. "Now?"

"Now."

She knelt in the angle of the building and the wall and rested her weapon on the grain bags. *Officers. The lizards spend all day and part of the night trying to kill us, and we send them breakfast. . . .*

FOURTEEN

The *ghartivatrampas* took a while to die although the delay was in no way due to a lack of enthusiasm on the part of the young Silsviss. Torin suspected that after failing to take the compound, their level of frustration was so high they were happy to kill anything. Although the smoke from a number of small fires had begun to smudge the sky, butchering the carcass and distributing the meat had barely begun.

Lieutenant Jarret's idea had indeed bought them some time.

Time enough for the Navy to return and pull them out? All Torin's instincts said probably not.

She turned so she could watch the lieutenant talking to the Dornagain ambassador by the remains of the well and smiled.

"You like him, don't you?"

"Morning, Mike. Platoon taken care of?"

Sergeant Glicksohn leaned against the building beside her. "Everyone's had their piss and porridge, and odd numbers along both walls are catching thirty. Except, of course, those who in the face of imminent death have to get it off one more time. You didn't answer my question."

"Do I like Lieutenant Jarret?" She shrugged. "Well, I haven't had to shoot him yet. For an untried second suddenly commanding in combat, that's saying *something*."

He scratched at the quarter inch of dark hair filling in the area between collar and cheekbones. "Say more."

"More?" Rolling up an empty food pouch, she shoved it in her pocket. "I think he's handled everything that's been thrown at him with remarkable aplomb. He gives orders like he means them, but he's been willing to try new things. He honestly cares about his people, but he doesn't let that paralyze him. He listens to those with more experience, then makes up his own . . . what?"

"You're gushing."

"I am not."

"Yes, you are. You don't think he's enjoying all this . . ." One hand swept out in an arc around his body. ". . . a little too much?"

"He's not enjoying the combat, but I'll give you that he's enjoying his chance to command."

"And?"

"And he's little more than a kid, Mike. He's getting a chance to prove himself, and he's doing a good job. Let him enjoy it."

"You like him."

Torin surrendered. "Yes, all right. Are you happy now? I like him. Given a little time, he'll be an officer worth serving under." It wasn't until Mike's brows rose to meet his hairline that she realized she was smiling again. "Never mind."

"Do I look like the sort to speculate on a friend's facial expressions? No."

Torin banished the memory and dimmed the smile. "What do *you* think of him?"

"The platoon's stopped glancing over at you when he gives them an order. That's good enough for me."

"Well, I'm happy if you're happy."

"I'd be happier if I had a couple of beers, twelve hours' sleep, and a chance to get Ressk in a game of five card draw."

"Why Ressk?"

"The Krai can't bluff for shit."

"Probably why they don't play."

"Odds are." Covering a yawn with the back of one hand, he gestured toward the center of the compound with the other. "Looks like you're wanted. Wonder why he's looking so cheerful."

"He's a morning person. It's one of his least endearing traits. If it turns out to be more than that, I'll let you know." Torin reluctantly pushed herself off the wall and limped out of the sliver of shade into the sun. The fine patina of sweat that covered her entire body by her second step reminded her to find a moment and have Juan Checya look at her environmental controls. Collapsing from heat stroke came under *setting a very bad example.*

*   *   *

"Staff Sergeant, the Dornagain think they can repair the well."

Torin looked down at the rubble-strewn, unstable piece of ground, then back up at her lieutenant. "With what, sir? Spit and luck?"

"With brute strength engineering, to hear the ambassador tell it. Point is, we're going to need that water." He glanced up at the section of sky that held the yellow-white circle of sun. "And soon."

"Yes, sir. What did you want me to do?"

"See that the Dornagain get all the materials they need. They can have everything excepting weapons, helmets, and vests."

"Stretchers?"

"Not all of them, but it won't hurt if they use a few. We're not going anywhere," he added in response to her silent question. "Win or lose."

She watched a muscle jump along the line of his jaw and knew exactly what he was thinking. "Win, sir."

It took him a moment and then he smiled. "You're sure?"

"Yes, sir. It's my job to be sure."

"Conn, what are you doing?"

"I'm looking at a vid of my daughter, what's it look like I'm doing?" The corporal snorted and settled back against the grain bags, his slate propped up on his knee. "I took it just before we left the station; she's showing me some kind of weird dance she made up."

The Marine on his other side glanced down and grinned. "Hey, cute. Let me see."

As Conn held out the slate, strong fingers closed around his wrist and augmented muscles dragged arm and slate back to his lap.

"Are you out of your mind?" the heavy gunner snarled. "Don't you ever watch war vids?"

"The what?"

She rolled her eyes. "Some poor sap shows off a picture of his darling family back on station, and the next thing you know his brains have been spattered all over his buddies and they have to pry the picture from rigor mortis fingers. It's guaranteed to get you bagged!"

"Guaranteed?"

"Yeah. It's got the same bag rate as announcing to the world that you're short. 'Gosh, fellas . . .'" She plastered on a goofy grin. ". . . 'just three more months and I'm a civilian again and I know exactly what I'm going to do. I'm going to go into partnership with my dad. He's old and he needs me.'" The grin disappeared and she drew a line across her throat. "Speech like that and next thing you know, bagged."

"But I am short."

She blinked. "What?"

"Two more months and I'm a civ . . ." It was Conn's turn to blink as her hand clamped over his mouth.

"I don't know why I even bother talking to you," she sighed.

"Staff? You've got to do something about Mysho."

"Do what?" Torin asked, looking up from an ammunition list. Then she took a closer look at the way the two men facing her were standing. That couldn't be comfortable. "Oh. I see."

"We didn't want to say anything, but she's got her masker turned up as high as it'll go, and it's still not helping. Even when we . . ." He met Torin's eyes, turned very red, and rushed on. ". . . you know, take care of it. It just comes right back and it's . . ."

He paused to search for a word and Torin hid a smile. "Distracting?" she offered at last.

"Yeah, distracting."

"And embarrassing," the other man muttered.

"I'll deal with it," she told them.

"But, Staff, why my tunic?" Binti asked a moment later.

"Because Humans can deal with this heat better than the di'Taykan can. Mysho's environmental controls are operating at no better than half capacity."

"But why *mine?*"

"Because mine's not working at all and yours will fit her."

"Oh. Do I get hers in return?" she asked, unfastening her vest. "I mean, half capacity's better than nothing."

"Do you really want to wear a tunic a di'Taykan's been pumping pheromones into all morning?"

"Uh . . ." She considered it.

"*And* deal with the next Silsviss attack?"

"I think I'll just sweat."

"Smart."

Sometimes, Torin said to herself as she came back from burying Mysho's tunic in the latrine, *I forget how young most of this lot is.*

"Staff Sergeant Kerr?"

"Dr. Leor." She turned to face him, noting how dull his eyes had become. "Are you all right?"

He raised a long-fingered hand as if to block her concern. "This one is merely tired." Unclipping her slate from his belt, he passed it over. "This one has found an antidote to the poison, although the Humans may die too quickly for it to do any good. And also, this one regrets to inform you that one of the Marines injured in the crash died in the night."

And sometimes you can only get through it by forgetting how young they are.

"*Fraishin sha aren. Valynk sha haren.*"

"*Kal danic dir kadir. Kri ta chrikdan.*"

"We will not forget. We will not fail you."

The bags flattened, and Torin added four more cylinders to the four she already carried. And all the others that she'd never entirely put down.

"Sir! Movement on the hill!"

Jarret hurried out into the compound and scanned the horizon, one hand shading his eyes from the noon sun. "Where?"

"Everywhere, sir!"

"Get off the roof, then, both of you! Before they start shooting."

"It's showtime, people!" Stopping by the lieutenant's side, Torin handed him his helmet.

He put it on without comment. "What's that coming over the hill to the north?"

Flipping down her scanner, she frowned. "I believe it's a rock, sir."

"Big rock."

"Yes, sir. I believe the word we're looking for is boulder."

Boulders, most taller than the Silsviss moving them, crested the hills to east, west, and south.

Jarret shook his head in disbelief. "How far did they have to go to get all those? That many boulders don't just happen to be lying around on top of the ground, ready to be moved."

"Yesss, they do," Cri Sawyes told him, arriving in time to hear the lieutenant's protest. "The area to the northeassst isss a glacial plain."

"Next to a swamp!"

"The swamp isss to the wesst, Lieutenant Jarret. And it hasss been a very long time sssince the glaciersss rolled through."

"Still . . ."

"There are a great many bodiesss out there, Lieutenant."

"I'm aware of that, Cri Sawyes."

"We have a sssaying, many handsss can move a mountain."

"And apparently did," Torin muttered.

"Yesss."

"With two more dead, there's going to be holes in the line," Hollice mused.

"Yeah, holes. Nice to have an effect. My death'll have no effect at all."

Hollice sighed. "If you're back in the depths of despair, I don't want to hear about it. In fact, I'm sick of hearing about it and . . ." He turned to glare at the di'Taykan. ". . . if I hear one melancholy comment out of you, I'll kill you myself."

The turquoise eyes blinked. "That's not . . ."

"I mean it, Haysole. I've had it with you. And I've had it with lying around here, too."

"You're in pieces."

"So?" His right arm had been taped tightly against his side to keep it from losing its tenuous hold on his shoulder, the remains of the shoulder had been packed in under sealant, and thanks to the pain blockers, he still didn't feel a thing. Dropping his left leg off the stretcher, he grabbed the edge with his left hand and hauled himself up into a sitting position. The world wobbled for a moment, then settled more or less level.

Reaching out cautiously, he scooped his helmet up off the floor and dropped it onto his head. "Staff Sergeant Kerr, Corporal Hollice. I have an idea that can free up two more Marines for the walls."

"Two more?" Haysole asked when he flipped away the mike.

"Why not? You're not holding your weapon with your toes."

"I can't *stand.*"

"Can you sit?"

"I don't know."

"So try."

"What if I can't?"

"We'll flip you over on your stomach, and you can fire prone."

The di'Taykan suddenly smiled. "It is a position I'm familiar with."

"Is there a position you *aren't* familiar with?" Hollice asked him wearily.

"This one does not believe it is a good idea."

"It's not my idea," Torin reminded him. "It's theirs. They seem to know what they're capable of."

"Do they? Do they know how movement and gravity act on their injuries? They think because they feel no pain they are not as damaged as they are. If the di'Taykan is not taken out of here soon, he will die of the injuries that keep his legs from working. Move him around, and he will die sooner rather than later." Dr. Leor ran both hands up and over his crest, smoothing the feathers down tight against his skull. "If you wish this one to continue doctoring your people, Staff Sergeant, you will not fight this one on this matter."

"Lieutenant Jarret . . ."

"Neither of you will fight." His shoulders sagged. "This one thinks there is fighting enough going on."

Torin looked past the doctor into the room where the two Marines were waiting for her word. *If the di'Taykan is not taken out of here soon, he will die of the injuries that keep his legs from working.*

"What about Corporal Hollice?"

"This one would prefer he remain on the stretcher; however, if you truly need him . . ." The shrug spoke volumes.

"We could certainly use him."

"Then you may. Do you want this one to tell the di'Taykan?"

Yes. "No, thank you, Doctor, it's part of my job."

"Corporal Hollice, I want you sitting, not standing; your weapon is to rest on the edge of the window, and the moment you feel you can't contribute to our defense you are to let me know immediately. I don't want any heroics, and I don't want any crap. Am I understood?"

"Yes, Staff."

"Good. North side window. Corporal Ng, outside on the south barricade."

"Yes, Staff."

"But before you go, Ng, give me a hand with this." Together, they lifted the grain bag under the window up on its end. "Now, go. Hollice, sit. They're caught in a crossfire on the north, so it won't matter much if your aim's a bit off. Haysole . . ." The look on his face stopped her cold. If she told him he had to just lie there, he'd be dead before sunset.

Fine. She bent and pulled his weapon out from under his stretcher and tossed it to him. "Hollice can't reload one-handed, and you can't get up or the doctor'll have my ass in a sling, so you'll be reloading for him."

"Wha . . ."

Both combat vests landed close by Haysole's stretcher. "Can you reach them here?"

"Well, yeah, but . . ."

"Good. Hollice needs a reload, he passes his weapon to you, you pass yours—with a full clip—to him, and reload his. Hang on." She dragged stretcher, di'Taykan, and vests closer to the window. "There." Arms folded, she stepped back and studied the two of them. Then she smiled, "I guess together you'll make one half-assed Marine."

For a moment she thought it wasn't going to work. The two able-bodied Marines on the east and south walls had turned to stare at her in astonishment. She glared their gaze back out the windows. The corpsman, trying to spoon some nourishment into a face ruined by the emmy's explosion, was not looking at her so intently that he might as well have been staring. They weren't the ones who mattered.

Hollice's expression she couldn't read, not with the light pouring in the window behind him, but he hadn't said anything, so he must've understood.

Haysole closed the fingers of one hand around the stock of his KC and lifted Hollice's vest by its ruined shoulder with the other. "I've got more clips left than he does, Staff. What happens when he runs out?"

Torin started breathing again. "Use yours."

"In his weapon?"

"The clips are interchangeable, Haysole. Or were you paying less attention in basic than I thought?"

He grinned up at her, and it almost masked the gray shadows on his face. "I don't think that's possible, Staff."

*   *   *

When she explained what she'd done to the doctor, more so he wouldn't undo it than because she felt he deserved an explanation, he shook his head.

"This one understands about the will to live, Staff Sergeant. You have devised an elegant solution."

"Thank you."

He stopped her before she made it out the door. "But what this one does not understand is why you seem to think you have—how do you Humans say?—put one over on the di'Taykan. He performs a necessary function."

Torin sighed. "No, he doesn't. If any of my people couldn't reload one-handed, either hand, I'd kick their butts back to basic training myself."

"But he accepted the function."

"No, Doctor. He accepted the hope."

"Settled?" Lieutenant Jarret asked when she returned to his side.

"Yes, sir."

"Good, nothing happened while you were . . ."

All around the hills the boulders began to roll forward, two or three Silsviss behind each keeping it moving down the slopes.

"Nice of them to wait for me," Torin muttered.

The lieutenant flipped his helmet mike down. "Fire at will but only if you've got a clear target. Don't waste ammo. What's the situation with the grenades?" he asked, turning to Torin.

"Insufficient quantity, sir, and they wouldn't stop those rocks anyway."

"Why not?"

"Well, they're rocks, sir."

As they watched, a Silsviss stumbled and was crushed by an errant bounce, his scream of pain lost in the shrieking of his companions.

"They're crazy!"

"They're only crazy if it doesn't work, sir."

"If *what* doesn't work?"

"I expect we'll find out in a minute, sir."

The first of the boulders reached the flat and slowed considerably, the heavy rain of the night before not yet baked out of the ground. Then the first stopped, captured by the soft ground. A second slammed into it, the impact moving them both only another few feet.

*   *   *

"Follow the fukking bouncing ball," Juan snarled, the muzzle of his weapon moving through jerky four-inch arcs. "Who can hit something moving that fast when you can't see anything but fukking bouncing boulders."

Beside him, sunlight gleaming darkly on her bare arms, Binti squinted through her sights and pulled the trigger.

Two hundred meters out, momentum moved a Silsviss through another three steps before he crumpled, a bloody hole where his chest had been.

The heavy gunner shook his head in admiration and grumbled, "Fukking show-off."

"They're not trying to get to us. They're building a barricade."

Torin watched the impact of another two boulders throw shards of rock up into the air and swore softly under her breath. The Silsviss now had shelter at the halfway mark. Race down from the top of the hills, charge in from the rocks. It would become a two-part attack and the part from rock to compound a fast dash instead of the end of a long run.

"That should mean we have twice as many chances to stop them," Jarret muttered.

"And wouldn't it be nice if it worked that way, sir?"

There were gaps in the ring of boulders. Some of the smaller ones had rolled closer to the compound, some of the larger had bogged down farther back. Most of the Silsviss running with the rocks had survived.

"If it was me," Lieutenant Jarret murmured, almost to himself, "I'd have moved the guns they took from the VTA down the hill with the boulders. Then I'd run as many people as possible to the rocks while the guns lay down a covering fire."

"And now they'll be close enough to hit us deliberately, instead of only by accident," Torin observed, flipping up her scanner. She couldn't see anything useful, and the glare had started a pounding headache. Just what she needed.

"You're not helping, Staff."

"Sorry, sir." Tone and delivery, that comment could have come from Captain Rose. Somewhat taken aback, she rubbed at a dribble of sweat running between her breasts and remembered how concerned she'd been that the polished diplomat working the *Berganitan* cocktail party wouldn't be able to handle combat. Her lips twitched. *They grow up so fast.*

"Once the Silsviss reach their barricade, can the heavies drop a grenade in behind?"

So much for the defensive battle he'd told Cri Sawyes they were fighting. Although, at this point, anything that helped keep them alive could pretty much be defined as defensive. They certainly weren't charging out anywhere.

Torin traced the trajectory from the piled grain bags to the boulders. "It might take them a shot to establish the angle, the heavies aren't exactly precision shooters, but it can be done."

"Are you sure?"

"It's my job to be sure, sir."

"Good. Tell them."

"Yes, sir."

The surrounding Silsviss started thrumming again before she finished speaking with Sergeants Glicksohn and Chou. By the time she got back to the lieutenant's side, they were at full volume and she could feel her teeth vibrating right out of her jaw.

"Another challenge?" Jarret was demanding of Cri Sawyes as she joined them.

"The sssame challenge, part two." His throat pouch had half inflated. "They're telling you they aren't going away."

"Really. Well, neither are we." To Torin's surprise, he took his slate off his belt and thrust it toward the Silsviss. "Tell them."

"Lieutenant, the dialect . . ."

"They aren't using words, just sounds, emotions given voice. You don't need to speak the language."

His inner lids flicked across, and he shook his head. "They won't be able to hear me, Lieutenant."

"Oh, they'll hear you."

After a quick glance at Torin, who kept her expression absolutely neutral, Cri Sawyes took the slate.

Heads turned as the Silsviss challenge boomed out in the compound. Under helmet rims, eyes were wide and hands moved nervously up and down the length of weapons.

The lieutenant scanned his perimeter, pointed and beckoned. As Ressk ran toward them, Torin flipped down her mike. "Eyes front, Marines!" Barely able to hear herself over the noise, she nodded in satisfaction as the gawkers spun back around.

Ridges flushed, Ressk skidded to a halt. "Yes, sir?"

"Can you take out the background noise so we just have Cri Sawyes' voice on the slate?"

"Yes, sir."

"Do it. Then use my code to transfer a copy of the recording to everyone in the platoon."

"Your code, sir?"

Jarret's eyes lightened. "Are you telling me you don't know it yet?"

"Uh, no, sir."

As Ressk's fingers danced over the lieutenant's slate, Torin took a step closer so she could be heard without shouting. "May I ask what you're doing, sir?"

"Certainly, Staff. We're about to tell the Silsviss that *we* aren't going away either."

Both older and larger, Cri Sawyes' voice had a deeper tone than the massed voices of the surrounding Silsviss. Booming out of every slate in the compound, it laid a bass line under their challenge that spoke not so much as defiance as contempt.

Half a dozen Silsviss broke cover and died, one of them hit nine or ten times.

"Let's be a little more frugal with the ammo," Torin advised sharply. "That's six down and two thousand, nine hundred, and ninety-four still out there."

"You counted?" Jarret asked as she flipped her mike back.

"Ballpark, sir."

Lilac brows drew in. "What?"

"An approximation," she corrected, making a mental note to smack Corporal Hollice upside the head if they both survived the day.

"I wonder what we're saying."

"Fuk you!" Haysole grinned as Hollice turned to scowl at him. "No, really, that's what we're saying!"

Weapon butt tucked under his good arm, he lifted his slate off the windowsill, listened for a minute, then nodded. "I think you're right."

"Not a phrase I'm usually wrong about."

The tempo of the thrumming changed.

Shots rang out from behind the boulders.

Torin glanced down at the new hole in the wall beside her, then up at the lieutenant, knowing he hadn't dropped only because she hadn't. "Good call, sir."

"Thank you, Staff. Tell them to turn off our reply and get ready."

"Yes, sir."

"You two are both crazy," Cri Sawyes hissed from the ground.

"Most of the targets will be coming down from the top of the hill. Some won't. Those are the ones not to miss." Torin rested her weapon on grain bags—once used for access to the roof, now built into a sort of command center. Given the angle of the buildings, they had as close to a full field of view as was possible. "Mark your targets and remember that they're shooting at us from a lot closer now."

"Here they come!"

No Silsviss reached the compound.

A great many reached the boulders.

As the first of the grenades arced up and over, Torin scanned the perimeter. No casualties, but that wasn't likely to last. She finished the circle and realized that all four Dornagain continued to work calmly at the side of the well.

How did we miss something that big?

"Sir! The Dornagain!"

Another grenade arced up and over.

"Get them under cover, Staff!"

"Yes, sir."

Juan stared out at the almost solid mass of bodies running for the south wall. He'd just dropped his last grenade behind the boulders. "I don't fukking believe it."

"You don't have to believe it," Binti snarled. "Just shoot!"

* * *

"Ambassador!" Torin had to grab at a fur-covered arm and pull to get his attention. "Get your people inside!"

"We are almost finished, Staff Sergeant." He effortlessly tugged his arm free. "We choose to continue working for the few moments more it will take. If we are injured, we absolve you from any blame."

"And if you're all dead, who's going to tell that to my superiors? Get your people inside. Now!"

His sigh fluffed out his whiskers. "A compromise, then. Strength of Arm will work from within the well, placing the last few pieces."

"She'll be within the well?"

"Yes."

All things considered, that didn't seem exactly safe, but at least it would move the others out of danger. "Fine. Do that. Just get inside!"

Biting her lower lip to prevent an undiplomatic outburst, she waited while the ambassador passed on his decision to his people. Shifted her weight from foot to foot, while they gathered up makeshift tools. Muttered under her breath while Strength of Arm climbed into the well, her movements surprisingly graceful although no faster than usual. And finally gave thanks to whatever gods were listening when all four Dornagain were safely under cover.

The lieutenant had moved to a position by the south wall while she was gone.

"Sir!" She had to shout to make herself heard. "The attack is strongest here!"

"I *had* noticed that, Staff Sergeant." He fired, adjusted his aim, and fired again.

Torin snapped off two quick shots of her own. While she admired the lieutenant's enthusiasm, leading from the front was not a good idea. If he died, she'd be stuck with Lieutenant Ghard—and she'd have to shoot him. "Sir! You're in command! We can't afford to lose you!"

"If the Silsviss get over this wall, there'll be nothing left for me to command!"

Dropping one of the front runners, she had to admit he had a point.

"What's happening on the north?"

One of the last grenades landed short of the rocks, but since there had to be more Silsviss in front than behind, it didn't much matter.

"There's a lot less of them on the north. They know they don't stand a chance running into the crossfire between the buildings, so they aren't. They're only trying to keep us busy enough that we can't reinforce the south."

Snapping another clip into his weapon, Jarret shot Cri Sawyes a tight glare. "Considering that until we arrived they'd been fighting with pointy sticks, they learn fast."

"For the sssake of my ssspeciesss, I accept the compliment. For the sssake of the sssituation, I apologissse."

"Apology accepted." He fired point-blank at a Silsviss, nearly to the wall, and took out the runner behind him as well. "Staff! Pull every third Marine off the north wall and send them to reinforce the south!"

"Yes, sir!"

The reinforcements weren't enough. The first Silsviss came over the wall.

Then the second . . .

Torin spun around as a Silsviss launched itself over her head and barely managed to block a spear thrust. Ducking under the point, she slammed the metal-reinforced butt of her KC up into an unprotected elbow, and when the arm flew wide, got the muzzle in under the chin and pulled the trigger.

A weight landed on her back.

She let it take her to the ground, rolled, and watched a spear point drive into the earth inches from her shoulder.

Not good.

Standing over her, the Silsviss paused to scream a challenge, and the center of his chest exploded with a soft, incongruous *phut*. Torin blinked away a spray of blood and rolled again as he toppled forward.

Up on one knee she fired twice more over the wall, and without even the seconds necessary to change the clip, swung the KC like a club, smashing in the head of a Silsviss about to stab Cri Sawyes in the back.

That seemed to clear the immediate area.

Breathing heavily, adrenaline sizzling along every nerve, she slapped in a new clip and looked around.

There were more Marines than the enemy standing.

Always a good thing.

Then she saw Ressk take a spear in the leg. He screamed, fell, and bit down on a tail that just happened to be too close to his mouth. The Silsviss seemed more surprised than hurt, but it delayed the second blow long enough for Torin to fire.

Chewing and swallowing the mouthful of flesh, Ressk shoved aside the dead Silsviss, got his good leg under him, and tried to stand without much success. Frowning, he glared down at the wound.

Most of the muscle had been carved off the side of his thigh and he could see bone.

It hadn't actually hurt until then.

The world became pain.

Blood welling up through his fingers, he squeezed everything back more or less where it went and curled protectively around it. He'd have screamed except he couldn't catch his breath.

When, inexplicably, he began to rise into the air, he whimpered.

"We do not wish to hurt you, Private Ressk, but we must move you."

He opened his eyes to see a Mictok eyestalk bent down by his face. "G'head," he gasped at his reflection as multiple forelegs laid him on the stretcher. "Get me out of here."

The eyestalk suddenly disappeared.

That was strange enough he found the strength to lift his head.

One of the Mictok—he didn't know which one, they all looked the same to him—had been flipped over on its back, all eight appendages in the air. No, seven. One was in the hand of the Silsviss standing over it. Given time, the Mictok could have righted itself, but a second Silsviss smacked it with its tail and sent it skidding across the compound.

The other three stood motionless around him.

"My weapon!" He swung at one, imprinting the mark of a bloody fist next to the red enamel cross. "Give me my weapon!"

No reaction.

The underside of a Mictok looked a lot softer than the top.

One of the Silsviss smacked it again.

Mandibles clacking, it bumped hard against the back of Sergeant Glicksohn's leg.

Half off the stretcher, fingers still inches from his weapon strap, Ressk watched Glicksohn turn.

Nearly trip over the Mictok.

Deflect the first spear thrust with the barrel of his KC.

Bend, get both hands under the body of the giant spider.

"Every time I see one, this little voice inside my head keeps screaming, Get it off me! Get it off me!"

Flip it back onto its feet.

Straighten.

Die.

The second spear went up in under the edge of his combat vest, slicing through soft tissue, up under the ribs, and into the heart.

He looked down at the rough wooden shaft angling out of his body.

His weapon fell from nerveless fingers.

His knees buckled, and he hit the ground.

"MIKE!"

Halfway across the compound, Torin saw him fall. Her first shot took out the Silsviss who'd speared him. The second Silsviss fell before she could get off her second shot.

As the world went black, Ressk closed his fingers around the KC. This time, he wasn't letting go.

By the time, Torin reached Glicksohn's side, the Mictok were clustered together and beginning to spin webbing around themselves. She didn't need his med-alert to tell her he was dead. Only the dead fell with that boneless disregard for gravity. She dropped to one knee and laid two fingers against his throat anyway.

No pulse.

But Ressk was still alive.

Lifting his upper body back onto the stretcher, she pulled her knife from her boot. Mictok webbing was supposed to be uncuttable. Torin got through it.

"You!" She grabbed an eyestalk below the bulge and turned it to face her. "Get the ambassador inside to the doctor. Now!" The loss of the leg had sent the whole collective into shock. She used her voice to bludgeon it aside. "And you!" Releasing the first eyestalk, she grabbed another. "Pick up that end of the stretcher!"

"We don't think . . ."

"Don't think! Do what you're told!"

Once they started moving, they moved fast. Even with only seven limbs. Torin had to run full out to keep up. Ressk wasn't getting the smoothest ride in, but at least he wasn't lying bleeding to death on the ground beside the dead sergeant.

They were almost to the med station when the largest Silsviss Torin had ever seen landed in front of them.

Landed?

He came off the roof!

The Mictok froze again. The end of the stretcher caught Torin in the stomach but she managed to stop. Unfortunately, the immobile Mictok on the other end continued to hold Ressk's feet up in the air.

The Silsviss throbbed out a challenge, throat pouch fully inflated. Torin was about ready to drop Ressk on his head and bring her weapon around when Strength of Arm rose up from the depths of the well. And kept rising.

At her full height, she towered over the Silsviss.

Her fur gleamed brilliantly gold in the sun.

A sharp, musky smell bludgeoned aside the smells of the battle.

Long, muscular arms spread out to their full extension, making her look even larger. Then she roared.

The sound echoed off the surrounding hills.

A moment of stunned silence followed from Marines and Silsviss both. Someone sneezed. Before the Silsviss in front of her could turn, Strength of Arm reached down, grabbed his tail, and flung him nearly six meters over the north wall.

Roaring again, she started for the next closest tail.

For a nonviolent species, she seemed to have caught on quickly.

A third Silsviss flew past about four meters off the ground.

Torin appreciated the help, but they had bigger problems.

There were Silsviss on the roof of the eastern building, the building holding the med station and the injured. And the thatch was on fire.

Fifteen

"There's hundreds of them out there!" Haysole tossed Hollice his reload and caught the empty KC one-handed, labored breathing rising and falling around every movement. "You hitting . . . any of them?"

"A few." Blinking sweat out of his eyes, Hollice squeezed off three more rounds. "Doesn't seem to be making any difference, though. Hit one and two more take his place."

A deep breath in and out; Haysole's voice steadied as he snapped in a new clip. "Sooner or later one'll get through."

"Not on my watch."

"Oh, yeah, I forgot. You're Corporal Hollice, super Mar . . ." He broke off and stared up at the line of falling dust, gleaming in a stray ray of light. His eyes darkened. "Hear that?"

Hollice snorted. They were less than a meter apart and shouting to hear each other. "You mean the shrieking?" he asked sarcastically.

"No." The line of dust broadened. Thickened. His hair spread, each end straining up toward the thatch. He drew air in slowly through his open mouth. "I smell smoke."

"I don't."

"Useless Human noses." The di'Taykan changed his grip on the KC, sliding a finger in through the guard. "I hear something on the roof."

"The pitter and patter of each tiny hoof?"

"What?"

"Never mind."

"You're weird, Hollice, even for a Human."

A spear point drove through the thatch, and the line of dust became a sudden fall of debris. Haysole smiled and fired nearly straight up.

The Silsviss that landed beside him, narrowly missing the stretcher, was dead.

The two who followed were uninjured.

Haysole shot one as he drove his spear into the back of the Marine on the east wall and winged the other as he turned. The thrown spear took him in the leg. Unable to do more than point the KC in the right direction, he fired again and again until the Silsviss danced backward and died.

Knocking the spear free of nerve-dead muscle, he had a whole heartbeat to enjoy his victory when the northeast corner of the roof fell in, spraying the room with pieces of burning thatch.

"Bloody great!" Hollice spun around and wished he hadn't as the world tilted. Teeth clenched, he forced it straight. "The roof! It's on fire!"

Haysole used the KC to knock an ember off his ankle. "No shit!"

"The wounded!" Including the di'Taykan, there were six occupied stretchers in the room. "We've got to get the wounded out!"

Haysole fired two short bursts as a Silsviss came up the unguarded east wall and in through the hole in the roof. "So do it! I'll cover you!"

"Dream on." Remembering how Staff Sergeant Kerr had moved both stretcher and occupant, Hollice reached for the same grip with his good hand but had it knocked aside. "Don't argue! Your legs . . ."

Another Silsviss appeared, wreathed in more burning thatch.

"Get the others out first!" Haysole fired two quick rounds and then a third for insurance as the body pitched forward. "You said it yourself, I don't need my legs to shoot!"

Given that the others couldn't shoot at all, couldn't do anything but lie there and die, it was a convincing argument. Coughing in the rising smoke, Hollice tossed his weapon onto Captain Daniels, grabbed the end of her stretcher and began dragging her toward the door, yelling at the Marine on the south wall to help.

"But my post . . ."

"Is on fire, jackass!"

At the door to the second room, someone grabbed the stretcher from him, but before they could grab him, he dove back into the smoke. There were four more stretchers in there. And Haysole. And the Silsviss were still attacking the compound. He'd have fallen over and let someone else deal with it, but there wasn't anyone else available.

A quick look around showed the corpsman dragging his injured partner clear and no sign of the Marine from the south wall, but as only two of the wounded remained, he hadn't gone empty-handed. Both stretchers were closer to the door than Haysole.

"What are you doing?"

"Moving you!" The protests wouldn't have stopped him, but as he got the di'Taykan even with the others, a Silsviss emerged suddenly out of the smoke at the far end of the room. "Have it your way! Shoot from here!" He transferred his grip to the next stretcher without actually stopping his backward shuffle toward the door, sucking air heavy with smoke in through his teeth. His chest felt as though it were being ripped apart by jagged lines of pain. Apparently the blockers extended only to the edge of his injured shoulder. Eyes streaming, he got the stretcher to the door, but this time the waiting hands grabbed him first.

"Are you insane?" the corpsman yelled, trying to hold him without doing more damage to his injured side. "The whole end of the roof's about to go!"

On cue, chunks of falling thatch drew lines of flame through the smoke.

Coughing too hard to argue, Hollice ripped himself free of the corpsman's grip and threw himself down on the floor. Where it wasn't a whole lot better.

Either the pain blockers had given up or his brain had figured out a way around them, but since everything hurt with equal intensity, he figured it couldn't get any worse. On his knees and good elbow, he scuttled forward, aiming for the sounds of di'Taykan profanity he could hear coming out of the smoke.

Hands closed around both his ankles.

He sprawled, full length, arm stretched out. As he began moving backward, his outstretched hand touched fingers. Then the fingers closed around his.

"Taking . . . too long," Haysole gasped. "Thought I'd . . . meet you . . . halfway."

Blood dribbled in two dark lines from the corners of his eyes, and his lips were nearly blue. Whatever he'd done to get this far had clearly added to the damage he'd taken in the crash.

Hollice felt as though his arm was about to come out of his socket when Haysole started moving as well. He couldn't have crawled more than three meters from the door; they'd be out of it soon.

The sudden stop forced a cry out through cracked lips. He'd been wrong about the pain not getting any worse. The pull intensified. Haysole didn't move.

"Something . . . on my legs." A falling line of sparks raised a blister along one cheek. He looked up. Looked down and smiled a charming di'Taykan smile. "Fuk it," he said clearly. Then he let go.

Hollice couldn't maintain the grip alone. His fingers were ripped free and he was hauled backward so fast only his outstretched hand was burned by the collapse of the roof.

The thatch had been over a meter thick on closely laid wooden beams. It burned with an intensity that ignited the fibers used as binding within the thick mud walls.

Perhaps the fire had been more than the Silsviss had bargained for.

Or perhaps Strength of Arm's sudden decision to get involved in the battle had turned the tide.

Torin didn't know and she didn't care. The Silsviss had withdrawn behind their boulders and that was good enough for her. As the fire roared unchecked and Strength of Arm returned, shaking and whimpering, to the astounded Dornagain, she started a bucket brigade to soak the western wall of the burning building, the wall that she needed to keep her perimeter whole. She made sure the med station got set up again, that the injured were tended. That the rest of her people got fed and watered and that they remained alert. That the bodies, Mike's and two others, were bagged and reduced. She was the calm that anchored every other emotion in the compound—regardless of how she herself felt—because that, too, was part of her job.

When the sun went down, the fire . . .

The pyre.

. . . was still so high there was no need to send up any of the few remaining flares.

As the sun rose, Torin splashed water on her face and bit into the second of the three stims all ranks above sergeant carried. Three, because they only delayed the need for sleep, they didn't replace it, and someone who'd never spent their nights trying to keep the remnants of a platoon alive against overwhelming odds had determined three was all that was safe.

Safe was a relative term.

She swallowed the bitter gel—purposefully bitter to keep them from becoming a habit—and walked dripping over to the remains of the eastern building. They'd saved the bottom three feet of the wall and enough rubble had fallen into the doorway to keep the line more or less unbroken. The grain bags the doctor had been using in the first room had exploded in the heat, leaving behind a smell reminiscent of burned toast. Compared to the stink of rotting bodies that surrounded them, it was almost pleasant.

Her stomach growled, and she ripped the strip off a food pouch, pushing the contents up into her mouth and swallowing without actually tasting.

"How many?"

"Three. Privates Eislor, Stovak, and Haysole. Two di'Taykan and a Human if you're keeping score."

"Staff."

She swallowed the last of the paste. "I'm sorry, sir. That was completely uncalled for."

Lieutenant Jarret tested the temperature of the wall with the palm of his hand, then leaned his forearms on it. "It's all right," he said after a long moment. "I understand where it's coming from."

It had come from places he'd never been, from battles he'd never fought. Torin turned, ready to challenge his assumptions, but his profile—carved out of the morning, too tight, too unmoving to be flesh—convinced her to hold her tongue. He couldn't understand it all, not at his age, not his first time out, but, unfortunately, he was on his way.

"Twenty-eight of us left; plus Lieutenant Ghard, two aircrew, and an unconscious Captain Daniels, and still hundreds of them." He sounded as though he were discussing the weather. Not good weather perhaps, but his voice held neither the self-pity nor the despair that Torin expected. That anyone might expect under the circumstances. "If we don't get out of here, do you think this'll be considered one of those legendary last stands like Carajys or Dalfour?" he wondered, crushing a rough pellet of baked mud under his thumb.

"Very probably, sir." Every military organization needed heroes; tragic heroes if they were the only type available. "But if it's all the same to you, I'd rather this became one of those amazing last-minute rescues, like Laysalifis."

"You were there."

She'd been on her first combat drop and so scared she'd tested just how waterproof combat uniforms were. "You checked my records."

"I checked everyone's records, Staff. General Morris insisted this mission was vital to signing the Silsviss, and I wanted everything to go well, to justify his trust in me." Without moving his head more than a fraction of an inch, he indicated the ring of bodies. "If the Silsviss aren't impressed, they should be." Then, pausing no more than a heartbeat, he added, "I don't want to die here."

"I don't want to die anywhere, sir."

The corner of his mouth moved toward a smile. "That's the trick, isn't it, Staff? Do you ever regret leaving the farm?"

She stared down into the ashes. "Every now and then, sir. Every now and . . ." Squinting into the rising sun, she let the words trail off. Something glittered out by the outline of the doorway that had led to the third room.

Something glittered.

Heart pounding, she took a step back and vaulted over the wall.

"Staff!"

Her boots and legs were covered in a fine coat of gray by the time she reached it.

A masker. Partially melted, covered in char, but unmistakable for all that.

Eislor had died by the far wall. It couldn't have been hers.

"If I die, take off the masker before you bag me."

She weighed it on her palm for a moment, then turned and threw it as hard as she could toward the Silsviss. It very nearly reached the rocks. Breathing heavily through her nose, she wiped her face clear before she turned back toward the perimeter.

Lieutenant Jarret said nothing until she was back on the other side of the wall. Then, as if she were another di'Taykan, he touched her lightly on the back of the wrist, fingers cool against her skin, and said, "Don't ever do that again."

"I won't, sir."

"If you died . . ."

"You'd manage without me, sir." She took a deep breath and straightened. "And it isn't every second lieutenant I'd say that of."

He was young enough that he couldn't help looking pleased, but he quickly sobered. "We won't survive another attack like yesterday's, will me?"

Mike Glicksohn was dead, so was Haysole. Ressk had taken a blow that would have removed the leg of anyone but a Krai. There couldn't *be* another attack like yesterday's. But that wasn't what he meant. "No, sir."

"They could have overwhelmed us then, but they didn't. Why?"

They turned together toward the ruin, and when he met her eyes a moment later, Torin knew they were thinking the same thing.

"Survival at what cost?" Jarret murmured.

She had no answer. She wouldn't be the one giving the order.

He looked away first. "Come on, we'll talk to the Dornagain."

"No."

"But, Ambassador, yesterday . . ."

"Yesterday was a terrible and unique situation, Lieutenant. Terrible and unique."

"And that same situation is likely to be repeated today."

The Dornagain ambassador cocked his head, a gentle breeze ruffling the fringe of fur along the curve of each ear. "I hear nothing from the Silsviss."

"Yet," Torin told him, shortly.

"Ah. Yes. Yet. And if they come, you would like the Dornagain to join your Marines in defense, Staff Sergeant?"

"In answer, Ambassador, I ask you what you once asked me, do you not think it would be better if you learned to fight your own battles?"

He sighed. "And I must answer what you answered me; it is a little late for that."

"So you won't help?"

He raised a hand and she noticed that the pad under the broken claw was red and inflamed. "Not won't, I'm afraid, can't." When he saw where her scowl was directed, he used the hand to brush his whiskers back. "No, not because of so minor an injury; we would literally not be able. Strength of Arm reacted without thought, impulsively if you would, and that is not a reaction we can replicate on command. As a species, we weigh everything we do, considering all possibilities. If we were to weigh our own death against the taking of another sentient life, I'm afraid we would die."

"But Strength of Arm . . ."

He glanced back over one massive shoulder to the building that sheltered the other three Dornagain. "Strength of Arm is now thinking, and her impulsiveness is causing her a great deal of pain. She is the first Dornagain in centuries to take a life. We fear for her sanity." He looked down at them both and spread his hands in surrender. "I am sorry, but if it comes to it, all we can do is die beside you." Rising up off his haunches, he turned and walked back to his people.

"Given their size, they'd be a lot more useful if they died in front of us," Torin muttered.

"Staff."

"Sorry, sir." She fell into step beside him, wondering why she was having so much trouble maintaining her detachment. *Maybe because this wasn't supposed to be a combat mission. Maybe . . .* She touched the cylinders she carried . . . *because no one was supposed to die.*

They'd barely gone three meters when the Silsviss began to thrum.

"Seems like we're out of options, Staff." He sounded calm, but the end of his hair had begun to flip about. "Get Sergeants Chou and Gli . . . sorry, get Sergeant Chou and the heavies. We haven't much time."

Frowning, Juan scratched at his wrist point. "You want us to fukking flame them, sir?"

"Yes."

"But we don't flame people, sir."

Standing just behind the lieutenant's left shoulder, Torin wasn't certain she'd ever heard Juan Checya complete a response without a profanity before.

Lieutenant Jarret managed to maintain an outward calm but they could all see the struggle under the surface. "It's all we have left," he said at last. "If any of you have a better idea . . ." He paused so they could hear the Silsviss gaining volume. ". . . now would be the time."

Only the Silsviss answered.

"I'm issuing the orders. I take full responsibility."

Juan glanced around at the other eight heavies grouped in a loose half circle in front of the lieutenant. Over half of them were fighting injured. Then he looked from the lieutenant to Torin. Then he sighed. "Just followin' orders has never been much of a fukking defense, sir. We'll take our own responsibility, if you don't mind." Leveling his weapon, he reached out and twisted the front receiver around so that the pressurized gas cartridge clicked into place. "We've only got two of these each," he said over the sound of eight other cartridges, "so it had better be enough."

* * *

They couldn't use the flamethrowers from the remaining building, so Torin doubled the number of KCs shooting through the walls. If the Silsviss moved toward the buildings to get away from the fire, they'd move into a fire of a different type.

"Here they come!"

"Steady." Torin dropped into position behind the wall and raised her weapon. "Wait for the lieutenant's order."

They'd distributed the ammo from the dead and from those too injured to contribute to the defense. It had to be enough.

Other days, other attacks, they'd started shooting by now. Torin squinted into her scanner. Did the Silsviss look confused? Were there moments of hesitation in the shrieked challenges? And since they kept coming closer, did it matter?

"Marines!"

Lieutenant Jarret's voice in her helmet sounded completely confident. If he had any doubts at all, she couldn't hear them. And if she couldn't hear them, no one could. Which was exactly how it should be. She drew in a deep breath and held it.

"Fire!"

A three-round burst slammed into the Silsviss from every KC in the compound. They rocked back but didn't stop.

"Fire!"

Another three-round burst.

"Heavies!"

She felt rather than heard the nine ready themselves to stand.

"Flame!"

The Silsviss were so close to the perimeter, they were almost shoulder to shoulder, too tightly packed for the sort of erratic defensive maneuvers they excelled at. The flame swept over them and back, and over and back, each of the heavies roasting their own arc of the circle.

The screaming didn't differ that much from the shrieking, but the smell . . .

Torin clenched her teeth and ignored it.

"Marines on the walls, fire at will!"

The Silsviss who broke forward died.

"Marines, in the building, fire!"

The Silsviss who broke away from the flames died.

"Fire!"

And kept dying.

"Fire!"

The smoke had begun to make it difficult to find a target. Sighting through her scanner, Torin kept firing.

A burning Silsviss crashed into the grain bags and died. The closest Marine reached over and pushed the body off the barricade.

An arrow rattled off her helmet, bounced off her shoulder, and hit the ground. Beyond hoping that the doctor had the antidote ready, Torin ignored it.

Then the first of the flamethrowers ran out of fuel. The rest lasted only a second longer.

The only Silsviss moving on the other side of the perimeter were writhing on the ground, keeping the smoke from settling. Wondering why the lieutenant hadn't called a cease fire, Torin turned. She knew exactly where he was supposed to be, but it took her a moment to find him. She hadn't expected him to be lying on the ground.

By the time she reached his side, his muscles had begun to tremble.

"Corpsman!"

He'd been on one knee to shoot and the arrow had gone almost an inch into the back of his left calf.

His eyes were half open and the palest lilac she'd ever seen.

"Corpsman!"

Hollice fell to his knees on the other side of the lieutenant's body and held out a small, snub-nosed syringe on a wrapped hand. "Legs work, not much else," he panted. "Doc says . . . wham it into one of the big blood vessels in the neck."

Pushing the lieutenant's chin up with one hand, Torin took the syringe with the other. Below the surface, Human and di'Taykan physiognomy was not exactly the same and the tremors weren't helping. If she injected the antidote into the wrong place . . .

He'll be as dead as if I don't inject it at all.

She ran her thumb along the column of his throat, found a pulse, and drove the syringe home.

Lieutenant Jarret jerked once, his eyes dilated almost black, and he went totally limp.

Ripping her slate free, Torin checked his med-alert, breathing as heavily as if she were running full out. "It says he's stable. This is stable?" A short nudge showed no response at all. "He's unconscious!" Glaring up at Hollice, she snapped, "This is an antidote?"

Sitting back on his heels, Hollice sighed wearily, cradling his burned hand in his lap. "At least he's not dead."

And the world came rushing back.

Breathe, Torin. She filled her lungs with smoky air and found calm. Or possibly denial, but at this point either would work. "You're right." Mirroring Hollice's position, she hooked her slate back on her belt. "Aren't you supposed to be lying down?"

"Corpsman needed help. The spi . . . Mictok webbed themselves into a corner."

"And the Dornagain?"

The disgusted expression answered for her.

Torin shook her head, not exactly in disbelief, because this information only reinforced something she'd believed all along. "Let's try and look at it like job security, Corporal. If it wasn't for us, the Others would overrun the Confederation in twenty minutes."

Hollice snorted. "Fifteen."

"Very likely. Can you stay with him?"

"Yes, Staff."

"Good." She flipped her helmet mike down as she rolled up onto her feet. "Cease fire! Let's have a look around."

Greasy smoke rose up from every point on the compass, drawing inky lines across a blue-white sky. There were Silsviss bodies everywhere, most stopped by fire, then shot. Against the south wall of the remaining building were places where the bodies were piled three deep. The smell of burning flesh could be ignored, but the smell of burning blood was very nearly overwhelming.

In the heavy silence, Torin could hear someone vomiting behind her, but she didn't turn to see who. It wasn't important, and it wouldn't be the last. All along the inside of the perimeter, Marines knelt facing the enemy, duty and adrenaline together overcoming exhaustion to hold them in place. In a few minutes, if nothing happened, they'd start to sag. The corpsman knelt by another casualty. It looked as though a Silsviss had made it over the wall and had fallen, burning, on a Marine. The Marine was alive. The Silsviss was dead.

The only living Silsviss in sight was Cri Sawyes, standing motionless by the well, a KC hanging limply from his hands.

Torin sent out a team to deal with any possible wounded, watched as Lieutenant Jarret was moved to a stretcher and inside. Then, finally, she walked over to Cri Sawyes.

"Are you all right?"

He shook his head. "Ssso many dead. I have ssseen battlesss before, Ssstaff Sssergeant. I have marched into citiesss after the bombersss have been there, but thisss . . . That ssso few of you could dessstroy ssso many of usss."

"For what it's worth, I'd have preferred it if the platoon could have survived another way."

"At the moment, that isss worth very little. Later, perhapsss . . ."

She didn't insult him by saying she understood. He either knew she did, or he didn't want to hear it. "I suppose this'll pretty much close the door on the Silsviss signing that treaty with the Confederation."

His tongue flicked out, just once. "On the contrary, it will ssseal it. Thisss isss the sssort of thing our governmentsss ressspect."

"And you . . ."

"Me?" He turned slowly in place, his eyes never leaving the circle of bodies and the Marines now walking among them. He flinched as a single shot rang out. "I am here, Ssstaff Sssergeant; the government is not. Lieutenant Jarret was injured?"

"An arrow. Dr. Leor's antidote stopped the poison, but he's unconscious." *At least he's not dead.* Torin shifted her weight onto her good leg. "I'd better go tell Lieutenant Ghard that he's in command."

"Should I be worried?"

She snorted. "I can handle him."

"Me?"

"Yes, sir." If there was another functional officer around, Torin had no idea where she or he was hiding. "Lieutenant Jarret was hit by an arrow."

"A poisoned arrow?"

"Yes, sir." By the time she finished explaining, Lieutenant Ghard's facial ridges had returned to their normal color.

"I wanted this command you know, back on the VTA." He turned, much as Cri Sawyes had. "I don't now."

Torin swallowed her first response. And her second, which was considerably longer and just as inappropriate. "The hard part's over, sir. It's only mopping up and waiting now."

"You think the Silsviss won't attack again?"

"There's no way of knowing, sir."

"Then what are we waiting for, Staff?"

"Whatever happens, sir. A Marine's expected to improvise."

Ghard stared up at her, eyes wide. "We're almost out of ammo, there's only a handful of us uninjured, we still don't know who shot us down or why, and you're saying we're expected to improvise!" His volume had risen with every word, and the surrounding Marines were turning to listen.

"Do you have a better idea, Lieutenant?" She held his gaze with hers and locked it down.

"No, no better ideas."

"Orders, sir?"

"Orders?"

Torin raised a single brow.

Ghard swallowed. "I, uh, guess you'd better get me a list of, uh, personnel and supplies."

"Yes, sir." She would, of course, obey every order he gave, but until he convinced her he knew what he was doing, he'd give the orders she *intended* to obey. Releasing him, Torin turned and walked away.

"What the fuk was that about?" Juan asked.

Binti tossed him a pouch of water, then dropped down with her back to the grain bags and laid her KC across her knees. "Staff was just telling Lieutenant Ghard he's in command."

"So we're down to that, are we? Fukking air support in command."

"Don't sweat it, Juan." Eyes closed, she let her head fall back. "Staff won't let him screw us over. Keeping twoie looies in line is what she does best."

"Good fukking point. She did a nice job on Jarret."

"Yeah, he's been doing okay. Nice buns, too."

Juan snorted. "Hadn't noticed. You think it's over?"

"I'm too tired to think."

"You see Ressk and Hollice when you went for the water?"

"Hollice looks like death warmed over, but he's going to make it. Ressk's got so much sealant holding him together he can't bend his leg."

"That's no fukking reason to leave us out here all alone."

Binti opened her eyes and stared up at the heavy gunner. "He can't bend his leg, how's he supposed to kneel behind these bags?"

"Let him stand," Juan snickered. "He's short."

A sigh followed close on the heels of her answering chuckle. "I must be tired, that wasn't funny. Anyway, Staff had him shooting from inside, propped up against the wall. And he says the smell of all this cooked meat is making him hungry."

"Fuk!"

"That's what he said you'd say."

They'd left the station with forty-one Marines plus six—the two pilots and four aircrew, forty-seven Marines altogether. There were fifteen dead—thirteen in cylinders and two aircrew in the VTA's engine room. Thirty-two live Marines. Of that thirty-two, nine were too badly injured to do anything but wait for rescue—and at least three of those had better not be kept waiting for long.

"We have twenty-three Marines able to stand the perimeter, sir." Although Ressk wasn't so much standing as propped. "Including you and me. The heavies have three flares left between them, nothing else. Combining all remaining ammo, we can give each of the twenty-three a little better than half a clip."

Lieutenant Ghard rubbed so hard at his lower ridge it paled. Torin barely managed to resist grabbing his wrist and pulling his hand away from his face. "And the good news?" he demanded, clearly expecting there to be none.

"We have plenty of rations still and the Dornagain did fix the well."

"So we won't starve while we're waiting to be slaughtered."

"Apparently not, sir." She hooked her slate back onto her belt. "Also, the Silsviss have retreated all the way to the top of the hill. The teams sent out to deal with the wounded report no one alive behind the boulders."

"How do you send people out to *deal* with the wounded, Staff Sergeant?"

"Without hesitating, sir, when the only other option was to let them die slowly in great pain."

He shuddered. "Better you than me, Staff."

"Yes, sir."

"They're not done with us. I can feel it. They're up there regrouping."

"Lieutenant, I don't think . . ."

From the top of the hill, the Silsviss started to thrum.

Torin turned away before she smacked the "I told you so" expression right off Lieutenant Ghard's face.

Sixteen

"What are they doing?" Torin curled both hands into fists to stop herself from grabbing Cri Sawyes by the shoulders and shaking him until he answered. "Why haven't they had enough?"

Cri Sawyes turned a dull, defeated gaze toward her. "Why should they? Becausssse you have?" Then he snorted and smacked his tail against the ground. "But you haven't, have you? You'll keep fighting until there'sss no one left sssstanding."

Arriving in time to hear that last bleak observation, Lieutenant Ghard stumbled to a stop and panted, "Would they give us an opportunity to surrender?"

"No."

"Then this is it. It's over." He swung his KC up, stared at it as if he'd never seen it before, and let it swing back against his side on its strap. "They'll show no mercy; we've been killing their wounded."

"They've been killing their own wounded, sir. A mercy death from us changes nothing." Torin found herself almost reluctantly pushed back into pragmatism by the lieutenant's reaction. A little hysteria would've felt good.

"But we won't survive another attack!"

"Begging your pardon, sir, but how the hell do you know?"

Looking confused, he opened and closed his mouth but was unable to find an answer.

"We survived the last attack. And all the attacks before that. We survived a crash landing, weeks of diplomatic posturing, and the incredible tedium of marching in straight lines. Why should we quit now?"

He stared up at her and, after a long moment when the only sound in the compound was the thrumming of the Silsviss, he sighed. "Marines don't quit, Staff Sergeant. We may retreat on occasion, but we don't quit. Was that the answer you were looking for?"

"It was the only answer, sir."

"You're a *serley* pain in the ass, you know that, Staff?"

"Just part of the job, sir."

The corners of his mouth curled up into a reluctant smile. He flipped down his mike. "Heads up, Marines, they're coming back for more. If you need me, Staff, I'll be in position on the perimeter."

"Sir."

"Do you really believe that you can sssurvive another attack?" Cri Sawyes asked quietly when Lieutenant Ghard was out of earshot.

"Not for a minute."

"But you convinced the lieutenant."

"I doubt it; he's a pilot, not a fool. Attitude, Cri Sawyes, is all we have left." She glared out at the surrounding hills, teeth clenched together so tightly her temples ached. Attitude wouldn't be enough. Then she frowned. But it might be the answer. "What if we decided to play it their way?"

"Their way?" Cri Sawyes repeated.

"I challenge their leader, one on one. Winner takes all." Her heart began to beat harder, faster.

"Do you think you could beat a young male in hisss prime? One whossse only thought isss to win?"

"Yes."

"Thessse young malesss are not like that pitiful creature you fought in the bar."

"That doesn't matter."

It was his turn to stare. "Perhapsss you could win, Ssstaff Sssergeant, but you are not the leader here. Lieutenant Ghard isss."

"Oh, yeah." It was a stupid idea anyway. She was a Confederation Marine, not some hormonally hopped-up teenager. Stupid, stupid idea. Her nails dug painful half moons into her palms. But it might have worked . . .

The thrumming changed suddenly, picking up a new rhythm and rising in pitch.

Torin swung her KC up and slid a finger behind the trigger guard. "You know, dying like this really annoys me."

"Dying like what, Ssstaff Sssergeant?"

"Dying for no good reason."

"It may not come to that."

Her first step back to the perimeter became her only step. Cri Sawyes had sounded almost as though he were in shock. "What?"

"That isss not a challenge. Look."

She looked out along the indicated path and saw three Silsviss coming down the hill, one carrying the bleached skull on the pole, one of the others carrying a wrapped object held out on both hands. "If it's not a challenge, what is it?"

"I think it'sss a sssurrender."

"I can take all three of them," Binti said softly, squinting through her sight and targeting each in turn.

"No." Standing behind the north wall, in line with the descending Silsviss, Lieutenant Ghard wiped his palms on his vest. "Let them come."

Barely turning her head, Binti glanced up at Torin, who nodded.

"They must know we can drop them," she murmured. "They've got balls, I'll give them that."

"Their ballsss are what got usss all into thisss messs," Cri Sawyes observed dryly.

Binti snickered. "Ain't that usually the case."

The three Silsviss split up to move through the boulders, then re-formed on the other side. Where they waited.

"Now what?" Ghard demanded.

"I suspect they want us to go out and meet them, sir."

"I don't trust them."

"Cri Sawyes and I will go if you want."

"Oh, yeah," he snorted. "Like it would be better to lose you than me. No chance of Lieutenant Jarret regaining consciousness in the next couple of seconds?"

If only. "No, sir."

"Pity." He shoved his feet into his boots and straight-armed himself over the grain bags. "Private Mashona."

"Sir?"

"If we fall, see that they fall right after us."

"Yes, sir!"

I notice you didn't check with me on that *order,* Torin thought, following the lieutenant.

"Keep your mike on, Staff. I want everyone to hear what's happening."

"Yes, sir."

Clouds of carrion flies rose up as they walked, settling almost immediately behind them. They had little enough time to feed before the sun baked all moisture out of the dead.

It took Torin a moment to realize that the faint hissing she could hear was Lieutenant Ghard sucking air through his teeth. The Krai sense of smell wasn't as acute as a di'Taykan's, but it beat out a Human's three to one. And his nose was about half a meter closer to the ground than hers was.

As the two Marines and Cri Sawyes stopped about nine meters from the three Silsviss, the thrumming from the hills softened until Torin could barely hear it. *Now what?*

Their backs against one of the boulders, the Silsviss stared, throat pouches inflating and deflating slightly with every breath.

Just kids, Torin realized. Next to Cri Sawyes, their physical immaturity was obvious. They were smaller, their faces were sharper, and they fidgeted constantly, tails jerking through agitated figure eights.

This is the first time they've gotten a good look at us. Probably the first time they've seen mammals our size. She remembered the first time she'd seen a Mictok and wondered at the lack of reaction. *Still, we've been killing each other for days now, I guess they feel like they know us.*

The Silsviss holding the skull stepped forward, shifted his grip, half turned, and smashed the bone against the rock.

Torin's finger was on the trigger by the time the shards settled. She couldn't hear the thrumming over the pounding of her heart.

No one moved.

Then the Silsviss holding the wrapped object stepped forward. Moving slowly, submissively, the third Silsviss unwrapped it.

Torin stared down at the bloody head and thought she'd never seen anything quite so pathetic.

"Their leader," Cri Sawyes murmured. "He dissshonored hisss pack by losssing—asss you hadn't killed him, they did. You're to mount hisss ssskull asss a sssymbol of your victory."

"We are?" Lieutenant Ghard sounded dubious about the honor. "Could you get that, Staff Sergeant Kerr?"

"Yes, sir."

It was surprisingly heavy.

*   *   *

The walk back to the perimeter seemed to take longer than the walk out. Carrying the rewrapped head in outstretched hands, Torin listened to Sergeant Chou's voice describe the Silsviss returning to the top of the hill and tried not to think about what she was stepping in. At the grain bags, she waited until both Lieutenant Ghard and Cri Sawyes were over. Then she set the head down and followed.

She could feel every eye in the compound on her as she picked it up again. *If that was a trick, now would be the time to attack.*

"They're back at the top of the hill," Sergeant Chou announced over the helmet relay. "Nothing seems to be happening."

The thrumming grew louder.

"Fuk!"

Torin had no idea which Marine had said it, but it seemed to sum up the situation.

Then the thrumming stopped.

"They're gone." Cri Sawyes blew out his throat pouch, then deflated it completely. "All of them."

Although he could no more see beyond the hills than any of them, there was something in his voice Torin had to believe. When there was no reaction, she remembered that only Sergeant Chou, Lieutenant Ghard, and herself had understood. She waited a moment, scanning the empty horizon, willing it to remain empty; then she translated Cri Sawyes' observation.

"They're gone. All of them."

The cheers and whistles were fifteen voices short, but they sounded good regardless.

"What are you going to do with the head?" Lieutenant Ghard demanded. When the noise in the compound suddenly stopped, he snatched off his helmet and scowled into it, muttering, "Forgot the *serley* thing was on."

Technically, the question should have been what was *he* going to do with the head, but since he seemed to be leaving it up to her . . . Torin grinned and, lifting the bloody package high into the air, raised her voice. Staff sergeants did not need microphones to make themselves heard. "I'm going to mount the skull as a symbol of our victory!"

This time, the cheers and whistles were loud enough that she could almost believe she didn't carry thirteen small metal cylinders in her vest. Conscious of Cri Sawyes' gaze, she lowered her arms and turned to face him.

"Will your Confederation allow you to hold sssuch a battle honor?" he asked.

"I'd like to see them try and stop me." The blood that had run down her wrists was beginning to itch as it dried.

Cri Sawyes' tongue flicked out. "Asss a matter of fact, Ssstaff Ssser-geant, ssso would I."

Torin slipped the head inside the doctor's largest specimen bag, sealed it, and activated the charge. In a matter of hours, there'd be nothing left of the soft tissue but a full molecular survey. *Time enough then to go looking for a stick to mount it on,* she reasoned, crossing to Lieutenant Jarret's stretcher. He was still stable and still unconscious, although Dr. Leor was working on an antidote to the antidote.

She squatted beside him and laid her hand over his. After a moment of watching his chest rise and fall, she sighed and stood. Nothing had oc-curred to her except half a dozen well-worn clichés.

One good thing about the kind of battle they'd just been through to-gether; it put that unfortunate night into the proper perspective. In compar-ison, it meant nothing at all. Which was exactly how it had to be.

In the next room, the Dornagain ambassador had somehow convinced the Mictok to emerge from their protective cocoon. Remaining seven limbs held tight to her body, Ambassador Krik'vir lay cradled in a nest of web-bing, her companions protectively grouped to either side and above her. As Torin approached, she swiveled an eyestalk around and broke off her con-versation with the Dornagain.

"Staff Sergeant Kerr, the Human who saved us; he has died?"

"Yes, Ambassador."

"We are sorry to hear that. We are sorry to hear of any death, but this one we feel responsible for."

"You're not. Sergeant Glicksohn chose to save you."

"Knowing that it put him at risk?"

"Yes, ma'am."

"We find it strange," the ambassador murmured, almost to herself, "how a species can be able to make such a sacrifice one moment and can kill another sentient being the next. This mix of caring and violence is most confusing—it must be a factor of bisymmetrical species." Then realizing whom she could count in her audience, she swiveled an eyestalk up toward the Dornagain. "We mean no offense."

He smiled. "We take none."

"Staff Sergeant Kerr, will you see to it that we receive the details of Sergeant Glicksohn's life? We will ensure that he is never forgotten and will live forever in Mictok memory."

"Every time I see one, this little voice inside my head keeps screaming, Get it off me! Get it off me!"

"You'll have the download as soon as possible," Torin assured her, thinking that Mike would appreciate the irony.

"We thank you for your assistance in this matter." Ambassador Krik'vir shifted position slightly, causing a ripple effect through her companions. "We understand the Silsviss have offered you the victory and retreated."

"Yes, ma'am."

"So it has ended. What happens now?"

Torin actually had her mouth open to answer when her implant chimed, letting her know she was back on-line.

"Staff!" Ressk hobbled in from the front room. "Lieutenant Ghard says the *Berganitan* is back! They're sending another VTA to evac!"

Feeling somehow separate from the nearly hysterical reaction of Marines and civilians alike, Torin found herself wondering why she wasn't more surprised by the Navy's sudden reappearance.

Med-op stripped the old sealant off Torin's arm and leg, pronounced the healing well under way, resealed only the leg wound, and released her. Scratching at the dry skin on her arm, she made her way through the crowded outpatient area to the quieter section reserved for those who'd need bed rest to recover.

"Hey, Staff! What's the word on the lieutenant?"

She stopped at the end of Hollice's bed. "He'll make a full recovery. They're bringing him up slowly, but he should be conscious by 1500."

"And Captain Daniels?"

"Tanked. But they're still running tests to determine the full extent of the damage."

"Maybe now Lieutenant Ghard'll stop acting like a hen with one chick."

"Maybe."

"You think they're getting it on?"

"I try not to think about the sex life of officers, thank you, Corporal. But since you ask, no. The lieutenant clearly worships the ground the captain flies over. If she should lose her mind and agree, he'd never be able to get it up." She nodded toward Hollice's heavily sealed shoulder. "I expect they'll be tanking you, too."

"Yeah. Full body immersion." He shuddered, dramatically. "I hate it. You come out with your fingers and toes all wrinkled, and while you're in there, it's like returning to the womb without the room service."

"The what?"

"Not important. Hey, Staff?" Eyes narrowed, Hollice lifted his head off the pillow, as though he had words for her ears alone. "Is it just me or is there one hell of a lot of medical personnel here? I mean, this is twice the size of what we usually get; they've added six med-op modules to the ship."

"It isn't just you," Torin told him shortly. No one had been able, or willing, to tell her why the remnants of a single platoon were getting so much grade-A attention. It wasn't that she was complaining, and it wasn't any more than her people deserved, but the whole thing added to the nebulous feeling she'd had since pickup that something wasn't exactly level.

Not, not just since pickup . . .

Circling the room, she spent a moment with everyone else, advising Ressk not to get any of the KC's cleaning solution on his bad leg. "That stuff'll dissolve the sealant, you know."

"I know." He showed her a missing patch about two centimeters square. "But it's the first chance I've had to strip it down, Staff. First time in days I haven't been actually using it. Although," he added, "if that chirpy Human medic says *'And how are we feeling?'* one more *serley* time . . ."

"You'll grin and bear it."

"Not my first choice," Ressk grumbled as she walked away.

Stepping outside the medical module, Torin noticed a lock that led out of the Marines' section of the ship. Not entirely certain why, she walked over to it and hit the release. Her implant chimed.

Access denied without proper clearances.

That was new. But somehow not unexpected.

Seemed like the brass didn't want word of their experience on Silsvah reaching unauthorized ears. Didn't want it discussed over a jar of beer in the Chief's and PO's mess. Interesting.

Rolling various bits of memory over to see the other side, she turned and made her way to the ladder leading down to the platoon's quarters. Those Marines who'd either come through miraculously unscathed or, like her, able to be patched and released, had cleaned their weapons, eaten a huge meal, and with only two exceptions, crawled into their bunks. Kleers was still eating, and Corporal Conn was deeply immersed in the vid from his wife and daughter he'd found waiting for him.

Torin took the report from Sergeant Chou, told her to get some sleep, and went into her own quarters, where she methodically wrote up the casualty reports, entered a recommendation that Corporal Adrian Hollice and Private First Class di'Stenjic Haysole receive the Medal of Honor, then sat and stared at her reflection on the desktop screen. When no answers were forthcoming from her other self, she called up the military news channel, half-expecting it to be blocked.

There were no reports of the *Berganitan* being in a battle, although the Others were moving quickly toward the sector. The Silsviss hadn't yet signed the treaty, and time was running out. The phrase *vitally important* was used seven times in a ten-minute report. It was vitally important the work on the defense grid begin immediately or it wouldn't be ready to activate in time. It was, therefore, vitally important the Silsviss sign the treaty. The remaining five occurrences were variations on the theme.

She keyed in the code for Ressk's slate and, when he responded, sent him an encoded text-only message.

At 1430 Twin's implant chimed.

General Morris would like to see you in his office at 1530.

So. General Morris was on board. Another nonsurprise.

She showered, changed into her service uniform, downloaded the reports into her slate, and paused at 1455, one hand raised to activate the door. If she was about to hear her suspicions confirmed, there were others who deserved to be there.

With the familiar weight of her combat vest resting on her shoulders, Torin made her way back to the med-op modules.

"The lieutenant is awake, Staff Sergeant. However, I don't feel that it's in his best interests to have visitors at this time."

"Sir, I am on my way to speak with General Morris about a . . ." The pause was deliberate and went on just long enough for the captain to begin frowning. ". . . situation where the lieutenant was in command. The general will want to know his condition."

"The general will find out Lieutenant Jarret's condition from me, Staff Sergeant."

"Yes, sir," Torin acknowledged. "But I also have casualty reports the lieutenant will need to see, and . . ."

"Let me speak plainly, Staff Sergeant. I have been given orders that no one is to talk to the lieutenant *before* the general debriefs him." The fuchsia gaze flickered around the room, alighting everywhere but on Torin. "That will be all, Staff Sergeant."

"Yes, sir." Wondering why the doctor should be feeling guilty about following what was, after all, a fairly common order, Torin made a quick visit to the general ward.

"Medical data now?" Ressk snorted. "Oh, come on, Staff, even you could hack into *those* files. But," he added quickly, as she caught his eye, "since I'm stuck in this bed with nothing to do, I'd be happy to do it for you. Can I ask why?"

"You've got all the pieces I have. Just put them together."

"Will I like what I find?"

"Probably not."

General Morris was not alone in his office module.

"Staff Sergeant Kerr, this is Cri Srah," he announced, nodding to the Silsviss standing by his desk after the barest of military formalities had been observed. "He represents the Silsvah World Council."

If the Silsvah had a functioning World Council, this was the first Torin had heard about it. As she understood it, their final destination had been intended to assist in the creation of such a body.

The Silsviss misunderstood her expression. "Cri Sssawyesss, whom I believe you know, isss of the sssame firssst egg."

Wishing she'd taken a moment to have the sibilants in her translation program repaired, Torin nodded.

General Morris cleared his throat, reestablishing himself as the center of attention. "In light of what your platoon went through, Staff Sergeant Kerr . . ." His gaze dropped down to her combat vest. Although his eyes narrowed slightly, he continued without mentioning her peculiar combination of uniforms. ". . . I thought you should know that the Silsviss have decided to join the Confederation."

He thought she should know? A general thought a staff sergeant should know? *Nice to be thought of, but that's not how it works.* Not usually anyway.

Cri Sawyes had said that the Silsviss governments would be impressed.

She looked from Cri Srah to General Morris and back again, and she remembered what Haysole had told her about the general after her first meeting with him. *I've heard the general's looking for a chance to be more than he is.* He had to have set things up so that he was certain the Silsviss would sign. But the only significant thing he'd actually done was to send the remnants of Sh'quo Company down to the planet.

"This was a test, wasn't it, sir?" The silence waited for her to continue. "The entire battle was a setup from the beginning. The Silsviss are a . . ." Cri Srah shifted position and Torin made a diplomatic edit. ". . . have a warrior culture and wanted to be certain that they weren't aligning themselves with the weak. That was the real reason why you sent a combat platoon on a ceremonial mission. The Silsviss decision to join was based on the way we performed when under attack."

"I'd be interested to know how you arrived at that theory, Staff Sergeant." The general leaned back in his chair, confirming her suspicions by not denying them.

"It was all just a little too convenient, sir." Although the muscles of her shoulders and back were rigid, training kept her growing anger from showing as she outlined all the little coincidences that could be piled into something that stank of a setup. Their Silsviss escort had gone back to base just before the missile shot them down, but the escort from their destination had never shown up. They'd been shot down not only over a wilderness preserve but over a swamp that would cushion the crash. The various small packs of Silsviss adolescents in the preserve had come together into what amounted to an army far, far too quickly. There had been a full platoon's worth of extra weapons on the VTA for no good reason.

A frown cracked the expressionless facade. "Was Lieutenant Jarret aware of the true nature of our mission, sir?"

"No. But his psychological profile was such that the odds were very high he'd not blow the armory. Or allow himself to be overruled by his NCOs." The general's tone was light, conversational, almost amused. "If you figured this out in the midst of that battle, I'm very impressed."

"No need to be, sir." And her inflection added, *because your opinion means less than nothing to me.* "Although I'd begun to doubt the string of coincidences early on . . ."

Where there're two viable theories, there could easily be a third or a fourth.

". . . my suspicions were fully aroused when the Silsviss in the reserve had no reaction to our appearance. The largest mammal on Silsvah is about the size of a Human infant and yet they showed no curiosity about us. They had to have seen, if not live mammals, some sort of representation previously." She remembered Cri Sawyes mentioning his fear of how an unscrupulous power could use the teenage males. General Morris had certainly proved his point. "My suspicions were strengthened when the *Berganitan* showed up so quickly after the battle was over. They solidified when I saw the medical facilities that had been added to the ship."

"The medical facilities?" For the first time the general looked surprised.

"Far too great a commitment of equipment and personnel for a single platoon, and the only possible reason for it could be guilt—at a very high level. So I did some checking." Technically, Ressk did the checking, but working on the military's need to know basis, that was something the general didn't need to know. "You ordered the *Berganitan* away from Silsviss and instructed the captain to lie." Which made General Morris not only responsible for the deaths of good people but for ensuring they died without knowing why. The first was something officers had to do every day, and the strength that took was one of the few things Torin respected them for as a group. The second was unforgivable.

The weight of Cri Srah's regard pulled her gaze from the general's face.

The Silsviss leaned forward, almost in anticipation. "Your general dis-sshonored your warriorsss by deliberately sssending them into an ambush."

No. Not almost in anticipation. Very definitely in anticipation.

Which was when Torin understood why she hadn't been allowed to see Lieutenant Jarret. According to his medical data, once the antidote had been neutralized, he'd made a nearly instantaneous recovery. He should be standing here, not her. He was the commanding officer.

But they needed her.

Because General Morris believed a mere second lieutenant wouldn't be able to do what needed to be done and she would.

What had they planned on doing to him had he not been injured? At least she knew why the doctor looked so guilty. Didn't they take oaths about that sort of thing?

Cri Srah was waiting for her reaction.

As Torin understood the Silsviss, it was unimportant that the general did not, could not, have made the original decision to sacrifice the platoon, that it had to have been made at the parliamentary level. For the Silsviss, it was enough that he had been responsible for giving the order to those actually doing the fighting and, as essential as the order may have been to keep the Others out of this sector, he had dishonored the platoon by doing so.

She had a skull in her quarters that defined the Silsviss' response to dishonor.

It was vitally important that the Silsviss sign the treaty.

This time, when Torin looked to the general, he met her eyes. What she saw there didn't surprise her. She'd begun to suspect that she was forever beyond surprise.

General Morris was prepared to die. He expected to die. She'd seen the same dark expression too many times over the years to mistake it now.

Whoever had decided that Lieutenant Jarret would be incapable of the necessary ending had been right. Could she end it? Yes. Would she?

She could see Cri Srah's tail beginning to lash back and forth, but all she could think of was an old joke.

Back before the Confederation combined their three newest members into one military organization, three officers, a Human, a di'Taykan, and a Krai, are standing in a shuttle bay, at the edge of a stasis field discussing the courage of their troops. To prove the courage of their race, the Krai officer calls over a Krai samal *and gives the order to jump through the stasis field. The* samal *snaps off a salute and leaps into space, decompressing messily.*

The di'Taykan sneers, and to prove the courage of the di'Taykan, calls over a di'Taykan fe'harr *and gives the same order. The* fe'harr *snaps off a salute and leaps into space, also decompressing messily.*

The Human raises a brow and calls over a Human private, giving the same order.

The private snaps off a salute and says, "Fuk you, sir."

"Now that," says the Human officer, turning to the others, "is courage."

Torin had no trouble following orders, but she really hated being manipulated.

General Morris' lip curled and she could hear him say, *Would you get on with it!* just as clearly as if he'd spoken out loud. He'd screwed his courage to the sticking point, and he clearly didn't know how much longer it would stick.

It was by no means a truism that insight into a species could be gained by wholesale slaughter, but Torin was willing to bet that, right at this particular point in time, no one in the Confederation knew the Silsviss as well as she did.

Her right foot caught Cri Srah solidly in the stomach. As he folded forward, gasping for breath, she dove onto his shoulders, slamming him down to the floor.

"Have you gone crazy?"

General Morris sounded a little shrill, but, preoccupied with maintaining her hold on a remarkably flexible lizard without being either brained by the tail or shredded by the claws, Torin ignored him.

Cri Srah got one arm around at an impossible angle and raked his claws across her back.

The combat vest took most of the damage. If she survived the fight, Torin figured there was more than enough room in med-op to take care of the rest.

"Staff Sergeant Kerr! Stop it immediately! That's an order, Staff Sergeant!"

The shouted, almost hysterical orders weren't a problem, but when the general grabbed her uninjured arm and tried to yank her away from Cri Srah's throat, she moved her leg just enough to release the tail on a narrow trajectory. She didn't see it hit, but the general grunted and staggered back, not so much releasing her arm as no longer being able to control his hand. *If he was ready to die,* Torin reasoned, struggling to trap the tail again before it broke bones, *he shouldn't complain about a slight concussion.*

She could feel Cri Srah struggling to inflate his throat pouch and she tightened her hold.

Fortunately, when he began to claw at her arm, fighting for air, he didn't have strength enough to do much more than shred skin.

"How dare you imply that we were dishonored," she shrieked, pain lending volume. "We were vastly outnumbered! We were under fire from our own weapons! And we fukking won!" If this worked, history could edit out the profanity. If not, it didn't much matter.

Gasping, Cri Srah clutched her arm and tried impotently to pull it away.

She eased up slightly—if he passed out, they'd have to do it all again. "You know the importance of this treaty! By sending us unknowing into battle, our general tells us that we're expected to win whatever the odds! That he believes us to be the best warriors of the Confederation!" Using her knee, with all her weight behind it, Torin threw the Silsviss away from her and then loomed over his prone body, dripping blood onto the floor. "You dishonor my general by suggesting he dishonors us! I demand that you yield!"

One hand clutching his bruised throat, Cri Srah began to yield.

Torin kicked him in the thigh. "Not to me! To my general!"

Cri Srah rose as the general staggered out from behind his desk, nose bleeding and no longer exactly straight. Still holding his throat, he bowed. "General Morris, I yield." Then turning to Torin, he bowed again, whistling his approval. "We insssisssted on the ambush and that you be so dramatically outnumbered. The packsss demanded accesss to at leassst a few of your weaponsss before they'd cooperate."

"You could have judged our skill from our history."

"Yesss," he admitted. "But it wasss more important we judge thossse usssing the ssskilllsss."

"Did Cri Sawyes know?"

"No. He doesss now." His tongue flicked out. "Hisss reaction wasss sssimilar to yoursss, although he actually killed the government member who informed him. He'll be promoted."

Good for him, Torin thought.

"Now, General . . ." As he turned, Cri Srah smacked his tail against the floor. "I believe I have a treaty to sign."

Torin decided to take that as her dismissal.

"So we were judged worthy, and they're going to sign."

"Yes, sir." This time, Torin hadn't asked to see the lieutenant. She'd used the code Ressk had given her to his room and walked right in. The doctor had taken his masker in order to keep him isolated, so she sucked air through her teeth and tried not to bleed on the bed.

"And the Others?"

"Not even in the neighborhood, sir."

Lieutenant Jarret's eyes were as dark as she'd ever seen them and his hair stood out like a lilac fringe around his head. "I don't like being used, Staff. And I don't like the Marines under my command being used to make a point."

And the politicians will note your protest, and it won't make a damned bit of difference.

He must have read the thought off her face; his hair suddenly flattened. "Was it worth it, Staff?"

Was it ever? Was it worth the loss of Haysole and Mike and all the dead Marines in all the different battles on all the different worlds? She had to believe that it was, or what was the point in continuing? She had to believe. "We needed the Silsviss to sign, sir."

"That doesn't answer my question, Staff."

"Best I can do, sir."

After a long moment, he nodded. "Go get yourself patched up, Staff Sergeant. I'd hate for you to bleed to death now that it's all over."

She looked down at the thick crimson stains that all but glued her left hand to her right arm and frowned. "Actually, sir, I'd hate to bleed to death at any point in the proceedings."

The doctor had just finished sealing her arm when General Morris walked into med-op. The two black eyes and the broken nose attracted the attention of everyone in the room, but he waved them all away.

"I need to speak with Staff Sergeant Kerr. Alone."

The room emptied. The general waited until both hatches had swung shut; then he walked over to stand by Torin's examining table. She sat up. She should have stood and come to attention, but she didn't much feel like it.

He didn't seem to notice. "I was supposed to die. I was never actually in combat, you know, but I *was* willing to die. My not very notable career had come to a full stop, but this, this would have ensured I was remembered. It would have given me a place in Confederation history."

"A noble sacrifice for the good of the many, sir?"

"Yes, exactly."

"And the Marines who died on Silsvah?"

He tried to frown, but the swelling had gotten too bad. "They were Marines, Staff Sergeant, and they died in battle like hundreds of Marines before them."

Torin weighed her options and decided it wasn't worth it. "Yes, sir."

The general visibly relaxed. "How did you know?"

"Sir?"

"How did you know I wasn't supposed to die? Why did you choose to attack Cri Srah?"

"The Silsviss have a pack mentality, sir. Each Silsviss knows where he fits into the, pack, and the strong fight to rise. They've just joined our pack, and they wanted to see how much they could push us around. If we'd fulfilled their expectations, they'd be running the Confederation by the end of the century."

His expression almost made the whole thing worthwhile. "They're not going to be an easy species to coexist with," he said after a long moment, trying to sound as though she didn't know he'd agreed to die for nothing.

"Yes, sir." Torin slid to the edge of the table and stood. "But that's not my problem."

"No," the general agreed, stepping back, "I don't suppose it is. Still," he added calculatingly, "it could be. If you wanted to apply for officer's training, I'd support your application." He chuckled encouragingly. "After what you did today, half of Parliament would support your application."

"Officer's training?" Torin lifted her combat vest off the chair where the medic had placed it.

"That's right."

"Thank you, sir, but no." One by one, she slid the cylinders out of her vest and indicated that the general should hold out his hands. "There's two very good reasons that I'd make a lousy officer." She dropped the thirteen Marines who'd paid for his place in history into his cupped palms. "First of all, I work for a living."

Stepping back, she gestured at his face. "You should have a doctor see to that, sir." The gesture snapped into a perfect salute that he was unable to return; there were too many cylinders for him to hold them with only one hand. Then she turned on her heel and walked toward the hatch.

"Staff Sergeant Kerr."

One hand on the hatch release, she paused.

"You said there were two reasons. What was the second?"

"The second reason, sir?"

"Yes."

"My parents were married."

Author's Note

Hands up everyone who recognized that battle.

Yes, it *was* loosely based on the battle of Rorke's Drift, one of the early battles of the Zulu War (January 22nd and 23rd, 1879). In this battle, a hundred and thirty-nine men and officers of the British Army, thirty-five of whom were sick or injured, held off what was later estimated to be a force of 4,000 Zulus. The movie *Zulu*, staring Michael Caine, was a fairly accurate dramatization of the battle, although none of the many historical records mention competitive singing.

For their efforts in saving the Rorke's Drift post, a total of eleven men were awarded with the Victoria Cross for conspicuous bravery, making this the highest number ever awarded for a single engagement in British military history.

Color-Sergeant F. Bourne, the senior NCO, was not among those eleven. He received instead a Distinguished Conduct Medal.

Why, although his bravery and courage under fire were unquestioned and he was instrumental in turning a number of the Zulu attacks, didn't Color-Sergeant Bourne receive the Victoria Cross?

Because he was only doing his job.

THE BETTER PART
OF VALOR

The worst of times brings out the best of people.

This is for the rescue workers who died going *up* the stairs.

ONE

"And the moral of the story: never call a two-star general a bastard to his face."

Stretching out his regenerated leg, Captain Rose leaned away from his desk and drummed his fingers against the inert plastic trim. "I'm a little surprised you didn't already know that."

"You and me both, sir." Staff Sergeant Torin Kerr stared down at the general's orders on her slate. "You and me both."

"Still, I suppose you could consider it a compliment that General Morris wants you on this reconnaissance mission."

"Yes, sir, but somehow when I think of 'an unidentified alien vessel drifting dead in space,' the word that tends to stick is *dead*. And I've barely recovered from the last time the general took a personal interest." Before looking up, she cleared her screen with more emphasis than was strictly necessary. "Considering how the *diplomatic* part of the last mission got redefined as getting our asses kicked, I just hope I can survive what he considers recon."

The captain smiled, pale skin creasing at the corners of both eyes. "You kicked some ass yourself, Staff."

"Yes, sir, I did. Although I admit I had help from a platoon of Marines and Lieutenant Jarret. Both of which," she added, "I wouldn't mind having with me this time."

"Should I authorize an armored unit as well?"

"I wish you could, sir." Hooking her slate onto her belt, Torin drew in a deep breath and accepted the inevitable. She'd made herself memorable to the top brass and would have to live with the consequences—although the little information she had made *survive* the consequences seem more accurate. "He wants me on the next Coreward shuttle. There'll be transportation arranged once I reach MidSector, but he doesn't actually say where I'm going."

"He's a general, Staff. He doesn't have to say. Ours is not to question why."

"Yes, sir. The next shuttle leaves in just under two hours. Unless the general's arranged for me to skip decontamination, I'll have to hurry."

The captain nodded, agreement and dismissal combined. "See that you hurry back, Staff Sergeant. I've got a new First, and he's got a shitload of new recruits he could use your help with. This is a lousy time for you to go gallivanting around the galaxy."

"I'll be sure to mention that to the general, sir."

"I'm hoping you're smarter than that, Staff."

"Yes, sir."

"Staff?"

She paused, just outside the door's proximity sensor.

"General Morris' parentage aside, it's entirely possible he recommended you for this mission because you're the best person for the job."

"General Morris' parentage aside, sir, I never doubted that."

And it started out as such a good day, Torin growled silently as she walked to the nearest vertical. Admin had finally cleared the files sending Binti Mashona to sniper school, Corporal Hollice was getting a well-deserved promotion to sergeant, a number of the new recruits actually seemed to have arrived with half their brains functioning, and, thanks to the situation on Silsviss, Sh'quo Company was so far down on the rotation that the Others would have to overrun the entire sector before they were sent back out. *I should have known something would happen to fuk it up.*

Report to shuttle bay twelve for decontamination in forty-six minutes.

Years of practice kept her from visibly reacting to her implant's sudden announcement. It hadn't taken Captain Rose long to post her orders to the station system.

A quick glance up and down the vertical showed a cluster of people descending but a clear fall below them all the way to C deck. With every intention of using General Morris' name not only in vain but in any way possible should the necessity arise, Torin dove headfirst down the shaft. The turn in mid-fall slowed her slightly, but she was still moving fast enough to set off the safety protocols when she grabbed the strap and swung out onto the deck.

Please exercise more caution in the verticals. This is a level one warning.

Torin tongued in an acknowledgment without breaking stride. She could live with a level one. It took three in a Tenday before the station reported them and she'd be gone long enough that this particular warning would be wiped by the time she returned.

Unhooking her slate, she began locking down her desk as she walked—sealing her personal folders and encrypting the rest to Sergeant Chou's access codes. Anne Chou would be senior noncom for the platoon while she was gone and would at least give Lieutenant Jarret someone he'd already . . .

"Is it true, Staff?"

She looked down at the Krai private who'd suddenly appeared beside her. Given their difference in height, all she could see was the mottled top of his hairless head, which gave no clue at all to the meaning of his question. "Is what true, Ressk?"

"That instead of a promotion and comfy tour at Ventris Station teaching *diritics* how to survive, General Morris has detoured you to a Recon mission."

"I'm impressed; those orders have been on system for less than ten minutes."

Ressk lengthened his stride to keep up, bare feet slapping against the floor. "I guess once you pull somebody's brass out of the fire they expect you to keep doing it."

"That is the way the universe tends to function." At the lock leading to SRQ, she paused. "You got a reason to be on this level, Ressk?"

"Sergeant Aman wants to see me, Staff. And when I saw you, I thought I'd say . . ."

The pause lengthened.

"Private?"

His nose ridges flushed. "Could you talk to the general, Staff? Exploring an unidentified alien vessel floating dead in space—that's always been my dream!"

Torin blinked. "You're kidding?"

"No, Staff, I'm not. You know there isn't a sys-op I can't get into. I could be useful on this kind of a mission."

"I don't doubt that, but I'm sure there'll be specialists . . ."

"I'm faster. If it's a matter of life and death, you're not going to want some specialist . . ." The word emerged somewhere between an insult and profanity. ". . . taking their time, doing everything by the book."

"Ressk . . ."

"I haven't even read the book!"

Report to shuttle bay twelve for decontamination in thirty minutes.

"If I can, I'll talk to Captain Rose before I go."

"Thanks, Staff. You're a real *chirtric*."

It wasn't every day she was called a delicacy, Torin reflected as she continued toward her quarters, but even if she managed to talk to Captain Rose he'd have no time to speak to the general before the shuttle left the station.

The captain's Admin clerk agreed to pass the message along. "You do know that captains aren't in the habit of paging two-star generals and suggesting they should make use of personnel with what amounts to illegal computing skills, don't you, Staff?"

"Not my problem." Torin thumbed her kit bag closed. "I told him I'd try to talk to Captain Rose. The captain was unavailable, I spoke to you. My conscience is clear." Her slate made a noise somewhere between a snort and a snicker. "You have something to add, Corporal?"

"Just my best wishes for a successful mission and a safe return, Staff Sergeant."

"Thank you. Kerr out."

The double tone closing the connection sounded as she glanced one last time around the room, noted both living and sleeping areas would pass at least a cursory inspection, and crossed to the door. The empty sockets of the Silsviss skull on the shelf over her entertainment unit seemed to follow her every move. A couple of the more politically correct Battalion NCOs had objected to having the skull of a sentient species mounted in the Senior Ranks' Mess, so rather than stuff it into a recycler, she'd brought it home.

"Don't look so concerned," she told it. "I'll be back."

Report to shuttle bay twelve for decontamination in twenty minutes.

In spite of a crowd on the lower beltway, she made it with seven minutes to spare and could walk across the lounge to the shuttle bay without challenging the belief, widely held by the lower ranks, that sergeants and above controlled time and therefore never had to hurry.

"Staff Sergeant Kerr!"

Torin checked her watch, then turned. His lilac eyes a couple of shades darker than his hair, Second Lieutenant di'Ka Jarret, her platoon commander, rushed around the end of an ugly gray plastic bench and hurried toward her. As incapable of looking awkward as any of his species, he didn't look happy. "Sir?"

"You were just going to leave?" He didn't sound happy either.

"The general's orders were specific, sir. I had forty-six minutes to get to decon and you were at Battalion. Captain Rose sent you a copy of the orders."

"I received the captain's transfer, Staff Sergeant," the di'Taykan informed her, drawing himself up to his full height. Torin stared at the pheromone masker prominently displayed at his throat and just barely resisted the urge to crank it up a notch. A small indiscretion some months prior had left her more susceptible to the lieutenant's chemical invitation than she should have been. One night he's a pretty young di'Taykan—one of the most enthusiastically undiscriminating species in the galaxy—and next morning he's her new second lieutenant. There were times Torin thought the universe had a piss poor sense of humor.

Had her time been her own, she could—and would—have waited indefinitely for him to continue. His last declaration had exhibited an indignation junior officers needed to be trained out of—the greater portion of the universe, not to mention the Marine Corps, ticked along just fine without them ever being consulted.

However, as she was currently on General Morris' clock . . .

"I sent a message as well, sir. Wrote it on the beltway. Station should have downloaded it to your slate by now."

She half expected him to check his inbox. When he didn't, she allowed herself a small smile. "I appreciate the chance to say good-bye, sir. You must have really hauled ass to make it all the way down from Battalion in time."

"Well, I . . ."

"Staff Sergeant Torin Kerr, report to decontamination at shuttle bay twelve."

"Tell the whole station," Torin muttered, as her name, rank, and destination bounced off the dull green metal walls of the lounge.

"I think they did." The lieutenant's hair and ears both had clamped tight to his skull. "You'll, uh . . ." When Torin lifted an eyebrow in his general direction, a skill that had been well worth the price of the program, he finished in a rush. ". . . you'll be coming back?"

"I always plan on coming back, sir." She took a step closer to the decontamination lock. "Every time I go out."

"I know. I mean . . ."

"I know what you mean, sir." One of the most important functions staff sergeants performed was the supporting of brand-new second lieutenants while they learned how to handle themselves in front of actual—as opposed to theoretical—Marines. The realization that this relationship wasn't necessarily permanent, that said support could be pulled out from under them at the whim of those higher up the chain of command, always came as a bit of a shock to the young officers. "During the time I'm temporarily detached from the company, you can have complete faith in Sergeant Chou's ability to handle the platoon."

"I do." He opened his mouth to continue, then closed it again. After a moment's thought, he squared his shoulders, held out his hand, and said only, "Good luck, Staff."

"Thank you, sir." When, like any di'Taykan, he tried to extend the physical contact, she pulled her hand free and moved into the decontamination lock's proximate zone.

"Staff?"

A half-turn as she stepped over the lip and into the outer chamber. The lieutenant was smiling, his eyes as light as she'd ever seen them.

"Is it true you called General Morris a bastard?"

Torin stowed her bag in the enclosure over her seat and took a look around the military compartment. Forward, a pair of officers sat on opposite sides of the aisle. The Human artillery captain had already slid his slate into the shuttle's system and, from the corner of the screen Torin could see, had accessed the hospitality file—although it wouldn't dispense his drink until they were in Susumi space. Her seat on full recline, it appeared that the di'Taykan major had gone to sleep. Torin wondered if she'd already made the captain an offer and was resting up. And if that's why the captain was drinking.

In the aft end of the compartment, half a dozen privates and a corporal were settling in. According to their travel docs—available to sergeants and above from the shuttle's manifest—the corporal from Crayzk Company's engineering platoon was heading Coreward on course and the six privates were on their way back to Ventris Station to be mustered out.

She had the NCO compartment to herself.

As the shuttle pulled away from the station, the walls separating the sections opaqued. Although the center aisle remained open along the length of the compartment, it was easy enough to maintain the illusion of privacy between the ranks—an illusion Torin was all in favor of. She as little wanted to be responsible *to* the officers as she wanted to be responsible *for* the junior ranks.

Half an hour later, the shuttle folded into Susumi space. Since little changed from trip to trip, they'd be spending only eight to fourteen hours inside, emerging four light-years away at MidSector at the same time they left. Torin pulled a pouch of beer from her alcohol allotment and settled back to watch the last three episodes of *StarCops*, one of the few Human-produced vids she hated to miss.

But neither Detective Berton's attempt to find the smugglers bringing the highly addictive di'Taykan *vritran* into Human space nor Detective Canter's search to find the murderer of a Krai diplomat could hold her attention. She might as well have been watching H'san opera. When the third episode featured a government official throwing his weight around, she thumbed it off and glared at her reflection on the screen.

If General Morris wanted a recon team to investigate an unknown alien spacecraft, the Corps had plenty of teams he could choose from. Torin didn't know whether he wanted her to replace the staff sergeant from an established unit or to be a part of a team he'd built from scratch, but either way she didn't much care for the idea. It was inefficient. And bordered on stupid.

She could do the job. She understood that as a member of the Corps, she was expected to pick up and move on as the Corps saw fit. And she took full responsibility for the actions that had lodged her in the memory of a two-star general.

But stupidity at high levels really pissed her off.

Because stupidity at high levels was the sort of thing that got people killed.

A Krai territorial cry sounded from the rear compartment, closely followed by a stream of happy Human profanity. Jerked out of her mood, Torin was startled to see she'd been brooding for almost an hour.

The profanity got a little less happy.

Not her problem.

She heard the corporal's voice rise and fall and then the unmistakable sequence of flesh to flesh to floor.

Now it was her problem.

Standing, she shrugged into her tunic and started down the aisle. *No point in letting a bad mood go to waste . . .*

The corporal was flat on his back. One of the Krai privates—probably the female given relative sizes—sat on his chest, holding his arms down with her feet. He wasn't struggling, so Torin assumed he'd taken some damage hitting the floor. The smaller Krai had a pouch of beer in the foot Torin could see and was banging both fists against the seat in front of him, nose ridges so dark they were almost purple. The di'Taykan were nowhere to be seen—all three of them had probably crammed themselves into the tiny communal chamber the moment the shuttle had entered Susumi space—which left, of the original six privates, only a Human who seemed to find the whole thing very funny.

He spotted Torin first. By the time she'd covered half the distance, his eyes had widened as the chevrons on her sleeves penetrated past the beer. By the time she'd covered the other half of the distance, he'd stopped laughing and had managed to gasp out something that could have been a warning.

Too late.

Transferring forward momentum, Torin wrapped her fist in the female Krai's uniform, lifted her off the corporal, and threw her back into a seat.

The sudden silence was deafening.

She reached down and helped the corporal to his feet.

Someone cleared his or her throat. "Staff, we . . ."

Her lip curled. "Shut up."

The silence continued.

"If I hear one word from any of you while Corporal Barteau . . ."

No one seemed at all surprised she knew the corporal's name.

". . . is telling me what the hell is going on back here, I will override your seat controls and you will spend the rest of the trip strapped in." Eyes narrowed, she swept the silent trio with a flat, unfriendly stare. "Do I make myself clear?"

"Yes, Staff Sergeant."

"Good. Corporal."

They walked back to the wall dividing the lower ranks from the NCOs.

Torin pitched her voice for the corporal's ears alone. "You all right?"

"Just a little winded, Staff. I didn't expect her to jump me. They'd been drinking, and I think she was showing off for Private Karsk. I was studying." He nodded toward the schematics spread out over the last two seats. "I asked them to keep it down. Next thing I knew . . ."

An unidentifiable sound from the back of the compartment pulled Torin's head around. All three privates, sitting exactly where she'd left them, froze, wide-eyed like they'd been caught in a searchlight. She held them there for a moment—half hoping they were drunk enough to cause more trouble—then turned slowly back to Corporal Barteau.

He shrugged. "They're on their way home, Staff."

"I know."

"Privates Karsk and Visilli were at Beconreaks and Private Chrac, she was aircrew, Black Star Evac. They flew at . . ."

"I know, Corporal, I was there. Your point?"

"I don't think they deserve to be put on report. Not for celebrating the fact that they're going home."

"I agree."

He looked surprised. "You do?"

Torin exhaled slowly and forced the muscles in her jaw to relax. From the corporal's reaction, she suspected she'd looked like she was chewing glass. "Yes. I do. I'll have a word with them and, *if* we get to MidSector without any more trouble, that'll be the end of it."

"You've already scared the piss out of them," the corporal acknowledged.

"Yeah, well, I'd say that was my intent except the shuttle service would make me pay for having the seats cleaned."

Feeling considerably more clearheaded, Torin accessed the hospitality screen and a moment later pulled the tab on a pouch of beer.

Ours is not to question why.

I'll do, she said silently, with a sarcastic toast to absent brass, *but I'll be damned if I'll die.*

The detoxicant Torin had taken when they folded out of Susumi space had done its job by the time the shuttle docked at MidSector. Although the

military and civilian passengers had been kept separate during the trip, exit
ramps emerged into the same crowded Arrivals' Lounge.

There were a lot fewer uniforms in the crowd than Torin was used to.

"Excuse me."

Torin had a choice. She could stop, or she could walk right over the
di'Taykan standing in front of her. She stopped. But it was a close decision.

The di'Taykan had lime green hair and eyes, the former spread out from
her head in a six-inch aureole, the latter so pale Torin wondered how she
could see since none of the light receptors seemed to be open. Her matching clothing was unusually subdued—in spite of the color—and the combined effect was one of studied innocence.

Torin didn't believe it for a moment. Anyone studying that hard had to
be working against type.

"One of my *thytrins* was supposed to be on that shuttle, Sergeant
di'Perit Dymone. I didn't see him get off so I was wondering if he, well,
missed his flight again." Her hair flattened a little in embarrassment. "He
missed the last flight he was supposed to be on."

Looking politely disinterested, Torin waited.

"I thought maybe, if he didn't miss this flight, he might still be on
board."

"No."

"Are you sure . . ." She dipped her head and her eyes went a shade
darker as she studied Torin's collar tabs. ". . . Staff Sergeant?"

"I'm sure."

"But . . ."

"I was the only NCO of senior rank on board. Your *thytrin* missed another flight."

"Oh." Her hair flattened farther as she stepped out of the way, one long-
fingered hand fiddling with her masker. "I'm sorry to bother you then."

Torin swung her bag back onto her shoulder. "No problem."

"Um, Staff Sergeant, would you like to . . ."

"No. Thank you." When a di'Taykan began a question with *would you
like to*, there was only ever one ending. And that was probably why the
girl's *thytrin* kept missing his flight.

By the time Torin reached the exit, she'd been delayed long enough for
the lines to have gone down at the security scanners. Wondering why the
Niln next to her was bothering to argue with the station sys-op—top of the
pointless activity list—she slid her slate into the wall and faced the screen.

In the instant before the scan snapped her pupils to full dilation, she saw a flash of reflected lime green. The di'Taykan? Scan completed, she turned.

On the other side of the lounge, now nearly empty of both the shuttle's passengers and those who'd come to meet them, the di'Taykan had crouched down to speak to a Katrien. Although conscious of being watched, they glanced up and smiled. For an omnivore, the Katrien had rather a lot of sharp-looking teeth in its narrow muzzle and although Torin couldn't see much of its face around an expensive-looking pair of dark glasses, something about its expression made her fairly certain she'd seen that particular Katrien before. She just couldn't put her finger on where.

You have been cleared to enter the station. Proceed immediately to docking bay SD-31. Your pilot has been informed of your arrival.

Torin tongued in an acknowledgment and stepped through the hatch, the Katrien's identity no longer relevant.

Facing the lounge exit was a large screen with a three-dimensional map of the station. As Torin stepped closer, a red light flashed over her corresponding place on the map and a long red arrow led to the legend: *"You are here."* Torin would have bet her pension that the graffiti scrawled next to it in a script she didn't recognize said, *"And your luggage is in Antares,"* or a variation thereof.

Shuttle departures were down one level. Unfortunately, SD-31 was not a shuttle bay. All MidSector and OutSector stations had a squadron of two-person fighters for station defense plus a few extra bays in case of fighters arriving without their ships. As no MidSector station had ever been attacked, their squadrons were on short rotation. There were few things more disruptive to a sentient society than a squadron of bored vacuum jockeys.

"Docking bay SD-31."

The map rearranged itself. A second red light appeared. A green line joined them.

Okay. That was going to take some time.

"Shortest route. Species neutral."

Not significantly shorter.

The MidSector stations had been in place longer than Humans had been part of the Confederation and over time they'd grown almost organically.

"Like a tumor," Torin muttered, heading for the nearest transit node. OutSector stations had been designed for the military after the start of the war and were a lot more efficient. She hoped that when informed of her arrival her pilot had kept right on with whatever it was a vj did when he wasn't flying or fighting with Marine pilots because they wouldn't be leaving any time soon.

At the node, she wasn't really surprised to find a link had just left. Given the way her day had been going, she wouldn't have been surprised to have found the links shut down for unscheduled maintenance and that she was supposed to cover roughly eight kilometers of station on foot.

Ours is not to question why.

A trite saying rapidly on its way to becoming a mantra.

By the time the next link arrived, the platform had become crowded. A trio of di'Taykan officers at the far end—pink, teal, and lavender hair—provided a visual aid for anyone who wondered why the Corps had switched to black uniforms, and about forty civilians filled the space in between, including four representatives of a species Torin couldn't identify.

There were also a number of Katrien. Hard to count because they were shorter than many of the other species but easy to spot since every single one of them appeared to be talking—sometimes to other Katrien, who were also talking. MidSector was close to their home system, which explained the numbers. Torin watched only the occasional broadcast coming out of the Core but she seemed to remember a Katrien news program announcing that their Trading Cartel had taken over a significant number of both X- and Y-axis routes.

When the link finally arrived, Torin took a center seat, plugged her slate into a data console, and ran "alien ship dead in space," then "ship of unknown origins," paying a little extra for a secure search. Nothing. *Great, the one time I could use a little help from the media, General Morris managed to keep the lid on.*

Impressive if only because the Marines had arrived in more than one contested system to find the media there first.

At her final node, Torin had her link to herself and at the end of the line stepped out onto an empty platform. Four Katrien bounced out of the link behind her and one out of the link behind that. Although she hadn't paid much attention to fur patterns, the dark glasses on the single Katrien, now hurrying to join the others, seemed familiar.

I'm in friendly territory, Torin reminded herself. *No reason to assume I'm being followed. Two different people could easily be wearing the same expensive eyewear.*

But she crossed the platform toward them anyway—paranoia and survival instinct were two sides of the same coin when the job description involved being targeted by projectile weapons. The single Katrien cut off a high-pitched and incomprehensible flow of sound as she reached the group, and all five turned toward her.

She scowled down at the source of her disquiet. "Do I know you?"

A heavyset individual—Torin didn't know enough about the Katrien to assume gender—spread hands that looked like black latex gloves extending from the sleeves of a fur coat, and replied in a friendly sounding torrent of its own language.

Translation not available.

"Do any of you speak Federate?"

A second torrent, even friendlier sounding than the first.

Translation not available.

All five were now smiling toothily, the Katrien who might or might not have been following her a little toothier than the rest. Torin knew better than to make cross-species generalizations, but it looked smug. If they were living on station, they spoke Federate; no question they were being deliberate pains in the ass. Maybe they disliked the military on principle. Many of the Elder Races were pacifists—to the point of extinction when the Others showed up, which was, after all, why the Humans, di'Taykan, and Krai had been invited in.

Maybe the Katrien *was* the same Katrien she'd seen in the lounge. Maybe it told the others to play dumb for the soldier. Fuk it. It was a free station. She was not going to get involved in the game.

But this time, she noted the fur pattern. If she saw this particular smugly smiling Katrien again, she'd know it.

Her answering smile was less toothy but more sarcastic: "Thank you for your time."

They shouted something after her as she left the platform. Torin tongued off her implant before it could tell her once again that a translation was unavailable. Some things didn't need to be translated.

There was a vacuum jockey leaning against the orange metal bulkhead outside SD-31. Torin wondered how the Navy flier could look so boneless and still remain upright. He straightened as she approached.

"Staff Sergeant Kerr?"

"Yes, sir."

"Lieutenant Commander Sibley. I'm your ride." He palmed the lock and stood aside as the hatch opened.

Torin peered into the tiny suiting chamber and looked back at the pilot in time to see him slide a H'san stim into his chest pocket. Humans chewed the sticks as a mild stimulant. They were nonaddicting and completely harmless although they had a tendency to stain the user's teeth and, in extensive use, turn subcutaneous fat bright orange. Although the sticks were frowned on, they weren't actually illegal, and Navy pilots, operating in three dimensions at high speeds, often chewed to give themselves an edge. Navy flight commanders, who preferred their pilots alive, usually looked the other way.

Lieutenant Commander Sibley followed her gaze and grinned. "I know, Staff, it's a filthy habit. And I'm not trying to quit."

"Not my business, sir."

"True enough." He stepped into the chamber. Torin followed. "We've got a one-size-fits-most flight suit for you. I take it your suit certifications are up to date?"

"Yes, sir. If either branch of the military uses it, I'm certified to wear it."

The suits were designed to fit loosely everywhere but the collar ring and the faceplate so one size fit well enough. Exposure to vacuum caused a chemical reaction which stiffened the suit and filled the spaces between it and flesh with an insulating foam capable of maintaining a constant temperature of 15°C for thirty minutes. Since the suits came with only twenty minutes of independent air, pilots who found themselves free of their fighter's life-support pod didn't have to worry about freezing to death.

Among themselves, Torin knew the vacuum jockeys referred to the suits as buoys—markers to make it easier for the Navy to find the bodies.

Theoretically, pilots weren't supposed to come out of their pods even with their fighters shot to hell all around them. In Torin's experience, theory didn't stand a chance up against reality. Theoretically, species achieved interstellar space travel after they'd put war behind them, but apparently no one had told the Others.

They checked each other's seals and packs, then Lieutenant Commander Sibley opened the outer door. SD-31 held, as expected, a two-person Jade although for the moment all Torin could see of it was the access to the pod.

"Ever ridden in one these jewels, Staff Sergeant?"

Torin's stomach flipped as she stepped out into the docking bay and the gravity suddenly lessened. "No, sir."

His hazel eyes held a gleam of anticipation as he showed her where and how to stow her bag, then he waved at the tiny rear section. "We're point five gees in here, Staff, so just step in, feet about this far apart . . ." He held out white-gloved hands. ". . . and settle into place. Your pack fits into the back of the seat and, if you do it right, all hookups are made automatically."

And if I do it wrong? Torin wondered as her feet hit the deck and she sat down on a disconcertingly yielding surface. Apparently, she'd have to find out another time as straps slid down around her shoulders and disappeared into the seat between her legs. *Great. We can fold space, but we can't improve on the seat belt my father uses on his tractor.* The screens to either side of her remained dark, but on the curved screen in front, half a dozen green telltales lit up.

"You're in." The pilot leaned up out of her section and dropped into his own, considerably faster than she'd done it. "Probably best if you keep your hands in your lap, Staff Sergeant. None of your controls are live, but you're in my gunner's seat and I'd just as soon we didn't shoot off bits of the station. Navy frowns at that."

Every time it happens, Torin snorted, but all she said aloud was, "Hands are in my lap, sir."

Almost before he was strapped in, the pod sealed. An instant after that, they dropped out into space.

Zero gravity flipped her stomach again. Torin swallowed hard as acceleration pressed her first against the straps and then down into the seat. Lieutenant Commander Sibley had cleared launch on his implant, probably so he could hit space without giving her warning. Two diagonal moves later, they were upside down relative to the station.

"Be about an hour and a half before we reach the *Berganitan*. I hope you're not claustrophobic."

Well, sir, if I was, I'd have probably found out years ago crammed into the troop compartment of a sled with a couple of dozen muddy Marines while the enemy tried to blow us the hell up. At least you've got windows.

But all she said aloud was, "Not that I know of, sir."

She spared a moment wondering if there was any significance in General Morris' apparent fondness for the *Berganitan*. Maybe it was the only ship the Admiralty would let him play with.

The Jade suddenly dropped away from the station. About thirty meters out, it flipped over.

Shouldn't have told him I'd never been in a Jade before. She'd probably thought a lieutenant commander was a little old to play "let's see if we can get the Marine to puke." More fool her. All vjs were crazy, from raw ensigns right up to Wing Admiral di'Si Trin herself—something she should have remembered. *Well, counting the ten hours and forty-seven minutes in Susumi space, it has been a long day.*

Lieutenant Commander Sibley added a few final flourishes as he brought the Jade up to cruising speed. "If you have to hurl, Staff Sergeant, bite the black tab at the base of your faceplate. It'll open a pouch."

No answer. Not even the sound of a lost lunch.

"Staff?"

Her telltales were green. She was conscious. Heart pumping at sixty/ sixty. Respiration slow and steady.

Then it dawned on him. While he'd been flying a pattern designed to test the limits of Human physiology, his passenger had gone to sleep.

TWO

"Staff Sergeant Kerr?"

"Yes, sir." The lieutenant waiting outside the fighter bay had hair and eyes the palest blue Torin'd ever seen on a di'Taykan. His Glass Cs had been perfectly creased, his boots and brass magnificently shined, even his masker gleamed.

He seemed momentarily disappointed that her spit and polish matched his.

"I'm Lieutenant Stedrin, General Morris' aide. The general wants to see you right away."

She'd been traveling for the last fifteen hours. What *she* wanted was a shower—although perhaps wanted wasn't the most accurate word.

Stedrin's eyes darkened, as though he were trying to see her expression in more detail. Then he stepped back and gestured to the right. "The Corps' attachment is this way."

They walked in silence, watched covertly by the *Berganitan*'s crew. Torin and a warrant exchanged nods as she passed his work party, but the lieutenant might as well have been moving through an empty ship. She wondered if he'd have shortened his stride had she not been tall enough to keep up and decided, after casting a quick glance at the rigid muscles of his jaw, he probably wouldn't. *Must make him real popular with the Krai. Why the hell didn't he just message my implant?*

"The general thinks highly of you." Stedrin made the sudden announcement in a tone that suggested the general was alone in that regard. "He says that without you, it's doubtful we'd have gained the Silsviss as allies." The pause was too short for a reply. Too long to have been anything but deliberate emphasis. "I think you've taken as much advantage of that as there is to be taken. Do you understand me, Staff Sergeant Kerr?"

"Yes, sir." And that answered the message versus personal touch question. He'd come all the way down to the fighter bay to warn her to play nice or she'd have him to deal with. The overachieving, armament-up-the-butt attitude was unusual for a di'Taykan. Willing to lay odds that he had a minimum of eight letters in the unmentioned half of his name—which would put his family low in the Taykan caste system—she kept her face expressionless under the weight of his regard.

"I get the impression you're not taking this seriously, Staff Sergeant."

Stepping forward, she checked that the lock lights were green and opened the hatch separating the Marine attachment from the *Berganitan* proper. "Sorry, sir."

"For what?" he demanded, walking over the seals with the self-conscious care of one who'd spent very little time in space.

"For your mistaken impression, Lieutenant." She dogged the hatch closed and turned to meet his eyes. "I take everything I do seriously. It's how I keep my people alive." After a moment, she let him look away.

Hair clamped tight to his skull, the lieutenant took a step back, opened his mouth, then snapped it closed again. Torin gave him credit for recognizing he was in a battle he couldn't win and waited patiently while he brought his emotions under control. The general's compartment was barely three meters down the passage, and the last thing he'd want was to have General Morris inquiring about his temper.

Or wondering where the hell he'd been.

Seconds before Torin was about to point that out, the di'Taykan turned on one heel and marched down the passageway, graceful in spite of a rigidity of spine that promised they weren't through.

"You're looking better than the last time I saw you, Staff Sergeant."

"Thank you, sir." So was he. Last time she'd seen the general, he'd had two black eyes, a broken nose, and a poleaxed expression—all of which she'd been essentially responsible for.

Given his current expression, he was thinking pretty much the same thing. "Yes, well, we've a new situation here, so let's put the past behind us, shall we?"

"Yes, sir."

It was more neutral noise than agreement, but General Morris took the words at face value, smiling and nodding—both of which put Torin on edge. Damn, she hated smiling generals.

"You're probably wondering why I had Lieutenant Stedrin bring you to me."

She was, but she wasn't expecting an explanation. The pause went on long enough so Torin began to think the general himself was also wondering. She was about ready to throw in another *Yes, sir*, to prod him forward, when he squared beefy shoulders and said, "You'll be Senior NCO for this mission and, as you were my personal choice, I felt I should be the one to introduce you to the officer commanding." He touched the edge of his comm unit. "Lieutenant."

"Sir." Stedrin's voice snapped out of the desk so crisply Torin knew he'd been hovering over it, waiting for the call.

"Have the captain report to my office immediately."

"Yes, sir."

Generals did not make introductions for staff sergeants.

Staff sergeants did not ask generals what the hell they were up to.

Unfortunately.

General Morris sat back in his chair and steepled his fingers, looking over their blunt ends at Torin. "How much do you follow politics, Staff Sergeant?"

"I don't, sir."

"You just do your job?"

Best to ignore two-star sarcasm.

"Yes, sir."

He nodded and continued. "As you're well aware, politics are a part of my job. The balance of power in Parliament is very tenuous right now. Many of the old races feel the Confederation isn't making enough effort to deal with the Others diplomatically—in spite of the fact that diplomacy so far has resulted in nothing but dead diplomats. There's a very real possibility that the arguments between the various factions could result in the same crippling of the government as happened back in '89 when, with defense spending stalled, the Others took over most of SD38, including the Ba'tan home world. It would be nice," he continued dryly, and Torin got the impression he was talking as much to himself as to her, "if this time, things could stabilize without such a drastic kick in the collective ass. Surprisingly enough, it's been the Krai who've been causing the most trouble of late, throwing one faction against the other so that the military will take notice of their complaints that there aren't enough of their people in top positions. They've been insisting Krai officers, Navy and Marine, receive more chances to serve in those places where promotions are most likely."

"The front lines, sir?"

The general looked startled by her question. "No, not the front lines. They're looking for a higher survival rate."

Aren't we all.

"Sir!"

Torin wondered if Stedrin stood at attention when he addressed the general over the comm. It certainly sounded like he did.

"Yes, Lieutenant?"

"The captain is here, sir."

"Send him in." General Morris stood, tugged his tunic into place, and came around the desk, shooting Torin a look that seemed almost apologetic.

Bugger it. That's not good. She'd been standing easy, so when the door opened behind her, she came around ninety degrees, presenting her back to neither the general nor the entering officer.

He looked vaguely familiar. Which wasn't necessarily relevant since the Krai as a whole had very little color or size variance and, to any species without a highly developed sense of smell, all seemed pretty much the same.

"Staff Sergeant Kerr, I'd like you to meet your commanding officer for this mission, Captain Travik."

Oh, crap.

Captain Travik's rescue of the besieged research station on Horohn 8, his reckless charge through the Others' perimeter recorded by the station's sensors, had captured the attention of the public and made him a celebrity. He'd been feted all through the sector, his image turning up every time the Corps got mentioned on any kind of a popular broadcast, his reputation growing as every new program fed on the one before it, his ego growing with his reputation.

Most of the Marines who landed under the captain's command hadn't survived.

To the public, that made him even more the hero.

To the Corps, particularly those who'd studied the recording, that made him a reckless hotshot who knew how to manipulate the media.

And here he was.

Because the Krai government wanted more Krai in top military positions.

Torin glanced over at the general and thought of a few more things to call him.

They folded into Susumi space early evening ship's time when the last two members of the recon team finally arrived. According to the data on the desk in Torin's small office, the twelve Marines had been detached from as many different units for security reasons. A decision had been made at the highest levels to keep the media away from the alien vessel and individual Marines moving about the Sector were deemed a lot less noticeable than a squad taken from one location.

From a combat perspective, it *was* inefficient, but Torin couldn't fault the security reasoning. She only hoped they'd be spending enough time in Susumi space to make the word *team* relevant. Even with specialized training in common, it was going to take a while to shake three different species and twelve different personalities into a smoothly functioning unit.

Although there'd be common ground the moment they knew who was commanding.

Might as well get it over with.

"That was Staff Sergeant Kerr giving us a ten-minute warning," Corporal di'Marken Nivry announced, upper body leaning through the hatch. "She wants us all. You two better get some clothes on and get in here."

The two dripping Marines on the shower platform exchanged glances as identical as Human and Krai physiognomy allowed.

"Briefing's tomorrow morning," Werst growled, turning the air jets on. "She can't wait?"

"She doesn't have to," Nivry reminded him and disappeared.

Lifting both heavily muscled arms over his head, Werst turned and scowled at the man standing next to him. "What?"

August Guimond scrubbed his fingers through the maximum amount of thick blond hair the Corps allowed, smiling broadly. "She was checking out my package."

"Dirsrick anbol sa serrik tanayn."

"That's Krai, isn't it?" Guimond turned off the air and stepped down. "What does it mean?"

"Roughly: who the fuk cares."

Torin glanced around the compartment. Five di'Taykan, five Humans, two Krai—pretty much the usual split for the Corps. The engineers, Lance Corporal Danny Johnston and Corporal Heer, were sitting together, slates out. The two highest caste of the five di'Taykan—Privates First Class di'Por Huilin and di'Wen Jynett—appeared to be playing "my family compound is bigger than yours," and looked as though they'd been interrupted in the midst of getting to know each other better. Which was pretty much standard operating procedure for di'Taykans and a heartbeat after she left all five would be in the communal compartment. For a moment it looked as though Pfc di'Sarm Frii was having a small spasm and then she saw the earphones almost covered by swinging ocher hair—although his hair seemed to be keeping a different beat than either hands or feet.

And Private First Class August Guimond, who was one of the biggest Humans Torin had ever seen, must have found something or somebody pretty funny given the size of his smile.

The rest were waiting more or less attentively for her to speak. The other Krai, who therefore had to be Pfc Werst, cradled a mug of *sah* in both hands. It took a security scan to release the stimulant to the Krai and, given the effect on Humans, Torin was glad to see Werst also wore an expression that promised critical damage should anyone try to take it from him.

She drew in a deep breath, noted that the silence became more attentive, waited for a blocky blonde—Lance Corporal Lesli Dursinski—to drive an annoyed elbow into Frii's ribs, and began. "My name is Staff Sergeant Kerr and I am your Senior NCO for this mission. Like you, I got dragged away from my team and my friends and the job I was doing and, like you, I know that doesn't matter one goddamned bit. The Corps calls—we answer. This is your new team . . ." A sweeping gesture with her right hand. ". . . these are your new friends . . ." Followed by a sweeping gesture with her left. "I don't care if you like each other, but you will respect each other's abilities and you will work together as Marines. Whenever that seems too difficult for you, remember there's sixteen of us and over two thousand sailors out here." Her left eyebrow lifted and her tone dried out. "I'm not saying that it's us against them, I'm just saying that sixteen Marines, working together, should have no trouble with two thousand sailors."

"Bring 'em on, Staff!" Pfc di'Benti Orla was on her feet. "I could do two thousand sailors myself before breakfast!"

One of the Humans, Corporal Harrop, snickered. "Yeah, I've heard that about you."

Orla flipped him the finger, a Human gesture the di'Taykan had adopted wholeheartedly. "Fuk you!"

"After breakfast."

"Deal."

When Harrop looked startled, Torin grinned and shook her head. "You *have* served with di'Taykan before, Corporal?"

"Sure, Staff. Hundreds."

"Then stop looking so damned surprised. At the moment," she continued, now that the room's attention had returned to her, "I know little more about this mission than you do; we'll be first on an alien deep-space craft found drifting by a civilian salvage operator. Briefing's tomorrow morning, 0900 hours, across in the *Berganitan*. General Morris would like us all to attend." Torin paused long enough for the expected rumble of complaint but not so long that the rumble turned into something more. "Whether he expects our presence to reassure or intimidate the civilian scientists who will also be in attendance remains unclear at this time."

Lance Corporal Ken Tsui snickered—there was one in every team who always got the joke—and several Marines smiled.

"At the briefing," Torin continued, "we'll meet our commanding officer, Captain Travik."

Johnston's slate squawked as he closed his fist around it. A heartbeat later, eleven of the twelve started talking at once.

". . . *serley* asshole couldn't command his way out of a wet . . ."

". . . had a *thytrin* with him at Horohn . . ."

". . . part of a fukking PR show . . ."

". . . bastard tries that 'hero' shit on me . . ."

". . . General Morris trying to get us fukking killed . . ."

Torin folded her arms and met Werst's eyes across the room. He took a long drink of his *sah*, expression no different than it had been before she'd started speaking. One by one the other Marines noted her position and their protests trailed off.

"All right, now that you've got that out of your system," she told the renewed silence, "let's get a few things clear. One, General Morris is not trying to get us killed. The Krai in Parliament want more senior officers, and Captain Travik was the politicians' choice. Unless the general wanted a repeat of '89, his hands were tied."

"Fuk the politicians," someone muttered.

Torin snorted. "Thank you, but no. Two, this is not a public relations show. Until we've determined exactly what we're dealing with, we're under level four security and a full media lockout—which is why they didn't move in an existing team. The media watches troop movements, they don't watch individual Marines."

"Staff?"

"What is it, Dursinski?"

"Why a full media lockout?" The lance corporal's frown fell into two well-defined vertical lines in the center of her forehead. "Is there something about this ship they're not telling us?"

"Probably. But I'm sure if you all put your little minds to it, you could come up with an infinite number of reasons for command to keep the discovery of this ship away from civilians until we've determined what it is."

"Well, if it's one of the Others' ships, they could get hurt."

"While I appreciate enthusiasm, Private Guimond, I wasn't actually asking for reasons."

Head cocked to one side, his lips moved as he silently repeated her previous statement. "Oh." His smile grew a little sheepish. "Sorry, Staff."

"It's okay. Three . . ." She swept the room with a flat, emotionless gaze. ". . . Captain Travik is a Marine Corps officer and his orders, passed to you through me, will be obeyed. What you think of him personally is irrelevant. Do I make myself clear?"

A ragged chorus of, "Yes, Staff." Scattered nods. Werst took another drink.

"Good. Form up in the passageway at 0830. I'll see you then." She paused, one hand on the hatch, and turned back to the room. "Private Orla."

"Staff?" The young di'Taykan looked startled to be singled out.

"I'm sorry to hear about your *thytrin*. For what it's worth, I expect your contact with the captain will be minimal." When Orla nodded, Torin stepped out of the compartment and closed the hatch behind her.

"You told them?"

Torin pivoted on a heel, just barely resisting an urge to ask Lieutenant Stedrin why he was lurking about the enlisted compartments. "Yes, sir. I did."

"Why?" The question held equal parts curiosity and challenge.

"If they found out about Captain Travik tomorrow at the briefing, that's all they would have found out. Now, it'll be old news, already dealt with, and they'll be able to concentrate on information that might keep them alive."

"I doubt the briefing will be that dangerous, Staff Sergeant. Good night."

"Good night, sir." Torin watched until the lieutenant turned the corner, trying to decide if he had the sector's driest delivery or the Corps' worst grasp of tactics.

"You've been pretty quiet, Werst," Guimond observed as the horror stories and complaints began to die down. "What do you think about serving under Captain Travik?"

"Why do you want to know?"

"I just . . ."

"You think because I'm Krai, I'm going to defend him?"

"No, I . . ."

"I think he's a grandstanding asshole at best and a murdering asshole at worst, but we won't be dealing with him." Werst scowled into the depths of his *sah*. "We'll be dealing with Staff Sergeant Kerr. He's her problem."

"Okay." Guimond grinned. "What do you think of her?"

Werst shrugged. *"Chrick."*

"What don't you find edible?" Ken Tsui demanded, getting himself another beer. "She's not recon."

"She was. She started out Fifth Re'carta, First Battalion, Recon. Went in half a dozen times, got wounded, made corporal, got transferred. What?" Nivry demanded of the room as whole. "I looked her up." The corporal held up her slate. "It's all in the attachment's database. You can bet she's downloaded everything in there on us."

No one took the bet.

"I heard the general picked her personally," Johnston offered, scratching at the faint shadow of whiskers across his chin.

"And we were randomly generated?" Nivry snorted. "With the whole sector to choose this team from, they'd have picked the best."

"And you think you're proof of that?"

"Damned right. Anyone in here think they're not?" She paused for effect and got an answer.

"He's not." Jynett jabbed her elbow into the ribs of the di'Taykan beside her.

"Suck up," Huilin grunted, rubbing at the damp patch of spilled beer on his shirt.

"Slacker."

"All right, let's be . . ."

"Relax, Corporal, we took our HE1 course together. This one . . ." Huilin raised the remains of his beer in an exaggerated toast. ". . . placed top in the class."

Jynnet's glass rose to touch his. "Which means poor Huilin had to settle for second."

"I was robbed."

Nivry's eyes lightened. "Which proves my point. We were picked because we're the best. Staff Sergeant Kerr was probably picked because she could get the job done even under the handicap of Captain Travik."

Across the room, Corporal Harrop said something that sounded distinctly rude in one of the remaining Human languages. With all eyes on him, he shrugged and translated. "No one's that good."

Werst drained his *sah*, stood, and tossed the cup into the recycler. "She'd better be."

Craig Ryder held a full house, kings over threes, when his ship, parked in one of the *Berganitan*'s shuttle bays, informed him it was 0600 hours. He tongued in an acknowledgment, then looked up and swept the table with his second best smile, the one designed to distract from the situation—which was, at the moment, the happy fact that he'd taken a month's pay or better off everyone at the table. "Afraid this'll have to be the last hand, mates. Duty calls."

"Duty?" One of the two watching di'Taykans, long since tapped out, stared up at him from under a moving fringe of lavender hair. "Calling *you?*"

"As it happens, I've got a briefing to attend in under two hours and— you know how it is—I'd like to make a good impression."

"On who?"

"On whoever it would do me the most good to impress, of course."

"Well, as it happens," Lieutenant Commander Sibley echoed, tapping his own cards on the edge of the table, "it's up to you."

Ryder allowed his smile to pick up a slight predatory edge as he aimed it directly at the vacuum jockey. "So it is. I see your hundred and I raise you . . ." Eyes locked on the opposition, he picked up a stack of markers and threw them into the pot. ". . . three hundred more."

The Krai between them glanced at the cards in her right foot, took a long draw on a pouch of beer, and shook her head. "I fold."

"Down to you and me, Sibley."

"You wish," he muttered, frowning at his hand.

The second di'Taykan made a suggestion.

Both Humans ignored him.

"Well?"

"Why not." Sibley looked up and grinned, pushing his last markers into the center of the table. "I call. What've you got?"

Ryder laid out his cards.

The grin slipped sideways but held. "Buh-bye," he sighed, throwing in two jacks, two tens, and a seven.

The Krai, who'd played cautiously all night, still had a few markers left; the rest Ryder scooped up and dumped into his belt pouch. "Always a pleasure doing business with the Navy." He lifted his beer in a flourishing salute, drained it, and tossed the empty pouch down on the table. "Hope you lads don't mind cleaning up . . ."

It was almost a question.

He was gone before anyone answered.

The markers were a comfortable weight against his hip as he made his way back to shuttle bay four—nothing like turning a profit to improve the time wasted in Susumi space. Later, he'd head down to QSM and cash in, but right now he needed to reach his ship before someone in Navy gray checked his pass and discovered his clearance didn't include this part of the *Berganitan*.

They—they being the anal retentives in uniform running the show—hadn't wanted him along. Too bad. He alone knew where they were going, and he had no intention of handing that information over gratis. Restricting his unescorted movements beyond the confines of the shuttle bay had been their way of taking a petty revenge. The sergeant at arms had made it quite clear they'd slap a security chip in him if they found him where he didn't belong.

That said, he still preferred to play on the other guys' turf—it made the opposition overconfident and kept the repair bills from coming out of his account if the game got out of hand. As friendly little games so often did.

A couple of techs on morning watch looked up from an open panel as he passed, but he made it back to the *Promise* without attracting any unwelcome attention. He'd refused the generous offer of access to the *Berganitan*'s system—and the reflective access that would give the *Berganitan* to him—and, because he'd always been a *cautious* man, he'd locked his implant and his ship down tight. A quick check after boarding proved the security protocols on both were intact; as far as anyone who might care would ever know, he'd spent the night sound asleep.

"And wouldn't that have been a waste of time?" Tossing the belt pouch onto his bunk, he stripped off for the shower.

He'd sincerely meant it when he'd said it was a pleasure doing business with the Navy—a vacuum jockey's idea of saving for retirement was drawing to an inside straight. Probably a result of too much time spent in zero gee.

He had a feeling the Marines weren't going to be half so much fun.

Torin had her team in place well before the briefing was due to start. The twelve Marines filled the last two rows, the double line of service uniforms creating a matte-black shadow at the back of the room. With the exception of Guimond, the rest—even the two engineers—wore the sort of blank expressions usually seen after the words, "We need a volunteer for. . . ." Guimond looked fascinated by everything he saw.

She had no doubt that each and every one of them had not only marked the exits but carried a complete mental map of the route back to the attachment and the armory—Marines being Marines and Recon even more so.

When General Morris, Captain Travik, and Lieutenant Stedrin entered, she brought them to attention. There was nothing of the parade ground about the movement, but they all ended up on their feet more or less at the same time. The general made a sotto voce suggestion to the captain, who then sauntered—there really could be no other word for it even given the natural gait of a species with opposable toes—back to Torin's side.

"So this is my reconnaissance team, is it, Staff Sergeant?"

He hadn't actually looked at them. Hadn't actually looked anywhere but at her. "Yes, sir."

"Excellent." His smile showed almost enough tooth to be considered a challenge—which would have been a lot more relevant had she been another Krai. "I assume you've gone through their records, checked them all out, made sure they're the best?"

"They were chosen for this mission because they *are* the best, sir."

"I know I was."

Jolly tones suggested he was making a joke. Torin decided not to get it. "Yes, sir."

"Well, I'm not sure why the general wants them here—that is, right here, right now. I'm quite sure you'd be capable of briefing them after it's all over, but ours is not to question why."

Torin managed not to wince. *Wonderful. Now, it's a theme.*

"Have them sit down. They can take notes if they feel it's necessary. I'll speak to you later."

"Yes, sir." After he'd turned and walked away, she turned herself, saying quietly, "As you were." Expressions as the team sat ranged from blank to bored. The one murmured observation had been too low for her to hear content, so she ignored it. All things considered, it hadn't gone badly.

Based on their two short meetings, Captain Travik seemed more an idiot than a murderous glory-hog. *Not*, she acknowledged, *that those personality traits are mutually exclusive.* She'd be able to form a more relevant opinion after she saw him in action.

A number of civilians filed in as she sat and the front rows filled quickly.

"We're not taking them *all* in with us, are we, Staff?" Guimond wondered, his voice a bass rumble by her left ear.

Torin sure as hell hoped not but all she said was, "We'll do what we're ordered to do, Guimond."

"Yeah, but . . ."

"We'll find out soon enough." She heard his seat creak as he sat back. He had reason to be concerned. There were eight or nine Katrien, all talking at once, a half a dozen Humans, three di'Taykan, three Krai, four Niln, and a Ciptran—sitting alone, antennae flat against his/her head, one mid-leg fiddling with the controls on the inhaler implanted over the gills on both sides of his/her carapace. The Katrien and the Niln were local to this sector, the Humans, di'Taykan, and Krai had probably been chosen because of the military presence in an effort to keep species numbers down. Torin had never seen a Ciptran before but had been told they were the exception to the rule that said only social species developed intelligence.

When Captain Carveg and two of her officers arrived to represent the *Berganitan* and things still didn't get started, Torin wondered who else they were waiting for.

He made his entrance at 0759, stepping through the hatch as though both the scientists and the Marines had been gathered in this room, at this time, for his benefit. A civilian, a Human male; just under two meters tall, with broad shoulders and heavy arms, almost broad and heavy enough to be out of proportion to the rest of a muscular body. Torin watched him cross to the general through narrowed eyes. She didn't know much about civilian styles, but she knew attitude when she saw it. And she was seeing it. In spades.

When he reached the officers, he smiled broadly, spread his hands, and said something too low for Torin to catch.

"The exact same thing happened to me." Captain Travik's voice carried clearly over the room's ambient noise. "That's the Navy for you, can't draw a straight line between two points. You ought to come stay with the Marines."

Torin glanced at Captain Carveg, who gave no indication she'd overheard the comment. If Parliament wanted to promote a Krai, why didn't they start with Carveg? A Navy captain held rank equivalent to a Marine colonel; Travik had a way to go to even catch up. *On the other hand,* Torin mused, her gaze flicking between the officers, *if they leave Carveg where she is, she can keep doing a job she's good at, and if we're very lucky, they'll stuff Travik where no one on the lines'll miss him.*

General Morris moved out beside the large vid screen at the front of the room and various conversations trailed off into an anticipatory silence. "We all know why we're here," the general began without preamble. "A vessel belonging to no known species has been discovered drifting in space. It is, or rather will be, our job to find out everything we can about this vessel. At this time, I will turn the briefing over to Mr. Craig Ryder, the CSO who made the discovery."

CSOs, civilian salvage operators, haunted the edge of battle zones where they dragged in the inevitable debris. Some they sold back to the military, the rest to the recycling centers. The overhead of operating in deep space being what it was, even the good ones never made much more than expenses.

Like all scavengers, they performed a valuable service and, like all scavengers, they profited by the misfortune of others. Since most of that misfortune happened in combat to people who were never strangers, Torin decided she didn't much care for the man now crossing to General Morris' side.

"Thank you, General." As the general moved back to the small knot of officers, Ryder turned to face his audience. His eyes were deep-set to either side of a nose that had clearly been broken at least once away from medical attention. Brown hair curled at his collar, and he wore a short beard—unusual in those who spent a lot of time in space and therefore expected to be suiting up regularly. He had a deep voice and an accent Torin couldn't quite place. "G'day. I hope you all understand why I'm unwilling to give out specific coordinates at this time but I can assure you, this ship is a good distance off the beaten paths. I found it by accident . . ." His smile suggested further secrets he wasn't ready to share. ". . . thanks to a small Susumi miscalculation . . ."

Torin heard several near gasps and even the Ciptran's antennae came up.

Susumi miscalculations usually ended in memorial services. *This guy's got the luck of H'san.*

". . . that popped me back into real space some considerable distance from the system I'd been heading for. After I got my bearings—and changed my pants . . ."

And the sense of humor of a twelve-year-old.

Behind her, Marines snickered.

He acknowledged the response like a seasoned performer and continued almost seamlessly. ". . . I thought I might as well have a look around. Imagine my surprise when I read a very large manufactured object a relatively short distance away. Which was, of course, nothing to my surprise when I went to have a look . . ." Half turning toward the screen, he ran his thumb down the vid control. ". . . and found this.

"That little shape down in the lower right is the *Berganitan.* I pasted it in to give you lot some idea of scale."

It was bright yellow. And it was big, close to the size of the OutSector Stations, longer than it was wide—20.76 kilometers by 7.32 kilometers—with a high probability of the dimpled end representing some kind of a propulsion system. The Confederation database had declared it alien, but—in spite of the color—Torin thought it looked a lot less alien than a number of ships she'd seen.

There were a number of identifiable air locks, one on each side up near the bow, one topside, one on the portside about two thirds of the way back, and one in the belly in the aft third. There were no identifiable exterior weapons. Unfortunately, air locks had limited design options, and weapons did not. They could be looking at enough firepower to rebang the big one and never know it.

Scans showed no energy signals—in fact they showed nothing at all inside the yellow hull although Ryder admitted his equipment was perhaps too small to penetrate.

Which brought the expected response from the di'Taykan present.

When the *Berganitan* arrived after four days in Susumi space, there'd be more scans, and then the Marines would be sent in to discover what the scans missed.

Simple. Straightforward.

Or it would have been had the scientists not argued every point—with each other, with Ryder, and occasionally with themselves. A half an hour later, when General Morris walked back out in front of the screen, now showing a dozen different views of the ship, his presence front and center had no noticeable effect on the noise level.

"Think he's going to order us to strangle them, Staff?"

Torin grinned at Guimond's cheerful question. "It would explain why we're here, but, somehow, I doubt it." She kept her attention locked on the general's face. When, eyes narrowed in irritation, he met her gaze and nodded, she stood.

"MARINES, ATTEN—SHUN!"

Her voice filled the room, wall to wall, deck to deck. It filled in every single space that wasn't already occupied by a physical form.

Twelve pairs of boots slammed down on the deck as twelve Marines snapped up onto their feet. This time, because it counted, it was a textbook maneuver.

The silence that followed was an unsure and tentative thing. Faces furred and bare stared from the general to the solid wall of black so suddenly behind them and back to the general again. Craig Ryder and the Navy officers had moved from Torin's line of sight, but Captain Travik was obviously amused by the scientists' discomfort. If Lieutenant Stedrin found the situation amusing, he didn't show it. The latter went up, the former down in Torin's regard.

General Morris swept a stern gaze across the first three rows of seats. "I would like to remind you all that until we are one hundred percent certain this vessel does not belong to the Others or one of their subject races, this will remain a military operation. Mr. Ryder's scans as well as information extrapolated from them have been downloaded into your laboratories or workstations where you may go over them in as much detail as you wish. When you have chosen the four scientists who will be first to board the vessel after it has been secured, have them report to Staff Sergeant Kerr so that she can ensure they will be neither a danger to themselves or to her team. That is all."

The Ciptran unfolded its lower legs and stalked out of the room.

The remaining scientists shuffled in place for a moment, then the Katriens—all trilling loudly—led the exodus.

A moment later Captain Travik waded through the stragglers and headed for the back of the room.

"Staff Sergeant Kerr."

"Sir."

"General Morris would like a word with you after you dismiss the team."

"Yes, sir."

"Nice to see the fear of the Corps in the eyes of those *serley chrika*. I told the general he should use the Marines to keep the civilians under control." He sounded like he believed it, too.

"Yes, sir."

She sent the team back to the Marine attachment under Corporal Nivry and followed the captain to the front of the room, where General Morris was speaking with Lieutenant Stedrin.

"Staff Sergeant Kerr?"

Most of her attention still on the general, she half turned to find Craig Ryder smiling at her. Up close, she could see that his eyes were very blue and the secrets in his smile had taken on a strangely intimate extension.

Intimate? Where the hell was that coming from? She'd never met the man.

"So, Captain Travik tells me you'll be helping him out on this little excursion."

Torin shot a look at the captain, who showed teeth. It was quite possibly exactly what the captain had told him. Verbatim.

"I'm Captain Travik's senior NCO, Mr. Ryder, if that's what you mean."

"Is it?" Both brows flicked up. "All right, then. Well, as Captain Travik's senior NCO, you should know that I'll be heading inside with you on that first trip."

"No, Mr. Ryder, you will not."

"Yes, Staff Sergeant, he will."

She slowly pivoted to face the general. "Sir?"

"It was one of the conditions Mr. Ryder imposed when he agreed to take us to the ship. And what I intended to speak with you about. As Mr. Ryder has beaten me to the punch, you two might as well carry on with your discussion." The general's expression made it clear, at least to Torin, that he appreciated the CSO's interference. "Lieutenant . . ."

"Sir." The di'Taykan fell into step beside the general as he left the room. After a moment's hesitation, Captain Travik hurried to catch up.

"Alone at last."

Torin pivoted once more, a little more quickly this time. "Are you out of your mind? You have no idea what's in that ship."

His eyes sparkled. "Neither do you."

"But *we* are trained to deal with the unexpected, the dangerous unknown." Torin held onto her temper with both hands. "You, Mr. Ryder, are not."

"I intend to protect my investment, Staff Sergeant."

"From what? We don't want your *salvage*."

"Nice try, but I've worked with the Marines before. You don't know you don't want my salvage until you've had a good look at it. Just to keep things on the up and up. I'll be looking at everything you do. Might as well accept it graciously."

"Graciously?"

"Kindly. Courteously."

"Mr. Ryder, if your presence endangers any of my people," Torin told him in as gracious a tone as she could manage, "I'll shoot you myself."

"Woo." He rocked back on his heels, both hands raised in exaggerated surrender. "I don't like to criticize, Staff Sergeant, but have you ever considered cutting back on your red meat?"

A moment later, watching the rigid lines of the staff sergeant's back disappear out the hatch, Ryder grinned. "Well, when I'm wrong, I'm right wrong—looks like I'll be having fun with the Marines after all."

THREE

The temperature in the narrow corridor had risen to just over 47°C, but the line of sweat running down Torin's neck had more to do with exertion—inside her suit, it remained a chilly 13°. For the last half hour, her suit had been maintaining di'Taykan conditions and couldn't be reset.

At least the environmental controls worked.

Early on, an electromagnetic pulse had knocked out her mapping program. Fortunately, the homing beacon had been unaffected and she'd been moving steadily back toward the air lock through a maze of corridors. The builders had gone in big for dead ends, rooms with no recognizable purpose, and huge pieces of machinery that seemed as much historical as alien. Torin had looked down a ladder into the heart of a steam turbine and, shortly after, on a long straightway, had raced against something that wouldn't have seemed out of place back on her family's farm—had any of the farm machinery ever tried to kill her.

The air lock was now only eight meters to her right.

Behind a wall.

She was standing at the bottom of an L-shaped area. Another dead end.

She had twenty-three minutes of air left.

There had to be a way.

Slowing her breathing, she mentally retraced her steps.

And smiled.

Three long strides toward the end wall and she released her boots. Momentum kept her moving forward. Feet up, she pushed off hard.

Negotiating the corner involved a bit of a ricochet, but she got twisted far enough around to hit nearly the right vector. "Nearly" equaling no more than a bruised shoulder. It wasn't pretty, but as long as it worked . . .

At the next T-junction, she flipped over, remagged her boots, and walked straight up the wall to a second-level gallery.

Visibility was bad. Particulates saturated what passed for atmosphere and had gummed up most of Torin's faceplate. It took her five long minutes to find the tube she'd remembered, seconds to confirm that it went in the right direction.

Air lock entry 22.86 meters away. One level down.

An earlier laser bounce had measured the tube at 16.3 meters. Which would put her on the other side of the wall she'd been staring at.

It was a tight fit.

Seven minutes of air left.

On the bright side, the tight fit allowed her to brace after impact, take up the shock with her knees, and keep from careening back the way she'd come.

Air lock entry 6.56 meters away. One level down.

Torin slapped down a shaped charge. It activated on impact.

With four minutes and twelve seconds of air, a thirty-second fuse delay took forever.

Stripping the suit of everything detachable, she jammed it in over the charge, and shuffled back.

Three minutes and forty-two seconds later, she shoved the rest of the debris through the hole, followed it, remagged her boots as she hit the deck, and jogged to the air lock.

As the door cycled closed behind her, she dug her gloves into the shoulder catches and dragged her helmet off the second the telltales turned green, sucking back great lungfuls of air less redolent of staff sergeant.

It took her a moment to identify the sudden sound through ringing ears.

Applause.

Torin turned, swept her gaze over the half circle of watching Marines and brought it to rest on Huilin and Jynett, who were looking like anxious parents. "You two are a pair of sadistic sons of bitches," she said, unhooking her empty tanks, too tired to think of a Taykan equivalent.

Their eyes lightened.

Jynett pounded Huilin on the shoulder and ducked his return swing. "Thank you, Staff."

"You're welcome."

"You had seventeen seconds' worth of air left, Staff," Nivry observed, coming forward to catch Torin's tanks as they dropped. "Why the rush?"

"Well, Corporal, it's like this . . ." She paused long enough to remove her left glove. "I didn't want anyone to think I was hogging the simulation."

"Very considerate."

"Aren't I." A hoot of laughter spun her around. Her thrown glove slapped against Guimond's chest. "You're next, laughing boy."

"All right!" The perpetual smile broadened and he waved the glove like a trophy. "Thanks, Staff."

You couldn't not laugh with him, Torin thought, as she unsuited against one side of the fake air lock and Guimond suited up by the other. With only two hours of air, they weren't bothering to hook in the plumbing, so the whole procedure took half the time it might have—and twice the time it would have had there not been so many people helping out.

The Corps' hazardous environment suits were high-tech marvels that allowed a full range of movement and protected the wearer against almost anything an unfriendly universe could throw against it—up to and including most personal projectile weapons, although a hit anywhere but the head or torso left a nasty bruise. The helmet co-opted H'san technology and held two different shapes. Dropped off the back toggle, it collapsed down the back of the suit like an empty bag; snapped back up over the head, it became a rigid, impenetrable sphere capable of polarizing to maintain any programmed light level.

Helmet up, if the outside atmosphere held oxygen and nitrogen in any combination, the suit could filter in something essentially breathable to support the tanks. It recycled fluids, all fluids, almost indefinitely. Self-contained, they were comfortable for six hours, livable for eight, and, if breathing was still an option, got progressively nastier after that. They glowed under a number of different light conditions in order to make it easier for S&R crews to find the bodies. Marines loved them and hated them about equally.

August Guimond was the first Marine Torin had ever seen who looked happy putting one on.

"All right . . ." She let the suit drop, stepped out of the boots, and rolled the kinks out of her shoulders. ". . . let's say a two-and-a-half-hour turnaround, a little longer if the subject doesn't survive and we need to debrief. Even simulated deaths are meaningless if we don't learn from them."

Nivry's eyes lightened. "That's deep, Staff."

"It'll get deeper as the day goes on. Pack a shovel." Her suit in one hand

and a cleaning kit in the other, Torin turned back to Huilin and Jynett. "Can that thing spit out another twelve programs?"

"No problem, Staff."

"Twelve *different* programs," she qualified.

"The Hazardous Environment Course 2 comes with an infinite number of nasties."

"How realistic. So"—her voice reached out to include the entire team—"we'll spend today and tomorrow running through singles and then break into squads. Guimond, you won't need that much ammo for your KC. We're playing variations on 'find your way home,' not 'search and destroy.'"

The big Human looked down at the double handful of clips he was loading into bulging leg pouches and then up at Torin. "It's simulated ammo," he reminded her with a grin.

"True."

"And you had explosives."

"I fail to see the connection. Demolition packs are standard Recon equipment." She draped her suit over one shoulder and tossed a pack across to him. "Don't leave home without it."

"And the ammo?" he asked, snapping the demo pack to his belt.

Torin sighed. "Take what you think you'll need."

"Thanks, Staff."

"But . . ." Her attention expanded to once again include the entire team. ". . . if I get the impression any of you are becoming too dependent on the suits, we'll run a couple of minimals."

About to settle his helmet, Guimond paused. "So, Staff, you're saying you'd rather send me in naked with a knife in my teeth?"

Torin waited out a pause almost di'Taykan in its implications, then said, "Knife in your hand, Guimond. I'd hate to see you cut your head off. Now, check your system and get in there; we're all getting older even if the universe isn't."

"A five percent death rate, Staff Sergeant?" Captain Travik shook his head in dismay. "I think you're making the simulations too easy."

"These Marines were specifically chosen, sir. They're good."

"Still, five percent. I don't want General Morris to think I'm not taking your training seriously."

As the captain's only contact with the team so far had been in the briefing room, Torin figured General Morris would have grounds. On the bright
side, if the captain wasn't involved, he wasn't screwing things up. "The
programs were taken from the HE2, sir."

"Two?" His brow furrowed until it met his upper nose ridges. "Did I
order you to run two?"

"You weren't specific about which simulations to run, sir. These were
the best we had on hand."

The extra ridges smoothed. "The best; I see." He beamed in approval.

Torin suspected he'd just edited reality and made the HE2s his idea
from the start—standard operating procedure for bad officers. As far as she
was concerned, he could claim to be the guy who'd dreamed up close order
drill just so long as he didn't put her people in unnecessary danger.

As for the HE2s: in the interest of getting a leg up on his next course,
Huilin had picked up a bootleg copy of the advanced simulations and, together, using information they'd acquired on their last course, he and Jynett
had managed to crack the instructor's code so it would run—nothing Captain Travik needed to know.

She glanced down at the report she'd just finished summarizing. "We'll
be running individual simulations tomorrow as well, sir."

"Excellent."

"Will you be coming by?"

"I don't think so, Staff Sergeant." Shifting forward in the chair, his chin
rose, his chest went out. "The troops'll stand a better chance if they're not
worried about me watching them."

"I was thinking you might want to run the simulation yourself, Captain."

"Me?"

Is there another captain in the room? Calmly meeting his indignant
gaze, she elaborated, "As your senior NCO, it's my responsibility to point
out that it's been a while since you've suited up."

"Your responsibility?"

"Yes, sir."

"To point out that it's been a while since I've suited up?"

"Yes, sir." It was like talking to a primitive translation program that
changed the pronouns and repeated everything said to it. Unfortunately, it
was like talking to a primitive translation program wearing a captain's
uniform.

"A while?"

"Yes, sir."

He stood, drawing himself up to his full height and jerking his tunic down in the same practiced motion. His shoulders squared, his head angled slightly, his lips curled back off his teeth. Torin couldn't shake the impression he was staring into a vid cam only he could see. "Horohn 8 was a hazardous environment, Staff Sergeant, and I'm sure you've heard that I suited up there. In fact, I spent four hours in that *serley* suit; four hours fighting for my life while, all around me, Marines were dropping like . . ." His nose ridges flushed lightly. "What is it that Humans have things dropping like?"

"Flies, sir."

"Yes, exactly. All around me, Marines were dropping like flies. When an officer comes out of that kind of a situation, Staff Sergeant, he doesn't need a hazardous environment course. He's survived the only course that means anything." The left half of his upper lip curled higher. "This mission is a mere moo two . . ."

"Sir?"

"A moo two." His ridges flushed darker. "Military operation other than war. MOOTW."

"Oh."

"Exactly. I won't be putting the mission in danger by not participating in your little drills, Staff Sergeant, and I resent the implication that you think I will. Continued insubordination will be reported to the general. Don't think it won't."

"Yes, sir."

He stared at her for a moment, trying to work out just what she was agreeing with. Torin gave him no help. "Good," he said at last, hiding his uncertainty in movement. Dropping down into his chair, he propped one foot up on his desk and reached for his slate with the other. "Now, if you actually want those simulations to do some good, go have a word with your friend Mr. Ryder. He hasn't the benefit of your training or my experience. I'd just as soon not have to include the details of his death in my report, and I'm sure you won't want to be encumbered by his body while securing the alien vessel."

With the bleed off from the Susumi drive giving her power to burn, the *Berganitan* used an internal transit system indistinguishable in every way but size from the links on the stations. Unable to go directly from the Marine attachment to the shuttle bays, Torin found herself waiting at an isolated transfer point. As much as she hated to agree with Captain Travik about anything, his observation on the Navy's inability to draw a straight line had merit.

When the link finally arrived, a pair of emerging vacuum jockeys nearly ran her down.

One paused, turned, and smiled. "Staff Sergeant Kerr."

"Lieutenant Commander Sibley."

"You're not lost, are you?" The vacuum jockey glanced around the corridor as though trying to figure out exactly where they were. "You're a little off your usual beaten paths. And you know what they say, no one beats a path like a Marine."

"Do they, sir?"

"Oh, yeah. Beats it into submission and plants a flag on it."

"They don't say that around me," Torin told him after a moment's consideration.

He nodded. "I can understand that. *Are* you lost?"

"No, sir." When he indicated a need for more detail, she added, "I'm on my way to shuttle bay six to speak with Craig Ryder."

"You want some advice? Don't play poker with him."

"Hadn't intended to, sir."

"Hey, Sibley!"

Torin and the pilot both turned toward the voice. The di'Taykan who'd emerged from the link at the same time was waiting down the corridor by an open hatch, citron hair a corona around his head. "You coming?"

"Not yet, still not even breathing hard."

Too much information, Torin decided. "Excuse me, sir, but I'm holding up the whole system here." She stepped onto the link at the lieutenant commander's good-natured wave. He must have said something she didn't catch because as the door closed she heard the di'Taykan officer say, "No, we're going to my quarters because your quarters are such a disaster I can't find my *kayti*!"

Way too much information . . .

Craig Ryder's ship, the *Promise*, nearly filled shuttle bay four. Torin found it hard to believe he'd managed to dock it cleanly, but both the hull and the edges of the *Berganitan* that she could see appeared to be free of scrapes. Whatever else Ryder was, he was one hell of a pilot.

Without the cargo pods extended, the *Promise* looked like a Navy ship-to-ship shuttle crouched under a stack of cross-slatted panels. Considering the dimensions of the most basic Susumi drive, Torin understood why CSOs tended to work alone—two people would have to be very friendly to share the remaining space.

The hatch was open, and the ramp was down.

Curiosity may have made her approach quieter than necessary, the only sound as she made her way up the ramp the soft and ever-present hum of Susumi space stroking the *Berganitan*'s outer hull.

May have.

The interior of the salvage ship was smaller than she'd imagined. To her left were the flight controls and the pilot's seat. Directly across from the hatch, a half-circle table butted up to a wall bench. To her right, across the blunt end of the oval, a bunk and a narrow opening leading to—she leaned through the tiny air lock—the toilet facilities. It looked as though taking a shower involved closing the door and the toilet seat and standing in the middle of the tiny room.

Bits of paper and plastic had been stuck to the bulkhead over the bunk and a single white sock lay crumpled on the deck. A blue plastic plate, cup, and fork had been left on the table next to a small, inset screen. The pilot's chair looked as though it had been built up out of spare parts and duct tape—clearly tailored to fit only the dimensions of the builder.

Approximately five meters from the edge of the control panel to the bunk and three, maybe three and a half meters, from side to side, Craig Ryder's entire world was smaller than the smallest Marine Corps APC.

How could anyone live like that? She found her gaze drawn back to the sock. *Or more specifically, what kind of person would choose to?*

"I don't recall inviting you on board, Staff Sergeant Kerr."

Torin glanced down at her boots before turning. "I'm not on board, Mr. Ryder."

"You're on my ramp."

"Granted. I apologize for intruding." Half a dozen long strides brought her back to the shuttle bay's deck and almost nose to nose with Craig Ryder, close enough to smell sweat and machine oil about equally mixed. Bare arms folded, a wrench held loosely in one hand, he clearly wasn't moving, so she took a single step away. Common sense suggested keeping a careful distance—if it came to it, she needed enough room to swing. "The hatch was down, and the door was open."

"I wasn't expecting visitors." Unfolding one arm, he scratched in the beard under his chin with the wrench and smiled charmingly. Strangely, the two actions didn't cancel each other out. "You're a long way from the Marine attachment. Can I assume you're here for the pleasure of my company?"

"No."

"No?"

It was like looking at two different men—the one who'd been standing at the end of the ramp watching her descent under lowered brows and the one who'd just repeated her blunt response in tones of exaggerated disbelief. Given a choice, Torin would have preferred to deal with the former.

"I'm here," she explained, "because you're not hooked to the *Berganitan*."

"I hook to the ship, the ship hooks to me." Ryder shook his head. "A little too much give and take for my tastes. Since you couldn't call, what did you walk all the way down here for?"

"I'm here to assess your hazardous environment status."

"Excuse me?"

"I'm not being funny, Mr. Ryder." Although he clearly thought she was. The urge to wipe the smirk off his face was nearly overwhelming. She wouldn't have taken that kind of attitude from a Marine, enlisted or commissioned, but she had no idea of how to handle it coming from a civilian. "Look, we have no idea of what we'll face inside the alien vessel . . ."

He snorted. "We have no idea whether we can even get the locks open."

"Excuse me?"

"It's an *alien vessel*, Staff Sergeant Kerr. We might not be able to crack it."

Torin shrugged. "That's an engineering problem, Mr. Ryder, not mine. If I can't stop you from boarding with the Recon team, I need to know you won't be a danger to my people—no matter what we face."

"Staff Sergeant, do you know how I operate?"

She managed to keep her lip from curling. "No, Mr. Ryder, I do not."

"When we claim salvage, we deploy specifically sized cargo pods made up of those panels." His gesture took in the stack on the *Promise* and his voice picked up a strange, mocking tone, as though he objected to the necessary explanation. "The number of panels depends on the size of the salvage. Each panel adds a specific set of factors to the Susumi equation. Do you know what happens to a ship when the Susumi equation is off by the smallest integer?"

"Oh, yeah; specifically, it pops out next to unknown alien vessels and complicates my life." When he turned to face her, she met the indignation in his eyes with mild exasperation.

After a moment, he blinked and grinned. "Condescending question?"

"You think?" Torin stared up at the panels, noting the signs of hard use. "You're telling me that every time you deploy, you vacuum trot?"

He followed her gaze. "Every time there's a questionable reading, yes."

"And that happens?"

"Oh, pretty much every time I deploy."

She shook her head and transferred her gaze to his face. "You're insane."

"Me? *You* get paid to be shot at."

"That's not why they pay me, Mr. Ryder. They pay me to see that we achieve our mission objectives without losing personnel."

"Military speak," he snorted. "You get the job done without anyone getting killed."

Seventeen tiny metal cylinders, each holding a Marine she'd brought home. "I try, Mr. Ryder."

He sighed and tossed the wrench down into his tool kit. "Look, Staff Sergeant, I can guarantee I've spent more time suited than your entire team. I will not be a danger to your people. And . . ." A crooked finger rose to emphasize the point. ". . . should we run into someone who objects to our presence, I have every intention of hauling ass out of there and, if that's not possible, hiding behind the professionals. I'm there protecting my salvage—which will be no use to me if I'm dead."

He'd sounded sincere. But he'd previously sounded annoyed, charming, amused, mocking, and sarcastic—all within their short conversation. What made this last emotion any more realistic than the rest?

And what difference does it make? Torin demanded silently. *You don't have to figure him out, you merely have to endure him.* "Okay, you know how to work in a suit. I'd still like to see you come out for the team simulations, if only to get my people used to having you hide behind them."

"When?"

"Day after tomorrow. In the afternoon." That would give them the morning to run the course without him, to shake down the squads, and make necessary changes to both personnel and equipment. She refocused to find him watching her from under the edge of thick lashes.

"So, what's happening tomorrow?"

"The remaining individual simulations—the ones you've convinced me you don't need."

"Maybe I'll come by anyway."

"You'd be a distraction."

"You find me a distraction, Staff Sergeant?" The question was almost coy.

"I find anything outside the mission parameters a distraction, Mr. Ryder." Weight back on her heels, Torin folded her arms and met his gaze. "You rank right up there with hangovers and hemorrhoids."

The skin around his eyes creased into laugh lines as his smile broadened. "You know, I was starting to think you didn't have a sense of humor."

"I don't. Day after tomorrow, afternoon; if you don't want to bring your own equipment, I'm sure we can find a suit to fit you."

Craig Ryder stood at the top of the ramp and took a couple of long steadying breaths before he stepped into the *Promise* and punched the inner hatch closed. That had been too close. Staff Sergeant Kerr had been one long stride away from being inside.

In his personal space.

His.

Bunk, bench, table, screen, dishes; he touched each in order, then spun the control chair once around and sat. The familiar sink and sway in reaction to his weight helped, but he still drifted a hand over each of the controls in turn before he leaned back and swung his feet up onto the precise place he'd rested them a thousand, a million times before—the place where his heels had worn the finish off the edge of the control panel.

His place.

After a long moment, he leaned back and closed his eyes. He hadn't quite made up his mind about attending the simulation although he suspected he'd go if only for the pleasure of continuing to annoy Staff Sergeant Kerr.

And to keep her from making a return visit.

"All right, then."

There didn't seem to be much else to say.

*   *   *

"Hey, Werst, Staff's sending me down to the armory to make sure the guys back at MidSector actually loaded what inventory says they loaded." Guimond grinned down at the top of the Krai's head. "She says I should take someone with me; you up?"

"No. I'm busy."

"Come on, you're sitting on your ass drinking *sah*, how busy is that?"

"I'm busy resting."

"Right, 'cause you'll be first through the sim in the morning, which is at least ten hours away." He slid a long step to his right, just far enough to bend and peer into Werst's face. "Come on."

Werst's attention remained on the contents of his mug. "Fuk off."

"I'll go with you, Guimond." Orla stood and tossed her empty beer pouch into the recycler in one lithe move. She crossed to the big Human's side and rubbed her shoulder against his. "Maybe we can find something else to count while we're down there."

"I've still got the same one I had yesterday." Guimond grinned. "But we have to do the inventory check first. Staff says MidSector's not used to loading for Recon and she doesn't want us going in with our asses hanging out."

"Staff said that?"

"Those very words."

Johnston glanced up from the circuit board he'd pulled out of the food dispenser, magnification lenses silvering his eyes to a di'Taykan monochrome. "Who'd have thought Staff would be so articulate?"

Golden brows drew in as Guimond turned to Orla, looking confused. "What's he talking about?"

She shrugged. "He's an engineer, who the fuk knows?"

"I, myself, am wondering," Dursinski put in from her place by the pool table, "if Staff's so worried about our asses, why's she not doing the inventory check?"

Nivry glanced up from her slate. "She got invited to dinner in the Chief's and PO's Mess."

"How do you know that?" Dursinski demanded.

"Harrop and I were going over squad assignments with her when the invite came in from some warrant officer. He's a friend from other trips on the *Berg*. Human, so, after dinner, they probably won't . . ." She dropped her attention back to her slate. ". . . have dessert."

"She doesn't really mean dessert, does she?" Guimond asked as he and Orla left the room. The hatch cut off the di'Taykan's laughter.

"What a fukking moron," Werst grunted.

Nivry caught Harrop's eye and shrugged. When making up the squads, the two corporals had decided to keep Werst and Guimond together—the Human's size and good nature making up for Werst's lack of either—and Nivry had drawn the short straw. "What do you have against him?" she demanded.

"You've got the double hooks," the Krai snorted, "you figure it out."

"Let's assume I got them for good looks—not brains—and you tell me."

"Whatever. Fine." Werst drained his mug, crushing it in one hand as he stood. "August Guimond's a big, sweet guy, good-looking by Human standards, and everyone likes him—why don't we just paint a fukking target on him now and get it over with? You all know he's exactly the sort of guy who gets shot first when his squad hits combat." His voice rose an octave. "They shot Guimond! That lousy *serley chrika* shot Guimond!" And dropped back down to a growl. "Then we spend the rest of the mission winning one for poor August. No, thank you." He slammed the crushed mug into the recycler hard enough for its bounce to be clearly audible then, growling inarticulately, stomped out of the room.

"What was that all about?" Harrop wondered.

Nivry shook her head. "I have no idea."

Chief Warrant Officer Dave Graham waited for the heckling to stop before raising his stein. "Thank you. And here's to the riggers of Black Star Squadron, the best in the fleet!"

Torin raised her stein with the rest. As Dave sat down amidst renewed noise, she leaned toward him and said, "Should I be grateful a brand-new, high and mighty chief warrant lowers himself to eat with a lowly staff sergeant?"

He grinned. "You should be grateful I lower myself to eat with a Marine."

"You know, I'd heard you were drinking accelerant again."

"How's the steak?"

"Great, thanks." She cut off another hunk of meat and chewed happily. The Navy ate well, that was for damned sure. "If I was your master chief, I'd be watching my back. You keep getting promoted at this rate and you'll have her job in five."

"I dunno, master chief's job gets pretty political. I think I'd rather keep my hands on the machinery. You can trust a thruster to be a thruster." He washed down a mouthful of braised *tabros* with a swallow of beer. "But people . . ."

"Speaking of, I think I met one of yours on the way in. I got a ride from MidSector with a Lieutenant Commander Sibley and I'm having a vague memory of black stars on his Jade."

"Yeah, Sibley's one of ours. Good pilot, but a little too fond of bad puns, if you ask me."

"I seem to have escaped unscathed."

"He must've been on his best behavior."

Torin remembered the multiple accelerations and angles as they left the station. "I wouldn't go that far."

"Well, he'll be out scouting for you when we reach the ship. Black Star and the Red Maces pulled flyby duty—orders came down this afternoon."

"Two squadrons?"

"It's a big ship. Brass wants to know as much as they can before they send you lot in."

"We lot appreciate that."

"Word is you're working with a patchwork team—no two Marines from the same unit."

"Word?"

Dave snorted and slathered butter over another thick slice of bread. "Fuk, Torin, gossip moves around a ship in Susumi faster than light. If you can't get the hockey scores, you've got to talk about something."

"Word's right, then. General Morris doesn't want the information that an alien ship's been discovered getting out to the media before we know what it is, so he decided moving individuals would be less noticeable. They're a good lot, though. With a whole sector to choose from, he could choose the best."

"Yeah, but you've only got four days, five tops, to build a team from scratch. Then you're heading into gods know what."

"Marines are infinitely flexible."

"Makes it easier to duck."

"I'm personally in favor of ducking."

"I personally am impressed your General Morris got Captain Travik away from MidSector without him alerting the media." Dave grunted. "You planning on bringing him back in one piece?" Tone made *his* preference perfectly clear.

"That's my job." Her tone pretty much matched his.

"Word has it you were the general's special choice." When Torin rolled her eyes, he added, "So what did you do to piss off General Morris enough for him to stick you with the ego that walks like a Krai?"

Unable to separate certain Krai specialties from the more prosaic Human provided varieties, she waved off a tray of mixed cheeses. "Believe it or not, he gave me the job because he wants it done right."

"No, really." He grinned. "Did it involve unspeakable acts?"

There were bodies everywhere, most stopped by fire, then shot. Against the south wall of the remaining building were places where the bodies were piled three deep. The smell of burning flesh could be ignored, but the smell of burning blood was very nearly overwhelming.

"You might say that."

Torin glanced down at her slate and shook her head. "Squad One, mission objective; find whatever it is that's sending out the BFFM signal and get back to the air lock with it, keeping Mr. Ryder alive while you do."

All heads turned toward the salvage operator.

"Mr. Ryder . . ."

"Staff Sergeant Kerr."

". . . your objective," she continued, ignoring the cheery interruption, "is to stay alive."

"I think I can do that." His smile had picked up that annoying intimate cast again.

"Corporal Harrop is squad leader. You will obey his orders. Corporal."

"Staff?"

"You will give those orders recognizing Mr. Ryder is a civilian."

"Civilian." Because of the helmet's faceplate, Harrop had to tilt his head to rake the other man head to toe with an unimpressed gaze. It took a while. "Right, Staff."

"Take them in, Corporal."

He'd come mostly out of boredom. And curiosity. And because he realized Staff Sergeant Kerr had been right. They had no idea what they were going to face inside that alien ship, and it was best to be prepared. But when she asked, he planned to make it clear that preparation was the least of his reasons.

She never asked.

She'd looked up, nodded, as though she'd never doubted her logic would convince him to show, reminded the roomful of black uniforms who he was, and told him he was with Squad One. No surprise. No happy smile of recognition. He hadn't expected either, but he wouldn't have minded a little credit for voluntarily walking into a hazardous environment with a group of armed strangers.

Shuffling into the simulator's air lock beside Heer, the Krai engineer, Ryder leaned down and tapped him on the shoulder. "What's a BFFM, mate?" he asked when the Marine glanced up.

"A Better Fukking Find Me."

"We're looking for a Better Fukking Find Me?"

"You having receiver trouble? It's a Flishing 117, isn't it? I can take it apart without cracking a seal on your suit . . ."

"Thanks, my receiver's fine." He blocked the reaching hand with the back of his forearm. "You Marines are a literal lot, aren't you?"

Heer snickered. "You have no idea."

"Play poker?"

"Does a *gruinitan* go better with red sauce?"

"I'm guessing . . . yes?"

Torin had been surprised to see Ryder come through the hatch, HE suit draped over his arm. He'd brought the basics, borrowed tanks, and now, as she watched the air-lock door close behind him, she wondered why he'd come.

Probably bored.

She knew more than one Marine back on OutSector who ran the simulation chamber just for the hell of it. Given what Marines did for a living, she always thought the di'Taykan way of filling spare time made a lot more sense.

"Hey, Staff, will Ryder be going through again or does Squad Two get a different objective?"

Nivry's question snapped her back to the here and now. "Squad Two," she told them, "gets a wounded comrade to carry out."

"Who?"

"You'll know when they know."

Every eye in the squad turned toward August Guimond, who was watching the action in the chamber like it was an adventure vid he'd heard good things about. None of the other Marines matched his size. Only Craig Ryder came close, and he wouldn't be there to carry the body.

After a moment, the pressure of half a dozen pairs of eyes drew his attention from the simulation. "What?"

"It won't necessarily be Private Guimond," Torin pointed out.

When those same eyes turned to her, she smiled.

Werst's upper lip came off his teeth. "Crap. Crap. *Serley* crap."

No one disagreed.

FOUR

Staff Sergeant Kerr, report to my office immediately.

Torin tongued in an acknowledgment, adding aloud for the pickup in her jaw, "We're in the midst of our last simulation, Captain, twenty minutes to endgame."

Captain Rose would have told her to take the twenty minutes. But then, in the same circumstances, Captain Rose would have been monitoring the simulation with her—after having run it once himself.

Immediately, Staff Sergeant Kerr.

"Yes, sir."

Squad Two had come up against enemy fire, and they were pinned down. Squad One was working their way through adjacent corridors trying to relieve them. Nothing in the briefing suggested the alien ship had to be empty. Granted, any aliens on board could be as cuddly as the H'san but a "hail fellow sentients, well met" kind of first contact didn't need to be practiced. Craig Ryder was currently flat on the deck—when the shooting started, Werst had dropped him down out of the target zone by simply kicking his feet out from under him and letting him fall. Torin made a mental note to commend Werst for his initiative.

Fuk; if they have to promote a Krai, why don't they promote Werst?

She punched in the simulation's override code, throwing open all channels as the lights in the training module came up. "Sorry, people, you were kicking simulated ass but the captain's called me away from the board. Get the gear stowed, then you can stand down. When I get back, we'll take a look at the vids; see if we can up our survival rate. Mr. Ryder, thank you for your participation; you're welcome to stay."

"Anything for the Marine Corps, Staff Sergeant."

Although she couldn't see his face through the reflections on the curve of the helmet, Torin could hear the charmingly supercilious smile in his voice as he pushed himself into a sitting position.

"But," he continued, "I'd better get back to my ship; I have a busy night planned."

"Fine." What made him think she cared what kind of a night he had planned? *Asshole.* "You're on your own, people."

"Good luck, Staff."

That had to be Guimond; from anyone else, it would have sounded like sucking up.

Wondering just what exactly Captain Travik had up his butt this time, she headed for the other end of the Marine attachment at a quick walk.

It hadn't sounded like an emergency.

The captain had sounded enthusiastic.

Experience had taught her that an enthusiastic officer was a bad thing; an enthusiastic idiot in a captain's uniform was a very bad thing.

"Staff Sergeant Kerr, what took you so long?" Captain Travik chewed, swallowed, and leaped up from behind his desk as she entered his office. "I've had a . . ." His lips curled back. "You're out of uniform."

Torin looked down at her combat fatigues and back up at the captain. "Simulations today, sir."

"I know that—but you were monitoring."

"Yes, sir."

"All right, then."

All right, then? Torin regarded him with some suspicion from behind a carefully neutral expression. The lights were at Krai levels, and the green filters made the mottling on his scalp look like lichen or moss—which she supposed was what it was meant to do from an evolutionary standpoint. It just looked damned weird in their present circumstances.

"What," he asked, nose ridges flushed with excitement, "do you think about a formal inspection?"

He really didn't want to know what she thought. Fortunately, he didn't want an answer to the question either.

"How often," he continued, "do combat Marines travel with a general? I want to give him the opportunity to see what we're made of."

"Due respect, sir, but combat Marines aren't usually made of anything that shows well in a formal inspection."

"Nonsense. A little applied spit and polish and they'll be fine."

Remembering the last time she'd heard that and what the ultimate result had been, Torin lost the next bit of the captain's announcement in the noise of battle, picking it up again at:

". . . dress uniforms, medals if they've got them."

He was salivating—which, given how fond Krai were of Human flesh, Torin found just a little disconcerting. Horohn 8 had netted him a Nova Cluster, and he clearly needed to show it off. She wanted to smack the condescending little bugger. "Sir, this mission was minimum kit; no one has their dress uniform with them."

"I do."

Of course he did.

"The rest of you can shine up your service uniforms. I'm sure the general will understand."

"You've already asked him, sir?"

"These are my Marines, Staff Sergeant, I don't have to ask the general's permission to hold an inspection and . . ." He stepped closer and poked a finger toward her chest. ". . . I certainly don't have to ask yours."

"Have you already asked the general to *attend*, sir?"

The finger withdrew. "Oh. I informed him of my intention. It's not like he has anything else to do on this tub. As I have no aide, myself, you can go over the details with his."

"Yes, sir."

Won't that be fun.

"Sir, it's irrelevant that the general is also traveling with a full dress uniform." And not really surprising. "The officers should be in service uniforms as well."

The ends of Lieutenant Stedrin's pale hair made short choppy motions in the still air. "But the general . . ."

Torin ignored the bristling. "The general doesn't need tassels and fringe, Lieutenant, he's a general—my people all know that. And the Marine Corps doesn't need to emphasize artificial divisions between the officers and the enlisted—not if we're going to function as a team when it counts." Maybe if this mission went in General Morris' favor, he'd be able to add a gunny to his staff. She shouldn't be the one explaining the facts of life to his aide. Closely following that thought came the sudden and horrible realization that she, herself, was due for a promotion to gunnery sergeant.

"But, Captain Travik . . ."

"Excuse me, sir . . ." Rattled by promotion possibilities, the interruption emerged a little sharper than she'd intended. ". . . but the general is mission CO, not Captain Travik."

"I'm aware of that, Staff Sergeant."

"And you're the general's aide, sir, not Captain Travik's." Torin banished an unknown future and shrugged. "But it's not my place to tell you how to do your job."

Stedrin met her gaze. After a moment, his eyes lightened. "That's a load of crap."

He was learning. "Yes, sir."

The inspection was a stupid idea, but not necessarily a bad one. Traditionally, Marines spent the time before their carrier emerged from Susumi space wondering if maybe *this* was the time the engineers had forgotten to carry the one and popped them out directly in front of an object too large for the bow wave to clear. They'd remember the *Sar'Quitain* and the battalion of Marines who'd slammed into the gas giant with her. They'd speculate about the *Sargara-West*, and the Marines who'd disappeared into Susumi space with her never to emerge—although twelve years later unconfirmed sightings continued to make the news.

They were helpless during a situation that could be terminal, and they hated that helplessness.

Captain Travik had given them all something new to think about.

No harm, no foul. Torin watched from her place in the rear as the three officers moved slowly past the dozen Marines. *It's not as if they liked him to begin with.*

The "all clear" sounded as the *Berganitan* blew out of Susumi space right on schedule.

The alien ship remained exactly where Craig Ryder's equations had placed it.

"You know, I can't help thinking of the HE suits," Torin muttered a short time later as the first pictures came down to the Marine attachment.

Nivry's eyes darkened for a closer look. "Why?"

"The bright colors." Torin nodded toward the screen at the tiny image of the brilliantly yellow ship. "It makes them easy to find."

Forty-six hours of deceleration later, the *Berganitan* came to a full stop one hundred and eighteen kilometers away from the alien ship, maintaining the minimum distance required by both defensive and offensive systems.

The two squadrons got their orders to hit vacuum.

"All I'm asking is that you *try* to remember you've got a fukking big surveillance system bolted to the front of your bird."

Lieutenant Commander Sibley swallowed the last of his stim stick and shot Chief Warrant Graham an incredulous look. "Bolted?"

"Figure of speech; just remember it's there."

He grinned and shrugged the flight suit up over his shoulders. "Vacuum, Chief, no resistance. Aerodynamic doesn't count."

"Yeah, sir, I know that. But if you have to fire . . ."

"Can't fire you, Chief, you're in the Navy. And there's nothing to fire at out there." An elbow waved more or less toward the air lock as he sealed his cuffs.

"Maybe some boffin'll want you to shoot off a sample, I don't know, but if you have to fire, that system's going to cut a chunk off your forward arc, port, *and* starboard."

"You get that, Shylin?"

His di'Taykan gunner settled her helmet over cadmium hair. "I got it."

"She's got it," Sibley informed the chief. "Probably not catching. And since Lieutenant Shylin's going to be jigging your system—not to mention doing the shooting should it come to it—maybe you ought to tell her what you've done to my baby."

Graham folded his arms. "The lieutenant knows, sir. As does the rest of your wing. Now, I'm telling you."

"You still haven't forgiven me for what happened at Sai Genist, have you? I brought most of her back, and you've got to admit I did some pretty flying."

"Considering what you had left to fly, sir . . ." The chief showed teeth in a reluctant smile. ". . . yeah, you did."

One hand on the air lock controls, Shylin twisted around to face her pilot. "You coming, Sib, or am I flying this thing from the back seat? Squadron's launching in five."

Dave Graham watched until the Jade dropped free of her bay and scratched at his cheek where the depilatory was beginning to wear off. No rigger, from the FNG to the master warrant, liked to see the fighters go out—they all spent too long waiting for them, and their crews, to come back.

"Chief?"

He recognized the voice of his newest petty officer. "I'll be there in a minute, Tristir."

"Bay's empty, Chief. She's gone."

"I know."

The Krai rigger walked over to stand by his side. "At least this time, we'll get her back in one piece."

"Fuk, Tris, I wish you hadn't said that."

"One hundred and eighteen kilometers, Captain Carveg?" Arms folded, eyes locked on the vast expanse of yellow ship filling the screen, General Morris shook his head. "Couldn't you bring us any closer?"

The *Berganitan*'s captain shot him a look Torin recognized. "Considering the size of my ship and the size of that ship and the relative size of the galaxy, one hundred and eighteen kilometers is plenty close enough, General. And just so you know, we get one ping off it, any energy indication at all, and I'm backing up so fast you'll taste yesterday's lunch."

Torin had always liked Captain Carveg—unlike some, she understood the meaning of orbital support. And, it turned out, she had a way with words.

The general stared down at the much shorter officer for a long moment; then he nodded. "You are, of course, in command of the *Berganitan*, Captain."

"Yes, sir, I am."

Torin heard the silent, *this time*, on the end of that agreement even if no one else in the room did.

With the exception of the enlisted Marines, the same people were back in the same briefing room for the first data from the flyby.

"The general wants you there for the flyby, Staff Sergeant."

"Why?"

Lieutenant Stedrin stiffened but had clearly been instructed to answer if asked. "Captain Travik will be there, and General Morris wants you to have the same information the captain has. Did you have something better to do?"

"No, sir. Squad Two challenged One to a boom ball game. I was going to watch."

"Why?"

He'd mimicked her tone exactly. She didn't bother hiding the smile. "You can learn a lot about people watching them play games, sir. Organized sports is like stylized warfare—only no one gets killed."

The lieutenant snorted. "You've never played in my old neighborhood, Staff."

He was standing a careful distance from the general, not so close he was crowding, close enough if he was needed. At best, half his attention was on the alien ship, the rest was on the general. He was still remarkably tight-assed—which was something Torin had never thought could be said about a di'Taykan—but he took his job seriously and did it well. Both were qualities she appreciated.

"I've never understood the Human attraction to the di'Taykan." Torin began to stand, but Captain Carveg waved her back into her seat. "To the Krai, they're too tall, too colorful, that pheromone thing is too annoying . . ." She rubbed a hand over her muzzle. ". . . and they're far, far too skinny. We like a people with a little more meat on their bones. Just in case."

Definitely, a way with words. "I'll be starting my diet tomorrow, ma'am."

Her smile showed no teeth. "I was glad to see you back on board, Staff Sergeant. I feel like I owe you—and your people—an apology."

"You were following orders, ma'am. Fortunes of war."

"War is one thing," she growled, "political expediency is something else again. I never heard exactly how things ended—I don't suppose you can tell me—but I do know you were the general's ace in the hole then and I suspect you're here now because you're his best bet at keeping Travik alive. Bottom line, the general's only here—with all his hopes for promotion tied up once again in one mission—because he couldn't trust Travik as senior officer. Now me, I run my ship and I don't follow politics, but you wouldn't believe the garbage I got sent when Captain Travik came on

board. The Krai need to stick together and that sort of *serley* shit. A number
of my people still think joining the Confederation wasn't the best idea.
Actually, a number of my people still think leaving the trees was a bad
idea." They turned together to watch the captain making a nuisance of
himself with one of the Krai scientists. "And the good news is," Captain
Carveg observed dryly, "if those food wasters in Parliament insist on promoting the species, at least they won't be taking a decent officer off the
line."

"I was thinking the same thing, ma'am."

Carveg didn't pretend to misunderstand. "Thank you, Staff Sergeant.
Now, I'd better get back before the general convinces my XO to stuff my
ship up that thing's bright yellow butt. I just wanted you to know that when
you go in, I'm not going anywhere." She waved off Torin's thanks and
headed back to the front of the room, pausing by Captain Travik to say a
few words as she went. Torin would have loved to have known what those
words were because they moved him back to Lieutenant Stedrin's side
PDQ.

Lieutenant Stedrin didn't look very happy about it.

"G'day, Staff Sergeant. Is this seat taken?"

Torin glanced pointedly around at the empty seats between her and the
clusters of people at the front of the room. Craig Ryder watched the motion, a smile creasing the corners of both eyes, and sat down anyway. She
was pleased to see he had the brains to leave a seat between them.

"I wasn't lurking around behind you or anything," he said, leaning back
and making himself comfortable. "I was just waiting until you finished
your conversation with the captain."

Maybe if she ignored him, he'd stop talking.

No such luck.

"So, what are you doing way back here? No, wait, let me guess; General Morris told you to find yourself a seat where you could see everything
and, for you, everything includes everyone. Am I right?"

"Does it matter?"

"Just wanted to prove I'm more than a pretty face, Staff Sergeant Kerr.
Or can I call you Torin?"

She turned to face him. "You can call me Staff Sergeant Kerr. Or just
Staff Sergeant if that's too much for you."

"The Marines call you Staff."

"They've earned the right."

"By doing a few simulations?" With exaggerated chagrin, he crossed both hands over his chest. "*I* did simulations."

"They earned it the moment they put on this uniform."

"Ouch." After a moment, he added, "Is this where you hand me the three white feathers?"

"The what?"

"You know, for cowardice because I'm not a Marine."

Torin sighed. "Mr. Ryder, you blind jump out of Susumi space in a vessel smaller than the average SRM. You secure potentially hazardous salvage in vacuum, with no backup, leaving you essentially screwed if something goes wrong. I do not think you're a coward."

He cocked his head and she could see a glint in the blue eyes. "You think I'm a scavenger who makes his living off the misfortune of people you call friends."

"It's like you were reading my mind, Mr. Ryder . . ."

"Call me Craig."

". . . but that doesn't make you a coward."

"Or a Marine."

"What makes you think we'd have you?"

"Ouch again."

"Lick your wounds a little quieter, please, they're starting."

"Are you smiling?"

She was. "No."

"Okay."

The two squadrons had set up in a grid pattern at one kilometer out. When the first flyby evoked no response from the ship, Captain Carveg had the flight commander bring Black Star Squadron in to five hundred meters while the Red Maces held their position.

"We might as well be circling a large yellow turd for all the notice it's taking," Sibley muttered, manually keeping his Jade an exact five hundred meters from every protrusion.

Shylin checked that the data stream was on its way back to the *Berganitan*. "Are we even sure this is a ship?"

"Scans say it's hollow inside."

"So's your head, but that only makes you a vacuum jockey with bad taste in men."

"Hey, did I know his family and yours have been feuding for generations? No."

"Coming up on alleged air lock coordinates."

"I've got it. Oy, mama." He flipped his ship so they could get a look at it from another angle. "That alleged air lock looks just like an air lock. You copy, Command? We've got a docking collar and, eyeballing it from here, it looks like it'll take a universal coupling."

"*We copy*, Black Star Seven. *Do you see anything that looks like external controls?*"

"Negative. You think they left the key under the mat?"

"*Could have. Find the mat.*"

They found the rest of the air locks—one larger, one smaller, three the exact same size, now marked in blue on the screen in the briefing room. Opposite the single aft air lock, portside, they found a ripple in the hull of the ship. The scientists receiving the data were momentarily excited until a continuing scan showed the ripple otherwise identical to the rest of the hull. They found no fighter bays, no shuttle bays, and nothing they could identify as an exterior sensor array. Close up, the ship did have a number of protrusions that looked more extruded than built, and these were now marked in red. Readings at the dimpled end confirmed it was indeed part of some kind of a propulsion system, but until those readings could be analyzed, not even the propulsion engineers could tell what kind.

"You know, I'm not one to cast disparaging remarks about the vast sums spent on military equipment and training, but you guys haven't found anything I didn't find with my two rubber bands and a gerbil."

That was just weird enough to merit a response. "What's a gerbil?"

"Small rodent."

"Okay. Two things: One . . ." Torin nodded toward the continuous stream of numbers rolling down one side of the screen. ". . . they've barely started analyzing the incoming data. And two, those aren't my guys, they're Navy. You send in the Marines, you get an immediate response."

"Someone tries to kill you."

"It's not that easy."

"And good on that, since I'll be going in with you."

Torin twisted in her seat. "What if I promise not to touch anything—will you stay back with the science group then?"

"If you promise not to touch anything?"

"Yes."

Smiling broadly, Ryder tucked his chin in and looked up at her through thick lashes. "No."

"Very pretty. But it's not going to get you anywhere."

He blinked. Then laughed, loudly enough to turn a few heads. "Are you always this direct, Staff Sergeant?"

"No. Usually, I'm armed."

"Am I in . . ."

Torin cut him off with a raised hand, her attention drawn back to the front of the room by the sudden agitated clumping of the Naval officers. Captain Carveg held a hurried conference with her flight commander, who snapped a series of orders into her headset, one hand raised to cover the line of sight to her mouth.

Whatever it was, she didn't want to panic any watching civilians— although as far as Torin could see, every scientist in the room but the Ciptran was involved in an argument of some kind. The big bug just sat holding his/ her version of a slate in his/her hand, attention apparently divided between it and the screen—apparently because it was pretty much impossible for any-one to tell where any of his/her compound eyes were focused.

On the screen, six of the bright lights representing the fighters peeled away from the ship and disappeared in a double wing formation off the edges of the screen.

Torin could feel Ryder watching her. "What is it?" he asked quietly.

"The ship's sensors have picked something up. It's nothing big, the flight commander only sent two wings and didn't pull the others back in, but it hasn't identified itself as a friendly or she wouldn't have sent any at all."

"Do you think it's trouble?"

Captain Carveg was now speaking to General Morris.

"Always."

The general turned to Lieutenant Stedrin, who unhooked his slate from his belt.

Staff Sergeant Kerr.

From his slate to her implant. Whatever was going on, they wanted it kept quiet. She tongued in an acknowledgment.

The general wants you to bring the Recon team up to combat readi-ness. You're to slip out quietly and join them.

So as not to panic the civilians.

She sent the affirmative, stood, and unhooked her own slate all in one smooth motion.

"What is it?" Ryder was standing as well, effectively blocking her way to the aisle. There'd be no trouble getting by him, but the result wouldn't be considered slipping out quietly.

About to input Corporal Nivry's code, Torin paused and adjusted her grip on the slate. "You'll know when they decide to tell you," she told him flatly. "I think you should get out of my way now."

He studied her expression for a moment longer, then, with a grin, spread his hands in surrender—a gesture he seemed fond of, Torin noted—and turned sideways, leaving room for her to get by but not without close contact.

One long stride put her very close to his left shoulder, where she said, so softly he had to cant his head to hear, "I could kill you and not make a sound doing it. They'd find your body sitting in this seat, looking surprised and beyond revivification. Get. Out. Of. My. Way."

For a big man, he could move quickly when he had to.

"Thank you."

The grin was gone. "Staff Sergeant, I'm sorry I . . ."

"Attention, **Berganitan,** *I are Presit a Tur durValintrisy of Sector Central News. I are needing immediate assistance!"*

Captain Carveg looked like she was about to take a bite out of something, preferably Presit a Tur durValintrisy. "Sector Central News, this is Captain Carveg of the *Berganitan,* narrow your bandwidth! You're jamming all ship's frequencies!"

"I are saying again. I are needing immediate assistance. My ship are having difficulties upon exiting Susumi space!"

There was no mistaking Katrien syntax. The Katrien scientists seemed excited by the contact and more excited when the captain strode over to them. Actually, as far as Torin was concerned, the Katrien always seemed excited about something.

Staff Sergeant Kerr, General Morris says that's a negative on combat readiness. Stand down the team.

Torin sent the lieutenant an affirmative and an expression that clearly asked, *It's the media; are you sure?*

After a moment's exaggerated consideration, he nodded as a call code sounded from her slate.

Hitting audio only, she brought it up by her mouth.

"Staff Sergeant Kerr? What the hell was that?"

"That was exactly what it sounded like, Corporal Nivry. The media appears to have breached a class four security. When I know more, you'll know more."

"You think it was Captain Travik?"

The general certainly seemed to, although the captain appeared to be vehemently denying the possibility. Torin looked pointedly at Craig Ryder, standing barely an arm's length away. "I think we have to consider all possibilities, Corporal. Find the best hacker on the team and have them go over the attachment's security. I don't want a further breach."

"I'm on it, Staff."

"You think I had something to do with this?"

Torin replaced the slate on her belt and, turning only her head, looked over at the salvage operator. "No. The more people who know about the ship, the better the odds someone'll try to jump your claim—and you're way too paranoid to let it slip."

"But you said . . ."

"That we had to look into all possibilities." She refocused her attention on the officers at the front of the room. "You are not the *only* possibility, Mr. Ryder."

His sigh had force enough to move a strand of hair against her cheek. "And here I thought we were getting along."

There wasn't any point in responding to that.

He sighed again. "I shouldn't have blocked your way, should I?"

"No."

"I said I was sorry."

"I know."

"I meant it."

"Okay." Answering a gesture from the general, Torin left him standing there—hopefully reevaluating his place in the current scheme of things, but she doubted it. An ego like his had to be resilient.

"Staff Sergeant, I want you to accompany Commander Verite and the security detail she'll be taking down to meet our unexpected visitor. I want to know everything that's said."

"Yes, sir." She shot a glance at Captain Travik—who was looking petulant—and slid it over to Lieutenant Stedrin.

General Morris read her question from the motion. "I'm not sending the lieutenant, because I don't want to give this representative from Sector Central News too much credence."

"Yes, sir."

He didn't bother explaining why he wasn't sending Captain Travik. But then, he didn't need to.

"Hey, Sib, that ship's particle trail leads right back to the exact point the *Berg* exited Susumi space."

Sibley frowned over at the tiny ship surrounded on all planes by the six fighters, their extended energy fields all that was holding it together. It was smaller than an STS shuttle, smaller than the *Promise* would be without her cargo panels. "Is there even room in that thing for a Susumi engine?"

"Well, they sure as *sanLi* didn't take the long way out."

"Good point. And good piloting. Given the readings coming off it, I'm amazed they're not sucking vacuum."

The nine members of the security team were wearing side arms. Neither Torin nor the commander were carrying weapons.

"Sensors read three Katrien in there," Commander Verite said softly as they took up positions at the air lock's inner door. "No weapon signature, but if this is some kind of an elaborate trick, Staff Sergeant, I want you to get out of the way and let my people handle it."

"Yes, ma'am."

"Telltales are green, Commander." The crewman by the door had one hand on his weapon, the other about a millimeter above the release pad.

"All right." She checked her masker and nodded. "Open it."

Torin had been on Sai Genist when the media had landed—it was like being attacked with both hands tied, with the Marines helpless to do anything in their own defense. Fortunately, it hadn't lasted long. The vid crews seemed to believe that, while they were shooting, they were immune to what everyone else was shooting. They weren't. And the signal from their equipment made it easy for the enemy to lock in. Torin's platoon had been covered in debris, but the enemy's aim was so exact no Marine was actually injured.

Vid crews got smarter after that. At least the vid crews from that particular news company. She didn't think they belonged to Sector Central News although a number of the crew had been Katrien.

The moment they had room enough between the door and the bulkhead, the three Katrien pushed out into the corridor, all talking at once.

Torin recognized the one in front. Recognized the silver fur edging the dark mask and running in single lines down each side of the muzzle. Recognized the way the black vee ran up the collarbone and over both shoulders to spread into a dark cape that ended in a narrow triangle halfway down the spine. *And if that's not enough, they're the same fukking dark glasses.*

"Staff Sergeant Torin Kerr." The Katrien pushed right by the commander. "I are Presit a Tur durValintrisy, Sector Central News. I are thanking you for your help in leading us to this story."

The next Katrien out was definitely recording.

Torin could feel the eyes of the entire security team now locked on her rather than on their visitors.

"Staff Sergeant?" The commander's voice was a low growl. Things were about to get ugly.

"One minute, Commander."

There was a slow way to get to the truth, and a quick way. Torin chose the latter.

Katrien were small, barely a meter high. They were, like all of the Elder Races, noncombatants. They were also very fast, but they had to know they were supposed to start running.

Torin dropped to one knee and leaned forward until her nose was almost touching the damp black tip of Presit a Tur durValintrisy's muzzle. Reaching up, she pulled off the dark glasses and locked eyes with the Katrien. "Please, explain," she said softly in a tone that had once caused a new recruit to piss himself in fear.

A wave rippled down the soft gray fur of the reporter's throat as she swallowed. "We are interviewing Captain Travik, and he are saying he are leaving on a top secret mission with General Morris. We are knowing General Morris are using you, Staff Sergeant Kerr, on his previous secret mission, so we are watching all shuttles from OutSector for Marines of your rank. Once we are finding you, we follow and find out you are going to *Berganitan*, then we are following *Berganitan*. You are not giving away the secret mission. We are not intending to cause you trouble."

"Thank you."

Pupils constricted to pinpricks, she put her hand on Torin's wrist. "Glasses?"

"Of course." Torin returned them and straightened.

Presit a Tur durValintrisy shook herself and spun around to face the Katrien who was recording. "Are you getting that? I are threatened!"

Ears flipped up and then down, the Katrien equivalent of a shrug. "Staff Sergeant are saying 'please' and 'thank you.'"

Torin got the distinct impression that Presit a Tur durValintrisy was less than popular with her crew. Hardly surprising if the near fatal trip had been her idea.

"Right. Well. Looks like you're in the clear, Staff Sergeant." The commander signaled her security team to fall in around the news team. "If you'll all come this way, Captain Carveg and General Morris would like to speak with you."

Torin stepped back as Presit a Tur durValintrisy swept forward and fell into step beside the commander, who was shortening her stride considerably. She found herself walking beside the third Katrien. Probably a male, but she didn't make assumptions. When she glanced down, it held up a hand.

"Durgin a Tar canSalvais. Call me Durgin."

She stroked her palm across his—a Tar, male. The skin was so soft it felt as though it had been dusted with powder.

"Nice you're not holding a grudge at least."

His ears flipped. "Hey, I are just her pilot. What are I caring if you are intimidating the *aururist*?"

The way the hair lifted off Presit a Tur durValintrisy's spine, Torin figured that had to be a very bad word. Now that she was getting a better look at it, that black triangle was too regular to be natural. It had to be dyed.

"Actually," Durgin continued, "I are thinking you are going to pick her up by the throat and shake her."

Torin's eyes narrowed as she watched the reporter mincing up the corridor. "Yeah. So was she."

FIVE

"General, General." The reporter raised a gently protesting hand, silvered claws glittering. "Protests are beside the point. Under laws of full disclosure if media are present, media must not be denied. If Marines are going into ship, we are going in with them."

"All three of you?"

"No. Durgin are pilot only. He are staying with my ship. I, Presit a Tur durValintrisy, and my crew, Cirvan a Tar palRentskik, are going in."

Her crew didn't look too happy about it.

"We don't know what's in there, Presit a Tur durValintrisy . . ."

She smiled winningly, showing many tiny points of teeth under the black line of her lip. "Call me Presit."

". . . but it will be dangerous. You'll be putting yourself and your crew in danger."

"I are not going in, in front, General Morris." The tiny points of teeth reappeared, and a purple tongue swept lightly over them. "But I are going in."

Teeth, tongue, body language; if the reporter had been Human, Torin would have said she was flirting with the general. She looked like she was about to rub against his leg.

By the time the security detail had escorted the three Katrien back to the briefing room, the scientists had been cleared out. Only the three Marine officers, Captain Carveg and two of her officers, and Craig Ryder remained. As far as Torin was concerned, they should have tossed Ryder out with the other civilians—having reached the alien ship, there was no longer a need to suck up in order to get his Susumi equations. The general had probably gotten used to including him and hadn't even noticed he was there.

Hands behind his back, General Morris frowned down at his reflection in the reporter's dark glasses. "All right. You and your crew may accompany the science group into the ship. You will not go in with the Recon team because I will not have you exposed to unknown dangers."

"A compromise, General? According to law, I are not having to compromise." She lifted one hand and combed her claws through her whiskers. Alien body language or not, Torin recognized a smug gesture when she saw one. "But I will."

"Good. And now, the other matter—you said you followed Staff Sergeant Kerr to the *Berganitan* . . ."

"No, no, no," Presit interrupted. Leaning around the general, she showed teeth at Torin. This time, it didn't look anything like a smile. "I are only following Staff Sergeant Kerr until I know what ship she are taking. Then I are following that ship to *Berganitan.*"

"Fine. You followed Lieutenant Commander Sibley's Jade to the *Berganitan.* How did you follow the *Berganitan* through Susumi space?"

Presit actually waved a tiny finger at the general. If Torin hadn't disliked the reporter so much, she'd have been enjoying this. "I are not having to tell you that, General Morris. Thanks to suspicious Parliament, full disclosure works only one way. You are having to disclose to me, but I are not having to disclose to you. But," she added as the general flushed puce, "it are no big thing. I are merely . . ."

Durgin trilled an interruption. Torin figured he objected to Presit's pronoun.

". . . locking on the tail end of the *Berganitan*'s Susumi signature," she continued, ignoring her pilot. "It are a tricky maneuver—we are having to be close enough to follow but not so close we are being swept up in the wake and destroyed—but are not a secret."

His broad cheeks lightening slightly to maroon, General Morris attempted to lock Durgin in a steely glare, but it kept sliding off the nearly black lenses of his glasses. "You're a pilot, you had to have known how insanely dangerous that was. You could have destroyed both ships. As it was, you nearly destroyed yourself and your passengers."

The pilot's ears flipped down and up. "Unfortunately," he began.

Presit cut him off, her glasses still pointed toward the general. "Durgin a Tar canSalvais are working for me. If he are intending to continue working for me, he are keeping certain things to himself."

Durgin's ears flipped again. "Yeah, what she are saying."

"Fine." Taking a deep breath, the general appeared to accept the situation the law had placed him in although his voice retained a snarl around the edges. "Owing to the unfortunate, near destruction of your vessel, Presit a Tur durValintrisy . . ."

"Please, Presit."

"Yes, Presit." He cleared his throat and continued through clenched teeth. "Captain Carveg has kindly offered all three of you quarters on the *Berganitan*."

"Where she are keeping an eye on us," Presit murmured, summing up exactly what Torin had been thinking. "Still . . ." The fingers of her left hand made three quick passes through her whiskers. ". . . I are graciously accepting."

Captain Carveg stepped forward. When a Krai showed that much tooth, the more edible species usually found some distance to put between them. "If you'll just accompany Yeoman Sanderson," she said politely, her tone in complete opposition to her expression, "he'll show you to the guest quarters. This is a warship and space is at a premium, so I'm afraid your pilot and your crew will have to share."

"They are not caring." Leaning around the other side of the general, Presit waggled silver-tipped fingers toward Captain Travik. "We are talking later, you and I."

The captain nodded graciously, "I'd be honored."

"You'd be honored?" General Morris asked, turning slowly to face his subordinate.

"Yes, sir. The full disclosure law may require my compliance, but if Presit a Tur durValintrisy of Sector Central News wants to speak with me, I would be honored."

He sounded sincere.

Torin couldn't decide what she wanted to do more, puke or smack him, but it certainly explained why he was so popular with the press.

"And this one, General." Presit's attention switched to Torin, who met her gaze with bland indifference. "You are intending to deal with how she are behaving to me?"

"That are . . . is, between myself and the staff sergeant." He nodded at the yeoman, who stepped forward.

"Ma'am."

"So polite." She smiled up at the young Human. "You are leading us, so go. We are following."

Looking slightly confused by the syntax, Yeoman Sanderson led the way from the briefing room, the reporter and her crew close on his heels, talking rapidly in their own language. Durgin fell in behind, occasionally interrupting. Cultural rules seemed to differ when communicating in Katrien as opposed to Federate.

General Morris rocked back on his heels as the door closed. "I don't suppose there's any way the locks on their quarters can malfunction until we're done here?" he snarled in Captain Carveg's direction.

Recognizing the snarl had nothing to do with her—which was lucky for the general—she shook her head. "Sorry, no."

"I can't believe they followed us through Susumi space."

"So it seems."

"That's insane."

"Yes."

"We have to get their equations. If they've actually found the sweet spot—and aren't merely the luckiest three S.O.B.s ever evolved—the information will have major military applications. Is there some way you can access their ship's logs?"

"Legally? No. Accidentally . . ." Captain Carveg smiled.

The smile suggested her people were already working on it.

"Good." Nodding, he repeated "good" to himself a couple more times, then turned toward Torin. "Now then, Staff Sergeant Kerr." His voice frosted over. "If I could have a moment of your time."

"Yes, sir."

They walked a short distance from the clump of officers.

"Is it true you threatened Presit a Tur durValintrisy?"

Torin met his gaze levelly. "No, sir. She made a statement, and I asked her politely for an explanation, saying both 'please' and 'thank you.' It's all on record."

"I'm not an idiot, Staff Sergeant." He clamped one hand down on a chair back. His knuckles whitened, his fingers sank into the upholstery. "I am well aware you're capable of saying *please* in such a way as to blister the finish off a tank."

"Yes, sir."

Sighing, he released the chair. "Don't do it again."

"No, sir."

"The scientists will want a day or so to interpret the data. See that our people are ready when they are."

"Yes, sir."

Recognizing a dismissal when she heard it, Torin waited until he'd rejoined the others, then she left the room. She was barely three meters down the corridor when she heard someone following, and a moment after that, Craig Ryder fell into step beside her.

"What?"

"Nothing. We're just going the same way. It's a free corridor. And"—he spread his arms—"it's the only way . . . excuse me . . ." Spinning sideways, he allowed two of the *Berganitan*'s crew to go by. ". . . to the links."

"What are you so happy about?"

"Well, I'm just basking in the knowledge that there's now a life-form on this ship you dislike more than me." He hit the link call a second before she could, but when the car arrived, Torin slid past him to claim it.

"For what it's worth," she said, as the door closed, "if you were also a reporter, I'd dislike *you* more."

Staring at the closed door, Craig grinned and hit the link call again.

"She wants me," he said conversationally to the crewman who'd arrived in time to hear the parting remark.

The crewman stared at him for a moment and then burst out laughing.

The next afternoon, Captain Travik, having spent the morning stroking his own ego with Sector Central News, arrived at the enlisted quarters for a surprise inspection.

Torin managed to get him out before much damage had been done. "I want this place spotless by the time I get back," she snapped, following the captain out the hatch. "And if it doesn't pass *my* inspection, you'll be doing it again."

"First, I'm reporting this incident to the general and then I'm putting them all on report," Captain Travik snarled as she caught up. "Every last one of them. When I'm done, the corporals will all be privates and the privates will be . . . privates for longer!"

"It was an accident, sir."

"Which was an accident, Staff Sergeant?" he demanded, cradling one hand against his chest. "The slammed locker or the spilled depilatory?"

Since Krai had minimal hair, the depilatory had been more of a waste of time in Torin's opinion. "Both, sir. You took them by surprise. You were the last person they expected to see."

"That was the point," he sneered. "It was a surprise inspection, and they attacked me."

"They *are* combat Marines, sir, and beyond that, they're Recon. First in, always facing the unknown, hair-trigger responses; if they'd actually attacked you, you'd be in Med-op right now. But you know about that, *you're* Recon." Amazed she'd managed to get that last bit out without gagging, she checked his expression.

The sulky look had vanished.

"Hair-trigger responses . . ."

"Yes, sir."

He tentatively flexed his fingers. "It was an accident?"

"Yes, sir."

"All right." They'd reached the door to his office. He turned and drew himself up to his full height—which would have been more effective had that not put the top of his head at Torin's collarbone. "For the sake of the team and because we're all Recon together, I will overlook their behavior."

"Thank you, sir."

"This time." His chin lifted, his nose ridges flushed. "But I'm still recording it, and if anything like it happens again, accident or no, I will not be so understanding."

"Sir, if anything like it happens again, I will personally hold the air lock open while you kick their collective asses into space."

Although she'd been gone only a short time, the enlisted quarters were gleaming when Torin returned. Standing just inside the hatch, fists on her hips, she swept her gaze up one side of the compartment and down the other, allowing it to freeze each member of the team indiscriminately. She didn't know exactly who'd done what, and she didn't care.

"Captain Travik has been convinced not to bring the whole lot of you up on charges." From the stiffening of certain shoulders, the fact that Captain Travik could bring charges hadn't occurred to everyone. "You lot are luckier than you deserve to be, and if you ever again put me in the position where I've got to kiss up to an officer—any officer—to save your sorry butts, I am going to make your lives so goddamned miserable you're going to beg to be dropped into the front lines stark naked and armed with a sponge just to get away from me. Do I make myself clear?"

"Yes, Staff Sergeant."

It wasn't exactly a unison response, but it was close enough.

"Something funny, Guimond?"

The big Human's smile disappeared. "No, Staff Sergeant."

"Good. The whole miserable lot of you are confined to the attachment tonight. No one goes into the *Berganitan.* Twenty minutes, simulation room, full HE gear." She stepped back through the hatch and slammed it closed.

"Problems, Staff?"

Only with lieutenants who lurk in corridors! Palm flat against the cool metal of the hatch, she counted to three before she turned. "No, sir."

"General Morris sent me to tell you that you're going in tomorrow morning."

"Thank God." It felt so good, she checked to see that Lieutenant Stedrin's masker was on.

He actually smiled, eyes light. "Natives getting restless, Staff?"

"That would be the polite way of putting it, sir."

"Well, they can keep busy tonight humping their gear to the shuttle. Navy's moving it to our lock ASAP. We should have full hookup in thirty," he added, glancing down at his slate.

"Do we have numbers on the scientists, sir?"

"We're still trying to get them to agree to six, but you can assume eight; plus Ryder and the two Katrien from the news vids. The general wants everyone on board and ready to go at 0830 tomorrow."

Nice to get the chance to sleep in. There were benefits to traveling with civilians. "Should I tell Captain Travik?"

"I've already done it." About to turn away, Lieutenant Stedrin paused, his eyes darkening. "You wouldn't happen to know why he tried to get the drop on me as I came into his office?"

Tried. Torin grinned. "He's Recon, sir. Hair-trigger responses."

"Weren't we supposed to be in the simulation room in twenty minutes anyhow?" Guimond wondered as the sound of the slammed hatch stopped ringing through the compartment.

"She's not as pissed about what happened as she's pretending," Nivry told him, yanking her locker open.

"Oh, yeah?" Heer pulled a sheaf of crumpled schematic diagrams out from under his mattress and began reattaching them to the bulkhead over his bunk. "Then why the CTA?"

"We're always confined to the attachment just before a mission," she reminded him. "And besides, she *is* pissed about the sucking up. Today's simulation is going to be fast and mean."

"And that's just the way Werst likes it." Frii tossed his headphones onto his bunk and made exaggerated kissing noises at the Krai.

Who responded with a curt, "Fuk you."

"Fast and mean."

"You've still got seventeen minutes," Guimond said helpfully.

The di'Taykan looked intrigued, but when Werst shot him an unmistakable gesture, he turned to the big Human instead. "What *were* you smiling about, Guimond?"

He shrugged, smiling again. "I just thought that whole naked with a sponge thing was funny."

Werst snorted.

"You didn't think it was funny?"

"Moron."

"Corporal Nivry!"

Waving the others quiet, Nivry opened the channel on her slate. "Staff?"

"Simulation's been scrubbed. We're out of here tomorrow. I want the whole team in the armory in fifteen."

"We'll be there in ten, Staff."

"No need to suck up, Corporal, I'm as anxious to get out of this tin can as you are."

At 0820 Torin stared down at her slate, read the contents again, then looked up at the general. "Sir, I still think the civilians should be on a second shuttle. Our STS can back off, and they can attach the moment we've secured the immediate area."

General Morris shook his head. "They've studied the coupling, and they're afraid that once an STS has detached, it'll need a complete overhaul before we attach another."

"With all due respect, sir, what about being afraid of a defense system that suddenly activates while we're inside and blows them into overeducated sticky bits?"

"Several factors indicate the need for an overhaul, but there's been no data collected indicating a defense system. Their argument, not mine," he added hurriedly. "Bottom line, Staff Sergeant, if they get themselves blown up, no one's going to blame you. And Captain Travik will be staying on the shuttle with them. For their protection."

And will thus have died valiantly should something happen.

It hung between them, unsaid but acknowledged.

"Too bad Sector Central News will have blown up with him," Torin muttered.

"I'm sure Lieutenant Stedrin will add a satisfactory obituary to his report."

The lieutenant's ears turned at the sound of his name. He crossed the compartment toward them, adding new information into his slate as he walked. "The pilot says they're clear to go, sir."

"Thank you, Lieutenant. Staff Sergeant . . ."

"Sir." Torin took a step back, snapped her slate into position on her HE suit, turned on one heel, and headed for the air lock. When she turned to cycle the inner door closed, Lieutenant Stedrin raised a hand in farewell. Although he remained the least di'Taykan-like di'Taykan she'd ever served with, she'd much rather have been commanded by him on this mission than Captain Travik.

Although, since I'd rather be commanded by a H'san's grandmother, that's not saying much . . .

The personnel compartments on ship-to-ship shuttles went straight back from the pilot's cabin. A double row of seats, back to back, ran down the center with a weapons station both port and starboard. Tsui and Jynett had proved to be the best shots during simulations, so Torin had assigned them the covering seats. With thirty seats to seat twenty-seven, they were almost at full configuration.

The scientists had filled the first ten. General Morris hadn't been able to hold them to eight—let alone the original six. In typical Confederation fairness-before-all-else, they consisted of two Katrien, two Niln, two Humans, two Krai, and two di'Taykan. The Ciptran had probably been left behind because there was only one of him/her. Because Presit and her crew had claimed seats side by side—although Cirvan was still standing and shooting vid—there were two empty places between the last starboard-side scientist and Torin's place in back of Captain Travik.

Military and civilians alike were wearing HE suits, helmets off, and the only one who seemed to be missing was Craig Ryder.

No loss. I've already got more deadwood than people I can use.

"G'day. Mind if I sit here?" He was suddenly at her left shoulder, nodding toward the empty seat next to hers.

Knew that *was coming.* "What if I said yes?"

"I'd sit here anyway."

"So why do you even ask?"

Ryder grinned up at her as he dropped into the seat and reached for his straps. "Just because you're a grumpy gus is no reason for me to be rude."

"I'm a what?"

Blue eyes gleamed. "But I'm sure you're very good at your job."

Torin opened her mouth and closed it again. There just really wasn't any point. "Guimond, Orla; check to see that the civilians are belted in properly."

The two Marines stood and clumped forward, their heavy soles ringing against the deck plates. Torin stopped Orla as she passed.

"Special attention to the Niln," she murmured. "They're never entirely comfortable with their tails stuffed down a suit leg, so they never strap tightly enough."

"Got it, Staff." The di'Taykan glanced down at Ryder and her eyes lightened. "You want me to check him, too?"

"No need," Ryder answered before Torin could. "The staff sergeant'll do it."

"Go on," Torin told her.

Smirking, she clumped off.

Torin leaned down, one hand on each side of Ryder's shoulders, their noses no more than ten centimeters apart. "You want me to check your straps?" she purred. His eyes widened as her right hand dropped between them. "They seem a little . . . slack." A quick yank brought out a strangled yelp and a roar of laughter from the watching Marines. "That's much better." She straightened as he pawed for the release catch. "I wouldn't want anything floating loose."

"If it floats loose, it'll only be because you've broken it off," he muttered to more laughter as the straps released.

Torin figured his relieved sigh would be the last she'd hear from him for a while.

On the other side of the seats, Guimond had finished with his five scientists and was trying, unsuccessfully, to get Cirvan into his seat.

"I are just needing a few more things on record," Presit explained. "It are so important to properly set the scene. Don't worry, Private Guimond, I are sitting and strapped in before we are detached." The reporter craned her neck and pointed toward the back of the compartment. "You are telling me, what are that back there?"

"That?" Guimond peered toward the green leather bunk built into the rear bulkhead. "That's the Med-op, ma'am."

"The Med-op?"

"It's the medical station," Captain Travik rushed to explain.

Poor boy. Doesn't want his reporter's attention on someone else.

"Ah." Presit went to claw her whiskers and frowned down at the heavy glove. "It are for Marines or for Navy?"

"Both Marines and Navy personnel have been laid there."

"And some of them were even wounded," Guimond added, ingenuously.

As the scientists craned around in their seats to see what the Marines were finding so funny, Torin waved Guimond away and leaned over the seat backs, her mouth by Captain Travik's ear. "Sir, we need everyone in their seats. If you could convince your news people to stop recording for a moment . . ."

"Wait." Presit's raised hand held Cirvan where he was. "This are a ship-to-ship shuttle, Staff Sergeant; why are it carrying weapons?"

"All STS vessels carry weapons, ma'am." Torin turned her head just enough to see her reflection in Presit's glasses. "Because sometimes that second ess doesn't stand for ship."

The reporter's brow creased, her fur folding into dark and light bands. "Ship to shi . . . Oh. You are being funny, Staff Sergeant. Marines are all being funny." The black line of her upper lip curled up. "You are taking your act on the road?"

"We're *trying* to, ma'am. Sir?"

"I think you'd better sit your crew down, Presit." Captain Travik touched the reporter lightly on the shoulder of her suit, clearly enjoying the thought that they were his news people. "I'd hate for anything to happen to the recording."

"Ah, yes, the recording." Presit trilled something in her own language and Cirvan howled something back as he sat down. Which incited the Katrien scientists to add their two credits' worth in a register that made Torin's teeth vibrate.

She straightened and somehow resisted the urge to beat her head against the bulkhead.

"Captain Travik, this is Lieutenant Czerneda. We're green for detach. Waiting for your go."

"Staff Sergeant Kerr."

"Yes, sir." Torin dropped into her seat and slaved her slate to the shuttle with one hand as she tightened her straps with the other. "Johnston, your left foot's not secured."

"Fuk. Sorry, Staff."

The last telltale flashed as she slid the toes of her boots under the plastic loops. "All personnel are secured, sir, air lock is sealed."

"Lieutenant Czerneda, this is Captain Travik. We're green for go."

"Roger, Captain. Detach in three, two, one . . ."

A familiar shudder ran down the length of the shuttle closely followed by a series of loud cracks. Torin had long suspected the Navy pilots of feeding sound effects through the comm system. In a universe that included furniture in a tube and spreadable broccoli, there was no other reason for the clamps to sound as though they'd been broken off rather than released.

She swallowed as they dropped into zero gee and swallowed again before saying, "If you're feeling queasy, take the suppressant. No one wants to be chasing puke through the compartment."

Behind her, she could hear someone shifting in his or her seat. Could be the captain, could be either of the Katrien, they were about the same size.

"This shuttle are having no gravity generator?" Presit asked, her voice pitched a little higher than usual and almost loud enough to echo off the facing bulkhead.

"I *am* sorry." The captain sounded more smug than apologetic. Krai were virtually immune to all negative effects of zero gee; no nausea, no disorientation, no decrease in red blood cells, no bone loss should the lack of gravity be maintained over time. When the Confederation made first contact, they were planning a trip to a star almost three light-years away in zero gee the whole trip.

A repeated pressure on Torin's left shoulder turned out to be Ryder's shoulder nudging against hers. When she glanced over, he had the shuttle's schematics on his slate. "This thing's *got* a gravity generator," he murmured for her ears alone—although as the Katrien were talking again, it wasn't a particularly soft murmur.

"Uses a lot of energy," Torin told him. "Navy won't waste it if it isn't necessary. Might need it for something else."

He nodded appreciatively. "And there's a lot of something else in here, too. This shuttle's got more lethal bells and whistles than a H'san toilet."

"I wouldn't know. And you're in files you shouldn't be able to access."

" 'Shouldn't' is such an interpretive word." Three fast screens went by; he lingered on performance variables. "Looks like the Navy bought next year's model. Do you Marines have this kind of fancy flight equipment?"

"Not likely. Marines just want the damned things to fly and drop explosives." She keyed her override code into her slate and his screen went blank. "If you survive this mission, I'm going to have to have you mind-wiped."

"You're joking."

She shrugged. "Okay."

"I mean about surviving the mission. What's to survive?"

"We won't know until we get there, will we?"

"Fair enough." He sighed, snapped his slate back on his suit, sagged within the confines of his straps, folded his arms, and stared at nothing in particular. After a moment, he focused his gaze on Torin's face. "Are we there yet?"

Torin ignored him.

"You're smiling, Staff Sergeant. I can see the corner of your mouth rise."

Oh, damn, she *was* smiling. There was nothing to do but continue ignoring him although she could feel his triumphant grin dancing between them. She pushed her chin against the collar of her suit, activating the HE's comm unit. Because the helmet detached, it carried almost no tactical equipment. "All right, Marines, suit check. Communications, first. Sound off by squad . . ."

They'd barely completed the checklist when Lieutenant Czerneda informed the compartment they'd be attempting first attach in ten minutes. Captain Travik unstrapped and stood, twisting in his foot loops to face the scientists.

"Doctor Hodges, *Harveer* Niirantapajee, I believe this is your area of expertise."

Torin figured he was being gracious for the news recording. Or sucking up for reasons of his own. He certainly seemed to manage better with civilians than with other Marines.

The two scientists, a Human and a Niln, unstrapped carefully. The Human, Dr. Hodges, pushed off the front bulkhead, flew the length of the compartment, turned just before Med-op, realigned himself, and snapped his boots down just before impact with the inside door of the air lock. A few Marines applauded, shouting out observations more or less complimentary, and Torin had to admit she couldn't have performed the maneuver much better herself.

Harveer Niirantapajee, her balance off with her tail down the leg of her suit, walked the entire distance hissing softly as she detached, swung, and reattached each booted foot.

Guimond dug his elbow into Werst's side as the Niln passed. "Looks like she tucks left." The snicker took him by surprise. "Hey, you're laughing."

"And you're pathetic."

"But funny."

Arms folded, slumped low in his straps, Werst growled something that could have been an agreement.

As the pair of scientists opened an instrument panel surface-mounted beside the airlock's emergency manual controls, Torin stood and leaned over the seat back toward the captain. Under normal circumstances, she'd have subvocalized over the implants, but with the Katrien still talking, she didn't see much point. She'd have to shout to be overheard.

"Sir, do you think you should order helmets on, just in case?"

Travik looked confused. "In case of what?"

"Vacuum."

He glanced toward the air lock and reached for his helmet. "Good idea, Staff. Make it so."

"Sir?"

"Just give the order, Staff Sergeant."

"Yes, sir."

The civilians followed the Marines' example.

"Check each other's seals, people. You have no idea of the size of the report I'll have to write if one of you pops an eyeball." She slipped her feet out of the loops and flipped up and over to the captain's side. "Sir."

"I am capable of securing my helmet, Staff Sergeant," he sniffed indignantly.

"Yes, sir, but regulations are clear on this matter. I check you, you check me."

"Well, we wouldn't want you to have any trouble." His smile was a patronizing pat on the head. "Would we?"

"No, sir."

"You should tighten your right shoulder connection."

"Yes, sir." She resisted the urge to crack the seal on his tank. To give credit where credit was due, however reluctantly, he'd put himself together perfectly. *High marks for self-preservation.* Flipping back over the seats, she found Craig Ryder waiting for her.

"Odd man," he reminded her as she slid her feet back in the loops. "If you wouldn't mind."

The man got in and out of his helmet half a dozen times a day when putting together a load of salvage. He no more needed his seals checked than she did. She checked them anyway. Hard vacuum was as unforgiving as it got.

Before she could move away, he checked hers.

"Just in case," he murmured, helmet to helmet. She nudged her comm system off group channel before he could continue. The pickup was sensitive enough to throw his opinion out to every Marine in the shuttle. "No offense, but I wouldn't trust that captain of yours to recognize a weak seal if it opened under his nose."

"Thank you." And back on again—no one had missed her. "Heer, that had better not be your emergency rations I hear you eating."

"Wouldn't think of it, Staff."

"I don't care what you're thinking about; stop it," Torin snapped, grabbing a di'Taykan scientist as he floated by, arms and legs flailing.

"It seemed significantly easier to navigate in zero gravity on the training vid," he complained, without even the expected double entendre about being grabbed. She sent him back toward his seat where two pairs of hands snagged him and dragged him back down to his straps.

Oh, this is *going to be fun.*

"Attempt first attach in three minutes."

"Weapons, people, we don't know what's coming through that door."

The Marines' weapon of choice was the KC-7, a fairly primitive, chemically operated projectile weapon, impervious to electrical disruptions and built solidly enough that even nonfunctioning, it made a deadly club. Every Marine, no matter what their specialty or trade, qualified on the KC-7 during basic training or they didn't qualify to be Marines. Unfortunately, projectile weapons were a bad idea in space, where shooting holes in the structure containing the life-support system was inevitably fatal.

On those rare occasions where the Marines were thrown into ship-to-ship fighting, they used a BN-4, a weapon which combined a cellular disrupter for antipersonnel use and a tight band laser operating off the same energy pack. The Marines called them bennys and those who preferred them to the KC never admitted it.

"Are weapons wise, Captain Travik?"

Torin's lip lifted. The full disclosure laws granted the reporter access to both the group and the command comm channels. The Others had forced Parliament to acknowledge the need for both Confederation-wide branches of the military but nothing could force them to like it.

"What," Presit continued, "if the aliens of the ship are coming in peace?"

"Then we won't shoot but we prefer to have the option."

Well, good for him.

"Did I ever tell you about the time I outshot half a dozen of the Others' top marksmen while I freed Horohn 8?"

"Yes, Captain. You are telling me three times already."

And good for her.

"Attempting first attach in three, two, one . . ."

If not for some creative cursing from *Harveer* Niirantapajee as she worked at the new control panel with a filament probe, contact would have been too smooth to notice.

The telltales flickered and turned green.

"We have a seal. Equalizing pressure."

Torin had put together a boarding plan that Captain Travik had approved and presented to the general as his own. She didn't give a damn who got the credit as long as she was able to implement it. "Squad Two, defensive positions."

"Opening inner door."

"Squad One; into the lock. Squad Two; maintain your positions, this side. If I can't talk you out of this, Mr. Ryder, stay with me."

"Oh, I'm right behind you, Staff Sergeant."

"And stay off the comm."

The air lock on a Navy shuttle held fifteen bodies—a few less if they were Dornagain, a few more if they were Katrien or Niln. Torin placed her people around the edges and waited. After a short argument with his colleague, Dr. Hodges joined them.

The shuttle's inner door closed.

Torin hated how loud her breathing sounded within the confines of the helmet.

After the atmosphere had been pumped out—so many things reacted badly with oxygen—Dr. Hodges walked across the lock to the outer door where the telltales were already green. "I am now opening the outer door."

"Sounds like he's talking for fukking posterity."

"Tsui."

"Sorry, Staff."

The outer door opened.

The alien ship was even more yellow up close. Torin's helmet polarized slightly.

"I am now laying the sensor band against the ship." As he spoke, Dr. Hodges placed a strip of something about thirty centimeters long and no more than five wide along the center axis of the ship's outer door. Tiny red and green lights flashed up and down the length.

Never underestimate the power of a flashing light. Torin resisted the urge to snort.

After a moment, the lights changed their pattern, and the doctor removed it. "The door is now ready to be opened. Commence opening, *Harveer.*"

The Niln made no reply the comm could pick up.

The solid yellow acquired a thin black line.

"Come on, baby," Ryder breathed. "Papa needs a new O_2 scrubber."

There was vacuum on the other side.

Torin strained to see what they were facing.

The line grew thicker, and became an opening into what was unmistakably another air lock.

Once again, she noticed that this alien ship wasn't very alien. The first time she'd seen a H'san air lock, she'd thought it was a large bag of lime jelly. Which, in a way, it was, given that lime was also a color.

Oblivious to any potential danger, Dr. Hodges carried his sensor band to the inner door. "We're making history, *Harveer.*"

He was also making himself an obvious target, but that wasn't Torin's problem. She moved the squad forward as first the shuttle's and then the ship's outer door cycled closed. They were now inside the alien air lock. It was also yellow.

"Don't touch the walls, people. Defense systems could be on a contact trigger."

"Amazing," Dr. Hodges murmured, crouched over almost familiar controls set into the floor. "Equalizing pressure."

Torin thought she could feel the slight purr of working machinery through her soles.

The inner door of the alien ship opened as easily as the outer.

"They knew we were coming, so they baked a cake," Johnston muttered.

There was a general consensus in the following silence.

Frozen in place, they stared into a dull gray corridor approximately three meters wide. The light levels were low but bright enough, Torin decided, not to have them switch on lights. Frii was on point and di'Taykans could adjust their vision to handle anything but total darkness.

Benny ready, Torin motioned for Corporal Nivry to grab the doctor—who'd made a try for the interior. She counted to ten, slowly, then checked the microfiber readout in her left sleeve. "Johnston, get your arm over here."

The engineer's readout was identical.

The atmosphere in the alien ship seemed to be exactly the same mix as the atmosphere in the shuttle had been. The temperature was off by point four of a degree, but that appeared to be correcting itself as they watched.

"What do you think, Staff?"

The corridor was empty.

"Scanners?"

"Readings show more empty corridors, Staff. No movement. No life signs."

"I think," Torin sighed, straightening, "that this is remarkably anticlimactic."

SIX

W hen it became clear the shuttle was in no immediate danger, Torin sent a protesting Dr. Hodges back to his colleagues and brought the other squad into the ship, splitting the entire team into pairs. Even numbers stood with weapon ready. Odds dropped to one knee, giving the evens a clear shot as they followed the scans downloaded from Torin's slate to theirs.

"All right, people, we're going to set up perimeters here"—Torin tapped her screen—"here, here, here, here, and here." The points indicated flared green. "And just because our scanners have picked up nothing but empty doesn't mean we . . . what the hell are you doing?"

Helmet hanging down his back, Ryder scratched at his beard with both hands. "Air's breathable, I didn't see any reason to stay sealed."

"The air may be breathable *here*, but we don't know what's around the next corner."

He shrugged. "I'm not going around the next corner, am I?" When she continued to scowl, he sighed. "Look, Staff Sergeant, someone had to be first. You do consider me expendable, don't you?"

"I don't consider anyone expendable," she snapped, "but you're as close as I've come in a while."

"Staff, should we . . . ?"

"No. We stay sealed until this area is secure."

"Is this great or what?" Guimond asked, staring down another hundred meters of gray and empty corridor identical to the hundred meters of gray and empty corridor just in from the air lock. "My whole battalion's been on station duty for two months now and I was so bored I almost requested a transfer to a sector where the Others were on the offensive." He glanced down at Werst, who was deploying a perimeter guard. "Good thing I didn't, eh? I'd have hated to miss this."

"Oh, yeah," Werst grunted, securing the guard to the deck. "It's a thrill." He adjusted the sensors to take in the full width of the corridor, then activated them. If anything turned on, if anything changed, if anything moved—they'd know about it.

"What do you think? The crew's abandoned ship or they're hiding deep, waiting to see what we're going to do?"

"What crew?"

"Well, come on"—Guimond swept the point of his benny from side to side—"you don't build these kind of halls in a drone, it'd be a waste of space." He switched back to group channel. "Staff, this is Guimond. Ready to test."

"Roger, Guimond. Test on my mark. Three, two, one, mark."

A small capsule tossed out in front of the guard hit the deck and shattered.

The area covered by the guard's sensors shimmered briefly blue and, had both Marines not been suited up, they'd have caught the faint smell of ozone.

"Guimond, this is Staff Sergeant Kerr. Perimeter test registered as capsule four; nitrogen and a nine-volt pulse."

"Roger, Staff. Perimeter point is secure."

"Head on back to the lock. Keep your eyes open."

"Roger, Staff. Guimond out. Not that there's anything much to see," he added, switching off as another pair began their test. "No doors. No panels. No light fixtures. Still, can't complain."

"You can't?" Werst checked the settings one last time and straightened. "Come on."

"You're expecting trouble?" Guimond wondered, shortening his stride to match the Krai's. "No, wait, let me guess." His smile gleamed inside the curve of his helmet. "You always expect trouble."

"Only when things are too fukking good to be true."

"Like this ship."

Werst glanced up at the big Human. "Yeah. That, too."

"Can I ask you something?"

"Can I stop you?"

"Who's Roger?"

"What?"

"Why does the Corps use Roger to mean, 'I hear and understand'? Why not Angela? Or Fred? Or Werst even?"

"How the fuk should I know? It's a Human thing."

"It is?"

"It's not a Krai thing. Humans joined first; we got it from you."

"So maybe it's a di'Taykan thing."

"Only if it starts humping your leg."

As their footsteps faded in the distance, the floor on the other side of the guard quivered and the remains of the test capsule disappeared. Nothing registered on any of the sensors.

". . . because you haven't given me any reason to keep them here, Staff Sergeant. Empty corridors can hardly be considered a danger."

"Sir, scans show the walls are full of things our engineers can't identify. We can't even tell where the light is coming from."

"But it is *light, and warm, and breathable over there?"*

"Yes, sir. And that's what concerns me." Torin nodded as Nivry indicated the last pair had appeared around the corner. "Alien ships don't maintain life support identical to that in a Confederation Navy shuttle. It doesn't happen."

"Why not?"

"Sir, a Krai ship and a Human ship don't maintain identical life support." Years of practice kept the implied, "you idiot" out of her voice. "Something had to have created this for us."

"A friendly gesture."

"Or a trap."

"You've secured the area around the air lock?"

"Yes, sir. But . . ."

"No 'buts,' Staff Sergeant. I am the officer commanding. I believe there's no danger and I'm bringing them over."

"Yes, sir." Torin switched off the command channel. "He's bringing them over, people! Johnston, Heer; I want you free to hook up with the scientists. Tsui, Jynett; pair up."

"Should we desuit, Staff?"

Torin glanced over at Ryder, who was leaning against the wall, arms folded, smiling broadly enough that fine lines bracketed both eyes. "No.

And keep your helmets on. We've got two more species coming over. We'll see how the ship reacts to them."

"Ship's not reacting to anything, Staff Sergeant."

"Then what's that you're breathing, Mr. Ryder?"

He checked his sleeve. "Appears to be predominantly an oxygen, nitrogen mix—22.3 and 76.6 percent respectively. The remaining 1.1 percent is made up of . . ."

"No one likes a smart ass, Mr. Ryder."

"You'd be surprised, Staff Sergeant."

Fully aware that any possible response would only serve to further amuse their audience, Torin beckoned for Nivry. "Corporal, I want you to take three Marines out to the T-junction. I want one of you in sight of the air lock and the others wandering no more than two meters down either corridor. I want actual eyes and ears out there, just in case."

Nivry studied the hundred meters of featureless passage leading to the junction. "In case of what, Staff?"

"Of whatever, Corporal. Move."

"Moving. Guimond, Werst, Frii—you're with me."

"We just got back," Werst protested, as the other two fell into step with the corporal.

"Yeah? Well, nothing changed while you were gone. Come on."

As the four Marines started down the corridor, Torin moved the rest of the Recon team away from the air lock. If anything happened, she wanted them to have maneuvering room.

"And where would you like me, Staff Sergeant?"

The salvage operator's question had a distinctly mocking undertone. "In the *Berganitan.* Failing that, stay out of the . . ." She frowned. Was that music? "Frii, if you've brought your player with you and if you should have an earphone in, I'd like to remind you about the regulations concerning the wearing of players while deployed and I'd like to point out that the captain's already got me in a bad mood."

Silence. An absence of music.

"Uh, it's turned off, Staff."

"Good. Keep it that way."

And the lock still hadn't opened.

"What's taking them so long?" Dursinski muttered, shifting her weight from foot to foot.

Beside her, Tsui snorted hard enough to momentarily fog the inside of his helmet. "Reporter's probably trying to set up the best shot."

"That's enough, people. Telltales are green, they're . . ." Torin frowned. What were the odds of an alien ship using the same color codes as the Human-organized Confederation Marine Corps?

"Staff?"

"Private Huilin, what color do those telltales look to you?"

Out of the corner of one eye, she saw him turn his head to look at her, turquoise hair spread out so that each blunt end touched the inside curve of his helmet.

"They're green, Staff."

"And that doesn't strike you as strange?"

"Telltales are always green."

"Human; yes. And because the Confederation found us first, so's the Corps' and the Navy's. di'Taykan telltales are orange . . ."

"Yuin."

"Orange to Human eyes." di'Taykans saw a much broader color spectrum although less fine detail.

"Staff, are you saying this is a Human ship?" Corporal Harrop asked as the inner doors began to open.

"I'm saying this ship is more than it seems. Odd numbers turn around and face down corridor." Torin could tell by the way they moved, they thought she was being overly cautious. She didn't care what they thought, as long as they did what they were told. If nothing happened, it'd give them something to bitch about later in the barracks.

Ryder, who'd been standing about two meters down corridor, hurriedly shifted position. "You know," he murmured, having moved closer to Torin's external pickups, "you're giving paranoids a bad name."

Several snappy comebacks went to waste as Cirvan backed out of the air lock closely followed by Captain Travik looking heroic for the benefit of Sector Central News. Heroic quickly turned to surprise.

"Staff Sergeant Kerr, why are these Marines still in their suits? The HE does stand for Hazardous Environment, doesn't it?" He gave the camera a three-quarter shot, chin slightly lifted, and continued before Torin could answer. "And I believe this is not a Hazardous Environment."

Neither the captain, nor the reporters, nor any of the scientists now spilling excitedly—and in the case of the Katrien, noisily—into the corridor were still in their suits.

"Sir, I have reservations about this ship."

"Reservations?" Presit pushed her way past the two Niln and wrinkled her muzzle at Torin. "Then I are wanting a corner suite with an extra deep nest and full links." When Torin stared down at her blankly, she sighed. "It are a play on the word reservations, Staff Sergeant. Reservations as misgivings and as a promissory booking for a room. Human humor. It are important I are appealing to many species," she added, stroking her whiskers.

Torin stared at the reporter for a moment longer, then she switched her gaze back to the captain. "Sir, I can't help feeling that this isn't all there is."

"I understand your disappointment, Staff Sergeant."

"Sir?"

"You're a Marine, and we prefer action."

Which was when she understood he was still performing for the camera.

"Not only that, but it's your job to be cautious, Staff Sergeant. As an officer, it's my job to see the big picture. And the big picture says, you don't need those suits. Take them off."

"Sir . . ."

"That's an order."

"Yes, sir. Respectfully request permission to maintain suits until all gear has been removed from the shuttle." Given what the scientists had brought from the *Berganitan* and what they didn't seem to be carrying with them as they spread out from the air lock, that ought to take some time. By then, the other shoe might have dropped.

It hadn't.

Sealing up the front of her combats, Torin watched the two Niln scientists spraying what smelled like cheap Scotch on a section of wall delineated by what looked like a single fiber-optic strand. She shrugged into her vest, snapped her slate into place, reached for her helmet, and paused.

"I know what you're thinking."

Did the man not have anyone else to bother? And did he have to stand so damned close? Her brows drew in, and he took half a step back but maintained his smile as he continued.

"You're thinking that if they—whoever the 'they' on this ship are— can't show up with a welcoming committee they can at least take a shot at you, just so you know where you stand." Before she could respond, he held up a pouch. "Corporal Nivry's got the mess kit up and running; I brought you a coffee."

"A coffee?"

"Nothing like a little caffeine to put the day in perspective."

Maybe he wasn't so bad. "Thank you."

He fell into step beside her as she crossed the section of corridor the Marines had claimed as their own. "I notice you didn't disagree with me— about the shooting."

"You brought me a coffee. I'm not totally unreasonable."

"Good." Ryder dropped his voice to a low purr as they drew closer to other ears. "In case you're curious, the captain has made a preliminary report to the general saying that the Recon team has found this section of the ship deserted but that he'll be sending two patrols out beyond the established perimeter as soon as everyone's eaten."

"A civilian has no business listening to a military . . ." And then she realized and sighed. "He said it on vid, didn't he?"

"Yes, he did."

"And the general's reply?"

"Came through loud and clear. 'Good work, Captain. Carry on.' I expect Presit will do a couple of cutaways with the general later. She's really very good at her job. You should give her a break."

"Oh, I should break something," Torin muttered under her breath. Fortunately a screaming match between the two Katrien scientists had drawn the news team away, leaving the captain standing by the mess kit, sucking down coffee and looking bereft.

"Everything all right, sir?"

"Why wouldn't it be?" he demanded, ridges flushing.

"No reason. You looked . . ."

"I looked like this is a colossal waste of my time, Staff Sergeant." He flapped his half-empty pouch toward half a dozen scientists sitting and staring at monitors. "That lot's accomplishing nothing much, and if the scans we took are right . . ."

"They are." Although Torin had no idea where the "we" came from.

". . . then this place is going to be *serley* boring to explore." Finishing his coffee, he stuffed the pouch in the kit's recycler and pulled another.

"I'm going to make major after this trip and, oh, aren't kilometers of gray corridor going to look exciting on the vids. It's not fair."

Okay, we've reached today's limit. "Don't whine, sir, it's unattractive in an officer."

Nose ridges moving through red to purple, Travik glared up at her, coffee pouch dangling from one corner of his mouth. "What?"

"Sets a bad example for the enlisted personnel. They're looking to you for leadership, sir." It took an effort but she managed to close her teeth before adding, *not that I should have to tell you that.*

"General Morris will hear about that insubordinate comment, Staff Sergeant."

"Yes, sir."

Travik stomped away, jerked his slate up off his vest, and turned his back before he began talking. From the angle of the bristles on the back of his head, he was seething. From inside the ship, contact with the *Berganitan* was patchy at best, so all communications were routed through the shuttle's system; Lieutenant Czerneda monitoring in case anything else attempted to make contact. Right about now, she was getting an earful.

"Was that wise?" Ryder asked. "I mean, it's none of my business, but he seems like he could be an officious little prick."

Torin shrugged. "You're right. It's none of your business."

"Looking on the bright side, you seem to have cured his boredom."

"All part of the job." Bending, she slid a tray out of the section marked with a big red H. Unlike field rations, designed to satisfy the nutritional requirements of all three military species, the mess kit's prepared meals were species specific. "I assume we're feeding you?"

"I tried to get my mom to pack me some sandwiches, but . . . thank you." He took the tray out of her hands and peered through the clear cover. "Mystery meat and vegetables in a pita. Cup of soup—best not to look too closely at the puree. Pouch of juice and a pudding cup. All maintained at their intended temperature provided their intended temperature is luke-warm."

Torin snorted. "You sure you've never been a Marine?"

"I picked up a surplus mess kit a couple of years ago," he explained, dropping down to the floor beside her. "I can load it at any station and this stuff'll last indefinitely as long as it's sealed."

"Just one of the differences between us," Torin noted, toasting him with her soup. "You pay to eat like this, I get paid to do it."

*   *   *

"Looks like Staff Sergeant Kerr and the civilian are getting along," Orla murmured speculatively, eyes darkening as she leaned past the Marine next to her in order to get an unimpeded look.

"Who else is she going to hang with?" Tsui asked. "If she hangs with us, we feel like we're being watched all the time, and I doubt she wants to hang with Captain Asshole. Besides, Ryder's okay, as long as you don't play cards with the son of a bitch." He poked a finger into his pudding, and the reaction by the di'Taykan took the conversation into a biologically unlikely direction.

STAFF SERGEANT KERR.

The bounce from the shuttle threatened to overwhelm her implant. Torin adjusted the volume then tongued in an acknowledgment.

You're pissing Travik off on purpose. Stop it. I don't want to hear any more complaints from him for the duration. Is that clear?

"Yes, sir." Not much point in subvocalizing since she didn't intend to say anything that couldn't be overheard. She glanced up at the captain. From his smug expression, he'd been expecting the general to contact her. "Sorry, sir."

Any problems?

"No, sir."

Good. Keep it that way and keep him alive. Morris out.

"Talking to yourself?" Ryder wondered, glancing from her to the captain and back again.

Corps business was none of his.

"Sometimes it's the only way to have an intelligent conversation," Torin told him.

"Corporal Harrop."

"Staff?"

"Take three Marines and relieve Nivry. I'll call you in as soon they finish eating. Captain wants to send out the entire team in two patrols."

"If we're coming back in so soon, why are we even going out?"

"You're going out because I told you to go out."

"But . . ."

"And in a minute you'll be cleaning out the recycler in the latrine because I told you to."

"Orla, Jynett, Dursinski, you're with me."

"This are Presit a Tur durValintrisy for Sector Central News reporting from a corridor inside a ship belonging to no Confederation species. With me are *Harveer* Niirantapajee, head of the Xeno-engineering department at Jinaf-fatinnic University on the Niln home world of Ciir. *Harveer* Niirantapajee, please tell our audience what you are discovered about this alien ship."

"Bugger all," the elderly engineer grunted, her nictitating membranes flicking across the golden orbs of her eyes.

Presit's smile tightened. "Could you elaborate?"

"We got in okay. Having established a door, there is, after all, a limited number of ways you can get a door to open. Once in, nothing. Scans show there's working parts in the walls but we can't get to them. We can't find panels, we can't make a hole. We can't even get a really good picture. The only thing we're fairly certain of is that the ship is at least partially constructed of PHA—polyhydroxide alcoholydes."

"Which are?"

"Essentially organic plastic. Certain bacteria use PHA to store energy much the way mammals use fat."

"So, you are saying bacteria are building this ship?"

"No. I'm not."

Her tone moved the reporter on. "Are you being discouraged, *Harveer*?"

The membrane flicked across her eyes again. "As you said, the ship belongs to no Confederation species. It doesn't belong to the Alliance . . ."

"The Alliance, that are being our allies, the methane breathers."

"Right. Given that and given that we've only been working at it . . ." Her tongue touched a spot on the shoulder of her overalls. ". . . a little under two hours, don't you think it's early yet to be discouraged? Now, if you'll excuse me, I have to get back to beating my tail against this *scrisin* wall."

"Captain Travik, we're ready to send out the patrols."

"Well?"

"Well, what, sir?"

"Well, send out the patrols, Staff Sergeant. Do I have to do everything?"

"No, sir."

"Corporal Nivry, you'll take your patrol to perimeter point six. Harrop, to perimeter point five. You'll be running parallel to each other and pretty much parallel to the hull. Logically, there should be compartments of some kind between you, so both teams will run deep scans on the walls every three meters. Don't let your guard down."

"Uh, Staff, what are we guarding against?" Tsui asked, his smile a millimeter from mocking.

"Right now?" Her smile flattened his. "Me. Tomorrow, we'll see how much corridor we can map and still make it back before the shuttle leaves. Today, we'll concentrate on protecting our specialists while they pull data for the science team."

"Hey, Johnston." Tsui poked Squad One's other lance corporal in the thigh with the butt of his benny. "You wish you were still back with the eggheads instead of getting ready to hump that thing through never-never land?"

The engineer snorted and flexed the exoskeleton supporting most of the scanner's weight. "Oh, yeah, I'd much rather be listening to a pair of frustrated Katrien argue about solitons. Sounds like a fukking cat fight."

Arms folded—which had to be a human posture he'd adopted as Torin had never seen another Krai use it—Captain Travik exposed most of his teeth. "You don't make plans about future assignments without consulting your commanding officer."

"General Morris made it clear he wasn't to be bothered, sir."

"I was referring to *myself.*"

"Yes, sir. When I spoke of tomorrow's plans, I was referring to the boarding plan you downloaded and approved on the *Berganitan.*" Torin brought up the file and read from her slate. "Day one, secure the area and, should no hostiles be encountered, support the science team. Day two, should no hostiles be encountered, map as much of the ship's interior as possible. Day three . . ."

"I want you to consult with me before you implement!"

"Yes, sir." Hooking her slate back on her vest, Torin calmly met the captain's apoplectic gaze. "Tomorrow—before I implement tomorrow's plan—I will consult with you."

Travik stood there for a long moment, as the blood gradually drained from his facial ridges. "Good," he said at last. Then he spun on one heel and strode purposefully away.

"You're armed," noted a quiet voice at Torin's shoulder. "How do you keep from killing him?"

She watched the captain head straight for the news team. "Captain Travik is the officer commanding, Mr. Ryder. Marines are not in the habit of killing their officers."

"Okay."

"It's an acquired skill."

"Mind if I ask you a question?"

"I don't seem to be able to stop you."

"Why the helmet? We're not under fire."

"Among other things, my helmet contains a PCU—personal communications unit. I use it to maintain contact with the patrols."

"But doesn't the whole unit snap out so you can just shove it in one ear? I'm not saying the helmet doesn't look good on you." He met her frown with a grin. "I just wondered why. Does it give a feeling of security?"

Torin's tone would have told even a raw recruit that the conversation was over. "I don't like things shoved in my ears, Mr. Ryder."

"Okay."

Unfortunately, Craig Ryder was not a Marine. "Stop saying that."

"Why?"

Also unfortunately, *because I said so*, wasn't good enough for a civilian. *More's the pity.* Before Torin could come up with a suitable reply, a sudden shout from Dr. Hodges froze everyone in place and in a moment brought most of the other scientists running to his workstation just inside the air lock. *Harveer* Niirantapajee and both Katriens, who were working closest to the Marines, glanced up from their equipment but continued working.

"I'm too old to go scampering off every time his analyzer farts," she muttered in answer to Torin's silent question. "And these two won't leave me alone with their pretty new toy. But don't let us stop you from joining the fun."

"Fun," Ryder repeated, matching his stride to Torin's. "Fun would be blowing through the walls with explosives."

She considered discouraging him from dogging her footsteps, but since there wasn't anywhere else for him to go . . . "The di'Taykan are planning that for later."

"That's because the di'Taykan know how to have fun."

They reached the edge of the group a moment later to see Captain Travik installed at Dr. Hodges' elbow looking as though he were personally responsible for any successes. Cirvan had climbed up onto a crate trying to get more in his shot than the elbows of the taller species, and Presit was asking questions of the scientist—who ignored her as he dealt with the incoming data.

"What's he actually doing?" Ryder asked, sidestepping a stack of packing crates to get a better look.

"Don't know, don't care." Torin pulled her helmet forward and flipped the microphone down. "Nivry, Harrop, hold up. Something's happening here."

"You want us to head back?"

Torin glanced at the display on her slate. Both patrols were in the corridor designated NS2, separate but still in sight of each other. "No. Wait there until we know what's actually going on."

"Roger, Staff. We'll wait."

Straightening, Dr. Hodges thrust both hands over his head in triumph. "I have the numbers!"

"And that means?" Torin muttered.

"Seems to mean something to them." Ryder nodded toward the excited scientists. There was hurried movement away from the younger Niln's uplifted tail.

Waving off questions, Dr. Hodges aimed two beams of blue light at the wall, then caught up a strip similar to the one he'd used on the air lock door and rushed around his apparatus, accepting congratulatory pats from his colleagues as he ducked between the beams.

Ryder took a step closer and was pushed back as Dr. Hodges returned to his data, the spectators surging back and forth with his movements. "So what's his machinery do?"

Torin shrugged. "No idea. I do know it's damned heavy and, apparently, it shouldn't be dropped."

"Did you drop it?"

"Not personally." The light strip, now on the wall, lit up. For all Torin knew it might have been the same strip Dr. Hodges had used in the air lock. As far as she was concerned, one set of red-and-green flashing lights looked like another. She dropped her benny down off her shoulder and brought it around to the ready, just in case.

"Dr. Hodges. Dr. Hodges!" Whiskers quivering, Presit pushed herself between the scientist and Captain Travik. "Are you please telling our viewers just what it is you are doing?"

"I'm about to open an access panel. Now get out of my way."

As the reporter stepped indignantly back, Captain Travik stepped forward. "As the officer commanding this mission, I'd like to . . ."

"I said, move!"

Enjoying the captain's discomfort, Torin didn't see the actual moment the panel opened. When the cheering drew her gaze, a three-or-four-centimeter crack already ran halfway down the wall between the two beams of light. As it widened farther, all the hair rose off the back of her neck.

The deck shivered under the soles of her boots.

Grabbing a handful of Ryder's shirt, she threw him down behind the packing crates and followed him to the floor just as an explosion filled the corridor with flying debris and plumes of smoke. Ears ringing, she rolled up tight against the lowest crate, shoulder pressed hard against Ryder's back.

"Staff! What the hell was that?"

She snapped her mike down against her mouth. "Explosion by the lock! Report!"

"Area rippled. No damage. No casualties."

A second blast slammed up against the pile, sending the upper crates flying. A hunk of meat still wearing a bit of sleeve splashed against her boot. "We've got both!" Coughing, she checked her sleeve. Combats had a lot of basic tech built in. "Pressure's holding; no hull . . . Craig!"

Twisting around, Ryder swept one arm up and swept the debris off his forearm. It crashed and bounced, missing them both by centimeters.

"Staff? Staff Sergeant Kerr?"

"I'm here." Her eyes burned and her nose streamed. She wiped her face on the back of one hand while pulling a filter mask out of her vest with the other. "I say again, pressure's holding; no hull breach." A flick of the wrist unrolled the mask and she slapped it over her nose and mouth. The edges sealed.

"We're on our way!"

Metal screamed against metal.

"Be careful, there's a lot of smoke and the whole area's un . . . Fuk!"
Her legs, Ryder's legs, the crate had all sunk into the floor.

And they were continuing to sink.

There was nothing she could grab. Nothing that wasn't sinking as fast
as she was.

"Son of a fukking bitch!" Instinct brought his hands down to shove against
the floor. They sank. And he couldn't pull them out again.

Something popped in his shoulder. He kept fighting.

Not like this. Not like this. Not like this.

"Mr. Ryder! CRAIG!"

Strong fingers turned his head.

"LOOK AT ME!"

The voice promised consequences worse than being swallowed by an
alien ship if he disobeyed. Torin's face swam into focus.

"Stop it! It's not doing any good and it's pissing me off."

"Oh, that's comforting," he panted, panic shoved aside by irritation.

"Good."

Now he'd stopped thrashing, Torin grabbed for Ryder's right arm with both
hands.

He jerked away.

"Staff Sergeant Kerr!"

"Nivry!"

"Staff! What's happening?"

"We're being sucked into the goddamned floor, that's what's happening!"

Still feeling a solid surface under her feet, she couldn't stand. She
couldn't change her position. The pressure against her lower body was so
slight, it couldn't possibly be holding her in place. But it was.

What had been the floor was now up around their waists.

The muzzle of her benny was under the surface. The trigger was up by
her right breast. The angle was bad, but she forced her thumb through the
trigger guard without touching her elbow to the floor.

"What are you doing?" Ryder coughed, eyes widening. He began to struggle again, leaning away from her.

"Fighting back!"

"You don't know what that'll do!"

"Well, I don't fukking like what's happening now!"

The weapon fired—she watched the charge drop—but it had no effect.

"Staff Sergeant Kerr!"

She stopped pulling the trigger. Took a deep breath. Coughed. Spat. Watched it sink.

"Listen up, Nivry: there were three scientists down by our gear. If anyone made it, they did." The floor was up by her shoulders. Torin could see a mark made by one of the pieces of heavy equipment, a black scuff against the gray. If she turned her head, she could see the piece of arm—di'Taykan or Human. It was too small a sample to tell for certain. Apparently, the ship didn't want it. "Deal with the civilian casualties, then get the team out." Her left arm was under, immobile. She held her right arm over her head.

"We're not leaving you behind, Staff."

"Glad to hear it, Corporal. Feel free to come back with the proper gear."

The floor touched her chin. It felt cool. She couldn't smell anything but the smoke she'd inhaled before she got the filter on. *What the hell does a floor smell like anyway?* Since she couldn't move her head, she stared into Ryder's eyes. They really were the most remarkable blue. Pity his nose had been running into all that facial hair.

"Take a deep breath," he advised.

"No shit."

She folded down all but one finger on her right hand.

The world went dark.

SEVEN

"**S** taff Sergeant Kerr!"
      No response.

Six running paces later, Nivry tried again. And six paces after that. Six paces after that brought them around the corner into NS1, the corridor leading to the air lock.

All twelve jostled for position.

"Fuk a duck," Guimond breathed.

It looked like the explosion had blown every piece of scientific equipment they'd humped off the shuttle into a barrier stretching wall to wall and very nearly ceiling high. Tendrils of gray-brown smoke pushed through the narrow opening and slowly dissipated. An HE suit had been fused across the front.

"Hey!" Orla took a step closer, her eyes darkening. "That's my suit!"

"We are so screwed," Dursinski murmured. "Those things aren't supposed to melt."

Johnston swung the scanner around. "It's not melted," he said after a moment. "Its molecules have been integrated into the molecules of the equipment behind it."

"And that's supposed to make me feel better how?"

The engineer shrugged. "It didn't melt."

"I don't care if it's stuck on with spit," Nivry snapped. "We're either going over or through. If there's anyone alive, they're on the other side of this thing."

"Not to mention," Werst grunted, "so is the air lock."

"Not to mention," the corporal agreed.

*   *   *

The darkness lasted thirty-one seconds—give or take the few seconds it took Torin to overcome panic and begin counting. The first twenty-eight seconds lasted forever; no sight, no sound, no smell, no touch, and only the bitter taste of burning chemicals in her mouth. At twenty-nine, she could move her legs. At thirty, her lower hand came free. At thirty-one, kicking and clawing for freedom, she dropped into dim gray light.

Her legs absorbed most of the impact. She rolled and would have come up on her feet had another body not slammed into the same space— knocking her flat and driving the breath out of her.

After a moment spent gasping, she slid her hand under a heavy, familiar shoulder and heaved.

Ryder flopped to one side, coughing out a curse as his head hit the floor, and Torin fought to catch her breath. *And wasn't that the perfect end to an unpleasant experience?* Still, it could have been worse. If the aliens did any probing during her trip through the flooring, they'd done it without her noticing and, as far as she was concerned, that was the preferable way to be probed—di'Taykan opinions on the matter aside. Hitting this new floor had left nothing more serious than bruises. Fortunately, Ryder's elbow had been moving fast enough that her vest had absorbed most of the impact.

The mask was gone. Wherever they were, the smoke hadn't come with them. The air was clear, odor free but for the stink of fear-sweat that clung to her and Ryder. Torin could hear Ryder's breathing and her own blood pounding in her ears but nothing else. As near as she could tell—given the light levels—the ceiling above her head was as featureless as the floor that had swallowed them. Rolling her head to the right, she could see a wall— looking like every wall they'd seen on the ship and, for that matter, like the floors and the ceilings. To her left, Craig Ryder's profile filled most of her line of sight but a few meters beyond him, she could see another wall.

Wherever they were, the scenery hadn't changed.

And where the hell's the packing crate? It had been sinking as fast as they had, but it wasn't with them now.

Groping for the weapon that should have been lying along her right side, Torin realized that, although the strap remained over her shoulder, the benny was gone. *H'san on fukking crutches!* Drawing in her legs, she touched the knife in her boot—more for reassurance than because she planned on immediately using it—and sat up. Slowly. If anyone—or any-thing—was watching, she didn't want to startle them.

They were alone in what was essentially a cross section of one of the corridors—three meters by three meters by three meters of uninterrupted gray.

A moan drew her attention to her companion. "You all right?"

"I just got swallowed by a fukking floor!"

Apparently civilians, like officers, were inclined to state the obvious. "And you survived it." An obvious observation back at him. "Are you injured?"

"Physically? No."

"Then move on." Crossing her ankles, she stood.

Ryder propped himself up on his elbows and glared at her. "Mind if I take a moment to have a freaking reaction to the experience?"

Torin shrugged; it wasn't like she needed his assistance. "Take all the time you want."

The shuttle had to have been destroyed by the explosion or Captain Travik's implant would have been sending her his vital signs—or lack of vital signs. Considering how close he'd been to ground zero, he and his implant had likely been blown to pieces. Her orders from General Morris had been to keep the captain alive, but she had no intention of beating herself up over a death she couldn't have prevented nor mourning an officer the Corps was inarguably better off without. *And on the bright side, Sector Central News probably went with him, so there's nothing to stop the general from having him die a hero's death and everybody's happy.*

Her helmet mike, snapped down before the explosion, still nestled against the corner of her mouth.

"Corporal Nivry. Nivry, this is Kerr. Acknowledge."

No response. Not even static.

"Corporal Harrop. Harrop, this is Kerr. Acknowledge."

"What are you doing?" Ryder groaned as he got to his feet.

"Attempting to contact my Marines." Lips pressed into a thin line, Torin slid her helmet off and checked the display. The telltale was green; if that still meant anything, the unit was working. It was possible that the internal structure of the ship was blocking the signal. It was also possible they could hear her, but she couldn't hear them.

Nivry's code in the slate brought no results. Neither did any of the other eleven.

Hooked into the *Berganitan*'s system, she could have used the tracking program to find anything with a familiar energy signature—other slates, comm units, weapons, living bodies. Without the *Berganitan*, she'd need one of the big scanners.

Her slate's mapping function had been disabled. Her own position was as unknown as the team's.

"What's wrong?"

"I'm not getting through."

"Why?"

"I don't know. You think it could have something to do with the alien technology we're surrounded by?"

"No need to be so sarcastic," he grumbled, staring up at the ceiling. "You sure they're alive?"

"Yes."

The inarguable response brought his attention back to her. "You don't know . . ."

"I know they were alive when we went out of contact, and that was less than five minutes ago."

"Look, I don't have to tell you that a lot can happen in five . . ."

"They're alive," Torin growled, daring him to argue.

Both hands lifted, he backed away.

She couldn't stop herself from taking another look around the cube.

No scanners. No weapons. No Marines. Just Craig Ryder, pacing from wall to wall, fists clenched as though he wanted to hit something. "We have to find a way out."

"No shit. What do you think I've been doing?"

"A piss-poor job. You're not even touching the walls."

"Well, excuse me for distrusting solid surfaces."

Torin rolled her eyes and crossed to his side. "All you have to do is . . ." Her hand stopped a centimeter from the surface. Muscles along her arm trembled; she couldn't bring herself to actually put flesh in contact with the wall. It felt as though she'd been stalled there for minutes, although it couldn't have been more than five or six seconds at the most. Breathing slowly and deliberately, she continued the motion back to her vest and pulled off one of the recharge bars for her missing benny. ". . . tap on the walls with this."

The wall seemed to absorb the sound but was otherwise solid enough.

She could feel him watching her, so she turned, one eyebrow lifted. "Did you need to borrow a bar?"

He knew. She could see it in his eyes. He knew she'd stopped and he knew why.

But all he said was, "No, thanks." He pulled a screwdriver out of a pouch on his belt. "I'll use this."

"What a fukking mess." His upper body sandwiched between the top of the barrier and the ceiling, Werst waved a hand to clear the smoke from his face. "Primary damage is at the far end of the corridor but the entire area between the barrier and the air lock's filled with rubble. I see no survivors, but I can smell blood." His facial ridges spread slightly behind the translucent filter covering the lower part of his face. "Human, di'Taykan, Krai, Niln . . . everyone took damage. I'm going down."

Feet holding a convenient piece of pipe, he dropped over the inside edge. "This side's warmer, all right."

"Hot enough to block the scanners from picking up a thermal signature?"

"Probably. Air temp reads 33.4°C, and the barrier's warmer than that." He grabbed a protruding corner, tested the stability, swung around, found another hold, swung again, and dropped to the floor. Facial ridges clamped shut, he froze, counted to ten, and slowly straightened, glancing down at his sleeve. "Nothing's moving."

"Sensors show nothing's moving." Corporal Nivry's correction was a quiet buzz in his ear. *"Sensors gave no warning of the explosion or of what happened to Staff Sergeant Kerr. Be careful."*

"Always."

"And no snacking."

"Up yours."

Joining a multispecies military had forced the Krai to change their battlefield eating habits.

A soft thud and Orla crouched beside him. "I don't care what Johnston says, Guimond's never going to fit through there."

"Not my problem. Go left."

They found *Harveer* Niirantapajee and one of the Katrien scientists alive but unconscious in a sheltered triangle made by their half-slagged piece of equipment and the mess kit.

"Clear to casualties, Corporal."

Nivry nodded at Tsui and Dursinski, who were carrying the patrol med kits. "Go."

As they reached the top, she sent the next two, then waved ahead the four Marines needed to move the scanners.

"We should leave the scanners," Harrop murmured, watching Heer follow Jynett over the barrier at the wider of the two points. "We can come back and get them."

Nivry shook her head. "No. If that air lock's been blown, we'll need them to find our way out of here. I don't trust this place enough to leave gear where we can't see it."

"If that air lock's been blown, we're fukked."

Neither corporal mentioned that the shuttle pilot would have contacted them by now had she been able to.

Harrop nodded at the barrier. "Command should be on the other side. I'll watch the rear."

The situation's serious, he thought as Nivry slid through the narrower point, *when that gets no comment from a di'Taykan.*

Too bulky to be worn, the scanners were passed over the barrier from hand to hand, most of the weight on both sides held by the augmentation worn by Johnston and Heer. Once the scanners were safely on the deck, Guimond climbed to the same space, looked dubiously through it, then back at Harrop.

"Hey, Corporal, maybe we should widen this."

"There's a three-centimeter difference between you and that space, Guimond. Now move."

Arms, head, shoulders . . .

Heer grabbed a double fistful of Guimond's combats while Johnston shoved from behind.

"Son of a . . ."

Chest.

Most of his descent was headfirst, then he swung in Heer's grip, and dropped.

Heads turned at the impact.

"Air lock's gone. Although Heer's still scanning it, looks like the shuttle went with it. There's a six-by-four-meter hole in the wall likely caused by the *something* Staff Sergeant Kerr mentioned. We've got two casualties—both unconscious—one dead Katrien and a whole lot of body parts that may or may not add up to the other civilians. What we don't have is either of our two missing personnel. Captain Travik wasn't in vest and helmet, but both the captain and Staff Sergeant Kerr were in combats and we've found no trace of uniforms. We all know this"—Nivry's gesture took in the destruction—"was not enough to obliterate . . ."

"Big word."

"Shut up, Tsui. This . . ." She repeated the gesture. ". . . was not enough to obliterate two MCCUs. Have I missed anything?"

There was a negative response around the circle.

Nivry stared down at the one clear section of floor, her eyes so dark they'd lost almost all color. "So, considering one of Staff's last transmissions said, and I quote, *'We're being sucked into the goddamned floor!'* does anyone have any better ideas about where the staff and the captain are?"

No one did.

Nivry bounced a piece of wreckage off the area in question. Then stepped out onto it. And back. And took the time to breathe before saying, "Johnston, start scanning."

"If they're more than a meter and a half down, I'm not going to find them," the engineer warned, squatting and setting the scanner facedown on the cleared bit. "We haven't been able to go more than a meter and a half through any of these walls."

"Good thing this is a floor."

"But what happens if they're more than a meter and a half down?" Dursinski demanded.

"We start digging. Johnston?"

"Give it time. It can't interpret half the data coming back and that . . . Got it! Just over a meter of something solid—same organic metal combo that the walls are made of—then some open space, then two thermal sigs. Except they're both Human. Captain Travik should be showing three to four degrees higher."

"Maybe he's wounded and his body temp has dropped."

"No. These are Human—and look at that hot spot there, and there." He tapped the display. "That's a slate and that's a helmet PCU. I'd say we've found the staff sergeant and one of the civilians but not Captain Travik."

"No *serley* loss."

"Werst."

He snorted unapologetically.

"What now?" Johnston asked, straightening.

"We make contact." Nivry stepped out beside the scanner. "Staff Sergeant Kerr, this is Corporal Nivry. Acknowledge."

The only sound in the ruined corridor was the hum of the mess kit turning the remaining food into field rations and the hiss of *Harveer* Niirantapajee's labored breathing.

After a moment, she stepped back. "I can't get through to her slate either. Can we adapt the scanner to signal her?"

"Sure. I could hit her with a couple of different things, and if she's running a scan protect, she'll even know I'm doing it. Other than that . . ." Lifting his helmet, Johnston ran a hand back over his scalp. "We could probably burn through with the bennys."

"It'd drain the lot of them," Dursinski pointed out. "We'd be disarming ourselves. I really don't think that's a good idea."

"Don't worry about it," Nivry told her dryly. "Given what happened the last time, we're not putting holes in these walls."

"How about a low-tech solution?"

Heads turned as Guimond slapped a metal bar into one palm.

"You're going to try and beat your way through?" Johnston asked, eyebrows nearly at his hairline. "Through a meter of a substance the entire science team couldn't get a scraping of?"

"No." Flipping the bar around, he tapped it against the floor. Three short. Three long. Three short.

Over the ambient noise came the sound of realization dawning.

Werst shook his head. "You're not as dumb as you look."

"Do you hear something?"

One ear cocked toward the ceiling, Torin frowned. "Tapping." They listened for a moment. Her frowned deepened. "It almost sounds like there's a rhythm to it." She snapped her slate off her vest.

Ryder snorted and began walking again, around and around the perimeter of their prison. "Vermin dancing in the pipes."

"Unlikely." Recording the ambient noise onto her slate, she boosted the gain and played it back.

"That was in the way of being a facetious observation."

"I know. Shut up."

Three short. Three short. Long short long.

"Son of a bitch . . ."

Her smile stopped Ryder in his tracks. "What?"

Smile broadening, Torin looked the civilian up and down. "You're what? A little taller than one point eight meters?"

"Why?"

"Because I'm a little shorter and I need to reach the ceiling."

"We already threw stuff at it," he protested. "It's solid."

"Yes, but we have a new situation." Slipping the strap of her benny off her shoulder, she uncoupled the ends. Holding the lighter piece, she whipped the heavier up against the ceiling. The thud sounded loud in the cube, but it wasn't enough to stop the pattern still tapping out of her slate. "Damn. They can't hear it."

Charging across to her, Ryder grabbed her shoulders and kept her from making a second attempt. "Who can't hear us?" he demanded. "Who?"

"The Recon team banging s-s-k, Staff Sergeant Kerr, into the floor up above."

"They're tapping out letters?"

She had to admire a man who didn't need a long explanation. "It's Morse code."

"They've found us?"

"Yes."

"They can get us out!"

No room for doubt, in spite of explosions and alien technology. Marines didn't leave their own behind. "Yes." He still had hold of her shoulders. She shrugged to remind him.

"Okay." Ryder took a deep breath, wiped his palms on his thighs, and started pacing again. "Okay," he said again, a little more calmly. Then he frowned. "What's Morse code?"

"A primitive communication system the anal retentives in the Corps have dragged through the last four centuries."

"Why?"

Easy answer. "For situations like this. I need you to get down on your hands and knees."

Ryder looked startled, then he grinned, blue eyes gleaming even brighter amidst the unrelieved gray. "What?"

"They can see us; that message is aimed at me. They're probably scanning energy sigs with one of the engineering units. The PCU in my helmet has a noticeable signature." While Ryder connected the dots she'd given him, Torin flipped up the microphone and took off her helmet. "If I hold it under your body, they can't see it. When I bring it out again, they can."

"Visual tapping."

"If you like."

"These vibrations aren't doing the scanner any good," Johnston grumbled as a sweating Guimond stopped pounding and the gathered Marines waited for a reply. "And we don't know that she can hear us."

Nivry glanced up from the scanner's display and frowned at the engineer. "A few more minutes."

"There's a good meter between the top of the staff sergeant's head and the ceiling. What's she going to do to answer, stand on the civilian?"

The corporal ignored him. "Guimond, try a . . . wait, something's happening."

Crouching, Johnston fiddled with the scan. "Looks like the thermal signals are joining."

"Now we know who the civilian is," someone snickered.

"Sig for the helmet PCU keeps disappearing and reappearing. There." He pointed. "Now you see it, now you don't."

"She's answering."

"Well, if she isn't, I'd like a closer look at what they *are* doing."

The tapping changed.

"Sounds like they got your message." Craig shifted his weight from one knee to the other and back and tried not to think about how ridiculous this had to look. "What're they saying?"

"Give me a minute, Mr. Ryder, it comes through one letter at a time."

The situation had clearly stabilized if she was Mr. Rydering him again. He had to hand it to the Marines, they had an interesting idea of a stable situation.

Air lock gob? No, gone . . . Torin reminded herself to send an apology to the gunny who'd taught communications back on Ventris. *Who knew I'd ever actually need to use this crap?*

When Ryder rose up onto his knees, she put a hand on his shoulder to stop him. He twisted out of her grip, the muscles across his back tight enough to march on.

"I need you for a few more minutes." She slid the words between the letters being pounded out above.

"No, I'm done . . ."

Torin understood his desire to do something, to not sit by and wait passively for rescue. Unfortunately, his options were limited, and if he started pacing again, she was going to have to break both his legs. "I can't do this without you," she reminded him.

"I don't . . ."

The tapping stopped.

Protest cut short, he looked up at the ceiling, then back at her, one corner of his mouth curling up. "Well?"

"Air lock's gone and the shuttle with it. And they've lost Captain Travik."

"Nice to get some good news with the bad." He stared down at his hands resting on his thighs and, exhaling with some violence, abruptly dropped forward. "What are you going to tell them?"

Torin forced herself to concentrate as he arched his back. "To look for another clean bit of floor."

"Found it."

Marines and the second scanner converged.

After a moment, Harrop straightened. "Nivry, ditch the small talk and tell the staff sergeant we've found Captain Travik and what could be another civilian."

"Could be?"

"Heer's reading five small separate sigs beside him."

"Four meters on the other side of that wall?"

Torin rocked back on her heels and stood. "That's what they tell me."

"On, that's just fukking great!" Ryder surged to his feet. "He might as well be four fukking kilometers away." He threw up his arms and spun around. "There's no way we can get to him. There's no way he can get to us. And even if your people up top had cutting tools, they couldn't get to us, so . . ." A thick finger jabbed toward Torin. ". . . don't bullshit me that they can because structural components around here don't seem to want . . ." He shouted a word at each wall. "To. Be. Fukked. With."

Settling her helmet back on her head, Torin walked forward. An arm's length from the wall, she paused and shouted.

By the time the noise faded, Ryder was at her side, arms folded. "What did you do that for?"

"No echo. When you were yelling, there was bounce off every wall but this one." Torin took a deep breath and stretched out her arm, holding her hand a steady centimeter from the wall's surface. Before she could think too hard about what she was going to do, she took a step forward. Her hand disappeared.

"Are you insane?"

"Could be." Given how much she wanted to scream, she wasn't going to rule it out.

Ryder grabbed her forearm and yanked. Nothing moved except a couple of small bones in her wrist.

She took another small step, and he snatched his hands away as her forearm disappeared.

"You're fukking kidding, right?"

Breathing heavily through her nose, she shrugged. "This seems to be an exit."

"It's a wall," he growled. "I'm staying right here."

They locked eyes for a long moment. Torin looked away first and shrugged again. "Suit yourself. If you change your mind, you know the way out."

"Take a deep breath."

Her heart was pounding so violently, she hardly heard him but she managed a smile. "No shit."

She'd intended to keep her eyes open, but at the last second, she closed them and threw herself forward.

It wasn't as bad as the first time but only because it was over a lot faster.

Momentum slammed her into another wall.

The bounce dropped her into a defensive position. A fast check confirmed everything working and no gear lost in transit.

Adrenaline buzzing, eyes flicking from point to point, she looked around. Another corridor, but no more than a meter and a half wide and the walls appeared to be made of welded steel. Stranger still, the welds were rusting. The same ridged black rubber used for traction in most station docks covered the deck. Strips in the ceiling emitted cold white light not quite strong enough to reach into the corners, throwing the first shadows Torin had seen on the ship. About a meter to her right, the corridor ended in a blank wall, but it continued another six, maybe seven, to her left before ending in what seemed to be an old manual hatch.

If she was under surveillance, it wasn't registering.

If she was in danger, it wasn't obvious.

The knife went back in her boot.

So where's a thousand Silsviss trying to kill you when you need them?

The great thing about an obvious danger was the option of fighting back.

The wall she'd come through was the same welded steel as the rest. Just as rusty. Just as solid.

Ryder came through a little faster than she had. Hit the steel a little harder. Took a swing at her on the way down.

Given the circumstances, Torin let it pass.

"What took you so long?" she asked, holding out a hand.

He hesitated a moment, breathing hard, then took it and let her help him to his feet. "Why so relieved? You think I wouldn't follow?"

She hadn't been sure. She'd seen the inside of his ship; he spent a lot of time alone in a small space, so it didn't take much to work out the reason for the pacing he had been doing in the cube. Two people in that small space and the ship runs out of resources a lot faster in an unforgiving environment. Having her in that cube with him had to have been working against years of survival conditioning. No wonder he'd been on the verge of panic. Given a choice between being alone in the cube and forcing himself through after her . . .

If he'd been one of her Marines, she'd have ordered him through and trusted training to overcome panic. As it was, she had to count on the fine Human tradition of not wanting to look like a coward in front of a crowd.

One shoulder lifted and fell. "You said you were staying."

"I changed my mind." He glanced down at their clasped hands, pulled free, stepped back, and swept the area with a disdainful gaze. "Oh, this is a big fukking improvement."

"There's a door."

Torin watched the tension go out of his shoulders as he turned. "Now, we're getting somewhere."

"It might be locked."

"I have a way with locked doors."

"No doubt."

"We seem to be heading in the general direction of your captain."

"Convenient." And it was. Torin began to have a distinct sense of déjà vu.

"Door looks low-tech. This looks like an older part of the ship."

"This looks like an entirely *different* ship. And if these walls are actually steel . . ."

"Corporal Nivry, this is Staff Sergeant Kerr. Acknowledge."

The silence was sudden and absolute as the staff sergeant's voice rang out over the group channel.

"This is Nivry." She could hardly hear herself over the shouting. "You disappeared off the scanner; first your signal, then Mr. Ryder's."

"We left the cube."

"How . . . ?"

"We went through the wall. We're now in what looks like a low-tech area and are advancing toward Captain Travik's position. Report."

"Harveer Niirantapajee has regained consciousness, but Gytha, the Katrien, is still out. We've patched up what damage we could see, but no one's really up on Katrien anatomy. The mess kit's still working; we're running everything edible through into field rations and we're bagging body parts. Most of the science team was at ground zero and there's not much of them."

"Careful with your labeling, then."

It got a bigger laugh than it would have under better circumstances.

"We've found four intact HE suits, and Heer and Johnston were checking to see that the air lock can attach another shuttle."

"Were?"

"We've got both scanners pointed at the floor."

"Point one back at the air lock, but keep the other on Captain Travik. We may need directions. See what can be done about boosting our comm signal—the sooner the Berganitan *knows we're alive, the better."*

Nivry stepped back as Johnston moved to reclaim his scanner. "We're on it, Staff."

"Good work. I'll check in when I've found the captain. Kerr out."

"She went through the wall," the engineer muttered as the exoskeleton took up the strain. Straightening his legs, he announced to no one in particular. "Sergeants and above, out of their fukking minds."

The hatch was locked. Ryder had it open before Torin snapped her mike up. She raised a hand to stop him from charging through and motioned for him to stand by the door, ready to slam it shut, while she checked the immediate area for unfriendlies.

He ignored her.

Which was when she remembered he wasn't a Marine.

It was a little too late to do it by the book, so she followed him through the hatch and stopped short.

If she hadn't known better, she'd have sworn she was standing in a dirtside warehouse. The kind that took advantage of the fact that the real estate came with an atmosphere and so there was never any need to clear the old crap out to make way for the new. Light levels were low, creating a shadow maze around the stacks of crates and pieces of equipment. The perfect location for an ambush.

She glanced at her sleeve. If her sensors were right, nothing was moving. They'd find out soon enough if her sensors were wrong.

"Holy fuk."

Ryder's voice held significantly more fear than that situation called for.

"What is it?"

"I've been here before." When Torin turned toward him, his eyes had nearly disappeared under the depth of his scowl. "It's Customs Storage 23 at Port Julion."

Environmental controls weren't enough to stop a chill from sliding down Torin's spine. "Dirtside warehouse?"

"Yeah."

"You're sure?"

"Dimensions, lighting, even the fukking shipping crates are in the same place. Except that." Ryder pointed toward a familiar box of gray plastic. "That sank with us. Our backs were right up against it. So, why did it land way over here when we got dropped inside the magic cube?"

"Good question. Here's a better one. My guys said it was just over a meter between their floor and our ceilings—a straight line from where we sank up there to where we ended up down here. But we were in darkness for just over thirty-one seconds. What else happened while we were in transit?"

He stared at her for a long moment. "Thank you for sharing that. You think the ship pulled this place out of my head?"

Torin shrugged. "Got a better answer?"

"And the corridor outside?"

"That could have come from either of us—it's pretty much a generic piece of old station or ship, but . . ." Again, she reached for the benny that wasn't there. "We'd better hope they decided to stick with what's in your head."

"And why would that be, Staff Sergeant?"

He sounded insulted. Tough. "Ever been in combat, Mr. Ryder? Trust me, I've been in places I don't ever want to go to again. Captain Travik should be over that way. Come on." Moving carefully around blind corners, she'd covered about half the estimated distance when the shriek of protesting hinges spun her around. Holding the lid up with one hand, Ryder was about to reach into a red octagonal case with the other. "What are you doing?" she snarled.

"This case was never in CS23. If the ship put it here, I want to know what's in it."

Torin closed the distance between them with three quick strides, slamming the lid down with both hands. "Are you out of your fukking mind?"

Breathing heavily, staring at his hands as though surprised they were still attached, Ryder snarled, "My salvage, Staff Sergeant. Don't forget it."

"Alien technology, Mr. Ryder. Quite possibly the same technology that's blown up once already. Anything you find will mean squat if we've been blown into greasy smears on the deck. Touch as little as possible. Open nothing." Lips drawn back off her teeth, she leaned toward him. "Am I making myself clear?"

He leaned in as well. "At the risk of sounding childish," he growled, his breath warm against her face, "you're not the boss of me."

"True." She held her position, their eyes locked.

After a long moment, Ryder jerked away. "All right. You win. I open nothing."

"Thank you."

"Yeah, yeah, you're welcome."

He stayed close on her heels after that, which was, she supposed, an improvement.

They found Captain Travik in an open area, one arm bent at an impossible angle, a triangular flap of skin peeled back over one eye and still bleeding sluggishly.

The five thermal points beside him turned out to be the muzzle, hands and feet of Presit a Tur durValintrisy—her fur too thick for the scanner to read body heat.

"And the day just keeps getting better," Torin sighed.

"Berganitan, this is *B7*. We're at the air lock and it's a mess. Looks like there's pieces of the ship missing and pieces of the shuttle still attached. I can't tell if parts are melted or melded." Frowning at the wreckage, Commander Sibley brought his Jade in closer. "Sending visuals and data stream now. You want my opinion, we're not going to be using this entrance again, and if the internal damage is half as extensive, I doubt there's anyone left alive."

EIGHT

It took seconds to seal Captain Travik's head wound. As she could do nothing about the triangular dent in the bone beneath the laceration, Torin ignored it. Familiarity with impact wounds suggested the explosion had flung a piece of debris at his head, and had he been anything but Krai, he'd have lost the top four inches of his skull. As it was, his med-alert had gone off, marking him for med-vac, so there was definite brain damage behind the dent.

Brand-new damage, Torin snorted silently, turning her attention to the arm.

Grateful that the captain remained unconscious—for her sake as much as his—Torin took a deep breath, then gripped his arm above and below the joint, slowly straightening it.

"I heard Krai bones were too tough to break," Ryder said quietly, his hands working nearly wrist-deep in Presit's fur.

"The bone's not broken; the joint's been shattered." She frowned down at the information on her slate and shifted her thumb until she felt something move beneath it. "The pieces are in roughly the right position, but he's going to need internal fusing to hold things together."

"And until he gets it?"

"We do the same thing we usually do."

Ryder snorted. "Because this sort of thing happens all the time?"

"Injuries are a side effect of battle, Mr. Ryder." Releasing the captain's arm, Torin picked up her slate and added the new data to his medical file. A moment later, his sleeve tightened, then stiffened, holding his arm immobile at a ninety-degree angle. "The main function of MCCUs—combats," she added at Ryder's expression, "is to keep the wearer alive. The fabric's got a dozen or so functions built into it."

"Or so?" Her attention back on the captain's head wound, she could hear the grin in Ryder's voice. "I'd have thought a staff sergeant of your caliber would know for certain."

"I know. You don't need to." She checked the sealant before rocking back on her heels and standing. "How's the reporter?"

"No broken bones, no lacerations, no dark glasses, so it's a good thing it's a little dim in here, and she definitely uses a conditioner when she shampoos."

"Ryder . . ."

"Other than that . . ." He sat back, hands on his thighs, and looked up at Torin, "I haven't the faintest idea. You don't have her specs in your slate?"

"Why would I? No Katrien in the Corps. Her heart's beating, she's breathing." Torin shrugged. "Other than that . . . Nivry, this is Kerr. Is your Katrien awake yet?"

"Negative, Staff. We've stopped the bleeding and her vitals seem steady, but she's still out."

"Roger that. Let me know when she comes to. Any progress on reaching the *Berganitan?*"

"Negative. The air lock's fused—completely unusable—and we've determined we can no more get an unassisted signal out through the hull than they can get one in. Heer thinks if we set a benny on narrow band and drain every charge we have, we might have juice enough to cut a pinprick hole through the hull: big enough so the Berganitan *could pick up the energy signal, not so big we'd decompress, and easy enough to patch."*

"Considering what happened to Dr. Hodges, let's try to avoid poking holes in the ship if it's at all possible. There's no chance of cobbling something together out of all that scientific equipment?"

"Not unless you or Mr. Ryder can make a comm unit with a mess kit; everything else has been slagged."

"I can't even make a decent pouch of coffee with a mess kit. And since we're down here and the mess kit's with you . . ."

"Johnston may have something on that, Staff."

"Staff Sergeant Kerr, Johnston here. I was checking the site of the explosion—it left one fuk of a hole in the wall and at the back of it, we're scanning six centimeters of solid and then an area that reads like a vertical shaft. I suspect it's what Dr. Hodges was aiming for. It seems to go down to your level. Do you want us to start through?"

"What part of 'avoid poking holes in the ship' are you having trouble understanding, Johnston?"

"Yeah, but the material at the back of the hole is different. It's still a mix of metal and organic, but the explosion changed the organic part."

"How?"

"Layman's terms—it cooked it. I'm extrapolating a bit from available data, but if we smack this stuff hard enough, it's going to shatter."

Torin considered implications for a moment. As much as it would simplify things to have the team in one place, another explosion was on no one's wish list. "Let's make sure the shaft actually reaches this far before we risk it. I'll take a look and recontact. Kerr out."

"Take a look at what?" Ryder asked as she snapped her mike up. He was standing so close, he'd clearly been attempting to overhear the other end of the conversation.

"One of our engineers may have found a vertical."

"Down to this level?"

"That's what I'm going to find out."

"I'll go with you."

"You'll stay with . . ." Catching sight of his expression, Torin bit off the rest of the order. *Not a Marine*, she reminded herself. "Look, Ryder . . ."

"You know, you called me Craig while we were being sucked through the floor."

Had she? "Extenuating circumstances."

He grinned. "Look, I don't care what you call me, just remember I'm not one of your soldiers and I'm not going to ask how high on the way up. You want me to stay with these two." Still grinning, he folded his arms and nodded toward the floor. "Then ask me nicely."

Torin lifted her upper lip off her teeth. "Mr. Ryder, as an investigation of the location of a possible vertical is not going to require both of us, and because I have the PCU and can therefore stay in contact with the Marine engineer who needs the information, would you mind staying with Captain Travik and the reporter while I check things out?"

"You're being sarcastic again."

"Just get out of my way before I knock you on your ass."

"Now *that*"—Ryder stepped back as she approached—"sounded sincere."

The good news, Torin reflected as she made her way around the crates toward the far wall, *is that our experiences thus far seemed to have caused no lasting trauma*—never a given with a civilian—*and he's regained his sense of humor. And the bad news is* . . . She froze as one of the lights flickered and then continued on more cautiously. . . . *he's regained his sense of humor.*

Directly below the point where the explosion had occurred there was an exact replica of the hatch they'd used to enter the room. More because it was procedure than because she thought it would do any good, Torin scanned for traps.

Nothing.

Yeah. Big surprise.

"Mr. Ryder, does CS23 have a hatch in this position?"

"Not that I remember. We've got one?"

"We do."

"Everything all right, Staff Sergeant?"

"Everything's fine, Mr. Ryder." She could hear him clearly although his voice had picked up a hollow, big-empty-room timbre. As the room was not empty, she assumed sound waves were being screwed with—certainly an effect well within the established tech level of the ship. Sound waves had shown them the way out of the cube. *We got to use them once; we don't get to use them again.* Which was either paranoia above and beyond the call or evidence of an emerging pattern. Since she could do nothing about either—yet—she wrapped her left hand around the bar latch and shoved it down. Metal hinges screamed.

"What the hell was that?"

"Bad maintenance. I've just opened the hatch."

"It wasn't locked?"

"No." No need. Her CSO had already shown them, whoever *they* were, that he could get through the lock.

The hatch opened into a vertical shaft a meter square made of the same rusted steel plates. There were no lights, but the spill from the storeroom was enough for Torin to see two more hatches, once again identical to the first. *It's like the ship pulled out one hatch pattern and decided it didn't need any others.* One was in the bulkhead to her right, the other straight ahead. To her left, metal rungs had been welded to the steel and painted yellow, the paint dabbed sloppily over the welds. Definitely not military. The ship seemed to be sticking to what it had pulled from Ryder's head.

Torin looked up, way up, eventually losing the shaft in darkness.

"Johnston, this is Kerr. You reading my thermal sig in the shaft you're scanning?"

"Affirmative, Staff. Do I kick the wall down?"

"You sure you can get through it safely?"

"Not one hundred percent sure, no. But close enough for government work."

No point in bringing a specialist along and then not listening to him. Torin looked up again and then back through the hatch toward Captain Travik and the two civilians. "Do it. Safety level three. Once you're through, there's a whole lot of vertical above you, so keep an eye topside."

"This'll take time, Staff."

"Keep me informed. I'm exiting the debris field. Kerr out." Flipping her mike up, Torin hurried back to find the captain and the reporter lying alone where she'd left them. *Oh, fuk.* She reached for her absent benny, swore again, opened her mouth to yell, and spotted the missing Ryder bent half inside the packing crate that had accompanied them through the floor. *Kicking his ass is looking better and better.* Crossing silently to the crate, she leaned over and, close enough that her breath moved a strand of his hair, said, "What are you doing?"

He jerked back, his head missing the edge of the lid by centimeters. "You want another body to lug around, do you? Because if you do, keep that up!"

"You were to stay with the injured."

"I was looking for something we could carry them on."

She folded her arms. "Really?"

He mirrored the movement. "Yeah. Really."

Maybe he had been. It was a good idea and it wouldn't kill her to give him the benefit of the doubt. "Find anything useful?"

"No!" And then a little more calmly, "Nothing we could use as a stretcher, but remember when you said the di'Taykan were going to use explosives after lunch?" Holding out his left hand, Ryder slowly opened the fingers. Lying across his palm were a pair of demolition charges. "You weren't kidding, were you?"

"Actually, I was." When she went to take the charges, he closed his fingers around them.

"Not Corps equipment, Staff Sergeant. My salvage."

"And if we need them to get off this thing?" If they'd all still been in HE suits, she'd be tempted to blow a hole in the hull and start tossing both the living and the dead out for pickup by the *Berganitan.* Space represented a known danger. This ship . . .

"I expect to be compensated. At the going rate."

"Which is?"

"Depends on where we're going."

"Funny."

A half smile barely showed within the beard. "I'm not kidding."

"You know how to use them?"

"Try to remember what I do for a living. Most days, the bits you can salvage need to be separated from the bits you can't." He tossed the four-inch ceramic cylinders one at a time to his other hand and slipped them both into his belt pouch. "I'd bet I'm better at setting demo charges than you are at getting second lieutenants to run their platoons your way."

Torin snorted. "I doubt that." Still, he had a point. More relevantly, she knew where they were if she needed them and could retrieve them if the situation called for it. Craig Ryder was a large, well-muscled man but, her own abilities aside, she had twelve Marines working for her. "Given the unexpected way things have of blowing up on this ship, the Corps appreciates your willingness to take the risk of providing storage."

Ryder stared at her for a moment then shook his head ruefully when she smiled. "Nice."

There was nothing else in the crate but packing intended to protect delicate equipment in transit.

Explosives and bubble wrap.

"Mixed messages," Torin sighed, straightening. "That's what's wrong with the universe."

A noise from the captain drew her back to his side. "Sir?" She dropped to her knees. "Captain Travik?"

His eyes flickered open. *"Fleruke ahs sa?"*

Torin's implant, keyed to automatically translate both Krai and di'Taykan, murmured an unnecessary, **Where am I?**

"We're a level below the air lock, sir. In . . ." An actual explanation was far too complicated. ". . . a storage facility."

"Explo . . . sion!"

"Yes, sir. There was an explosion. Then the floor opened up and we went through it."

"Telling . . . Gen . . . eral Morris."

Torin ignored the whiny tone. "I wish you would, sir. I'd be a lot happier if the *Bergani* . . . God damn it!" She sighed and looked up at Ryder. "He's gone again."

"You think there's brain damage under that dent?"

"Not for me to say."

"Brain damage *caused* by the dent?"

She sat back on her heels. "I know what you meant."

"Okay. So, how can he contact the big *B* if you can't?"

"Officer's implants are a couple of grades higher than mine." Torin's left hand rose involuntarily to her jaw. "More memory and more power— maybe enough to get a signal through the hull."

Ryder squatted and studied the captain's face, pulling thoughtfully on the edge of his beard. "I've got an external mike in mine, tucked in under a molar . . . and what?"

"You have an implant."

"Yeah. Won the installation in a poker game."

Torin kept her voice quiet and nonthreatening. She had a feeling she should pace herself. "Have you tried to reach the *Promise?*"

"Nope. I figure this is your problem." His hands rose into a protective position at her expression. "Kidding. I've tried, no luck—not even static. It's only a seven-aught-four. So I was wondering," he continued when To- rin didn't respond, "why can't you just reach in and activate the captain's implant and talk loud enough to be picked up?"

"Because Captain Travik is a Krai."

"So?"

Using only one finger, Torin pushed against the captain's chin just hard enough to open his mouth. Then she leaned back and picked up the broken arm of Presit's dark glasses.

"What are you doing?"

"Making sure you'll believe what I'm about to tell you. This is some- thing we show the Human and di'Taykan recruits. Most of them have never worked with Krai."

The moment the end of the arm passed between the captain's teeth, his mouth snapped shut. As he chewed and swallowed the plastic, Torin held up what was left. "Never stick your finger in a Krai's mouth. You stand a slightly better chance of keeping the finger if they're conscious, but only slightly."

Ryder looked impressed. "How do they get the implant in there?"

"No idea; I'm not tech."

"He swallowed that plastic."

"And if there's anything organic about it, he'll digest that and pass the rest."

"So his implant's useless to us?"

"Unless he dies, then we have a three-minute window until it powers down."

"So, our best chance to contact the *Berganitan* involves holding a piece of bubble wrap over the captain's face?"

"Yes."

"Okay." Sighing, Ryder stood. "We're not going to do that, are we?"

"No."

The sound of debris hitting the floor of the shaft occurred simultaneously with Johnston's voice announcing he was through. After that, the debris came thick and fast, huge pieces falling and shattering. Then a moment of silence. Then Johnston again.

"We've got access, Staff. Waiting for orders."

"All right, everybody listen up. Given that the explosion destroyed the air lock and blew her shuttle to shit, Captain Carveg will assume that survivors will make their way to the next air lock and wait for pickup. My download of the *Berganitan*'s scan of the exterior put the next air lock down on the belly of the beast—maybe another seven levels and about four klicks aft and three and a half inboard. Since we're going down anyway, I want supplies and the injured brought to this position. Any questions?"

"Dursinski, Staff. Captain Carveg doesn't know we're alive, does she?"

"That's correct. Unless they've come up with something that can read through the hull since we left this morning, Captain Carveg has no way of knowing if anyone survived the explosion."

"Then how do we know she'll wait for us to get to the other air lock? We'll be moving injured personnel through unfamiliar territory inside an alien vessel—it's going to take time."

"You're Recon, Dursinski, moving through unfamiliar territory is what you do."

"But Captain Carveg . . ."

"Will have a shuttle waiting by that air lock until she knows we're dead."

"Speaking of the dead, Staff, what do we do with them?"

Body bags were standard equipment on combat vests. Every Marine carried one. Activated, the bag would use the single charge it carried to reduce its contents to fit inside a narrow cylinder less than two inches long. Marines didn't leave their own behind. Since she'd made sergeant, Torin had carried more cylinders than she wanted to remember—every one was one dead Marine too many.

Of the ten scientists, there were eight dead. Plus Cirvan a Tar pal-Rentskik. Nine.

"You said you bagged them, Nivry; what in?"

"Depends on the size of the piece."

"Send someone down, I'm on my way up."

She'd taken only a single step toward the hatch when Ryder's hand on her arm pulled her up short.

"Are you going to tell them?"

"That they've designed this part of the ship around bits they pulled from your head? Yes," Torin added when he nodded. "I don't hold back information that might help keep my people alive."

"You don't think it'll distract them?"

"They're trained to stay focused while penetrating into enemy territory, Mr. Ryder. As long as it doesn't pin them down under a withering cross fire before calling in an air strike, I don't think your head will offer them much of a challenge."

"Bottom line, Staff Sergeant, if they get themselves blown up, no one's going to blame you."

Begging the general's pardon, Torin thought, staring at the dead, *but sure as shit someone's going to blame me if I just leave them here.*

"It's not like you were under fire, Staff Sergeant." She could hear the Board of Inquiry as clearly as if she was standing before them. *"You took the time to make field rations."*

Field rations. That would certainly solve the problem. And they probably wouldn't taste any worse.

"Staff?"

"What is it, Heer?"

"Werst and I would like to do ritual for the two Krai. They were spread around a bit, but if we run them through the mess kit, we can probably get four meals each out of them."

She frowned down at the engineer. "Did I say field rations out loud?"

Seven bags.

Torin ran her thumb along the edges the explosion had ripped in the wall. If more than five Marines died on the way to that other air lock . . .

"No one dies."

"Staff?"

"Bag them, Nivry. We'll carry them out."

"*Harveer* Niirantapajee." Torin looked down at the scientist sitting slumped against the wall, noting three field dressings and, through a singed hole in her lab coat, a glistening blister on one shoulder that had turned gray-green skin a muddy yellow. "I'm Staff Sergeant Kerr. Do you think you'll be able to climb down a vertical ladder or should we lower you?"

The elderly Niln got slowly to her feet and peered up along the line of her nose, nictitating membrane flicking across both eyes. "Not going to ask how I'm feeling, Staff Sergeant Kerr?"

All right. "Do you feel like you'll be able to climb down a vertical ladder, or should we lower you?"

They stared at each other for a moment, then the *harveer* snorted. "How far?"

"One level. About three meters."

"We're making our way to the next air lock?"

"Yes, ma'am."

"Where's your officer? Didn't you lot have an officer when we came in here?"

"Captain Travik is unconscious."

"And you're in charge." It wasn't a question, so Torin didn't bother answering it. "Just so we're clear, you're not in charge of me. It was agreed that the science team would operate independent of the military presence on this ship." Her tail, which had been moving slowly back and forth, began to speed up. "Our investigations were not to be interfered with. I did not agree with Dr. Hodges' procedure. Molecular unzipping . . ." Nostrils flared, her breathing had sped up to match the rhythm of her tail. "Dr. Hodges was a fine scientist. They were all fine scientists—although I believe the di'Taykan team's structural fluidity theory was way off the curve. Way off the curve!"

Anger in the face of death, Torin understood. She pulled one of the seven cylinders from her vest and held it down to the Niln. "If you'd prefer to carry this, *Harveer* . . ."

"What is it?"

"*Harveer* Ujinteripsani."

"*Harveer* Ujinteripsani?" Tail and breathing stopped together. An instant later, just as Torin was running through the little she knew of Niln physiology, breathing began again. Reaching out a trembling hand, *Harveer* Niirantapajee ran a vestigial claw down the length of the cylinder. "Returned to the egg. You did this?"

"Yes, ma'am."

"Thank you." Scooping it up, she slipped it into one of the many pockets in the overalls she wore under her coat, murmuring, "May the First Egg protect and enclose him." Then she sighed and looked around, as though she were actually seeing the extent of the disaster for the first time. "May the First Egg protect and enclose them all. Well, then, about that vertical descent." Leaning around Torin, she pointed an imperious finger toward Guimond. "You can put the big Human at the bottom to catch me, but I expect I'll manage."

They moved the gear down first, and then the injured. Torin would have moved *Harveer* Niirantapajee first, but the Niln had wanted to stay with Gytha a Tur calFinistraven, the Katrien scientist. Torin wanted Gytha moved last. The longer they waited, the greater the chance that she'd wake up and they'd have a better idea of what was wrong—not to mention the best way to drop her down nine meters and do the least additional damage.

Both med kits carried stretchers, a rectangle of smart fabric with a handle at each corner. In the end, they snapped it out rigid, using it as a backboard and immobilizing her for the descent in a webbing of rope.

Recon packs carried fifty feet of near weightless rope as part of standard gear. Spun by Mictok—Torin had no intention of asking how, only partly because it seemed obvious to anyone who'd met a Mictok—the rope didn't stretch, didn't bind, and damn near didn't tangle.

"How's it going, Werst?"

Hanging from his feet above the stretcher, one hand steadying the edge—the only way a Marine and the injured Katrien could descend the shaft at the same time—Werst carefully moved his right foot a rung down. "Keep her coming."

Braced on either side of the hole, Harrop and Jynett played out another bit of line.

A meter and a half from the bottom of the shaft, the stretcher came to rest across the inside of Guimond's forearms.

"You know, there's nothing to her under all that fur," he murmured as Werst reached down and unhooked the ropes. "She's so tiny and helpless."

"And quiet," Werst grunted. "I've never seen one quiet before."

"She's only quiet because she's unconscious."

"No shit."

They tipped stretcher and Katrien slightly to get them through the hatch, then Guimond reclaimed her.

"Remember, sentient species; no scratching her behind the ears."

"Shut up, Tsui."

He carried her through the maze of cases, emerging in the temporary infirmary to see Huilin kneeling beside Captain Travik with a pouch of water. The captain swallowed and grabbed the di'Taykan's arm. "It wasn't my fault," he said distinctly and slumped back down, head lolling to one side.

Huilin rocked back on his heels and caught sight of Guimond. "Just put her beside the other one," he sighed, shoving his helmet back far enough to allow a few strands of turquoise hair to escape.

"Where's *Harveer* Niira . . . Nyri . . . Where's the Niln?"

"Staff's got her and Ryder checking out packing crates on a 'look, don't touch' basis. She wants to know how good this reconstruction is and if there's stuff in here that couldn't have come from Ryder's memory, she wants to know if either of them recognize it. She says if we can get an idea of who else this barge has been in contact with, we can get an idea of where it's been and we'll have a better idea of whose side it's on."

"Okay, but what if they don't recognize anything?"

"Then the civilians are still out of the way while we make ready to move out. Win-win situation." Tilting the helmet over one ear, Huilin granted momentary freedom to new bits of hair. "Fuk, I hate these things. She as light as she looks?" he added as Guimond squatted and set the scientist on the deck beside the reporter.

"Lighter."

"Good. 'Cause the captain's got that Krai bone density thing going, and he's gonna be no fun at all to hump around."

The rope holding the injured Katrien to the stretcher had been pulled tight enough that thick tufts of fur poked up through the spaces. It didn't look comfortable. Guimond freed one edge, then frowned over a second set of knots. Unable to tell which way they went, he moved the scientist's arm out from her body to allow him a better angle.

Her hand brushed Presit's shoulder.

Two sets of black eyes snapped open.

Guimond barely got out from between them in time.

"Staff? Guimond. The Katrien are awake."

"Good. Is that them I can hear?"

"Yeah, that's them."

"What the hell are they doing?"

"Uh, they were, I uh, guess . . . grooming?" He winced at a particularly high-pitched burst. "Now, they're talk . . ."

A small black hand clutched suddenly at a handful of his uniform.

"Was that you, *Guimond?"*

"Yeah, Staff." Ears burning, he tried to ignore Huilin snickering.

A second hand joined the first although about ten centimeters to the left and in a significantly less sensitive region.

"Why is Gytha a Tur calFinistraven tied down?" Presit demanded imperiously.

"We're being tested." Torin made the statement in a tone so flatly inarguable, her entire audience blinked in near unison. "When Mr. Ryder and I sank through the floor, we spent more time in transit than the depth of the floor would allow for. During that time, the ship clearly lifted information from Mr. Ryder's mind." A truncated jerk of her head directed their attention to the surrounding storehouse. "We don't yet know if information was also taken from myself, Captain Travik, or Presit a Tur durValintrisy, but I expect we'll find out soon enough."

Perched near the top of the pile of gear, Orla shuddered dramatically, hair fanning out in a fuchsia halo. "No offense, Staff, but given your simulations, I'd rather not end up somewhere out of your head."

"Better her head than the captain's," Tsui snorted.

Inclined to agree but not letting it show, Torin cut the general agreement off and continued. "Once we solved the communication problem, we got comm contact back. Mr. Ryder and I found our way through a seemingly solid wall . . ." She couldn't stop her gaze from drifting toward him. One corner of his mouth quirked up in appreciation of the understatement. "Since then, we've been given hatches. The first hatch was locked. Mr.

Ryder dealt with it, and the rest have been merely latched. If holing the wall caused the explosion, Johnston found a place where the wall could be knocked down conveniently over a shaft enabling us to join up."

"That are all being coincidence," Presit scoffed from the edge of the group where she and Gytha were sitting so close their fur intermingled.

"No." Torin shook her head. "It doesn't feel like coincidence."

"And you are being who so that what you are feeling means so much?"

"What?"

"She wants to know why *your* feelings should define the situation," *Harveer* Niirantapajee sighed, shooting an exasperated look at the reporter.

"I are *speaking* Federate," Presit snapped, actually showing teeth.

Torin caught Werst's eye and he carefully covered his own.

The Niln slapped her tail against her leg. "You're speaking the Katrien idiosyncratic version of Federate. If you're going to learn a language, why don't you learn the syntax, that's what I've always wondered. Egocentric mammals."

"Enough!" The whip snap of Torin's voice sat both Katrien down again and cut off half a dozen other comments. "*Harveer*, thank you for the translation but there will be *no* interspecies conflict. And to answer the question, I'm defining the situation because I'm in charge."

"Who are saying . . ."

"They are." She jerked her head toward the twelve Marines.

Heads pulled almost reluctantly around, the two scientists and the reporter stared up at the mass of black uniforms.

Tsui waved.

"You want to wander around this vessel on your own," Torin told them, pretending she couldn't see Ryder grinning his stupid head off over on the other side of the team, "be our guest. You want a hope in hell of getting off this thing, you stay with us, you do as you're told, and I don't want to have to keep telling you that."

"We are not Marines," Presit muttered.

"That's for damn sure." Folding her arms, she swept her gaze over the remains of the boarding party, uniting them again. "Our mission objective is simple; we need to get to the next air lock as quickly as possible and pick up our ride back to the *Berganitan*."

"You're sure the *Berganitan* will still be there?"

"I am." Which she was, and her certainty was all they needed. "The closest air lock is seven levels down, a little over four klicks aft, and about three and a half klicks starboard. Hatch one opens into a passageway that goes forward a hundred meters, then drops into a descending vertical with no bounce and no disruption of airflow that'd indicate an egress—not to mention standard gravity and no visible rungs. Hatch two opens into an identical passageway heading starboard for seventy-five meters, then turns ninety degrees to head forward. This passageway, now paralleling the first, shows no bounce, no egress. Either *could*, eventually, lead us where we want to go, but I'd just as soon not wander randomly around—we need a map."

"Staff, what makes you think the ship'll give us what we need?" Nivry's hair was flicking back and forth. "I mean, maybe we'll solve the puzzle in this room and it'll give us . . . uh . . ."

"Piped-in music," Frii offered.

Nivry shot the other di'Taykan an irritated look but let the suggestion stand.

"It's given us what we've needed so far."

"Yeah, after it exploded and killed most of the science team."

"I don't think it meant to do that," Ryder said suddenly. "I think it saved your captain and the reporter because they were the only two not killed instantly. And I think it removed me and the staff sergeant because we were in danger. And now I think it's trying to figure out who and what we are."

Expressions changed as the assembled company considered new possibilities. Finally, brows knitted into a deep vee over the bridge of her nose, Dursinski shook her head. "It won't know we need to go out an air lock."

"It knows we came in an air lock," Torin said flatly.

"You're making this up as you go along, aren't you, Staff?"

"You got a better suggestion, Lance Corporal? Because if you do, I'll listen to it." Tsui ruefully shook his head and, arms folded, Torin watched the twelve Marines consider all that had been said. Heer and Johnston, the two engineers, looked intrigued. Nivry, Harrop, Frii, and Huilin looked reluctantly convinced. Dursinski looked worried and Werst pissed off, but both, Torin had come to realize, were pretty much a given regardless. Tsui, Orla, and Jynett seemed doubtful, but as long as they had no better ideas, they could do as much doubting as they liked. Guimond was smiling broadly. Torin decided she'd rather not speculate about the reason.

"Orla, you'll be staying with the captain. He regains consciousness, try and get him to contact the *Berganitan*."

"Why me?" the di'Taykan protested.

"Because if I remember correctly, which I do, you're pretty much the only one left who hasn't done something to piss him off. Heer, Johnston, you start scanning the cases. Mr. Ryder didn't know what was in them in the original storehouse so there could be anything in them now. Squad One, check the perimeter for anything resembling an access panel. Squad Two, sweep the room looking for anything that doesn't seem to fit. You find something, you check it against Mr. Ryder's memory." She stepped back and half turned, gesturing dramatically into the room. "Let's move, people; you really don't want to be around me when we run out of coffee."

She was surprised to find the three non-Human civilians beside her when the rush ended.

"We have very little equipment," *Harveer* Niirantapajee began without preamble, "but what we have we will use in an attempt to communicate directly with the ship." She held up a slate about half again as large as the military version. "I suspect that by your standards, I'm carrying nothing of practical value in here, but I do have a large memory and a great deal of processing ability as well as about half of the data I'd collected before the explosion."

"You said, we?"

Gytha leaned forward, muzzle wrinkled in what Torin assumed was a smile. "I are carrying a second degree in fractal communications. Presit are being a professional communicator."

"And the three of you can work together?"

Presit looked dubious, but the Katrien scientist patted *Harveer* Niirantapajee on the shoulder. "I are working with her many times before. She are having—how are you Humans saying?—worse bark than her bite?"

"Close enough. Communicating with the ship would be very helpful, thank you." Torin watched them walk away, the Katrien keeping up a running commentary in their own language. As far as being stuck with civilians went, she supposed it could have been worse.

On cue, she turned to find Ryder standing behind her. "You walk too damn quietly."

"Sorry."

"Listen, I want to thank you for the support."

"Craig."

"What?"

"Thank you for the support, *Craig*."

"Don't push it." But she was smiling, and with the smile some of the muscles in her back relaxed.

"You know, I hate to put a damper on things, but we could be wrong. There could be no puzzle to solve in this room."

Torin took a deep breath and let it out slowly. At just past 1740 it had already been a very, very long day. "There has to be, because the alternative is trying to find a way to that air lock by wandering around inside an enormous ship that can change its configuration at will while carrying a wounded officer, escorting three civilians, with only three field rations and a little over a liter of water each."

"Four."

"What?"

"Four civilians." He smiled broadly and his eyes twinkled. "Although I'm flattered that you seem to be counting me among your people."

She had. And if he hadn't been so damned amused by it, she'd have let it go.

"I wouldn't be flattered," she told him, pulling her slate to check Captain Travik's vitals. "I'd forgotten to count you entirely."

"Ouch."

But a half glance toward him showed he was still smiling, and still twinkling. Annoying son of a bitch.

NINE

"We plan to attach this comm unit directly to the side of the ship . . ." The science officer touched the screen and the image rotated one hundred and eighty degrees on the X-axis and ninety on the Y. ". . . with these pads here. Once attached, it will, in essence, act in the same manner as the shuttle's comm unit, boosting the signals of the Marines' PCUs and enabling us to communicate with your people."

"Seems simple enough," General Morris grunted, glaring at the three-dimensional rendering. "What's taking so long?"

Captain Carveg waved the science officer back and answered herself. "We don't just pick one of these off the shelf and slap it onto an RC drone, General. I've had engineers working since the explosion to adapt both the comm unit and the delivery system. We're talking about only a matter of hours here, so you've got little to complain about."

"I've got an officer in there who represents the entire Krai vote in Parliament, Captain. You'll excuse me if I'm impatient."

"You've got fourteen Marines in there, General. Not one."

He turned slowly, broad face flushed nearly maroon. "I don't much like your tone, Captain Carveg."

Her upper lip lifted. "I'm sorry to hear that, sir."

The tension in the room rose to near palpable levels. Four Naval officers and Lieutenant Stedrin froze in place—eyes locked on their respective leaders, Lieutenant Stedrin, at least, willing to shield his CO with his own body.

"Captain Carveg, we're picking up Susumi leakage at that portal we spotted earlier. Educated guess says it's about to reopen."

The voice of the watch officer over the ship's internal comm snapped the captain's attention off the general as though he no longer existed. "On screen in here, Commander Versahche."

The modified comm unit disappeared to be replaced by a familiar star field. The only thing missing was the alien ship usually hanging motionless in front of it.

"This is coming in from the buoy we set on the other side of the ship, Captain. When I emphasize the aurora . . ."

Soft green rays spread out against the stars. At their center was a shimmering green circle.

"I see it, Commander." Carveg stepped closer to the screen, facial ridges spread. "How far back behind the ship is that thing?"

"About one hundred and thirty-six thousand kilometers."

"Dangerously close."

"Yes, ma'am. Given the estimated size of the portal, there's no way the vessel coming through will be able to decelerate in time."

"Which means?" the general snapped.

"Which means," Captain Carveg repeated grimly, "that the vessel coming through is going to smack into the other side of the alien ship at a high speed, blowing themselves and very likely the alien ship, as well, into fragments. Commander Versahche, do we have any fighters out?"

"No, ma'am."

"Good. Get us to a safe distance and ready defense systems." With a last look at the screen, she pivoted on one heel and moved quickly toward the nearer of the room's two exits, bare feet slapping purposefully against the deck. "Yellow alert. I'm on my way to Combat Command Center."

After a stunned moment spent staring at the rapidly retreating back of the captain's head, General Morris charged after her, Lieutenant Stedrin at his heels. They caught up outside the conference room, the moving clump of three officers sending ship's personnel on their way to duty stations hard up against the bulkheads. "Captain! I will not allow you to abandon my Marines."

"General, one of two things is about to happen." Without breaking stride, or removing her gaze from the link station at the end of the passageway, Captain Carveg lifted her left hand into the air, first finger extended. "Either that ship is made of stronger stuff than anything in the Confederation and the incomer will bounce off its hide, in which case, we'll go back for your Marines because I assure you I am not abandoning anyone. Or . . ." A second finger joined the first, the three joints allowing it to snap erect with an emphasis a Human finger could never achieve. ". . . your Marines are about to become part of a large debris field traveling toward us at high velocity, and as much as I have no intention of abandoning those Marines, neither do I have any intention of joining them in death." Reaching the link station, she slapped her hand over the call pad. "Captain's override, *car sanute di halertai.*" With her back against the access hatch, she looked up at the general, her expression carefully neutral. "You'll be able to watch the whole thing from the Marine attachment, which is where I respectfully suggest you go. Now."

"And do what?" General Morris snarled as the link arrived.

"Try prayer," she suggested, stepping back through the hatch. "Because that portal's going to open, and there's not a *serley* thing we can do about it."

Crimson hair keeping up a steady sweep from side to side, Commander Versahche fell into step beside the captain as she stepped off the link and onto C3. "We've got a problem, Captain."

"Does it have to do with the main engines being off-line?" she snarled.

"You noticed."

"Inertial dampers aren't that good, Commander. What's happening?"

"We don't know. For no apparent reason, we're as dead in space as our big yellow friend."

"We can't move?"

"Not a centimeter. Engineering's working on it, but there's nothing to actually work *on.* All available data indicates the engines should be working."

"But they aren't."

"No, ma'am."

"Wonderful." She took her place behind the captain's station, one hand resting over the communications touch pad. Each finger opened a channel to a specific area of the ship; pressure from her palm opened a channel shipwide. Her thumb dipped, then lifted. No need to urge engineering to work faster; if anyone knew the result of a vessel exiting Susumi space too close to another solid object, they did. The three screens in front of the commander showed five-second sections of the surrounding star field, the alien ship, and the portal. Its aurora had brightened. "All right; any idea of what's coming through?"

"No, ma'am. Only thing we can tell for certain is that it's not one of ours."

"Not Navy."

"Not from the Confederation at all unless someone's put something new in vacuum and no one gave us the specs for it."

"Like that's never happened before," Carveg snorted. "You'd think we weren't involved in a shooting war out here. What about the Methane Alliance?"

"Again, if it is, it's something new. They use essentially the same Susumi drive we do, and this is subtly different."

The captain froze in place. "In what way?"

Before he could answer, another member of the C3 crew broke in.

"Captain Carveg, we just picked up a signal from the alien ship."

"From the ship or from the Marines, Ensign?"

"It was very brief, ma'am." Scalp darkly mottled, the young Krai had hands and feet both working his board. "I'm analyzing the little we got."

The aurora had grown so bright, the *Berganitan*'s screens dimmed automatically.

"Engineering?" Asking, not urging. Because she knew engineering was already busting their collective asses.

"Still nothing, Captain."

"Captain, we have a seventy percent probability that the signal came from Captain Travik's implant."

"And the message?"

"What little there was, was completely scrambled."

"Unscramble it."

The lieutenant monitoring the buoy cut off the ensign's reply. "Portal opening, Captain!"

"Engineering!"

"Engines are still off-line!"

"Vessel emerging from Susumi space! Speed registering as fifty-one thousand, four hundred and three point seven seven kilometers per second."

Screens flared, then went blank almost immediately.

"Buoy's fried. Vessel's bow wave has reached the alien ship."

Captain Carveg slapped her palm down on the touch pad. "All hands! Brace for impact!"

Except that at those speeds, impact should have happened before the words left her mouth. When it still hadn't happened a heartbeat later, she took a moment to breathe. "Anyone know why we're still alive?"

"Ma'am, last data from the buoy indicates that the alien vessel was absorbing the energy from the incomer."

All eyes turned to the lieutenant.

"You think the alien ship—what did you call it, Commander?—Big Yellow?—absorbed the incomer?"

"No, ma'am." Eyes on her screen, the lieutenant's voice held equal parts disbelief and awe. "I think it stopped it."

"Stopped it?"

"Yes, ma'am. Data fragments support the theory that the incomer's just sitting there, on the other side of the alien ship."

"All right." Palm back on the touch pad, a little more gently this time. "All hands, stand down from impact!" Palm up. "Lieutenant, let's get some unfragmented data; launch another buoy. Stealth mode."

"Aye, aye, ma'am, buoy away."

"Commander Versahche, have General Morris informed that his votes in Parliament are alive."

"Yes, ma'am."

"And until we know what's out there . . ." Palm down once again. "All hands, red alert!"

". . . heading for nearest air lock and . . . son of a bitch. He's gone again."

"You think they heard you, Staff?"

"No way to tell." Torin straightened and pushed Captain Travik's mouth carefully closed. "We don't know if his implant's strong enough to breach the hull. We don't know if he actually turned the damned thing on."

Orla's eyes lightened. "If you'd told me to activate *my* implant in that tone, I'd have come back from the dead to do it."

"Thank you. Should you get an implant, I'll keep that in mind." She rocked back on her heels and stood. "What made you put him in the HE suit?"

"It was his, and I thought it would be easier than carrying them separately. He's not hooked in, so I left him in his combats and got the arm of the suit to conform."

"Good thinking. Let me know if he comes to again."

The rest of the Recon team stood a cautious distance from the only sealed container in the room that hadn't scanned as a solid object, watching Werst direct the beam of his benny along the seam between box and lid. Without hinges, without a hasp, it was the only way in. As Torin returned from attempting to contact the *Berganitan*, he was just finishing the last side.

As she slid back into the position she'd vacated at Orla's summons, Guimond half turned and flashed her a welcoming smile. "Any luck, Staff?"

Other heads turned until there were as many eyes on her as on Werst.

"Well, I could offer you possibilities and speculation—but I won't. This much I know for certain; Captain Travik was conscious long enough to activate his implant. Unfortunately, he lost consciousness before he could tell me if the *Berganitan* replied."

Guimond's smile broadened. "That's great! They know we're alive."

"They know Captain Travik's alive," Tsui snorted. "But why would they wait around for *him?*"

Torin leaned far enough forward to spear the lance corporal with an icy glare. "Tsui, I don't really give a crap what your opinion of our OC is and that means, I don't want to hear it. Do you understand?"

"Yes, Staff Sergeant."

"Good."

"I'm through," Werst grunted in the sudden silence that had replaced the constant background noise of the benny. "Charge is down to twelve point four percent."

Standard operating procedure called for power packs to be replaced when the charge hit ten percent, not before. Packs carried in were to be carried out and inspected by the senior NCO who was responsible for ensuring both that all packs were accounted for and under the minimum charge. NCOs who consistently came up either under count or over charge were written up. Combat officers who recognized the reports were a load of crap tended to lose them, but they were exactly the sort of thing Captain Travik would enjoy passing on.

Captain Travik was unconscious.

Not that it would have made any difference.

"Open it," Torin told him. "Take cover, people. Huilin, Jynett, Dursinski . . ."

As Marines ducked behind other cases, the two di'Taykan stepped forward wearing their HE suits, helmets up. Dursinski, also in her suit, held her benny pointed toward the crate. If anything unpleasant came out of it, the suits would keep them alive long enough to get it closed again.

Or at least they lengthened the odds.

"You're just not much of a risk taker, are you, Staff Sergeant?"

"It's my job to keep these people alive, Mr. Ryder."

"And, sometimes, doesn't that mean riding the whirlwind?"

Torin turned just far enough to meet his gaze. "I don't ride whirlwinds, Mr. Ryder. I beat them into submission."

One corner of his mouth lifted. "And just thinking of you doing that is turning me on."

"Turn yourself off again."

The lid slid clear.

Nothing emerged.

Inside, were thirty-six medium gray, empty boxes. The interior of the case showed only smooth gray walls identical in color and texture to the walls in both the original corridor and the cube.

After removing the boxes, the entire company, with the exception of Orla and the captain, stared at the empty case.

Torin sighed. "Son of a fukking bitch."

"You're thinking that's the way out?" Ryder asked in much the same tone.

"Yes, I am."

Tossing one of the boxes from hand to hand, Guimond shook his head. "Uh, no disrespect, Staff, this thing's solid. See?" He tossed the box back into the crate where it bounced noisily.

"Solid is a relative term around here," Torin reminded him wearily. Before she could tell him to remove the box, the lights dimmed and an earsplitting burst of static evoked some creative profanity in three languages as helmets were snatched off.

"What was *that*?" Nivry demanded, hair an emerald aurora around her head.

"Let's assume it was a suggestion from Big Yellow that we move on."

"Big Yellow?"

"There's a limit to how long I can refer to something as 'the alien ship' and that seemed the obvious name." Replacing her helmet over hair nearly as wild as the di'Taykan's, Torin nodded toward Guimond. "Take the box from the crate."

The big Marine shrugged good-naturedly, grabbed the edge with his left hand, leaned in, stretched, slipped a little, and froze. "Staff . . ."

It was the first time Torin had heard him sound anything but cheerful. From the sudden surge forward, it was the first time for all of them. By the time she reached the crate, she had to shove Marines out of her way in order to get a place by Guimond's side. The fingers of his right hand had sunk into the floor up to the first joint. When he turned to face her, his eyes were huge in a flushed face, pupils so dilated the irises had all but disappeared.

"I can't . . . I can't get them out."

"Stop trying; you'll hurt yourself." She reached in and gripped his arm, stopping the constant jerk, jerk, jerk as he tried to pull free. The muscles under her fingers felt more like stone than flesh. "It's all right, Guimond, you've just found the way to the next level."

"I have?" He managed a wan smile. "Good for me. You want me to keep going?"

"I don't think you have a choice."

"We could cut his fingers off."

Giving Guimond's arm a last squeeze, Torin straightened. "Shut up, Tsui."

"No, really; six months or so with his arm in a regen sleeve and he'll grow a whole new se . . ." The last word got lost in a strangled squawk as Werst grabbed a fistful of combats at Tsui's waist and lifted the larger Marine off his feet.

"What part of shut up," he growled, "do you not understand?"

"Werst, drop him."

"Unfortunate choice of words," Ryder murmured by Torin's ear as Tsui hit the deck, both hands yanking fabric away from his crotch.

"Deliberate choice of words," Torin told him, aiming her reply under the covering shouts of laughter and at least three voices telling Guimond what had happened. "All right, people," she cut the noise off as Tsui got to his feet, "listen up. This is our way out. Private Guimond is on point." A touch on his shoulder and she was pleased to hear a chuckle from within the crate. "But I want two Marines in there immediately, and I mean immediately after him. Tsui, Werst, you just volunteered. Huilin, Jynett, Dursinski, stay in your suits. Frii, you help Orla with the captain. Johnston, go find our civilians and get them over here. Someone bring me Guimond's pack. I'll take it through." A pause and she raised her voice just a little. "Let's *go*, Marines, we're moving out."

Clutching the edge of the crate so tightly that silver polish flaked off her claws, Presit stared down at the visible two thirds of Guimond's hand. "I are not going through there."

"Yes, you are," Torin told her absently, catching the end of the line connecting Tsui and Werst to Guimond and tossing it back into the group of Marines who secured it. "You ready?"

Tsui looked anything but ready. Werst grunted an affirmative.

"Heer, Johnston?"

"Scanners up and running, Staff."

Both scanners were reading a big fat nothing under the crate, as though reality ended halfway up Guimond's right hand. But that was about to change. Because it had to change. It had to become the way out. It had nothing to do with faith. It had everything to do with putting all the pieces together in the right order.

"Just relax, Guimond."

"Trying to, Staff."

There didn't seem to be any way around Guimond going through to the next level headfirst.

"You won't drop until your entire body is in the open so you'll actually fall no more than a meter." *Provided this works like it did the last time*, amended a snide voice in her head. Torin ignored it. "Tuck and roll and you'll be fine."

"Tuck and roll," Guimond repeated. "Right."

Under the circumstances, he sounded remarkably cheerful.

Stepping back, Torin nodded to Tsui and Werst. "Go."

Bending, they each lifted one of Guimond's legs. The moment they released the pressure against the crate, he began to sink.

He sank very fast.

Seconds later, Tsui and Werst hit the bottom together, and were almost instantly ankle-deep.

"Let the line play out," Torin snapped, as it began to tighten, "we've got plenty." Watching the line run into the crate, she began to count under her breath, ignoring the watch on her sleeve. It was more important that she *do* something than that the count be accurate to the nearest nanosecond. "One MidSector Station. Two MidSector Station." The top of Werst's helmet disappeared. "Three MidSector Station." The crate was empty again. "Four MidSector Station. Five MidSector Station. Six Mid . . ."

"Staff Sergeant Kerr, this is Private Guimond, do you read?"

The cheering was a little premature but she let it run anyway. "I hear you, Guimond."

"We came through fine and you were right."

"It's part of the job description." Never let the relief show. They had to believe she never worried. "But what—specifically—was I right about this time?"

"We're standing in what looks like a station corridor heading fore and aft and there's one of those three-dimensional signs on the bulkhead."

"One of *what* signs, Guimond?"

"The kind that tell you where you are. You know: you are here and this is how you get to docking bay seventeen."

Torin sighed. "Guimond, are you trying to tell me there's a map down there?"

"Uh, affirmative, Staff."

A map.

"Is the air lock marked on it?"

"Seems to be."

Things were looking up.

"Corporal Nivry." Torin motioned toward the crate.

"They're your squad."

Nivry, Frii, Johnston . . .

"Staff, we have a problem."

"What is it, Corporal?"

"Johnston's scanner and the exoskelton didn't come through."

"Did he lose any body parts?"

"No, he's fine."

"Then it's a problem we can live with."

With Squad One on the lower level and their immediate area secured, Torin had the captain passed carefully down through the floor into Guimond's waiting arms. She'd half hoped, half feared that the trip would bring him back to consciousness but Nivry reported no change.

Both scientists attempted to take readings as they went through the floor. Although they were unsuccessful, at least *they* got to keep their equipment.

As Guimond announced he was back in position, Torin turned to the remaining Katrien. "Your turn."

"No." Presit stared into the crate, black eyes narrowed suspiciously. "I said, I are not going through there."

"You can't stay here all alone," Torin pointed out reasonably.

"I are not wanting to stay here all alone. You are getting me out a different way."

Waving away a cloud of shed fur, Torin stepped closer. "There is no other way."

"You are not knowing that!"

"I know it's frightening." She was using the voice she used on new recruits. The one that gave comfort and no options in equal measure. "But everyone else went through all right."

"I are not caring about everyone else. I are not going through that."

"Yes, you are." Abandoning reason, Torin grabbed the Katrien under the arms and swung her up over the edge of the crate. "Guimond, incoming at speed."

"Ready, Staff."

The reporter nearly folded in half, trying to get out of Torin's grip. Torin let go.

"I are going to do you FOR THI . . ."

"Got her, Staff."

Squad Two stood grouped in an admiring half circle as she turned.

"If this situation comes up again," Orla murmured, her eyes so light they looked pale pink, "can I do that?"

"Sure." Torin held up a bleeding wrist. "She scratches. Mr. Ryder . . ."

He stared at her for a long moment, then nodded and jumped.

"Corporal Harrop . . ." The edge of the crate had been melted smooth by the benny. Torin ran her thumb up and down one of the curves. "Send your squad through on my word. Leave the line tied where it is; I'd rather lose it than risk . . ." She didn't want to think of what they might be risking; she certainly didn't want to say the words out loud. Not right before . . .

She tightened her grip. Adjusted the straps of Guimond's pack. Wondered why she hadn't just dropped it down.

And jumped.

Her gaze went straight to Craig Ryder when she landed, one hand against the new deck, her knees absorbing the shock. He looked like she felt. She very carefully arranged her features so that she looked like nothing at all.

A few seconds later, Heer came through stripped of scanner and exoskeleton. Torin's best guess was that the ship disliked being probed. No one else lost a benny, leaving her the only one without a weapon. At the moment, it was merely embarrassing. She could only hope it didn't become something more.

Corporal Harrop was the last through the crate. The rope dropped with him.

In a silence so complete even the Katrien had stopped talking, Torin lifted a loop off Harrop's shoulder and saluted the ceiling with it. "Thanks."

Then she tossed it to the corporal. "Get this packed up again, we may need it later."

He glanced at the ceiling, shrugged, and began rolling the line as half a dozen conversations were resumed.

Torin hid a smile as she turned back toward the map; Recon didn't much worry about a line of retreat at the best of times. Which these weren't. *Although*, she admitted, tracing a mental line from "you are here" to "closest available air lock," *things* are *looking up.*

"Buoy in place, Captain Carveg."

"Thank you, Lieutenant." Returning to her position, she stared down at the screens. "Let's see what we've got."

The first screen showed a distant image of a ship similar to the *Berganitan* in that there was nothing streamlined about it. Built for the frictionless vacuum of deep space, it was never intended to go into atmosphere.

"Distance from the incomer to Big Yellow?"

"One hundred and eighteen kilometers, Captain."

"One hundred and eighteen?"

"Yes, ma'am. The incomer is not only exactly the same distance we are from the alien ship, it's in the same position relative to the ship."

The captain's lip curled. "Interesting."

"Yes, ma'am. Receiving second data stream."

The incomer now filled the next screen.

Commander Versahche's hair had flattened against his skull. *"Ablin gon savit."*

"Indeed. And how fortunate we're already at red alert." Visible armaments equaled the *Berganitan*'s. No way of knowing what they had hidden. "I think we must assume this is one of the Others' ships. Mister Potter, do the Others know we're here?"

"No, ma'am." The lieutenant answered without taking his eyes off his screen. "Big Yellow is directly between us and the enemy. They've launched no buoys and—should they have recently acquired tech capable of either penetrating or circumventing the alien ship—we haven't been scanned. Nor are they running any of the standard defense sweeps."

"Maybe their sudden deceleration has slapped the entire crew against the bulkheads hard enough to turn them to jelly." She took a deep breath and exhaled forcefully. "Lucky day for us. Not so lucky for them."

After a number of fatal attempts at diplomacy, the Rules of Engagement had been adjusted to allow for the destruction of any enemy vessel found in Confederation space—although enemy vessels weren't usually *found* so much as interrupted in the midst of destroying or co-opting Confederation property. Neither were they easy to destroy.

Her forefinger touched the pad. "Missile Control Room. I want four of the PGM-XLs, the ship smasher missiles, programmed to round Big Yellow every ninety degrees, targeted on the Others' ship."

Targeting data on enemy vessels went automatically to the MCR the moment one was sighted, although missiles were most often used to soften up a Marine landing site.

"Four PGM-XLs to round Big Yellow every ninety degrees. Aye, aye, Captain."

"Even if an ADS comes on," she noted to no one in particular, "it won't be able to stop four missiles impacting simultaneously."

"The battle'll be won before the Others know they're in a fight," Commander Versahche agreed.

"Best kind of battles to be in. When they send out a buoy, Mister Potter, I want to know about it before it clears the launch tube."

"Aye, aye, Captain."

"Without a buoy, would they be able to pick up the drone taking the modified comm unit to Big Yellow?"

"No, ma'am."

"All right." An open channel to communications led to the discovery that attaching the unit to the drone was not going well. "I don't care if you have to stick it on with spit. Get it done and get it moving!"

"Yes, ma'am."

She drummed the fingers of her right hand against the edge of the console and spent a moment wrapped in the reassuring hum of her ship. Propulsion remained off-line, but thousands of other pieces of machinery were working perfectly. Then, because she had the time, a luxury not often given in battle, she pressed her palm down on the touch pad and let the rest of the *Berganitan* know what was going on. Rumors traveled through the closed environment of a ship faster than a head cold and usually caused more damage.

"Captain Carveg, this is MCR. Four PGM-XLs programmed and ready to launch."

"Fast work, MCR."

"Not exactly complicated trajectories, Captain, but thank you."

"Weapons officer . . ."

The lieutenant commander at the station stiffened slightly.

". . . launch missiles."

"Aye, aye, Captain. Missiles away."

"Buh-bye." Lieutenant Commander Sibley waved glumly at the monitor mounted high on the wall of the "Dirty Shirt" as the ship plotted a graphic of the missile launch. "Now, doesn't that just take all the fun out of war?"

A number of the other pilots in the flight officers' wardroom nodded glumly. On red alert, two squadrons of Jades were held launch ready, leaving two squadrons moaning about drawing the short straw. With the captain using missiles rather than fighters, they were even farther out of rotation.

The missiles rounded Big Yellow. The wardroom held a collective breath waiting for them to turn toward the target.

They didn't turn.

Instead, they continued on their original trajectory, bracketing the Others' ship at a distance before heading off into deep space.

"I bet that's made them a little curious about what's on this side of the fence," Sibley murmured, as the silence gave way to a cacophony of speculation and profanity about equally mixed.

"No bet." Shylin raised her mug in a mocking salute. "Looks like war is fun again."

"MCR, what the *chreen* happened?"

"As near as we can figure, Captain, Big Yellow wiped the program as the missiles passed."

"Captain Carveg, the Others have launched a buoy!"

"Well, so much for the decelerate into jelly theory. Stealth or open, Mister Potter?"

"Open, ma'am."

"No real reason for stealth, I suppose." Her lip curled up off her teeth. "They know we're here."

In a nose-to-nose fight, the *Berganitan* could hold her own with anything but the largest of the Others' ships, those that Command had dubbed Dreadnoughts. They weren't facing a Dreadnought and with the alien vessel playing silly bugger between them, that was the first good news she'd had today.

Any battle would now depend mostly on small fighters. The question: would they be allowed to fight? With that question unanswered, she wasn't going to risk the lives of pilots and crews.

"Mister Potter, can we use our buoy to fry their buoy?"

"We *should* be able to, ma' am . . ."

"And from your choice of words, can I assume we *can't*?"

"Yes, ma'am."

Drumming her fingers again, she watched the Others' buoy arc toward the top of the alien ship.

"I wonder what they're up to."

"The Others, Captain?"

"No, the Big Yellow aliens."

His hair beginning to move again, the commander turned far enough to see her face. "Do they have to be up to anything?"

"I doubt it's coincidence that they stopped that ship"—she nodded toward the screen—"exactly one hundred and eighteen kilometers out. They redirected our missiles and now they're allowing the Others' to take a look at us. My people have a saying, Commander, if it looks like a vertrek, and it sings like a vertrek, roast it with a nice red sauce."

"Which means?"

"Which means, they're up to something."

"Captain Travik, sir, I need you to activate your implant. Now."

He blinked up at her, facial ridges spread wide as he struggled to breathe. "You don't tell me what to do . . . Staff Sergeant. I . . . am the Officer Commanding. Me. You aren't even . . ." His ridges fluttered and his eyes closed.

Torin glanced down at the medical data on her slate. It didn't look good.

"Staff, what do you think?"

Heer had attached the captain to the stretcher by tying his personal fifty feet of rope into a loose net. Rural Krai were still largely arboreal and Heer's family were farmers.

"Nice to know all that specialist training didn't wipe out your more useful skills."

He beamed. "The last year I was home, my net took first prize at the Vertintry Fair."

She managed an answering smile. He couldn't know he'd evoked a cascade of memories, each more *country* than the last—pigs and poultry, plowing and preserves—thank God, the Corps had given her a way out.

It would take four Marines to carry the captain, one at each corner. The passageway they were currently in was just wide enough and, with any luck, would stay that way.

Crossing to the map, Torin turned to face the group, most of whom were finishing up the last dregs of their field rations. A quick glance at her sleeve told her it was now 20:14. It felt later. Barring any unforeseen circumstances, they'd be at the air lock in about three hours and back on the *Berganitan* an hour after that—an observation she had no intention of making aloud, nothing being more likely to bring on unforeseen circumstances.

"Listen up, people. I want Squad One on point." Glancing over, she met Nivry's eyes. "Corporal, place your people as you see fit. As neither Mr. Ryder nor myself have a weapon, we'll be taking two of the places around the captain—if Mr. Ryder agrees."

He flashed her a disarming smile—less effective in Torin's opinion because he clearly knew it was a disarming smile. "Happy to help out the Corps."

"Corporal Harrop, in an attempt to keep the captain relatively level, I'll want Huilin and Orla on the other two spots. The rest of your squad will cover the rear. You've got ten minutes to finish eating and use the facilities."

"Facilities?" Presit scoffed, from directly across the passage. "There are being no facilities."

Torin held up an empty ration bag. "They reseal."

"I are not using a food container to . . . to . . ."

"You won't be eating out of it again, ma'am," Guimond told her helpfully.

"Go in pairs," Torin reminded them over the laughter, "and don't go far. Three meters forward of the map and that's it. And, ma'am . . ."

Even with her eyes squinted nearly shut, the reporter was unmistakably glaring.

"If you think you can hold it for another three hours, be my guest."

*　　*　　*

Back against the bulkhead, Guimond peered around a ninety-degree turn, then waved Werst forward. "So you still think there's no crew on this thing?"

"I never said there was no crew." Finger through the trigger guard, Werst went around the corner and up against the opposite bulkhead.

"Yeah, you di . . . Okay, maybe you didn't." They started moving up the new length of passageway, boots making almost no sound on the black rubber flooring. "So where do you think the crew is?"

"What crew?"

"So then you don't think there's a crew?"

"I don't *care.*"

"I just think that if there's a crew, we should try communicating with them."

"We are. They set puzzles. We solve them. That's communicating."

"But it's not talking."

"Maybe we should all sit down and have a beer together."

"I think that's a perfectly valid way of solving problems."

"I think you're an idiot." He stopped and motioned Guimond forward.

The big Human nodded and slipped to the other side of what looked like a standard vertical opening. Then he leaned forward and looked.

"Oh, that's smart," Werst grunted. "Lead with your head."

Flipping down his mike, Guimond ignored him.

"Corporal, we've reached the first vertical."

"Roger that. Wait for backup before attempting a descent."

So far, the floor plan matched the map in her head.

"Cred for your thoughts?"

So she told him.

"You memorized the map? I thought you had . . . what? uh . . . *even* numbers scan it into their slates?"

"That's right." Even numbers only. Should something go wrong, it would leave half the team's slates unaffected. She hadn't told the rest of the Marines to memorize the map. They were Recon. She expected it as a matter of course. "The Corps issues slates that are pretty much indestructible, but they can't do anything to prevent, say, a strong electromagnetic pulse from wiping the memory. Fortunately, Mr. Ryder, Marines are trained to use technology, not to be dependent on it. The Corps has always believed that the most powerful weapon its people possesses is between their ears."

"So you're saying you could charge naked into battle and triumph?"

She could hear the grin in his voice and replied with flat sincerity. "That, Mr. Ryder, depends on what I'm fighting."

From not five feet behind her, the soft-voiced di'Taykan conversation grew suddenly speculative. Torin ignored them with the ease of long practice.

"You really think we're going to make it out of here in three hours?"

"If that map's right, there's no reason why we shouldn't."

"How about them?" He nodded toward the three civilians walking ahead of them. "The *harveer's* quite a few years out of the egg, and I doubt either of our furry friends have ever walked seven kilometers in their lives."

Even more than the Krai, the Katrien's feet were designed for climbing. Although Torin doubted either the scientist or the reporter had ever climbed the equivalent of seven kilometers either.

"They're not very big." The scratches on her wrist throbbed. "We can carry them if we have to."

"Still, maybe you should have the lads up front looking for a defensible place to catch some kip."

"If it comes to it, a passageway will do fine. There're only two approaches in a passage, making it easy enough to defend. I don't know about you, but I'm hesitant to lock myself into anything on this ship."

"Even after the map, you don't trust it?"

"I don't trust anything I don't understand."

"What am I looking at?" Captain Carveg leaned over the screens at one of the science stations.

"These are the last views Lieutenant Commander Sibley took of the air lock, Captain. And these are our most recent images."

"It looks like it's healing."

"The ship is partially organic, ma'am. The science team was able to determine that much before . . ."

"Before they blew that air lock and killed one of my shuttle pilots?" the captain snorted.

"Yes, ma'am."

"And what's so important about what I'm looking at?"

"This area here. Where the ship has, for lack of a better word, healed. Notice the beginnings of a ripple in the hull. A ripple like . . ." The screen split. "This. This is the ripple on the opposite side of the hull, pretty much exactly in the same relationship to the Others' ship as the destroyed air lock is to us."

"So it's possible that the Others were here previously—while making one of their smash-and-grab forays into Confederation space—landed a boarding party, left—because they didn't want to hang around in Confederation space where a stationary target is likely to get its ass blown off—and are now back to pick up their people who are stuck inside having also blown their air lock?"

"That's one theory, ma'am."

"I'm open to any others."

The silence stretched and lengthened.

"All right." She ran one hand back over her scalp. "Let me guess this next part. The closest air lock the Others can now use is the same air lock the Marines are heading for."

"Yes, ma'am."

By the time Staff Sergeant Kerr—and it would *be* Staff Sergeant Kerr because on a good day Captain Travik was a *serley chrika* with delusions of grandeur—got her people to the next available air lock, there had to be a shuttle waiting for them. Unfortunately, the next available air lock was dead center on the belly of the beast, visible to the Others. The *Berganitan*'s gunners could shoot an enemy shuttle off the spot without even trying. Captain Carveg had to believe the Others' could as well.

Unless Big Yellow made arrangements for a peaceful pickup.

Hopefully, there'd be someone left alive to pick up.

"So." Hands locked behind her, she rocked back on her heels. "There's an unknown number of the enemy inside Big Yellow with the Marines."

"There's an eighty-seven point two percent probability of it, ma'am."

"Then we need to tell them that. Where's that *serley* comm unit now?"

A graphic of the drone approaching the alien ship replaced rippled yellow hull. "Almost there, Captain. We should be able to open communications in seventeen minutes, twelve seconds."

"Good. Let's just hope we're the first to give them the news."

The next level down had red and green lights running randomly along the bulkheads.

"I wonder whose head these came out of."

"Who cares?"

The passage was about to end in a T-junction. According to the map, six meters starboard there was another vertical that would take them two levels down and into a passage that ran aft for a full kilometer.

"You know," Guimond murmured as they moved up on the junction, "they could have reconfigured this thing into one long corridor aft, and a single four level drop. I wonder why they didn't?"

Werst shot the big Human a look that suggested he'd like to see him on a serving platter with an apple in his mouth.

"Maybe they wanted you to have something to chat about."

Guimond grinned. "Maybe."

A quick look showed the corridors empty both to port and starboard and a moment later they stood on either side of the vertical. About to lean into the shaft, Werst froze, and looked up at Guimond. Voice barely clearing his facial ridges, he muttered, "Did you hear something?"

TEN

"You're sure?"

"*Werst recognized the language. The Others used bugs when they took Drenver Mining Station; Werst was there.*"

"Okay, have them hold just to this side of the vertical. Secure the entrance to the shaft and establish perimeters in the passageway; we'll regroup there."

"*Roger, Staff.*"

Torin pulled her slate free and, one-handed, thumbed in the next level of the map. "And why am I not surprised," she muttered, switching to group channel. "Werst, take a quick look at the map from the bottom of the vertical."

"*It's changed.*"

"Yes, it has." Instead of an essentially straight path, they now had options. Several corridors. Cross corridors. Chambers. Access . . . tunnels? Galleries? Shafts? Whatever the hell they were called, they were registering as about a meter square. "This isn't the interior of Drenver Mining Station, is it?"

"*No.*"

"Good." Because they'd lost at Drenver. Not badly, 2nd Recar'ta, 1st Battalion, Delta Company had managed to rescue most of the station's workforce and not lose many Marines doing it, but the Others had taken the station. And still held it. Torin assumed it was on somone's list of things to get back. Trouble was, the bugs were good in enclosed spaces and— although they'd have to strip off most of their gear in order to fit—they could move like shit through a H'san in passages a meter square.

"Johnston, Heer, I want you to replace me and Frii on the captain's stretcher." The thought of the height difference brought a reluctant smile, but if there were bugs around they needed to free up as many weapons as possible and carrying the captain in comfort took a backseat to winning any potential firefights. Although the youngest on the team, the di'Taykan scored better than both the engineers in combat skills and she needed to be free to move around. The moment one of the engineers arrived, she'd make sure the civilians—a particularly shrill bit of Katrien conversation bounced off the walls and around the inside of her skull—didn't give their position away.

"Harrop, keep your Tailends sharp," she added, taking another look at the map. "The way this bastard layout's changing, the bugs could end up behind us."

"Roger, Staff. How the hell you figure they got in here in the first place? You think Big Yellow could be an enemy ship after all?"

"No. I don't." She could hear the entire team waiting for her response. "We all know their tells and we haven't seen any of them—outside or in. As to how the bugs got in here—" Nodding her thanks to Johnston, she handed over her arm of the stretcher. "That, people, is not our problem."

"All I can say is, it's about time!" General Morris stomped into the small ready room off the Combat Command Center and rocked to a stop, face flushed, in front of Captain Carveg's desk. "You have a situation here, Captain, and I very much resent being kept out of the loop."

"You're *in* the loop, General. All the main monitors are linked through to your office and you've been kept informed of any developments."

"I have been locked in!"

"Marines are always locked in their attachment during a red alert. If we have to drop you off, we like to know we're dropping all of you." It took an effort, but she managed to keep from sounding like she'd prefer to drop him out an air lock at the earliest opportunity. "As there's only the two of you, I'll lift the restrictions if you give me your word you'll stay out of the way."

"I do not get in the way," the general sputtered, cheeks darkening.

Captain Carveg lifted her upper lip, just a little. "Your word, General."

"Fine!" He spat it across the desk at her. "You have my word!"

"Thank you. Access extends to Lieutenant Stedrin as well, of course."

"And do you want his word, too, or will my assurances suffice?"

"Your word will be quite sufficient, General." As the di'Taykan lieutenant had been locked in with only the general for company, she very much doubted *getting in the way* would be on the top of his to do list. "I requested your presence just now because the modified comm unit has been attached to Big Yellow and we're about to contact your Marines."

"Finally!"

As lives were at risk, she decided to ignore the implication that members of her crew hadn't been working to the general's standards. "My people felt that, even amplified, implant to implant would be the most secure." She stood. "If you'll come with me, we've decided to bring the signal through to the communications station in C3."

Taking a deep breath, he fell into step beside her. "I apologize for my bad temper, Captain, but I'm sure you'll understand the stress I'm under here. Had I lost Captain Travik, the war effort would have lost the support of your people in Parliament."

"My people are on board this ship, General. I don't really care what a group of idiot politicians from my home world do."

"Those idiot politicians can see to it that the *Berganitan*'s docked indefinitely," he snorted, following her through the hatch into C3. "And that you spend the rest of your career watching the borders of the Confederation grow ever smaller."

Before she could answer—before she was even certain *what* she'd answer—the science officer in charge of the contact project crossed the room toward them, looked from her to the general, and finally decided where to deliver his news. "I'm sorry, General, but although Captain Travik is still alive and his implant is functioning, we can't raise him. You'll be speaking to Staff Sergeant Kerr."

"Thank God."

The general's response was quiet, almost prayerful, and Captain Carveg found herself smiling as she returned to her station. *Just when I'm convinced there's nothing to like about the man, he goes and says something like that.*

". . . and Presit a Tur durValintrisy."

The reporter is alive?

"Yes, sir."

Then, for God's sake, keep her happy, Staff Sergeant.

Torin glanced down the passage to where Presit sat sulking. She'd had to finally threaten to gag both Katrien before they'd shut up.

The last thing we need, the general continued, *is for this to look worse than it is in the media.*

"Yes, sir." Which could be, when necessary, a polite way of saying, "Fuk you." Torin couldn't remember it ever being quite so necessary before.

General Morris missed the subtext. *Remember, Staff Sergeant, it is vitally important to the war effort that Captain Travik come out of this mission looking good.*

"Sir, right at the moment, he'll be lucky if he gets out alive."

Alive's not good enough, Staff Sergeant.

"I'm sorry, sir, I didn't catch that. You're breaking up. The Others must be jamming the sig . . ." She tongued her implant off. "Asshole." After a moment, when it became clear he wasn't going to use the command codes to override, she moved silently up the passage to join the rest of the Marines. Gathering them close, she quietly filled them in on the situation. "They have the list of survivors, they know we're heading for the air lock, they know we have bugs. Conversely, we now know they're being held in place, there's an Others' ship being held on the opposite side of Big Yellow, and they aren't allowed to shoot at it. On the upside, they *will* pick us up at the air lock. On the downside, they tell me this is going to look really bad on the vids."

Tsui snickered first, then it swept the circle.

After a moment of low-voiced but inventive profanity—mostly having to do with where General Morris could stick his PR problem—Torin raised a hand for silence. "Listen up, people, this is what we're going to do. The perimeter pin's reading no movement in the shaft, so I'm taking Jynett and Werst down with me to see where the bugs actually are. Werst." She turned to the Krai. "I know you've been working point, but you're the only one with any actual bug experience."

He nodded, his expression so neutral it bordered on blank. "And the simulation?"

"Jynett and I are the only ones who've qualified."

"How do you know that?" Jynett whispered. "It never came up."

"I know everything, Jynett. Get used to it. The rest of you stay sharp. This area is secure now, but it may not stay that way. Maintain PCU silence and do your best to keep the civilians quiet. You might want to take a crack at that last bit, Guimond. They seem to like you."

He flashed her a dazzling smile. "Everyone likes me."

"Oh, puke," Werst grunted.

The vertical was no different than verticals on any station Torin had ever been on except that the low-gravity cylinder was only two levels long—far too small to be cost effective on a station. Holding a borrowed benny, she dropped in headfirst and caught herself on a loop just above the lower exit, her body swinging around until her boots touched the deck. Given the ship's on-again-off-again solids, she maintained her grip on the loop.

Werst landed beside her, Jynett to the other side of the exit.

Over the years, the Corps' R&D had developed a number of small drones that could be sent in advance of personnel to search for the enemy. And over the years, the enemy had found every one of them. Once or twice, the drones had been the first the enemy had known there were Marines deployed in the area. Eventually, R&D had discovered what Marines in the field already knew—it was impossible to replace an informed set of eyes and ears.

On the other hand, there was no point in being stupid about it.

Torin flipped down her helmet scanner and unhooked the narrow cable that ran around the inside of the rim. Holding it about six inches back from the camera end, she crouched and poked it around the corner just off the deck.

No bugs. No movement.

Nothing but an empty corridor, a junction, and two closed hatches. Illumination seemed even spottier than it had up above, but at least this level had no red and green running lights.

Werst's facial ridges flared, Jynett's hair flattened, and even Torin could smell the lingering bug scent. Approximately a third of their language was scent based and to Human noses the dominant notes were cinnamon and formaldehyde—not exactly unpleasant but unmistakable in combination. The scent trail raised the odds the bugs weren't in suits, which meant they'd have to be just as careful about shooting holes in bulkheads or releasing toxins into the life-support system. Two definite pluses if it came to combat.

With any luck, it wouldn't.

Taking a perimeter pin from her vest, Torin set it so that it covered the approach from the bow and pointed the other two members of the team toward the first hatch.

No bugs.

The compartment looked like a repair shop as much as it looked like anything. Tools, accurate enough in their rough shapes but lacking details, hung from the walls, and disassembled equipment had been spread over the center bench. A fast glance showed nothing they could use. About to turn away, Torin's eye caught a familiar shape. It took her less than a minute to find all the pieces of her missing benny and less even than that to check it and reassemble it.

She checked it for traps, then she wrapped her hand around the grip. It responded instantly, showing a full charge—which was interesting because she distinctly remembered firing into the floor. At an interrogative lift of Jynett's hair, she shook her head and transferred the strap of the borrowed benny to the returned weapon, slinging it across her back. Until she knew for certain it had been returned unchanged, she was taking no chances.

"And put your damned helmet on," she growled at the di'Taykan as they left.

The second compartment was a mirror image of the first. The parts on the bench had all been shoved to one side, and the room reeked of an animated discussion.

Looked like the ship had borrowed a bug's weapon as well. And returned it.

So the ship knows what both sides are carrying. Would that be a problem? *And it allowed us to know that it knows.* Was that even relevant? *One thing's for sure,* Torin acknowledged as they covered the last few meters to the T-junction, *a good old-fashioned firefight is going to come as a relief after all this does-it-or-doesn't-it crap.*

Twelve meters up the starboard arm of the T-junction, they found a dead bug. Although it was always dangerous to extrapolate with an unfamiliar species, the sticky patch on one side of its abdomen looked remarkably like a field dressing. A bug's vital organs—heart, lungs, brain—were in its abdomen behind not only the thickest bits of exoskeleton but body armor as well. In order to gain access to the wound, two pieces of armor had been removed. From the position of the entry hole, it looked as if something had gotten in a lucky shot, angling up in through both armor and exoskeleton at the break where the first section of millipedelike legs appeared. The carapace had been cracked; fluids had been seeping out.

"She probably took the hit during the explosion that destroyed *their* air lock. They carried her this far; she died. When they moved on, they took her weapon but left her body armor because"—Torin flipped a finger into

the air—"they want to travel quickly and because"—a second finger—
"they don't know we're in here."

"How do you figure that second one, Staff? We can't use this stuff."

"We can use this." Torin knelt and peered down at a section of the thorax cover. "In the simulation, this was a comm unit."

"No translation program," Werst reminded her. "Even if we can get it
to work."

"And it doesn't look like it comes off."

"It won't have to." Ignoring Jynett's silent request for more information, she rocked back on her heels and stood. "I think we can safely say the
bugs have left this area. Put a perimeter pin around that corner facing aft,
another on this hatch here, and let's bring the rest down."

"You've got a little time if you'd like to examine the bug, *Harveer* . . ."

"Do I look like a biologist?" the elderly Niln snapped, cutting Torin off.
Leaning heavily on Gytha's arm, her tail dragging, she shuffled past. "If
there's time to *examine*, there's time to sit and contemplate the stupidity of
leaving a comfortable lab in a highly regarded university in order to deny
one's age by throwing oneself into an intriguing bit of fieldwork. I want
that as my epitaph," she added as the younger scientist carefully lowered
her to the deck.

"Yes, *Harveer.*"

"You're not going to argue with me? Tell me I don't need an epitaph?"

"Everyone are needing an epitaph, *Harveer.*"

"And no one likes a fluffy smart-ass," she snorted, sagging back against
the bulkhead.

"It are not unattractive," Presit declared thoughtfully. "At least it are having
a shell and are not a species looking like it are skinned." A glance and a
lifted lip made it quite clear what species she'd been referring to.

"Please keep your voice down, ma'am." Guimond told her earnestly.
"There's more of them around, and we don't want you to get hurt."

She patted his arm, her hand looking even tinier than usual against his
bulk. "I are thanking you for your concern, and I are remembering it for
later."

"Are you blushing?" Nivry demanded as the reporter moved down the passage to join Gytha and the two Katrien began what was for them a quiet conversation. di'Taykan didn't blush; their circulatory system wasn't set up for it, and they found it a fascinating Human response.

The pink in Guimond's cheeks deepened. "I can't help it, Corporal. They're just so damned cute."

"All right, Frii, hand it over."

"Staff . . ."

"Now."

Sighing deeply, he reached down in under the collar of his combats and pulled out his music card. After a last lingering look, he dropped it into Torin's outstretched hand. "It's the best on the market," he told her mournfully. "Best sound, most memory, great range. They could turn it on from the *Berganitan.* The Corps'll reimburse me, right? I mean, it's personal property destroyed during a military operation."

"Tell you what, Private, if this actually works . . ." Torin handed the card in turn to Johnston, who began attaching it to the input end of the bug's exposed comm unit. ". . . I'll ignore all three regs you broke bringing it along and I'll personally file the reimbursement request with your company clerk."

Frii's eyes lightened. "And if it doesn't work?"

"We'll have bigger problems than you breaking regs."

Propped against a bulkhead, carefully situated to see both where they were going and where they'd been, Craig Ryder watched the Marines moving purposefully around the bug. Besides the staff sergeant, one of the engineers and a di'Taykan—*who looks remarkably depressed for a species who invented flavored massage oil before the wheel*, he snorted silently—three others were peering through their helmet scanners and keying information into their slates. It seemed that time taken to turn the bug's comm unit into a weapon was also being used to gather information on the enemy. Now, had *he* been in charge, they'd be breaking speed records hauling ass to the air lock, but clearly the staff sergeant believed that whole gram of prevention thing. Not to mention, better safe than sorry.

Since sorry in this instance meant dead, he supposed he had to appreciate her thoroughness.

Not the only thing about her that he appreciated, either.

Although most of the rest of it was the standard stuff he appreciated on most women.

Actually, it had been a long while since he'd spent enough time with a woman to appreciate anything else. Sex and gambling both had a pretty narrow focus.

I've got to get out more.

Provided, of course, I get out of here.

Funny thing, though, he didn't feel trapped, hadn't felt the growing pressure of sharing limited resources in an unforgiving environment. Maybe it was the size of the ship. Maybe it was because they were actively moving toward a destination. Whatever the reason, he hadn't felt the familiar panic since Torin had led the way out of that cube.

His heart began to pound, and he hurriedly reburied the rising memory.

Maybe it was Torin.

She turned away from the bug and started toward him. As she passed, he fell into step beside her.

"Mind if I ask you something?"

He had a strange, speculative look in his eyes Torin wasn't sure she trusted.

"What's with all the sneaking around and whispering? You lot have state-of-the-art PCUs on your heads, why not use them instead?"

Not the question Torin had expected. *And I expected what?* "We in the Corps prefer to call it reconnaissance—not sneaking."

"No offense intended."

"None taken. To answer your question, we're not entirely certain the bugs can't pick up our PCU signals. We don't want them eavesdropping; even if they don't understand us—and we're not entirely certain about that either—they could use the signal to acquire our position."

The left corner of Ryder's mouth curled up, creasing laugh lines around his eyes. "And what *are* you entirely certain of?"

"That if they're close enough to hear a whisper, they're close enough to shoot," Torin snorted. *And what the hell am I doing looking at his laugh lines? Let's try to remember he's a civilian, shall we?* Emphatically not looking, she dropped to one knee beside Captain Travik. "Any change?"

Orla's gaze flicked between the staff sergeant and the salvage operator, then she glanced back down at the captain and shook her head. "Not really. He mumbled something about wasters of food out to ruin him—I think. My Krai doesn't go much beyond *gre ta ejough geyko.*"

"Sit on it and rotate?" Ryder translated, smiling broadly. "I wouldn't have thought you lot considered that an insult."

The di'Taykan grinned up at him. "We don't."

Torin attempted to ignore their continuing exchange but with little success. The years of practice she'd put in honing her skills at selective listening seemed suddenly insufficient. *I must be more tired than I thought.*

The captain's vitals were low but holding steady. There'd been only minor changes since the last time Torin checked his medical program, and his heart rate had even improved slightly. As she stood, she patted him on the leg almost fondly. Not the hero the general expected him to be, but he was doing a lot less damage unconscious than if he'd been up and giving orders.

Johnston had finished up at the bug.

The *harveer* seemed to have gotten her breath back.

The moment Harrop's squad returned . . .

As if summoned, Harrop, Dursinski, and Huilin rounded the corner.

"Everything still matches the map, Staff. Passage is heading aft, and we get a bounce at 570.3 meters. There's a vertical at 569, accessed through the starboard bulkhead. It goes down one level, ladder only."

Torin followed on her slate as Harrop made his report and tried to stop worrying about why the ship had changed the original configuration. Nothing she could do about it; not worth wasting wetware on.

"There's a cross corridor every 95.05 meters," the corporal continued. "Six in total. They bounce out at 80 meters ending in the passage, here . . ." He touched the map. ". . . that runs parallel to our main passage. No sign of bugs."

"Although that doesn't mean they're not down here," Dursinski muttered as he finished.

"We *know* they're down here," Torin sighed. A gesture brought the Recon team together, another sent them to their positions, ready to move out. She turned to the civilians, expecting to find them on their feet.

"Guimond?"

He shrugged. "I can't make them stand up, Staff."

"You're twice the size of all three of them put together, so, yeah, you can."

"We are still resting," Presit declared, folding her arms. "It are getting late, we are having a *very* full day." Her lip curled up off sharp points of teeth. "We are not moving until we are ready."

The two scientists looked more resigned than enthusiastic but had obviously been convinced to support the mutiny.

"And if we were alone on this ship, we could take our time. But we aren't. And if they"—Torin jerked her head toward the body—"return, they will kill you."

"We are being killed, walked off our feet!"

"Ma'am, you need to understand that there is a difference between being killed and walking." Dropping her benny off her shoulder, Torin squeezed a burst off into the bug's head. It didn't make much noise as it blew, but rusty brown fluid covered both bulkheads and dripped from the ceiling. "That," she said, turning back to her astounded audience, "is being killed and I'm trying to prevent it from happening. We're leaving. Now!"

A few moments later, as the entire company began making its way to the next vertical, she felt Ryder's familiar presence at her side.

"Good shot."

"Not really."

"Well, I suppose the odds were in your favor that it wasn't going to duck," he allowed thoughtfully. "You learn about using visual aids in NCO school?"

"No, just something I picked up on my own."

"You knew it was going to do that?"

"Obviously." Then, because he was waiting, she added, "The helmet scans of Drenver Mining Station, the last place the Others brought in bugs, are part of the training simulation. After they've been dead for a while, the stuff in their heads becomes unstable. The scans are piss-yourself-laughing type funny . . . if you can disregard the fact that we're losing."

Harrop, back on point, had reached the first cross corridor. Raising his weapon to cover the new approach, he held his position and waved the march on.

The far end seemed darker than the distance would allow, Torin noted as she crossed. Not good. The light levels were already low. It wouldn't take much more dimming before only the nocturnal Katrien and the di'Taykans could see clearly. Torin had no idea how well the bugs could see in the dark, nor did she want to find out.

The second cross corridor was identical to the first.

No. Torin paused for a heartbeat. Not identical but she couldn't put her finger on the difference.

Her feeling of unease grew at the third corridor.

And the fourth.

As they approached the fifth, she moved up on point, waving Dursinski back.

Raising her benny to her shoulder, she peered through the targeting scope and sent a quick bounce.

Harrop had bounced all six cross corridors at eighty meters. Corridor five showed barely twenty. *Son of a fukking bitch!* The ship had changed the floor plan again.

Hand signals sent Nivry and Jynett on the run to the sixth and final corridor. As they raced off, she moved Werst and Tsui into position covering corridor five and got the rest of the march moving double time toward the vertical.

Then she turned back to the shadows.

The bugs racing out of them were almost expected.

The benny's cellular disrupter had to actually hit organic matter to work. Fortunately, it "splashed" on impact, widening the target area. Torin squeezed off two quick bursts, aiming for the shoulder joint in the lead bug's body armor, then as it jerked back, arm and weapon dangling, she dropped prone and began trying for their legs, forcing the bugs to either fold them in under their abdominal armor—becoming stationary targets— or to retreat. No fools, they chose the latter.

Tsui and Werst stood behind the slight cover offered by the corners, on opposite sides of the corridor, shooting diagonally. Under their covering fire, Torin scrambled back until she shared Werst's space.

The two engineers carrying the captain between them were past. Guimond pounded by carrying a Katrien under each arm, closely followed by Ryder holding *Harveer* Niirantapajee.

How nice he's making himself . . . She fired as a head and thorax suddenly appeared, driving the bug back. . . . *useful. And who the hell took him off stretcher duty?*

As the last Marine crossed, Torin tapped Werst on the shoulder. "Go!"

The moment he was clear, she followed.

It still seemed to be ninety-five point five meters to cross corridor number six.

Thirty paces along, Torin stopped and spun around, back against the wall, benny extended out from her right side. "Tsui! Break off!"

The lance corporal squeezed off another half dozen shots, then whirled and ran.

Torin held her position as Tsui raced past, waiting for the first bug.

"Staff! Break off!"

Thirty paces farther up the passage, Tsui held the wall.

They'd managed to leapfrog nearly all the way to the sixth corridor when the first bug appeared out of corridor five.

Torin dropped to her stomach and fired.

The bug threw itself back out of range.

A quick glance over her shoulder and Torin noted Captain Travik had nearly reached the vertical.

At corridor six, Nivry and Jynett had taken a bug out, although from nine meters away, it was impossible to tell for certain if it was dead. Eventually, its head would explode and remove any doubt, but Torin had no intention of remaining around for the spectacle.

Jynett's right arm was smoking.

"Chemical weapon," she explained, firing at the sudden appearance of a bug in the shadows. "Tried to fukking eat through my suit. Couldn't quite. Suit's neutralized it now, I think."

"Make sure of it the moment you can." Over the years, Torin had taken a number of injuries and, in her experience, nothing delivered old-fashioned, scream-until-hoarse pain like a chemical burn. She jerked her head in the direction of the vertical. "Go. I'll hold here."

With two corridors to watch, the next set of leapfrogs became more complicated. Ten meters from the drop, the bugs swarmed out of corridor six.

Firing one-handed, Torin dropped her microphone. "Do it, Frii!"

His music card was everything he'd said it would be. Blasted through the dead bug's comm unit at full volume, the attack ran into a solid wall of sound.

The passage smelled suddenly of burned cork.

The final three Marines sprinted for the ladder.

Torin slid last, and as her head dropped below the level of the deck, the sound switched off. *Found another channel. Smart bugs.*

Almost before her boots hit the deck, she was moving out into the new passage.

Before she could speak, the hatch slammed, the two engineers were laser welding the seal, and Presit had a handful of Torin's combats.

"You are getting me out of here, now!"

"Guimond!"

"Sorry, Staff."

"Was anyone besides Jynett hit?" Torin snarled, glaring at the Katrien as Guimond led her away.

"Huilin and Dursinski. Aid kit stuff. Nothing to . . ." Something rattled in the vertical.

"Fire in the hole!"

Johnston and Heer dove out of the way as a muffled explosion buckled the hatch.

"Something to remember, people," Torin announced as she stood. "They've got ordnance with them. Did the welds hold?"

"Enough of them, Staff."

"And the hatch is jammed in its track now," Heer added. "They're not coming through here."

"Unless they've got a couple more of what they just dropped?"

"Well, yeah."

"Then let's not linger, people. We're on the right level, it's just a matter of getting to the air lock before the bugs." She checked the charge on her benny, noted that Guimond seemed to be keeping his bulk between her and the reporter, and finally took a moment to look around. "What's with all the fukking pipes?"

"Captain! The Others appear to be opening their launch bays!"

"Appear to be, Mister Potter, or are?"

"The Others *have* opened launch bays."

"Flight Commander."

"Launch bays open, Captain. Squadrons standing by."

"Captain!"

"I see it." Fighters, longer and narrower than the Jades, were dropping into space. *What would happen if we didn't respond?* the captain wondered as the enemy fighters began to gather into flights of three. *What would happen if we just sat here, and let them come at us? Would Big Yellow stop them?*

Maybe.

Maybe not. It wasn't something she could risk.

"Flight Commander, launch squadrons."

"Aye, aye, Captain. Launching squadrons."

"Buh-bye scientific support," Lieutenant Commander Sibley chortled as he dropped his Jade with the rest. "Let's hear it for being back in the saddle."

"It," Shylin muttered. "You think we're going to be allowed to do any shooting, Sib?"

"Allowed?"

"Big Yellow stopped the missiles. Could as easily stop us."

"Could. Won't."

"You know something I don't?"

"Lieutenant, the amount I know that you don't could overload the *Berg*'s memory core."

"And you're modest, too."

"Aren't I?" Grinning, he turned to his wing frequency. *"Black Eight, Black Nine*, form up on me."

"Roger, B7. Eight *taking position to port."*

"Nine *to starboard. Ready to move in."*

"All fighters, enemy is advancing around the full 360 of Big Yellow." The flight commander's voice filled the double cockpit like the voice of God and Sibley hurriedly adjusted the volume. *"All fighters, advance pattern zeta."*

"Eight wings of them, eight wings of us, all evenly spaced out in two pretty, pretty circles. Oy, mama, I get the feeling someone's selling tickets to this." Sibley moved his wing into the forty-five-degree mark. "Step right up, ladies, gentlemen, and species undecided. Get a front row seat as we fill the skies with pyrotechnics."

"They're more ellipses than circles, Sib."

"I'm not going to argue with you, Shy."

" 'Cause I'm right."

"Fighters are about to clear Big Yellow, Captain."

"Ours or theirs?"

"Both."

ELEVEN

"When I find out whose head *this* came out of, I'm going to kick their ass."

When no one claimed responsibility, Torin snorted and ducked another pipe. The only passage leading away from the last vertical headed starboard in a series of fifty-six-meter diagonals no more than a meter wide, crossed and recrossed by pipes in a variety of diameters and colors. The lowest pipes were about shoulder height on Torin, the highest disappeared into darkness two or three levels up. Some of them were warm to the touch. Some of them made noise.

The lack of space had taken them down to two stretcher-bearers. At each corner, they had to lift Captain Travik's head until his body was nearly vertical in order to get him around the forty-five-degree angle. Various vital signs would fluctuate during the maneuver, but as they always returned to more or less the same position afterward, Torin figured they weren't doing much damage. Not that they had any choice.

On the upside, the civilians, now behind the stretcher party, got a series of short rests. *Harveer* Niirantapajee was visibly flagging and even the Katrien were saving most of their breath for walking. Sooner or later, they'd have to be carried, but Torin wanted to delay the inevitable as long as she could. Many Marines had trouble taking the smaller species seriously, and she didn't want to reinforce bad attitudes. Nor, however, did she plan on allowing the march to be overrun by bugs because the civilians couldn't keep up.

"Why won't he just fukking die," Johnston muttered, inching backward, both hands at shoulder height gripping the forward stretcher handles. The captain sagged forward against the net. "Then we could bag him. Dust him and he'd be a lot easier to carry."

"A good officer would die," Heer grunted agreement at the other end of the body. "Fukking figures Travik would linger."

"You call that an *abquin*?"

Johnston jerked and narrowly missed hitting his head on a random "u" of yellow pipe. "Staff! Captain Travik's awake."

The captain's eyes rolled around in their sockets independent of each other while the two engineers lowered him carefully back to a horizontal position. "Sergeant, put that Marine on report."

"Captain?" Torin waved the stretcher carriers forward so the rest of the march could get around the corner then bent and wrapped one hand around the captain's chin. His skin felt cold and slightly clammy. "Sir? Can you hear me?"

For an instant, his eyes focused on hers. "I won't," he snarled, upper lip curled. "And you can't make me." Then he blinked twice and his features sagged back into oblivion.

She sighed and straightened. "He's gone again, let's move on."

"They are wishing he is dead," Presit declared, emerging into the new length of passage. "I are hearing them."

"Ma'am, fair warning." Torin waved the engineers and their burden forward. "No one likes a snitch." Rather than waiting for a response, she turned and shuffled sideways past the captain, shooting Johnston and Heer both a silent warning as she passed. Griping was a grunt's right, but they needed to keep their voices down unless they wanted every word repeated on Presit a Tur durValintrisy's *Voice from the Front*. The torrent of chittering that followed her to her previous place in the march sounded less than complimentary even given the language barrier.

"Staff! Dursinski. We got bugs cutting us off!"

According to the map, the switchbacks opened up into a wide passage that would take them the remaining 1.79 kilometers aft. Which would do them no good at all if they couldn't get to it.

"Dursinski, which direction are they coming from?"

"Both directions. I think they know we're in h . . ." The sound of weapons fire sounded clearly over Dursinski's PCU. *"That's a big affirmative on them knowing we're here! We can't get out!"*

Fuk. Only one thing to do. "Fall back. We'll retreat to that last vertical and head back up a level." Provided Big Yellow hadn't changed the floor plan, they'd have room to maneuver up there.

"Roger, Staff. Falling . . . Goddamn it, Huilin! Cover your left side! . . . back."

"Staff."

"What is it, Johnston?"

"We sealed the hatch at the bottom of the vertical."

"I know. Now, you'll have to unseal it because they could hold us indefinitely at these goddamned angled corners. You heard what's happening, people. Nivry, you've just moved from tail end to point."

"Roger, Staff."

"So, now we are walking back," Presit sneered. She pointed an ebony finger up at Torin with such force the thick fur fringe folded back off her wrist. "You are having no idea what you are doing!"

"Shut up, you idiot. I'm so tired of hearing you complain." The scales on the Niln's throat began to flush a deep gold. "In fact, I'm just generally tired of hearing you."

Presit whirled on her, teeth bared. "You are not silencing the media!"

"No, I'm not. I'm silencing an annoyance with more hair than brains."

"We are needing to get along," Gytha began, but Torin cut her off with a touch on the shoulder and a quick shake of her head. When the Katrien stepped back, Torin stepped between the two combatants, her relative bulk impossible to ignore. "I've run out of dead targets to shoot in order to make a point," she said quietly.

"You are not meaning . . ." Presit's voice trailed off as she met Torin's eyes.

Torin raised a brow.

"Fine. We are walking back." She spun around and stomped off in a cloud of shed fur. "But I are registering a complaint with General Morris the instant we are rescued."

"You know," the *harveer* murmured to Gytha as they passed, the younger scientist having given an arm to the elder, "I'm thinking freshmen would be a lot easier to control if they let us carry weapons."

Ryder wanted to say something, she could feel it in the air, but a pointed look got him moving after the others. Grinning, Guimond followed.

"And what are you two smiling at?"

Johnston and Heer exchanged essentially identical expressions as they carried the captain back to the corner.

"Nothing, Staff."

She stepped back as Harrop paused by her shoulder. "Go on, Corporal. I'm going to beat my head against a bulkhead for a moment."

"The general'll stand by you, Staff. No matter what the little hairball says."

"Thanks." Given their history, Torin figured the odds were about even that he wouldn't. "Now, get moving."

"Staff, Nivry. We got bugs at this end, too!"

As all eyes turned toward her, Torin allowed only mild annoyance to show.

They'd maneuvered their way back around three corners. If the map was right, and if the ship hadn't decided to rearrange the architecture, they were exactly halfway between in and out.

No way to avoid a firefight.

"How many bugs, Nivry?"

"Can't tell. Tsui took a hit trying to get around that last corner for a look."

"Is he bad?" Torin ducked around a pipe looping down from the tangle up above, paused, flipped down her helmet scanner, and tilted back her head.

"He's bleeding, but he'll live. We can hold them here indefinitely, Staff."

"Just like they can hold us." At maximum magnification, the light she'd spotted became a recognizable pattern. "Everyone fall back on my position."

"Roger, Staff."

"Dursinski, you copy that?"

"Roger, Staff. Falling back."

"Harrop. Take a look up there and tell me what you see?"

"Lotta pipes. No way out."

She reached over and thumbed an adjustment into his scanner. "Look again."

"It's a . . . well, it *could* be an access grille."

"Let's find out, shall we? Werst!"

He stepped back from the corner, benny remaining in firing position until Frii stepped into his place. By the time he reached Torin's side, he'd already slid his pack down off his shoulders. "Fukking obvious," he grunted at her raised brow. "We're trapped, and you're looking up. Where do I climb to?"

Torin pointed.

"Right." He wrapped a hand around the pipe Torin had ducked and swung himself up. Yellow, to blue, to red, to yellow to . . .

"Serley chrika!"

"Werst? You okay?"

"Yeah. Mostly. This pipe, it's fukking cold!"

"Which pipe?" Torin snapped. All she could see was the lower half of his right leg.

"Pinky-purple one." His tone suggested he was as much insulted by the color as hurt by the cold. "I'm moving on."

He disappeared and reappeared a moment later, a shadow against the light. "You were right, it's an access grille. Double toggles holding it in place. Should I go in?"

"Carefully."

Since she wasn't supposed to hear his grunted "No shit," she didn't.

After a few moments, he returned and dropped as much as climbed back to the passage. "You're not going to fukking believe it, Staff. Tube comes out in one of the Ventris Station wardrooms. Pool table, bar, big comfy chairs—and the door's been barred from the inside."

"And the bugs?"

"Not a whiff."

The door barred from the inside suggested a sanctuary—or would have were they not running around the changeable guts of a whacked alien ship. Still, it had to have taken the wardroom from Captain Travik's mind—there was nothing to say it hadn't taken the symbolism as well.

"Staff!" Dursinski threw herself into the passage after Huilin. "We got bugs one corner back." She wiped a dribble of sweat off her face and shook her head. "We're trapped. Trapped like rats."

"Cork it, Dursinski." Torin decided she didn't need to see the quick glances directed at the Katrien—who looked nothing at all like rats but were the only fur-bearing species present. "Nivry, where are you?"

"Two corners out. We'll be there in a . . . Tsui!"

"Got her!"

Up was their only option.

Although their hands and feet looked uselessly tiny poking out from the bulk of their fur, the Katrien, like the Krai, were natural climbers. *Harveer* Niirantapajee was not.

"And I'm old. And I'm exhausted."

"We're not leaving you behind," Torin told her, indicating that Guimond should lift her to the first pipe.

"Who asked you to?" she snapped. "You there, Worst! Don't just hang there. Give me your hand."

"It's *Werst*."

"Worst, best . . . what difference does it make? Just give me your hand!"

"You're going to be just like her when you're old." Ryder had moved back into place by Torin's shoulder.

Torin snorted. "Except I'll be taller. And tailless."

"And not half as smart."

"Ma'am, just climb."

Guimond was already halfway up, blocking the view but not the steady stream of sound.

"Is that the pipe you were burned on? It's considerably more pink than purple to my mind. How well does your species see that part of the spectrum? An educated guess says it's transporting some kind of liquid gas and . . . Young man, get your hands off my tail!"

The Katrien were strangely silent.

Maybe they just need someone *to be talking*, Torin reasoned as Werst took a rope attached to the captain's stretcher up over a pipe and dropped the free end back down into the passage. Heer took up a position only a Krai could hold, approximately halfway between the passage and the hatch.

Captain Travik remained unconscious while they hoisted him up into the access tunnel.

"Staff! He's jammed!"

"Unjam him!" Bruises would heal. Or he'd be dead before they had a chance to. Either way, no one else could make the climb while the captain remained stuck between two pipes.

"Staff!" Nivry's voice had picked up a shrill edge. "They just tossed a smoker! I think they're going to try to rush us this side."

"*Both* sides!" Dursinski yelled.

"Maintain a continuous fire along the floor! Frii, Huilin, steady bursts at a meter!"

"I can't see!"

"You don't need to *see*, the passage is only a meter wide!"

"What are they trying to prove?" Ryder demanded. With no room to pace, he stood shifting his weight from foot to foot. "They hold us here and they keep themselves from getting to the air lock. It makes no fukking sense!"

"Welcome to war. Start climbing."

"Tsui's hurt, he should . . ."

Torin grabbed his arm and shoved him toward the pipe. "Go!"

When the smoke cleared, Dursinski's passage held a small clump of still twitching legs.

"Nivry?"

"I don't know, Staff. They were making so much noise we must've hit something, but they've cleared any bodies." The corporal adjusted her grip on the vid cable and waved a hand under her nose. "Smells like roasted nuts."

"Do bugs *have* nuts?" Huilin wondered beside her.

"Maybe they roasted yours."

He laughed but made a fast, one-handed grab for his crotch. Just in case.

The packs went up quickly, Orla to Heer to Werst to Guimond. Once they were clear, Torin called the two Krai down and sent Tsui and Orla up.

"You're the fastest climbers. You'll be the last two on the corners. If I put Huilin by the liquid gas pipe, can you get by?"

Heer looked dubious. "It'll be tight."

"Just tell him not to grab anything," Werst grunted, "and we'll manage."

As Johnston, Harrop, and Jynett made the climb, the Krai replaced the two di'Taykan on the corners.

"Frii, up. Huilin, seal your helmet; you'll be covering our tracks."

"You want me to laser a hole in that pipe?"

He was smarter than he looked, but then most di'Taykan were. "No, I want you to use your cutters on that pipe. We're not using lasers on an unknown gas."

"Okay, but why not just use a grenade? I mean, you made us carry them all this way."

"Because it'd be a waste of a smoker and we don't use the gas if we're not all in suits. We're in a closed environment, and I don't want us running into it later. Besides, it'd be rude not to use the free alternative kindly provided."

"Yeah, but, Staff, my cutters went up with my p . . ."

Torin held out the pair she'd pulled as the packs went by. "I'd do it myself, but you're in the suit. Nivry, Dursinski, now!"

Nivry squeezed off two more shots, but Dursinski whirled and ran for the pipes.

"What'll keep them from following us?" she demanded, as Torin boosted her to the first handhold.

"They don't climb for shit. They don't like the cold. And they've chased us up a level away from the air lock. Pick one."

She half twisted to stare down at Torin. "It's not cold."

"Yet. Climb!"

Nivry's foot had barely left the pipe when Torin grabbed it. "Huilin, right behind me. Heer, Werst, wait for my word and then haul ass." She squeezed her shoulders through between a red and a blue pipe, wondered how Guimond and Ryder had fit, and pulled herself up to the pipe above the gas line. It was, indeed, a pinky-purple regardless of the *harveer*'s contrary opinion.

"In there, Huilin." Leg wrapped around a vertical, she bent and checked his seals as he wedged himself as far out of the way as possible. "If you're not through the pipe by the time Werst and Heer are at the access tunnel, leave it. This is just insurance; like I said, bugs don't climb for shit."

He grinned at her through his faceplate. *"What happened to the rule about not putting holes in the ship?"*

"It got beat by the desire to not have bugs put holes in us. Werst, Heer! Now."

She could feel them on the pipes as she dragged herself into the tunnel, two pairs of hands and feet slapping out a staccato rhythm. Benny across her back, she crawled forward on elbows and knees. It was a familiar means of locomotion—join the Marines, crawl around the universe. Uncountable sums budgeted for tech and somehow it always came down to that. Usually, it also came with mud.

"Blade's not making much of an impression."

"Then leave it."

"No, it's cutting. It's just slow."

"And on a flat surface the bugs aren't." She could hear Werst and Heer in the tunnel behind her. "I said leave it, before they start shooting at you."

"Almost got . . ."

It was a small explosion, strangely muffled. A ripple ran down the length of the tunnel.

"Huilin! Goddamn it, Huilin, answer me!"

"I'm okay. Mostly okay. I'm in the tunnel."

Torin's heart slowed closer to its normal rate as she crawled off the metal onto carpeting, rolled to one side, and stood.

Heer and Werst crawled past; then, a long moment later, the top of Huilin's helmet appeared. Torin helped him the last meter with a white-knuckled grip on his tank, hauling him up onto his feet and popping his seals before he was fully standing.

"First, what the fuk does mostly okay mean?"

His eyes were as pure a turquoise as his hair—every light receptor closed tight. "I got caught looking at the flash." His arm trembled under her hand.

"Well, it's a good thing you're di'Taykan then; it's a better ocular system for stupidity." She tightened her grip and shook him gently. "They'll open up again, just give them time. And until then, you've got an excuse to grope your way through the team." His hair started to lift but before he could reach for her, she snapped, "Second, what happened?"

"Gas started to pour out. It split the pipe and flooded down into the passage just when one of the bugs got off a shot." He shrugged. "Boom."

"Yeah. I got that part. And third . . ." This time when she shook him, it was a lot less gently. "What part of *leave it* did you not understand?"

"I wanted to get the job done."

"Admirable sentiment. Except when I'm telling you to do something else."

"Sorry, Staff."

"You're just lucky you didn't get yourself killed 'cause that would have really pissed me off." Still holding his arm, she turned the two of them toward the room. "Come on, let's . . . H'san on fukking crutches."

It really was one of the wardrooms on Ventris Station. It said so over the door. *Ventris Station. Wardroom Three.*

It held a bar big enough for captains to drink at without having to rub elbows with lieutenants—although the bottles of booze behind it seemed to be part of the wall. There were a dozen big comfy chairs and four sofas. A pool table. Carpeting. Soft, indirect lighting. Deep burgundy curtains covered the wall opposite the bar.

"Don't tell me there's a window behind there," she sighed.

"Okay." Grinning broadly, Ryder opened the curtains instead.

They were looking out toward the *Berganitan*, impossibly tiny one hundred and eighteen kilometers away. *Could Human eyes even see one hundred and eighteen kilometers?* Torin wondered. *Even through empty space?*

Space . . . She ran over the distance they'd traveled. "It can't be a window, we're nowhere near the hull."

"It doesn't seem to matter."

A Jade spun by, one of the Others' fighters in close pursuit.

Her eyes narrowed. "I've had just about enough of this crap. Has anyone taken a look at what's outside that door?"

"Corridor," Harrop told her. "Just like on the map."

Handing Huilin over to Frii, she checked her slate. According to the map, the corridor ran a quarter of a kilometer aft, then ended in a T-junction. The port arm ran a hundred meters then cornered and headed back forward. The starboard arm went two hundred meters then through a series of compartments. The next vertical appeared to be in the middle of the fourth compartment.

Aft. Starboard. Down. Just where they needed to go.

"I checked the door," Harrop continued. "It can't be locked from the outside. I think the ship wants us to take a break, Staff."

"The *ship* wants us to take a break?"

He shrugged.

"And since when do we do what the *ship* wants?"

"Pretty much from the moment the air lock blew," Ryder snorted.

"No one asked you." Torin glanced down at her sleeve. 2343. Another two hours and seventeen minutes and it would be tomorrow. It *had* been a long day. Unfortunately . . . "If the bugs get to the air lock first, they'll use it and then destroy it so that we can't use it, trapping us on board."

Harveer Niirantapajee stared up at her from the corner of a couch. "Why would they do that?"

"Every enemy they take out of the fight is one less they'll have to face later."

"And you know this because?"

"Because it's what I'd do."

"If we are just talking to them . . ."

"You'd say what?" Torin asked the younger scientist. "Why can't we all just get along? Well, ignoring the immediate bug/Federate language barrier, if we could get an answer to that, we wouldn't be fighting this war. Or any other wars for that matter."

"Then why are we not using another air lock?" Presit demanded. "There are more than one. So this air lock are closer; let the bugs have it!"

In answer, Torin held up her slate. "The maps we were given—before we knew we were heading into bugs—have all gone aft of our original position. If we start for another air lock now, we'll be wandering blind. We have limited food and, more importantly, limited water." A sweep of her arm directed everyone's attention to the window. "Also, there's a whole different battle going on out there and we need to get off this thing while the *Berganitan* is still able to protect the shuttle." She swept an uncompromising gaze around the room. "Fifteen minutes, people, then we're moving out."

"Do you want someone on the door, Staff Sergeant?" Harrop asked before any of the civilians could make another protest.

He was so obvious, Torin grinned. "You lock it behind you when you came back in?"

"I did."

"Then I think we can ignore it for fifteen minutes." Crossing the room, she dropped to one knee by the end of the sofa where Tsui was sitting. "You okay?"

"I'm fine, Staff." He flexed the arm. "Bug just creased me; lots of blood but no real damage."

A gesture turned him in the seat so she could take a look at his field dressing. "Nice work. Who . . . What the hell is wrong with this thing?" Although the cushions looked soft, there was no give under her hand and the surface had the familiar slickness of the original walls.

"I think Big Yellow doesn't quite get it," Nivry offered, dropping onto the other end of the sofa and rapping it with her knuckles. "The stuff behind the bar is one big molded piece, too. It's like it took the visual part of the captain's memory but nothing else."

"Probably didn't want to go any deeper into the captain's head," Tsui snorted. "I mean, talk about a gross . . . invasion of an officer's privacy."

"Nice save," Torin told him, smacking his leg lightly as she straightened. The chemical burn *had* been neutralized before it breached the integrity of Jynett's suit—given the amount of damage it had done, without the suit it would have gone right through her arm. Huilin's light receptors were beginning to reopen. Dursinski was complaining of a charley horse. Captain Travik's condition seemed unchanged. All things considered, they were in pretty good shape.

A full circuit of the room brought her to the window. Coincidence only that Ryder was standing by it, arms folded, looking out.

"I don't see any more fighters," he said as she stopped beside him.

"There." Torin pointed at a distant moving point of light. "And there. At this distance and at their speeds, they're hard to spot unless you know what you're looking for."

One of the points flared suddenly.

"Saw that," Ryder said softly. "Any idea if it was us or them?"

"Them."

"How do you know?"

"I don't." She could feel his gaze on the side of her face but she kept her own eyes locked on the stars. "So as far as I'm concerned, it's always them."

"Shylin!"

The lieutenant kept her attention on her screen as the Jade flipped one eighty to come up behind an enemy fighter. "I see him."

"Then you think maybe you could do something about him?" Although there was no way to tell for certain, Lieutenant Commander Sibley thought there were bugs flying the fighters as well as bugs inside Big Yellow. They flew with a certain style that suggested non-binocular vision.

"Give me a minute, he's jamming the targeting computer."

"And isn't that the reason I bring you along on these little outings?"

"I thought it was for my witty repar . . . Got it! PGM away and . . . Sib, he's shooting back!"

Sibley slipped the Jade sideways and down. "Looks like his bug buddy's taking out our ordnance."

"He's shooting at it; hasn't hit it yet."

"B7 *this is* B8, *I've got a double tail wagging; you think you could get one of them?*"

"On our way." Leaving their smart bomb to its own devices, Sibley pulsed full lower thrusters. "Ready, Shy . . ."

They popped straight up a fast hundred meters. Full upper thrusters to kill momentum. Energy burst back along the X-axis meeting the enemy missile dead on.

The canopy polarized at the sudden flare, but by then the Jade had already moved forty-five degrees forward and down, away from the debris field.

"Thanks, B7, *we can handle the other one."*

"You sure, Boom Boom?"

"If you hadn't just saved my ass, I'd find that question highly insulting. Looks like your guy's getting away."

The Jade flipped in time to see their PGM taken out before reaching its targeted fighter. "Crap. Hey, bug buddy, those things are expensive! The Navy likes us to hit stuff with them!"

"He can't hear you."

"I think most bugs are roughly female."

"Whatever. Looks like she's trying to get in under the guns."

"B9! Herd dogs!"

"Roger, Seven."

The moment it had become apparent that Big Yellow wasn't going to prevent fighters from either side crossing its axes, the flight commander had divided the squadrons into offense and defense—half to try and take out the Others' ship, half to defend the *Berganitan* against enemy fighters.

Simultaneously—or so close to it there was little point in clocking the difference—the Others had done the exact same thing.

Black Star Squadron had drawn the defensive end of the stick.

As *Black Nine* moved to intercept the enemy fighter, Sibley tucked in behind, bobbing and weaving to avoid being target locked. Together, they herded it toward the *Berganitan*'s big guns. At the last possible instant, it sped up, slid in and down, flipped, and nearly skimmed the surface of the *Berganitan* as it raced away, firing at both fighters, secure in the knowledge they couldn't fire back without hitting their own ship.

"Fuk. That bug can fly."

"Good thing she was more interested in hitting us than the *Berg*." Sibley brought the Jade around. "At that range, even a bug couldn't have miss . . . Boom Boom! You're double tailed again!"

"Tell me something I don't know! A little help?"

"The second missile must've split." Shylin's fingers danced over the pad. "Get me closer."

"I'm trying. Boom Boom, level out so my gunner can lock!"

"I level and I'm toasted."

"No. We take one, your gunner takes the other."

"He won't have time to lock!"

"Tail's be right up your ass, he won't need to lock. He can reach out and smack it away."

The pause took them forty meters in three directions.

"B8 *leveling. Just don't fukking miss!*"

"Now, *I'm* insulted," Shylin muttered. "Got the lock!"

This time, they went right through the debris field. No way to tell for a long moment what or who the pieces had belonged to.

Then something big hit them all along the portside.

"B7! B7 *this is* B8, *respond!*"

"I'm a little busy right now, Boom Boom."

"Looks like that serley *piece of shit took out your port thrusters!"*

"You think?" As the galaxy spun wildly around him, Sibley locked his eyes on his instruments and fired the starboard thrusters, canceling their rotation and bringing the Jade more or less level—a position that lasted less than a heartbeat as Shylin fired one of the starboard guns and they were suddenly engulfed by another debris field. An unidentifiably soft object slapped into the canopy and stuck.

"Damn it, Shy!" There were days when he'd kill for a little air resistance. This was clearly going to be one of them.

"No choice; spin took us into the path of a bug. Us or them situation. I voted for us."

"That's because you're not flying this thing!" His fingers danced over the keyboards. "Give a two H'san burst on your PFU."

She squeezed the trigger. "One H'san, two H'san." And then she released it. "Better?"

"Much." This time when he got them straightened they were more or less facing the *Berganitan*, both wingmen hovering close.

"B7, *this is* Eight. *You need a hand.*"

"No, thanks, Boom Boom." Sibley glanced up at the body part stuck to the canopy. "Got one."

"B7, *this is* B9. *Can you make it back to mother?*"

"It won't be pretty but I think so."

"Sib . . ."

"I see it. Boom Boom, we've got an enemy fighter moving in. Looks like they're going to try and finish us off."

"I'm on it. B9, *I'll chase off the bug, you get* Seven *back to the ship."*

"Roger, B8. *Will tuck* Seven *in safe and sound."*

"Unless you'd rather take out that second fighter."

"What sec . . . Fuk, Sibley, you've got eyes like a hurnatic."

"Yep, keep them in a jar on my desk. Don't worry about us, we'll get ourselves back. You go deal with the bad guys."

"Roger, B7. Dealing."

As both his wingmen peeled away, Sibley tried not to think of how vulnerable the loss of a quarter of his maneuvering thrusters made his Jade. They'd be sitting ducks if an enemy attacked while they were on their final approach to the launch bay.

Something flared in the distance, the pattern unmistakable against the stars.

Even without knowing, it hurt.

"One of theirs?"

Shylin checked her positioning data, her hair flattening. "No."

"What I don't understand," General Morris growled, glaring at the long view of Big Yellow on the center screen, "is why you don't launch another squadron, have them blow through the enemy fighters around the *Bergani-tan*, and then attack the Others' ship with superior numbers."

"General, the moment we set to launch, the Others will know and they'll do the same, blowing through *our* fighters, and in the end we'll be in the same position only we'll both be short a squadron. As long as Big Yellow's holding us in place and keeping us from using our heavy ordnance, neither of us will commit all our fighters."

"The Others are an alien enemy, Captain. How can you possibly know what they're thinking?"

Captain Carveg's teeth came together with an audible snap, but before she could answer, the flight commander turned from his station, eyes narrowed. "They're fliers, sir."

"Are you trying to tell me that cognitive patterns follow function?"

One shoulder rose and fell in a motion that might have been a shrug had it not been directed toward a full general. "How do you anticipate what the enemy will do on the ground, sir?"

"It looks bad, Chief. *Black Seven*'s coming in with no port thrusters and he's coming in fast. Seems like they're shooting at him out there and he can't fire back without losing his approach. Which you, of course, already knew," Tristir amended as the squadron's senior NCO turned a basilisk stare on her. She hurriedly added, "Emergency crews are ready—the fire team and two corpsmen are standing by."

"What's his ET . . ." A loud crunch and shudder that ran through the deck plate and up into his boots cut off the last letter. "Never mind."

It wasn't the worst landing Chief Graham had ever seen—worst was reserved for those landings when a crippled Jade smashed home so hard it took out some of the crew waiting there trying to help it. Worst was reserved for the Jade whose pilot found out when they reached the docking bay that the braking thrusters were slag and they hit so hard the fighter went right through into the ship and they had to seal off the section to prevent decompression—pilot, gunner, half a dozen of the emergency crew, and two poor bastards who'd just been passing by dead.

By those standards, this landing was merely messy.

Four canisters of foam sealed the bay along Black Seven's damaged side. Chief Graham popped the hatch the moment the compartment had been repressurized and entered in time to see Lieutenant Commander Sibley climbing out of his pod refusing the corpsman's offer of help.

"We sucked a little smoke, but we're fine. Aren't we fine, Lieutenant?"

"Oh, yeah." Shylin crawled from the rear section, eyes still watering, hair flat against her head. "We're fine."

The corpsman folded her arms. "You still have to go to medical, sirs."

"Not a problem, we know the . . . Chief!"

"Lieutenant Commander Sibley." Chief Graham crossed the bay and squatted by the Jade's damaged side.

"So, how fast do you think you can get it fixed?"

He straightened slowly and turned to glare at the pilot. "How fast can I get it fixed?"

"Well, yeah, there's . . ."

"*How fast can I get it fixed?* You didn't scratch the paint, sir; you had your port thrusters blown away and you're leaking enough radiation to scramble sperm you haven't thought of spilling yet. Get to decontamination, then get to medical, and stop being so goddamned anxious to get back out there and get yourself killed!"

Sibley opened his mouth, took a closer look at the chief's face and closed it again. Gathering up his gunner, he headed for the hatch. As it closed behind them, Chief Graham sighed.

"Would you fukking look at that; they *also* scratched the paint."

TWELVE

"CC Hydroponics Garden, Paradise Station. It was the first HpG I'd ever seen—blew me away that you could grow things without dirt." Torin leaned over the familiar/subtly wrong railing, and stared up at the central column with its rings of plants' roots hanging down in nutrient sprays, growing tips supported by fine filaments. Six levels high, it was an aesthetic design, not a practical one. The shallow ramp that circled the outside of the atrium was also edged with plants—the greens were too uniform to be real, but she had to give Big Yellow an "A" for effort.

"And you were worried about what would come out of your head," Ryder murmured by her left ear. "Me, I knew it couldn't all be death and destruction."

Torin looked just far enough over her shoulder to meet his gaze and asked flatly, "How?"

"Well, it's . . . uh . . ."

Behind them, a Marine snickered.

Pivoting on one heel, Torin swept her gaze over the gathered Recon team. "Listen up, people, we need to go down a level and this looks like the only chance we're going to get. Huilin, eyes?"

He squeezed them tightly shut and opened them again. The right looked darker than the left. "About seventy percent. Maybe seventy-five."

"Stay in the middle of the march. Harrop, your squad takes point. Keep alert; at the bottom of the ramp you'll be in a park of sorts and there's about two dozen places the bugs could be shooting from on that level alone. You hear or smell anything that could be bugs, you assume it is. Heer, don't eat that. It's not a real *gitern*, it's a part of the ship."

The engineer looked sheepishly down at the fruit in his hand. "Ship's partly organic, Staff."

"And it could be trying to get you to ingest it as a way to infiltrate the Confederation. You have no idea what you'd be shitting."

"You really think so?"

"No. Get rid of it."

Heer sighed and tossed it back into the tank with its parent plant.

A quick glance at Werst showed the other Krai staring challengingly back at her. His jaw might have been moving. Nothing she could do about it now if he'd eaten something and, besides, if it came down to a one on one, Big Yellow against a Krai digestive tract, smart money would be on the colon.

"At the bottom of the ramp, we head across the atrium on a diagonal. Keep moving until we're out of all this cover. Maintain PCU silence unless there's no other option, and keep the dialogue to a minimum. We clear?" Heads nodded. "Orla, get your goddamned helmet on." The patch of fuchsia amidst the gray disappeared. "Go."

The back of Torin's neck crawled as they moved down the ramp. The public HpGs were *always* crowded. There should have been hundreds of people, dozens of races, every size and age, all milling about in a space that now held fourteen Marines, two scientists, a reporter, and a salvage operator. She should have been able to smell a dozen things but mostly the gardens. There should have been noise.

It was the lack of noise that bothered her the most. Unlike the Krai and to a lesser extent the di'Taykan, Humans relied a lot more on their sense of hearing than on their sense of smell, and silence was a warning more often than not.

It's too quiet.

And she was well aware that there was often truth in old clichés.

Exhaustion had momentarily shut up the Katrien although Presit seemed to be mumbling to herself as she followed Guimond down the ramp.

They were strung out across the park in a staggered diagonal when someone sneezed, someone else made a sound like wet fingers rubbing glass, the air filled with the smell of cinnamon and, an instant later, with weapons' fire. As Johnston and Heer raced for the dubious cover of a copse of tarrow—Captain Travik making them almost fatally slow—Torin dropped to one knee and began firing back along the incoming trajectory, hoping to buy them some time.

The moment the spiky, broad-leaved plants closed behind them, she dove and rolled, gouging through the pebble bed that provided the illusion of a traditional garden but still allowed the liquid nutrients to reach the roots. Under normal circumstances, leafy vegetation would not have been her first choice in a firefight, but these weren't normal circumstances, and Big Yellow apparently had no more actual knowledge of plants than it did of sofa cushions—which made the tarrow difficult to get through but not totally useless as a protective barrier.

As she scrambled behind the triangular leaves, an energy bolt exploded in the pebbles by her right leg, throwing a hundred or so tiny missiles against her. Her combats absorbed most of the impact, but Torin could feel bruises rising along the length of her calf.

Heer bled sluggishly from a nick in the edge of his outer ridge and the back of Johnston's left hand had been scored in a cross-hatched pattern— probably by a leaf tip. The captain remained unconscious. Bright side to everything. Craig Ryder and *Harveer* Niirantapajee had actually dug down into the pebbles.

Smart. She wasted an instant wondering which of them had come up with the idea.

Torin could see Guimond, the Katrien, Orla, and Jynett in the next clump of garden—Jynett's HE suit a brilliant and unmistakable orange against the green—looking back, she could pick out Nivry, Huilin, and Werst. If Tsui had been walking as tail end, he should be . . . yes; the unmistakable spit of a benny came from up a branched palm.

Up was good. It gave him the best line of sight.

"Tsui, were they waiting for us?"

"Negative, Staff. I think they were just crossing the park at the same time."

Just? Torin doubted that very much. It wasn't coincidence that put both groups here—heading out of different passages, heading into different passages—at exactly the same time.

"Has anyone taken a look at the passage behind us?" Not the way they needed to go but preferable to a firefight.

"Way ahead of you, Staff. It's been sealed."

She'd be willing to bet that the passage behind the bugs had been sealed, too. The ship was dicking them around again. In the vids, this would be the moment both sides would realize it and decide to work together against a common enemy.

Torin jerked as a shot fried the edge of a leaf.

Unfortunately, they were in a war, not a vid.

"I see you've got each other pinned down again."

"Ryder, get back in your goddamned hole!" Shoving him to one side, she stayed reclining half over his torso as she took a quick shot at the glint of bug armor across the park.

"You know, you're not light."

"Not now, Ryder." About to roll off, she froze, eyes locked on the center column.

Two Marines up the column could provide enough cover for the rest to get out of the park. If the bugs were smart, they wouldn't stick around to get shot at from the high ground, they'd make a run for the closest open passage. If the two Marines were in suits, they could drop smokers to keep the bugs in the passages and to cover their own fallback.

Two bugs up the column could do the same thing and the door was out in the open, exactly between the two lines. Inset into the column, it offered shelter once it was reached. Reaching it would be the problem.

And she had the shortest run on it.

"Dursinski, where are you?"

"Behind a bench about two and a half meters from the passage."

"I need you back here. I want two suits in the central column."

"Huilin and Jynett are closer."

"Huilin's half blind."

"It's not that bad, Staff."

"I'm not asking for your opinion, Private. Dursinski, move your ass. Drop back to Jynett's position and then move to the column on my signal."

"Why didn't the ship fry my fukking suit . . ." Dursinski's complaint trailed off as the pattern of firing changed.

While the bugs were distracted by the movement, Torin pushed off Ryder's chest, ignoring his grunted protest. "Keep their heads down, people. I'm going over to open the door." Clearing the plants with only minor damage, she tucked her benny close and sprinted across the open area. No point in ducking; the bugs tended to fire low. The column would keep the bugs on the far end of their position from getting off shots but the rest . . .

An energy bolt nearly took her knee off.

"Sniper on the upper ramp!"

"I see him!"

"So stop looking and try fukking hitting him!"

Torin forced herself to dive and slide as her hindbrain kept insisting she wanted minimal contact with shiny, gray floors. She rammed shoulder first into the tower and flipped into the setback just ahead of a chemical impact. A single drop splashed up and hit under the edge of her right shoulder flash. Her combats had been woven from the same material the Confederation used to build ship parts and Torin had to believe they'd maintain their physical integrity long enough for her to get the job done.

Way back in the real HpG on Paradise Station, she'd tried the door and it had been locked, a sign announcing *Authorized Personnel Only* in the three local languages as well as Federate. Odds were good that the copy was also locked. Not a problem. Last time, she hadn't been armed.

Another shot splashed against the edge of the door as she switched her benny to laser and began cutting the lock.

"Keep their damned heads DOWN!"

"Bugs know where you are, Staff. And they know what we're trying to do. They're not bothering to aim."

Wonderful. If they got lucky . . .

Fortunately, the lock had only been designed to stand up to inquisitive teenagers.

After the next splash—evidence suggested they needed time to reload—Torin backed out a step and put her boot to the door. It slammed open just as an energy bolt went wild past her shoulder and up toward the atrium ceiling.

"Got her! Bug couldn't resist taking a shot at your ass."

"Must've been a di'Taykan bug."

"Shut up, Tsui!"

"Can the chatter," Torin snapped, tucked into the setback's one safe angle. "Dursinski, Jynett, you ready to run?"

"Ready, Staff!"

She spun out and aimed toward the bug position, squeezing the trigger as she yelled, "Go!"

No one moved at their top speed in an HE suit. Fully aware they were bright orange targets, both Marines gave it their best shot as the rest of the team hit the bugs with everything they had. Jynett's longer legs reached the setback two strides ahead of Dursinski, but they pounded up the interior stairs in unison.

"Fuk, there's a lot of them!"

"How many's a lot, Dursinski?"

"Uh, seventeen, twenty-three . . . thirty give or take. Some of them are so close together they're hard to count."

"So shoot them twice."

"Roger, Staff."

Sent in by General Morris to be pinned down by an enemy with a numerical advantage while attempting to keep a group of civilians alive.

Déjà vu all over again.

"We've got them pinned, Staff."

"You heard her, people. Move. Everyone into that passage before the bugs figure out a way around this." At least, this time, it wasn't turning into a bloodbath.

"I'm hit!"

If there was one thing in the universe Torin truly hated, it had to be irony.

"How bad?"

"Not good." Tsui's voice held as much anger as pain. *"And I'm hung up on this fukking tree!"*

"Going back for him, Staff."

"Roger, Nivry." Torin could hear the corporal moving behind her. Somehow the gravel ground out a different sound than it did for those moving out of the battle.

"Staff. Dursinski. Bugs are on the ru . . . fuk!"

A flurry of shots rang both up and down the column.

"Bug on the way to your position, Staff! She's inside our range!"

"I'm on it."

Actually, it was anyone's guess as to who was on whom.

Trying for the legs under the armor, Torin threw herself out of the setback and slid round the curve of the column on her belly. The bug was up on her side sliding toward her, legs safely pointed away, torso folded back nearly flat against the abdomen. Torin's first shot ran harmlessly above the floor. The bug's hit high on the column—right about where Torin's head would have been had she been standing.

Torin flipped onto her side and kicked out hard as she passed.

The bug started to spin but managed to get the curved claws on her lower arm around Torin's ankle as the upper arms swung her weapon around.

The helmet scans from the Marines on the Drenver Mining Station had shown that in hand-to-hand with a bug, the bug always won. But this was a new position for them, and as the claws closed, Torin realized that in bending so far back, she'd opened the waist joint in her armor. A thumb switched the benny to laser.

A moment later, torso and head fell free of the abdomen.

Torin kicked again with her free leg and took out the brain-case on the next spin.

Eyes watering from the overpowering stink of cinnamon, she cut the claw off her boot.

"Staff! I can't get to Tsui. That ablin gon savit *of a sniper's got us both pinned down."*

"Dursinski?"

"Yeah, I can see her. She's moved to a one-eighty from the door, Staff, second level. But the angle's fukked for us. We can't hit her."

"I've got her."

"How?"

Another time, she'd have a chat with Dursinski about that tone. "I'm going to give her a target she'll have to break cover for. Nivry, get ready." Flipping her helmet scanner around to the side, Torin rose from behind the dead bug, studying the fake plants on the second level from the corner of one eye. The bugs on the mining station had been derisive of binocular vision. As far as the sniper was concerned, the stupid mammal was looking the wrong way.

There. A glitter in the green as she rose to aim.

Nivry's first shot appeared to catch her under the upper armpit. The second spun her head around.

Torin didn't wait to see if there was a third; she was already sprinting for Tsui's position.

He was missing his left foot, sheared off clean just above the boot. Fortunately, the wound had cauterized—so it hadn't been the bugs emitting the smell of burned pork. When he'd fallen, the strap of his benny had got hung up, twisting him around so that his good leg had been jammed in the deep vee of a lower branch. The only way he could free himself would have involved pushing off from the trunk with the bloody remains of his other leg.

He was about to do just that as Torin reached him. She grabbed his calf as gently as possible and swung his leg out from the tree while freeing the spray tube of emergency sealant from her vest with her other hand. Nivry arrived an instant later, benny still covering the sniper's position.

"I hit her high, Staff, both times. I can't be sure she'll stay down."

"We'll have to risk it." The tube empty, Torin tossed it aside, snapped off Nivry's tube, and kept spraying. The two together wouldn't seal things as tightly as she'd like, but they'd have to do.

"I can't feel my foot." Tsui sounded mildly put out by the realization.

"Because it's not there." The second tube hit the gravel, and Torin motioned Nivry around the other side of the tree. At 1.87 meters, the di'Taykan corporal had height enough to free the trapped leg.

"Oh. So I guess you're telling me I'm a foot shorter."

"Shut up, Tsui."

He snickered, then moaned as the shock suddenly wore off.

"Now, Nivry." Digging her boots into the gravel, Torin braced herself, not so much catching the injured Marine as directing his fall onto her left shoulder, minimizing the chance of his injured leg hitting her body. Two careful strides took her back out onto solid deck.

Panting and swearing softly in three languages, Tsui struggled to get down.

Left arm between his legs, Torin tossed her benny to Nivry and smacked him on the ass with her right. "Stop it! Or you can walk to the painkillers."

"Fukking hurts . . ."

"I know." Shifting his weight across her back, she started for the passage. Three steps to get her balance and then she was running. As she passed the column, she snapped, "Dursinski, Jynett; give me a ten count and then smoke them."

"Roger, Staff."

Torin counted strides. One, two . . . Nivry fired at something behind them. *Goddamned bugs just don't give up.* Under normal circumstances, she appreciated tenacity but this was becoming too fukking much. Five, six . . . Tsui'd stopped swearing, but he was holding fistfuls of her combats tighter than he needed to keep from falling. Seven, eight . . . *Where the hell is that passage?* Nine, ten. . . .

The smoke canisters hit and blew.

Firing ahead of her now and behind, the sound of HE boots slapping deck.

She almost stumbled on the lip of the hatch but caught herself and Tsui at the last moment, then straightened and rolled the injured Marine into waiting arms. Breathing heavily, she slumped back against the wall, one hand held out to Nivry for her benny.

"We have a way out of here?" she demanded of no one in particular.

"Passage conforms to the map, Staff."

"Perimeter pins set?"

"At the first corner."

Nice thing about working with Recon, they had the right answers to those kind of questions.

Dursinski and Jynett pounded by a moment later, then Werst and Guimond backed into the passage in a swirl of smoke.

"Close it."

Facial ridges shut tight, Werst shoved Guimond behind him and slapped the hatch controls.

Torin half expected the doors not to work, but with a familiar purr they slid into place. Big, open spaces in stations made people nervous, so builders always set decompression doors into the exits. Big Yellow had reproduced them here and, dogged down from inside, they provided a barrier the bugs didn't have the ordnance to get through.

Probably didn't . . .

She drew in a deep breath and let it out slowly as the adrenaline buzz of combat began to die. Her gaze slid over the captain—any relevant change meant he was either conscious or dead. The former would be obvious, the latter . . . He was a Marine and she'd fight to get him out alive because of that, but only because of that, and General Morris could just deal. She continued scanning down the passage. Kneeling on the deck beside the med kit, Frii had Tsui's stump up over his thigh and was applying painkillers directly to the raw tissue. The rest of the team were checking their weapons, changing charges if necessary—still edgy, still psyched. Huilin had his benny a little close to his eyes, but his hands snapped the old charge out and the new one in with confidence. The Katrien had rushed for Guimond as soon as he came in and were both pressed up against his side grooming with short swipes of curved fingers and chattering almost quietly to each other. *God help me, it's becoming a comforting sound. Harveer* Niirantapajee appeared to be asleep. "Anyone else hurt?"

Harrop shook his head. "The plant life did more damage than the bugs."

"I'm sweating like a pig in this thing, Staff." Dursinski pulled at a fold in her HE suit. "Can I take it off?"

"No. If Jynett hadn't been in hers, that chemical burn would have taken off her arm. Be thankful for the extra protection."

"I'd be more thankful if I wasn't sitting in a puddle," she muttered as Torin dropped down by Tsui's side.

Ryder watched Torin murmur words of encouragement to the wounded Marine and shook his head. Back against the wall, he slid down until his ass touched the deck, then he stretched out his legs. "Okay," he muttered, just loud enough for the Marines on either side of him to hear, "first she ran across open deck to the column. Then, having set up cover for our retreat, she took out a bug in hand to whatever the hell those things the bugs have are. *Then* she set herself up as a sniper target, ran toward the sniper, and carried that man pretty much the length of the park, saving his life. And yet, no one seems too impressed."

"She'd say she's just doing her job," Harrop grunted, draining the charge from a nearly empty power pack into another.

"That's what she says. But what do you guys say?"

"About her doing her job?"

"Yeah, about that."

Orla exchanged a glance with the corporal and shrugged. "She's pretty good at it." Her eyes suddenly lightened as a thought occurred. "You like her, don't you?" The accompanying gesture made the di'Taykan's definition of "like" obvious and mildly obscene.

"Staff?" Tsui wet his lips, and Torin braced herself for one of the "what's it all mean" questions that always seemed to follow a major injury. "How come whenever we meet up with the bugs we're in a configuration out of one of our heads?"

It took her a moment to regroup. "Configuration?" She smiled down at him. "Big word."

"I'm serious."

"You're stoned on painkillers."

"Well, yeah, but it's still a good question. How come?"

"I don't know. Those switchbacks may have been made by the bugs or, since they've got the advantage of numbers, maybe Big Yellow's giving us the terrain."

He sighed. "I don't think I want to play this game anymore." Dark brows suddenly snapped in, and he clutched at her arm. "Staff, where's my foot?"

She closed her fingers over his. "Totally disintegrated. Not even a toe-nail left."

"Good." Muscles visibly relaxed. "It's just, I don't want this ship to have it. You know?"

"I know." And with any luck it was a lie that wouldn't come back to haunt her. Torin had no idea where Tsui's foot was. Finding it hadn't been high on her to-do list at the time, and she sure as hell wasn't going back out to look for it. *Let's just hope it's not waiting for us at the air lock.*

As his eyes began to unfocus, she lifted his hand off her arm and laid it on his chest. His fingers were warm, his injury not as bad as it looked. He'd spend a few weeks with a regen tube around his leg, and then brand-new foot. Thing was, she had to get him to a regen tube. *And to do that, I have to get him to the air lock and off this fukking ship.* Fourteen Marines. Two of them on stretchers. Four stretcher carriers. Thank God, Tsui was Human and not another Krai. Eight Marines. Against thirty bugs, give or take.

Coming to a decision, Torin picked Tsui's weapon off the deck where Nivry had left it and stood. With the amount of painkillers careening around his system, he wouldn't be using it any time soon.

Ryder was sitting between Harrop and Orla about twelve meters from the closed hatch. There were deep circles under his eyes and a few lines she hadn't noticed earlier. *So. We're all tired.* Stepping over Orla's outstretched legs, she held the benny out toward the CSO. "I want you to learn to use this."

He looked startled. "The gun?"

"Yes, the gun."

Orla snickered—no surprise, di'Taykans could turn a court-martial in-quiry into innuendo—but even Harrop looked amused. Torin decided she didn't want to know.

"Isn't it against the law for a civilian to carry a Marine Corps weapon?" Ryder asked, scrambling to his feet.

Torin stepped back to give him room. "Yes."

"Okay." He seemed a little taken aback by the blunt response. "I figured I'd be carrying a stretcher."

"You will be, but if we're in another firelight, I want the weapons with the people who can use them. Tsui's out, and even if the other three were bigger, I couldn't ask them." Her lip curled slightly as she glanced over at the pair of Katrien and the Niln. Funny how easily those species who'd evolved past violence had been convinced to allow the less evolved to commit violence for them the moment diplomacy had failed with the Others. "Which leaves you."

"Me?"

"Unless I'm talking to myself and Orla . . ." Her gaze slapped down on the di'Taykan. "What's so damned funny?"

"Nothing, Staff."

"Harrop?"

"It's him." The corporal jerked his head toward Ryder's back, implication clear: *It's him, it's not you.*

"I see. Well, as much as I hate to remove Private Orla's source of amusement . . ."

Orla suddenly became very interested in her boots.

". . . I think maybe we should talk over here." Grabbing Ryder's arm, she pulled him diagonally across the passage to the other wall, which didn't put enough distance between him and the di'Taykan but did, at least, mean she could ignore whatever it was they had going on. "Have you ever fired one of these?"

"No. Not going to ask me if I'm willing to?"

"No. I think you're smart enough to realize that reaching and holding the air lock is going to take every weapon we've got, and if it came to it, you'd rather be unevolved and alive."

An eyebrow rose at *unevolved*, but all he said was, "That's the nicest thing you've ever said to me."

"Don't let it give you a swelled head." She shoved the benny into his hands and twisted the barrel. "This is the laser, it functions pretty much like every cutting tool you've ever used." Reaching out, she tapped a small screen. "This is your remaining charge. The MDC is point and shoot." She twisted the barrel again. "This is your charge for that."

"MDC?"

"Molecular Disruption Charge."

"I can see why you use the short form. What's it do?"

"Simple explanation?"

"Yeah, please."

"It causes organics to explode at a cellular level. We use them in situations like this, so we don't inadvertently hole a bulkhead and die sucking vacuum."

Ryder frowned down at the benny, then up at Torin. "Isn't Big Yellow partly organic?"

So it was. And it had definitely been hit on a number of occasions. She had a sudden flash of her benny spread out over the "workbench." "The ship found out what we were shooting—us and the bugs—and did something to protect itself."

"What?"

"How the hell should I know? Can we continue?" When he nodded, she lifted her weapon and thrust a finger through the trigger guard. "Same trigger works for both. If it's locked, and that one is, press on the pad just ahead of the trigger guard; it's species-keyed to Human, di'Taykan, and Krai. Don't forget to check the lock, don't forget to check the charge; empty, these things make crappy clubs. This is how you change the power pack."

Ryder snapped his pack in and out, gave the barrel a couple of experimental turns, and stared at the data stream. "That's it?"

"Essentially."

When he looked up, his eyes had crinkled at the corners. "How come they spend so much training you lot if that's it?"

"How to shoot's the easy part," Torin snorted. "They train us to know when."

"Okay. When?"

"When I tell you to." Body still squared off against Ryder, she turned her head. "Frii?"

"We can move him now, Staff."

"Then let's go, Marines. Air lock's not getting any . . ."

She was looking at Heer, saw his facial ridges clamp shut an instant before she smelled the cinnamon. When the panel popped out above her head, she'd already pivoted more than halfway around. The grenade came as a bit of a surprise—it didn't look like a smoker.

She caught it one-handed, swore at the heat, saw Ryder go to one knee, stepped up on his raised leg, and threw it back down the vent. It hit the retreating bug in the face and rolled under her thorax.

Good guess that *Oh, fuk* in bug smelled like lemon furniture polish.

Torin dropped, grabbing Ryder's shoulder, taking him to the ground with her.

"FIRE IN THE HO . . ."

The deck lifted, slamming them together. Then it lifted again, throwing them against the bulkhead. Teeth clenched to keep from biting her tongue, Torin felt the bulkhead buckle under her shoulder. Then she was falling. They were falling.

A bounce. A hand grabbed at her arm. A blow against her helmet canted it forward over her eyes.

She landed without ever being totally out of contact with the ship—or engulfed by the ship. Both were an improvement on the last time.

A feather touch against her cheek made her think of antennae, but grabbing for it, she stubbed her fingers through Ryder's beard. Which explained the yielding surface she'd impacted against.

Her helmet was jammed tight. Torin jerked her head back out of it and shifted around, ignoring the grunts from beneath her until she was sitting half astride Craig Ryder's hips. She could just barely make out his face in the spill of light from above. He seemed to be grimacing. "YOU OKAY?"

The ringing in her ears drowned out all but the question. When he nodded, she stood. The wall or possibly the deck had fallen in after them, leaving a jagged hole half the diameter of her head about four meters up. An easy climb but nowhere to go.

Harrop's face appeared, plunging the area into total darkness. Before Torin could use several choice words she'd been saving, his helmet light came on. His eyes were wide, and his lips were moving.

"I CAN'T HEAR YOU!" Touching both ears, Torin shook her head. "WAIT!" Bending around Ryder, who chose that moment to stand, she braced one boot on a twisted support beam and yanked her helmet free. Most of the photoelectric coating would have to be replaced, but the PCU seemed to be working fine. She cranked the receiver's volume and tried not to shout.

"What's the situation, Harrop?"

"Orla's nose is bleeding and Tsui slammed his stump into the deck—no other casualties."

"And the civilians?"

"Gytha's having hysterics, but Presit's calming her down."

That didn't change Torin's opinion of the reporter, but it was a nice surprise. The universe had been short of those lately. "No sign of the bugs?"

"None."

She heard him that time around the PCU, so she took off her helmet and blew out her ears.

"You guys are never going to make it out of this hole, Staff. Hang on; Johnston wants to scope it out."

The engineer's opinion matched Harrop's. "Unless there's another way up, we'll have to cut—if the ship'll allow it."

Torin took a good look around. They appeared to be in a one-by-three-meter hole in the wreckage. "Cut," she growled.

"And if the ship's got a complaint, it can take it up with me."

"So, what did the general say?"

Torin tongued off her implant and sagged back against a bent piece of bulkhead. "He said we should get to the air lock as fast as possible. Man's a military genius."

"Could be worse; he's not using the override codes and insisting on a play-by-play."

"He's probably forgotten he has the override codes. I doubt he's used his implant much, if at all, in the last few years—that's what aides are for."

"He tell you what's been happening out there."

"Oh, yeah, generals always take the time to keep staff sergeants fully informed. I got the impression the fighters from both ships are still going at it, though. If they weren't playing with live ammo, the vacuum jockeys would probably be pissing themselves with joy. The whole breed's insane." Reaching out, she grabbed the hand tapping against his thigh. "Stop it."

"I don't do well sharing a small space."

"I know. Stop it anyway."

He jerked his hand away. "And you're doing so well yourself."

Biting back a profane suggestion, Torin spread her hands. "Sorry." Not a gracious apology, but he was right. *And if I'm not out of this hole soon, I'm going to start fukking shooting my way out.*

"I have the feeling you don't do well with being helpless."

Letting her hands drop, she closed her eyes. "And I have the feeling you wouldn't do well with a boot to the head."

"So what about Marine Corps vacuum jockeys?" Ryder asked after a moment's silence.

Torin opened her eyes. She couldn't see his expression. *Okay. If he wants to make polite conversation . . .* "What about them?"

"They insane, too?"

"Oh, yeah. It's a whole vj thi . . . Son of a fukking bitch!" Jerking away from the bulkhead and up onto her knees, she ripped open the seal on her vest, scrambling beneath it for the tab that would open her combats. Given the myriad bruises she'd been collecting, it had been easy to ignore the itching on her upper arm; not until the itch suddenly, painfully became a burn did she remember the chemical spill. "God fukking damn it!"

The tab finally lifted. She yanked it down to her waist and dragged her right arm clear. "JOHNSTON!"

The engineer's laser shut off.

"AID KIT! NOW!"

It had taken over an hour for the chemical to work through her sleeve. It was moving a lot faster through flesh.

"Torin, what's wrong?"

Right hand clutching a fistful of fabric, teeth clenched, forcing herself to breathe—in and out, in and out, filling her lungs each time—she turned just enough for him to see. A chemical burn was worth a thousand words.

"Son of a fukking bitch!"

"Yeah." In and out. In and out. "Said that."

Boots pounded against deck plates.

"Staff! Kit's too big for the hole."

"Chem kit!" They could drop it into her left hand or . . . "Ryder."

He surged up onto his feet. "I've got it." She heard it hit his hands. He dropped to his knees beside her and shoved the kit into her line of sight. "What do I do?"

"Rip the film off. Slap the unit, sticky side down over the burn."

"It may not fit."

"Then fukking hurry!" Contact was a minor pain lost in nearly overwhelming sensation. Analysis and treatment were supposed to be instantaneous. Instantaneous turned out to be a relative term, depending on which side of the treatment defined it.

When the neutralizing agent finally hit, the sudden absence of pain was so intense Torin swayed into a warm, solid barrier, realized what it was as an arm rose to steady her, and swayed out again.

"It would kill you to collapse for a minute?"

Beginning to breathe more normally, she swung her head around and up to meet his gaze. "I get to collapse when the job's done. Not before." A few drops of neutralizer ran out from under the unit and down her bare arm, pulling her attention with it. She noticed that the handful of fabric her right hand clutched wasn't covering her leg. She had no idea when she'd shifted her grip. Opening her fingers, Torin patted the crumpled handful smooth and looked up to find Ryder staring at her. "When the job's done," she repeated.

"What if we die in here?"

"Not going to happen."

"Because you say so?"

Torin snorted. If he'd been a Marine, he wouldn't have had to ask. "Yeah. Because I say so."

"Staff! You okay?"

"We're fine. Keep cutting."

THIRTEEN

Torin scrubbed both hands over her face and looked back down at the map. "You're sure?"

"Positive." Nivry tapped the screen. "We follow this passage to here, then there's some kind of weird engine room shit to cross and the air lock's right here."

"No bugs?"

"None."

"How are you sure?"

Nivry glanced down at the small hand clutching her sleeve. "It's what we in Recon do, ma'am. We go out and we find the enemy."

"How?"

"How do we find them?" When Presit nodded, she grinned. "Well, usually, we know we're close when they start shooting at us."

The reporter snatched her hand away and stared up at Nivry with accusing eyes, her ears flat to her skull. "That are not being funny!" she snapped, and flounced off, the silver tips of her fur trembling indignantly.

"Shouldn't have asked the question if she didn't want to hear the answer." Torin watched her go with as close to a neutral expression as she could manage, then looked back up at Nivry. "ETA on the air lock?"

Emerald hair flicked back and forth, then . . . "Even with the stretchers and the civilians, we're no more than an hour away."

"I'll let the *Berganitan* know."

". . . and Captain Travik?"

He's alive, sir.

"Good. Arrange it so that he's first onto the sh . . . Staff Sergeant Kerr?

Staff Sergeant Kerr! Damn it." General Morris rubbed his left hand over his forehead and glared at the science officer. "You've lost the signal again; find it."

"Sir, it's gone out at the other end."

"And isn't that signal booster of yours supposed to stop that?"

"Yes, sir, but . . ."

"I don't want excuses, Lieutenant. I want to talk to my Marines."

Who don't want to talk to you. Taking pity on her officer—who faced a choice between telling the general that Staff Sergeant Kerr had cut the signal or outright lying to a direct question from a superior—Captain Carveg stepped down from her station and said, "We'll launch the shuttle now, General."

She thought he might push the matter, but after a long moment, he turned to face her.

"I want your best STS pilot flying it," he growled.

"Sorry. You'll have to settle for second best. Lieutenant Czerneda was my best STS pilot, but she's dead—along with three fighter crews."

"Four, Captain," a voice announced grimly from one of the stations monitoring the battle.

"Thank you, Ensign." She took a step closer and stared up at his face. "Four."

His face began to darken. "And your point, Captain?"

"My point, General . . ." Her toes worked to find purchase on the deck and she forced them to relax before she continued, ". . . is that my people have been doing their best, and we don't need you to ask for it. Flight Commander, launch squadron."

"Aye, aye, Captain. Squadron away."

"Any response from the bugs?"

"No, ma'am."

"Launch shuttle."

Fingers drumming against the table, Sibley locked his eyes on the monitor currently showing the signal coming in from the buoy.

"Sib, stop it."

"Stop what."

Shylin put her hand over his and flattened it. "Stop that."

"They're going to respond." He jerked his chin toward the image of the

Others' ship. "There's no way they'd fight so hard and then just let us pick up our grunts and go home."

"They're still fighting. The Marauders and the *Katray Sants* are still out there."

"Not what I meant. They're going to attack the shuttle."

"It's got a full squadron riding shotgun."

"I know."

"You don't think they'd have launched by now if they were going to try something?"

"Yeah, I do. And that's what bugs me." Sibley pulled his hand out from under his gunner's and, without taking his gaze from the monitor, pulled a stim stick from the breast pocket of his flight suit.

"Don't you think you've had enough of those?"

"No."

"Your fingers are turning orange, and you're never going to get to sleep."

He looked down at that. "Sleep?"

"Yeah, you remember, it's what you do when you're in bed and not fukking. You know, the stuff you do between crash landings and going out again."

One eyebrow rose. "Not a lot of sleeping going on right now, Shy."

She looked around. With the exception of the three squadrons currently deployed, most of the *Berganitan*'s vacuum jockeys were in the "Dirty Shirt." The flight officer's wardroom wasn't exactly crowded, but it bordered on full. Crews from the two squadrons that had already been out were mostly staring into coffee or talking quietly about the empty places at their tables. Some, like Boom Boom, sitting beside her with a mug of *sah* held loosely in one foot, had their slates out and were writing home. Just in case. The virgin crews were watching the monitors. Waiting for their turn.

"Forget I said anything," she sighed.

"Captain! The Others have opened missile tubes one through six! Firing missiles!"

"Unless the rules have changed, missiles aren't a problem." She glared down at the relevant screen and muttered, "Anyone know if the rules have changed?"

"Yes, ma'am."

C3 went completely silent and, if only for an instant, all eyes flicked away from monitors and data streams.

"That was a rhetorical question, Ensign."

His ears flushed crimson. "Yes, ma'am, but I'm reading life signs in the missiles. I think they're actually specialized fighters."

"And Big Yellow allows fighters."

"Yes, ma'am."

"Good work, Ensign. Flight Commander, alert your squadrons!"

All eyes were on the monitors now, coffee and letters home forgotten.

"These are new," someone muttered. "Fuk, they're fast."

"And it ain't like the fighters were slow," someone else added.

The Marauders and the *Katray Sants* had been pulled away by the Others' fighters, leaving the shuttle and her escorts alone in space.

"Maces are moving to intercept."

Fifteen to six, Sibley thought, stim stick forgotten in the side of his mouth. *Oy, mama, why don't I like those odds?*

The missile/fighters closed the gap rapidly and made no attempt to avoid the Jades swooping in at them. They roared on by, maintaining the same close diamond formation.

"A hit!"

One of the diamond's outer points spun away from the rest, leaving a trail of debris. Three Jades raced in for the kill. Another point was hit with the same result. Another wing peeled off after it to cheers in the "Dirty Shirt," but somehow Sibley didn't feel like cheering, although other times, other missions, he'd been yelling advice and bad puns at the screens with the rest of them.

Nine Jades; one wing holding position around the shuttle, the other two racing after the four missile/fighters.

"They're going to take out the shuttle." He almost didn't recognize his own voice.

"Well, they're going to try," Shylin snorted, her hair flicking back and forth. "But if they want to survive the attempt . . ."

"They don't."

One of the pilots seemed to realize the same thing; a Jade moved directly into the path of the enemy. Both ships were destroyed, but the three remaining enemy fighters were through the debris field so fast it did no damage.

The shuttle was taking evasive action but, given the comparative speeds between hunter and hunted, it needn't have bothered.

All three enemy fighters detonated on impact.

The explosion stopped all conversation, all speculation. The brilliant white light blanked out all but two of the monitors and the entire wardroom held its collective breath until they came back on-line. The shuttle and the two closest Jades were gone without even debris enough to mark their passing.

"Stupid fukking bugs," Boom Boom said at last.

Shylin leaned in closer to her pilot's shoulder and muttered, "You know, I really hate it when you're right."

"Yeah." Sibley fished out another stim stick and bit down without tasting it. "Me, too."

"Captain Carveg! The Others launched an STS shuttle of their own just before their missile/fighters impacted."

Her fingers clutched the edge of her panel, grip tightening with every flash that told her two more of her people weren't coming home. "No fighter escort?"

"No, ma'am. The shuttle has been covered in a stealth material; it's almost impossible to see unless you know what you're looking for."

Her lip curled. "They thought we wouldn't see it until too late."

"Yes, ma'am."

"They think they can get it to the air lock while we're preoccupied with our losses. Flight Commander, move the remainder of the Red Maces to the attack. If you can't blow the damned thing up, cripple it. Keep it from getting to Big Yellow. And keep a better watch on the Others. Even if we couldn't see the shuttle, those things aren't small and there should be an energy spike when they open the shuttle bay doors. If it happens again, I want to know about it." She glanced around C3, but General Morris wasn't in the room. He had a definite knack for being around when he wasn't wanted and vanishing when he was. "Yeoman White, find the general and tell him he should contact his people and let them know the bugs are probably close on their collective ass. Only say it politely."

"Aye, aye, Captain."

"Communications, punch through to the staff sergeant's implant, but don't let the general know you did it. Or that you can do it."

"Aye, aye, Captain."

*Due respect, General . . . * The sound of weapons' fire nearly drowned out her next words. * . . . but we already knew that.*

"Listen up, people; the good news is, we won that round. The bad news is, we're running low on ammo."

"Staff? I volunteer to go to the *Berganitan* and get more."

Torin moved a little ahead so she could see Tsui's face as she walked. "And you'd just be completely screwed if I had a way to send you, wouldn't you?"

He let his head fall back down onto the stretcher. "Wouldn't have volunteered if you had a way to send me," he pointed out faintly. "But I could use a beer."

"Couldn't we all."

They'd run into the bugs again on their way to Nivry's "weird engine room shit." The lights were low enough that the Marines had helmet scanners in place, the passage had begun to look like a mechanical access route, and the front of the march was halfway across a T-junction when the sudden smell of furniture polish had let them know they weren't alone.

The bugs had been the more startled. Torin suspected it was because Big Yellow was also screwing around with their maps, moving corridors, shortening passageways, joining two sections that hadn't been joined before. They'd probably thought they were on a direct route to the air lock with no chance of running into the enemy.

There'd been a fast flurry of shots exchanged, and the bugs had retreated.

No casualties.

As fights went, it was one of the better ones.

"How's your arm?"

In moving up beside Tsui, Torin'd also moved up by Ryder, who carried the foot of his stretcher. She slowed until he caught up, then matched his stride. "It's all right."

"Really? It didn't look *all right*."

The gleam of the field sealant showed through the hole in her sleeve—the burn had been deep enough that had it been on either the front or the back of her arm instead of the side, it would have taken out a muscle group. "It aches, but I can use it."

"You were very brave."

Eyebrow raised, Torin turned to face him. It could have been a condescending remark, but after spending the last few hours in his company, she didn't think it was. "You're not used to seeing people get shot, are you?" she asked dryly.

"No, I'm not." One corner of his mouth lifted into a wry smile. "You know, most people aren't."

She considered that for a moment, then nodded. "Good."

A decompression hatch at the end of the passage opened into the upper wall of a well-lit, two-level chamber. Six-by-six grates covered the ceiling, allowing glimpses of a maze of pipes and wires through their mesh. Metal stairs led down to a textured deck. Four large tanks sat along one fifteen-meter wall in black cradles, digital readouts of pressure, temperature, and volume flashing on each. Large pieces of gray machinery that no one could actually identify squatted in rows down the center of the deck.

"Area's clear," Werst announced from an identical platform on the other side of the room.

"You heard him, Marines. Let's move. Air lock's twenty meters on the other side of Private Werst."

The deck vibrated as they crossed it, as though they were near the combustion chamber. A faint smell of ozone hung over the whole space.

Torin kept her people moving as quickly as possible; the last thing she wanted was prolonged exposure to what appeared to be four hydrogen tanks. She had no doubt this was just another scenario created for them—the system appeared far too primitive to be an actual working part of the ship—but, because of its availability, hydrogen *was* the default fuel and should anything happen, should the bugs reappear, the last thing she wanted was a stray shot damaging one of those tanks. Big Yellow had proved willing to blow part of itself up before.

They were three quarters of the way across when Werst yelled, "Enemy above!"

Above? *It's a fukking drop ceiling. Those things aren't weight bearing!*

Sliding along on a piece of armor, only arms and head visible around its edges, the bug was a moving shadow behind the grates.

"Take cover!"

Marines and civilians dove under and behind the big gray machines. They didn't look likely to explode, but then, neither had that original section of wall.

The MDCs were defused by the grate. Anything that got through hit the armor.

"Stop firing! You're just wasting your fukking ammo!" Who was tallest and closest to the stairs? "Huilin, Frii; get to Werst and boost him high enough to get through the grate!" She could hear the two di'Taykan moving.

The bugs had fired energy bursts in the hydroponics. *They can't be stupid enough to fire that weapon in here.*

A short burst dropped everyone to the deck.

Okay. They can.

When Torin looked up again, a metallic blue cylinder, small and familiar, was falling through a smoking hole in the grate.

The grenade hit one of the gray machines and bounced.

Torin spun around in time to see it roll past Guimond and the three civilians and disappear under a tank.

Time slowed to a crawl as Dursinski dropped to her stomach and batted it out with the muzzle of her benny. She grabbed for it with her free hand but it skittered away, taking an odd bounce on the textured deck, spinning around and almost disappearing again into the thick fur of the reporter flank's. Presit reluctantly shuffled her leg aside and picked up the grenade, holding it in both hands, her eyes squinted nearly shut as she tried to see what she had.

Guimond had his pack off and combat vest undone.

Standard operating procedure for a grenade in a sensitive area. *If you can't throw it back at the bastards, wrap it in your vest then get some distance. The vest will contain most of the explosion.*

Cinnamon.

Presit sneezed.

Guimond grabbed the grenade from her hands and threw himself down to the deck on top of it.

The explosion lifted his body, shaking it like a small animal in a predator's jaws.

On Torin's slate, his med-alert went off, then settled down to the steady beep of the locator. She keyed in the code that would turn it off. She knew where the body was.

Time sped up again.

"NO!"

Somebody had to yell it; the only question had ever been who.

The rage in Werst's voice spun all heads around. From the handrail around the platform, he leaped out onto the grate. Gripping with fingers and toes, he raced toward the bug.

Torin didn't waste breath calling him back. He wouldn't have listened. *Rage, but no denial*, she thought as he crawled across the ceiling. *He expected this, or something like it.*

Werst reached the hole the bug had blown through the grate and shoved his benny into it, pulling the trigger again and again.

Another energy burst went off.

"If that bug's got more than one grenade . . . !" Dursinski yelled.

"She'd have dropped it already." Torin's voice filled all the spaces in the room, leaving no place for panic. If the bug had more than one grenade, she'd have tossed them down in a pattern, one right after the other, and they'd *all* be dead.

The grate Werst clung to peeled away from the ceiling, screaming a protest. Hanging upside down, he reached around the jagged edge and fired one more time. The bug made much the same sound as the grate and pitched forward through the hole, all four arms flailing wildly.

One caught Werst across the small of the back.

She missed the machines and hit the deck with a wet crunch.

Hanging from his feet, Werst swung, once, twice, his helmet flying off his head to clatter against a tank. The grip of his toes alone wasn't enough to support his weight. He twisted in the air, hit the top of a machine on all fours, and slid off to the deck.

"Harrop, the bug! Nivry, Guimond!"

Torin was at Werst's side a heartbeat later but, even so, he was already on his hands and knees crawling toward the remains of the bug, pushing his weapon ahead of him, his finger still hooked around the trigger. "She's dead, Werst. You got her. Let it go."

He snarled a Krai profanity and kept crawling.

"Werst!" When he jerked to a stop, she wrapped her hand around his right wrist, pinning his weapon to the floor. When he tried to roll out of her grip, when his left fist jabbed out toward her face, she was ready for him. "That's. Enough."

And it was because she said it was. She used the words to fill him as she used them to fill a room, leaving no space for questions or doubt.

His facial ridges flared once and with a sound halfway between a growl and a whimper, he collapsed into the circle of her arms.

A heartbeat later, when Torin felt muscles begin to tense, she let him push away. He had his own places to store grief, just as she did. Just as they all did.

"Wasn't enough he had the *nice guy* fukking target painted on him," Werst growled, glaring at nothing over Torin's shoulder, "he had to go like a fukking hero."

"Guimond saved a lot of lives."

"And that makes it better?"

Torin snorted. "Only time makes it better and there never seems to be enough of it."

She wasn't telling him anything he didn't know, but the snort drew his focus to her face. He stared into her eyes for a moment, then he nodded and looked away. "You're a big *serley* comfort, you know that, Staff Sergeant Kerr?"

"Just doing my job." His meaning had been clear on his face, the words used were irrelevant. "When you're ready to talk about it . . ."

He nodded.

"And otherwise; are you all right?"

"Yeah, I'm . . ." As he moved a leg, his ridges clamped shut and the mottling on his skull suddenly stood out in bold relief. "I broke a *serley* toe!"

"You're lucky you only broke one," Torin told him, standing. Huilin had been carrying one of the med kits, but he was still on the far platform. He—or he and Frii—had cut a section free near the hatch and, standing on the handrail, he was tall enough to make sure any other bugs trying that route would find an unpleasant welcome. The other kit . . . "Dursinski!"

"Right here, Staff."

"Werst's broken a toe."

"That's what he gets for not landing on his head." But she was on her knees with the med kit out before she'd finished talking.

"If there's one broken . . ."

"Yeah, yeah, I'll check the others."

The bug was next. Harrop poked it with a boot as she approached. "Not that I'm an expert on these things, Staff, but I'm pretty sure it . . ."

"She."

"What?"

When you forget the enemy is a person, you react to their weapons not them. That's dangerous. The little we know suggests the bugs are female. Not the time for a lecture, so Torin merely repeated, "She."

"Okay. I'm pretty sure *she* was dead before *she* hit the deck. Werst did a lot of MDC damage on the lower thorax. That windmilling as she fell was a last hurrah. She could have finished us if she'd dropped three or four grenades." He pushed back his helmet and glanced toward Guimond's body. "Why do you figure she only dropped one?"

"Maybe they thought the ship would endure one grenade but not two. Maybe, it's a bug honor thing, strip off your armor . . ."

"She was on a piece of armor."

"Yeah, but she wasn't in it. Maybe you win points by stripping down and dropping a grenade on the enemy—this *is* the second time they've tried it."

"Seems to be a bit of a suicide mission."

"That might be the point." Torin shrugged, suddenly not so much tired as weary. "Maybe they've had budget cuts back home and they can only afford one grenade each."

"Fukking budget cuts," Harrop grunted. "So what do we do with her?"

"Leave her. If her people want the body, they know where it is. Take her weapon, though. R&D'll want it."

"Give me a break, Staff, it's covered in bug guts!"

"Welcome to another glorious day in the Corps, Corporal Harrop."

And, finally, Guimond.

Welcome to another glorious day in the Corps.

She pushed past the wailing Katrien and dropped to one knee through the cloud of shed fur. Fortunately for them, they expressed their grief at a lower decibel level than regular conversation. Nivry had turned Guimond over, still had one hand on his shoulder. His combats had contained the explosion although the force of it had collapsed his chest and forced blood from every visible pore. The blue of his eyes was strangely untouched amidst all the red. *And isn't that a fukking cliché.*

"If he'd had his vest done up . . ." Nivry murmured.

Torin shook her head. "It wouldn't have mattered."

Small fingers dug into her shoulders. "You are not going to him immediately! You are letting him die!"

"He was dead the moment he grabbed the grenade from your hands," Torin told the reporter bluntly as someone, she neither knew nor cared who, pulled her away.

The ring of Marines split to let Werst limp in to Guimond's side.

"The *serley* bastard's still smiling," he grunted.

Which seemed like as good an epitaph as any. Torin brushed Guimond's eyes closed, rocked back, and slid her hand into an inner pocket in his vest. The body bags were a smarter fabric than the stretchers and, unfolded, held what amounted to one massive MDC. Even given Guimond's weight, it took only moments to get the body into the bag. Torin wiped the blood off her thumb and ran it down the seal. *We're just too fukking good at this.*

She sighed deeply and stood.

"We will not forget. We will not fail you."

"Fraishin sha aren. Valynk sha haren."

Although Heer was the ranking Krai, no one was surprised when Werst spoke. *"Kal danic dir kadir."* Leaning on Heer's shoulder, he bit a small piece from the back of his forearm. *"Kri ta chrikdan."*

The bag stiffened, then flattened.

Torin bent, picked up the tiny canister of ash, closed her fingers around it, and looked down at her sleeve. From the moment the grenade had fallen until the moment she could hold Private First Class August Guimond in the palm of her hand—seventeen minutes, twenty-three seconds. Bracing herself against the weight, she slipped the canister into her vest, then bent and picked up Guimond's pack. "All right, people, let's haul ass to that air lock."

"This are it? So efficient you are dealing with death! You are not care . . ."

Torin had a fair indication of what her expression must have been when Ryder stepped between her and the Katrien.

"Let it go, Torin. Presit doesn't mean what she's saying. She's grieving."

She could feel the Marines behind her. "And we're not?"

"I didn't say that."

They locked eyes. Torin looked away first, making it quite clear she conceded *his* point, not the Katrien's.

A short choppy wave got the march moving, Nivry, Werst, Johnston, and Heer carrying the captain, Presit and Gytha, clinging so closely to each other fur merged between them, *Harveer* Niirantapajee, whose visible scales had turned a yellow-gray, Orla and Ryder carrying Tsui, Jynett, Dursinski, and Harrop bringing up the rear. Torin moved along the line between the two corporals, her gaze never resting for more than a moment in one place. The bugs had proved they were resourceful, the ship had proved it was not to be trusted; she had a lot to watch for.

She reached the metal stairs just after Werst, let the two Katrien pass, caught the *harveer* as she stumbled stepping onto the lowest tread.

"Can you make it?"

"Do I have a choice?"

"I can have someone carry you."

"No," she snapped, fingers hooked around the handrail, both feet placed carefully on one step before she tried the next. "Your lot are carrying enough."

It might have been sympathy, but it might as easily have been criticism—neither tone nor facial features gave Torin any indication of which. Empty air where Guimond should have been passed next, then Orla and Tsui's stretcher. She beckoned Jynett forward to take one of Orla's handles and moved into place beside Ryder herself. Until she noticed the di'Taykans' smirks, it didn't even occur to her it would have made more sense to do it the other way.

On the other hand, di'Taykans were known to smirk at weather reports, so fuk it.

Ryder looked from one Marine to the other. All four were wearing similar blank expressions. He'd seen men die before but he'd never seen a return to business-as-usual quite so quickly. Made sense, he supposed. *Can't have a war stop to acknowledge every new dead guy; damn thing'd never end.*

And he supposed the four Marines around him, Torin particularly, had had a lot of practice carrying on with big empty holes where people used to be.

He hadn't.

"Did he have any family?"

At that moment, *he* could only mean one person.

"His parents run an import/export business off New Horizon." Torin would be writing them a letter when she got the rest of the team safely back to the *Berganitan*. Another one of Captain Travik's jobs she'd be doing.

"He has a younger brother who's studying to be a teacher," Orla offered in the pause.

"People said his mother must've spent her whole pregnancy in the centrifuge," Jynett said, grinning. "No one could believe he was station born."

"Big boy."

"Mmmm."

This time the smirks were closer to satisfied smiles.

"He had this joke," Tsui snickered, hanging white-knuckled onto the sides of the stretcher as it rose up another step. "How many dirtballs does it take to screw in a lightbulb? Dirtballs don't screw in lightbulbs, they screw in gravity wells."

"What's a lightbulb?" Orla wondered.

"Hey, I never said it was a good joke. It was just his."

"He was going to re-sign at the end of his three years. He said he was happy in the Corps."

"He was happy cleaning the crappers."

"He was always happy."

Struggling to keep the stretcher level as they reached the top platform, Ryder shook his head. "You guys only knew him for a week."

"No." Torin waited until Ryder had hold of both handles, then she stepped away. "We knew him his whole life."

"Captain Carveg!" Face flushed, General Morris pounded into C3 and up to the captain's station, gripping the edge of the console with beefy fingers. "What's taking so damned long to launch that next shuttle? I ask your people a simple question and they shoot me a line of crap about constructing new defense systems. If I had a couple of Marine pilots here . . ."

"You'd be welcome to risk their lives in whatever way you pleased. But you don't. You have Navy pilots, my pilots, and before I tell them to launch, I'm going to see to it they have a fighting chance." She frowned down at the left screen. "Lieutenant, rotate B section of the grid twenty percent and run the simulation again."

"Aye, aye, Captain."

A satisfied nod and then she glanced up at the general. "Besides, General, this is the last STS shuttle we have and we thought you might like it to actually arrive at the air lock."

"What do you mean, it's the last shuttle you have?"

"Under normal circumstances, we carry four, but Mr. Ryder's *Promise* is using one of the bays. We've lost two, one at the first air lock, one on the way to the second. We have one shuttle remaining. It's not that difficult, General." A flick of her wrist turned a screen toward him. "Now that we know what we're up against, we can protect ourselves. We've deployed two dozen linked drones to fly in a defensive pattern round the shuttle, half a kilometer out. All six of those missile/fighters could impact simultaneously with minimal effect and they could keep doing it at thirteen-minute intervals all the way to Big Yellow and back."

"Why thirteen minutes?"

"That's the maximum time the drones need to reboot. It takes the missiles twelve minutes to cover the distance between their own launch tubes and Big Yellow, so unless they're going to throw a steady line of those things, we've got it covered."

"And at the air lock? Which seems to be inside your thirteen-minute maximum?"

"They won't blow the air lock, they need it to get their own people off. And before you ask, they need to get their own people off because they've got the only information about Big Yellow. I'm betting the Others can no more scan it than we can."

The general's eyes narrowed. "Based on what?"

"Based on them being as dead in the water as we are."

"Then what about their regular fighters? Couldn't they shoot out the drones?"

She wouldn't have minded so much if she'd thought he was asking for information, but his whole bearing insisted he was asking to find fault. It had been years since she'd wanted to bite someone this badly. "They could, General, but we'll have Jades out there stopping them."

"All right. Fine. Good work." He rearranged his features into an expression resembling composure, clasped his hands behind him, and rocked back on his heels. "But when do you launch, Captain? That's the question."

"Flight Commander?"

"Ready to launch now, Captain."

Her lips curled off her teeth in a Human approximation of a smile. General Morris should know what it really meant. "We're ready to launch now, General. Flight Commander, launch fighters, launch shuttle, deploy defensive drones."

"Aye, aye, Captain. Fighters away. Shuttle . . ." The pause went on just a little too long.

"Flight Commander?"

He raised his hand, listened intently for another long moment, then slid one side of the headphones back. "The shuttle controls are unresponsive, Captain."

"Unresponsive?"

"Yes, ma'am. Crews are running diagnostics now, but . . ."

"But you expect they have the same problem the engines have?"

"Yes, ma'am."

"What?" General Morris glared from one to the other, his face beginning to flush again. "What's wrong?"

"Big Yellow is fukking us around again. The shuttle will no more launch than the main thrusters will fire."

Arms folded, the general put himself squarely in Captain Carveg's line of sight. "You're taking this very calmly."

Captain Carveg glared up at him, lips curled. "Trust me, General, if screaming and biting would do any good, I'd be screaming and biting. Engineering's been working all hands since the beginning, but nothing's changed. If that *serley* ship's frozen the launch controls, that shuttle's not going anywhere."

"These things don't have a manual override?"

"What?" she snorted. "A big crank to open the launch door and some greased logs to help roll the shuttle out into space? No, the only manual override these things have involves pushing an actual sequence start switch instead of sitting back and letting the computer do it." She ran one hand back over her scalp. "Not that a big crank and greased logs aren't looking good right now."

"Captain! Buoy picking up an energy spike. The Others are opening . . ." His voice trailed off as he peered down at his screens.

"Opening, Lieutenant?"

"Nothing, ma'am. But there was a spike."

"The Others attempted to launch another shuttle, and Big Yellow shut them down, too."

"There's, uh, no way to know that, ma'am."

"We'll know if they never launch another shuttle. General Morris, you're going to want to talk to your Marines in private. Do you need someone to take you to Communications?"

"No. I can find my way."

"I'll have the comm officer begin trying to get through now. He should have contact by the time you arrive." The edge of the forward screen creaked, and she reluctantly loosened her grip. "Tell them this is a temporary setback. I'm not giving up."

"You'll go get them yourself?"

"If I have to."

"Captain! The Others are launching more fighters."

"Match them ship for ship, Flight Commander."

"Aye, aye, Captain."

She glared down at the screens, at the image fed from the buoy. Knowing it was foolish to put motivations on the movements of fighters two hundred and thirty-six kilometers away, something in how they were being spit out of the launch bays gave the impression that someone inside was intensely pissed off. "And I know exactly how you feel," she growled.

"What do you mean, she's not ready?"

Chief Graham tossed a tester down to the Krai working inside the Jade and turned, one hand gripping the edge of the open panel. "What I mean, Lieutenant Commander Sibley, is that we're replacing all your port thrusters, plus all the couplings, rebooting your whole goddamned propulsion system, and hopefully convincing your new thrusters to fire when you want them to and turn off when you don't."

"Chief, the squadron's going back out."

"And until your ride's fixed, you're not."

Hands deep in the pockets of his flight suit, Sibley stared at the parts of his Jade spread out on the mech deck. "How long?"

"That depends, sir." Dark brows drew in. "How long do you plan on standing here taking up my time?"

"Well?" Shylin fell into step beside him as Sibley came out into the passage. "How long?"

"Would you believe eight inches?"

"No."

"As big as a baby's arm?"

"Sib."

"Chief says it'll be done when it's done."

"Did you tell him the rest of the squadron's going out?"

"He knows."

"Did you pull rank?"

"On a chief warrant officer?" They'd reached the link, and he slapped the call button. "Do I look suicidal?"

FOURTEEN

"This makes no spatial sense."

"This whole day's made no sense," Torin reminded the engineer. "Not spatially, not any other 'ly' you care to suggest. What's the specific nonsense this time?"

"The air lock opens out into space. This"—Johnston rapped his knuckles against the pale gray bulkhead—"is the hull. Except that the air lock is on the belly of the beast, so this"—he stomped on the deck—"should be the hull. Except that the room where Guimond bought it is a level below. We came up a flight of stairs to get here."

"Yeah, I remember. What's your point, Johnston?"

"My point, Staff, is that this isn't right."

"Neither was the window in the wardroom. Hell, neither was the wardroom. Is this a working air lock?"

"As far as we can tell."

"Then don't sweat the weirdness, Lance Corporal Johnston. Can you get it open?"

"Me? No. But the *harveer* seems pretty confident. She worked with Dr. Hodges on the program that opened the first air lock, and she says the minimal readings she can take here are exactly—to the decimal point—the same. All she has to do is reproduce the codes on her slate and then use her filament probe to interface with the lock."

"*All* she has to do?" Torin glanced down at the elderly Niln, oblivious to the discussion going on above her head as she worked. "She has to get a Confederation slate to interface with an unknown alien technology. I can't even get this year's slate to interface with last year's desk." She clapped him lightly on the shoulder as she left. Tsui was resting comfortably, but Captain Travik's life signs were slipping. He hadn't regained consciousness since the switchbacks, and Torin had a strong feeling he never would.

Keep the captain alive. Make him look like a hero. She'd pretty much screwed the pooch on both mission objectives. General Morris wasn't going to be too happy with her.

General Morris can kiss my noncommissioned ass.

August Guimond was worth a dozen Captain Traviks.

The two Katrien were slumped against the wall in an exhausted heap. At first Torin thought they had their eyes closed against the light, then she realized they were sleeping, the edges of their blended ruffs rising and falling. As she watched, Presit whimpered. Without waking, Gytha combed at her fur until she settled. No surprise they were tired, they'd now been up and at a high stress level for about twenty-three straight hours.

Poor little thi . . . Torin cut the thought off short. They were not poor little things, they were adult members of a sentient species both of whom had considerably more formal education than she did. *And if even* I'm *falling into the cute furry darlings trap, it's no wonder they get away with being so obnoxious.*

Although in all honesty, Gytha was a sweetheart and Presit wasn't any more obnoxious than any other reporter Torin'd had the misfortune to meet.

You're doing it again.

If the shuttle wasn't there in half an hour, she was taking one of the three stims provided to sergeants and above. She'd need a clear head if the bugs attacked and fuzzy thoughts about the Katrien indicated anything but.

Leaving the civilians, Torin moved out to check the perimeter. Emptying out the remaining food and water, the ropes and the med kits, they'd snapped all the packs together into two barricades three packs wide and two high coming out from both bulkheads twenty meters down the passage from the air lock. Made of the same fabric as the combats, they were a small but psychologically necessary protection. Harrop and Dursinski had pulled the watch. The hatch leading back to the tank room had been welded shut.

Laser charges were holding; MDCs were nearly spent.

Ryder sat, back to a bulkhead, talking quietly with Orla and Huilin. Given they were di'Taykan who'd been forced to go twenty-three whole hours without sex, Torin could guess the content of their conversation.

Directly across from the air lock, Heer was patting the wall with one hand, and holding his slate up to his face with the other. "There's something here," he said when Torin asked. "The *harveer* copied one of her programs to my slate and had me running auxiliary scans around the lock. When I turned with the scan still running, I got one strange reading off this wall."

"A *strange* reading? What would you consider a normal reading on this ship?"

"Not strange in that way, Staff. Strange in that it resembled a piece of the code defining the air lock."

The section of wall looked as gray and blank as any on the ship. "It can't be a second air lock." She pointed across the passage. "Not if that's the hull."

"I don't think it's a second lock, I think it's a . . ."

A two-meter-by-a-meter-and-a-half piece of the bulkhead slid sideways. Behind it was a small access tunnel and a ladder leading down.

Heer looked up at Torin and grinned. "I think it's an access tunnel."

"And one without a bug in it. Nice change." She dropped a perimeter pin. It stuck to the deck as it landed and registered no movement on the lower level. "Spatially, this ought to make Johnston happy."

"Staff?"

"Never mind." A half-turn checked out the available Marines. "Orla, Huilin, got a job for you."

Ryder shot her an indecipherable glance which she ignored. Not everything was about him. In fact, not much of anything was about him.

"Staff, Orla. You've got to see this."

"On my way."

The lower level had four hatches and four control panels built into the bulkhead defined as the hull by the air lock up above. "Escape pods?"

"Well, they're not like any we've ever seen, but it's our best guess. Look." Orla pressed her hand against one of the hatches and a section twelve centimeters by eight cleared.

Torin leaned forward, staring through the window into a gray padded interior. It looked like no escape pod she'd ever seen either, but—in a weird way—it looked like all of them. They could probably fit both Katrien in it with no difficulty, but of the larger species there'd be room only for two di'Taykan and their total lack of issues concerning personal space. To get two Humans or two Krai into them, they'd have to be under heavy fire with no other chance of survival. In Torin's experience, no other chance of survival settled *issues* pretty damned quick.

Given the way the last twenty-plus hours had gone, too few escape pods to save all her people were high on the list of things she didn't want to see. The one thing she knew for certain was that Big Yellow had an agenda, and this didn't look good.

"Should we get the *harveer* and see if she can open them, Staff? Just in case?"

"No, not right now. She's still working on the lock, and after that, I'd like her to have her rest a bit before she has to face a vertical ladder. She's old, and it's been a long day. And, Huilin, put your goddamned helmet on."

He sighed deeply but obeyed. "It doesn't fit under the HE's helmet, Staff."

"When you've got the HE's helmet on, you can take your combat gear off, but not before."

"We going to guard these things, so the bugs don't get them?"

"No, the air lock's more important. They try to rush us and we'll need all weapons. We'll set 2Ps at twenty meters both directions keyed to my pin at the foot of the shaft. The bugs show up, we'll know it."

"I'm out of pins, Staff."

"And this is my last."

"All right, hang on." She flipped her mike. "Heer, drop a perimeter pin down the shaft."

"You not sure you're moving, Staff?"

"Just do it."

Nearly out of 2Ps, nearly out of MDCs. If the shuttle didn't get there soon they'd be out everything but smart-ass remarks.

"The new thrusters are DK-7s, your old ones are sixes. The new ones are a fraction of a second more responsive. Try to remember that."

Sibley sealed his flight suit and grinned up at Chief Graham. "It's on my list and I'm checking it twice."

"A fraction of a second means something at the speeds you're traveling."

"I know that, Chief."

"I should be replacing *all* the sixes with sevens, but for some reason the FC wants to give you another chance to get your ass shot off."

"Well, you know what they say, ass not what you can do for the Confederation."

The chief sighed and folded his arms over a barrel chest. "No one says that, sir."

"I just did." Sibley slapped the hatch release and motioned Shylin ahead of him into the docking bay, continuing the gesture and turning it into a jaunty wave back at the chief.

"Try to bring your ride back in one piece this time," Graham growled as the hatch closed.

Because if the Jades came back in one piece, so did the crews flying them.

"Think we can catch the squadron, Sib?"

His fingers danced over the thruster pad. "As easy as catching crabs on shore leave."

"And thank you for that image."

The rest of Black Star Squadron were nearly under the belly of the alien ship, having been sent to guard the air lock.

"Why would the Others destroy the air lock?" Shylin muttered, eyes locked on her tracking screens. "They want to use it, too."

"Why did the Others invade in the first place? Why do the H'san and the Mictok keep getting themselves blown to rat-shit attempting a diplomatic end to the war? Why did I get that tattoo on my ass? Answer these and other skill testing questions, and you've solved the secrets of the universe."

"Just how many of those stim sticks did you have?"

"Not enough. Looks like the rest of the team's seeing some action up close and personal."

An enemy squadron had joined the Black Stars outside the air lock. Maneuvering under the four-kilometer breadth of the ship, both sides tried for a clean target lock that would keep them from blowing up their own fighters.

"Sib! Unfriendly, starboard, four o'clock!"

"Got her. Moving to engage. She's not reading us yet."

"Target locked and . . . she's firing!"

A pair of missiles streaked out from the enemy fighter.

"Taking evasive action!"

"She's not firing at us."

Both missiles raced toward the fight under Big Yellow.

And then she fired again and there were four.

"Fuk! She's got as much chance of hitting her guys as ours! Can you get them?"

Each missile split into three smaller warheads.

"What, all *twelve*?"

"Black Group, this is *Black Seven*! Disengage! Incoming ordnance! Repeat, incoming ordnance! Bugs are firing into melee."

"Black Seven, *this is* Black Leader. *Bugs can't be firing into melee; they'll hit their own people.*"

"They don't care, Skipper! You've got a dozen little bangers moving in fast. Get out of there, now!"

"*Black Group, this is* Black Leader. *You heard the man! Move.*"

"Must've looked out his fukking window," Sibley muttered.

"Evasive action, Sib. This time she's aiming at *us*!"

By the time they straightened out, most of the squadron had cleared out of the blast zone.

"Boom Boom! Disengage!"

"*Don't tell me, tell the bu . . .*"

Something slammed into the hull and bounced. The double impact filled the passage with sound. The Katrien woke shrieking. Fingers slid under trigger guards as bennys rose looking for an enemy.

"What the fuk was that?" Werst demanded when the sound faded.

All eyes turned to Torin. "That was opportunity knocking." She shoved the last empty coffee pouch into her pack. "You didn't answer, so it's buggered off to find someone who appreciates it."

"Oh, I'll fukkin' appreciate it," Werst growled.

"And would the universe end if you just told them you didn't know?" Ryder asked under cover of the snickering.

Torin stared at him for a long moment. "Theirs would," she said at last.

"We only lost one of the Jades, Captain. *Black Star Eight.*"

Captain Carveg sighed deeply and drummed her fingers against the edge of the screen. "Good thing Lieutenant Commander Sibley was where he was when he was."

"Yes, ma'am."

"And the enemy fighters?"

"One of the enemy fighters was destroyed with *Black Eight*. Another took damage but got clear."

"So they can also thank Lieutenant Commander Sibley." She looked down at her fingers as though she didn't recognize them and forced them to still. "What did they think they were doing?"

Those of the C3 crew who could look up from their screens exchanged uncertain glances.

"Risking collateral damage to win," a lieutenant commander offered when the continuing silence seemed to indicate it hadn't been a rhetorical question.

"Win what?" the captain demanded. "They destroy some magic number of our fighters and get their engines back? Have they got information about Big Yellow that we don't? This makes no *serley* sense!"

"This whole war makes no more sense than a H'san opera."

Captain Carveg spun around in her chair and glared at the general. He was smiling, and she had to work very hard at not taking it personally. "Have you spoken to your people, sir?"

"No. I had an idea." When he paused, the room paused with him. "The *Promise*. The CSO's ship." When no one seemed enthused, he continued more forcefully. "It's using up one of your shuttle bays, I say we use it to get my Marines. Hell, we'll use it to get Ryder, so he'll certainly have no grounds for complaint." Brows drawing in, his smile faded as he took a closer look at her face. "What? You've got to have pilots left; how hard can it be to fly?"

"Flying it isn't the problem, General." *And thank you for that sensitive assessment of my flight crew.* "Craig Ryder's got his ship locked down so tight we might not even be able to break the cipher to get the air lock open. And, if we could get in, preliminary investigation suggests we'll blow the engines if we try to start them without his code."

"You've had your people working on it."

It wasn't exactly a question, but since he seemed to resent the preempting of his idea, and the last thing she needed on top of everything else was a sulky general, she said only, "Yes."

"So have your ship override his system! Goddamn it, Captain, you're sitting on a Confederation destroyer—use it!"

"Ignoring for the moment, General, that you do not give orders concerning my ship while on *my* ship, the *Promise* is not hooked up to the *Berganitan.*"

"Why the hell not?"

She spun her chair around to face him full on and got to her feet, the dais giving her enough height to look him in the eye. "Why the hell should it be? I certainly didn't anticipate having to use it and, frankly, sir, if *you* did, I wish you'd told me back when it would have done some *serley* good!"

"Standard Operating Procedures . . ."

"Do not cover civilian ships in military shuttle bays because civilian ships aren't permitted to use military shuttle bays." She drew in a deep breath and slowly released it. "If there's any way we can use the *Promise*—and my people are continuing to work on it—we will. I no more want to leave those Marines there than you do. And believe me, sir, it's not because I give a fuk about what the Krai in Parliament will say about the loss of Captain Travik."

"I believe you, Captain Carveg."

Something had occurred to him. He couldn't possibly be looking so *serley* happy because she'd thrown in a *sir.*

"And now, if your communications officer will see about raising Staff Sergeant Kerr, I'll see what I can do about having her get those codes from Mr. Ryder."

"Well?"

Ryder shook his head. "The air lock and the control panel both need a retina scan as well as the codes."

"Yours?"

"No, my mother's. I keep her left eye in a jar under my bunk. You know, you ought to bottle that look, you could sell it to weapons manufacturers."

"Ryder."

"Yeah, mine." He rubbed a hand over his face. "I'm sorry. I'm tired."

"Your mother's eye would be more useful," Torin muttered, and passed the bad news on to General Morris.

We'll keep working on it, Staff Sergeant. There has to be someone on this ship who can bypass a civilian security system.

Ressk's voice rose out of memory. *"You know there isn't a sys-op I can't get into. I could be useful on this kind of a mission."*

Except he'd be trapped on Big Yellow with the rest of the team.

Staff Sergeant Kerr?

"Sorry, sir. I was trying to think of a way to get Ryder's eye to you."

Yes. Well. How's Captain Travik?

The urge to ask "Who the fuk cares?" was intense. "He's alive, sir."

Good. We'll let you know if anything changes at this end. Don't worry, Staff Sergeant, I have complete faith in your ability to maintain discipline under these trying circumstances.

"Yes, sir." Torin tongued off her implant and lifted an eyebrow in Ryder's direction. "And they say I'm paranoid." No point in mentioning that his paranoia had just got them killed; he knew it. She could see the realization on his face. "It's not your fault; you couldn't have anticipated this when you locked up."

He shrugged and a corner of his mouth curled up in a self-mocking smile. "I just don't like people touching my stuff."

"Who does?"

"Staff, we got bugs!"

"On my way." She hurried down the passage to the rhythm of weapons' fire, wondering why the perimeter pins they'd left at the corner hadn't given them more warning. "Frii."

He glanced up as she passed.

"What the hell are you singing?"

"It's di'Taykan electro pop, Staff."

"Well, pop it back where you found it."

He grinned. "It sounds better with the music."

"Let's hope." She dropped behind the left barricade with Harrop. "Hold your fire until you're sure you can hit them," she ordered, loud enough to be heard by Dursinski as well. "We're going to need more than bad language to stop them when they make their try for the air lock."

"So far they're just keeping our heads down," Harrop told her, checking the charge on his benny. "Letting us know they're there."

"How many?"

"Hard to say but two definitely; one shooting high, one low."

"They took out the perimeter pin," Dursinski added. "We had no warning."

"They did or the ship did. It doesn't much matter." A sudden vision of a perimeter pin sinking into a previously solid deck flashed through Torin's head. Lifting her hand, she rocked forward onto the balls of her feet, wishing she could lift those as well.

"How long are we going to have to hold them, Staff?"

"Good question." Harrop shot her a questioning look and Torin switched to the group channel. "Listen up, people: Big Yellow has decided to prevent the *Berganitan* from launching her last shuttle. Which means they're going to have to come up with another way to get us off this thing. Which means we'll be here a while yet."

"Goddamned Navy."

"I doubt they're happy about it either, Dursinski. Huilin, Orla, you two get up here and double our strength on the barricades. The rest of you, stay sharp."

"Staff, we got something going on back here, too."

"What is it, Nivry?" The other corporal was standing by the sealed hatch to the tank room. "We got bugs cutting through?"

"I can't tell."

Neither could Torin when she laid her hand against the hatch and felt the faint vibration. "Could be some kind of sonic cutter, I suppose. All we can do right now is keep an eye on it."

"Staff . . ."

"Captain Carveg told me she wasn't leaving without us," Torin said, answering the question Nivry didn't ask. "She'll find a way."

"Why do you think Big Yellow let one evac shuttle launch but not the other?"

"Probably took it that long to figure out how to jam the controls."

Or both ships only got one chance and they blew it. But although that felt more likely, she wasn't planning to say it out loud.

And who said they only got one chance?

"Mr. Ryder, leave the benny and come with me."

She walked past, assuming that he'd follow, and the strength of that assumption pulled him to his feet.

"They're escape pods," Ryder said, studying the interior.

"Yes, they are. And you're going to get in one, get to the *Berganitan*, get into your ship, then come back and get us."

He straightened so quickly, he had to reach out and steady himself against the hatch. "You're insane."

Torin folded her arms. "What makes you think so?"

"What makes me think so?" When she made it clear she was waiting for an answer, he sighed. "Okay, to begin, there's two stretchers, eleven standing Marines and three civilians—I have a one-man operation. You've seen the inside of my ship." One hand slapped his chest. "*I* barely fit inside."

"You're right, I saw inside your ship and there's plenty of room for the stretchers and the three civilians."

Which wasn't the problem and they both knew it, but they had a way to go before they needed to pick at psychological scabs.

"And the eleven standing Marines?"

"Grab enough HE suits from the *Berg* and we'll ride in the salvage pens."

Ryder stared at her for a moment. Then he spun on one heel, walked six paces out, spun again, walked six back. "Okay, I was just talking before, but you really are insane."

"It's one hundred and eighteen kilometers; a little under half an hour's travel time in an STS. From what I saw of the *Promise*, you should be able to do it in an hour. We'll be fine."

"No inertial dampers."

Torin shrugged. The space between Big Yellow and the *Berganitan* buzzed with enemy fighters; inertia would be the least of their problems. "You've got straps, don't you? To keep the salvage from crashing around? We'll strap in."

Six out, six back. He wiped his hands on his thighs. "All right, given that we've established your lack of sanity, what makes you think Big Yellow will allow me to launch? I could easily be locked down, just like the shuttle."

"Won't happen."

"What makes you so fukking sure? And, God help me, Torin, if you say it's your job to be sure, I won't be responsible for my actions."

"You won't be locked down because Big Yellow was in your head." She kept talking as he walked away, and back, and away. "Based on that visit, the intelligence behind this ship wouldn't assume for an instant that you'd do something like this. Even after you launch, it would never believe that you'd willingly share your cabin with five people. You could hook up to the air lock and open the doors and it would know that at the last minute, as the first tiny Katrien foot stepped into your space, you'd freak and run away."

And back. "How the hell do you know that?"

"That you'd freak and run away?"

He opened his mouth. Closed it. Finally said, "No. How do you know what Big Yellow believes?"

A partial smile. "Because that's what I'd believe if I'd gone into your head."

"But you don't believe it, or you wouldn't be suggesting I ride to the rescue." Six paces away, seven back. A step into her personal space. Not threatening, although Torin suspected that was how he'd intended it. "So what makes you think that I wouldn't have done it then but I'll do it now? I'm a civilian, remember. You can't order me into that padded coffin. You think I'll do it for you? Just because you're asking me to?"

"No." She locked her gaze on his and held it. He was standing so close she could feel his breath on her face. "Because I expect you to."

One corner of his mouth curved up in a mocking smile. "And you find people live up to your expectations?"

"Yes."

She meant it. It wasn't bullshit, it wasn't bravado. Ryder found himself searching her face for any doubt, for the tiniest indication that she didn't think he could pull this off.

All he saw was a frightening certainty. A complete faith. In him.

And he saw that she believed that would be enough.

"You know, you really have a fukking huge ego." Seven paces away, six back. "I mean, you expect me to change a basic, intrinsic part of who I am . . ." Six away, six back. ". . . of who I've been for years—based on the strength of your personality alone and the vague possibility that when all this is over . . ."

Protests trailed off as one of Torin's eyebrows slowly rose.

"Fine." He threw up his hands in surrender and turned to the nearest escape pod, ignoring the voice of reason that kept asking what the hell he thought he was doing. "Do you know how to operate these things?"

"Actually," she admitted, and he found himself wishing she'd smile like that more often, "I haven't the faintest goddamned idea."

Opening the pods turned out to be relatively simple.

"Fortunately," Heer muttered, peering at the pressure pad running across the bottom of the control panel, "it defeats the purpose of escape pods if they're too complicated to get into."

"And to operate?" Ryder demanded.

"Usually you don't operate them. You just pop out and drift until someone rescues you, or you lock onto the nearest planet you can exist on."

"You mean live on."

"Nope." Heer punched a sequence into the pod's control panel and didn't elaborate.

Torin figured it was time she stepped in. "You'll be picked up by one of the Jades and taken to the *Berganitan;* no drifting, no rescues, no planets."

He shook his head, although what precisely he was denying remained unclear. "We don't even know if I can breathe in there."

"We'll know that as soon as Heer gets the hatch open. If you can't, you'll wear Huilin's HE suit."

"It'd never fit."

"Or you can hold your breath until they pick you up. Your choice." There'd be further argument; Torin could see it in Ryder's eyes, but Heer postponed it.

"Got it." Stepping aside, Heer pushed his thumb against the same place on the contact pad three times. With a wet, sucking noise, the walls around the hatch folded in. "Okay. Maybe not."

"Maybe not," Ryder repeated to Torin. "You hear that?"

"He'll figure it out. Won't you, Heer?"

"It's *chrick.*" He flashed Ryder a broad smile. "Trust me."

"Nice try, but I know what it means when you guys show teeth."

The wall had closed entirely over the hatch. A faint shudder vibrated through boot soles, and Torin thought she heard a distant pop.

"Command, this is *Black Seven*; there's something being extruded from Big Yellow not far from the air lock."

"*Extruded*, Black Seven?"

"Roger, Command. Extruded. Popped out like a big yellow zit." Sibley corkscrewed the Jade to avoid an enemy fighter and swung around for a closer look. "There's a section of hull suddenly rising up in a half circle a little less than two meters across at the point where it joins the . . . Shit! Shylih!"

"I see it." She counterfired to take out a PGM almost locked on their tail.

"B7, *does this half circle of hull appear to be a weapon?*"

He rolled his eyes. "It appears to be a half circle. That's it. Nothi . . . Hang on, it's still coming."

"B7, *we repeat, does it appear to be a weapon?*"

"Not unless they're setting up for a game of zero gee dodgeball."

"*Say again*, B7."

When the round section of hull remained attached to the ship with only a thin umbilical cord, the yellow coating suddenly slid off a gray sphere and remerged with the ship. Floating freely, the sphere moved slowly out into space.

"It could be a mine," Shylin said thoughtfully. "I'm reading energy but no life signs."

"I need better than a 'could be,' Shy."

"Then get me closer."

They were moving in when an enemy fighter swooped in off their Y-axis and hit the sphere with two energy bolts at close range, destroying it.

There wasn't so much an explosion as a sudden brilliant absence of sphere.

"B7, *are you hit?*"

"That's a negative, Command." Blinking rapidly to clear his vision, tears running from eyes still seeing a full spectrum of spots, Sibley managed to match course with the enemy fighter although he had no idea how.

"Target locked."

"Let's blow up a bug for Boom Boom."

This time, the force of the explosion threw the debris field into the belly of the alien ship.

The impact was gentler than the last one had been, but there were more of them. The constant patter, patter of heavy items hitting the ship's hull almost sounded like rain.

Working on the second pod, Heer ignored it, but Ryder grabbed Torin's uninjured arm. "They blew it up."

"Sounds like."

"This may come as a surprise to you, but I don't want to die."

"No one does." She dropped her voice to match his. "But we all will unless we get off this ship. The bugs'll kill us quickly, or thirst will do it slowly, but we *will* die. You're our only chance."

"But no pressure, right? Torin, we don't even know who blew up the pod. It could have been the vacuum jockeys from the *Berganitan*."

"Yeah, it could have been, but that means they saw it and know it came from near our position. General Morris will contact me to find out what I know about it, and I'll make sure that our side, at least, doesn't blow you up."

"That's not very comforting."

Torin shrugged.

"This is where you tell me I don't *have* to go."

"Waste of breath; you had to go from the moment I made it clear you were our only hope. You have to go because you couldn't live with yourself if you didn't."

He stared at her for a long moment. "You actually believe that, don't you?"

Smiling, Torin shrugged.

One corner of his mouth twitched. Then the other. "You know," he said conversationally, "you're very good at your job."

"And which part of that job would you be referring to?"

"Inspiring the troops to get their collective asses blown off."

He was still holding her left arm just above the elbow and a deep breath would be enough to bring their bodies together.

Staff Sergeant Kerr?

Torin jerked back, pulling her arm from Ryder's grip, trying unsuccessfully not to feel like her father had just caught her making out on the couch. "Sir?" She mouthed, *General Morris*, at Ryder, who seemed to be trying not to laugh. The bastard.

One of Captain Carveg's pilots has reported a sphere extruded from the ship near your position.

Extruded? "Yes; sir. It's an . . . General? General Morris? Sir?" The implant remained unresponsive.

"So the booster unit is gone?"

"Yes, Captain. Engulfed by the alien ship."

"Engulfed?" When the communications officer nodded, the captain sighed and rubbed a hand across the back of her neck. That wasn't good. "And we still don't know what that sphere was or if we can expect more of them."

"No, ma'am. We lost contact before the staff sergeant could pass on that information."

"But it could have been a mine?"

"Yes, ma'am."

She stared down at the screen where Big Yellow blotted out twenty kilometers of stars and tiny red and white lights zipping back and forth represented the fighters from both sides. "Mines are definitely just what we need floating around out there. Flight Commander?"

He shrugged, the movement worn down to almost nothing by the last few hours. "It might be smarter to blow them while they're still attached to the ship."

The captain sighed again. "It very well might."

"But you don't know *why* General Morris stopped transmitting."

"No, I don't." Her arms folded, Torin watched Ryder pace. "Maybe the *Berganitan* blew up. Maybe the galaxy got sucked into the ass end of a black hole, and we're all that's left. I do know that if we sit here with our thumbs in our mouths we *will* die, and I will *not* allow that. You give me a retina on a stick, and I'll get in the escape pod myself but otherwise . . ."

He stopped pacing in what had become a familiar position; face-to-face and too close for comfort. "I never said I wasn't going."

"Good."

"I wouldn't trust one of those ham-handed Navy pilots to fly the *Promise* anyway."

"Okay, this time, I've got it."

Torin turned gratefully toward her engineer. In another moment they were going to start smiling at each other again, and she honestly didn't think she was up to it. The subtext was rapidly becoming a distraction. "Show me."

Heer pushed his thumb against the contact pad three times.

"And how was that different from the last time?" she asked, one eyebrow rising as the pod's hatch sighed open.

"This time, I pressurized it." Arm stuck into the pod, he checked the readout on the sleeve. "Pod has the same atmosphere as the ship, which had the same atmosphere as the shuttle—a compromise mix for all species present. Which means," he continued, removing his arm and turning to the CSO, "you won't freeze or asphyxiate before they blow you up."

"That's a big help," Ryder muttered.

"Hey, look at the bright side. If you'd been stuffed into a di'Taykan's

HE suit you'd be humping the first sailor you saw at the end of the trip. Not necessarily a bad thing but . . ."

"Heer."

"Right." The Krai engineer twisted around until his feet were on the deck, both hands holding the upper lip of the opening, and his body arced back, allowing him to examine the pod without putting any weight inside. "There appears to be a self-contained air supply and a scrubber, but other than that, there're only two controls. Logically, the big button launches the pod, and the T-bar unlocks the hatch when you get where you're going."

"You're assuming one fuk of a lot."

"Not much choice." Heer straightened. "He can go any time, Staff."

Ryder looked from the pod to Torin. "You know, if you'd say, 'Don't go,' then I could say something like, 'A man has to do what a man has to do,' and leave a hero."

"Or there's always that retina on a stick option."

"I might have known she'd get all mushy on me," he muttered to Heer as he folded himself through the hatch. "It's not exactly roomy in here."

"You won't be in there long."

When he reached for the hatch, Torin was already there. She wanted to say something as she closed it but couldn't think of anything that wouldn't sound trite—he knew he was their only chance to live, he knew he might die—but she watched him through the window as the walls around the hatch folded in. And stood there until she heard the distant popping sound of the pod being extruded from the ship.

"Staff, we're getting a little more action from the bugs."

"On my way." Spinning around, she glared down at Heer. "What are you grinning about?"

"Not a thing, Staff Sergeant."

All the way up the ladder, Torin listened for pieces of an escape pod impacting against the hull.

FIFTEEN

Bouncing against the padded interior of the pod, Ryder looked for straps and couldn't find any. He didn't mind the bouncing; he worked in zero gee most of the time and, to save money, ran the artificial gravity generator in the *Promise* only enough to maintain muscle tone and bone mass. Considering he was floating out to an uncertain fate, as likely to be blown up by a vacuum jockey supposedly protecting his way of life as he was to reach the *Berganitan* and save the day, he had to admit he felt remarkably relaxed.

Probably because he was on his own.

Granted, Big Yellow was the size of most stations but deep down, he'd always known it was still a ship. He turned a slow somersault. He did better on his own. No big deal.

But the trip back . . .

"*. . . as the first tiny Katrien foot stepped into your space, you'd freak and run away.*"

The muscles across his shoulders knotted as tension returned.

Being blown up on the way to the *Berganitan* would almost be preferable. Almost.

His fingers sank deep into the padding, and he felt something give.

"I think this definitely proves it," he muttered, pulling his hand away from the five impressions he'd gouged into the wall. "Some guys'll do anything to impress a girl."

And some girls were pretty damned hard to impress.

Torin threw herself up the last few rungs of the ladder and out onto the upper deck. "Talk to me, Harrop!"

"*The good news is, they haven't thrown any ordnance. Either they're afraid they'll damage the lock, or they're out. Bad news, they're doing a lot more firing. I think they're getting ready for a charge."*

"I agree. Heads up, people. Bugs incoming. The packs aren't much of a barrier, but we can't let them get by. Jynett, Frii, join the others at the barrier. Johnston, Werst, get the captain off his stretcher and add it to the barrier. Heer, help me with Tsui."

The injured Marine was up on his elbows fumbling for his returned benny.

Torin took a quick look into his eyes. His irises were so dark a brown it was difficult to tell, but his pupils appeared to be at a normal dilation. "Neural blockers working?"

"I hope so; I can't feel my whole fukkin' leg."

"Good." She grabbed one end of the stretcher and motioned Heer to the other. "Let's get him down by the tank room. He can guard the hatch."

"It's sealed!" Heer protested as they ran crouched over, trying to stay under stray energy bursts coming from the bugs.

"Now," Torin amended. They slid to a stop by Nivry and set the stretcher down. "Sitting or lying, Tsui?"

"Sitting."

She slipped her hands into his armpits. "Heer, get his legs. Mind the stump. Nivry, the stretcher. On three."

A quick glance showed Johnston and Werst were being a lot less careful with Captain Travik. Johnston hoisted the top end, Werst the bottom, and they both kicked the stretcher clear. The captain didn't quite bounce as he hit the deck.

Torin sent Nivry forward with Tsui's stretcher.

"You hear anything coming through, you let me know!" she told him as Heer propped Tsui's stump up and he checked the charge on his benny. "You see anything, you shoot it *and* you let me know!"

His teeth were a brilliant white arc, slightly chipped on the right side. "You worry too much, Staff."

"Yeah, it's what I do. Heer . . ." She grabbed the engineer by the arm and dragged him to the edge of the open hatch leading to the lower level. "You and Johnston are in charge of the civilians." Three quick strides took her across the corridor; half a dozen shorter ones brought her back with the Katrien, who clung silently to each other. As much as she'd come to hate the sound of their voices, the silence was disconcerting. Johnston crossed behind her, one arm half guiding, half carrying *Harveer* Niirantapajee.

"The bugs break through, you get them down below and into an escape pod."

"What if they come up from below?"

"If they could, they'd be there now, flanking us. No one charges a fixed position, even a piss poor one if they have an option. Once the pods are launched . . ."

"We're back up here to help kick bug butts."

Torin looked from the Human to the Krai and saw identical expressions. "Your choice," she told them. "But don't spend your lives stupidly or you'll answer to me—if not in this life then the next."

"Staff Sergeant Kerr, I are not . . . are not . . ." Presit stared down toward the barricade, now stronger by the stretchers but still a fragile bulwark.

"It'll be okay." Torin pulled the reporter's attention back to her. "We do this for a living."

"I are not wanting to die."

"Well, I are not intending to."

Presit bristled at Torin's mocking tone and looked better than she had in hours.

Some people just prefer being annoyed. And annoying civilians seemed to be a big part of her job. "Stay low," Torin reminded the two Marines, as she turned. "The bugs seem fixated on this whole brain in the head thing and keep shooting high."

As she reached the barricade, a flurry of shots slapped into the packs and sizzled overhead.

"Here they come!"

"Command, this is *B7*. We have another extrusion out of Big Yellow."

"Roger, B7. *Is this second extrusion identical to the first?"*

"Shy?"

"Not exactly." The lieutenant bent over her screens, cadmium hair flicking back and forth. "But until you stop flinging us around, I won't be able to identify the difference."

He dropped the Jade fifteen meters, forty-five degrees to the Y-axis. "When I stop flinging us around, we go boom."

The yellow coating slid off the sphere and back into the ship.

"B7, we repeat, is the second extrusion identical to the first?"

"That's a good question, Command." Straight up. Full port thrusters for six seconds. "And as soon as we know, we'll let you know. Shy!"

"I've got her."

The bug fighter went spinning out of control and as the other fighters concentrated on getting out of her way, Sibley brought his Jade in for a tight swoop around the sphere.

"I'm reading life signs inside!"

"You catch that, Command?"

"Roger, B7. What species?"

"Insufficient data."

"Get the data!"

"Oh, yeah, easy for you to say," Sibley muttered, slipping his Jade under the arc of two incoming bugs. "It's getting a little crowded out here."

His maneuver threw one bug off enough that her shot merely skimmed the sphere.

"Oh, crap!" Ryder spit the words out through clenched teeth. His inner ear told him he was spinning and damned fast, too, given the pressure pushing him into the walls.

Sibley locked onto the tail of the second bug swinging into the attack and she broke it off before they could get a lock.

"Command, this is *B7*. I don't know who's inside, but the bugs don't seem to like them much."

"The bugs are shooting at the sphere?"

"Well, duh."

"B7, *we didn't copy that last transmission.*"

Grinning, Sibley spun his Jade one-eighty to give Shylin a clear shot at an enemy fighter. "I said, that's an affirmative. The bugs are shooting at the sphere."

"Lieutenant Commander Sibley, this is Captain Carveg."

"Now you're in for it," Shylin muttered.

"If the bugs want that sphere destroyed, I want it picked up and brought in."

"Aye, aye, Captain." He burned upper thrusters for three seconds, dropping straight down out of a missile lock. "Uh, got any ideas how we can do that without getting our asses burned?"

"B7, *this is* Red Mace One. *We're moving in to cover you.*"

"*Does that answer your question, Mr. Sibley?*"

"Yes, ma'am."

Maneuvering over the sphere wasn't the problem. Canceling its spin, however, was a little trickier.

"Equal and opposite force?"

Shylin shook her head. "Given the way the first one went up, I wouldn't want to risk a shot."

"Okay, we extend an energy field, let it transfer momentum, and I correct our spin."

"We'll be sitting *rinchas* while we're spinning," Shylin reminded him. "I won't be able to get a shot off, and the Maces'll have our lives in their hands."

Sibley barely touched the starboard thrusters, then goosed portside to bring them into position. "What's the point of having friends if you can't take advantage of them? Right, *Red One?*"

"*Don't worry about it, Shy. We'll keep you in one piece; your bastard pilot owes me money.*"

"Extending field . . ."

Double impact against opposite sides of the pod.

Ryder rubbed at a dribble of sweat running into his beard. All of a sudden, he desperately had to piss.

"Round and round and round she goes." Stars, bug fighters, Jades, and Big Yellow circled by; once, twice, three times. Sibley's fingers danced over the controls canceling the spin without sending them around the other way. "Where she stops nobody knows—but me."

"*Ablin gon savit,*" Shylin muttered as they slowed. "You actually figured out how to fly this thing."

They hung motionless in space for a moment, then he locked onto the *Berganitan*'s coordinates and hit the thrusters.

"*Red One*, this is *B7*. I'm taking my ball, and I'm going home."

"*Roger*, B7. *We have you covered.*"

*   *   *

MDCs gone, Torin switched to laser and dove out from behind the barricade under the reaching arms of the incoming bug. Slicing through the joint in the armor where the thorax joined the abdomen, she hit the deck, rolled, slid, and kicked out hard. To her surprise, the top half of the bug separated from the bottom half. As she rose to her knees, dripping with bug blood and stinking of cinnamon, Dursinski and Huilin took out the pieces.

The sudden silence made her ears ring.

The bugs had made it almost all the way to the Marine position. They'd been advancing behind their own dead.

"Good thing they're so explosive," Torin muttered, crawling back behind the barricade. "And I gotta say *that's* an observation I never thought I'd make."

When she went to stand, an energy bolt sizzled past her right ear, close enough so her PCU reacted with a painful burst of static.

"They've retreated, but they're not giving up."

Torin dropped to a crouch. "I noticed. Anyone have numbers on remaining unfriendlies?"

Dursinski scratched at the chemical neutralizer dribbling down her cheek. "I saw six go back."

"Yeah, six." Werst grunted, ridges flared. "And there's nine, maybe ten bodies."

Fifteen, maybe sixteen. Half of the thirty they'd faced in the garden. And if the bugs were willing to keep spending lives, they weren't going to last through many more charges. And there would be more charges, she was certain of that. Once the bugs regrouped, they'd try again.

"Stay sharp, people."

No need to tell them to consolidate the dregs of their ammo into a single power unit. No need to tell them to stay sharp either, but they needed her to say something.

Huilin had Frii tucked into the crease between bulkhead and deck. Blood stained the chest of the younger di'Taykan's combats almost black.

"How is he?"

Huilin shrugged. "I've got a tube in and he's breathing okay, but this is way beyond first aid. When we get back to the *Berganitan* they're going to have to rebuild the whole front of his throat."

He looked up at her as he said it and Torin read the challenge in his eyes.

"We'll get back to the *Berganitan*," she told him, her fingers wrapping around Frii's for a moment. "You have my word on it."

"All of us?"

She let Frii's limp hand slide from hers and fought the urge to touch Guimond's cylinder. "All of us," she answered grimly.

The captain's vitals were unchanged.

The Katrien were talking again, a series of high-pitched, overlapping short shrieks and howls. It could have been Katrien hysterics. It sounded like Katrien conversation. The *harveer* appeared to be in shock, her leg joints drawn up against her stomach, motionless but for the trembling in the tip of her tail. There wasn't any comfort Torin could offer, so she moved on.

Tsui licked his lips as she crouched beside him. "I'm having an intense craving for a cinnamon donut."

"Yeah?" Torin scraped a congealed bit of bug off her thigh with her thumbnail. "I, personally, may never eat French toast again. You said the vibration's getting stronger?"

"That was a while ago, Staff."

"I was busy." Palm pressed against the hatch, she frowned. "There's a throbbing under the vibration?"

"Yes, there is." Tsui frowned. "It seems familiar. It's like a sound I've heard a thousand times, but I can't put my finger on what it is."

"It *is* a sound you've heard a thousand times."

And it was the reason the bugs were so riled up and ready to die.

Big Yellow had started up its engines.

"B7, *this is Command. Cut fields and release the sphere into shuttle bay one.*"

"Roger, Command. Shuttle bay one, it is. If we get there in one piece," he added under his breath. "What the hell's bugging the bugs?"

The one hundred and eighteen kilometers back from Big Yellow had nearly doubled. In spite of his escort, Sibley had needed to use every flying trick he had to keep from being destroyed. Normally, the bugs would have pulled back when they came within range of the *Berganitan*'s guns, but the mass of Jades and fighters were so intermixed, the big guns were useless.

"Now would be the time for a few Jades to peel off and take out the Others' ship," Shylin noted grimly.

"And which of our escort would you like to lose?" Sibley asked her. "I myself would just as soon not get my ass blown off."

Up ahead, the shuttle bay doors were opening.

"I guess as long as they're not launching a rescue mission, Big Yellow's willing to release control. *Red Leader*, this is *B7*; am flipping ninety degrees to release."

As the sphere seemed to have no propulsion system, the only way to get it into the *Berganitan* was to line it up on the doors and give it a push—hard enough to get inside before one of the bugs got in a lucky shot, not so hard it was moving too fast for the emergency docking equipment.

As he began the flip, he caught sight of something out of the corner of one eye and trying for another look, cranked his head around so hard he nearly self-inflicted more damage than the bugs had managed.

"Uh, Command, is that a big net?"

"*Affirmative, B7.*"

"You want me to toss this thing into a big net?"

"*The item is too smooth for the docking clamps. Is it a problem?*"

"Uh, negative, but I'm outside the foul line, so it's a three-point shot." He juiced the top thrusters, released the grapples, and vectored away. The sphere continued along its original course. "And an object in motion will remain in motion unless acted upon by an equal or opposite force."

"Sib, are you all right?"

"Me?" A quick slip sideways took them out between *Red Three* and *Four.* "I'm having a ball."

"Captain, we have the sphere in the shuttle bay. Pressurizing now."

She surged up out of her chair. "Tell them I'm on my way."

"Aye, aye, Captain."

"Captain!" Lieutenant Potter's voice stopped her at the hatch. "Security reports General Morris and Lieutenant Stedrin on their way to the shuttle bay."

A little tired of having the general show up in C3 without warning, she'd had security tracking him. "Delay him," she snapped. "I don't want him there first."

*   *   *

Totally featureless and smoothly gray, the sphere hung in the net about a meter off the deck. Half a dozen technicians crowded around it with hand-held scanners and portable science stations, and behind them an equal number of security personnel stood with weapons drawn.

"Can I assume proper quarantine procedures were followed?" Captain Carveg snorted, glancing around.

The senior science officer jumped at the sound of her voice and hurried over. "It's absolutely clean, Captain," he assured her. "Not so much as a micro on it. And, if we compare it to the preliminary reports of the science team on Big Yellow, it's the same combination of metals and polyhydroxide alcoholydes as the original corridor just inside the air lock."

"Then I suggest we don't use cutting tools on it."

"We weren't planning to, ma'am."

"Good." She walked forward until she stood a body-length away, security and science alike moving aside for her. "What's in it?"

"An excellent question."

The science officer jumped again as General Morris' comment boomed out and echoed around the shuttle bay.

"You might think about switching to decaf, Commander," the captain muttered as she turned.

If General Morris was annoyed she'd arrived first, he wasn't allowing it to show. He crossed quickly to her side, Lieutenant Stedrin behind his left shoulder, and stood rubbing his hands together expectantly. "Well, is it Captain Travik?"

The commander glanced from his captain to the general to his slate. "It's, uh, Human, ma'am. Sir."

The general smiled broadly. "No Human scientists survived, so it's got to be one of my Marines. Now, we'll find out what's happening. Might even be Staff Sergeant Kerr."

"The staff sergeant would never leave the Recon team, sir," Lieutenant Stedrin murmured, leaning toward the general's ear.

Captain Carveg's estimate of the lieutenant rose.

"Well, whoever it is, it's a Marine. Get it open, Commander."

"I'd be happy to, sir, but I don't know how."

With the return of gravity came the unwelcome realization that the hatch was now on the bottom of the pod. Straddling it, Ryder stared down at the T-bar. He had no way of knowing which ship he was on. If he'd been taken prisoner by the Others, being upside down was the least of his problems.

Unfortunately, there was only one sure way to find out.

He bent, took hold of the bar, and twisted it counter-clockwise a hundred and eighty degrees. It snapped into place. Releasing it, he straightened.

A tech kneeling under the sphere threw herself backward. "Commander!"

"I see it." A dark crack now outlined an area about a meter square. "Filters, everyone. Captain."

"Thank you." As she slapped the disposable filter over her mouth and ridges, she turned to check the watching Marines. The lower half of both faces bore an unmistakable sheen. General Morris might have a knack for showing up and being a pain in the ass, but at least he came prepared. Although the odds were better Lieutenant Stedrin had come prepared.

The hatch sighed open.

Ryder stared down at a familiar square meter of deck. It looked exactly like the deck he'd parked the *Promise* on. *So I'm either on the* Berganitan, *or the North Fleetrin Shipyards really do have the lowest prices in the universe.*

He was probably no more than a meter and a half up. Less than his own height. So he jumped.

"You!"

Ryder moved out from under the sphere and straightened. "And g'day to you, too, General," he replied, adding, as the other man pushed past him to look up into the sphere, "You're shit out of luck if you think I brought friends."

"Nothing!"

"Told him," Ryder remarked conversationally to the area at large.

General Morris slapped the side of the sphere with enough force to start it swinging. "Why you?" he demanded.

Before Ryder could answer, Captain Carveg stepped forward, her expression suggesting she'd had about as much of General Morris as she could handle and was about ready to chew a piece out of him. "You're going back for them in the *Promise*, aren't you?"

He was safe and he was going back. He was out of his mind. "Yes, Captain, I am."

The first energy bolt in some minutes hit the packs, was partially absorbed by the fabric, arced over an area that had been previously fried, and fizzled out to nothing.

"When we get out of this, remind me to send a nice thank you note to the company that makes these packs," Harrop muttered, picking himself up off the deck.

"I hate to discourage good manners," Torin told him, "but I suspect the bugs are nearly out of juice. That shot had nothing behind it."

Dursinski sat slumped on the deck, head between her knees. "So, when they run out, do they give up or what?"

"What," Torin answered calmly. "A final flurry of shots to keep our heads down, then it's hand-to-hand."

"Hand-to-claw." Dursinski's lower lip went out. "That is so unfair."

"Claw-to-laser," Werst snarled.

She glanced down at her charge. "Yeah, and in thirty seconds when that runs dry?"

Werst snapped his teeth together with enough force so the sound jerked Huilin up out of sleep.

"Oh, sure. Easy for you. And then what? What if Ryder doesn't get back before Big Yellow finishes warming up? What if the ship takes off with us still in it? What then?"

Torin reached over and took the younger woman's chin between the thumb and forefinger of her left hand, lifting her head until they were eye to eye. "Then, we find the control room and learn to fly this thing. We turn it around. We bring it home."

"We can do that?"

"We're Marines. We can do whatever the fuk we put our minds to."

The packs jerked three times in quick succession and one of them started to smoke.

"It's your flurry of shots, Staff!"

"Marines! Incoming!"

*　　*　　*

"You want to put my Marines in your salvage . . ." Flushing, General Morris searched for the word, finally spitting out, "Enclosure?"

"Yeah, my enclosure; and we haven't got time to discuss it." It had been a long day, and he was pretty much running on pure adrenaline. In another minute he was going to shove the general out of his way. "Unless you can think of a better way to bring them home, I need eight HE suits and I need them twenty minutes ago."

"That's insane!"

"Look, I don't need your blessing, I just need the damned suits! Or a better idea." He paused pointedly, leaning in closer. "No? Fine." A half pivot, another officer. "Captain Carveg?"

"The Navy will supply you with as many suits as you need, Mr. Ryder."

"The Corps can look after its own, Captain. Lieutenant!"

"Sir." Lieutenant Stedrin pushed through the crowd of Naval researchers.

"Get Mr. Ryder those suits."

Power struggle. Use it wisely, Ryder thought. "Three di'Taykan, three Human, two Krai. Bring them to the *Promise*."

Stedrin glanced at the general who, lips pressed into a thin line, nodded. He watched Stedrin's retreating back for a moment, then stepped back deliberately out of Ryder's way. Body language clearly saying, *You leave because I allow it.*

And he can just keep thinking that.

He was almost to the hatch when the general stopped him.

"Mr. Ryder, Captain Travik . . . ?"

"Is still unconscious," he said, turning and walking backward. "Which puts a limit on how much your pet gnome can fuk this up." Which was when he realized that referring to the captain by the derogatory description might not have been a good idea. He flashed Captain Carveg his most charming smile. "No offense."

She shrugged and the Krai around her relaxed. "None taken. I met him, remember? As it stands right now, we can still open the launch doors to let you out, but I'd hurry before Big Yellow figures out what you're up to."

"Yes, ma'am." One hand on the hatch.

"Mr. Ryder . . ."

This time, he didn't bother turning. "General, write me a fukking note."

"You can't talk to me like that!"

"Yeah, I can." Through the hatch. His hands braced on either side, he leaned back into the shuttle bay and locked eyes with the general. "I don't work for you. I'm not doing this for you. I'm doing this because . . ." Which was when he realized that he didn't owe General Morris an explanation and he grinned. ". . . Staff Sergeant Kerr told me to."

The *Promise* wasn't exactly as he'd left her, but then, he hadn't expected her to be.

"You weren't exactly subtle about trying to get in, were you, mate?"

The sailor shrugged. "Yeah, well, sorry about the scorch marks. After the last shuttle got locked down, we got a little desperate."

"And before?"

"Security doesn't like question marks."

Ryder ran his fingers down five parallel scratches. "You lot ever hear of privacy or personal rights?"

"Not on a warship, buddy. You want privacy you've got to get it cleared by three levels of noncoms and signed off by an officer." As she turned to go, she raised her wrench in a sloppy salute. "Fukkin' impressive security system."

"Yeah, well, I don't like people messing with my stuff," he muttered, punching in his personal code. At first he was afraid they'd damaged the lens on the retinal scanner, but after a moment, the hatch swung open.

The tiny air lock's inside door was also closed and locked, but it, at least, had only the dents he'd put in it himself.

The doors stayed open behind him to save time when the HE suits arrived. And because he was afraid if he closed them, he'd never open them again.

As he stepped into the cabin, the lights came up, air circulation increased and his implant announced it was 0312. He'd been up for just over twenty hours. No wonder he felt like he'd been pureed. Three long strides took him across to the small galley. He reached for the coffee and pulled out a pack of caffeine lozenges instead. Same boost, fewer pit stops.

Which reminded him.

When he stepped out of the head, there was a Katrien standing in his air lock, peering curiously around the cabin.

". . . *first tiny Katrien foot stepped inside and you'd freak.*"

Fuk off, Torin.

"You want something, mate?"

The pointed face swiveled around, close enough that Ryder could see his reflection in the dark glasses.

"You Craig Ryder?"

"That's right." He crossed to his chair and gripped the back, stopping himself from advancing and forcing the much smaller male out of the air lock, down the ramp, and off his ship. If he couldn't handle one of them . . . His fingers sank through worn vinyl and deep into old foam.

"Durgin a Tar canSalvais. Call me Durgin." He started to step forward, his nose wrinkled, and his foot went back down where it had been. "I are Presit's pilot. They are telling me Cirvan was killed?"

"Sorry."

Durgin's ears drooped. "He are putting up with a lot from that . . . how are you Humans calling it?"

"Prima donna?"

"Bitch." A flash of teeth. "You are bringing her back?"

"'Fraid so."

He grinned—showing a lot more teeth—and reached into his belt pouch. "I are bringing this for her. It are her small recorder. You are giving her this when she comes on board and she are in a corner talking and not chewing on you."

"Good." If she was outside in a corner of the cargo corral, even better.

Holding out the recorder, Durgin slowly stepped into the cabin.

A trickle of sweat rolled down Ryder's back. He had a Katrien foot . . . two feet . . . an entire Katrien in his ship and although he could feel the familiar panic rising, he hadn't *freaked.*

And a very military word, by the way, Torin.

His heart began to pound and he tightened his grip. The back of the control chair creaked. *Air lock's open. Either one of us can leave any time.*

That helped. It'd mean piss all later on, but right now, it helped.

Setting the recorder down by the coffeepot, Durgin glanced over at the control panel. "You are having a panel of H'san controls?"

"Yeah, well, I got them cheap. It's not that much of a size difference."

The Katrien snorted and held up a hand. "Not for you." Back in the air lock . . .

Almost off my ship.

Durgin paused. "You fly alone?"

Ryder managed a tight grin. "Usually."

Durgin's ears rose and fell, but all he said was, "Good luck."

Lieutenant Stedrin paused at the door to the general's office. From the condition of the room, he'd taken out his anger on a few inanimate objects. "General Morris, sir?"

The general slowly turned his chair to face the door. He looked more weary than angry. The second stim must have been wearing off. *Once Mr. Ryder's left, I'll see if I can get him to sleep.*

"Sir, the HE suits are on their way over to Mr. Ryder's ship. I need your permission to give him the codes for the PCUs."

General Morris frowned. "For the PCUs?"

"Yes, sir. When he's close enough, he'll need to contact Staff Sergeant Kerr."

"Captain Travik is still in command."

"Due respect, sir, Captain Travik is unconscious: He won't be much help when it comes to docking or loading."

"He hasn't been much help just generally, has he?" Leaning back in his chair, the general dragged both hands over his face, pulling the skin down into temporary jowls. "He's been unconscious through the whole damned mission and in front of a reporter, too. Oh, she'll have a great story, won't she?" Eyes narrowed, he glared up at the lieutenant. "Do you have any idea how much political trouble this thing's going to cause?"

"A lot, sir?"

"A lot, Lieutenant. What do you figure the odds are that Travik'll regain consciousness and do something heroic before he's dragged back here in disgrace by a goddamned civilian salvage operator? A civilian."

"It's no disgrace to be wounded, sir."

"Well, it's not a great honor either." Both hands slapped down on his desk. "If he was dead, at least it would be a tragedy instead of a farce. You have my permission to give Mr. Ryder the PCU codes. In fact"—his lip curled—"give him the codes for Staff Sergeant Kerr's implant as well. Who knows what else she'll tell him to do if given the opportunity."

*   *   *

"What's taking so long?" Dursinski demanded, scratching at the sealant over the chemical burn on her cheek. "We're going to be taken halfway across the fukking galaxy any minute!"

"First, stop scratching. Your fingers are covered in bug guts and you're going to get that thing infected." Torin glared at the shorter woman until her hand dropped back to her side. "Good. And second, odds are the *Berganitan* doesn't know the engines have started up. Right from the beginning their scans have been worthless, and I doubt they're suddenly working now."

Dursinski snorted. "Goddamned Navy."

"Stedrin's probably got Ryder filling out forms in triplicate before he'll issue the suits," Huilin snickered. "Fuk, there's probably a 'civilian request to rescue Marines' form."

"Yeah, I'd laugh," Nivry sighed, sliding down the bulkhead and landing awkwardly on the deck, "but there probably is."

Graceless di'Taykan were exhausted di'Taykan. The Humans were in much the same shape. Only Werst and Heer showed any kind of energy. Torin suspected they'd been snacking on bugs, but she didn't want to know for sure.

"Bugs have withdrawn," Nivry continued. "I don't think there's more than seven or eight left."

"I can't believe we're kicking bug ass."

Tsui, Frii, and Harrop had all taken major wounds. Torin had stopped counting the minor ones. And Guimond was dead. "I think we took out their command structure early on. There's been no direction to their attacks."

"You mean besides straight at us," Nivry snorted.

"Yeah, besides that. Still, nice to know we've got something under control."

The vibrations could be felt through the decks, through the bulkheads—probably through the ceiling although Torin had no intention of checking. A small puddle of blood, from where a bug's claw had cut through an artery along with half of Harrop's thigh, trembled constantly.

"Ryder'll tell them about the engines," Orla murmured, her eyes dark. "Ryder'll hurry back."

Which would have been comforting except that Ryder didn't know.

SIXTEEN

The suits were on board. The *Promise* was sealed. He could leave any time.

He was sweating so heavily, the controls felt greasy under his hands.

"*. . . the intelligence behind this ship wouldn't assume for an instant that you'd do something like this.*"

"Yeah, and it might be right."

"*What was that, Promise?*"

"Nothing." He took a deep breath. Dried his palms on his thighs. Told himself he was their only chance. Torin's only chance. Torin, who expected him to get the job done. *So let's not think about the trip back until we fukking get there.*

"*Berganitan*, this is Craig Ryder on the *Promise;* open the launch doors."

"*Promise*, this is *Black Star Seven*. I'll be your point man for the trip back to Big Yellow. Follow me and ignore the rest of the squadron; they'll be out there trying to keep you alive."

"*I'm on you. And thanks for the pep talk*, BS7."

"He's got your number, Sib," Shylin snickered.

"*B7*'s fine, *Promise*. No BS out here."

"*My mistake, mate.*"

Sibley flicked the comm channel closed and snorted. "I wonder what he's up to."

"What do you mean?"

"He has to know he'll get sweet fuk all for doing this."

"If it works, they'll give him a medal."

"Yeah. That and a thumbprint'll get you a cup of coffee." Sibley shook his head. "He's got something in the bag."

"Cynic."

"Not even; I've played poker with him."

The trip back to Big Yellow turned out to be as uneventful as the trip into the *Berganitan* with the sphere had been busy. The bugs still had three full squadrons of fighters out, but they had no real interest in the salvage vessel. Even their one-on-one encounters were more for appearances.

"Our lot's no better," Sibley noted when Shylin pointed it out. "There's a limit to how long you can keep it up when nothing changes. Both ships are locked down and we're too evenly matched for anyone to get the upper hand. No one, not even a bug, wants to risk being killed for no reason."

"That's more philosophical than usual, Sib."

"Yeah, well, I'm tired. I'm out of stim sticks." He shifted inside his webbing. "And my damned flight suit is crotching me."

"Lucky flight suit."

"That's the best you can do? And you call yourself a di'Taykan."

"Hey, I'm tired, too." Hair barely moving, she checked her screens. "You'd think the bugs'd find the energy to go after the *Promise*."

"I doubt they see the point. With that Susumi engine taking up all the room, the cabin's not much more than two meters square, so it can't be going in on a rescue. Fuel and ammo are finite. At this point the bugs'll wait to see what he does when he gets where he's going before they commit."

"What *is* he going to do when he gets where he's going?"

"Damned if I know."

Torin snatched her slate off her vest as the low, pulsing tone began.

"The captain," she answered when she looked up and saw Nivry's unspoken question. "I'm heading back to check on him. Keep an eye on things up here."

Nivry turned and stared toward the corner with the one emerald eye that hadn't swollen shut. The bugs were still there—they could both hear and smell them talking—but no one had fired so much as a warning shot in almost half an hour. "You think they're going to try something the moment your back is turned?"

"Always," Torin snorted.

In spite of the blood loss, Frii's and Harrop's vital signs were holding steady. Tsui's blockers wouldn't last much longer, but he was fine except for the missing foot.

When Torin sank carefully down beside Captain Travik, favoring the knee a bug had clipped, he looked no different, but all of his numbers had redlined.

"And?"

She glanced up to see Werst crouched across the captain's body. No. Not body. Not yet. "He's dying."

Werst nodded. "Smells like he's dying. Mind you, he's smelled like he was dying from the beginning."

"Thanks for telling me."

He snorted. "You knew."

She supposed she had. Any blow hard enough to damage a Krai skull had to have pulped the brain behind it. Immediate med-evac might have saved him. The vibrations had very likely finished off the jellied parts of his brain.

"If you wanted to make him a hero for General Morris, you should've thrown his body on the grenade."

"Believe me," Torin sighed, "if I'd had time, I'd have done it. He'd be a lot more useful as a dead hero than just dead."

"*Marines, this is the* Promise. *Come back.*"

Ryder's voice blaring out of every PCU snapped people out of sleep up and down the passage. A sudden burst of formaldehyde and cinnamon seemed to indicate that even the bugs had heard.

"Ryder, this is Kerr. What the hell took you so long?"

"*What?*" She could hear the smile in his voice. "*You started starving in an hour and a half?*"

Was that all it had been?

"It's a little more serious than that." The bugs were all in a day's work, but the engines . . .

"*You sure they're engines?*" he demanded after she filled him in.

"Ryder, I've got two engineers in here and a Niln with a fukking armload of degrees. They're engines. Get us off this thing."

"*That's what I'm here for. But I'm going to need some help hooking up.*"

The *Promise* came with what the manufacturers advertised as a universal lock—a flexible, ribbed tube guaranteed to seal to any solid surface on contact. Unfortunately, the four small thrusters on the end of the tube came with a safety feature that kept them from firing within three meters of organics—which was how their software recognized Big Yellow.

"You're going to have to throw something out, hook onto the tube, and drag it in. Once there's contact, it should seal."

"Should?" Dursinski protested loudly.

"And what are we supposed to throw?" Nivry demanded from the barricade. "Bug parts?"

"Too organic."

"Good. 'Cause that's called indignity to a body and they charge you for stuff like that."

"So you're allowed to shoot them, but you can't toss them around?"

"Everyone shut up."

"Torin, we don't . . ."

"You, too, Ryder." She tapped her fingers against the edge of her slate and worked through the variables again. It might work. It should work. "All right." A deep breath and she straightened, shaking off the last couple of hours. *"Harveer,* can Johnston use your slate to open the lock?"

The elderly scientist peered from Torin to the engineer and back. "He's a bright boy. Probably."

"Good. Jynett, Orla, take the civilians down to the escape pods. If worse comes to worst, launch all three of them."

"No." Her fur dull, Presit pulled away from Gytha's grip, showing a hint of her old animation for the first time since Guimond died. "I are not moving away from a story. I are not even hearing the other half of . . ." When words failed her, she waved a tiny hand toward Torin's helmet. ". . . that."

"Ma'am, if it's a choice between having you carried away from your *story* or watching your eyeballs explode as you spontaneously decompress, I know what I'd choose." The pause lasted just long enough for Presit to begin to bristle. "If you'll go to the pods, you can take Private Frii's helmet with you and listen to everything on group channel."

"Uh, Staff . . ."

"She deserves to get the end of the story." Torin scooped up the helmet and offered it to the reporter. "Well?"

"I don't think eyeballs explode during spontaneous decompression," Johnston muttered away from his microphone when the civilians were safely out of sight.

Torin flicked her mike up. "Who cares? Get the lock pressurized and the door open."

Her slate began a steady hum.

"The rest of you stay where you are. Werst, you're with me."

The hum stopped.

They stared at each other over the captain's body.

"You refuse," Torin told him, her voice so low he leaned forward to hear, "and we use the suit without the captain. You agree, and we may be able to make him the kind of hero General Morris needs."

"We'd be doing this for the general?"

"Fuk him. We'd be doing this to keep Parliament from tying the Corps' hands. Be nice to achieve something worthwhile today," she added when he frowned. *Be nice if we could salvage something from Guimond's death.* But she didn't have to say that out loud.

Werst's ridges clamped shut. "If it goes wrong?"

"I'll take the heat."

"Fuk that, too. And the rest of the team?"

"They just have to play dumb."

He snorted. "Shouldn't be too hard for most of them." All at once, he grinned, showing an ivory slash of teeth. "Hope I can get the *serley* accent right."

Her own teeth clenched together, Torin pushed down on the captain's jaw and reached into his mouth. It was beginning to cool. She found the ridge that ran under his left molars and activated the implant.

Microphone down, Werst bent over the captain's mouth, their lips almost touching in a parody of tenderness.

*No! I will not allow one of my Marines to take that kind of risk. I will . . . *

". . . be the one to get that tube."

"But, sir, you've been unconscious . . ."

"Krai are tougher than you think, Staff Sergeant."

"Yes, sir, but . . ."

"Don't argue with me, Staff Sergeant Kerr. I'm the one giving the orders. I'm in command here, not you."

"Yes, sir."

They flipped up their mikes at the same time and sat back.

"Nailed the accent," Torin told him, pushing the captain's jaw shut. "We lost the implant after the *I will* but that was plenty. It's only important that Presit hear the whole speech; we just need the general to believe he's alive.

Get him sealed up and ready to go." She rocked back on her heels, stood, turned, and found, as she knew she would, every pair of eyes in the passage locked on her.

Moving deliberately, so they all could see her do it, she flipped her mike back down. Long silences would not help the story. "Huilin, get out of your HE suit. There's nothing to tie off to in the air lock, and Captain Travik wants me to anchor him."

Huilin's eyes were dark and under the edge of his helmet his hair was in constant motion. "The captain's regained consciousness?"

Torin slowly raked her gaze over the Marines, her expression silencing any other questions. "You heard him. He seems to feel it's his duty to get the tube. He also seems to think if he's going to risk his ass, so should I. Get out of the suit. Now."

Her voice moved his hands to the seals . "Why . . ."

"Because it's the only one I have a hope in hell of fitting in. Dursinski's too short and Jynett's integrity has been compromised. Move it, Marine. Time's wasting."

The suit puddled around his legs. Huilin glanced toward the vertical that led to the escape pods and back to Torin.

He knew.

They all knew. Although Torin suspected the whispering she'd heard had been Nivry filling Dursinski in.

They'd known her for eight days in Susumi space and for thirty hours on Big Yellow. They trusted her to get them through battles alive, but trusting her in this was a whole different ball game.

"It's my suit, Staff," Huilin said, at last. "I should go."

"Did I ask for volunteers? Just give me the damned suit."

I won't involve you lot any more than I have to.

They heard the subtext. It echoed around the suddenly quiet passageway so loudly, Torin was afraid Presit would hear it one level down.

After a long moment, Johnston made the decision for all of them. "I'll have the lock open by the time the captain's ready, Staff Sergeant Kerr."

"Good. And I'll need someone's rope." She stripped off her combats and held out her hand for Huilin's suit.

Torin, what the fuk is going on in there?

The sudden blaring of her implant made her drop the captain's body. It was a damned good thing he only had to sound alive. Hauling him back up again, she half turned and nodded to Werst.

"Close the inner door, Lance Corporal Johnston."

Johnston scowled in Werst's direction, but all he said was, "Closing the inner door, Captain."

Torin? Answer me, damn it. Captain Travik is not seriously heading out to save the day? He was a fukking vegetable when I left.

She tongued her implant on and subvocalized so the suit mike wouldn't pick it up. *Trust me.*

Trust you? The heavy sigh came through loud and clear. *Do I have a fukking choice?*

No. Stay on group channel. And then aloud, "Ryder, Captain Travik and I will be working on command channel for clarity. Were you given the codes?"

"I have the codes. What I don't have is all day; move your collective ass."

"Keep your goddamned pants on," she muttered, watching the panel of lights as the air lock depressurized. Which was not an image she needed. Stuffed into an HE suit a di'Taykan had been wearing for hours had her so horny that Ryder's voice alone was nearly enough to overload the circuitry. The series of lights Johnston had told her to watch for flashed green, and she laid her glove against the pressure pad.

The door slid open the way a thousand air lock doors had slid open all her life.

Moving carefully, she centered herself and Captain Travik in the opening and set her boot magnets at full power.

"I see you." A short pause, and he added, "Both of you."

Torin smiled and adjusted her grip on the captain. *And thank you for playing.*

It was good to see the stars.

"Torin, Sibley says you might want to think of hurrying. Bugs are moving in."

"Roger that." She resisted the urge to look for the bugs. It wouldn't make a damned bit of difference if she knew where they were.

With the bulk of Big Yellow behind her, the Promise looked absurdly small. The floating end of the universal lock was smaller still.

With one end of the rope tied around the captain's waist and the other around hers, Torin flipped him over so his boots were pointing toward the universe and threw the already stiffening body toward the tube. Her aim didn't need to be exact. When he was closer to the tube than Big Yellow, she punched his boot codes into her slate. Part of her job was ensuring that the captain's equipment functioned properly.

Magnetic soles worked fine.

"What the *sanLi* are they doing?"

Sibley took a look straight up through the canopy. "Putting their best foot forward? Booting up the air lock? Proving they've got sole?"

"You done?" Shylin sighed.

"For now."

"Well, I don't know about soul, but the little guy's got balls the size of . . . Bugs!"

The Jade slid to the left, dropped six meters, and fired as a shot streaked by their portside. A touch on the upper right thruster flipped them around. Another touch on the lower left stopped the spin.

"Target's taking evasive action."

"Let it. We've got two more closing on the *Promise.*" He goosed the Jade up and in. "Ryder, you want to remind your Marines they're not alone in the universe?"

"No shit. You think that's why people keep shooting at us?"

All Ryder could see was the middle bulge of the tube, but the instruments showed the end had nearly reached Big Yellow. "Could be your sparkling personality."

"Mine?" Torin wondered. *"Or the Corps'?"*

"Is there a difference?" A bug fighter streaked past almost too quickly to identify. It was amazing how the old panic, the panic he could feel bubbling and roiling beneath the forced, teeth-clenched surface calm, kept new panic at bay. At least if he got blown to component atoms by something that looked like a cross between an ant and a cockroach, he'd die alone in his ship.

His one-man ship.

Alone.

The way it was supposed to be.

"Securing first point of UAL and manually activating the seal. You sure this thing'll stretch to fit?"

Torin's voice helped.

"The brochure said 'one size fits all.' "

"Yeah, well let's hope it wasn't written by the same moron who sizes lingerie."

A sudden vision of what Staff Sergeant Torin Kerr wore under her combats caused an involuntary smirk. "You never struck me as the lingerie type."

"I have hidden depths."

"That, I never doubted." The UAL controls greenlined. "We've got a seal." He stared down at his hand on the panel. An inch to the right were the main thruster controls. He wouldn't even have to move his arm.

"Craig?"

And it came as no surprise she could read his thoughts in the silence.

"Tell your people to pressurize." He watched his fingers curl into a fist. "I'll deploy the salvage pen."

"Roger. I'm switching back to group channel. Any time you think you can't do this, contact me."

"I can do this."

"Glad to hear it. Kerr out." Torin propped the captain up against the inside of the lock and stepped in front of him to keep him from falling. "Marines, we are leaving. Johnston, get this thing pressurized. I want wounded and civilians moving, and moving fast, the instant the door opens."

"I'm sorry, General, we still can't raise Captain Travik."

"Why not?"

"He's not answering, sir."

General Morris placed both hands on the edge of the console and leaned into the comm officer's space. "I heard him not ten minutes ago!"

"Yes, sir. But he's not answering now."

"If you're still being blocked, why don't you blast the signal through that salvage ship the way you did with the first shuttle? It's practically sitting right there on the hull."

"We can't, sir. It's a civilian vessel and its comm unit isn't set up to handle that kind of amplification."

"Why the hell not? Why wasn't it set up before it launched?"

"We didn't have time, sir."

"So you're telling me I still can't speak to the officer commanding?"

"Yes, sir."

"Goddamned Navy." General Morris rocked back on his heels and fixed the comm officer with a basilisk glare. "Fine. If you can't raise the captain's implant, I suppose it's too much to hope you can raise the staff sergeant's—so get me Ryder," he continued without waiting for an answer. "Unless your tin can and piece of string don't reach that far!"

"I'm a little busy, General." Ryder swiveled his chair around so that he was staring at the air lock. "What do you want?"

"What do I want? I want a full report on the situation!"

Both inner and outer doors were still closed. The lock itself was unpressurized. He was alone in the cabin. A full report to General Morris would keep things that way for a good long time.

"Ryder! Goddamn it, answer me!"

One hand reached back for the comm controls.

"I think you're forgetting that I don't work for you, mate."

"Remember, the ship's AG field stops at the outer hull. I want one Marine to a civilian, one helping Tsui, two carrying each of the stretchers. You drop your baggage, you grab an armload of suits, you haul ass back to Big Yellow." A shadow flickered over the thin membrane of the tube. No way to tell if it was a bug fighter or a Jade. "I want a minimum of time spent in this worm casing." And what was taking the goddamned pressurizing so long?

"Staff Sergeant Kerr, we are not being carried . . ."

"Yes, you are. We don't have time for sloppy maneuvering in zero gee."

"Captain Travik! I are asking you . . ."

"The captain can't answer you, ma'am." Torin glanced back at the corpse. "Saving all our lives took everything he had. He's drifting in and out of consciousness again."

"Black Seven, *this is* Red Three. *We've got bugs heading toward your position.*"

"So stop them," Shylin muttered, her fingers dancing across her targeting data.

"They appear curious rather than hostile. We see no attack patterns."
"Yet."

"Roger, *Red Three. B7* out." Sibley took the Jade down over the tube, around and under the deploying salvage pen. "You know, Shy, you're starting to be a real downer."

Clutching her helmet in both hands, Presit surged forward as the air lock door opened, took one look at eighteen meters of ribbed tube stretching out to the *Promise*'s lock, and her toes clamped down on the edge of the deck.

"I are not . . ."

Before Torin could speak, Nivry grabbed the reporter from behind. "Yeah, you are."

Three long strides took her to the edge of the hull, and a graceful dive—made less graceful than di'Taykan norm by an armload of squirming Katrien—took them both out of the AG field and to the *Promise* just as the outer lock opened. She caught herself on the edge of the lock and practically threw a vehemently protesting Presit into Ryder's arms.

Torin grinned at his expression and began to strip out of Huilin's suit.

Nivry back. Huilin and Gytha.

Huilin back. Orla and the *harveer.*

Two shadows passed over the tube almost too fast to register.

"Keep it moving, people."

Orla back.

Heer and Werst with Tsui on the first stretcher, Tsui protesting all the way that he could manage without a foot in zero gee.

"Tsui."

He tilted his head enough to see her around Heer.

"Make sure nobody touches Mr. Ryder's stuff and"—she raised her voice loud enough to be heard inside *the Promise*—"gag that reporter if she doesn't shut the fuk up!"

The torrent of Katrien protests shut off.

Tsui grinned into the sudden silence. "You got it, Staff."

Still standing at the outer edge of his air lock, Ryder tossed a smile in Torin's direction. Torin, in turn, tossed Huilin his suit. And blamed any visceral reactions on residual pheromones.

Frii.

Of the serious casualties, only Harrop remained on Big Yellow.

*   *   *

"They're going for the tube, Sib!"

"I'm on them!"

A hard burst with both left and right upper thrusters, intended to drop the Jade down behind the bug, put them into a spin. Sibley swore, corrected, and raced to intercept.

"What happened?"

"Forgot about the new lefties. I hit them too hard."

Fingers gripping the edge of the panel, right thumb a whisper above the fire control, Shylin shook her head. "We may not get a lock."

"We have to."

Her hair flipped forward. "You got anything encouraging to say that's not a cliché?"

"At this hour? I doubt it." He fought to get everything he could out of the Jade. "Goddamned bug is not getting away."

"Target has flipped one-eighty. She's coming back at us, Sib."

"Good." Teeth clenched, he headed the Jade right down the bug's throat. "We'll use less fuel catching her."

One piece of the debris hit the *Promise.* The others passed to the left of the tube.

"Son of a . . . ! Torin!"

Nivry, Orla, and the stretcher holding Harrop were between them, but there was no mistaking the terror now in Ryder's voice.

"This thing won't take a direct hit from a thrown turd. If it punctures . . ."

If it punctured with both air locks open, it would at the very least decompress the smaller ship, killing everyone on it and probably sucking two or three Marines into space before the emergency protocols closed the inner doors.

She kept her own voice vaguely disinterested. "What do you suggest we do about it, Mr. Ryder?"

Nivry and Orla had Harrop inside. She could see him now. More importantly, he could see her. When she locked her gaze to his and lifted a deliberate brow, he grinned and shook his head. "I suggest we don't throw any turds."

Torin nodded. "I can support that idea."

"So." He leaned against the ship and folded his arms. "The Marines teach you to be calm in the face of disaster, or are you naturally like this?"

"The Corps believes in making use of natural ability."

He flinched as another shadow passed the tube, but it was a minor movement. Had she not been watching him so closely, she'd have missed it.

"And what do you believe in?" he wondered.

Then the two di'Taykan were pushing past him and launching themselves down the tube. Nivry landed, took three running steps to kill momentum and was safely inside Big Yellow.

Another shadow closely followed.

Orla hit the AG field with her feet still in the tube, turned the landing into a shoulder roll, and bounced upright. "I meant to do that," she muttered as she went inside.

"Captain Travik, you are coming inside now!"

About to tell Ryder to get his door closed and the tube cast off, Torin tried to remember why it had seemed like a good idea to give Presit that helmet. A quick glance at the body reminded her. The Corps had also taught her to make use of available resources. She flipped down her mike. "Presit's right, sir. You can't ride in the cargo pen, you're injured. There's room inside."

"I ride with my Marines." The voice was barely audible; the upper class Krai accent unmistakable. If this backfired, Werst could always join her in a fulfilling career in musical theater.

"But, sir . . ."

"I'm the officer, Staff Sergeant. I give the orders."

"Yes, sir."

The mike went back up. She looked down the tube toward Ryder, ignoring the Katrien who continued to babble about or to Captain Travik. "Thanks for coming back." She couldn't see past him, but she knew how crowded the small cabin had to be. Even if she hadn't known how he felt about sharing the space, she'd have seen it in the way he rocked back and forth, muscles rigid. A muscle had to be damned rigid to see it from eighteen meters away. "And as much as I'd enjoy standing here talking to you all day, get your ass inside." She reached out and tapped the tube. "Dump this. Get the salvage pen below the lock and as close to the hull as you can. Once we're in, just concentrate on getting us back to the *Berganitan* in one piece."

"Just?" He looked like he was about to launch himself toward her.

"Just keep doing what I tell you, and everything'll be fine."

Half a smile showed in the shadow of his beard. "Words to live by, then?"

"People do. I've been thinking . . ."

"When did you have time?"

"Shut up. Did you give your implant codes to anyone on the *Berg*? Then run mine into the program the *Promise* uses to contact you," she continued quickly when he shook his head. "You can talk to me any time you need to with no one else being the wiser."

"How did you know I . . . ?" He shook his head again, more in wonder this time. "Never mind. Stupid question. It's your job to know."

"You're not part of my job—but I think I'll keep you alive anyway." Stepping back, she reached for the lock controls. "Inside. Now." The tone that had terrified a thousand recruits pushed him into the ship as effectively as if she'd reached out a hand and shoved. "Close up and go." Hand raised, she didn't touch her controls until she saw his door close.

And that was all she could do for him right now. He had to get through the next bit without her.

She had problems of her own.

"Uh, Staff. You better come see this."

Already suited, Dursinski had remained on guard at the barricade.

Sealing the front of a mercifully pheromone-free suit, Torin ran to join her.

The bug was standing in the center of the passage. She wore no armor. She carried no weapons. All four arms were spread. The air smelled of cinnamon and melted butter.

"What the fuk's she doing?" Dursinski's benny took a bead on the bug's head.

Torin pushed it down. "She's surrendering."

Werst limped up beside them and snorted derisively. "The Others don't let their soldiers surrender."

"Granted, but this lot has lost contact with their ship. They have no leaders left alive. They recognize the sound of an engine and they know what it means as well as we do. They're desperate. They don't want to die."

"Who does?" Dursinski sighed.

Two more bugs came out into the passage, armorless, weaponless, carrying vaguely familiar gear across their arms. Behind them, two more.

"And," Torin continued, "they've got their own suits."

"You can't trust them, Staff." Nivry's voice came from behind her left shoulder.

"They're the enemy," Werst agreed.

"I don't trust them." She handed her benny to the corporal and stepped beyond the barricade. "But I'm not leaving them here."

"This is fukkin' weird," Johnston muttered, shrugging his suit up over his shoulders.

Settling his tank, Heer glanced over at the five surviving bugs getting into their own suits under the supervision of Dursinski's and Jynett's weapons. "This is fukkin' history," he amended, ridges flared.

"I flunked history."

"And now you're part of it. Weird or what?" He tucked his head into the collar ring and came up with his emergency rations tube in his mouth. "Soup's on and life is good."

Johnston grimaced as the other engineer swallowed with every indication of enjoyment. "You want to talk about weird . . ."

"Salvage pen's in place. Any time, Torin."

"First group's on their way."

The first group consisted of four Marines and two bugs. Torin, the captain's body still propped behind her, opened the outer doors and motioned them forward. The bugs' reaction transcended both the lack of a common language and the bulk of their suits. They took one look and backed up, pushing Marines and weapons both out of their way.

"We don't have time for this. Nivry."

Torin grabbed the back of the corporal's suit as she stepped out into space. A push and release sent her angling down into the pen.

"Johnston."

"But . . ."

"Now."

Two Marines safely loaded reassured the bugs.

When we get a minute, I'll have to find out what "you guys are fukking idiots" smells like, Torin mused, pitching the last of the first group. "Half done, Ryder. We're . . ."

As she closed the outer doors, the background vibrations moved suddenly to the foreground. "Fuk!"

"Torin?"

"Not now!"

Inner doors open.

"Get in here! Move!"

Everyone remaining in Big Yellow surged forward.

Inner doors closed.

"Here!" Torin tossed the loop of rope still connecting her and Captain Travik. "Grab hold!"

The three bugs imitated the Marines.

Torin slapped the outer control panel.

"Staff! The pressure hasn't . . ."

"Just hang on!"

The outer doors opened. Five Marines, three bugs, and the rope sucked past her into space. Torin's boots held but only just. "Another chance for you to be a hero," she muttered, grabbing Captain Travik's body with both hands, aiming him toward the clump of Marines now tethered in the pen, and throwing him as hard as she was able.

The outer door began to close.

Torin released her boots as the rope around her waist jerked her out through the rapidly disappearing opening. She swore as the door slammed her injured arm and spun her around, Marines, bugs, pen, *Promise*, all spinning against a background of stars.

"Get your thumbs out of your butts and pull us in!" she snapped. "Ryder! Get moving!"

"But you're . . ."

"Six meters from a ship that's about to fire main engines!"

The first two bodies on the rope were in the pen.

"My engines . . ."

"Are one thousandth the fukking size!"

Three. Four.

She'd stopped spinning and was now moving steadily toward the pen.

Two bugs holding as much to each other as the rope slipped inside.

They were probably thinking they should have stayed with Big Yellow. Not that she blamed them.

Below her, below the salvage pen, the *Promise* began to move.

Too goddamned slow! Her breath sounded unusually loud in her ears.

The rope jerked violently.

Someone screamed.

Torin threw out her arms and instinctively grabbed the body that slammed into her.

"I thought I told you to hold on!" she gasped, hoping the rib had cracked and not actually broken.

"*Sorry . . . Staff . . .*" Orla's voice sounded wet and bubbling.

"You hurt?"

Her boots touched the outside of the pen.

"*I . . . don't . . . I don't . . . I . . . I . . .*"

There was no mistaking the sound of someone puking into a comm unit.

As the rope dragged them down into the pen, Torin reached around and hit the external controls for Orla's cleanup suction, passing her off to reaching hands in almost the same move.

"We lose anyone?" she asked as Nivry pulled her to a strap beside the captain's body. The bugs were strapped along the back wall, the Marines to the sides just above the angled sections that kept the pen from being rectangular.

"Acceleration drove the edge of the pen into Huilin's thigh. Bone snapped, but it didn't break the skin and his suit's fine. He'll . . ."

The universe became brilliant yellow-white light.

Torin's helmet polarized instantly, going completely opaque. Still, she could see nothing but glowing blotches burned into her eyes. The temperature inside her suit began to rise. "Marines! Sound off by number!"

Only eight of the original twelve, but she heard from all eight. Huilin and Orla both sounded like shit, but they were alive.

She had no way of checking on the bugs.

She was sweating now. Squinting, she could just make out the readout on the left curve of her collar. Environmental controls placed the highest temperatures where her suit was touching the pen. "Marines, loosen your straps. Move out from the sides but do not, I repeat, do *not* unstrap completely."

One of the great things about vacuum, it didn't hold heat.

"*Torin!*"

Her helmet beginning to clear, still tied to the captain, and unable to tell the bugs to move away from the pen, she headed back to physically shift them. "We're still here." One bug was totally unresponsive; alive or dead,

Torin couldn't know. One clutched at her in terror. Pain shooting along her left side, she barely managed to break free.

"What the hell happened out there?" she demanded, dragging herself back one-handed along the rope to her place between Nivry and the captain.

"Big Yellow's gone."

And that meant the rules had changed.

SEVENTEEN

"Captain Carveg! Our engines are back on-line!"

"Captain Carveg! The Others' ship has simultaneously sent a message to every fighter!"

"Captain Carveg! Mr. Ryder reports he has surviving Marines, scientists, and bugs on board."

The last report shut off the noise in C3—from chaos to quiet in an instant. All eyes lifted from monitors and data streams and turned to the captain.

She alone was looking at the lieutenant charged with monitoring the *Promise*. "Mr. Ryder has bugs on board?"

"Yes, ma'am. He says the last five bugs surrendered and are in suits in the salvage pen with the Marines."

"Prisoners of war."

Not entirely certain it was a question, the lieutenant answered anyway. "Yes, ma'am."

"Right." Captain Carveg straightened in her command chair, adrenaline banishing exhaustion. Those species who fought for the Others—or *were* the Others, no one knew for certain—never surrendered. And now Staff Sergeant Kerr was returning to the *Berganitan* with five. Things were about to get interesting. "Engineering, I want full maneuverability five minutes ago!"

"Aye, aye, Captain."

"Flight Control, let our pilots know the bugs are likely to attempt some kind of unified attack."

"Aye, aye, Captain."

"Lieutenant Demoln, see that Mr. Ryder is kept informed." She reached out and slapped her palm down on the touch pad. "All hands, battle stations!"

*   *   *

Torin was really beginning to miss the quiet inside Big Yellow. "Sir, Captain Travik saved the life of Presit a Tur durValintrisy, Sector Central News' star reporter. She'll make sure everyone knows it. Even without Big Yellow, you've got what you needed. Captain Travik is a hero."

"And he commanded the mission that captured five of the enemy," the general added thoughtfully.

"They weren't exactly captured, sir. They surrendered."

"Perhaps."

Perhaps? Torin sagged back against the side of the pen, the material no longer hot enough to damage her suit. The stim she'd taken had cleared her head and washed the fatigue from her body but it hadn't changed the fact that it had been a very long day.

"As far as the public needs to know, they were captured. We don't need to tell all we know, Staff Sergeant."

She glanced over at the captain's body, her tone carefully neutral. "Yes, sir."

"We can count on the captain to say anything he feels is in his best interest."

She could see the general, sitting at his desk, fat fingers spread on either side of the raised comm unit.

"Pity that reporter's crew person got killed."

"As well as nine scientists, Navy Lieutenant Czerneda, and Private First Class August Guimond. Sir."

"All deaths are . . ."

"Strap in tight, mates!" Ryder's shout over the group channel cut the general off in mid-platitude. *"We're about to be swarmed."*

"Never a bug zapper around when you need one," Sibley muttered, slamming on his thrusters and moving away from the salvage pen to give himself more room to maneuver. "Looks like every bug out here's heading this way."

"B1 to squadron. Heads up, team, we're about to be visited by every goddamned bug with wings."

"Didn't I just say that?" He switched to the squadron's frequency. "You got a number on every goddamned bug, *B1?*"

"Five squadrons minus the ones we've taken out. A whole fukking lot of bugs."

"Roger that. Tell me, how did we get so popular?"

"Maybe they're attracted to your sparkling personality, Sib. Defensive pattern 12-4-2, people. We let the bugs come to us and hope the rest of the group knocks a few out before they get here."

"They're not having much luck," Shylin observed dryly.

Although the Jades were significantly more maneuverable, the bug fighters flew a lot faster in a straight line and they were heading right for the *Promise*.

Black Star Squadron had lost three Jades—Boom Boom's *B8* had been destroyed, *B2* and *B11* had been grounded; *B2* with no loss of life, but *B11*'s gunner had taken a jagged edge of the control panel in the throat. The twelve Jades remaining in the squadron moved into a two-on defensive pattern, four pairs defending the *Promise*'s four main axis points, two pairs free to go where they were most needed.

Sibley found himself beside *B6*, matching the *Promise*'s speed a half a kilometer out from the stern of the cargo pod.

"I've got fifty-two bugs on my screen, Sib. There's no way twelve of us will be able to stop them."

"Well, not with that attitude."

Light flared in the distance.

"Now there's fifty-one." Sibley grinned. "Piece of cake."

"They're moving too fast to be locked."

"Then they're moving too fast to lock—they'll have to slow down to get a shot off." Lifting his hand, he ran through a quick series of finger exercises, then laid them over the complex keypads that controlled the Jade's thrusters. "I'm ready. Bring 'em on."

"Maybe not," she declared with more energy than he'd heard in hours. "Sib, I need Flight Command."

"Group, this is Flight Command! Gunners who have a shot, lock missiles on the bug fighters' trajectories. Repeat, lock missiles on the trajectories, not the fighters."

*　　*　　*

"We know where they're going, and we know they're taking the shortest way there, so we let missiles and bugs run into each other—very smart, Shy. There's gonna be pats on the head for you."

"How nice for me," Shylin replied absently, feeding the last of the data into her targeting computer. "Permission to fire two remaining PGMs."

Sibley grinned. For a regulation question it had sounded a lot like a statement. "Permission granted. Fire away."

Forty-eight. Forty-two.

The flares of light made a pattern of destruction against the stars.

"You'd think seeing other fighters blow would bug them just a little. Enough to try something else."

"They know there's more of them than there are PGMs remaining."

"Would they be . . ."

"Ablin gon savit!"

"What?" He jerked against the restriction of his webbing.

"We lost a Jade in a debris field." A moment later on the small side monitors that showed Jades in the field, a call sign began flashings. *"Red Nine.* Jan Elson and Dierik."

The webbing felt like it was getting tighter with every second that passed. "I fukking hate waiting. You know, I once saw Dierik eat half a dozen pouches of that crap the grunts call field rations."

"Probably enjoyed them, too."

"Said it reminded him of his *jernil's* funeral."

More flares. Closer now.

Thirty-seven.

"And why the hell can't I take evasive action?" Ryder demanded, his screens showing three dozen bug fighters plus one still heading right for him.

"You're easier for the Jades to protect if they know where you are. You start changing your trajectory, and half their attention switches to you. Just let our people deal with this, Mr. Ryder. It's what they do."

Yeah, well, under normal circumstances, he'd be heading for Susumi space and the hell with sucking small fighters in with him. Unfortunately, he had live cargo in salvage pens and although the field would extend to cover them, they wouldn't survive even a short jump.

Not that the odds of them surviving thirty-seven enemy fighters were a lot better.

We are all going to die.

Too late to stop himself from thinking about exactly how many "we all" were.

Crap.

Denial was a wonderful thing—while it worked.

His muscles had knotted so tightly it felt as though daggers had been driven into the back of his neck, and every time he had to move his arms, pain shot from his spine to his shoulders. He *knew* he had six people in the cabin with him, but as long as they were quiet, he'd been able to ignore them. The Katrien had helped by locking themselves in the head with Presit's small recorder when he'd told them they were going out the air lock if they didn't shut the fuk up about the light levels.

Two of the Marines were unconscious. The Niln was sleeping, snoring anyway. He could feel Ken Tsui's gaze on the back of his head.

Carbon dioxide levels were rising.

He couldn't breathe.

He had to turn around. Had to. Not a good idea.

The only thing he could hear was his own heartbeat.

His fingers were trembling as he had the *Promise* contact Torin's implant. Never very good at subvocalizing, he had no idea what was about to come out of his mouth and no desire to have either the general or the *Berganitan*'s comm station listening in. The eavesdroppers behind him were plenty.

"Torin."

I'm here.

All at once, the situation didn't seem so dire. Her voice gave him a new focus. He wished he knew how she did it but, for now, it was enough to be able to draw a full breath. "Jades took out nearly a third of the bugs. Still three dozen coming in, though."

We can see them.

She sounded bored. As if being strapped into a salvage pen while three dozen enemy fighters blasted through a mere dozen defenders was something she did every day. Ryder grinned. Maybe it was.

"Navy says we should trust them to do their jobs."

As Dursinski would say, Goddamned Navy.

Dursinski. He had a sudden vision of her, blonde brows drawn tight into a worried frown. Since she seemed happiest with something to worry about, she was probably ecstatic right about now.

"Is everyone okay?"

Yeah, most of them are sleeping.

"Sleeping?"

*Why not? You get those bugs to climb in here with us and we'll kick ass; until then, it's been a long . . . *

The *Promise*'s small port polarized too slowly to prevent purple-white dots from dancing across his vision. "Torin!"

"We're fine," she snorted, switching back to group channel for her answer, her tone making it quite clear she had no intention of allowing her people to be anything but fine. "You might not be aware of this, but it takes more than bright lights to damage a Marine. We've been highly trained to deal with loud noises, too."

Someone snickered. It sounded like a di'Taykan. Nivry probably. The Corps had to have put her through at least one leadership course and this situation was tailor-made for that last lesson in Combat Morale, *"If you're going to die anyway, see to it that your people die with dry underwear and a smile."*

"We don't usually get to watch the vacuum jockeys work from such good seats," Torin continued before Ryder could respond. "Maybe we'll finally find out why they get the big . . ."

Not so bright this time, although the salvage pen rocked.

". . . bucks."

"So if there's three bugs for each of us, why the fuk are there five bugs on me!" Unable to take either hand from the thruster controls, Sibley jerked his head toward the stars.

"At least they haven't got a clear shot off." Shylin's hair stood out from her head in a cadmium nimbus. "And . . . I've . . . got . . . Damn it, Sib." The salvage pen was now straight up. "How am I supposed to take them out when you keep . . ."

The Jade slid down forty-five degrees to port and flipped ninety degrees.

"Saving our collective ass?"

"Yeah. That. I need a clear target; we've only got small stuff left."

"The AR-67s?"

"One."

"We had four!"

"Now we have one. And after that it's PFUs only."

"And after that we throw cocktail weenies—get ready."

A one-eighty flip and a short burst on the rear thrusters.

Shylin's shot hit the bug fighter a glancing blow, spun it into another fighter's path, and sent the two of them careening out of control.

"You know for a cadmium-haired sex maniac, you're a decent shot."

"Thanks. For a . . ."

"Superior officer."

". . . Human, you're a decent pilot."

"Was that an insult?"

"Up to you."

Starboard thrusters. Full topside. The bottom of the Jade skimmed the side of the pen.

"Fuk!" Dursinski twisted around in her strapping. "I could read 'made by the H'san coalition' on the bottom of that thing!"

"You can read?" Werst snorted.

"Up yours."

Morale seemed fine, Torin noted.

"Squadron's down to ten. *B5* lost starboard thrusters, *B3* lost power. She's drifting, but the bugs are ignoring her."

"Great time to be an odd number." Sibley slid them between two fighters, throwing one off course. The other got by. "Ryder! Heads up!"

"Heads up? Oh, that's helpful, mate. Just bloody helpful." An early shot had fried a rack of the *Promise*'s processors. Fire control was now manual. So was the coffeemaker, but with green smoke gathering under the ceiling, that didn't seem as crucial somehow. *Not that I'd turn down an offered double double . . .*

One of the port thrusters had taken a direct hit from debris, and although it continued to fire, its angle had to continually be adjusted.

If he'd been an inch shorter, he wouldn't be able to handle the board.

"Can I help?"

Goddamn it! He didn't have enough going on—what with being the fukking center of attention and all? He had to have someone breathing down the back of his neck? Breathing his oxygen. Limited oxygen.

"Ryder!"

He jerked, realized two new trouble lights were flashing red, that the two systems he'd been monitoring were fluctuating wildly, that he was sitting frozen in place by a panic attack.

And he realized that he didn't want to die, that the odds of being killed by the *Promise* blowing apart around him were significantly better than by half a dozen unwelcome passengers sucking up his oxygen, that he needed help.

Turning, he found Tsui gripping the back of the control chair, balanced on his one remaining foot.

Fuk! The Marine really had been breathing down the back of his neck.

And so what? Ryder surged up out of the seat and practically threw the smaller man down into it, grabbing his wrist and slapping his hand down by the thruster control. "Keep that between seventy-five and seventy-nine degrees! Use your other hand to code in seven-slash-slash-three every time that bar lights up red."

"What am I doing?" Tsui demanded as Ryder moved to the other side of the board.

"Does it matter?" He glanced down at the stump of the Marine's left leg. "Doesn't that hurt?"

"Neural blockers," Tsui explained. "I'm good for another twenty minutes. After that . . ."

". . . we'll be in the clear or we'll be in pieces."

"A great big hunk of the *Promise* just blew by."

"Important hunk?" Shylin asked without looking up.

"Apparently not."

Ninety-degree flip, two seconds of forward thrusters; a last instant deflection of one of the enemy's small missiles from the salvage pen.

"I'm guessing they don't care there's also bugs in that pen."

"I think that's the point, Sib."

"Take out the prisoners before they talk?"

"Or whatever it is that bugs do."

He brought them around for another run. "You ever get the feeling we're playing by different rules?"

"You and me?"

"Us and . . ."

The bug fighter didn't bother slowing down to take a shot. It hit the side of the salvage pen farthest from the *Promise*, cutting through the metal latticework, shearing off the last third of the pen.

Torin had been the last one into the pen, the closest—but for Captain Travik—to the end and the bugs. She didn't see the fighter approach, but the impact jerked the strap up against her cracked ribs and turned her bones to jelly. The universe slowed. The pen began to tear. The fighter slammed past. She saw stars through the deck plates. Realized her boots were attached to the piece breaking away.

The universe sped up again.

Boot release.

Boot release.

Boot release!

Pain.

Fingers of her right hand locked around a broken strap, Torin dangled into space, the rope around her waist only a meter long and ending in a charred fray.

The bugs were gone. The end of the pen was gone. Captain Travik's body was gone. The piece of deck that had been under her boots was also gone and had nearly taken her with it. Fortunately, the straps had held until she got the magnetic field off. On the down side, the ribs that had been cracked were now definitely broken and every breath was agony.

She brought her head around so she could stare into the ruin of the pen.

Only the captain and the bugs seemed to be missing.

"You lot must fukking live right. Well, don't just stand there staring," she added through clenched teeth. "Pull me in." The only response was a continuing stunned silence as every eye stared out at the stars wheeling by as the *Promise* continued the spin begun by the impact. "NOW!"

Shock fled, chased off by a more immediate danger.

Her boots firmly locked, Nivry leaned out to the extent of her straps, grabbed Torin's lifeline and yanked.

The pain Torin'd been feeling in her upper arm exploded.

"Staff?"

She didn't remember making a noise, but it seemed she had. "The chemical burn. Should've grabbed on with my other hand."

"Your other hand?" Nivry set her into the pen. "You should be *dead.*"

"Well, thank you, Corporal."

"No. I mean . . . Look!" A gloved hand gestured past Torin's shoulder.

"I don't think so." She couldn't open the fingers of her right hand. Her brain knew that she was safe, that her boots were remagged and firmly connected to the deck, that Nivry had pulled out new straps and she'd been resecured, but her body wasn't taking any chances. *Fine. Good. Smart body.*

A quick glance at the readouts running along her collar showed Huilin was unconscious—"Johnston, you're showing a small leak. Find it and patch it! Heer, give him a hand." Everyone's respiration and heartbeat was up, and most of the suits were dealing with extra liquids.

No surprise.

"Staff Sergeant Kerr! What's going on out there! I want a full repor . . ."

"With all due respect, sir . . ." Standing stiffly at attention, Lieutenant Stedrin lifted his hand from the general's desk. ". . . this is not the time."

General Morris stared from his inoperative comm unit to his aide. "What the hell do you think you're doing, Lieutenant?"

"Preventing Staff Sergeant Kerr from telling you to get . . . stuffed. Sir."

Torin!

Torin didn't know what miracle had cut off the general, but this was a voice she wanted to hear.

Torin, are you all right?

"More or less. We lost the bugs, and the captain. Everyone else is still here. You?"

AG field's out. We got knocked around, but no one's badly hurt. I don't have the kind of external visuals you lot do, but it looks like the bugs are trying something new!

The skin between her shoulder blades tightened.

"Oh, that's just fukking great."

*   *   *

"Now that's more like it! Think you can outfly me? Dream on, bug breath!"

"Sib! All the fighters are moving away from the *Promise*. The squadron's following!"

"And we're driving them right into the rest of the group!"

"That doesn't make sense!"

"They took out the bug POWs! You saw the bits go spinning into space."

"They can't know they've got all of them."

"Then . . . Oy, mama." The Jade flipped one-eighty. They came around just as a large hunk of debris hit its thrusters and turned into a fighter.

It began to accelerate straight toward the broken end of the pen.

"I'm not reading any weapons."

Sibley raced disaster back toward the salvage ship. "It doesn't need a weapon. Remember how they took out the shuttle."

"They're going to ram . . ."

"Rams eat oats and does eat oats and little lambs eat ivy."

"What?"

"Human thing."

"Uh, Staff. I think you'd better turn around."

Something in Nivry's voice overcame the fear paralysis—part of it anyway. Fingers still clutching the broken strap, Torin turned.

The bug fighter was some distance away but closing fast.

"Ryder, now would be a good time for evasive action."

Love to, but I've lost most of my power relays.

"So use the rest."

Hey, if you don't like the way I'm driving, you can get out and walk.

"It might be safer," Torin acknowledged as the fighter grew rapidly larger. And just because she couldn't stand and do nothing, she swung her benny around onto her hip.

"Sib, we don't have anything big enough to stop it! And we're low on fuel. If we've got to do much maneuvering . . ."

"Won't be a problem," he interrupted, "'cause I've got a plan."

"Which is?"

He dropped the Jade into the bug's trajectory and hit all thrusters.

"Oh. Good plan. And we're ejecting at the last minute?"

"You are. I'm staying in case she blinks."

"Compound eyes don't blink, Sib."

"I know." Amazed by how calm he sounded, he reached out and hit the release for Shylin's half of the pod. As it blew clear, sealing him into his own small space, he forced his hands away from the thruster controls as the bug fighter filled his forward port. "Buh-bye . . ."

"Vacuum jockeys; goddamned show-offs," Dursinski muttered, her voice cracking with emotion.

"Convinced me they're worth what they're paid," Werst grunted.

Torin nodded and opened her eyes. She'd see that final explosion every time she closed them for months. But that was how it should be—sacrifice should be remembered. Honored.

Torin! All fighters have flipped one-eighty and are heading back!

She sighed. She could feel the Marines around her thinking, *"A single ship attempting to ram failed. They'll ram with everything they've got now."*

And the Others' ship is . . . Fuk!

Which, in Torin's professional opinion, was a fairly accurate assessment of the situation.

The Others' ship loomed suddenly to the rear of the pen, blocking out an impossibly huge section of the stars.

"This is it. We're going to die."

Eyes narrowed, Torin glared out at the ship. "Not until I say so, we aren't."

"Get real, Staff, you can't stop . . ."

The *Berganitan* swooped in over the *Promise*, angling her bulk between the surviving Marines and the enemy. While she might have been small next to Big Yellow, she was immense at this range and kept coming for what seemed like hours although it couldn't have been more than minutes.

"Saw 'made by the H'san coalition' on the bottom of that, too," Dursinski muttered.

Torin's temperature and radiation gauges shot into the black, and her suit began to overheat.

Then the destroyer was past and the Others were on the run.

"Staff Sergeant Kerr, this is Captain Carveg. Sorry we had to come in so close, but we wanted to hit the Others where they wouldn't expect it. You lot all right?"

The temperature gauge began to drop as empty space wrapped around them again.

"We got a little cooked, but we're okay."

"They're running for Susumi, so we'll be back in a few minutes to pick you up."

"We'll be here, ma'am." And so much for the one loose end. There was nothing like the backwash from a destroyer to wipe the memory off a slate. And off the suits . . . "Marines, check your environmental controls."

"Staff, my clock's out."

"You got an appointment somewhere, Jynett?"

"I'd like to have a chat with my recruiting sergeant," the di'Taykan sighed, her hair fanning out to connect with the reflected stars on her helmet. "But I guess it can wait."

"Glad to hear it."

By the time Torin stood on the *Berganitan*'s shuttle deck and pushed her helmet back, she could hardly stand the smell of herself. The panting she'd had to do in order to breathe around her broken ribs was probably the only thing keeping the stink bearable.

Stripping carefully out of the suit, she was pleased to note Captain Carveg had made sure that the closest Navy personnel when the di'Taykan Marines broke seal were other di'Taykans. The release of trapped pheromones was so strong it roused Huilin out of his stupor as they laid him on a stretcher, and he grabbed the nearest corpsman's ass.

Fortunately, the *Berganitan*'s scrubbers cleared the air before much of it reached the Humans and the Krai.

Tsui, Harrop, and Frii were already in Med-op, the *Promise* having been a lot easier to unload than a salvage pen with no air lock.

"Staff!"

She turned, took too deep a breath, realized the problem the instant the fog cleared from her vision. "Go with the corpsman, Werst."

"I'm fine!"

"You broke your toe. Go."

"You're next, Staff Sergeant."

Another turn. A more careful breath. And the sudden realization that long lines of red ran out from the cracks in the seal over the chemical burn, down her arm, and dripped off her fingers. She could see that the pair of corpsmen, an AG stretcher between them, were waiting for an argument. It didn't seem worth it to give them one.

Torin?

It seemed the backwash hadn't wiped her codes from the *Promise*. Activating her implant, she subvocalized, *Fine. You?*

The medical officer working on her arm glanced up, assumed Torin was talking with one of her own officers, and continued repairing the damage done by the chemical burn.

They won't let me see you. Some crap about both of us needing to be debriefed.

No crap. Policy.

More crap. I'm a civilian.

Later.

"Can I take it from your smile that your general is pleased with you?" the doctor asked as she tongued off her implant.

Was she smiling? She was.

"Too bad he's not pleased enough to give you more time in here," he continued, stepping back. "I've bonded the ribs, but they'll be tender for a while, so no rough stuff. And lots of fluids—you may be a little light-headed from the loss of blood."

Light-headed. Good. There was a medical explanation.

Ken Tsui was being fitted for a regeneration tank that would extend down from his left knee; Torin couldn't get in to see him. Frii and Harrop had been fully tanked the moment they'd arrived in Medical. The doctors were cautiously optimistic they'd both make it. Huilin's leg had been bonded, and he'd been given a sedative that should keep him under until the *Berganitan* reached Susumi space. The rest were being checked over, cuts and bruises and minor injuries attended to.

Torin motioned the corpsman out of Werst's cubicle and stepped in.

"They hosed us down first," he grunted, bare feet swinging half a meter above the deck. "You'd think they'd build these fukkers Krai size."

"That is Krai size," Torin snorted. "On a Human table, I can't touch the deck."

"You're here to tell me I can change my mind, aren't you?"

She opened her mouth and closed it again as he kept talking without pausing for a reply.

"I can read it on your face, Staff." He scratched up under his robe and shook his head, facial ridges clamped shut as he locked his eyes on hers. "You do what you have to to get the job done—you don't like that you had to involve me. Don't worry about it. The captain's a hero, the mission was a success, we weren't where Guimond could throw himself on a grenade to save eighteen people for no good reason." His facial ridges began to slowly open as the words spilled out, more words than Torin had heard him speak the whole time she'd known him. "I had a buddy once. Knew him most of my life. We joined up together, went through Ventris together. He was Krai, not Human, but big and friendly and didn't have a bad thing to say about shit. He died our first time out. Antipersonnel missile took his big, fukking, friendly head right off.

"Why is it the big, fukkin', friendly ones who die, Staff?"

"They're not the only ones who die, Werst, it's just we miss them more than the short, fukkin', cranky ones."

He grinned reluctantly. "So you're not going to miss me when I get it?"

Torin tightened her fingers around the cylinder in her hand. "No more than everyone else I lose."

Lieutenant Stedrin glanced up as Torin entered the outer office. "General Morris will be with you in a minute, Staff Sergeant. The reporter is still with him."

"Thank you, sir." She walked over to the edge of the desk. "I'd like to also thank you for taking General Morris off the comm unit."

He jerked and his pale eyes darkened. "How did you know . . . ?"

She hadn't. Not until this instant. Which she was not going to mention. "It's my job to know these things."

"What things?"

"What officers can be depended on, sir. I hope you didn't get in too much trouble on my behalf."

"He was annoyed," the lieutenant admitted reluctantly, pale blue hair flipping back and forth over the points of his ears.

Torin raised a single brow.

"Okay, he was furious." Stedrin shrugged, the graceful motion pure di'Taykan. His small rebellion seemed to have loosened his body language.

"But there's just him and me out here and he needs me, so, hopefully, he'll get over it before . . ." He surged up to his feet as the door opened.

"I are happy I are having had this talk with you, General." Presit—her fur brushed, her nails repainted, her dark glasses back in place—minced out of the inner office. "I are looking forward to integrating earlier vids of the brave Captain Travik into our full story."

Face wreathed in smiles, the general followed close behind. "The resources of the Corps are at your disposal, ma'am."

"I are thanking you, so much." Her head turned and Torin found herself staring at her reflection in the reporter's glasses. "And the Staff Sergeant?" she asked, her tone as pointed as her teeth.

"Will be dealt with."

"Good."

"Lieutenant Stedrin, if you could escort our guest out of the Marine attachment?"

"Yes, sir!"

Torin had never heard a response snapped off with such perfect military delivery. Lieutenant Stedrin was reinforcing his chances of forgiveness with a little spit and polish.

When the outer door closed, General Morris stepped back, clearing access to his office. "Staff Sergeant Kerr . . ."

Torin took up the usual position in front of his desk, staring at the usual spot on the wall.

"At ease, Staff Sergeant. I hate it when you do that."

"Yes, sir." She dropped into a perfect parade rest—the lieutenant wasn't the only one who knew when to smooth off any rough edges. "Do what?"

"Stare at the damned wall. Makes me feel like I'm not in the room." He sighed deeply, dropped into his chair, and laid both hands flat on his desk. "Why did I bring you on this mission, Staff Sergeant?"

Hers was not to question why. *Because you're my own, personal, two-star pain in the ass.* "To keep Captain Travik alive, sir."

"Yes, to keep Captain Travik alive. Which he isn't. Still, his final acts of heroism were enough to generate an amazing amount of good PR—essentially keeping him alive."

The general seemed pleased and he'd damn well better be—it wasn't every day Torin *essentially* raised the dead.

"Presit is more than willing to put the captain back onto his media pedestal and then crank it up a few levels. I suspect she's motivated as much by his actions as by her dislike of you and her belief that elevating the captain is the best way to get under your skin."

Interesting. Although the statement could certainly be taken at face value, it was possible the reporter knew more of what was really going on than Torin had thought. *You are thinking you are so smart, Staff Sergeant. I are making sure you are getting none of the credit.*

Not that it much mattered what her motivations were as long as the result was the same.

Leaning forward, General Morris' voice dropped into a low growl. "Did you actually threaten to blow her head off, Staff Sergeant Kerr?"

"No, sir."

"Not in so many words, sir," he mocked. "Fortunately for you, she seems content to have me deal with you." The fingers of his right hand drummed out a slow beat. "Don't do it again. The Corps is not in the habit of making idle threats."

Idle threats. No doubt the general's word choice came out of a few hours spent in the Katrien's voluble company.

"As welcome as the media coverage is," the general continued, "it won't bring Captain Travik back to life and that means he can't be promoted to command rank."

"Yes, sir. The way I see it, we all win."

"Explain yourself, Staff Sergeant."

"I have every confidence that the general can use the amazing amount of good PR to placate the Krai in Parliament to the extent that the captain's intended promotion will be forgotten."

"Yes." The single syllable dripped suspicion. Torin was willing to grant he had precedent for the emotion. "But how do *you* win?"

"Captain Travik would have been promoted for political reasons." She dipped her head just enough to meet his gaze. "Political officers in command positions aren't good for the Corps. Sir."

He stared at her for a long moment. His eyes narrowed. "Are you *sure* your parents were married, Staff Sergeant?" he asked at last.

Torin kept her face expressionless. "Yes, sir."

"When we get back, I suggest you check the paperwork. For now, tell me why—Captain Travik's heroism aside—this whole mission wasn't a total waste of time."

"Two reasons, sir. First—as regards the enemy. We kicked ass."

"And that would be your professional, combat NCO's opinion?" the general snorted.

"Yes, sir." Answer the question not the tone. "We learned more about how the bugs fight and how they think. How they react when they've lost their leadership. Intelligence can use the data to extrapolate cultural practices. We brought back one of their weapons. Next time we meet them, we'll be better prepared and they'll have nothing but the knowledge of getting their ass kicked. Second—as regards Big Yellow; granted, we learned very little about the ship or the species who built it. We don't know why it was here, where it came from, or where it was going. But . . ." She drew in a deep breath and let it out slowly. "But I think it was on a fact-finding mission and I think it learned the best about us."

"The best?"

"Yes, sir." She held out her arm, opened her fingers over his desk, and let Guimond's cylinder fall from her hand. "One life, freely given, so that eighteen could live. I can't think of anything I'd rather have an alien intelligence learn."

The general picked up the cylinder and turned it over and over between his fingers. Maybe he was remembering the thirteen she'd handed him at the end of the last "special" mission he'd sent her on. Maybe he was just staring at his reflection. Torin couldn't know.

"All right, Staff Sergeant." He closed his fingers, enclosing the cylinder in his hand much as she had. "Let's go over the whole thing from the moment the shuttle blew."

"Yes, sir."

"Dave."

Chief Warrant Officer Graham looked up from his phase welder, waved, and powered down. "Torin." He pulled off his safety glasses as he walked over to the hatch. "What brings you into the depths?"

She nodded past him at the empty docking bay. "That. Well, not that specifically, but I wanted to thank the pilots who saw to it we got home. But Marine Corps staff sergeants don't just walk in on Navy pilots, so I hoped you would pass it on for me."

"*That* specifically, then. This was Lieutenant Commander Sibley's bay. He's the one who slammed his Jade down the bug's throat."

The explosion played out again on the back of Torin's eyes. It was never a stranger. "We saw a half pod eject."

"His gunner. We picked her up just before we got you. She's still tanked—di'Taykan." He shifted his glasses from one hand to another. "They feel these things more, you know."

The two noncoms locked eyes for a long moment—grieving, anger, understanding, shared.

The *Promise* no longer quite filled shuttle bay four. The damaged salvage pen was one bay over—without the stacked panels the ship had a little more headroom. Considering the damage she'd taken, she didn't look bad. Or good, for that matter.

The hatch was open and the ramp was down.

The only sound as Torin made her way up the ramp was the soft and ever-present hum of Susumi space stroking the *Berganitan*'s outer hull. Which was drowned out as she reached the top of the ramp by a stream of inventive profanity.

She stopped, her boots carefully on the ramp side of the tiny lock, and leaned inside. "You need some help?"

Ryder was lying on his back, half under the control panel, both muscular arms raised and buried elbow deep. She almost expected him to jerk up and crack his head, but he just lifted it enough to be able to see her and grinned. "Why aren't I surprised that you can fix one of these things?"

"Sorry, I can't. But I have friends on the *Berganitan*." Friends who right now were mourning the losses of their Jades and the crews who flew them. "If you want me to put a word in . . ."

"Thanks, but Captain Carveg has already offered to send over any help I need."

"Captain Carveg's a good captain, but I doubt she knows who the best mechanics are."

"'Cause she's not a staff sergeant?"

"Sad but true. I'd have been by sooner, but this is the first downtime I've had."

"Me, too."

"I know, the *Promise* told me. You've haven't taken my codes out of her system."

"Son of a bitch, I knew I was forgetting to do something." He slid out into the limited floor space, stood, and held out his hand. "Come in."

In his place, she'd have thought it insulting to be asked if he was sure, so she didn't ask. The cabin was small enough to put them very close. Small enough to force the issue. She could smell the mix of sweat and grease coming off him and it seemed to be having the same effect as di'Taykan pheromones.

"So." Blue eyes gleaming, he scratched his beard with the charred edge of the processor rack. "What would you have done with the captain's body if the bugs hadn't conveniently removed him for you?"

Torin shrugged. "Brought him back to a hero's welcome."

"A dead hero's welcome."

"You can't tell the exact time of death without a molecular autopsy and they don't put heroes under the knife. That implies something might be wrong, that he might not be the hero a two-star general desperately needs him to be." She spread her hands. "He died to save us all."

"Your slate had his medical information in it." His teeth were brilliantly white in the shadow of his beard.

"True." Shifting her weight to one hip, she folded her arms. "You know, it's not that easy doing a vacuum trot from a damaged salvage pen into an unpressurized shuttle bay."

"A terrible accident?"

Another shrug. "Who can say what would have happened?"

"I'm betting you could."

The beginning of a smile to answer his. "I was just doing my job."

To her surprise, he stepped back and glanced around the cabin, his expression suddenly serious. "You think I'm a coward? Because of . . . you know?"

"No. You overcame your fear. Isn't that the definition of bravery?"

"You're the Marine," Ryder snorted. "You tell me."

"I *am* telling you."

"And what are you afraid of?" he asked after a long moment.

All things considered, he deserved an honest answer. "Failure."

"Not being able to do your job?"

"I get it wrong and people die."

"You said, back in that hole on Big Yellow, that when the job's done . . ." His smile returned as suddenly as it left. "It *is* done, isn't it? I mean, I wouldn't want to start anything that'll get me whacked. You probably know twenty-five ways to kill a man with your bare hands."

"Twenty-six," Torin told him as he closed the distance between them. "But you'll like the last one."

Bitching amongst themselves, a maintenance crew worked to clear the huge net out of the shuttle bay. No one seemed to know why it had been put there or on whose order, although a couple of the di'Taykans had a few athletic suggestions for its use.

No one noticed the twelve large gray canisters stacked along one bulkhead.

Author's Note

In September, 1944, the 1st Marine Division attacked the small, "wretched" Pacific island of Peleliu. The westernmost of the Carolines, Peleliu had an oven-hot climate, a convoluted terrain, an *"ungodly scramble of coral cliffs,"* mangrove swamps, and 10,000 dug in and well-armed Japanese soldiers.

Lack of both time and ammunition made the Navy's preliminary bombardment short and essentially ineffective. As the amphibious landing craft approached the beach, the enemy opened fire with antiboat guns and heavy machine guns.

It was said to be as deadly a landing as the Marines would ever face.

After the slaughter on the beach, Colonel Lewis "Chesty" Puller led his men in a *"gallant but fruitless series of frontal assaults"* on the cliffs and sharply angled hills the Marines called Bloody Nose Ridge.

At one point during the six-day battle for the ridge, an excited subordinate reported to Colonel Puller, "We've had such heavy losses we have nothing better than sergeants to lead our platoons!"

"Let me tell you something, son," Puller replied calmly, "in the Marines, there *is* nothing better than a sergeant."

—from A FELLOWSHIP OF VALOR, THE BATTLE HISTORY OF THE UNITED STATES MARINES by Col. Joseph H. Alexander, USMC (Ret.), published by Lou Reda Productions for The History Channel and A&E Television Networks, 1997